D0556744

David Armstrong

## *About the Author*

CLIVE BARKER is the internationally bestselling author of more than twenty books for adults and children. He is also a widely acclaimed artist, film producer, screenwriter, and director. He lives with his partner, the renowned photographer David Armstrong, in Beverly Hills.

# ALSO BY CLIVE BARKER

### NOVELS
*The Damnation Game*
*Weaveworld*
*The Great and Secret Show*
*The Hellbound Heart*
*Imajica*
*Everville*
*Sacrament*
*Coldheart Canyon*
*Mister B. Gone*

### SHORT STORIES
*The Books of Blood, Volumes I–III*
*In the Flesh*
*The Inhuman Condition*
*Cabal*

### PLAYS
*Forms of Heaven: Three Plays*
*Crazyface · Paradise Street · Subtle Bodies*
*Incarnations: Three Plays*
*Colossus · Frankenstein in Love · The History of the Devil*

### ANTHOLOGIES
*Revelations* (contributor)
*The Essential Clive Barker*

### FOR CHILDREN
*The Thief of Always*
*Abarat*
*Abarat: Days of Magic, Nights of War*

# CLIVE
# BARKER

# GALILEE

### A NOVEL OF THE FANTASTIC

HARPER

NEW YORK · LONDON · TORONTO · SYDNEY

*To Emilian David Armstrong*

# HARPER

A hardcover edition of this book was published in 1998 by HarperCollins Publishers.

FIRST HARPER PAPERBACK PUBLISHED 2008.

Designed by Alma Hochhauser Orenstein

Library of Congress Cataloging-in-Publication data has been applied for.

ISBN 978-0-06-168427-2

08 09 10 11 12 RRD 10 9 8 7 6 5 4 3 2 1

# CONTENTS

# PART ONE

# The Time Remaining

# I

## i

At the insistence of my stepmother Cesaria Barbarossa the house in which I presently sit was built so that it faces southeast. The architect—who was no lesser man than the third President of the United States, Thomas Jefferson—protested her desire repeatedly and eloquently. I have the letters in which he did so here on my desk. But she would not be moved on the subject. The house was to look back towards her homeland, towards Africa, and he, as her employee, was to do as he was instructed.

It's very plain, however, reading between the lines of her missives (I have those too; or at least copies of them) that he is far more than an architect for hire; and she to him more than a headstrong woman with a perverse desire to build a house in a swamp, in North Carolina, facing southeast. They write to one another like people who know a secret.

I know a few myself; and luckily for the thoroughness of what follows I have no intention of keeping them.

The time has come to tell everything I know. Failing that, everything I can detect or surmise. Failing that, everything I can invent. If I do my job properly it won't even matter to you which is which. What will appear on these pages will be, I hope, a seamless history, describing deeds and destinies that will range across the world. Some of them will be, to say the least, strange events, enacted by troubled and unpalatable souls. But as a general rule, you should assume that the more unlikely the action I lay upon this stage for you, the more likely it is that I have evidence of its having happened. The things I will invent will be, I suspect, mundane by comparison with the truth. And as I said, it's my intention that you should not know the difference. I plan to interweave the elements of my story so cunningly that you'll cease to even care whether an event happened out there in the same world where you walk, or in here, in the head of a crippled man who will never again move from his stepmother's house.

✲     ✲     ✲

This house, this glorious house!

When Jefferson labored on its designs he was still some distance from Pennsylvania Avenue, but he was by no means an unknown. The year was 1790. He had already penned the Declaration of Independence, and served in France as the US Minister to the French government. Great words had flowed from his pen. Yet here he is taking time from his duties in Washington, and from work in his own house, to write long letters to my father's wife, in which the business of constructing this house and the nuances of his heart are exquisitely interlaced.

If that is not extraordinary enough, consider this: Cesaria is a black woman; Jefferson, for all his democratic protestations, was the owner of some two hundred slaves. So how much authority must she have had over him, to be able to persuade him to labor for her as he did? It's a testament to her powers of enchantment—powers which in this case she exercised, as she was fond of saying, "without the juju." In other words: in her dealings with Jefferson she was simply, sweetly, even innocently, human. Whatever capacities she possesses to supernaturally beguile a human soul—and she possesses many—she liked his clear-sightedness too well to blind him that way. If he was devoted to her, it was because she was worthy of his devotion.


They called the house he built for her L'Enfant. Actually, I believe the full name was L'Enfant de les Carolinas. I can only speculate as to why they so named it.

That the name of the house is in French is no big surprise: they met in the gilded salons of Paris. But the name itself? I have two theories. The first, and the most obvious, is that the house was in a sense the product of their romance, their child if you will, and they named it accordingly. The second, that it was the infant of an architectural parent, the progenitor being Jefferson's own house at Monticello, into which he poured his genius for most of his life. It's bigger than Monticello by a rough measure of three (Monticello is eleven thousand square feet; I estimate L'Enfant to be a little over thirty-four thousand) and has a number of smaller service buildings in its vicinity, whereas Jefferson's house is a single structure, incorporating the slave and servant quarters, the kitchen and toilet facilities, under one roof. But in other regards the houses are very similar. They're both Jeffersonian reworkings of Palladian models; both have double porticoes, both have octagonal domes, both have capacious high-ceilinged rooms and plenty of windows, both are practical rather than glamorous houses; both, I'd say, are structures that bespeak great confidence and great love.

Of course their settings are radically different. Monticello, as its name suggests, is set on a mountain. L'Enfant sits on a plot of low-lying ground forty-seven acres in size, the southeastern end of which is unredeemable swamp, and the northern perimeter wooded, primarily with pine. The house itself is raised up on a modest ridge, which protects it a little from the creeping damps and rots of this region, but not enough to stop the cellar from flooding during heavy rain, and the rooms getting damnably cold in winter and humid as hell in summer. Not that I'm complaining. L'Enfant is an extraordinary house. Sometimes I think it has a soul all of its own. Certainly it seems to know the moods of its occupants, and accommodates them. There have been times, sitting in my study, when a black thought has crept into my psyche for some reason, and I swear I can feel the room darken in sympathy with me. Nothing changes physically—the drapes don't close, the stains don't spread—but I nevertheless sense a subtle transformation in the chamber; as if it wishes to fall in rhythm with my mood. The same is true on days when I'm blithe, or haunted by doubts, or merely feeling lazy. Maybe it's Jefferson's genius that creates the illusion of empathy. Or perhaps it's Cesaria's work: her own genius, wedded with his. Whatever the reason, L'Enfant knows us. Better, I sometimes think, than we know ourselves.

## ii

I share this house with three women, two men, and a number of indeterminates.

The women are of course Cesaria and her daughters, my two half-sisters, Marietta and Zabrina. The men? One is my half-brother Luman (who doesn't actually live in the house, but outside, in a shack on the grounds) and Dwight Huddie, who serves as majordomo, as cook and as general handyman: I'll tell you more about him later. Then, as I said, there's the indeterminates, whose number is, not surprisingly, indeterminate.

How shall I best describe these presences to you? Not as spirits; that evokes something altogether too fanciful. They are simply nameless laborers, in Cesaria's exclusive control, who see to the general upkeep of the house. They do their job well. I wonder sometimes if Cesaria didn't first conjure them when Jefferson was still at work here, so that he could give them all a practical education in the strengths and liabilities of his masterpiece. If so, it would have been a scene to cherish: Jefferson the great rationalist, the numbers man, obliged to believe the evidence of his own eyes, though his common sense revolted at the idea that creatures such as these—brought out of the ether at the command of the mistress of L'Enfant—could exist. As I said, I don't know how many of them there are (six, perhaps; perhaps less); nor whether they're in fact projections of Cesaria's will or things once possessed of souls and volition. I only know that they tirelessly perform the task of keeping this vast house and its grounds in a reasonable condition, but—like stagehands in a theater— do so only when our gaze is averted. If this sounds a little eerie, maybe it is: I've simply become used to it. I no longer think about who it is who changes my bed every morning while I'm brushing my teeth, or who sews the buttons back on my shirt when they come loose, or fixes the cracks in the plaster or trims the magnolias. I take it for granted that the work will be done, and that whoever the laborers are, they have no more desire to exchange pleasantries with me than I do with them.

There's other occupant of the place that I think I should mention, and that's Cesaria's personal servant. How she came to have him as her bosom companion will be the subject of a later passage, so I'll leave the details until then. Let me say only this: he is, in my opinion, the saddest soul in the house. And when you consider the sum of sorrow under this roof, that's no little claim.

Anyway, I don't want to get mired in melancholy. Let's move on.

Having listed the human, or almost human, occupants of L'Enfant, I should make mention perhaps of the animals. An estate of this size is of course home to innumerable wild species. There are foxes, skunks and possums, there are feral cats (escapees from domestic servitude somewhere in Rollins County), and a number of dogs who make their home in the thicket. The trees are busy with birds night and day, and every now and then an alligator wanders up from the swamp and suns itself on the lawn.

All this is predictable enough. But there are two species whose presence here is rather less likely. The first was imported by Marietta, who took it into her head some years back to raise three hyena pups. How she came by them I don't recall (if she ever told me); I only know she wearied of surrogate motherhood quickly enough, and turned them loose. They bred, incestuously of course, and now there's quite a pack of them out there. The other oddities here are my stepmother's pride and joy: the porcupines. She's kept them as pets since first occupying the house, and they've prospered. They live inside, where they roam unfettered and unchallenged, though they prefer on the whole to stay upstairs, close to their mistress.

We had horses, of course, in my father's day—the stables were palatially appointed—but none of them survived an hour beyond his passing. Even if they'd had choice in the matter (which they didn't), they were too loyal to live once he'd gone; too noble. I doubt the same could be said of any of the other species. They grudgingly coexist with us while we're here, but I doubt there would be much grieving among them if we all departed. Nor do I imagine they'd long respect the sanctity of the house. In a week or two they'd have taken up residence: hyenas in the library, alligators in the cellar, foxes running riot under the great dome. Sometimes I wonder if they're not eyeing it already; planning for the day when it's theirs to shit on from roof to foundations.

# II

My suite of rooms is at the back of the house, four rooms in all, none of which were designed for their present purpose. What is now my bedroom—and the chamber I consider the most charming in the house—was originally a dining room used by my late father, Hursek Nicodemus Barbarossa, who did not once sit at the same table as Cesaria all the time I lived here. Such is marriage.

Adjacent to the study where I am sitting now, Nicodemus put his collection of keepsakes, a goodly portion of which was—at his request—buried with him when he died. There he kept the skull of the first horse he ever owned, along with a comprehensive and outlandish collection of sexual devices fashioned over the ages to increase the pleasure of connoisseurs. (He had a tale for every one of them: invariably hilarious.) This was not all he kept here. There was a gauntlet that had belonged to Saladin, the Moslem lover of Richard the Lionheart. There was a scroll, painted for him in China, which depicted, he once told me, the history of the world (though it seemed to my uneducated eyes simply a landscape with a serpentine river winding through it); there were dozens of representations of the male genitals—the lingam, the jade flute, Aaron's rod (or my father's favorite term: *Il Santo Membro*, the holy cock)—some of which I believe were carved or sculpted by his own priests, and therefore represent the sex that spurted me into being. Some of those objects are still here on the shelves. You may think that odd; even a little distasteful. I'm not certain I would even argue with that opinion. But he was a sexual man, and these statues, for all their crudity, embody him better than a book of his life, or a thousand photographs.

And it's not as if they're the only things on the shelves. Over the decades I've assembled here a vast library. Though I speak only English, French and a halting Italian, I read Hebrew, Latin and Greek, so my books are often antiquated, their subjects arcane. When you've had as much time on your hands as I've had, your curiosity takes obscure turns. In learned circles I'd probably be counted a world expert in a variety of subjects that no person with a real life to live—children, taxes, love— would give a fig about.

My father, were he here, would not approve of my books. He didn't like me to read. It reminded him, he would tell me, of how he'd lost my mother. A remark, by the way, which I do not understand to this day. The only volume he encouraged me to study was the two-leaved book that opens between a woman's legs. He kept ink, pen and paper from me when I was a child; though of course I wanted them all the more because they were forbidden me. He was determined that my real schooling be in the art and craft of horse breeding, which, after sex, was his great passion.

As a young man I traveled the world on his behalf, buying and selling horses, organizing their transportation to the stables here at L'Enfant, learning how to understand their natures as he understood them. I was good at what I did; and I enjoyed my travels. Indeed I met my late wife, Chiyojo, on one of those trips; and brought her back here to the house, intending to start a family. Those sweet ambitions were unfortunately denied me, however, by a sequence of tragedies that ended with the death of both my wife and that of Nicodemus.

But I'm getting ahead of myself. I was talking about this room, and what it housed during my father's occupancy: the phalli, the scroll, the horse's skull. What else? Let me think. There was a bell which Nicodemus claimed had been rung by a leper healed at the Crucifixion (he took the bell to his grave), and a device, no bigger than the humidor in which I keep my havanas, which plays a curious, whining music if touched, its sound so close to the human voice that it's possible to believe, as my father insisted, that its sealed interior contains a living mechanism.

Please feel free to make of these claims what you will, by the way. Though my father has been dead almost a hundred and forty years, I'm not about to call him a liar in print. Such men as my father do not take kindly to having their stories questioned, and though he is deceased I do not entirely believe I am beyond his reach.

Anyway, it is a fine room. Obliged as I am to sit here most of the day I have become familiar with every nuance of its form and volume, and were Jefferson standing before me now I would tell him: sir, I can think of no happier prison than this; nor any more likely to inspire my slovenly mind to fly.

If I am so very happy here, sitting with a book in my hands, why, you may ask, have I decided to put pen to paper and write what will be inevitably a tragic history? Why torment myself this way, when I could wheel myself out onto the balcony and sit with a copy of St. Thomas Aquinas in my lap and watch life in the mimosas?

There are two reasons. The first is my half-sister Marietta.

It happened like this. About two weeks ago she came into my room (without knocking, as usual), partook of a glass of gin, without asking, as usual, and sitting down without invitation in what used to be my father's chair said: "Eddie . . ."

She knows I hate to be called Eddie. My full name's Edmund Maddox Barbarossa. Edmund is fine; Maddox is fine; I was even called The Ox in my younger day, and didn't find it offensive. But *Eddie?* An Eddie can walk. An Eddie can make love. I'm no Eddie.

"Why do you always do that?" I asked her.

She sat back in the creaking chair and smiled mischievously, "Because it annoys you," she replied. A typically Mariettaesque response, I may say. She can be the very soul of perversity, though to look at her you'd never think it. I won't dote on her here (she gets far too much of that from her girlfriends), but she is a beautiful woman, by any measure. When she smiles, it's my father's smile; the sheer appetite in it, that's an echo of him. In repose, she's Cesaria's daughter; lazy-lidded and full of quiet certitude, her gaze, if it rests on you for more than a moment, like a physical thing. She's not a tall creature, my Marietta—a little over five feet without her boots—and now the immensity of chair she was sitting in, and the silly-sweet smile on her face, diminished her almost to a child. It wasn't hard to imagine my father behind her, his huge arms wrapped around her, rocking her. Perhaps she imagined it too, sitting there. Perhaps it was that memory that made her say:

"Do you feel sad these days? I mean, *especially* sad?"

"What do you mean: especially sad?"

"Well I know how you brood in here—"

"I don't brood."

"You shut yourself away."

"It's by choice. I'm not unhappy."

"Honestly?"

"I've got all I need here. My books. My music. Even if I'm desperate, I've got a television. I even know how to switch it on."

"So you don't feel sad? Ever?"

As she was pressing me so hard on the subject, I gave it a few more moments of thought. "Actually, I suppose I have had one or two bouts of melancholy recently," I conceded. "Nothing I couldn't shake off, but—"

"I hate this gin."

"It's English."

"It's bitter. Why do you have to have English gin? The sun went down on the Empire a long time ago."

"I like the bitterness."

She pulled a face. "Next time I'm in Charleston I'm going to bring you some really nice brandy," she said.

"Brandy's overrated," I remarked.

"It's good if you dissolve a little cocaine in it. Have you ever tried that? That gives it a nice kick."

"Cocaine dissolved in brandy?"

"It goes down so smoothly, and you don't get a nose filled with grey boogers the next morning."

"I don't have any need for cocaine, Marietta. I get along quite well with my gin."

"But liquor makes you sleepy."

"So?"

"So you won't be able to afford so much sleepiness, once you get to work."

"Am I missing something here?" I asked her.

She got up, and despite her contempt for my English gin, refilled her glass and came to stand behind my chair. "May I wheel you out onto the balcony?"

"I wish you'd get to the point."

"I thought you Englishmen liked prevarication?" she said, easing me out from in front of my desk and taking me around it to the french windows. They were already wide open—I'd been sitting enjoying the fragrance of the evening air when Marietta entered. She took me out onto the balcony.

"Do you miss England?" she asked me.

"This is the most peculiar conversation . . ." I said.

"It's a simple question. You must miss it sometimes."

(My mother, I should explain, was English; one of my father's many mistresses.)

"It's a very long time since I was in England. I only really remember it in my dreams."

"Do you write the dreams down?"

"Oh . . ." I said. "Now I get it. We're back to the book."

"It's time, Maddox," she said, with a greater gravity than I could recall her displaying in a long while. "We don't have very much time left."

"According to whom?"

"Oh for God's sake, use your eyes. Something's changing, Eddie. It's subtle, but it's everywhere. It's in the bricks. It's in the flowers. It's in the ground. I went walking near the stables, where we put Poppa, and I swear I felt the earth shaking."

"You're not supposed to go there."

"Don't change the subject. You are *so* good at that, especially when you're trying to avoid your responsibility."

"Since when was it—"

"You're the only one in the family who can write all this down, Eddie. You've got all the journals here, all the diaries. You still get letters from you-know-who."

"Three in the last forty years. It's scarcely a thriving correspondence. And for God's sake, Marietta, use his name."

"Why should I? I hate the little bastard."

"That's the one thing he certainly isn't, Marietta. Now why don't you just drink your gin and leave me alone?"

"Are you telling me *no*, Eddie?"

"You don't hear that very often, do you?"

"*Eddie* . . ." she simpered.

"Marietta. Darling. I'm not going to throw my life into turmoil because you want me to write a family history."

She gave me a sharp little look and downed her gin in one throatful, setting the glass on the balcony railing. I could tell by the precision of this motion, and her pause before she spoke, that she had an exit line in readiness. She has a fine theatrical flair, my Marietta.

"You don't want to throw your life into turmoil? Don't be so perfectly pathetic. You don't *have* a life, Eddie. That's why you've got to write this book. If you don't, you're going to die without having done a damn thing."

# III

### i

She knew better of course. I've lived, damn her! Before my injury I had almost as great an appetite for experience as Nicodemus. I take that back. I was never as interested in the sexual opportunities afforded by my travel as he was. He knew all the great bordellos of Europe intimately; I preferred to wander the cathedrals or drink myself into a stupor in a bar. Drink is a weakness of mine, no question, and it's got me into trouble more than once. It's made me fat too. It's hard, of course, to stay thin when you're in a wheelchair. Your backside gets big, your waistline spreads; and Lord, my face, which used to be so well made I could walk into any gathering and take my pick of the female company, is now pasty and round. Only in my eyes might you glimpse the magnetism I once exercised. They are a peculiar color: mingled flecks of blue and gray. The rest of me's just gone to hell.

I suppose that happens to everybody sooner or later. Even Marietta, who is a pure-blooded Barbarossa, has said that over the years she's noticed some subtle signs of aging; it's just much, much slower than it would be for a human being. One gray hair every decade or so isn't anything to bitch about, I remind her, especially when nature had given her so much else: she has Cesaria's flawless skin (though neither she nor Zabrina are quite as black as their mother) and Nicodemus's physical ease. She also shares my delight in getting drunk, but as yet it's taken no toll on her waist or her buttocks. I digress; again. How did I get onto the subject of Marietta's backside? Oh yes, I was talking about how I traveled as my father's envoy. It was wonderful. I stood in the shit in a lot of stables over the years, of course, but I also visited some of this planet's glories: the wilds of Mongolia, the deserts of North Africa, the plains of Andalusia. So please understand that though I'm now reduced to being a voyeur, this wasn't always the case. I don't write as a theorist, pontificating on the state of a world that I only knew from my newspapers and my television screen.

As I get deeper into the story I'll no doubt season it with talk of the sights I saw and the people I knew on my journeys. For now, let me just talk of England, the country where I was conceived. My birth mother was a woman by the name of Moira Feeney, and, though she died a short time after my birth, of a sickness I've never quite comprehended, I passed the first seven years of my life in her native country, looked after by her sister, Gisela. It was not by any means a cosseted existence; Gisela was enraged when she discovered the father of her sister's child did not intend to bring us into his charmed circle, and rather than accept the substantial sums he offered her to help raise me, she proudly, and foolishly, refused all subsidy. She also refused to see him. It wasn't until Gisela also died (she was struck, somewhat suspiciously, by lightning) that my father appeared in my life, and took me with him on his travels. In the next five years we lived in a number of extraordinary houses, the guests of great men who wanted my father's advice as a horse breeder (and Lord knows what else besides; I think he was probably shaping the destinies of nations behind the scenes). But for all the glamour of those years—two summers in Granada, a spring in Venice; so much more that I can't recall—it is my years in Blackheath with Gisela that I still return to most fondly. Gentle seasons these; and my gentle human aunt, and milk and rain and the plum tree at the back of the cottage, from the topmost branches of which I could see the dome of St. Paul's.

I have a pristine memory of what it was like to perch in those gnarled branches, where I would linger for hour upon hour, lulled into a happy trance by rhymes and songs. One of those rhymes I remember to this day.

> It seems I am,
> It seems I was,
> It seems I will
> Be born, because
> It seems I am,
> It seems I was,
> It seems I will
> Be born because—

And so on, round and round.

Marietta's right, I *do* miss England, and I do what I can to keep remembrance of it. English gin, English syntax, English melancholy. But the England I yearn for, the England I dream of when I doze in my chair, no longer exists. It was just a view from a plum tree, and a happy child. Both went into history a long time ago. It is, however, the *second* reason why I am writing this book. In opening the floodgates of memory, I hope to be carried, at least for a little while, back into the bliss of my childhood.

## ii

I should tell you, just briefly, about what happened the day I told Mari-etta I'd begun this book, because you'll understand better what it's like to live in this house. I had been sitting on my balcony with the birds (there are eleven individuals—cardinals, buntings, soldier-wing black-birds—who come to feed from my hand and then stay to make music for me), and while I was feeding them I heard her down below having a furious argument with my other half-sister, Zabrina. As far as I could gather Marietta was being her usual imperious self, and Zabrina—who keeps out of everybody's way most of the time, and when she does encounter one of the family doesn't say much—was for once standing up for her own opinions. The gist of the exchange was this: Marietta had apparently brought one of her lovers into the house the previous night, and the visitor had proved to be quite the detective. Apparently she'd got up while Marietta was asleep, had gone wandering around the house and seen something she should not have seen.

Now she was apparently in a state of panic, and Marietta was quite out of patience with her, so she was trying to cajole Zabrina into cook-ing up some spiked candy that would wipe the woman's memory clean. Then Marietta could take her back home, and the whole untidy busi-ness could be forgotten.

"I told you last time I don't *approve*—" Zabrina's voice is normally reedy and thin; now it was positively shrill.

"Oh *Lord*," said Marietta wearily. "Don't be so high-handed."

"You know you should keep ordinary folks away from the house," Zabrina went on. "It's asking for trouble, bringing somebody here."

"This one's special," Marietta said.

"So why do you want me to wipe her memory?"

"Because I'm afraid she's going to lose her mind if you don't."

"What did she see?"

There was a pause. "I don't know," Marietta finally admitted. "She's too incoherent to tell me."

"Well where did you find her?"

"On the stairs."

"She didn't see Mama?"

"No, Zabrina. She didn't see Mama. If she'd seen Mama—"

"She'd be dead."

"—she'd be dead."

There was a pause. Finally Zabrina said: "*If* I do this—"

"Yes?"

"*Quid pro quo.*"

"That's not very sisterly," Marietta groused. "But all right. *Quid pro quo*. What do you want?"

"I don't know yet," Zabrina said. "But I'll think of something, don't worry. And you won't like it. I'll make sure of that."

"How very petty of you," Marietta observed.

"Look. Do you want me to do it or don't you?"

Again there was a pause. "She's in my bedroom," Marietta said. "I had to tie her to the bed."

Zabrina giggled.

"It's not funny."

"They're *all* funny," Zabrina replied. "Weak heads, weak hearts. You're never going to find anyone who can really be with you. You know that don't you? It's impossible. We're on our own, to the very end."

About an hour later Marietta appeared in my room. She looked ashen; her gray eyes full of sadness.

"You heard the conversation," she said. I didn't bother to reply. "Sometimes that bitch makes me want to hit her. Hard. Not that she'd feel it. Fat cow."

"You just can't bear to be in anybody's debt."

"I wouldn't mind with you," she said.

"I don't count."

"No, I guess you don't," she replied. Then, seeing the expression on my face. "*Now* what have I said? I'm just agreeing with you, for God's sake! Why is everybody so damn *sensitive* around here?" She went to my desk and examined the contents of the gin bottle. There was barely a shot remaining. "Got any more?"

"There's half a case in the closet in the bedroom."

"Mind if I—?"

"Help yourself."

"You know we should talk more often, Eddie," she called back to me while she dug for the gin. "Get to know one another. I don't have anything in common with Dwight and Zabrina's been in the foulest mood for the last couple of months. She's so *obese* these days, Eddie. Have you seen her? I mean, she's grossly fat."

Though both Zabrina and Marietta insist that they're completely unlike—and in many regards this is true—they have some essential qualities in common. At their cores they're both willful, stubborn, obsessive women. But whereas Marietta, who's eleven years Zabrina's junior, has always prided herself on her athleticism, and is as lean as a woman can get and still have a lushness about her body, Zabrina gave into her cravings for praline brittle and pecan pie years ago. Occasionally I'll see her from my window, wandering rotundly across the lawn. At the last sighting she was probably three hundred and fifty pounds. (We are, you've doubtless begun to grasp, a profoundly wounded group of people. But trust me, when you better know the circumstances of our lives, you'll be astonished we're as functional as we are.)

Marietta had emerged with a fresh bottle of gin, and, unscrewing the top, poured herself an ample measure.

"Why do you keep all those clothes in the closet?" she said, knocking back a mouthful. "You're never going to wear most of them."

"I presume that means you have your eye on something."

"The smoking jacket."

"Take it."

She leaned forward and kissed my cheek. "I've underrated you all these years," she said, and went back into the bedroom to fetch the jacket in case I changed my mind.

"I've decided to write the book," I told her when she emerged.

She tossed the jacket at Nicodemus's chair and fairly danced with excitement. "That's so wonderful," she said. "Oh my God, Eddie, we're going to have *such fun.*"

"We?"

"Yes, *we.* I mean, you'll be writing it most of the time, but I'll be helping. There's a lot you don't know. Dirt about Cesaria that she told me when I was little."

"Maybe you should keep your voice down."

"She can't hear me. She's always in her chambers these days."

"We don't know what she can hear," I said. There was a story that she'd had Jefferson design the house so that it funneled sounds to her chambers (which I've never entered, by the way; nor has Marietta). The story may be apocryphal, but I wonder. Though it's many, many months since I caught sight of the woman I don't have difficulty believing she sits there in her boudoir listening to her children, and her husband's children, conniving and weeping and slowly losing their minds. She probably enjoys it.

"Well if she can hear me, so what? She should be happy we're going to all this trouble. I mean, it's going to be a history of the Barbarossas. It'll make her immortal."

"If she isn't already."

"Oh no . . . she's getting old. Zabrina sees her all the time and she says the old bitch is failing."

"I find that hard to imagine."

"It was her saying that which started me thinking about our book."

"It's not *our* book," I insisted. "If I'm going to do it, it's going to be done my way. Which means it's not going to simply be a history of the Barbarossas."

She emptied her glass. "I see," she said, with a little chill in her voice. "So what's it going to be?"

"Oh, it'll be about the family. But it'll be about the Gearys too."

Now she fell silent and stared out of the window at the place where I sit with the birds. It took her fully a minute to bring herself to speak again. "If you write about the Gearys, then I'm having nothing to do with the fucking thing."

"How can I write—"

"Or indeed you."

"*Let me finish*, will you? How can I write about this family—particularly the recent history of this family—and *not* write about the Gearys?"

"They're scum, Eddie. *Human scum.* And vicious. Every one of them."

"That's not true, Marietta. And even if it were, I say again: what kind of bowdlerized account would this damn book be if I didn't include them?"

"All right. So just mention them *in passing.*"

"They're part of our lives."

"They're not part of mine," she said fiercely. Her gaze came back in my direction and I saw that she wasn't so much enraged as sorrowful. I was revealing myself as a traitor with my desire to tell the story this way. She measured her next words with great care, like a lawyer making a pivotal argument.

"You realize, don't you, that this may be the only way people out there get to know about our family?"

"All the more—"

"Now you let *me* finish," she snapped. "When I came in here suggesting you write this fucking book, it was because I had this feeling—I *have* this feeling—that we haven't got very long. And my instincts are rarely wrong."

"I realize that," I said quietly. Marietta has prophetic talents, no question. She gets them from her mother.

"Maybe *that's* why she's looking so haggard these days," Marietta said.

"She's feeling what you're feeling?"

She nodded. "Poor bitch," she said softly. "And that's another thing to consider. Cesaria. She hates the Gearys even more than I do. They took her beloved Galilee."

I snorted at this nonsense. "That's one sentimental myth I intend to lay to rest, for a start," I said.

"So you don't believe he was taken?"

"Absolutely not. I know what happened the night he left better than anyone living. And I intend to tell what I know."

"Of course, nobody may give a damn," Marietta observed.

"At least I'll have set the record straight. Isn't that what you wanted?"

"I don't know what the hell I was thinking," Marietta replied, her distaste at what I had proposed now resurfacing. "I'm beginning to wish I'd never suggested a fucking book."

"Well, it's too late now. It's begun."

"You began already?"

This was not entirely true. I hadn't yet laid pen to paper. But I knew *where* I was going to begin: with the house, and Cesaria and Thomas Jefferson. The work was as good as started.

"Well don't let me delay you," Marietta said, going to the door. "But I'm not guaranteeing you my help."

"That's fine. I'm not asking for it."

"Not now you're not. But you will. You'll have to. There's a lot of pieces of information I've got that you'll need. Then we'll see what your integrity's worth."

So saying, she left me to my gin. I didn't doubt the significance of this last remark: she intended to make some kind of bargain. A section of my book she didn't approve of excised in return for a piece of information I needed. I was absolutely determined she wasn't going to get a single word removed however. What I'd told her was true. There was no way to tell the story of the Barbarossas without telling that of the Gearys, and thus also the story of Rachel Pallenberg, the one name I do not ever expect to hear crossing Marietta's lips. I had deliberately not mentioned the Pallenberg woman myself, because I was certain as soon as I did so Marietta would be screaming inventive obscenities at me. Needless to say, I intend to devote a substantial portion of this story to the vices and virtues of Rachel Pallenberg.

That said, this narrative will be somewhat impoverished if I don't get Marietta's help; so I intend to be selective in the way I talk about what I'm doing. She'll come round; if only because she's an egotist, and the idea of not having her ideas in the book is going to be far more painful to her than my talking about the Gearys. Besides, she knows very well there are so many matters that I'm going to trust to my instinct on, matters that cannot be strictly *verified*. Matters of the spirit, matters of the bedroom, matters of the grave. These are the truly important elements. The rest is just geography and dates.

### iii

Later that day, I saw Marietta escorting from the house the woman I'd heard her talking to Zabrina about. She was, like almost all of Marietta's lovers, blonde, petite and probably no more than twenty years old. By the look of the clothes, I'd guess she was a tourist, perhaps a hitchhiker, rather than a local woman.

Zabrina had plainly done as Marietta had requested, and relieved the poor woman of her panic (along with any memory of the experience that had induced that panic). I watched them from my balcony through my binoculars. The blank expression on the girl's face disturbed me. Was this really the only way human beings could deal with the appearance of the miraculous: panic rising to insanity; or, if they were lucky, a healing excision of the memory, which left them like this woman, calm but impoverished? What pitiful options they were. (Which thought brought me back to the book. Was it too grand an ambition to hope that in these pages I might somehow prepare the way for such revelations, so that when they came the human mind didn't simply crack like a mirror too frail to reflect the wonders before it?) I felt a kind of sadness for the visitor, who had been washed, for her own good, of the very experience that might have made her life worth the living. What would she be after this, I wondered. Had Zabrina left deep inside her a seed of the memory, which, like the irritant mote in an oyster's flesh might with time become something rare and wonderful? I would have to ask.

Meanwhile, under the cover of the trees, Marietta had halted with her companion, and was saying a more than fond goodbye. Having promised to tell the truth, however unpalatable, I can scarcely remain silent on what I saw: she bared the woman's breasts while I watched; she teased the woman's nipples and kissed her lips, while I watched, and then, while I watched, she whispered something, and the woman went down on to her knees, unbuckled and unbuttoned Marietta's pants, and put her tongue into Marietta, flicking it so cunningly I heard Marietta's yelps from my balcony. Lord knows I'm grateful for whatever pleasures come my way, and I'm not about to pretend that I'm deeply ashamed of watching them make love. It was perfectly wonderful to watch, and when they were finished, and Marietta escorted the woman to the path

that winds away from L'Enfant and back into the real world, I felt—
though this may seem absurd—a pang of loneliness.

# IV

Though Marietta had mocked my belief that the house is a kind of
listening device, which brings news from all its rooms to the ears of
one soul in particular, that very night I had that belief confirmed.

I do not sleep well; never have, never will. It doesn't matter how
weary I am, as soon as I put my head on my pillow all manner of
thoughts, most of them utterly without merit, circle in my skull. So it
was last night; fragments of my conversation with Marietta, all
rearranged so as to be nonsensical, and punctuated with her libidinous
yelps, constituted the soundtrack. But the images were from some
other store entirely. Neither Marietta's face nor form appeared in my
mind's eye; rather the faces and forms of men and women I did not
even recognize. No, I take that back. I recognized them; I simply
couldn't *name* them. Some seemed grotesquely happy with their lot;
going naked, some of them, on the streets of what I think was
Charleston, darting along the sidewalks and defecating from the chestnut trees. But there were others I dreamed of who were far less happy:
one moment blank-faced brothers and sisters to Marietta's concubine,
the next moment shrieking like tortured animals—as though their forgetfulness had been snatched away, and what they were remembering
was unbearable. I know there are some psychoanalysts who theorize
that every creature which appears in a dream or waking dream is an
aspect of the dreamer. If so, then I suppose the naked beasts in the
streets of Charleston are the part of me that's my father, and the other,
the terrified souls sobbing incoherently, are that human part which my
mother made. But I suspect the scheme's too simple. In search of a pattern, the theorist ignores all that's ragged and contradictory, and ends
with a pretty lie. I'm not two in one; I'm many. This self has my
mother's compassion and my father's taste for raw mutton. That one
has my mother's love of murder stories and my father's passion for sun-
flowers. Who knows how many there are? Too many for any dogma to
contain, I'm certain of that.

The point is, these dreams had me in a terrible state. I was close to
tears, which is rare for me.

And then, in the darkness, I heard the sound of shuffling, and of clicking on the wooden floor and, looking down toward the noise, saw in a lozenge of moonlight a prickly silhouette waddling toward my bed. It was a porcupine. I didn't move. I simply let the creature come to me (my arm was hanging off the bed, my hand close to the floor) and put its wet nose in my palm.

"Did you come down here on your own?" I said softly to the creature. Sometimes they did just that, particularly the younger, more adventurous ones; came shuffling down the stairs in the hope of finding a snack. But I'd no sooner asked the question than I had my answer, as my body responded to the entrance of the quill-pig's mistress, Cesaria. You see, this pitiful anatomy of mine, wounded beyond all hope of repair, was quickening. It was uncanny. I was in the presence of this woman, my father's wife, very rarely, but I knew from past experience the effect of this visit would last for days. Even if she were to leave the room now I would feel spasms in my lower limbs for a week or more, though the muscles of my legs were atrophied. And my cock, which had been just a piss-pipe for far too long, would stand up like an adolescent's and demand milking twice an hour. Lord, I thought, was it any wonder she'd been worshiped? She could probably raise the dead if it pleased her to do so.

"Come away, Tansy," she said to the porcupine.

Tansy ignored the instruction, which I will admit pleased me. Even *she* might be disobeyed.

"I don't mind it," I said.

"Just be careful. The spines—"

"I know." I still had the scars where one of her quill-pigs, as she preferred to call them, had taken against me. And I think it had distressed Cesaria to see me bleed. I remember the look on her face quite clearly: her eyes like liquid night in that obsidian head of hers; her sympathy terrifying to me, because I suppose I feared her touch, her healing. Feared it would transform me, make me her devotee forever. So we'd stood, neither one of us moving, both distressed by something essential to the other (her power, my blood) while the quill-pig had sat on the floor between us and scratched its fleas.

"This book . . ." she said.

"Marietta told you about it?" I said.

"I don't need telling, Maddox."

"No. Of course not."

What she said next astonished me. But then of course she would never be who she is—she could not trail the legends she trails—if she were not a constant astonishment.

"You must write it fearlessly," she said. "Write out of your head and out of your heart and never care about the consequences."

She spoke more softly than I'd ever heard her speak before. Not weakly, you understand, but with a kind of tenderness I'd always assumed she would never feel toward me. In truth, I hadn't believed she felt it toward anybody.

"So the business about the Gearys—?"

"Must go in. All of it. Every last detail. Don't spare any of them. Or any of us, come to that. We've all made our compromises over the years. Treated with the enemy instead of stopping their hearts."

"Do you hate the Gearys?"

"I should say no. They're only human. They know no better. But yes, I hate them. If they didn't exist I'd still have a husband and a son."

"It's not as though Galilee's dead."

"He's dead to me," she said. "He died the moment he sided with them against your father." She snapped her fingers lightly, and her quill-pig turned round and waddled back to her. Throughout this entire conversation I'd seen only glimpses of her, but now, as the porcupine approached her, she bent down to gather it up into her arms, and the moonlight, washing up off the boards, momentarily showed me her entirely. She was not, as Marietta had reported, frail or sickly; far from it. She looked like a young woman to my eye; a woman prodigiously gifted by nature: her beauty both refined and raw at the same time, the planes of her face so strong she seemed almost the idol of herself, carved out of the silver light in which she stood. Did I say that she was beautiful? I was wrong. Beauty is too tame a notion; it evokes only faces in magazines. A lovely eloquence, a calming symmetry; none of that describes this woman's face. So perhaps I should assume I cannot do it justice with words. Suffice it to say that it would break your heart to see her; and it would mend what was broken in the same moment; and you would be twice what you'd been before.

With the quill-pig in her arms, she was moving toward the door. But as she reached it she halted (all this I only heard; she was again invisible to me).

"The beginning is always the hardest," she said.

"Well actually I've already begun . . ." I said, a little tentatively. Despite the fact that she'd neither said nor done anything to intimidate me, I was still—perhaps unfairly—anxious that she'd blindside me with some attack or other.

"How?" she said.

"How did I begin?"

"Yes."

"With the house, of course."

"Ah . . ." I heard the smile in her voice. "With Mr. Jefferson?"

"With Mr. Jefferson."

"That was a good idea. To begin in the middle that way. And with my glorious Thomas. He was, you know, the love of my life."

"Jefferson?"

"You think it should have been your father?"

"Well—"

"It was nothing like love with your father. It became love, but that's not how it began. When such as I, and such as he, mate, we do not mate for the sake of sentiment. We mate to make children. *To preserve our genius,* as your father would have said."

"Perhaps I should have begun there."

She laughed. "With our *mating?*"

"No I didn't mean that." I was glad of the darkness, to cover my blushes—though with her eyes she probably saw them anyway. "I . . . I . . . meant with the firstborn. With Galilee."

I heard her sigh. Then I heard nothing; for such a time I thought perhaps she'd decided to leave me. But no. She was still there in the room.

"We didn't baptize him Galilee," she said. "He took that name for himself, when he was six."

"I didn't know that."

"There's a great deal you don't know, Maddox. A great deal you can't even guess. That's why I came to invite you . . . when you're ready . . . to see some of the past . . ."

"You have more books?"

"Not books. Nothing so *tangible* . . ."

"I'm sorry, I don't really understand."

Again, she sighed, and I was afraid this offer, whatever it was, would be snatched away again because I was making her impatient. But she sighed not out of irritation, rather out of a heaviness of the heart.

"Galilee was everything to us," she said. "And he became nothing. I want you to understand how that came about."

"I'll do my best, I swear."

"I know you will," she said gently. "But it may take more courage than you have. You're so *human,* Maddox. I've always found that hard to like."

"I can't do much about it."

"Your father loved you for that very reason, you know . . ." Her voice trailed away. "What a mess it all is," she said. "What a terrible, tragic mess. To have had so much, and let it go through our fingers . . ."

"I want to understand how that happened," I replied, "more than anything, I want to understand."

"Yes," she said, somewhat distractedly. Her thoughts were already elsewhere.

"What do I need to do?" I asked her.

"I'll explain everything to Luman," Mama replied. "He'll watch over you. And of course if it's too much for your human sensibilities—"

"Zabrina can take it away."

"That's right. Zabrina can take it away."

# V

### i

I had a different vision of the house thereafter. Everything was expectation. I was looking for a sign, a clue, a glimpse of this mysterious source of knowledge that Cesaria had invited me to share. What form would it take, if it wasn't books? Was there somewhere in the house a collection of family heirlooms for me to sift through? Or was I being entirely too literal? Had I been invited into a place of spirit rather than substance? If so, would I have the words to express what I felt in that place?

For the first time in perhaps three months I decided to leave my room and go outside. For this, I need somebody's help. Jefferson didn't design the house anticipating the presence of a crippled occupant (and I doubt that Cesaria ever thought she'd entertain such frailty) so there are four steps in the passageway that leads out to the front hall; steps which are too deep for me to negotiate in a wheelchair even with help. Dwight has to carry me down, like a babe in arms, and then I wait, laid prone on the sofa in the hallway, until he brings down the chair and sets me in it.

Dwight is quite simply the most amiable fellow I have ever known; though he has every reason to hate the God who made him and probably every human being in the state of North Carolina. He was born with some kind of mental defect that made self-expression difficult, and was therefore thought to be an idiot. His childhood and early adolescence were a living hell: denied any real education, he languished, abused by both his parents.

Then, one day in his fourteenth year, he wandered into the swamp, perhaps to kill himself; he says he doesn't exactly recall the reason. Nor does he know how long he wandered—though it was many days and nights—until Zabrina found him at the perimeters of L'Enfant. He was in a state of complete exhaustion. She brought him back to the house, and for reasons of her own nursed him to health in her rooms without telling anyone. I've never pressed Dwight as to the exact nature of his relationship with Zabrina, but I don't doubt that when he was younger she used him sexually; nor do I doubt that he was quite happy with the arrangement. She wasn't then quite the scale she is now, but she was still substantial; for Dwight this was no hardship. He has several times mentioned to me in passing his enthusiasm for plentitude in a woman. Whether that taste predated his time with Zabrina, or was formed by it, I don't know. I can only report that she kept him a secret for almost three years, during which she apparently made it her business to educate him; and well. By the time she introduced him to Marietta and myself, all but the faintest trace of his speech impediment had disappeared, and he had become the fledgling form of the man he was to become. Now, thirty-two years later, he is as much a part of this house as the boards beneath my feet. Though his relationship with Zabrina soured for reasons I've never been able to pry out of him, he still speaks of her with a kind of reverence. She is, and will always be, the woman who taught him Herodotus and saved his soul (which services, by the way, are in my opinion intimately connected).

Of course, he's aging far faster than any of the rest of us. He's forty-nine now, and crops his thinning hair to a gray stubble (which gives him a rather scholarly look) and his body, which used to be lean, is getting pudgy around the middle. The business of carrying me around has become much more of a chore for him, and I've told him several times that he's soon going to have to go looking for another lost soul out there; someone he can train to take over the heavy duties in the house.

But perhaps now that's academic. If Marietta's right, and our days here are indeed numbered, he won't need to train anyone to follow in his footsteps. They, and he, and we all, will have disappeared from sight forever.


We ate together that day, not in the dining room, which is far too large for just two (I wonder sometimes what kind of guests Mama had intended to invite), but in the kitchen. Jellied chicken loaf, and chives and sesame seed biscuits, followed by Dwight's dessert specialty, a Hampton polonaise: a cake made with layers of almond and chocolate, which he serves with a sweet whipped cream. (His skills as a cook he got from Zabrina, I'm certain. His repertoire of candies is remarkable: all manner of crystallized fruit, nougat, pralines, and a tooth-rotting wonder he calls divinity fudge.)

"I saw Zabrina yesterday," he said, serving me another slice of the polonaise.

"Did you speak to her?"

"No. She had that *don't come near me* look on her face. You know how she gets."

"Are you just going to watch me make a hog of myself?"

"I'm so filled up I'll not stay awake this afternoon as it is."

"Nothing wrong with a little siesta. Good ol' Southern tradition. It gets hot, you go snooze till it cools down." I looked up from my plate to see that Dwight had a glum expression on his face. "What's wrong?"

"I don't like sleep as much as I used to," he said softly.

"Why not?" I asked him.

"Bad dreams . . ." he said. "No, not bad. Sorrowful. Sorrowful dreams."

"About what?"

Dwight shrugged. "I don't rightly know. This and that. People I knew when I was little." He drew a deep breath. "I've been thinkin' maybe I should go out . . . you know . . . back where I come from."

"Permanently?"

"Oh Lord, no. I belong here an' I always will. No, just go out one more time to see if my folks are still alive, an' if they are, say my goodbyes."

"They must be getting old."

"It's not them that's goin', Mr. Maddox, an' we both know it. It's us." He ran his finger through the remaining cream on his plate and put his finger on his tongue. "That's what I'm dreamin' about. Us goin'. Everythin' goin'."

"Have you been talking to Marietta?"

"Now and again."

"No, I mean about this."

He shook his head. "This is the first I've told anybody."

There was an uneasy silence. Then he said: "What do you think?"

"About the dreams?"

"About going to see my folks an' all."

"I think you should go."

## ii

Though I attempted to take my own advice and have a siesta that afternoon, my head, despite the melancholy exchange with Dwight—or
perhaps because of it—was buzzing like a stirred-up hive. I found
myself thinking about certain parallels that existed between families
that were in every other way unlike. The family of Dwight Huddie, for
instance, living in a trailer park somewhere in Sampson County: did
they ever wonder about their child, whom they lost to a place they
would never see, never even know existed? Did they think of seeking
him out all those years ago, when he was first lost, or was he as good as
dead to them, as Galilee was to Cesaria? And then there was the Gearys.
That family, for all its fabled clannishness had also in its time cut off
some of its children as though they were gangrenous limbs. Again: *as
good as dead.* I was sure that as I went on, I was going to find connections like these throughout this history: ways in which the sorrows and
the cruelties of one bloodline were echoed in another.

The question that still lay before me, and I had so far failed to
answer, was the way these connections might best be expressed. My
mind was filled with possibilities but I had no real sense of how all that
I knew was arrayed and dispersed; no sense of the pattern.


To distract myself from anxiety I made a slow exploration of the house.
It was many years since I'd gone from room to room as I did now, and
everywhere I looked this newly curious gaze of mine was rewarded. Jefferson's extraordinary taste and passion for detail was in evidence all
around me, but married to a wildness of conception that is, I'm certain,
my mother's gift. It's an extraordinary combination: Jeffersonian
restraint and Barbarossian bravura; a constant struggle of wills that creates forms and volumes utterly unlike any I have seen before. The great
study, for instance, now fallen into neglect, which seemed the perfect
model of an austere place of intellectual inquiry, until the eye drifted to
the ceiling, where the Hellenic columns grew sinewy and put forth a
harvest of unearthly fruit. The dining room, where the floor was set with
such a cunning design of marble tiles that it seemed like a pool of blue-
green water. A long gallery of arched alcoves, each of which contained
a bas-relief so cunningly lit that the scenes seemed to shed their own
luminescence, which spilled out as from a series of windows. There was
nothing, it seemed to me, that had been left to chance; every tiny sub-
tlety of form had been planned so as to flatter the greater scheme, just
as the great scheme brought the eye back to these subtleties. It was all,

it seemed to me, one glorious *invitation:* to pleasure in the seeing, yes; but also to a calm certainty of one's own place in all of this, not over-powered, simply enjoined to be here in the moment, feeling the way the air flowed through the rooms and brushed your face, or the way the light came to meet you from a wall. More than once I found my eyes filling with tears at the sheer beauty of a chamber, then soothed from my tears by that same beauty, which wanted only my happiness.

All this said, the house was not by any means unspoiled. The years, and the humidity, have taken a terrible toll; scarcely a single room has escaped some measure of decay, and a few—particularly those which lay closest to the swamp—are in such a poor state of disrepair that I was obliged to have Dwight carry me into them, the floors were too rotted for my wheelchair. Even these chambers, I should say, had an undeni-able grandeur to them. The creeping rot on the walls resembles the charts of some as yet unnamed world; the small forests of fungi that grow in the sodden boards have a fascination all of their own. Dwight was unpersuaded. "These are bad places," he said, determined that their deterioration was due to some spiritual malaise that hung about them. "Bad things happened here."

This didn't make a lot of sense to me, and I told him so. If one room had rot in the walls and another didn't, it was because of some vagary in the water table; it wasn't evidence of bad karma.

"In this house," Dwight said, "everything's connected."

That was all I could get him to say on the subject, but it was plain enough, I suppose. Just as I had come to appreciate the way the house played back and forth between spirit and sight, so Dwight seemed to be telling me the physical and moral states of the house were connected.


He was right, of course, though I couldn't see it at the time. The house wasn't simply a reflection of Jefferson's genius and Cesaria's vision: it was a repository for all that it had ever contained. The past was still present here, in ways my limited senses had yet to grasp.

# VI

I encountered Marietta once or twice during these days of reacquaintance with the house (I even glimpsed Zabrina on a few occasions, though she shared no interest in conversing with me; only hurried away). But of Luman, of the man Cesaria had promised could help educate me, I saw not a hair. Had my stepmother decided not to allow me access to her secrets after all? Or perhaps simply forgotten to tell Luman that he was to be my guide? I decided after a couple of days that I'd seek him out for myself, and tell him how badly I wanted to get on with my work, but that I couldn't do so; not until I knew the stories Cesaria had told me I could not even guess at.

Luman, as I've said, does not live in the main house, though Lord knows it has enough rooms, empty rooms, to accommodate several families. He chooses instead to live in what was once the Smoke House; a modest building, which he claims suits him better. I had not until this visit ever come within fifty yards of the building, much less entered it; he has always been fiercely protective of his isolation.

My mounting irritation made me bold, however. So I had Dwight take me to the place, wheeling me down what had once been a pleasant path, but which was now thickly overgrown. The air became steadily danker; in places it swarmed with mosquitoes. I lit up a cigar to keep them at bay, which I doubt worked, but a good cigar always gets me a little high, so I cared rather less that they were making a meal of me.

As we approached the door I saw that it was open a little way, and that somebody was moving around inside. Luman knew I was here; which probably meant he also knew *why* I called out to him.

"Luman? It's Maddox! Is it all right if Dwight brings me in? I'd like to have a little talk!"

"We got nothing to talk about," came the reply out of the murky interior.

"I beg to differ."

Now Luman's face appeared at the partially opened door. He looked thoroughly rattled, like a man who'd just stepped away from not one but several excesses. His wide, tawny face was shiny with sweat, his pupils pinpricks, his cornea yellowed. His beard looked as though it hadn't been trimmed, or indeed even washed, in several weeks.

"Jesus, man," he growled, "can't you just let it be?"

"Did you speak to Cesaria?" I asked him.

He ran his hand through his mane and tugged it back from his head so violently it looked like an act of masochism. Those pinprick eyes of his suddenly grew to the size of quarters. This was a parlor trick I'd never seen him perform before; I was so startled I all but cried out. I stifled the yelp, however. I didn't want him thinking he had the upper hand here. There was too much of the mad dog about him. If he sensed fear in me, I was certain he'd at very least drive me from his door. And at worst? Who knew what a creature like this could do if he set his perverse mind to it? Just about anything, probably.

"Yes," he said finally, "she spoke to me. But I don't think you need to be seeing the stuff she wants you to see. It ain't your business."

"She thinks it is."

"Huh."

"Look, can we at least have this conversation out of the way of the mosquitoes?"

"You don't like bein' bit?" he said, with a nasty little grin. "Oh I like to get naked an' have 'em at me. Gets me goin'."

Perhaps he hoped he'd repulse me with this, and I'd leave, but I was not about to be so easily removed. I simply stared at him.

"Do you have any more of them cigars?"

I had indeed come prepared. Not only did I have cigars, I had gin, and, by way of more intellectual seduction, a small pamphlet on madhouses from my collection. Many years before Luman had spent some months incarcerated in Utica, an institution in upstate New York. A century later (so Marietta told me) he was still obsessed with the business of how a sane man might be thought mad, and a madman put in charge of Congress. I dug first for the cigar, as he'd requested it.

"Here," I said.

"Is it Cuban?"

"Of course."

"Toss it to me."

"Dwight can bring it."

"No. Toss it."

I gently lobbed the cigar in his direction. It fell a foot shy of the threshold. He bent down and picked it up, rolling it between his fingers and sniffing it.

"This is nice," he said appreciatively. "You keep a humidor?"

"Yes. In this humidity—"

"Got to, got to," he said, his tone distinctly warming. "Well then," he said, "you'd better get your sorry ass in here."

"It's all right if Dwight carries me in?"

"As long as he leaves," Luman said. Then to Dwight: "No offense. But this is between my half-brother and me."

"I understand," said Dwight, and picking me up out of my wheel-chair carried me to the door, which Luman now hauled open. A wave of stinking heat hit me; like the stench of a pigpen in high summer.

"I like it rank," Luman said by way of explanation. "It reminds me of the old country."

I didn't reply to him; I was too—I don't know quite what the word is—astonished, perhaps appalled, by the state of the interior.

"Sit him down on the ol' crib there," Luman said, pointing to a peculiar bed-cum-coffin set close to the hearth. Worse than the crib itself—which looked more like an instrument of torture than a place of repose—was the fact that the hearth was far from cold: a large, smoky fire was burning there. It was little wonder Luman was sweating so profusely.

"Will this be all right?" Dwight said to me, plainly concerned for my well-being.

"I'll be fine," I said. "I could do with losing the weight."

"That you could," Luman said. "You need to get fightin' fit. We all do."

He had lit a match, and with the care of a true connoisseur, was slowly coaxing his cigar to life. "My," he said, "this *is* nice. I surely do appreciate a good bribe, brother. It's a sign o' good breedin', when a man knows how to offer a good bribe."

"Speaking of which . . ." I said. "Dwight. The gin."

Dwight set the bottle of gin on the table, which was as thickly strewn with detritus as every other inch of Luman's hellhole.

"Well that's mighty kind of you," Luman said.

"And this—"

"My, my, the presents jus' keep comin', don't they?" I gave him the book. "What's this now?" He looked at the cover. "Oh, this is *interestin'*, brother." He flipped through the book, which was amply illustrated. "I wonder if there's a picture of my li'l ol' crib."

"This came from an asylum?" I said, looking down at the bed on which Dwight had set me.

"It sure did. I was chained up in that for two hundred and fifty-five nights."

"Inside it?"

"Inside it."

He came over to where I sat and tugged the filthy blanket out from under me, so I could better see the cruel narrow box in which he had been put. The restraints were still in place.

"Why do you keep it?" I asked him.

"As a reminder," he said, meeting my gaze head-on for the first time since I'd entered. "I can't ever let myself forget, 'cause the moment I forget then I've as good as forgiven them that did it to me, and I ain't never going to do that."

"But—"

"I know what you're going to say: they're all dead. And so they are. But that don't mean I can't still get my day with 'em, when the Lord calls us all to judgment. I'm going to be sniffin' after 'em like the mad dog they said I was. I'm going to have their souls, and there ain't no saint in Heaven's goin' to stop me." His volume and vehemence had steadily escalated through this speech; when it was done I said nothing for a moment or two, so as to let him calm down. Then I said:

"Seems to me you've got reason to keep the crib."

He grunted by way of reply. Then he went over to the table and sat on the chair beside it. "Don't you wonder sometimes . . . ?" he began.

"Wonder what?"

"Why one of us gets put in a madhouse an' another gets to be a cripple an' another gets to go 'round the world fuckin' every beautiful woman he sets his eyes on."

This last, of course, was Galilee; or at least the Galilee of family myth: the wanderer, pursuing his unattainable dreams from ocean to ocean.

"Well don't you wonder?" Luman said again.

"Now and again."

"See, things ain't fair. That's why people go crazy. That's why they get guns and kill their kids. Or end up in chains. Things ain't fair!" He was beginning to shout again.

"If I may say . . ."

"Say what the fuck you like!" he replied, "I want to hear, brother."

". . . we're luckier than most."

"How'd you reckon that?"

"We're a special family. We've got . . . *you've* got talents most people would kill to have . . ."

"Sure I can fuck a woman then make her forget I ever laid a finger on her. Sure I can listen in on one snake's sayin' to another. Sure I got a Momma who used to be one of the all time great ladies and a Poppa who knew Jesus. So what? They still put me in chains. And I still thought I deserved it, 'cause in my heart I thought I was a worthless sonofabitch." His voice dropped to a whisper. "An' that ain't really changed."

This silenced me utterly. Not just the flow of images (Luman listening to snakes? My father as a confidante of Christ?) but the sheer desperation in Luman's voice.

"We ain't none of us what we should've been, brother," he said. "We ain't none of us done a thing worth callin' important, an' now it's all over, and we ain't never goin' to *have* that chance."

"So let me write about *why.*"

"Oh . . . I knew we'd get back to that sooner or later," Luman replied. "There ain't no use in writin' no book, brother. It's just goin' to make us look like losers. 'Cept Galilee, of course. He'll look fine an' fancy an' I'll look like a fuckwit."

"I'm not here to beg," I said. "If you don't want to help me then I'll just go back to Mama—"

"If you can find her."

"—I'll find her. And I'll just ask her to have Marietta show me the sights instead of you."

"She doesn't trust Marietta," Luman said, getting up and crossing to crouch in front of the fire. "She trusts me because I've stayed here. I've been loyal." His lip curled. "Loyal like a dog," he said. "Stayed in my kennel and guarded her little empire."

"Why do you stay out here?" I asked him. "There's so much room in the house."

"I hate the house. It's entirely too civilized. I find I can't catch my breath in there."

"Is that why you don't want to help me? You don't want to go in the house?"

"Oh, shit," he said, apparently resigned to this torment, "if I have to I have to. I'll take you up, if you want to go that badly."

"Up where?"

"To the dome, of course. But once I've done that, buddy, you're on your own. I ain't staying with you. Not in that place."

# VII

Ibegan to see that one of the curses of the Barbarossa family is self-pity. There's Luman in his Smoke House, plotting his revenge against dead men; me in my library, determined that life had done me a terrible disservice; Zabrina in her own loneliness, fat with candy. Even Galilee—out there under a limitless sky—writing me melancholy letters about the aimlessness of his life. It was pathetic. We, who were the blessed fruit of such an extraordinary tree. How did we all end up bemoaning the fact of living, instead of finding purpose in that fact? We didn't deserve what we'd been given: our glamours, our skills, our visions. We'd frittered them all away while we bemoaned our lot.

Was it too late to change all of that, I wondered? Was there still a chance for four ungrateful children to rediscover why we'd been created?

Only Marietta, it seemed to me, had escaped the curse, and she'd done so by reinventing herself. I saw her often, coming back from her visits to the world, dressed like a trucker sometimes in low-slung jeans and a dirty shirt, sometimes like a torch-song singer in a slinky dress; sometimes barely dressed at all, running across the lawn as the sun came up, her skin as dewy as the grass.

Oh Lord, what am I admitting to? Well, it's said; for better or worse. To my list of sins (which isn't as long as I'd like it to be) I must now append *incestuous desires*.

Luman had arranged to come and fetch me at ten. He was late, of course. When he finally turned up, he had the last inch of his havana between his teeth, and the last inch of gin left in the bottle. I suspect he didn't indulge himself with hard liquor very often, because he was much the worse for wear.

"Are you ready?" he slurred.

"More than ready."

"Did you bring something to eat and drink?"

"What do I need food for?"

"You're going to be in there a long time. That's why."

"You make it sound like I'm being locked up."

Luman leered at me, as though he was making up his mind

whether to be cruel or not. "Don't be shittin' yourself," he said finally. "The door'll be open all the time, you just won't feel like leaving. It's very addictive once you get going." With that he started off down the passageway, leaving me to trundle behind him.

"Don't go too fast," I told him.

"Afraid of gettin' lost in the dark?" he said, "Brother, you are one nervous son of a bitch."

I wasn't afraid of the dark, but there was good reason to be concerned about getting lost. We turned a couple of corners and I was in a passageway I was pretty certain I'd never visited before, though I'd thought myself familiar with the entire house, barring Cesaria's chambers. Another corner, and another, and a passageway, and a small empty room, and another, and another, and now I knew this was unknown terrain. If Luman decided to play the mischief maker and leave me here, I doubted I could find my way back to anywhere familiar.

"You smell the air here?"

"Stale."

"Dead. Nobody comes here, you see. Not even *her*."

"Why not?"

"Because it fucks with your head," he said, casting a glance back in my direction. I could barely see his expression in the musk, but I'm certain he had that yellow-toothed leer back on his face. "Of course, you're a saner man than I ever was, so maybe it won't bother you so much 'cause you got better control of your wits. On the other hand . . . maybe you'll crack, and I'll have to put you in my li'l crib for the night, so's you don't do yourself harm."

I brought the chair to a halt. "You know what?" I said. "I've changed my mind."

"You can't do that," Luman said.

"I'm telling you I don't want to go in there."

"Well ain't this a flip-flop, huh? First I don't want to take you, and now I brought you here, you don't want to go. Make up your fuckin' mind."

"I'm not going to risk my sanity," I said.

Luman drained the gin bottle. "I can see that," he said. "I mean, a man in your condition ain't got but his mind, right? You lose that you ain't got nothin'." He came a step or two toward me. "On the other hand," he said, "if you don't go in, you ain't got no book, so it's a kind of toss-up." He lobbed the gin bottle from hand to hand, and back again, to illustrate his point. "Book. Mind. Book. Mind. It's up to you."

I hated him at that moment; simply because what he said was true. If he left me under the dome and I lost my sanity, I wouldn't be capable of putting words in any sensible order. On the other hand, if I didn't risk the lunacy, and I simply wrote from what I already knew, wouldn't I always wonder how much richer, how much *truer*, my work would have been if I'd had the courage to see what the room had to show me?

"It's your choice," he said.

"What would you do?"

"You're asking me?" Luman said, sounding genuinely surprised at my interest in his opinion. "Well it ain't pretty being mad," he said. "It ain't pretty at all. But the way I see it, we don't have a lot of time left. This house ain't goin' to stand forever, an' when it comes down, whatever you might see in there . . ." he pointed along the passageway ahead of me, towards the stairs that led up to the dome ". . . is going to be lost. You won't be seeing no more visions when this house falls. None of us will."

I stared at the passageway.

"I guess that's my answer then," I said.

"So you're goin' to go in?"

"I'm goin' to go in."

Luman smiled. "Hold on," he said. Then he did a remarkable thing. He picked up the wheelchair, with me in it, and carried us both up the stairs. I held my breath, afraid he was either going to drop me, or topple back down the flight. But we reached the top without incident. There was a narrow landing, and a single door.

"I'm goin' to leave you here," Luman said.

"This is as far as you go?"

"You know how to open a door," he said.

"What happens when I get inside?"

"You'll find you know that too." He laid his hand on my shoulder. "If you need anything, just call."

"You'll be here?"

"It depends how the mood takes me," he said, and sauntered off down the stairs. I wanted to call him back; but I was out of delaying tactics. Time to do this, if I was going to do it.

I wheeled my way to the door, glancing back once to see if Luman was still in sight. He'd gone. I was on my own. I took a deep breath, and grasped the door handle. There was still a corner of me that hoped the door was locked and I'd be denied entry. But the handle turned, and the door opened—almost too readily, I thought, as though some overeager host stood on the other side, ready to usher me in.

I had some idea of what I thought lay on the other side, at least architecturally speaking. The dome room—or "sky room" as Jefferson had dubbed his version at Monticello—was, I'd been told by Marietta (who'd crept up there once to do the deed with a girlfriend) a somewhat strange but beautiful room. At Monticello it had apparently been used as a child's playroom, because it was hard to access (a design deficiency which also applied to L'Enfant) but here, Marietta had told me, there was a whisper of unease in the room; no child would have been happy playing there. Though there were eight windows, after the Monticellian model, and a skylight, the place seemed to her "a little on the twitchy side," whatever that meant.

I was about to find out. I pushed the door wide with my foot, half-expecting birds or bats to fly in my face. But the room was deserted. There was not so much as a single piece of furniture to spoil its absolute simplicity. Just the starlight, coming in from nine apertures.

"Luman," I murmured to myself, "you sonofabitch . . ."

He'd prepared me for something fearful; a delirium, an assault of visions so violent it might put me out of my wits. But there was nothing here but murk and more murk.

I ventured in a couple of yards, looking everywhere for a reason to be afraid. But there was nothing. I pressed on, with a mingling of disappointment and relief. There was nothing to fear in here. My sanity was perfectly secure.

Unless, of course, I was being lulled into a false sense of security. I glanced back toward the door. It was still open; still solid. And beyond it the landing where I'd stood with Luman, and debated the wisdom of coming in here. What an easy mark I'd made; he must have been thoroughly entertained at the sight of my discomfort! Cursing him again, I took my eyes from the door and returned them to the murk. This time, however, much to my astonishment, I discovered that the sky room was not *quite* as empty as I'd thought. A few yards from me—at the place where the lights of the nine windows intersected—there was a skittering pattern in the gloom, so subtle I was not certain at first it was even real. I kept staring at it, resisting the urge to blink for fear that it would vanish. But it remained before me, intensifying a little. I wheeled my way toward it; slowly, slowly, like a hunter closing on his quarry, fearful of alarming it into flight. But it didn't retreat. Nor did it become any the less mystifying. My approach had become less tentative now; I was very soon at the center of the room, directly under the skylight. The patterns were in the air all around me; so subtle I was still not absolutely certain I was ever seeing them. I looked up to my zenith: I could see stars through the skylight, but nothing that would be likely to create these shifting shadows. Returning my gaze to the walls, I went from one window to the next, looking for some explanation there. But I found none.

There was a little wash of light through each of them, but no sign of motion—a wind-stirred branch, a bird fluttering on a sill. Whatever was creating this shifting shadow was here in the room with me. As I finished my study of the windows, muttering to myself in confusion, I had the uncomfortable sense my befuddlement was being watched. Again, I looked toward the door, thinking maybe Luman had crept back to spy on me. But no; the landing was deserted.

Well, I thought, there's no use my sitting here, getting dizzy and paranoid. I may as well spit out my reasons for coming, and see if that elicited some response.

I drew an anxious breath, and spoke.

"I came . . . I came to see the past," I said. My voice sounded tiny, like a child's voice. "Cesaria sent me," I added, thinking that might help whatever forces occupied the room understand that I was a legitimate presence, and that if they had something to show me, they should damned well do it.

Something that I'd said—whether it was talking about the past or about Cesaria I can't say—brought a response. The shadows seemed to darken around me, and their motion grew more complex. Some portion of the pattern twitched like a living thing, and rose up in front of me—up, up toward the skylight. Another flew off toward the wall at my left, trailing more fragments of dark air, whipping like the tail of a kite. A third dropped to the polished boards and spread across the floor.

I believe I breathed some words of astonishment. "Oh my Lord," or some such. I had reason. The spectacle was growing by the moment, the writhing motions of these shadows, and their scale, expanding as if by some logarithmic progression. Motion was inspiring motion; forms were inspiring forms. In the space of perhaps forty-five seconds the walls of the dome room had been all but eclipsed by these roiling abstractions; gray on gray, yet filled with subtle intimations of visions to come. My eyes were darting everywhere, of course, astonished by all this, but even as my gaze went on from one cloudy cluster of shapes to the next, it moved with the impression that something was *almost* visible here. That I was moments away from understanding how these abstractions worked.

And yet, even in their protean condition they moved me. Watching these roilings and cavortings I began to understand why Luman had been so reluctant to enter this room. He was a man of great vulnerability, despite his manner: there was simply too much *feeling* here for a soul so tender. Watching the unfolding spectacle, I felt as though I were listening to a piece of music; or rather several at the same time.

Those grand shapes moving overhead, like columns of smoke passing across the sun had all the gravity of a requiem; while the forms that moved close to me reeled and swaggered as though to a drunken polka. And in between, circling me as they climbed, were sinuous ropes of ether that seemed to express lovely, rising music, like the bright line of a rhapsody.

To say I was enchanted does not begin to express my beguilement. It was all so perfectly mysterious: a seduction of eye and heart that left me close to tears. But I was not so enthralled that I didn't wonder what powers lay so far undisclosed. I had invited this vision with my own readiness to accept it. Now it was time to do the same thing again; to open my spirit, as it were, a little wider, and see what the shadows would show me.

"*I'm ready*," I said softly, "whenever you are . . ."

The forms before me continued to profligate, but made no visible response to my invitation. There was still a sense of evolution in their motion, but I sensed that it had slowed. I was no longer seeing the heart-quickening changes that had astonished me a minute or two before.

Again, I spoke. "I'm not afraid," I said.

Did I ever say anything so foolish in my life as to boast fearlessness in such a place as this?

The words were no sooner out of my mouth than the shadows before me convulsed, as though some seismic shock had shaken the dome. Two or three seconds later, like thunder coming a heartbeat after lightning, the shock wave struck the only nonethereal form in the room, which is to say, myself. My chair was propelled backward, tipping over as it went. I vainly tried to regain some measure of control, but the chair sped over the boards, its wheels shrieking, and struck the wall close to the door with such violence that I was pitched out of it.

I felt something crack as I landed face down, and the breath was completely knocked out of my body. Had I possessed the wherewithal I might have attempted a plea for clemency at that moment; might have attempted to withdraw my too-brave words. But I doubt it would have availed me much.

Gasping, I tried to haul myself up into a semirecumbent position so that I could find out where my chair had landed. But there was a sharp pain in my side. I'd plainly snapped a rib. I gave up trying to move, for fear of doing myself still greater damage.

All I could do was lie where I'd been so unceremoniously dropped, and wait for the room to do its work. I had invited the powers here to show me their splendors, and I was quite certain they weren't about to deny themselves the pleasure.

# VIII

Nothing happened. I lay there, my breaths quick and shallow, my stomach ready to revolt, my body sticky with sweat, and the room just waited. The unfixable forms all around me—which had by now entirely blotted out every detail of windows and walls, even carpeted the floor—were almost still, their evolutionary endeavors at an end, at least for the moment.

Had the fact that I'd been injured shocked the presence, or presences, here into reticence, I wondered? Perhaps they felt they'd overstepped the bounds of enthusiasm, and now wanted nothing more than for me to crawl away and tend my wounds? Were they waiting for me to call down to Luman, perhaps? I thought about doing so, but decided against it. This was not a room in which to speak a simple word unless it was strictly necessary. I would be better lying still and quiet, I decided, and let my panicked body calm itself. Then, once I had governed myself, I would try to crawl back to the door. Sooner or later, Luman would come up and fetch me; I felt certain of that. Even if I had to wait all night.

Meanwhile I closed my eyes so as to put the images around me out of the way. Though the pain in my side was by now only a dull throb, my head and eyes were throbbing too; indeed it was not hard to imagine my body had become one fat heart, lying discarded on the floor, pumping its last.

*I'm not afraid* I'd boasted, moments before the bolt had struck me. But now? Oh, I was very much afraid now. Afraid that I would die here, before I'd worked my way through the catalog of unfinished business that sat at the back of my skull, awaiting my attention and of course never getting it, while all the time growing and growing. Well, it was most likely too late; there would not be time for me to flagellate myself for every dishonorable deed in that list, nor any chance to make good the harms I'd done. Minor harms, to be sure, in the scheme of things; but large enough to regret.

And then, on the back of my neck, a touch; or what I believed to be a touch.

"Luman?" I murmured, and opened my eyes.

It wasn't Luman; it wasn't even a human touch, or anything resembling a human touch. It was some presence in the shadows; or the shadows themselves. They had swarmed upon me while my eyes were closed, and were now pressing close, their intimacy in no way threatening, but curiously *tender*. It was as though these roiling, senseless forms were concerned for my well-being, the way they brushed my nape, my brow, my lips. I stayed absolutely still, holding my breath, half expecting their mood to change and their consolations to turn into something crueler. But no; they simply waited, close upon me.

Relieved, I drew breath. And in the instant of drawing, knew I had again unwittingly done something of consequence.

On the intake I felt the marked air about my head rush toward my open lips, and down my throat. I had no choice but to let it in. By the time I knew what was happening it was too late to resist. I was a vessel being filled. I could feel the marks on my tongue, against my tonsils, in my windpipe—

Nor did I want to choke them off, once I felt them inside me. At their entrance the pain in my side seemed instantly to recede, as did the throbbing in my head and eyes. The fear of a lonely demise here went out of my head and I was removed—in one breath—from despair to pleasurable ease.

What a maze of manipulations this chamber contained! First banality, then a blow, then this opiated bliss. I would be foolish, I knew, to believe that it did not have more tricks in its repertoire. But while it was content to give me some relief from my pains I was happy to take what was offered. Greedy for it, indeed. I gulped at the air, drawing in great draughts of it. And with every breath I felt further removed from my pain. Nor was it just the hurt in my flank and the throb in my head that was becoming remote; there was a much older ache—a dull, wretched pain that haunted the dead terrain of my lower limbs—that was now, for the first time in almost two human spans, relieved. It wasn't, I think, that the pain was taken away; only that I no longer knew it as pain. Need I say I gladly banished it from my mind, sobbing gratitude to be relieved of an agony that had attended me so closely I'd forgotten how profound a hurt it was?

And with its passing my eyes—which were more acute than I could ever remember their being, even in my youth—found a new sight to astonish them. The air that I was expelling from my lungs had a bright solidity of its own; it came from me filled with flecks of delicate brilliance, as though a fire was stoked in me, and I was breathing out shards of flame. Was this some representation of my pain, I wondered? The room—or my own delirium's—way of demonstrating the expulsion? That theory floated for ten seconds, then it was gone. The motes were about to show me their true nature, and it had nothing to do with pain.

They were still flowing from my mouth with every breath, but I wasn't watching those I'd just exhaled. It was those that had flown from me first which drew my startled sight. They were seeding their luminescence in the shadows—disappeared into the cloudy bed around me. I watched with what I'd like to think was almost scientific detachment. There was a certain logic to all that happened to me here; or so I now supposed. The shadows were only half the equation: they were a site of possibilities, no more than that; the fertile mud of this chamber, waiting for some galvanizing spark to bring forth—to bring forth *what?*

That was the question. What did the marriage of fire and shadow want to show me?

I didn't have to wait more than twenty seconds to discover the answer. No sooner had the first of the motes embedded themselves than the shadows surrendered their uncertainty, and blossomed.

The limits of the dome room had been banished. When the visions came—*and oh, how they came!*—they were vast.

First, out of the shadows, a landscape. The most primal of landscapes, in fact: rock and fire, and a flowing mass of magma. It was like the beginning of the world; red and black. It took me only a moment to make sense of this scene. The next, I was besieged with images, the scene before me transforming with every beat of my heart. Something flowered from the fire, gold and green, rising into a smoky sky. As it rose the blossoms it bore became fruit, and fell back onto the laval ground. I didn't have time to watch them be consumed. A motion in the smoke off to my right drew my gaze. An animal of some kind—with pale, scarred flanks—galloped through my field of vision. I felt the violence of its hooves in my bowels. And before it had passed from sight came another, and another, then a herd of these beasts—not horses, but something close to them. Had I made these creatures? I wondered. Had I exhaled them with my pain; and the fire too, and the rock and tree that rose from the rock? Was all this my invention, or perhaps some remote memory, which the enchantments of the room had somehow made visible?

Even as I shaped that thought the pale herd changed direction and came pounding at me. I instinctively covered my head, to keep my brains from being beaten out. But for all the fury of their hooves, the passage of the herd did me no more harm than a light breeze; they passed over me, and away.

I looked up. In the few seconds I'd had my eyes averted the ground had given prodigious birth. There were now sights to be seen on every side. Close by me, sliding through the very air from which it was being carved, a snake came, bright as a flower. Before it was even finished with its own creation another creature snatched it up, and my eyes rose to find before me a form that was vaguely human, but winged and sleek. The snake was gone in an instant, swallowed down the throat of this thing, which then settled its fiery eyes on me as though wondering if I too were edible. Plainly I looked like poor fare. Pumping its massive wings the creature rose like a curtain to reveal another drama, stranger still, behind it.

The tree I'd seen born had spread its seeds in every direction. In a few seconds a forest had sprung up, its churning canopy as dark as a thunderhead. And flitting between the trees were all manner of creatures, rising to nest, falling to rot. Close by me, an antelope stood in the dapple, shitting itself in terror. I looked for the cause. There; a few yards from the creature, something moved between the trees. I glimpsed only the glint off its eye, or tooth, until it suddenly broke cover, and came at its prey in one vast bound. A tiger, the size of four or five men. The antelope made to dart away, but its hunter was too fast. The tiger's claws sank into the antelope's silken flank and finished its leap with its prey beneath it. The death wasn't quick or pretty. The antelope thrashed wildly, though its body was torn wide open, and the tiger was tearing out its stringy throat. I didn't look away. I watched until the antelope was steaming meat, and the tiger sank down to dine. Only then did my eyes wander in search of new distractions.

There was something bright between the trees, I saw; brighter by the moment. Like a fire in its appetite, it climbed through the canopy as it approached, its advance above outpacing its steadier progress below. There was chaos in the thicket, as every species—hunter and hunted alike—fled before the blaze. But above me there was no escape. The fire came too fast, consuming birds in their flight, the chicks in their nests, monkeys and squirrels on the bough. Countless corpses fell around me, blackened and smoking. White hot ash came with them, powdering the ground.

I wasn't in fear for my life. By now I knew enough about this place to be confident of my immunity. But the scene appalled me nevertheless. What was I witnessing? Some primal cataclysm that had scoured this world? Undone it from sky to ground? If so, what was its source? This was no natural disaster, I was certain of that. The blaze above me had made itself into a kind of roof, creating in the moment of destruction a fretted vault, in which the dying were immortalized in fire. Tears started into my eyes, the sight moved me so. I reached to brush them out, so as not to miss whatever new glories or horrors were imminent, and as I did so I heard in my heart the first human utterance—other than my own noise—to come my way since I'd entered this chamber.

It was not a word; or if it was it was no word I knew. But it had meaning; at least that was my belief. To my ear it sounded like an open-throated shout raised by some newborn soul in the midst of the blaze; a yell of celebration and defiance. *Here I am!* it seemed to say. *Now we begin!*

I raised myself up on my hands to see if I could find the shouter (whether it was man or woman I couldn't yet decide) but the rain of ash and detritus was like a veil before me: I could see almost nothing through it.

My arms could not support me for more than a few moments. But as I sank back down to the ground, frustrated, the fire overhead—having perhaps exhausted its fuel—went out. The ash ceased falling. And there, standing no more than twenty yards from where I lay, the blaze surrounding her like a vast, fiery flower, was Cesaria. There was nothing about her attitude or her expression that suggested the fire threatened her. Far from it. She seemed rather to be luxuriating in its touch; her hands moving over her body as the conflagration bathed it, as though to be certain its balm penetrated every pore. Her hair, which was even blacker than her skin, flickered and twitched; her breasts seeped milk, her eyes ran silvery tears, her sex, which now and then she fingered, issued streams of blood.

I wanted to look away, but I couldn't. She was too exquisite, too ripe. It seemed to me that all I had seen before me in the last little while—the laval ground, the tree and its fruit, the pale herd, the hunted antelope and the tiger that took it; even the strange, winged creature that had briefly appeared in my vision—all of these were *in* and *of* the woman before me. She was their maker and their slaughterer; the sea into which they flowed and the rock from which they'd sprung.

I'd seen enough, I decided. I'd drunk down all I could bear to drink, and still keep my sanity. It was time I turned my back on these visions, and retreated to the safety of the mundane. I needed time to assimilate what I'd seen—and the thoughts that the sights had engendered.

But retreat was no easy business. Ungluing my eyes from the sight of my father's wife was hard enough; but when I did so, and looked back toward the door, I could not find it. The illusion surrounded me on every side; there was no hint of the real remaining. For the first time since the visions had begun I remembered Luman's talk of madness, and I was seized with panic. Had I carelessly let my hold on sanity slip, without even noticing that I'd done so? Was I now adrift in this illusion with no solid ground left for my senses?

I remembered with a shudder the crib in which Luman had been bound; and the look of unappeasable rage in his eyes. Was that all that lay before me now? A life without certainty, without solidity; this forest a prison I'd breathed into being, and that other world, where I'd been real and in my wounded fashion content, now a dream of freedom to which I could not return?

I closed my eyes to shut out the illusion. Like a child in terror, I prayed.

*"Oh Lord God in Heaven, look down on your servant at this moment; I beg of you . . . I need you with me.*

*"Help me. Please. Take these things out of my head. I don't want them, Lord. I don't want them."*

Even as I whispered my prayer I felt a rush of energies against me. The blaze between the trees, which had come to a halt a little distance from me, was on the move again. I hastened my prayer, certain that if the fire was coming for me, then so was Cesaria.

*"Save me, Lord—"*

She was coming to silence me. That was my sudden conviction. She was a part of my insanity and she was coming to hush the words I'd uttered to defend myself against it.

*"Lord, please hear me—"*

The energies intensified, as though they intended to snatch the words away from my lips.

*"Quickly, Lord, quickly! Show me the way out of here! Please! God in Heaven, help me!"*

"Hush . . ." I heard Cesaria say. She was right behind me. It seemed to me I could feel the small hairs at the nape of my neck fizzle and fry. I opened my eyes and looked over my shoulder. There she was, still cocooned in fire, her dark flesh shining. My mouth was suddenly parched; I could barely speak.

"I want . . ."

"I know," she said softly. "I know. I know. Poor child. Poor lost child. You want your mind back."

"Yes . . ." I said. I was close to sobbing.

"But here it is," she said. "All around you. The trees. The fire. Me. All of it's *yours.*"

"No," I protested. "I've never been in this place before."

"But it's been in you. This is where your father came looking for me, an age ago. He dreamed it into you when you were born."

"Dreamed it into me . . ." I said.

"Every sight, every feeling. All he was and all he knew and all he knew was to come . . . it's in your blood and in your bowels."

"Then why am I so afraid of it?"

"Because you've held on to a simpler self for so long, you think you're the sum of what you can hold in your hands. But there are other hands holding you, child. Filled with you, these hands. Brimming with you . . ."

Did I dare believe any of this?

Cesaria replied as though she'd heard the doubt spoken aloud.

"I can't reassure you," she said. "Either you trust that these visions are a greater wisdom than you've ever known, or you try to rid yourself of them, and fall again."

"Fall where?"

"Why back into your own hands, of course," she said. Was she amused by me? By my tears and my trembling? I believe she was. But then I couldn't blame her; there was a part of me that also thought I was ridiculous, praying to a God I'd never seen, in order to escape the sight of glories a man of faith would have wept to witness. But I was afraid. Over and over I came back to that: *I was afraid.*

"Ask your question," Cesaria said. "You have a question. Ask it."

"It sounds so childish."

"Then have your answer and move on. But first you have to ask it."

"Am I . . . safe?"

"Safe?"

"Yes. Safe."

"In your flesh? No. I can't guarantee your safety in the flesh. But in your immortal form? Nothing and nobody can unbeget you. If you fall through your own fingers, there's other hands to hold you. I've told you that already."

"And . . . I think I believe you," I said.

"So then," Cesaria said, "you have no reason not to let the memories come."

She reached out toward me. Her hand was covered with countless snakes: as fine as hairs but brilliantly colored, yellow and red and blue, weaving their way between her fingers like living jewelry.

"Touch me," she said.

I looked up at her face, which wore an expression of sweet calm, and then back at the hand she wanted me to take.

"Don't be afraid," she said to me. "They don't bite."

I reached up and took her hand. She was right, the snakes didn't bite. But they *swarmed;* over her fingers and onto mine, squirming across the back of my hand and up onto my arm. I was so distracted by the sight of them that I didn't realize that she was pulling me up off the ground until I was almost standing up. I say *standing* though I can't imagine how that's possible; my legs were, until that moment, incapable of supporting me. Even so I found myself on my feet, gripping her hand, my face inches from her own.

I don't believe I had ever stood so close to my father's wife before. Even when I was a child, brought from England and accepted as her stepson, she always kept a certain distance from me. But now I stood (or seemed to stand) with my face inches from her own, feeling the snakes still writhing up my arm, but no longer caring to look down at them: not when I had the sight of her face before me. She was flawless. Her skin, for all its darkness, was possessed of an uncanny luminescence, her gaze, like her mouth, both lush and forbidding. Strands of her hair were lifted by gusts off the blaze around us (to the heat of which I seemed invulnerable) and brushed against my cheek. Their touch, though it was light, was nevertheless profoundly sensual. Feeling it, and seeing her exquisite features, I could not help but imagine what it would be like to be received into her arms. To kiss her, to lie with her, to put a child into her. It was little wonder my father had obsessed on her to his dying day, though all manner of argument and disappointment had soured the love between them.

"So now . . ." she said.

"Yes?" I swear I would have done anything for her at that moment. I was like a lover standing before his beloved; I could deny her nothing.

"Take it back . . ." she said.

I didn't comprehend what she was telling me. "Take what back?" I said.

"The breath. The pain. Me. Take it all back. It belongs to you Maddox. *Take it back.*"

I understood. It was time to repossess all that I'd attempted to put away from myself: the visions that were a part of my blood, though I'd hidden them from myself; the pain that was also, for better or worse, mine. And of course the very air from my lungs, whose expulsion had begun this journey.

"*Take it back.*"

I wanted to beg a few moments' grace, to talk with her, perhaps; at least to gaze at her, before my body was returned into its agony. But she was already easing her fingers from my grip.

"*Take it back,*" she said a third time, and to be certain I obeyed her edict she put her face close to mine and drew a breath of her own, a breath so swift and strong it emptied my mouth, throat and lungs in an instant.

My head reeled; white blotches burnt at the corners of my vision, threatening to occlude the sight before me. But my body acted with a vigor of its own, and without instruction from my will, did as Cesaria had demanded: it took the breath back.

The effect was immediate, and to my enchanted eyes distressing. The fabled face in front of me dissolved as though it had been conjured out of mist and my needy lungs had unmade it. I looked up— hoping to snatch a glimpse of the ancient sky before it too dissolved, but I was too late.

What had seemed unquestionably real moments before came to nothing in a heartbeat. No; not to nothing. It unknitted into marks such as had haunted the air when I'd first entered the room. Some of them still carried traces of color. There were smudges of blue and white above, and around me, where the thicket had not been consumed by fire, a hundred kinds of green; and ahead of me glints of gold from the flame and scarlet-flecked darkness where my father's wife had stood. But even these remains evaporated in the next heartbeat, and I was back in the arena of gray on gray which I had mistaken for a maze of stained walls.

All of the events that had just unfolded might have seemed a fiction but for one simple fact: *I was still standing.* Whatever force my mind had unleashed here, it had come with power enough to raise me up off the ground and set me on my feet. And there I stood, amazed; and of course certain I would fall down again at any moment. That moment passed, however; so did the next and the next and the next, and still I stood.

Tentatively I glanced back over my shoulder. There, not six yards from me, was the door through which I'd stepped all these visions ago. Beside it, overturned, lay my wheelchair. I fixed my gaze upon it. Dared I believe it was now redundant?

"Look at you . . ." said a slurred voice.

I glanced back from the wheelchair to the door, where Luman was now leaning. He'd found another source of liquor while I'd been occupied in the room. Not a bottle but a decanter. He had the glazed look of a well-soused man. "You're standing," he said. "When did you learn to do that?"

"I didn't . . ." I said. "I mean, I don't understand why I'm not falling down."

"Can you walk?"

"I don't know. I haven't tried."

"Well, Lordie, man. Try."

I looked down at my feet, which had not taken any instruction from me in a hundred and thirty years. "Go on then," I murmured.

And they moved. Not easily at first, but they moved. First the left, then the right, turning me around to face Luman and the door.

I didn't stop there. I kept moving, my breath quick and fast, my arms stretched before me to break my fall should my legs suddenly give out. But they didn't. Some miracle had occurred when Cesaria had raised me up. Her will, or mine, or both combined, had healed me. I could walk; stride. In time, I would run. I would go all the places I'd not seen in my years in the chair. Out into the swamp, and the roads beyond; to the gardens beyond Luman's Smoke House; to my father's tomb in the empty stables.

But for now, I was happy to reach the door. So happy indeed that I embraced Luman. Tears were coming, and I could not have held them back if I'd cared to.

"Thank you," I said to him.

He was quite happy to accept my embrace. Indeed he returned it with equal fervor, burying his face in my neck. He too was sobbing, though I didn't quite know why. "I don't see what you have to thank me for," he said.

"For making me brave," I said. "For persuading me to go in."

"You don't regret it then?"

I laughed, and took his bleary face in my hands. "No, brother, I do not regret it. Not a moment."

"Were you nearly driven mad?"

"Nearly."

"And you cursed me?"

"Ripely."

"But it was worth the suffering?"

"Absolutely."

He paused, and considered his next question. "Does that mean we can sit down and drink till we puke, like brothers should?"

"It would be my pleasure."

# IX

## i

*What must I do, in the time remaining? Only everything.*
I don't yet know how much I know; but it's a great deal. There are vast tracts of my nature I never knew existed until now. I lived, I sup-

pose, in a cell of my own creation, while outside its walls lay a landscape of unparalleled richness. But I could not bear to venture there. In my self-delusion I thought I was a minor king, and I didn't want to step beyond the bounds of what I knew for fear I lost my dominion. I daresay most of us live in such pitiful realms. It takes something profound to transform us; to open our eyes to our own glorious *diversity*.

Now my eyes were open, and I had no doubt that with my sight came great responsibility. I had to write about what I saw; I had to put it into the words that appear on the very pages you are reading.

But I could bear the weight of that responsibility. Gladly. For now I had the answer to the question: what lay at the center of all the threads of my story? It was myself. I wasn't an abstracted recanter of these lives and loves. I was — *I am* — the story itself; its source, its voice, its music. Perhaps to you that doesn't seem like much of a revelation. But for me, it changes everything. It makes me see, with brutal clarity, the person I once was. It makes me understand for the first time who I am now. And it makes me shake with anticipation of what I must become.

I must tell you not only how the living human world fared, but also how it went among the animals, and among those who had passed from life, yet still wandered the earth. I must tell you about those creatures God made, but also of those who made *themselves* by force of will or appetite. In other words, there must inevitably be unholy business here, just as there will be sacred, but I cannot guarantee to tell you — or even sometimes to know — which is which.

And in my heart I realize I want most to *romance* you; to share with you a vision of the world that puts order where there has been discordance and chaos. Nothing happens carelessly. We're not brought into the world without reason, even though we may never understand that reason. An infant that lives an hour, that dies before it can lay eyes on those who made it, even that soul did not live without purpose: this is my sudden certainty. And it is my duty to sweat until I convince you of the same. Sometimes the stories will recount epic events — wars and insurrection; the fall of dynasties. Sometimes they'll seem, by contrast, inconsequential, and you'll wonder what business they have in these pages. Bear with me. Think of these fragments as the shavings off a carpenter's floor, swept together after some great work has been made. The masterpiece has been taken from the workshop, but what might we learn from a study of some particular curl of wood about the moment of creation? How here the carpenter hesitated, or there moved to complete a form with unerring certainty? Are these shavings then, that seem at first glance redundant, not also part of the great work, being that which has been removed to reveal it?

I won't be staying here at L'Enfant, searching for these shavings. We have great cities to visit: New York and Washington, Paris and London; and further east, and older than any of these, the legendary city of Samarkand, whose crumbling palaces and mosques still welcome travelers on the Silk Road. Weary of cities? Then we'll take to the wilds. To the islands of Hawaii and the mountains of Japan, to forests where the Civil War dead still lie, and stretches of sea no mariner ever crossed. They all have their poetry: the glittering cities and the ruined, the watery wastes and the dusty; I want to show you them all. I want to show you everything.

*Only everything:* prophets, poets, soldiers, dogs, birds, fishes, lovers, potentates, beggars, ghosts. Nothing is beyond my ambition right now, and nothing is beneath my notice. I will attempt to conjure common divinities, and show you the loveliness of filth.

Wait! What am I saying? There's a kind of madness in my pen; promising all this. It's suicidal. I'm bound to fail. But it's what I want to do. Even if I make a wretched fool of myself in the process, it's what I want to do.

I want to show you bliss; my own, amongst others. And I will most certainly show you despair. That I promise you without the least hesitation. Despair so deep it will lighten your heart to discover that others suffer so much more than you do.

And how will it all end? This showing, this failing. Honestly? I don't have the slightest idea.

Sitting here, looking out across the lawn, I wonder how far from the borders of our strange little domain the invading world is. Weeks away? Months away? A year? I don't believe any of us here know the answer to that question. Even Cesaria, with all her powers of prophecy, couldn't tell me how fast the enemy will be upon us. All I know is that they will come. *Must* come, indeed, for everybody's sake. I no longer cling to the idea of this house as a blessed refuge for enchantment. Perhaps it was once that. But it has fallen into decadence; its fine ambitions rotted. Better it be taken apart, hopefully with some measure of dignity; but if not, not.

All I want now is the time to enchant you. After that, I suppose I'm history, just as this house is history. I wouldn't be surprised if we didn't both end up at the bottom of the swamp together. And truth to tell, that prospect doesn't entirely distress me, as long as I've done all I need to do before I go.

*Which is only everything.*

## ii

And so at last I come to the beginning.


What place *is* that? Should I start, perhaps, with Rachel Pallenberg, who was lately married to one of the most handsome and powerful men in America, Mitchell Monroe Geary? Shall I describe her in her sudden desolation, driving around a little town in Ohio, utterly lost, even though this is the place where she was born and raised? Poor Rachel. She has not only left her husband, but several houses and apartments, along with a life that would be considered enviable by all but perhaps one percent of the populous (which percentage already lives that life, and knows it to be largely joyless). Now she has come home only to discover that she doesn't belong here either, which leaves her asking herself: where do I belong?

It's a tempting place to begin. Rachel's so human; her confusions and contradictions are easy to comprehend. But if I begin with her I'm afraid I'm going to get distracted by modernity. I need first to strike a mythic note; to show you something from the distant past, when the world was a living fable.

So, it can't be Rachel I begin with. She'll come into these pages soon enough, but not yet.

It must be Galilee. Of course, it must be Galilee. My Galilee, who has been, and is, so many things: adored boy-child, lover of innumerable women (and a goodly number of men), shipwright, sailor, cowboy, stevedore, pool player and pimp; coward, deceiver and innocent. My Galilee.

I won't begin with one of his great voyages, or one of his notorious romances. I will begin with what happened the day of his baptism. I would not have known any of this before I entered the room beneath the dome. But I know it now, as clearly as my own life. More clearly perhaps, because it's only a day since I walked out of that chamber, and these memories seem to me but a few hours old.

# PART TWO

# The Holy Family

# I

Two souls as old as heaven came down to the shore that ancient noon. They wandered, accompanied by a harmonious baying of wolves, out of the forest which in those days still spread to the very fringes of the Caspian Sea, its thicket so dense and its reputation so dire that no sane individual ventured into it more than a stone's throw. It was not the wolves that people feared meeting between the trees, nor was it bears, nor snakes. It was another order of being entirely; one not made by God; some unforgivable thing that stood to the Creator as a shadow stands to the light.

The locals had legends aplenty about this unholy tribe, though they told them only in whispers, and behind closed doors. Tales of creatures that perched in the branches devouring children they'd tempted out of the sun; or squatted in foetid pools between the trees, adorning themselves with the entrails of murdered lovers. No story-teller along that shore worth his place at the fire failed to invent some new abomination to enrich the stew. Tales begot tales, bred upon one another in ever more perverted form, so that the men, women and children who passed their brief lives in the space between the sea and trees did so in a constant state of fearfulness.

Even at noon, on a day such as this, with the air so clear it rang, and the sky as polished as the flanks of a great fish; even today, in a light so bright no demon would dare show its snout, there was fear.

As proof, let me take you into the company of the four men who were working down at the water's edge that day, mending their nets in preparation for the evening's fishing. All were in a state of unrest; this even before the wolves began their chorus.

The oldest of the fishermen was one Kekmet, a man of nearly forty, though he looked half that again. If he had ever known joy there was no sign of it on his furrowed, leathery face. His warmest expression was a scowl, which he presently wore.

"You're talking through your shithole," he remarked to the youngest of this quartet, a youth called Zelim, who at the tender age of sixteen had already lost his cousin to a miscarriage. Zelim had earned Kekmet's scorn by suggesting that as their lives were so hard here on the shore, perhaps everyone in the village should pack up their belongings, and find a better place to live.

"There's nowhere for us to go," Kekmet told the young man.

"My father saw the city of Samarkand," Zelim replied. "He told me it was like a dream."

"That's exactly what it was," the man working alongside Kekmet said. "If your father saw Samarkand it was in his sleep. Or when he'd had too much wine . . ."

The speaker, whose name was Hassan, raised his own jug of what passed for liquor in this place, a foul-smelling fermented milk he drank from dawn to dusk. He put the jug to his mouth, and tipped it. The filthy stuff overran his lips and dribbled into his greasy beard. He passed the jug to the fourth member of the group, one Baru, a man uncommonly fat by the standards of his peers, and uncommonly ill-tempered. He drank from the jug noisily, then set it down at his side. Hassan made no attempt to reclaim it. He knew better.

"My father . . ." Zelim began again.

"Never went to Samarkand," old Kekmet said, with the weary tone of one who doesn't want to hear the subject at hand spoken of again.

Zelim, however, was not about to allow his dead father's reputation to be impugned this way. He had doted on Old Zelim, who had drowned four springs before, when his boat had capsized in a sudden squall. There was no question, as far as the son was concerned, that if his father claimed he'd seen the numberless glories of Samarkand, then he had.

"One day I'll just get up and go," Zelim said. "And leave you all to rot here."

"In the name of God *go!*" fat Baru replied. "You make my ears ache the way you chatter. You're like a woman."

He'd no sooner spat this insult out than Zelim was on him, pounding Baru's round red face with his fists. There were some insults he was prepared to take from his elders, but this was too much. "I'm no woman!" he yelped, beating his target until blood gushed from Baru's nose.

The other two fishermen simply watched. It happened very seldom that anyone in the village intervened in a dispute. People were allowed to visit upon one another whatever insults and blows they wished; the rest either looked the other way or were glad of the diversion. So what if blood was spilled; so what if a woman was violated? Life went on.

Besides, fat Baru could defend himself. He had a vicious way with him, for all his unruly bulk, and he bucked beneath Zelim so violently the younger man was thrown off him, landing heavily beside one of the boats. Gasping, Baru rolled over on to his knees and came at him afresh.

"I'm going to tear off your balls, you little prick!" he said. "I'm sick of hearing about you and your dog of a father. He was born stupid and he died stupid." As he spoke he reached between Zelim's legs as though to make good on the threat of unmanning, but Zelim kicked out at him, and his bare sole hit the man in his already well-mashed nose. Baru howled, but he wasn't about to be checked. He grabbed hold of Zelim's foot, and twisted it, hard, first to the right, then to the left. He might have broken the young man's ankle—which would have left Zelim crippled for the rest of his life—had his victim not reached into the shallow hull of the boat, and grasped the oar lying there. Baru was too engaged in the task of cracking Zelim's ankle to notice. Grimacing with the effort of his torment, he looked up to enjoy the agony on Zelim's face only to see the oar coming at him. He had no time to duck. The paddle slammed against his face, breaking the half dozen good teeth left in his head. He fell back, letting go of Zelim's leg as he did so, and lay sprawled on the sand with his hands clamped to his wounded face, blood and curses springing from between his fat fingers.

But Zelim hadn't finished with him. The young man got up, yelping when he put weight on his tortured leg. Then, limping over to Baru's prone body, he straddled the man, and sat down on his blubbery belly. This time Baru made no attempt to move; he was too dazed. Zelim tore at his shirt, exposing great rolls of flesh.

"You . . . call me a woman?" Zelim said. Baru moaned incoherently. Zelim caught hold of the man's blubbery chest. "You've got bigger tits than any woman I know." He slapped the flesh. "Haven't you?" Again, Baru moaned, but Zelim wasn't satisfied. "*Haven't you got tits?*" he said, reaching up to pull Baru's hands away from his face. He was a mess beneath. "Did you hear me?" Zelim demanded.

"Yes . . ." Baru moaned.

"So say it."

"I've . . . got tits . . ."

Zelim spat on the man's bloody face, and got to his feet. He felt suddenly sick, but he was determined he wasn't going to puke in front of any of these men. He despised them all.

He caught Hassan's lazy-lidded gaze as he turned.

"You did that well," the man remarked appreciatively. "Want something to drink?"

Zelim pushed the proffered jug aside and set his sights beyond this little ring of boats, along the shore. His leg hurt as though it were in a fire and burning up, but he was determined to put some distance between himself and the other fishermen before he showed any sign of weakness.

"We haven't finished with the nets," Kekmet growled at him, as he limped away.

Zelim ignored him. He didn't care about the boats or the nets or whether the fish would rise tonight. He didn't care about Baru or old Kekmet or drunken Hassan. He didn't care about himself at that moment. He wasn't proud of what he'd done to Baru, nor was he ashamed. It was done, and now he wanted to forget about it. Dig himself a hole in the sand, till he found a cool, damp place to lie, and forget about it all. A hundred yards behind him now, Hassan was shouting something, and though he couldn't make sense of the words there was sufficient alarm in the drunkard's tone that Zelim glanced back to see what the matter was. Hassan had got to his feet, and was gazing off toward the distant trees. Zelim followed the direction of his gaze, and saw that a great number of birds had risen from the branches and were circling over the treetops. It was an unusual sight to be sure, but Zelim would have paid it little mind had the next moment not brought the baying of wolves, and with the wolves, the emergence of two figures from the trees. He was about the same distance from this pair as he was from the men and the boats behind him, and there he stayed, unwilling to take refuge in the company of old Kekmet and the others, but afraid to advance towards these strangers, who strode out of the forest as though there was nothing in its depths to fear, and walked, smiling, down towards the glittering water.

# II

To Zelim's eyes the couple didn't look dangerous. In fact it was a pleasure to look at them, after staring at the brutish faces of his fellow fishermen. They walked with an ease that bespoke strength, bespoke limbs that had never been cracked and mismended, never felt the ravages of age. They looked, Zelim thought, as he imagined a king and a queen might look, stepping from their cool palace, having been bathed in rare oils. Their skins, which were very different in color (the woman was blacker than any human being Zelim had ever set eyes upon, the man paler), gleamed in the sunlight, and their hair, which both wore long, seemed to be plaited here and there, so that serpentine forms ran in their manes. All this was extraordinary enough; but there was more. The robes they wore were another astonishment, for their colors were more vivid than anything Zelim had seen in his life. He'd never witnessed a sunset as red as the red in these robes, or set eyes on a bird with plumage as green, or seen with his mind's eye, in dream or daydream, a treasure that shone like the golden threads that were woven with this red, this green. The robes were long, and hung on their wearers voluptuously, but still it seemed to Zelim he could see the forms of their bodies beneath the folds, and it made him long to see them naked. He felt no shame at this desire; just as he felt no fear that they would chasten him for his scrutiny. Surely beauty like this, when it went out into the world, expected to be doted on.

He hadn't moved from that place on the bank where he'd first spotted the couple, but their path to the water's edge was steadily bringing them closer to him, and as the distance between them narrowed his eyes found more to beguile them. The woman, for instance, was wearing copious ornaments of jewelry—anklets, wristlets, necklaces—all as dark as her skin, yet carrying half-concealed in their darkness an iridescence that made them shimmer. The man had decoration of his own: elaborate patterns painted or tattooed upon his thighs, which were visible when his robe, which was cut to facilitate the immensity of his legs, parted.

But the most surprising detail of their appearance did not become clear until they were within a few yards of the water. The woman, smiling at her mate, reached into the folds of her robe, and with the greatest tenderness, lifted out into view a tiny baby. The mite bawled instantly at being parted from the comfort of its mother's tits—nor did Zelim blame the thing; he would have done the same—but it ceased its complaints when both mother and father spoke to it. Was there ever a more blessed infant than this, Zelim thought. To be in such arms, to gaze up at such faces, to know in your soul that you came from such roots as these? If a greater bliss were possible, Zelim could not imagine it.

The family was at the water now, and the couple had begun to speak to one another. It was no light conversation. Indeed from the way the pair stood facing one another, and the way they shook their heads and frowned, there was some trouble between them.

The child, who had moments before been the center of its parents' doting attentions, now went unnoticed. The argument was starting to escalate, Zelim saw, and for the first time since setting eyes on the couple he considered the wisdom of retreat. If one of these pair—or God Almighty help him, *both*—were to lose their temper, he did not care to contemplate the power they could unleash. But however fearful he was, he couldn't take his eyes off the scene before him. Whatever the risk of staying here and watching, it was nothing beside the sorrow he would feel, denying himself this sight. The world would not show him such glories again, he suspected. He was privileged beyond words to be in the presence of these people. If he went and hid his head, out of some idiot fear, then he deserved the very death he would be seeking to avoid. Only the brave were granted gifts such as this; and if it had come to him by accident (which it surely had) he would surprise fate by rising to the occasion. Keep his eyes wide and his feet planted in the same spot; have himself a story to tell his children, and the children of his children, when this event was a lifetime from now.

He had no sooner shaped these thoughts, however, than the argument between the couple ceased, and he had cause to wish he had fled. The woman had returned her gaze to the baby, but her consort, who'd had his back to Zelim throughout most of the exchange, now cast a look over his shoulder, and fixing his eyes upon Zelim, *beckoned* to him.

Zelim didn't move. His legs had turned to stone, his bowels to water; it was all he could do not to befoul his pants. He suddenly didn't care whether or not he had a tale to tell his children. He only wanted the sand to soften beneath him, so he could slide into the dark, where this man's gaze could not find him. To make matters worse the woman had bared her breasts and was offering her nipple to the babe's mouth. Her breasts were sumptuous, gleaming and full. Though he knew it wasn't wise to be staring past the beckoning husband and ogling the wife, Zelim couldn't help himself.

And again, the man summoned him with the hook of his fingers, but this time spoke.

"*Come here, fisherman,*" he said. He didn't speak loudly, but Zelim heard the command as though it had been spoken at his ear. "*Don't be afraid,*" the man went on.

"I can't . . ." Zelim began, meaning to tell the man his legs would not obey him.

But before the words were out of his mouth, the summons moved him. Muscles that had been rigid a few heartbeats before were carrying him toward his summons, though he had not consciously instructed them to do so. The man smiled, seeing his will done, and despite his trepidation Zelim could not help but return the smile, thinking as he walked toward his master that if the rest of the men were still watching him they would probably think him courageous, for the casual measure of his stride.

The woman, meanwhile, having settled the infant to sucking, was also looking Zelim's way, though her expression—unlike that of her husband—was far from friendly. What radiance would have broken from her face had she been feeling better tempered Zelim could only guess. Even in her present unhappy state she was glorious.

Zelim was within perhaps six feet of the couple now, and there stopped, though the man had not ordered him to do so.

"What is your name, fisherman?" the man said.

Before Zelim could reply, the woman broke in. "I'll not call him by the name of a fisherman."

"Anything's better than nothing," the husband replied.

"No it's not," the wife snapped. "He needs a warrior's name. Or nothing."

"He may not *be* a warrior."

"Well he certainly won't be a fisherman," the woman countered.

The man shrugged. The exchange had taken the smile off his face; he was plainly running out of patience with his lady.

"So let's hear your name," the woman said.

"Zelim."

"There then," the woman said, looking back at her husband. "Zelim! Do you want to call our child Zelim?"

The man looked down at the baby. "He doesn't seem to care one way or another," he remarked. Then back at Zelim. "Has the name treated you kindly?" he asked.

"Kindly?" Zelim said.

"He means are you pursued by women?" the wife replied.

"That's a consideration," the husband protested mildly. "If a name brings good fortune and beautiful women, the boy will thank us for it." He looked at Zelim again. "And have you been fortunate?"

"Not particularly," Zelim replied.

"And the women?"

"I married my cousin."

"No shame in that. My brother married my half-sister and they were the happiest couple I ever met." He glanced back at his wife, who was tenderly working the cushion of her breast so as to keep the flow of milk strong. "But my wife's not going to be content with this, I can see. No offense to you, my friend. Zelim is a fine name, truly. There's no shame in Zelim."

"So I can go?"

The man shrugged. "I'm sure you have . . . fish to catch . . . yes?"

"As it happens, I hate fish," Zelim said, surprised to be confessing this fact—which he had never spoken to anyone—in front of two strangers. "All the men in Atva talk about is *fish, fish, fish*—"

The woman looked up from the face of the nameless child.

"Atva?" she said.

"It's the name of—"

"—the village," she said. "Yes, I understand." She tried the word again, several times, turning the two syllables over. "At. Va. At. Vah." Then she said: "It's plain and simple. I like that. You can't corrupt it. You can't make some little game of it."

Now it was her husband's turn to be surprised. "You want to name my boy after some little *village?*" he said.

"Nobody will ever know where it came from," the woman replied. "I like the sound, and that's what's important. Look, the child likes the sound too. He's smiling."

"He's smiling because he's sucking on your tit, wife," the man replied. "I do the same thing."

Zelim could not keep himself from laughing. It amused him that these two, who were in every regard extraordinary beings, still chatted like a commonplace husband and wife.

"But if you want Atva, wife," the man went on, "then I will not stand between you and your desires."

"You'd better not try," the woman replied.

"You see how she is with me?" the man said, turning back to Zelim. "I grant her what she wants and she refuses to thank me." He spoke with the hint of a smile upon his face; he was clearly happy to have this debate ended. "Well, Zelim, *I* at least will thank you for your help in this."

"We all of us thank you," the woman replied. "Especially Atva. We wish you a happy, fertile life."

"You're very welcome," Zelim murmured.

"Now," said the husband, "if you'll excuse us? We must baptize the child."

# III

L ife in Atva was never the same after the day the family went down to the water.

Zelim was of course questioned closely as to the nature of his exchange with the man and woman, firstly by old Kekmet, then by just about anybody in the village who wanted to catch his arm. He told the truth, in his own plain way. But even as he told it, he knew in his heart that recounting the words he had exchanged with the child's mother and father was not the whole truth, or anything like it. In the presence of this pair he had felt something wonderful; feelings his limited vocabulary could not properly express. Nor, in truth, did he entirely wish to express them. There was a kind of possessiveness in him about the experience, which kept him from trying too hard to tell those who interrogated him the true nature of the encounter. The only person he would have wished to tell was his father. Old Zelim would have understood, he suspected; he would have helped with the words, and when the words failed both of them, then he'd have simply nodded and said: "It was the same for me in Samarkand," which had always been his response when somebody remarked upon the miraculous. *It was the same for me in Samarkand . . .*

Perhaps people knew Zelim was not telling them all he knew, because once they'd asked all their questions, he began to notice a distinct change in their attitude to him. People who'd been friendly to him all his life now looked at him strangely when he smiled at them, or looked the other way, pretending not to see him. Others were even more obvious about their distaste for his company; especially the women. More than once he heard his name used loudly in conversation, accompanied by spitting, as though the very syllables of his name carried a bitter taste.

It was, of all people, old Kekmet who told him what was being said.

"People are saying you're poisoning the village," he said. This seemed so absurd Zelim laughed out loud. But Kekmet was deadly serious. "Baru's at the heart of it," he went on. "He hates you, after the way you spoiled that fat face of his. So he's spreading stories about you."

"What kind of stories?"

"That you and the demons were exchanging secret signs—"

"Demons?"

"That's what he says they were, those people. How else could they have come out of the forest, he says. They couldn't be like us and live in the forest. That's what he says."

"And everyone believes him?" Here Kekmet fell silent. "Do *you* believe him?"

Kekmet looked away toward the water. "I've seen a lot of strange things in my life," he said, the coarseness going from his voice. "Out there particularly. Things moving in the water that I'd never want to find in my net. And in the sky sometimes . . . shapes in the clouds . . ." He shrugged. "I don't know what to believe. It doesn't really matter what's true and what isn't. Baru's said what he's said, and people believe him."

"What should I do?"

"You can stay and wait it out. Hope that people forget. Or you can leave."

"And go where?"

"Anywhere but here." Kekmet looked back at Zelim. "If you ask me, there's no life for you here as long as Baru's alive."

That was effectively the end of the conversation. Kekmet made his usual curt farewell, and left Zelim to examine the two available options. Neither was attractive. If he stayed, and Baru continued to stir up enmity against him, his life would become intolerable. But to leave the only home he'd ever known, to stray beyond this strip of rock and sand, this huddled collection of houses, and venture out into the wide world without any clue as to where he was going—that would take more courage than he thought he possessed. He remembered his father's tales of the hardships he claimed to have suffered on his way to Samarkand: the terrors of the desert; the bandits and the djinns. He didn't feel ready to face such threats; he was too afraid.

Almost a month passed; and he persuaded himself that there was a softening in people's attitudes to him. One day, one of the women actually smiled at him, he thought. Things weren't as bad as Kekmet had suggested. Given time the villagers would come to realize how absurd their superstitions were. In the meantime he simply had to be careful not to give them any cause for doubt.

He had not taken account of how fate might intervene.

It happened like this. Since his encounter with the couple on the shore he had been obliged to take his boat out single-handed; nobody wanted to share it with him. This had inevitably meant a smaller catch. He couldn't throw the net as far from the boat when he was on his own.

But this particular day, despite the fact that he was fishing on his own, he was lucky. His net was fairly bursting when he hauled it up into the boat, and he paddled back to the shore feeling quite pleased with himself. Several of the other fisherman were already unloading their catches, so a goodly number of villagers were down at the water's edge, and inevitably more than a few pairs of eyes were cast his way as he hauled his net out of the boat to study its contents.

There were crayfish, there were catfish, there was even a small sturgeon. But caught at the very bottom of his net, and still thrashing there as though it possessed more life than it was natural for a creature to possess, was a fish Zelim had never set eyes on before. It was larger than any of the rest of his catch, its heaving flanks not green or silvery, but a dull red. The creature instantly drew attention. One of the women declared loudly it was a demon-fish. Look at it looking at us, she said, her voice shrill. Oh God in Heaven preserve us, look how it looks!

Zelim said nothing: he was almost as discomfited by the sight of the fish as the women; it did seem to be watching them all with its swiveling eye, as if to say: you're all going to die like me, sooner or later, gasping for breath.

The woman's panic spread. Children began to cry and were ushered away, instructed not to look back at the demon, or at Zelim, who'd brought this thing to shore.

"It's not my fault," Zelim protested. "I just found it in my net."

"But why did it *swim* into your net?" Baru piped up, pushing through the remaining onlookers to point his fat finger at Zelim. "I'll tell you why. Because it wanted to be with you!"

"Be with me?" Zelim said. The notion was so ridiculous, he laughed. But he was the only one doing so. Everybody else was either looking at his accuser or at the evidence, which was still alive, long after the rest of the net's contents had perished. "It's just a fish!" Zelim said.

"I certainly never saw its like," said Baru. He scanned the crowd, which was assembling again, in anticipation of a confrontation. "Where's Kekmet?"

"I'm here," the old man said. He was standing at the back of the crowd, but Baru called him forth. He came, though somewhat reluctantly. It was plain what Baru intended.

"How long have you fished here?" Baru asked Kekmet.

"Most of my life," Kekmet replied. "And before you ask, no I haven't seen a fish that looks like this." He glanced up at Zelim. "But that doesn't mean it's a demon-fish, Baru. It only means . . . we haven't seen one before."

Baru's expression grew sly. "Would you eat it?" he said.

"What's that got to do with anything?" Zelim put in.

"Baru's not talking to you," one of the women said. She was a bitter creature, this particular woman, her face as narrow and sickly pale as Baru's was round and red. "You answer, Kekmet! Go on. You tell us if you'd put *that* in your stomach." She looked down at the fish, which by some unhappy accident seemed to swivel its bronze eye so as to look back at her. She shuddered, and without warning snatched Kekmet's stick from him and began to beat the thing, not once or twice, but twenty, thirty times, striking it so hard its flesh was pulped. When she had finished, she threw the stick down on the sand, and looked up at Kekmet with her lips curled back from her rotted teeth. "How's that?" she said. "Will you have it now?"

Kekmet shook his head. "Believe what you want," he said. "I don't have the words to change your minds. Maybe you're right, Baru. Maybe we *are* all cursed. I'm too old to care."

With that he reached out and caught hold of the shoulder of one of the children, so as to have some support now that he'd lost his stick. And guiding the child ahead of him, he limped away from the crowd.

"You've done all the harm you're going to do," Baru said to Zelim. "You have to leave."

Zelim put up no argument. What was the use? He went to his boat, picked up his gutting knife, and went back to his house. It took him less than half an hour to pack his belongings. When he went back into the street, it was empty; his neighbors—whether out of shame or fear he didn't know or care—had gone into hiding. But he felt their eyes on him as he departed; and almost wished as he went that what Baru had accused him of was true, and that if he were to now curse those he was leaving behind with blindness they'd wake tomorrow with their eyes withered in their sockets.

# IV

Let me tell you what happened to Zelim after he left Atva. Determined to prove—if only to himself—that the forest from which the family had emerged was not a place to be afraid of, he made his departure through the trees. It was damp and cold, and more than once he contemplated retreating to the brightness of the shore, but after a time such thoughts, along with his fear, dissipated. There was nothing here that was going to do harm to his soul. When shit fell on or about him, as now and then it did, the shitter wasn't some child-devouring beast as he'd been brought up to believe it'd be, just a bird. When something moved in the thicket, and he caught the gleam of an eye, it was not the gaze of a nomadic djinn that fell on him, but that of a boar or a wild dog.

His caution evaporated along with his fear, and much to his surprise his spirits grew lighter. He began to sing to himself as he went. Not the songs the fishermen sang when they were out together, which were invariably mournful or obscene, but the two or three little songs he remembered from his childhood. Simple ditties which brought back happy memories.

For food, he ate berries, washed down with water from the streams that wound between the trees. Twice he came upon nests in the undergrowth and was able to dine on raw eggs. Only at night, when he was obliged to rest (once the sun went down he had no way of knowing the direction in which he was traveling), did he become at all anxious. He had no means of lighting a fire, so he was obliged to sit in the darkened thicket until dawn, praying a bear or a pack of wolves didn't come sniffing for a meal.

It took him four days and nights to get to the other side of the forest. By the time he emerged from the trees he'd become so used to the gloom that the bright sun made his head ache. He lay down in the grass at the fringe of the trees, and dozed there in the warmth, thinking he'd set off again when the sun was a little less bright. In fact, he slept until twilight, when he was woken by the sound of voices rising and falling in prayer. He sat up. A little distance from where he'd laid his head there was a ridge of rocks, like the spine of some dead giant, and on the narrow trail that wound between these boulders was a small group of holy men, singing their prayers as they walked. Some were carrying lamps, by which light he saw their faces: ragged beards, deeply furrowed brows, sunbaked pates; these were men who'd suffered for their faith, he thought.

He got up and limped in their direction, calling to them as he approached so that they wouldn't be startled by his sudden appearance. Seeing him, the men came to a halt; a few suspicious glances were exchanged.

"I'm lost and hungry," Zelim said to them. "I wonder if you have some bread, or if you can at least tell me where I can find a bed for the night."

The leader, who was a burly man, passed his lamp to his companion, and beckoned Zelim.

"What are you doing out here?" the monk asked.

"I came through the forest," Zelim explained.

"Don't you know this is a bad road?" the monk said. His breath was the foulest thing Zelim had ever smelt. "There are robbers on this road," the monk went on. "Many people have been beaten and murdered here." Suddenly, the monk reached out and caught hold of Zelim's arm, pulling him close. At the same time he pulled out a large knife, and put it to Zelim's throat. *"Call them!"* the monk said.

Zelim didn't understand what he was talking about. "Call who?"

"The rest of your gang! You tell them I'll slit your throat if they make a move on us."

"No, you've got me wrong. I'm not a bandit."

"Shut up!" the monk said, pressing his blade into Zelim's flesh so deeply that blood began to run. *"Call to them!"*

"I'm on my own," Zelim protested. "I swear! I swear on my mother's eyes, I'm not a bandit."

"Slit his throat, Nazar," said one of the monks.

"Please, don't do that," Zelim begged. "I'm an innocent man."

"There are no innocent men left," Nazar, the man who held him, said. "These are the last days of the world, and everyone left alive is corrupt."

Zelim assumed this was high-flown philosophy, such as only a monk might understand. "If you say so," he replied. "What do I know? But I tell you I'm not a bandit. I'm a fisherman."

"You're a very long way from the sea," said the ratty little monk to whom Nazar had passed his lamp. He leaned in to peer at Zelim, raising the light a little as he did so. "Why'd you leave the fish behind?"

"Nobody liked me," Zelim replied. It seemed best to be honest.

"And why was that?"

Zelim shrugged. Not too honest, he thought. "They just didn't," he said.

The man studied Zelim a little longer, then he said to the leader: "You know, Nazar, I think he's telling the truth." Zelim felt the blade at his neck dig a little less deeply into his flesh. "We thought you were one of the bandits' boys," the monk explained to him, "left in our path to distract us."

Once again, Zelim felt he was not entirely understanding what he was being told. "So . . . while you're talking to me, the bandits come?"

"Not *talking*," Nazar said. His knife slid down from Zelim's neck to the middle of his chest; there it cut at Zelim's already ragged shirt. The monk's other hand slid through the shirt, while the knife continued on its southward journey, until it was pressed against the front of Zelim's breeches.

"He's a little old for me, Nazar," the monk's companion commented, and turning his back on Zelim sat down among the rocks.

"Am I on my own then?" Nazar wanted to know.

By way of answering him, three of the men closed on Zelim like hungry dogs. He was wrested to the ground, where his clothes were pulled seam from seam, and the monks proceeded to molest him, ignoring his shouts of protest, or his pleas to be left alone. They made him lick their feet and their fundaments, and suck their beards and nipples and purple-headed cocks. They held him down while one by one they took him, not caring that he bled and bled.

While this was going on the other monks, who'd retired to the rocks, read, or drank wine or lay on their backs watching the stars. One was even praying. All this Zelim could see because he deliberately looked away from his violators, determined not to let them see the terror in his eyes; and equally determined not to weep. So instead he watched the others, and waited for the men who were violating him to be finished.

He fully expected to be murdered when they were done with him, but this, at least, he was spared. Instead the monks had the night with him, on and off, using him every way their desires could devise, and then, just before dawn left him there among the rocks, and went on their way.

The sun came up, but Zelim closed his eyes against it. He didn't want to look at the light ever again. He was too ashamed. But by midday the heat made him get to his knees and drag himself into the comparative cool of the rocks. There, to his surprise, he found that one of the holy men—perhaps the one who had been praying—had left a skin of wine, some bread, and a piece of dried fruit. It was no accident, he knew. The man had left it for Zelim.

Now, and only now, did the fisherman allow the tears to come, moved not so much by his own agonies, but by the fact that there had been one who'd cared enough for him to do him this kindness.

He drank and ate. Maybe it was the potency of the wine, but he felt remarkably renewed, and covering his nakedness as best he could he got up from his niche among the rocks and set off down the trail. His body still ached, but the bleeding had stopped, and rather than lie down when night fell he walked under the stars. Somewhere along the way a bony-flanked she-dog came creeping after him, looking perhaps for the comfort of human company. He didn't shoo her away; he too wanted company. After a time the animal became brave enough to walk at Zelim's heel, and finding that her new master didn't kick her, was soon trotting along as though they'd been together since birth.

The hungry bitch's arrival in his life marked a distinct upturn in Zelim's fortunes. A few hours later he came into a village many times larger than Atva, where he found a large crowd in the midst of what he took to be some kind of celebration. The streets were thronged with people shouting and stamping, and generally having a fine time.

"Is it a holy day?" Zelim asked a youth who was sitting on a door-step, drinking.

The fellow laughed. "No," he said, "it's not a holy day."

"Well then why's everybody so happy?"

"We're going to have some hangings," the youth replied, with a lazy grin.

"Oh . . . I . . . see."

"You want to come and watch?"

"Not particularly."

"We might get ourselves something to eat," the youth said. "And you look as though you need it." He glanced Zelim up and down. "In fact you look like you need a lot of things. Some breeches, for one thing. What happened to you?"

"I don't want to talk about it."

"That bad, huh? Well then you should come to the hangings. My father already went, because he said it's good to see people who are more unfortunate than you. It's good for the soul, he said. Makes you thankful."

Zelim saw the wisdom in this, so he and his dog accompanied the boy through the village to the market square. It took them longer to dig through the crowd than his guide had anticipated, however, and by the time they got there all but one of the men who were being hanged was already dangling from the makeshift gallows. He knew all the prisoners instantly: the ragged beards, the sunburned pates. These were his viola-tors. All of them had plainly suffered horribly before the noose had taken their lives. Three of them were missing their hands; one of them had been blinded; others, to judge by the blood that glued their clothes to their groins, had lost their manhoods to the knife.

One of this unmanned number was Nazar, the leader of the gang, who was the last of the gang left alive. He could not stand, so two of the villagers were holding him up while a third slipped the noose over his head. His rotted teeth had been smashed out, and his whole body covered with cuts and bruises. The crowd was wildly happy at the sight of the man's agonies. With every twitch and gasp they applauded and yelled his crimes at him. "Murderer!" they yelled. "Thief!" they yelled. "Sodomite!" they yelled.

"He's all that and more, my father says," the youth told Zelim. "He's so evil, my father says, that when he dies we might see the Devil come up onto the gallows and catch his soul as it comes out of his mouth!"

Zelim shuddered, sickened at the thought. If the boy's father was right, and the sodomite robber-monk had been the spawn of Satan, then perhaps that unholiness had been passed into his own body, along with the man's spittle and seed. Oh, the horror of that thought; that he was somehow the wife of this terrible man and would be dragged down into the same infernal place when his time came.

The noose was now about Nazar's neck, and the rope pulled tight enough that he was pulled up like a puppet. The men who'd been supporting him stood away, so that they could help haul on the rope. But in the moments before the rope tightened about his windpipe, Nazar started to speak. No; not speak; *shout*, using every last particle of strength in his battered body.

"*God shits on you all!*" he yelled. The crowd hurled at him. Some threw stones. If he felt them breaking his bones, he didn't respond. He just kept shouting. "*He put a thousand innocent souls into our hands! He didn't care what we did to them! So you can do whatever you want to me—*"

The rope was tightening around his throat as the men hauled on the other end. Nazar was pulled up on to tip-toe. And still he shouted, blood and spittle coming with the words.

"*—there is no hell! There is no paradise! There is no—*"

He got no further; the noose closed off his windpipe and he was hauled into the air. But Zelim knew what word had been left unsaid. God. The monk had been about to cry: *there is no God.*

The crowd was in ecstasies all around him; cheering and jeering and spitting at the hanged man as he jerked around on the end of the rope. His agonies didn't last long. His tortured body gave out after a very short time, much to the crowd's disapproval, and he hung from the rope as though the grace of life had never touched him. The boy at Zelim's side was plainly disappointed.

"I didn't see Satan, did you?"

Zelim shook his head, but in his heart he thought: maybe I did. Maybe the Devil's just a man like me. Maybe he's many men; all men, maybe.

His gaze went along the row of hanged men, looking for the one who had prayed while he'd been raped; the one Zelim suspected had left him the wine, bread, and fruit. Perhaps he'd also persuaded his companions to spare their victim; Zelim would never know. But here was the strange thing. In death, the men all looked the same to him. What had made each man particular seemed to have drained away, leaving their faces deserted, like houses whose owners had departed, taking every sign of particularity with them. He couldn't tell which of them had prayed on the rock, or which had been particularly vicious in their dealings with him. Which had bitten him like an animal; which had pissed in his face to wake him when he'd almost fainted away; which had called him by the name of a woman as they'd ploughed him. In the end, they were virtually indistinguishable as they swung there.

"Now they'll be cut up and their heads put on spikes," the youth was explaining, "as a warning to bandits."

"And holy men," Zelim said.

"They weren't holy men," the youth replied.

His remark was overheard by a woman close by. "Oh yes they were," she said. "The leader, Nazar, had been a monk in Samarkand. He studied some books he should never have studied, and that was why he became what he became."

"What kind of books?" Zelim asked her.

She gave him a fearful look. "It's better we don't know," she said.

"Well I'm going to find my father," the youth said to Zelim. "I hope things go well with you. God be merciful."

"And to you," Zelim said.

# V

## i

Zelim had seen enough; more than enough, in truth. The crowd was working itself up into a fresh fever as the bodies were being taken down in preparation for their beheading; children were being lifted up onto their parents' shoulders so they could see the deed done. Zelim found the whole spectacle disgusting. Turning away from the scene, he bent down, picked up his flea-bitten dog, and started to make his way to the edge of the assembly.

As he went he heard somebody say: "Are you sickened at the sight of blood?"

He glanced over his shoulder. It was the woman who'd spoken of the unholy books in Samarkand.

"No, I'm not sickened," Zelim said sourly, thinking the woman was impugning his manhood. "I'm just bored. They're dead. They can't suffer any more."

"You're right," the woman said with a shrug. She was dressed, Zelim saw, in widow's clothes, even though she was still young; no more than a year or two older than he. "It's only us who suffer," the woman went on. "Only us who are left alive."

He understood absolutely the truth in what she was saying, in a way that he could not have understood before his terrible adventure on the road. That much at least the monks had given him: a comprehension of somebody else's despair.

"I used to think there were reasons . . ." he said softly.

The crowd was roaring. He glanced back over his shoulder. A head was being held high, blood running from it, glittering in the bright sun.

"What did you say?" the woman asked him, moving closer to hear him better over the noise.

"It doesn't matter," he said.

"Please tell me," she replied, "I'd like to know."

He shrugged. He wanted to weep, but what man wept openly in a place like this?

"Why don't you come with me?" the woman said. "All my neighbors are here, watching this *stupidity*. If you come back with me, there'll be nobody to see us. Nobody to gossip about us."

Zelim contemplated the offer for a moment or two. "I have to bring my dog," he said.

## ii

He stayed for six years. Of course after a week or so the neighbors began to gossip behind their hands, but this wasn't like Atva; people weren't forever meddling in your business. Zelim lived quite happily with the widow Passak, whom he came to love. She was a practical woman, but with the front door and the shutters closed she was also very passionate. This was especially true, for some reason, when the winds came in off the desert; burning hot winds that carried a blistering freight of sand. When those winds blew the widow would be shameless—there was nothing she wouldn't do for their mutual pleasure, and he loved her all the more for it.

But the memories of Atva, and of the glorious family that had come down to the shore that distant day, never left him. Nor did the hours of his violation, or the strange thoughts that had visited him as Nazar and his gang hung from the gallows. All of these experiences remained in his heart, like a stew that had been left to simmer, and simmer, and as the years passed was more steadily becoming tastier and more nourishing.

Then, after six years, and many happy days and nights with Passak, he realized the time had come for him to sit down and eat that stew.

It happened during one of these storms that came off the desert. He and Passak had made love not once but three times. Instead of falling asleep afterward, however, as Passak had done, Zelim now felt a strange irritation behind his eyes, as though the wind had somehow whistled its way into his skull and was stirring the meal one last time before serving it.

In the corner of the room the dog—who was by now old and blind—whined uneasily.

"Hush, girl," he told her. He didn't want Passak woken; not until he had made sense of the feelings that were haunting him.

He put his head in his hands. What was to become of him? He had lived a fuller life than he'd ever have lived if he'd stayed in Atva, but none of it made any sense. At least in Atva there had been a simple rhythm to things. A boy was born, he grew strong enough to become a fisherman, he became a fisherman, and then weakened again, until he was as frail as a baby, and then he perished, comforted by the fact that even as he passed from the world new fishermen were being born. But Zelim's life had no such certainties in it. He'd stumbled from one confusion to another, finding agony where he had expected to find consolation, and pleasure where he'd expected to find sorrow. He'd seen the Devil in human form, and the faces of divine spirits made in similar shape. Life was not remotely as he'd expected it to be.

And then he thought: I have to tell what I know. That's why I'm here; I have to tell people all that I've seen and felt, so that my pain is never repeated. So that those who come after me are like my children, because I helped shape them, and made them strong.

He got up, went to his sweet Passak where she lay, and knelt down beside the narrow bed. He kissed her cheek. She was already awake, however, and had been awake for a while.

"If you leave, I'll be so sad," she said. Then, after a pause: "But I knew you'd go one day. I'm surprised you've stayed so long."

"How did you know—?"

"You were talking aloud, didn't you realize? You do it all the time." A single tear ran from the corner of her eye, but there was no sorrow in her voice. "You are a wonderful man, Zelim. I don't think you know how truly wonderful you are. And you've seen things . . . maybe they were in your head, maybe they were real, I don't know . . . that you have to tell people about." Now it was he who wept, hearing her speak this way, without a trace of reprimand. "I have had such years with you, my love. Such joy as I never thought I'd have. And it'd be greedy of me to ask you for more, when I've had so much already." She raised her head a little way, and kissed him. "I will love you better if you go quickly," she said.

He started to sob. All the fine thoughts he'd had a few minutes before seemed hollow now. How could he think of leaving her?

"I can't go," he said. "I don't know what put the thought in my head."

"Yes you will," she replied. "If you don't go now, you'll go sooner or later. So go."

He wiped his tears away. "No," he said. "I'm not going anywhere."

So he stayed. The storms still came, month on month, and he and the widow still coupled fiercely in the little house, while the fire muttered in the hearth and the wind chattered on the roof. But now his happiness was spoiled; and so was hers. He resented her for keeping him under her roof, even though she'd been willing to let him go. And she in her turn grew less loving of him, because he'd not had the courage to go, and by staying he was killing the sweetest thing she'd ever known, which was the love between them.

At last, the sadness of all this killed her. Strange to say, but this brave woman, who had survived the grief of being widowed, could not survive the death of her love for a man who stayed at her side. He buried her, and a week later, went on his way.

He never again settled down. He'd known all he needed to know of domestic life; from now on he would be a nomad. But the stew that had bubbled in him for so long was still good. Perhaps all the more pungent for those last sad months with Passak. Now, when he finally began his life's work, and started to teach by telling of his experiences, there was the poignancy of their soured love to add to the account: this woman, to whom he had once promised his undying devotion—saying what he felt for her was imperishable—soon came to seem as remote a memory as his youth in Atva. Love—at least the kind of love that men and women share—was not made of eternal stuff. Nor was its opposite. Just as the scars that Nazar and his men had left faded with the years, so had the hatred Zelim had felt for them.

Which is not to say he was a man without feeling; far from it. In the thirty-one years left to him he would become known as a prophet, as a storyteller and as a man of rare passion. But that passion did not resemble the kind that most of us feel. He became, despite his humble origins, a creature of subtle and elevated emotion. The parables he told would not have shamed Christ in their simplicity, but unlike the plain and good lessons taught by Jesus, Zelim imparted through his words a far more ambiguous vision; one in which God and the Devil were constantly engaged in a game of masks.

There may be occasion to tell you some of his parables as this story goes on, but for now, I will tell you only how he died. It happened, of course, in Samarkand.

# VI

Let me first say a little about the city, given that its glamour had fueled so many of the stories that Zelim had heard as a child. The teller of those tales, Old Zelim, was not the only man to dote on

Samarkand, a city he had never seen. It was a nearly mythical place in those times. A city, it was said, of heartbreaking beauty, where thoughts and forms and deeds that were unimaginable in any other spot on earth were commonplace. Never such women as there; nor boys; nor either so free with their flesh as in Samarkand's perfumed streets. Never such men of power as there; nor such treasures as men of power accrue, nor such palaces as they build for ambition's sake, nor mosques they build to save their souls.

Then—if all these glories were not enough—there was the miraculous fact of the city's very existence, when in all directions from where it stood there was wilderness. The traders who passed through it on the Silk Road to Turkistan and China, or carried spices from India or salt from the steppes, crossed vast, baking deserts, and freezing gray wastelands, before they came in sight of the river Zarafshan, and the fertile lands from which Samarkand's towers and minarets rose, like flowers that no garden had ever brought forth. Their gratitude at being delivered out of the wastes they'd crossed inspired them to write songs and poems about the city (extolling it perhaps more than it deserved) and the songs and poems in their turn brought more traders, more beautiful women, more builders of petaled towers, so that as the generations passed Samarkand rose to its own legendary reputation, until the adulation in those songs and poems came to seem ungenerous.

It was not, let me point out, simply a place of sensual excesses. It was also a site of learning, where philosophers were extolled, and books written and read, and theories about the beginning of the world and its end endlessly debated over glasses of tea. In short, it was altogether a miraculous city.

Three times in his life Zelim joined a caravan on the Silk Road and made his way to Samarkand. The first time was just a couple of years after the death of Passak, and he traveled on foot, having no money to purchase an animal strong enough to survive the trek. It was a journey that tested to its limits his hunger to see the place: by the time the fabled towers came in sight he was so exhausted—his feet bloody, his body trembling, his eyes red-raw from days of walking in clouds of somebody else's dust—that he simply fell down in the sweet grass beside the river and slept for the rest of the day there outside the walls, oblivious.

He awoke at twilight, washed the sand from his eyes, and looked up. The sky was opulent with color; tiny knitted rows of high cloud, all amber toward the west, blue purple on their eastern flank, and birds in wheeling flocks, circling the glowing minarets as they returned to their roosts. He got to his feet and entered the city as the night fires around the walls were being stoked, their fuel such fragrant woods that the very air smelt holy.

Inside, all the suffering he'd endured to get here was forgotten. Samarkand was all that his father had said it would be, and more. Though Zelim was little more than a beggar here, he soon realized that there was a market for his storytelling. And that he had much to tell. People liked to hear him talk about the baptism at Atva; and the forest; and Nazar and his fate. Whether they believed these were accounts of true events or not didn't matter: they gave him money and food and friendship (and in the case of several well-bred ladies, nights of love) to hear him tell his tales. He began to extend his repertoire: extemporize, enrich, invent. He created new stories about the family on the shore, and because it seemed people liked to have a touch of philosophy woven into their entertainments, introduced his themes of destiny into the stories, ideas that he'd nurtured in his years with Passak.

By the time he left Samarkand after that first visit, which lasted a year and a half, he had a certain reputation, not simply as a fine story-teller, but as a man of some wisdom. And now, as he traveled, he had a new subject: Samarkand.

There, he would say, the highest aspirations of the human soul, and the lowest appetites of the flesh, are so closely laid, that its hard sometimes to tell one from the other. It was a point of view people were hungry to hear, because it was so often true of their own lives, but so seldom admitted to. Zelim's reputation grew.

The next time he went to Samarkand he traveled on the back of a camel, and had a fifteen-year-old boy to prepare his food and see to his comfort, a lad who'd been apprenticed to him because he too wanted to be a storyteller. When they got to the city, it was inevitably something of a disappointment to Zelim. He felt like a man who'd returned to the bed of a great love only to find his memories sweeter than the reality. But this experience was also the stuff of parable; and he'd only been in the city a week before his disappointment was part of a tale he told.

And there were compensations: reunions with friends he'd made the first time he'd been here; invitations into the palatial homes of men who would have scorned him as an uneducated fisherman a few years before, but now declared themselves honored when he stepped across their thresholds. And the profoundest compensation, his discovery that here in

the city there existed a tiny group of young scholars who studied his life
and his parables as though he were a man of some significance. Who
could fail to be flattered by that? He spent many days and nights talking
with them, and answering their questions as honestly as he was able.

One question in particular loitered in his brain when he left the
city. "Do you think you'll ever see again the people you met on the
shore?" a young scholar had asked him.

"I don't suppose so," he'd said to the youth. "I was nothing to them."

"But to the child, perhaps . . ." the scholar had replied.

"To the child?" said Zelim. "I doubt he even knew I existed. He
was more interested in his mother's milk than he was in me."

The scholar persisted, however. "You teach in your stories," he
said, "how things always come round. You talk in one of them about the
Wheel of the Stars. Perhaps it will be the same with these people.
They'll be like the stars. Falling out of sight . . ."

". . . and rising again," Zelim said.

The scholar offered a luminous smile to hear his thoughts com-
pleted by his master. "Yes. Rising again."

"Perhaps," Zelim had said. "But I won't live in expectation of it."

Nor did he. But, that said, the young scholar's observation had lingered with him, and had in its turn seeded another parable: a morose
tale about a man who lives in anticipation of a meeting with someone
who turns out to be his assassin.


And so the years went on, and Zelim's fame steadily grew. He traveled
immense distances—to Europe, to India, to the borders of China,
telling his stories, and discovering that the strange poetry of what he
invented gave pleasure to every variety of heart.

It was another eighteen years before he came again to Samarkand;
this—though he didn't know it—for the last time.

# VII

By now Zelim was getting on in years and though his many journeys
had made him wiry and resilient, he was feeling his age that
autumn. His joints ached; his morning motions were either water or
stone; he slept poorly. And when he did sleep, he dreamed of Atva; or

rather of its shore, and of the holy family. His life of wisdom and pain had been caused by that encounter. If he'd not gone down to the water that day then perhaps he'd still be there among the fishermen, living a life of utter spiritual impoverishment; never having known enough to make his soul quake, nor enough to make it soar.

So there he was, that October, in Samarkand, feeling old and sleeping badly. There was little rest for him, however. By now the number of his devotees had swelled, and one of them (the youth who'd asked the question about things coming round) had founded a school. They were all young men who'd found a revolutionary zeal buried in Zelim's parables, which in turn nourished their hunger to see humanity unchained. Daily, he would meet with them. Sometimes he would let them question him, about his life, about his opinions. On other days— when he was weary of being interrogated—he would tell a story.

This particular day, however, the lesson had become a little of both. One of the students had said: "Master, many of us have had terrible arguments with our fathers, who don't wish us to study your works."

"Is that so?" old Zelim replied, raising an eyebrow. "I can't understand why." There was a little laughter among the students. "What's your question?"

"I only wondered if you'd tell us something of your own father."

"My father . . ." Zelim said softly.

"Just a little."

The prophet smiled. "Don't look so nervous," he said to the questioner. "Why do you look so nervous?"

The youth blushed. "I was afraid perhaps you'd be angry with me for asking something about your family."

"In the first place," Zelim replied gently, "I'm far too old to get angry. It's a waste of energy and I don't have much of that left. In the second place, my father sits before you, just as all your fathers sit here in front of me." His gaze roved the thirty or so students who sat cross-legged before him. "And a very fine bunch of men they are too." His gaze returned to the youth who'd asked the question. "What does your father do?"

"He's a wool merchant."

"So he's out in the city somewhere right now, selling wool, but his nature's not satisfied with the selling of wool. He needs something else in his life, so he sends you along to talk philosophy."

"Oh no . . . you don't understand . . . he didn't send me."

"He may not think he sent you. You may not think you were sent. But you were born your father's son and whatever you do, you do it for

him." The youth frowned, plainly troubled at the thought of doing anything for his father. "You're like the fingers of his hand, digging in the
dirt while he counts his bales of wool. He doesn't even notice that the
hand's digging. He doesn't see it drop seeds into the hole. He's amazed
when he finds a tree's grown up beside him, filled with sweet fruit and
singing birds. But it was his hand did it."

The youth looked down at the ground. "What do you mean by
this?" he said.

"That we do not belong to ourselves. That though we cannot know
the full purpose of our creation, we should look to those who came
before us to understand it better. Not just our fathers and our mothers,
but *all* who went before. They are the pathway back to God, who may
not know, even as He counts stars, that we're quietly digging a hole,
planting a seed . . ."

Now the youth looked up again, smiling, entertained by the notion
of God the Father looking the other way while His human hands grew
a garden at His feet.

"Does that answer the question?" Zelim said.

"I was still wondering . . ." the student said.

"Yes?"

"Your own father—?"

"He was a fisherman from a little village called Atva, which is on
the shores of the Caspian Sea." As Zelim spoke, he felt a little breath of
wind against his face, delightfully cool. He paused to appreciate it.
Closed his eyes for a moment. When he opened them again, he knew
something had changed in the room; he just didn't know what.

"Where was I?" he said.

"Atva," somebody at the back of the room said.

"Ah, yes, Atva. My father lived there all his life, but he dreamed of
being somewhere quite different. He dreamed of Samarkand. He told
his children he'd been here, in his youth. And he wove such stories of
this city; such stories . . ."

Again, Zelim halted. The cool breeze had brushed against his
brow a second time, and something about the way it touched him
seemed like a sign. As though the breeze was saying *look, look* . . .

But at what? He gazed out of the window, thinking perhaps there
was something out there he needed to see. The sky was darkening
toward night. A chestnut tree, still covetous of its leaves despite the season, was in perfect silhouette. High up in its branches the evening star
glimmered. But he'd seen all of this before: a sky, a tree, a star.

He returned his gaze to the room, still puzzled.

"What kind of stories?" somebody was asking him.

"Stories . . . ?"

"You said your father told stories of Samarkand."

"Oh yes. So he did. Wonderful stories. He wasn't a very good sailor, my father. In fact he drowned on a perfectly calm day. But he could have told tales of Samarkand for a year and never told the same one twice."

"But you say he never came here?" the master of the school asked Zelim.

"Never," Zelim said, smiling. "Which is why he was able to tell such fine stories about it."

This amused everyone mightily. But Zelim scarcely heard the laughter. Again, that tantalizing breeze had brushed his face; and this time, when he raised his eyes, he saw somebody moving through the shadows at the far end of the room. It was not one of the students. They were all dressed in pale yellow robes. This figure was dressed in ragged black breeches and a dirty shirt. He was also black, his skin possessing a curious radiance, which made Zelim remember a long-ago day.

"Atva . . . ?" he murmured.

Only the students closest to Zelim heard him speak, and even they, when debating the subject later, did not agree on the utterance. Some thought he'd said *Allah*, others that he'd spoken some magical word, that was intended to keep the stranger at the back of the room at bay. The reason that the word was so hotly debated was simple: it was Zelim's last, at least in the living world.

He had no sooner spoken than his head drooped, and the glass of tea which he had been sipping fell from his hand. The murmurings around the room ceased on the instant; students rose on all sides, some of them already starting to weep, or pray. The great teacher was dead, his wisdom passed into history. There would be more stories, no more prophecies. Only centuries of turning over the tales he'd already told, and watching to see if the prophecies came true.

Outside the schoolroom, under that covetous chestnut tree, two men talked in whispers. Nobody saw them there; nobody heard their happy exchange. Nor will I invent those words; better I leave that conversation to you: how the spirit of Zelim and Atva, later called Galilee, talked. I will say only this: that when the conversation was over, Zelim accompanied Galilee out of Samarkand; a ghost and a god, wandering off through the smoky twilight, like two inseparable friends.

Need I say that Zelim's part in this story is far from finished? He was called away that day into the arms of the Barbarossa family, whose service he has not since left.

In this book, as in life, nothing really passes away. Things change, yes; of course they change; they must. But everything is preserved in the eternal moment—Zelim the fisherman, Zelim the prophet, Zelim the ghost; he's been recorded in all his forms, these pages a poor but passionate echo of the great record that is holiness itself.

There must still be room for the falling note, of course. Even in an undying world there are times when beauty passes from sight, or love passes from the heart, and we feel the sorrow of partition.

In Samarkand, which was glorious for a time, the lozenge tiles, blue and gold, have fallen from the walls, and the chestnut tree under which Zelim and Galilee talked after the prophet's passing has been felled. The domes are decaying, and streets that were once filled with noise are given over to silence. It's not a good silence; it's not the hush of a hermit's cell, or the quiet of dawn. It's simply an absence of life. Regimes have come and gone, parties and potentates, old guards and new, each stealing a portion of Samarkand's glory when they lose power. Now there's only dirt and despair. The highest hope of those who remain is that one of these days the Americans will come and find reason to believe in the city again. Then there'll be hamburgers and soda and cigarettes. A sad ambition for the people of any great city.

And until that happens, there's just the falling tiles, and a dirty wind.

As for Atva, it no longer exists. I suppose if you dug deep in the sand along the shore you'd find the broken-down walls of a few houses, maybe a threshold or two, a pot or two. But nothing of great interest. The lives that were lived in Atva were unremarkable, and so are the few signs that those lives left behind them. Atva does not appear on any maps (even when it thrived it was never marked down that way), nor is mentioned in any books about the Caspian Sea.

Atva exists now in two places. Here in these pages, of course. And as my brother Galilee's true name.

I have one additional detail to add before we move on to something more urgent. It's about that first day, when my father Nicodemus and his wife Cesaria went down to baptize their beloved child in the water.

Apparently what happened was this: no sooner had Cesaria lowered the baby into the water than he squirmed in her hands and escaped her, diving beneath the first wave that came his way and disappearing from view. My father of course waded in after him, but the current was particularly strong that day and before he could catch hold of his son the babe had been caught up and swept away from the shore. I don't know if Cesaria was crying or yelling or simply keeping her silence. I do know she didn't go in after the escapee, because she once remarked to Marietta that she had known all along Galilee would go from her side, and though she was surprised to see him leaving at such a tender age she wasn't about to stop him.

Eventually, maybe a quarter of a mile out from the beach, my father caught sight of a little head bobbing in the water. By all accounts the baby was still swimming, or making his best attempt at it. When Atva felt his father's hands around him he began to bawl and squirm. But my father caught firm hold of him. He set the baby on his shoulders, and swam back to the shore.

Cesaria told Marietta how the baby had laughed once he was back in her arms, laughed until the tears ran, he was so amused by what he'd done.

But when I think of this episode, especially in the context of what I'm about to tell you, it's not the child laughing that I picture. No, it's the image of little Atva, barely a day old, squirming from the hands of those who created him, and then, ignoring their cries and their demands, simply swimming away, swimming away, as though the first thing on his mind was escape.

# PART THREE

# An Expensive Life

# I

## i

You remember Rachel Pallenberg? I spoke about her briefly several chapters back, when I was figuratively wringing my hands about whose story I was first going to tell. I described her driving around her hometown of Dansky, Ohio—which lies between Marion and Shanck, close to Mount Gilead. Unpretentious would be a kind description of the town; banal perhaps truer. If it once had some particular charm, that charm's gone, demolished to make room for the great American ubiquities: cheap hamburger places, cheap liquor places, a market for soda that impersonates more expensive soda and cheese that impersonates milk product. By night the gas station's the brightest spot in town.

Here, Rachel was raised until she was seventeen. The streets should be familiar to her. But she's lost. Though she recognizes much of what she sees—the school where she passed several miserable years still stands, as does the church, where her father Hank (who was always more devout than her mother) brought her every Sunday, the bank where Hank Pallenberg worked until his sickness and early demise—all of these she sees and recognizes; and still she's lost. This isn't home. But then neither is the place she left to drive here; the exquisite apartment overlooking Central Park where she's lived in the bosom of wealth and luxury, married to the man of countless women's dreams: Mitchell Geary.

Rachel doesn't regret leaving Dansky. It was a claustrophobic life she lived here: dull and repetitive. And the future had looked grim. Single women in Dansky didn't break their hearts trying for very much. Marriage was what they wanted, and if their husbands were reasonably sober two or three nights a week and their children were born with all their limbs, then they counted themselves lucky, and dug in for a long decline.

That was not what Rachel had in mind for herself. She'd left Dansky two days after her seventeenth birthday without giving it so much as a backward glance. There was another life out there, which she'd seen in magazines and on the television screen: a life of possibilities, a movie-star life, a life she was determined to have for herself. She wasn't the only seventeen-year-old girl in America who nurtures such hopes, of course. Nor am I the first person to be recounting in print how she made that dream a reality. I have here beside me four books and a stack of magazines—the contents of most of which don't merit the word reportage—all of which talk in often unruly metaphor about the rise and rise of Rachel Pallenberg. I will do my best here to avoid the excess and stick to the facts, but the story—which is so very much like a fairy tale—would tempt a literary ascetic, as you'll see. The beautiful, dark-eyed girl from Dansky, with nothing to distinguish her from the common herd but her dazzling smile and her easy charm, finds herself, by chance, in the company of the most eligible bachelor in America, and catches his eye. The rest is not yet history; history requires a certain closure, and this story's still in motion. But it is certainly something remarkable.

How did it come about? That part, at least, is very simple to tell.

Rachel left Dansky planning to begin her new life in Cincinnati, where her mother's sister lived. There she went, and there, for about two years, she stayed. She had a brief but inglorious stint training to be a dental technician, then spent several months working as a waitress. She was liked, though not loved. Some of her fellow workers apparently considered her a little too ambitious for her own good; she was one of those people who didn't mind voicing their aspirations, and that irritated those who were too afraid to do so for themselves, or simply had none. The manager of the restaurant, a fellow called Herbert Finney, remembers her differently from one interview to the next. Was she "a hardworking, rather quiet girl?" as he says to one interviewer, or "a bit of a trouble-maker, flirting with the male customers, always looking to get something for herself?" as he tells another. Perhaps the truth is somewhere in between. Certainly waitressing didn't suit her for very long; nor did Cincinnati. Twenty-one months after arriving there, in late August, she took a train east, to Boston. When she was later asked by some idiot magazine why she'd chosen that city, she'd replied that she'd heard the autumn months were pretty there. She found another waitressing job, and shared an apartment with two girls who were, like her, new to the city. After two weeks she was taken on by an upscale jewelry store on Newbury Street, and there she worked through the fall—which was indeed beautiful, crisp and clean—until, on December 23rd, late in the afternoon, Christmas came visiting in the form of Mitchell Geary.

## ii

It began to snow that afternoon, somewhere around two, the first flurry coming as Rachel returned from lunch. The prediction for the rest of the day, and into the night, was worsening by the hour: a blizzard was on its way.

Business was slow; people were getting out of the city early, despite the fact that they could calculate the shopping hours left to Christmas morning on their fingers and toes. The manager of the store, a Mr. Erickson (a forty-year-old with the wan, weary elegance of a man half his age again), was on the phone in the back office discussing with his boss the idea of closing up early, when a limo drew up outside and a young dark-haired man in a heavy coat, his collar pulled up, his eyes downcast as though he feared being recognized in the ten-yard journey from limo to store, strode to the door, stamped off the snow on the threshold and came in. Erickson was still in the back office, negotiating closing times. The other assistant, Noelle, was out fetching coffee. It fell to Rachel to serve the customer in the coat.

She knew who he was, of course. Who didn't? The classically handsome features—the chiseled cheekbones, the soulful eyes, the strong, sensual mouth, the unruly hair—appeared on some magazine or other every month: Mitchell Monroe Geary was one of the most watched, debated, swooned-over men in America. And here he was, standing in front of Rachel with flakes of snow melting on his dark eyelashes.

What had happened then? Well, it had been a simple enough exchange. He'd come in, he explained, to look for a Christmas gift for his grandfather's wife, Loretta. Something with diamonds, he'd said. Then, with a little shake of his head: "She *loves* diamonds." Rachel showed him a selection of diamond pin brooches, hoping to God Erickson didn't come off the phone too soon, and that the line at the coffee shop was long enough to delay Noelle's return for a few minutes longer. Just to have the Geary prince to herself for a little while was all she asked.

He declared that he liked both the butterfly and the star. She took them from their black velvet pillows for him to examine more closely. What was her opinion, he asked. Mine? she said. Yes, yours. Well, she said, surprised at how easy she found it to talk to him: if it's for your grandmother, then I think the butterfly's probably too romantic.

He'd looked straight at her, with a mischievous glint in his eyes. "How do you know I'm not passionately in love with my grandmother?" he'd said.

"If you were you wouldn't still be looking for someone," she'd replied, quick as silver.

"And what makes you think I am?"

Now it was she who smiled. "I read the magazines," she said.

"They never tell the truth," he replied. "I live the life of a monk. I swear." She said nothing to this, thinking she'd probably said far too much already: lost the sale, lost her job too, if Erickson had overheard the exchange. "I'll take the star," he said. "Thank you for the advice."

He made the purchase and left, taking his charm, his presence, and the glint in his eye away with him. She'd felt strangely cheated when he'd gone, as though he'd also taken something that belonged to her, absurd though that was. As he strode away from the store Noelle came in with the coffees.

"Was that who I think it was?" she said, her eyes wide.

Rachel nodded.

"He's even more gorgeous in the flesh, isn't he?" Noelle remarked. Rachel nodded. "You're drooling."

Rachel laughed. "He is handsome."

"Was he on his own?" Noelle said. She looked back out into the street as the limo was pulling away. "Was *she* with him?"

"Who's she?"

"Natasha Morley. The model. The anorexic one."

"They're all anorexic."

"They're not happy," Noelle remarked with unperturbable certainty. "You can't be that thin and be happy."

"She wasn't with him. He was buying something for his grandmother."

"Oh that bitch," Noelle sniped. "The one who always dresses in white."

"Loretta."

"That's right. Loretta. She's his grandfather's second wife." Noelle was chatting as though the Geary family were next door neighbors. "I read something in *People* where they said she basically runs the family. Controls everybody."

"I can't imagine anybody controlling him," Rachel said, still staring out into the street.

"But wouldn't you *love* the opportunity?" Noelle replied.

Erickson appeared from the back office at this juncture, in a foul temper. Despite the rapidly worsening storm they had been instructed to keep the store open until eight-thirty. This was a minor reprieve: two days before Christmas they were usually open till ten at night, to catch what Erickson called "guilty spouse business." The more expensive the present, Erickson always said, the more acts of adultery the customer had committed during the preceding year. When in a particularly waspish mood, he wasn't above quoting a number as the door slammed.

So they dutifully stayed in the store, and the snow, as predicted, got worse. There was a smattering of business, but nothing substantial.

And then, just as Erickson was starting to take the displays out of the window for the night, a man came in with an envelope for Rachel.

"Mr. Geary says he's sorry, he didn't get your name," the messenger told her.

"My name's Rachel."

"I'll tell him. I'm his driver and his bodyguard, by the way. I'm Ralph."

"Hello, Ralph."

Ralph—who was six foot six if he was an inch, and looked as though he'd had a distinguished career as a punching bag—grinned. "Hello, Rachel," he said. "I'm pleased to meet you." He pulled off his leather glove and shook Rachel's hand. "Well, goodnight folks." He trudged back to the door. "Avoid the Tobin Bridge, by the way. There was a wreck and it's all snarled up."

Rachel had no wish to open the envelope in front of Noelle or Erickson, but nor could she stand the idea of waiting another nineteen minutes until the store was closed, and she was out on the street alone. So she opened it. Inside was a short, scrawled note from Mitchell Geary, inviting her to the Algonquin Club for drinks the following evening, which was Christmas Eve.

Three and a half weeks later, in a restaurant in New York, he gave her the diamond butterfly brooch, and told her he was falling in love.

# II

This is as good a place as any to attempt a brief sketch of the Geary family. It's a long, long drop from the topmost branch, where Rachel Pallenberg was poised the moment she became the wife of Mitchell Geary, to the roots of the family; and those roots are buried so deep into the earth I'm not sure I'm quite ready to disinter them. So instead allow me to concern myself—at least for now—with that part of the family tree that's readily visible: the part that appears in the books about the rise and influence of the Geary engine.

It quickly becomes apparent, even in a casual skimming of these volumes, that for several generations the Gearys have behaved (and have been treated) like a form of American royalty. Like royalty, they've always acted as though they were above the common law; this in both their private and their corporate dealings. Over the years several members of the dynasty have behaved in ways that would have guaranteed incarceration if they hadn't been who they were: everything from driving in a highly intoxicated state to wife-beating. Like royalty, there has often been a grandeur to both their passions and to their failures which galvanized the rest of us, whose lives are by necessity confined. Even the people that they'd abused over the years—either in their personal lives or in their corporate machinations—were entranced by them; ready to forgive and forget if the gaze of the Gearys would only be turned their way again.

And, like royalty, they had their feet in blood. No throne was ever won or held without violence; and though the Gearys were not blessed by the same king-making gods who'd crowned the royal heads of Europe, or the emperors of China or Japan, there was a dark, bloody spirit in their collective soul, a Geary daemon if you will, who invested them with an authority out of all proportion to their secular rights. It made them fierce in love, and fierce still in hatred, it made them iron-willed and long-lived; it made them casually cruel and just as casually charismatic.

Most of the time, it was as though they didn't even know what they were doing, good, bad or indifferent. They lived in a kind of trance of self-absorption, as though the rest of the world was simply a mirror held up to their faces, and they passed through life seeing only themselves.


In some ways love was the ultimate manifestation of the Geary daemon; because love was the way that the family increased itself, enriched itself.

For the males it was almost a point of pride that they be adulterous, and that the world know it, even if the subject wasn't talked about above a whisper. This dubious tradition had been initiated by Mitch's great-grandfather, Laurence Grainger Geary, who'd been a cocksman of legendary stamina, and had fathered, according to one estimate, at least two dozen bastards. His taste in mistresses had been broad. Upon his death two black women in Kentucky, sisters no less, claimed to have his children; a very well respected Jewish philanthropist in upstate New York, who had served with old man Geary on a committee for the Rehabilitation of Public Morals, had attempted suicide, and revealed in her farewell letter the true paternity of her three daughters, while the madam of a bordello in New Mexico had showed her son to the local press, pointing out how very like a Geary child he looked.

Laurence's wife Verna had made no public response to these claims. But they took their toll on the unhappy woman. A year later she was committed to the same institution that had housed Mary Lincoln in her last years. There Verna Geary survived for a little over a decade, before making a pitiful exit from the world.

Only one of her four children (she'd lost another three in their infancy) was at all attentive to her in her failing years: her eldest daughter, Eleanor. The old woman did not care for Eleanor's constant kindness, however. She loved only one of her children enough to beg his presence, in letter after letter, through the period of her incarceration: that was her beloved son Cadmus. The object of her affections was unresponsive. He visited her once, and never came again. Arguably Verna was the author of her own son's cruelty. She'd taught him from his earliest childhood that he was an exceptional soul, and one of the manifestations of this specialness was the fact that he never had to set eyes on any sight that didn't please him. So now, when he was faced with such a sight—his mother in a state of mental disarray—he simply averted his eyes.

"I want to surround myself with things that I enjoy looking at," he told his appalled sister, "and I do *not* enjoy looking at *her.*"


What was pleasing the twenty-eight-year-old Cadmus' senses at that time was a woman called Katherine Faye Browning—Kitty to those close to her—the daughter of a steel magnate from Pittsburgh. Cadmus had met her in 1919 and courted her fiercely for two years, during which time he had begun to work his financial genius on his father's already considerable wealth. This was no chance collision of circumstances. The more Kitty Browning toyed with his feelings (refusing to see him for almost two months in the autumn of that year simply because—as she wrote—"*I wish to see if I can live without you. If I can, I will, because that means you're not the man who rules my heart*") the more frustrated love fueled young Cadmus's ambition. His reputation as a financial strategist of genius—and a demonic enemy if crossed—was forged in those years. Though he would later mellow somewhat, when people thought of Cadmus Northrop Geary it was the young Cadmus they brought to mind: the man who forgave nothing.

In the process of building his empire he acted like a secular divinity. Communities dependent upon industries he purchased were destroyed at his whim, while others flourished when he looked upon them favorably. By his early middle age he had achieved more than most men dream of in a hundred lifetimes. There was no place of power in which he was not known and lionized. He influenced the passing of bills and the election of judges; he bought Democrats and Republicans alike (and left them at the mercy of their parties when he was done with them); he made great men look foolish, and—when it suited him, as it occasionally did—elevated fools to high office.

Need I tell you that Kitty Browning finally succumbed to his importunings and married him? Or add that he committed his first act of adultery—or *philandering*, as he preferred—while they were on their honeymoon?

A man of Cadmus's power and influence—not to mention looks (he was built after the classic American model, his body graceful in action and easy in repose, his long, symmetrical features perpetually tanned, his eyes sharp, his smile sharper still)—a man such as this is always surrounded by admirers. There was nothing languid or dull about him; nothing that bespoke doubt or fatigue: that was the heart of his power. Had he been a better man, his sister once remarked, or a much worse one, he might have been president. But he had no interest in wasting his attributes on politics. Not when there were so many women to seduce (if seduction was the word for something so effortless). He divided his time between his offices in New York and Chicago, his houses in Virginia and Massachusetts, and the beds of some several hundred women a year, paying off irate husbands when they found out, or employing them.

As for Kitty, she had a life of her own to lead: four children to raise, and a social calendar of her own which was nicely filled. The last thing she wanted was a husband under her feet. As long as Cadmus didn't embarrass her with his shenanigans, she was perfectly content to let him go his way.

There was only one romance—or more correctly a failed romance—that threatened this strange equilibrium. In 1926, at the invitation of Lionel Bloombury, who was then the head of a small independent studio in Hollywood, Cadmus went west. He considered himself quite the connoisseur when it came to movies, and Lionel had suggested he could do worse than invest some of his capital in the business. Indeed he would later do so; he put Geary money into Metro-Goldwyn-Mayer, and saw, during its golden years, a substantial return on his investment; he also purchased sizable parcels of land in what would later become Beverly Hills and Culver City. But the only deal he really wanted in Hollywood he failed to make, and that was with an actress called Louise Brooks. He met her first at the premiere of *Beggars of Life*, a Paramount picture she'd made, starring opposite Wallace Beery. She'd seemed to Cadmus an almost supernatural presence; for the first time, he'd said to a friend, he believed in the idea of Eden; of a perfect garden from which men might be exiled because of the manipulations of a woman.

The subject of this metaphysical talk, Louise herself, was without question a great beauty: her dark sleek hair cut almost boyishly to frame a pale, exquisitely sculptured face. But she was also an ambitious and intellectually astute woman, who wasn't interested in being an *objet d'art* for Cadmus or anybody else. She left for Germany the next year, to star in two pictures there, one of which, *Die Büchse de Pandora*, would immortalize her. Cadmus was by now so enraptured that he sailed to Europe in the hope of a liaison, and it seems she was not entirely scornful of his advances. They dined together; and took day trips when her filming schedule allowed. But it seems she was dallying with him. When she went back to filming she complained to her director, a man called Pabst, that the presence of Geary on set was spoiling her concentration and could he please be removed? There was some kind of minor fracas later that week, when Cadmus—who had apparently attempted to purchase the studio that was making *Die Büchse de Pandora* in the interim, and failed—forced his way onto the set in the hope of talking to her. She refused to speak to him and he was forcibly removed. Three days later he was on a ship headed back to America.

His "folly," as he would later call this episode, was over. He returned to his business life with a sharpened—even rapacious—appetite. A year after his return, in October of 1929, came the stock market crash which marked the beginning of the Great Depression. Cadmus rode the calamity like a broncobuster from one of his beloved Westerns; he was unshakable. Other men of money went into debt and penury or ended up dead by their own hand, but for the next few years, while the country suffered through the worst economic crisis since the Civil War, Cadmus turned the defeats of those around him into personal victories. He bought the ruins of other men's enterprises for a pittance; putting out lifeboats for a lucky few who were drowning around him, thus assuring himself of their fealty once the storm was over.

Nor did he limit his business dealings to those who'd been relatively honest but had fallen on hard times; he also dealt with men who
had blood on their hands. These were the last days of Prohibition; there
was money to be made from supplying liquor to the parched palates of
America. And where there was profit, there was Cadmus Geary. In the
four years between his return from Germany and the repeal of the Eigh-
teenth Amendment, he funneled Geary family funds into several illicit
booze and "entertainment" businesses, raking off monies that no tax-
man ever saw, and ploughing it back into his legitimate concerns.

He was careful with his choice of business partners, avoiding the
company of individuals who took too much pleasure in their own notoriety. He never did business with Capone or his like, preferring the qui-
eter types, like Tyler Burgess and Clarence Filby, whose names didn't
make it into the headlines or the history books. But in truth he didn't
have the stomach for criminality. Though he was reaping enormous
sums of money from these illicit dealings, in the spring of 1933, just
before the repeal was passed by Congress, he broke all contact with
"The Men in the Midwest," as he called them.

In fact it was Kitty who forced his hand. Normally she kept herself
out of financial affairs, but this, she told him, was not a fiscal matter: the
reputation of the family would be irreparably harmed if any association
with this scum could be proved. He readily bowed to her pressure; he
didn't enjoy doing business with these people anyway. They were peasants, most of them; a generation ago, he'd said, they'd have been in
some Godforsaken corner of Europe eating scabs off their donkeys. The
remark had amused Kitty, and she took it for her own, using it whenever
she was feeling particularly vicious.


So Prohibition and the grim years of the Great Depression passed, and
the Gearys were now one of the richest families in the history of the continent. They owned steel mills and shipyards and slaughterhouses. They
owned coffee plantations and cotton plantations and great swaths of land
given over to barley and wheat and cattle. They owned sizable portions
of real estate in the thirty largest cities in America, and were the land-
lords of many of the towers and fancy houses and condominiums that
were built on that land. They owned racehorses, racetracks, and racing
cars. They owned shoe manufacturers and fish canneries and a hot dog
franchise. They owned magazines and newspapers, and distributors who
delivered those magazines and newspapers, and the stands from which
those magazines and newspapers were sold. And what they could not

own, they put their name on. As though to distinguish his noble family from the peasants with whom he had ceased to do business in '33, Cadmus allowed Kitty to use tens of millions of Geary dollars in philanthropic endeavors, so that in the next two decades the family name went up on the wings of hospitals, on schools, on orphanages. All these good works did not divert the eyes of cynical observers from the sheer scale of Cadmus's acquisitiveness, of course. He showed no sign of slowing up as he advanced in years. In his middle sixties, at an age when less driven men were planning fishing trips and gardens, he turned his appetites eastward, toward Hong Kong and Singapore, where he repeated the pattern of plunder that had proved so successful in America. The golden touch had not deserted him: company after company was transformed by Cadmus's magic. He was a quiet juggernaut, unseen now for the most part, his reputation almost legendary.

He continued his philandering, as he had in his younger days, but the hectic business of sexual conquest was of far less significance to him now. He was still, by all accounts, a remarkably adept bed partner (perhaps consciously he chose in these years women who were less discreet than earlier conquests; advertisements for his virility, in fact); but after the Louise Brooks episode he never came so close to the blissful condition of love as when he was in full capitalist flight. Only then did he feel alive the way he had when he'd first met Kitty, or when he'd followed Louise to Germany; only then did he exalt, or even come close to exaltation.

Meanwhile, of course, another generation of Gearys was growing up. First there was Richard Emerson Geary, born in 1934, after Kitty had suffered two miscarriages. Then, a year later, Norah Faye Geary, and two years after that George, the father of Mitchell Garrison.

In many ways Richard, Norah, and George were the most emotionally successful of any of the generations. Kitty was sensible to the corruptions of wealth: she'd seen its capacity to destroy healthy souls at work in own family. She did her level best to protect her children from the effects of being brought up feeling too extraordinary; and her capacity for love, stymied in her marriage, flowered eloquently in her dealings with her children. Of the three it was Norah who was most indulged; and Cadmus was the unrepentant indulger. She rapidly became a brat, and nothing Kitty could do to discipline her did the trick. Whenever she didn't get what she wanted, she went wailing to Daddy, who gave her exactly what she requested. The pattern reached grotesque proportions when Cadmus arranged for the eleven-year-old Norah—who had become fixated upon the notion of being an actress—to star in her own little screen test, shot on the backlot at MGM. The long-term effects of this idolatry would not become apparent for several years, but they would bring tragedy.

In the meanwhile, Kitty dispersed her eminently practical love to Richard and George, and watched them grow into two extraordinarily capable men. It was no accident that neither wanted much to do with running the Geary empire; Kitty had subtly inculcated into them both a distrust of the world in which Cadmus had made a thousand fortunes. It wasn't until the first signs of Cadmus's mental deterioration began to show, in his middle seventies, that George, the youngest, agreed to leave his investment company and oversee the rationalization of what had become an unwieldy empire. Once in place, he found the task more suited his temperament than he'd anticipated. He was welcomed by the investors, the unions, and the board members alike as a new kind of Geary, more concerned with the welfare of his employees, and the communities which were often dependent upon Geary investment, than with the turning of profit.

He was also a successful family man, in a rather old-fashioned way. He married one Deborah Halford, his high school sweetheart, and they lived a life that drew inspiration from the kind of solid, loving environment which Kitty had tried so hard to provide. His older brother Richard had become a trial lawyer with a flair for murderers and rhetoric; his life seemed to be one long last act from an opera filled with emotional excess. As for poor Norah, she'd gone from one bad marriage to another, always looking for, but never finding, the man who would give her the unconditional devotion she'd had from Daddy.

By contrast, George lived an almost dull life, despite the fact that he ruled most of the Geary fortunes. His voice was quiet, his manner subdued, his smile, when it came along, beguiling. Despite his skills with his employees, stepping into Cadmus's shoes wasn't always easy. For one thing, the old man had by no means given up attempting to influence the direction of his empire, and when his health crisis was over he assumed that he'd be returning to his position at the head of the boardroom table. It was Loretta, Cadmus's second wife, who persuaded him that it would be wiser to leave George in charge, while Cadmus took up an advisory position. The old man accepted the solution, but with a bad grace: he became publicly critical of George when he disapproved of his son's decisions, and on more than one occasion spoiled deals that George had spent months negotiating.

At the same time, while Cadmus was doing his best to tarnish his own son's glories, other problems arose. First there were investigations on insider trading of Geary stocks, then the complete collapse of business in the Far East following the suicide of a man Cadmus had appointed, who was later discovered to have concealed the loss of billions; and, after half a century of successful secrecy, the revelation of Cadmus's Prohibition activities, in a book that briefly made the bestseller list despite Richard's legal manipulations to have it withdrawn as libelous.

When things got too frantic, George took refuge in a home life that was nearly idyllic. Deborah was a born nest-builder; she cared only to make a place where her husband and her children would be cared for and comfortable. Once the front door was closed, she would say, the rest of the world wasn't allowed in unless it was invited; and that included any other member of the Geary clan. If George needed soli-tude—time to sit and listen to his jazz collection, time to play with the kids—she could be positively ferocious in her defense of her threshold. Even Richard, who had persuaded juries of the impossible in his time, couldn't get past her when she was protecting George's privacy.

For the four children of this comfortable marriage—Tyler, Karen, Mitchell, and Garrison—there was plenty of affection and plenty of pragmatism, but there was also a string of temptations that had not been available to the previous generation. They were the first Gearys who were regularly followed around by paparazzi during their adolescence; who were squealed on by classmates if they smoked dope or tried to get laid; who appeared on the cover of magazines when they went skinny-dipping. Despite Deborah's best efforts, she could not protect her chil-dren from every sleazehound who came sniffing around. Nor, George pointed out, was it wise to try. The children would have to learn the pain of public humiliation the hard way, by being hurt. If they were smart, they'd modify their behavior. If not, they'd end up like his sister Norah, who'd had almost as many tabloid covers as she'd had analysts. It was a hard world, and love kept no one from harm. All it could do, sometimes, was speed the healing of the wounds.

# III

## i

So much for my promised brevity. I intended to write a short, snappy chapter giving you a quick glimpse of the Geary family tree, and I end up lost in its branches. It's not that every twig is pertinent to the story at hand—if that were the case, I'd never have undertaken the task—but there are surprising connections between some of what I've told you and events to come. To give you an example: Rachel, when she smiles a certain way, has something of Louise Brooks's wicked humor in her eyes; along with Louise's dark, shiny hair, of course. It's useful for you to know how devoted Cadmus was to Louise, if you're to understand how the presence of Rachel will later affect him.

But even more important than such details, I suspect, is a general sense of the patterns these people made as they passed their behavior, good and bad, on to their children. How Laurence Grainger Geary (who died, by the way, in a prostitute's bed in Havana) taught his son Cadmus by example to be both fearless and cruel. How Cadmus shaped a creature of pure self-destruction in Norah, and a man subtly committed to his own father's undoing in George.

George: we may as well take a moment here to finish George's story. It's a sad end for such a good-natured man; a death over which countless questions still hang. On February 6th, 1981, instead of driving up to his beloved weekend house in Caleb's Creek to join his family, he went out to Long Island. He drove himself, which was strange. He didn't like to drive, especially when the weather was foul, as it was that night. He did call Deborah, to tell her that he'd be late home: he had an "annoying bit of business" he needed to attend to, he told her, but he promised to be back by the early hours of the morning. Deborah waited up for him. He didn't come home. By three a.m. she had called the police; by dawn a full scale search was underway, a search which continued through a rainy Saturday and Sunday without a single lead being turned up. It wasn't until seven-thirty or so on Monday morning that a man walking his dog along the shore at Smith Point Beach chanced to peer into a car that had been parked there he'd noticed, close to the sand, for three days. Inside was the body of a man. It was George. His neck had been broken. The murder had taken place on the shore itself—there was sand in George's shoes, and in his hair and mouth—then the body had been carried back to the car and left there. His wallet was later found on the shore. The only item that had been taken from it was a picture of his wife.

The hunt for George's killer went on for years (in a sense, I suppose, it still continues; the file was never closed) but despite a million-dollar reward offered by Cadmus for information leading to the arrest of the murderer, the felon was never found.

## ii

The major effects of George's demise—at least those relevant to this book—are threefold. First, there was Deborah, who found herself strangely alienated from her husband by the suspicious facts of his death. What had he hidden from her? Something vital; something lethal. For all the trust they'd had in one another, there had been one thing, one terrible thing he had not shared with her. She just didn't know what it was. She did well enough for a few months, sustained by the need to be a good public widow, but once the cameras were turned in the direction of new scandals, new horrors, she quickly capitulated to the darkness of her doubts and her grief. She went away to Europe for several months, where she was joined by (of all people) her sister-in-law Norah, with whom until now she'd had nothing in common. Stateside, rumors began to fly again: they were living like two middle-aged divas, the gossip columnists pronounced, dredging the gutters of Rome and Paris for company. Certainly when the pair got back home in August 1981, Deborah had the look of a woman who'd seen more than the Vatican and the Eiffel Tower. She'd lost thirty pounds, was dressed in an outfit ten years too young for her, and kicked the first photographer at the airport who got in her way.

The second effect of George's death was of course upon his children. Fourteen-year-old Mitchell had become a particular focus of public attention after his father's demise: his looks were beginning to deliver on their promise (he would be, by general consensus, the handsomest Geary yet) and the way he dealt with the invasiveness of the press spoke of a maturity and a dignity beyond his years. He was a prince; everyone agreed; a prince.

Garrison, who was six years his senior, had always been far more retiring, and he did little to conceal his discomfort during this period. While Mitchell stayed close to his mother throughout the period of mourning, accompanying her to philanthropic galas and the like in his father's stead, Garrison retreated from the limelight almost completely. And there he would remain. As for Tyler and Karen, both of whom were younger than Mitchell, their lives were left unexamined by the columnists, at least for a few years. Tyler was to die in 1987, along with his Uncle Todd, Norah's fourth husband, when the light aircraft Todd was piloting came down during a sudden storm near Orlando, Florida. Karen—who in hindsight probably most closely resembled her father in the essential gentility of her nature—became an archeologist, and rapidly distinguished herself in that field.

The third consequence of George Geary's sudden demise was the reascension of Cadmus Geary. He had weathered the physical and mental frailty that had been visited upon him just as he'd weathered so much else in his life, and now—when the Geary empire needed a leader, he was there to take charge. He was by now in his eighties, but he behaved as though his little sickness had been but a palate cleanser, a sour sorbet that had sharpened his appetite for the rare meat now set before him. In a decade of naked acquisitiveness, here was the triumphant return of the man who'd written the modern rules of combat. At times he seemed to be at pains to compensate for his late son's humanity. Anyone who stood against him (usually for principles espoused by George) was summarily ousted; Cadmus didn't have the time or the temper for persuasion.

Wall Street responded well to the change. *Old Man Cadmus Back in Charge,* ran the headline of *The Wall Street Journal,* and in a couple of months there were profiles running everywhere, plus the inevitable catalogues of Cadmus's cruelties. He didn't care. He never had and he never would. This was his style, and it suited the world into which he had resurrected himself more than a little well.

## iii

There'll be more about Old Man Geary later; a lot more. For now, let me leave him there, in triumph, and go back to the subject of mortality. I've already told you how Laurence Geary died (the whore's bed, Havana) and Tyler (Uncle Todd's plane, Florida) and of course George (in the driving seat of his Mercedes, Long Island) but there are other passages to the great beyond that should be noted here. Did I mention Cadmus's mother, Verna? Yes, I did. She perished in a madhouse, you'll remember. I didn't however note that her passing was almost certainly also murder, probably at the hands of another inmate, one Dolores Cooke, who committed suicide (with a stolen toothpick, pricking herself so many times she bled to death) six days after Verna's demise. Eleanor, her rejected daughter, died in hearty old age, as did Louise Brooks, who gave up her career in cinema in the early thirties, finding the whole endeavor too trivial to be endured.

Of the significant players here, that only leaves Kitty, who died of cancer of the esophagus in 1979, just as Cadmus was emerging from his own bout of frailty. She was two years younger than the century. The next year, Cadmus remarried: the recipient of the offer a woman almost twenty years his junior, Loretta Talley, (another sometime actress, by the way: Loretta had played Broadway in her youth, but, like Louise, tired of her powerlessness).

As for Kitty, she has little or no part in what follows, which is a pity for me, because I have in my possession a copy of an extraordinary document she wrote in the last year of her life which would fuel countless interesting speculations. The text is utterly chaotic, but that's not surprising given the strength of the medications she was on while she was writing it. Page after page of the testimony (all of which is handwritten) documents the yearnings she felt for some greater meaning than the duties of mother, wife, and public philanthropist, a profound and unanswered hunger for something poetic in her life. Sometimes the sense of the text falls apart entirely, and it becomes a series of disconnected images. But even these are potent. It seems to me she begins, at the end of her life, to live in a continuous present: a place where memory, experience and expectation are all folded together in one delirious stream of feeling. Sometimes she writes as though she were a child looking down at her own wasted body, fascinated by its mutinies and its grotesqueries.

She also talks about Galilee.

It wasn't until I read the document for the third time (combing it for clues to her beliefs about George Geary's murder) that I realized my half brother was present in the text. But he's there. He enters and exits Kitty's account like the breeze that's presently ruffling the papers on my desk; visible only by its effect. But there's no question that he somehow offered her a taste of all that she'd been denied; that he was, if not the love of her life, at least a tantalizing glimpse of what changes a love of real magnitude — reciprocated love, that is — might have wrought in her.

## iv

Let me now give you a brief guided tour to the Geary residences, since so many of the exchanges I will be reporting occur there. Over the years the family has accrued large amounts of real estate and, because they never needed to realize the capital, seldom sold anything. Sometimes they renovated these properties, and occupied them. But just as often Geary houses have been kept for decades — regularly cleaned and redecorated — without any member of the family stepping over the threshold. As of this writing, I know of houses and apartments the family owns in Washington, Boston, Los Angeles, Montana, Louisiana, South Carolina, and Hawaii. In Europe they own properties in Vienna, Zurich, London, and Paris; and further afield, in Cairo, Bangkok, and Hong Kong.

For now, however, it's the New York residences that I need to describe in a little detail. Mitchell has a *pied à terre* on the fringes of Soho, far more extravagantly appointed inside, and far more obsessively guarded, than its undistinguished exterior would suggest. Margie and Garrison occupy two floors close to the top of the Trump Tower, an apartment which commands extraordinary views in all directions. The purchase was Margie's suggestion (at the time it was some of the most expensive space in the world, and she liked the idea of spending so much of Garrison's money) but she never really warmed to the apartment, for all its glamour. The decorator she hired, a man called Jeffrey Penrose, died a month after finishing his transformation, and posthumous articles about him mentioned the Trump Tower apartment as his "last great creation; like the woman who employed him—kitschy, glitzy, and wild." So it was; and so was Margie, back then. The years since haven't been kind, however. The glitter looks tawdry now; and what seemed witty in the eighties has lost its edge.

The one truly great Geary residence in the city is what everyone in the family refers to as "the mansion"; a vast, late nineteenth century house on the Upper East Side. The area's called Carnegie Hill, but it might just as well have been named for the Gearys; Laurence was in residence here twenty years before Andrew Carnegie built his own mansion at 5th and 91st. Many of the houses surrounding the Geary residence have been given over to embassies; they're simply too large and too expensive for one family. But Cadmus was born and raised in the mansion, and never once contemplated the notion of selling it. For one thing, the sheer volume of possessions the house contains could not be transferred to a more modestly scaled space: the furniture, the carpets, the clocks, the *objets d'art*; there's enough to found a sizable museum. And then there are the paintings, which unlike much of the other stuff were collected by Cadmus himself. Big canvases, all of them; and all by American painters. Magnificent works by Albert Bierstadt, Thomas Cole, and Frederick Church, enormous paintings of the American landscape at its most awe inspiring. To some, these works are regressive and rhetorical; the products of limited talents overreaching themselves in pursuit of a sublime vision. But hanging in the mansion, sometimes occupying entire walls, the paintings have an undeniable authority. In some ways they define the house. Yes, it's dark and heavy in there; sometimes it seems hard to draw breath, the air is so dense, so stale. But that's not what people remember about the mansion. They remember the paintings, which almost look like windows, letting onto great, untamed wildernesses.

The house is run by a staff of six, who work under Loretta's ever judgmental eye. However hard they labor, however, the house is always bigger than they can manage. There's always dust gathering somewhere; they could work twenty-four hours a day, seven days a week, and still not tame the enormity of the place.

So: that's the New York City residences. Actually, I haven't told you everything. Garrison has a secret place that even Margie doesn't know he owns, but I'll describe that to you when he visits it, along with an explanation as to why he's obliged to keep its existence to himself. There's also a house upstate, near Rhinebeck, but that also has a significant place in the narrative ahead, so I'll delay describing it until then.

The only other residence I want to make mention of here is a long way from New York City, but should be mentioned here, I think, because in my imagination it forms a trinity with the mansion and L'Enfant. That house is a far more humble dwelling than the other two. In fact it's probably the least impressive of any of the major residences in this story. But it stands a few yards from the blue Pacific, in a grove of palm trees, and for the lucky few who've spent a night or two beneath its roof, it evokes Edenic memories.

That house we'll also come to later, and to the secrets it contains, which are sweatier than anything Garrison hides away in his little bolt-hole, and yet so vast in their significance that they would beggar the skills of the men who painted the wildernesses in the mansion. We are a while away from being there, but I want you to have the image of that paradisiacal spot somewhere in your head, like a bright piece of a jigsaw puzzle which doesn't seem to fit in the scheme, but must be held on to, contemplated now and again, until its significance becomes apparent, and the picture is understood as it would not have been understood until that piece found its place.

# IV

## i

I must move on. Or rather back; back to the character with whom I opened this sequence, Rachel Pallenberg. The last two chapters were an attempt to offer some context for the romance between Rachel and Mitchell. And I hope as a consequence you'll feel a little more sympathy for Mitchell than his subsequent actions might seem to deserve. He was not, at least at the beginning, a cruel or reprehensible man. But he had lived most of his life in the public eye, despite his mother's best efforts. That kind of scrutiny creates an artificiality in a person's behavior. Everything becomes a kind of performance.

In the seventeen years since his father's funeral, Mitchell had learned to play himself perfectly; it was his genius. In all other regards — excepting his looks — he was average, or below average. An uninspired student, a so-so lover, an indifferent conversationalist. But when the subject of the exchange vanished and charm alone held the air, he was wonderful. In the words of Burgess Motel, who'd spent half a day with him for a profile piece in *Vanity Fair*, "The less substance there was to what he was saying, the more at ease he seemed; and, yes, the more perfect. If this seems to tread perilously close to nonsense, it's because you have to be there, watching him perform this Zen-like trick of being in nothingness, to believe just how persuasive and sexy it is. Do I sound entranced? I am!"

This wasn't the first time a male writer had swooned girlishly over Mitchell in print, but it *was* the first time somebody had successfully analyzed the way Mitchell ruled a room. Nobody knew charm like Mitchell, and nobody knew as well as Mitchell that charm was best experienced in a vacuum.

None of this, you may say, reflects well upon Rachel. How could she have fallen for such triviality? Given herself over into the arms of a man who was at his best when he had nothing of consequence to say? It was easy, believe me. She was dazzled, she was flattered, she was seduced, not just by Mitchell but by all he stood for. There had never been a time when the Gearys had not been a part of her idea of America: and now she was being invited to enter their circle; to become a part of their mystique. Who could refuse an offer like that? It was a kind of waking dream, in which she found herself removed from the gray drudgery of her life into a place of color and comfort and plenty. And she was surprised at how well she fitted into this dreamscape. It was almost as though she'd known in her heart that this was the life she'd one day be living, and had unconsciously been preparing for it.

All of which is not to say there weren't times when her palms got a little clammy. Meeting the whole family for the first time on the occasion of Cadmus' ninety-fifth birthday party; the first time down a red carpet, at a fund-raiser at the Lincoln Center, just after the engagement had been announced; the first time she was flown somewhere in the family jet, and turned out to be its only passenger. All so strange, and yet so strangely familiar.

For his part Mitchell seemed to read her anxiety level instinctively in any given situation, and act appropriately. If she was uncomfortable, he was right there at her side, showing her by example how to fend off impertinent questions politely and ease the flow of small talk if somebody became tongue-tied. On the other hand if she seemed to be having a good time he left her to her own devices. She rapidly gained a reputation as lively company; at ease with all kinds of people. The chief revelation for Rachel was this: that these power brokers and potentates with whom she was now beginning to rub elbows were hungry for simple conversation. Over and over again she would catch herself thinking: they're no different from the rest of us. They had dyspepsia and ill-fitting shoes, they bit their nails and worried about their waistlines. There were a few individuals, of course, who decided she was beneath them—generally women of uncertain vintage—but she rarely encountered such snobbery. More often than not she found herself welcomed warmly, often with the observation that she was the one Mitchell had been looking for, and everyone was glad she was finally here.

As to her own story, well she didn't talk about it much at first. If people asked about her background, she'd keep the answers vague. But as she began to trust her confidence more, she talked more openly about life in Dansky, and about her family. There was a certain percentage of people whose eyes started to glaze over once she mentioned anywhere west of the Hudson, but there were far more who seemed eager for news from a world less sealed, less smothering than their own.

"You will have noticed," Garrison's garish and acidic wife Margie—whose tongue was notoriously acidic—remarked, "that you keep seeing the same sour old faces wherever you go. You know why? There's only twenty important people left in New York, twenty-one now you're here, and we all go to the same parties and we all serve on the same committees. And we're all very, very bored with one another." She happened to make the remark while she and Rachel stood on a balcony looking down at a glittering throng of perhaps a thousand people. "Before you say anything," Margie went on, "it's all done with mirrors."

Inevitably on occasion a remark somebody would make would leave her feeling uncomfortable. Usually such remarks weren't directed at her, but at Mitchell, in her presence.

"Wherever did you find her?" somebody would say, meaning no conscious offense by the question but making Rachel feel like a purchase, and the questioner fully expected to go back to the same store and pick up one for themselves.

"They're just amazed at how lucky I am," Mitchell said, when she pointed out how objectionable she found that kind of observation. "They don't mean to be rude."

"I know."

"We can stop going to so many parties, if you like."

"No. I want to know all the people you know."

"Most of them are pretty boring."

"That's what Margie said."

"Are you two getting on well?"

"Oh yes. I love her. She's so outrageous."

"She's a terrible drunk," Mitchell said curtly. "She's been okay for the last couple of months, but she's still unpredictable."

"Was she always . . . ?"

"An alcoholic?"

"Yes."

"Maybe I can help her," Rachel said.

He kissed her. "My Good Samaritan." He kissed her again. "You can try but I don't hold out much hope. She's got so many axes to grind. She doesn't like Loretta at all. And I don't think she likes me much."

Now it was Rachel who offered the kiss. "What's not to like?" she said.

Mitchell grinned. "Damned if I know," he said.

"You egotist."

"Me? No. You must be thinking of somebody else. I'm the humble one in the family."

"I don't think there's such a thing—"

"—as a humble Geary?"

"Right."

"Hm." Mitchell considered this for a moment. "Grandma Kitty was the nearest, I guess."

"And you liked her?"

"Yeah," Mitchell said, the warmth of his affection there in his voice. "She was sweet. A little crazy toward the end, but sweet."

"And Loretta?"

"She's not crazy. She's the sanest one in the family."

"No, I meant, do you like her?"

Mitchell shrugged. "Loretta's Loretta. She's like a force of nature."

Rachel had met Loretta only two or three times so far: this was not the way the woman seemed at all. Quite the contrary. She'd seemed rather reserved, even demure, an impression supported by the fact that she always dressed in white or silvery gray. The only theatrical touch was the turbanish headgear she favored, and the immaculate precision of her makeup, which emphasized the startling violet of her eyes. She'd been pleasant to Rachel, in a gentle, noncommittal sort of way.

"I know what you're thinking," Mitchell said. "You're thinking: Loretta's just an old-fashioned lady. And she is. But you try crossing her—"

"What happens?"

"It's like I said: she's a force of nature. Especially anything to do with Cadmus. I mean, if anyone in the family says anything against him and she hears about it she tears out their throats. 'You wouldn't have two cents to rub together without him,' she says. And she's right. We wouldn't. This family would have gone down without him."

"So what happens when he dies?"

"He isn't going to die," Mitchell said, without a trace of irony in his voice. "He's going to go on and on and on till one of us drives him out to Long Island. Sorry. That was in bad taste."

"Do you think about that a lot?"

"What happened to Dad? No. I don't think about it at all. Except when some book comes out, you know, saying it was the Mafia or the CIA. I get in a funk about that stuff. But we're never going to really know what happened, so what's the use of thinking about it?" He stroked a stray hair back from Rachel's brow. "You don't need to worry about any of this," he said. "If the old man dies tomorrow we'll divide up the pie—some for Garrison, some for Loretta, some for us. Then you and me . . . we'll just disappear. We'll get on a plane and we'll fly away."

"We could do that now if you want to," Rachel said. "I don't need the family, and I certainly don't need to live the high life. I just need you."

He sighed; a deep, troubled sigh. "Ah. But where does the family end and Mitchell begin? That's the question."

"I know who you are," Rachel said, drawing close to him. "You're the man I love. Plain and simple."

## ii

Of course it wasn't that plain and it wasn't that simple.

Rachel had entered a small and unenviable coterie: that group of people whose private lives were deemed publicly owned. America wanted to know about the woman who had stolen Mitchell Geary's heart, especially as she'd been an ordinary creature so very recently. Now she was transformed. The evidence was there in the pages of the glossies and the weekly gossip rags: Rachel Pallenberg dressed in gowns a year's salary would not have bought her six months before, her smile that of a woman happy beyond her wildest dreams. Happiness like that couldn't be celebrated for very long; it soon lost its appeal. The same readers who were entranced by the rags-to-riches story in February and March, and astonished by the way the shop girl had been made into a princess in April and May, and a little tearful about the announcement of an autumn wedding when it was made in June, wanted the dirt by July.

What was she *really* like, this thief who'd run off with Prince Mitchell's eligibility? She wouldn't be as picture-perfect as she seemed; nobody was that *pleasant*. She had secrets; no doubt. Once the wedding was announced, the investigators went to work. Before Rachel Pallenberg got into her white dress and became Rachel Geary, they were going to find something scandalous to tell, even if they had to turn over every rock in Ohio to do it.

Mitchell wasn't immune from the same zealous muckraking. Old stories about his various liaisons resurfaced in tarted-up forms. His short affair with the drug-addicted daughter of a congressman; his various trips around the Aegean with a small harem of Parisian models; his apparently passionate attachment to Natasha Morley, who'd lately married minor European royalty, and (according to some sources) broken his heart by so doing. One of the sleazier rags even managed to find a classmate from Harvard who claimed that Mitchell's taste for girls ran to the barely pubescent. "If there's grass on the field, play ball, that's what he used to say," the "classmate" remembered.

Just in case Rachel was tempted to take any of this to heart, Margie brought over a stack of magazines that her housekeeper, Magdalene, had hoarded from the early years of Margie's life with Garrison, all of which contained stories filled with similar vitriol. The two women were in almost every way dissimilar: Rachel petite and stylish, reserved in her manner; Margie big-boned, overdressed, and voluble. Yet they were like sisters in this storm.

"I was really upset at the time," Margie said. "But I've begun to wish ten percent of what they were saying about Garrison was true. He'd be a damn sight more interesting."

"If it's all lies, why doesn't somebody sue them?" Rachel said.

Margie offered a fatalistic shrug. "If it wasn't us it'd be some other poor sonofabitch. Anyway, if they stopped writing this shit I might have to go back to reading *books*." She gave a theatrical shudder.

"So you read this stuff?"

Margie arched a well-plucked eyebrow. "And you don't?"

"Well . . ."

"Honey, we all love to learn about who fucked who. As long as we're not the who. Just hold on. You're going to get a shitload of this thrown at you. Then they'll move on to the next lucky contestant."

Margie, God bless her, hadn't offered her reassurances a moment too soon. The very next week brought the first gleanings from Dansky.

Nothing particular hurtful; just a willfully depressing portrait of life in Rachel's hometown, plus a few pictures of her mother's house, looking sadly bedraggled: the grass on the lawn dead, the paint on the front door peeling. There was also a brief summary of how Hank Pallenberg had lived and died in Dansky. Its very brevity was a kind of cruelty, Rachel thought. Her father deserved better than this. There was much worse to come. Still sniffing after some hint of scandal, a reporter from one of the tabloids tracked down a woman who'd trained with Rachel as a dental technician. Giving her name only as "Brandy," because she claimed not to want the attention of the press, the woman offered a portrait of Rachel that was beyond unflattering.

"She was always out to catch herself a rich man," Brandy claimed. "She used to cut pictures out of newspapers—pictures of rich men she thought she had a hope of getting, you know—but rich, always real rich, and then she pinned them all up on the wall of her bedroom and used to stare at them every night before she went to sleep." And had Mitchell Geary been one of Rachel Pallenberg's hit-list of eligible millionaires, the reporter had asked Brandy. "Oh sure," the girl had replied, claiming she'd got a sick feeling when she'd heard the news about how Rachel's plan had worked. "I'm a Christian girl, born and raised, and I always thought there was something weird about what Rachel was doing with those pictures up there. Like it was voodoo or something."

All idiotic invention, of course, but it was still a potent mixture of elements. The headline, accompanied by a picture of Rachel at a recent fund-raiser, her eyes flecked with red from the photographer's flash, read: "Shocking Sex-Magic Secrets of Geary Bride!" The issue was sold out in a day.

## iii

Rachel did her best with all this, but it was hard—even accepting that she'd been a consumer of this nonsense herself, and thoroughly enjoyed it. Now it was her face people were staring at as they waited at the supermarket checkout, her life they were half-believing these lies about. All the detachment she was able to muster didn't spare her the hurt of that.

"What are you doing even *looking* at that shit?" Mitchell asked her when she raised the subject over dinner that night. The establishment was Luther's, an intimate restaurant round the corner from Mitchell's apartment on Park Avenue.

"They could be saying *anything*," Rachel said. She was close to tears. "Not just about me. About my mother or my sister or *you*."

"We've got lawyers watching them all the time. If Cecil felt they were going too far—"

"Too far? What's too far?"

"Something worth fighting over," Mitchell said. He reached over and took hold of her hand.

"It's not worth crying about, baby," he said softly. "They're just stupid people who don't have anything better to do than try and tear other people down. The thing is: they can't do it. Not to us. Nor to the Gearys. We're stronger than that."

"I know . . ." Rachel said, wiping her nose. "I want to be strong, but—"

"I don't want to hear *but*, baby," he said, his tone still tender despite the toughness of the sentiment. "You've got to be strong, because people are looking at you. You're a princess."

"I don't feel much like a princess right now."

He looked disappointed. He pushed the plate of kidneys away, and put his hand to his face. "Then I'm not doing my job," he said. She stared at him, puzzled. "It's my job to make you feel like a princess. My princess. What can I do?" He looked up at her, with a kind of sweet desperation on his face. "Tell me: *what can I do?*"

"Just love me," she said.

"I do. Honey, I do."

"I know you do."

"And I hate it that those sleazeballs are giving you grief, but they can't touch you, honey. Not really. They can spit and they shout but they can't touch you." He squeezed her hand. "That's my job," he said. "Nobody gets to touch you but me."

She felt a subtle tremor in her body, as though his hands had reached out and stroked her between her legs. He knew what he'd done too. He passed his tongue, oh-so-lightly, over his lower lip, wetting it.

"You want to know a secret?" he said, leaning closer to her.

"Yes, please."

"They're all afraid of us."

"Who?"

"Everybody," he said, his eyes fixed on hers. "We're not like them, and they know it. We're Gearys. They're not. We've got power. They haven't. That makes them afraid. So you have to let them give vent once in a while. If they didn't do that they'd go crazy." Rachel nodded; it made sense to her. A few months ago, it wouldn't have done, but now it did.

"I won't let it bother me any more," she said. "And if it does bother me I'll shut up about it."

"You're quite a gal, you know that?" he said. "That's what Cadmus said about you after his birthday party."

"He barely spoke to me."

"He's got eyes. '*She's quite a gal,*' he said. '*She's got the right stuff to be a Geary.*' He's right. You do. And you know what? Once you're a member of this family, *nothing* can hurt you. Nothing. You're untouchable. I swear, on my life. That's how it works when you're a Geary. And that's what you're going to be in nine weeks. A Geary. Forever and always."

# V

Marietta just came in, and read what I've been writing. She was in one of her willful moods, and I should have known better, but when she asked me if she could read a little of what I'd been writing, I passed a few pages over to her. She went out onto the veranda, lit up one of my cigars, and read. I pretended to get on with my work, as though her opinion on what I'd done was inconsequential to me, but my gaze kept sliding her way, trying to interpret the expression on her face. Occasionally, she looked amused, but not for very long. Most of the time she just scanned the lines (too fast, I thought, to really be savoring the prose) her expression impassive. The longer this went on the more infuriated I became, and I was of half a mind to get up, go out onto the veranda. At last, with a little sigh, she got up and came back in, proffering the pages.

"You write long sentences," she remarked.

"That's all you can say?"

She fished a book of matches out of her pocket, and striking one, began to rekindle her cigar. "What do you want me to say?" she shrugged. "It's a bit gossipy, isn't it?" She was now studying the book of matches. "And I think it's going to be hard to follow. All those names. All those Gearys. You don't have to go that far back, do you? I mean, who cares?"

"It's all context."

"I wonder whose number this is?" she said, still studying the book. "It's a Raleigh number. Who the hell do I know in Raleigh?"

"If you can't be a little more generous, a little more constructive . . ."

She looked up, and seemed to see my misery. "Oh, Eddie," she said, with a sudden smile. "Don't look so forlorn. I think it's wonderful."

"No you don't."

"I swear. I do. It's just that weddings, you know," her lip curled slightly. "They're not my favorite thing."

"You went," I reminded her.

"Are you going to write about that?"

"Absolutely."

She patted my cheek. "You see, that'll liven things up a bit. How are your legs by the way?"

"They're fine."

"Total recovery?"

"It looks that way."

"I wonder why she healed you after all this time?"

"I don't care. I'm just grateful."

"Zabrina said she saw you out walking."

"I go to see Luman every couple of days. He's got it into his head that we should collaborate on a book when I'm finished with this."

"About what?"

"Madhouses."

"What a bright little sunbeam he is. Ah! I know! This is Alice." She tossed the book of matches into the air and caught it again. "Alice the blonde. She lives in Raleigh."

"That's a very dirty look you've got in your eyes," I observed.

"Alice is adorable. I mean, really . . . sumptuous." She picked a piece of tobacco from her teeth. "You should come out with me one of these days. We'll go drinking. I can introduce you to the girls."

"I think I'd be uncomfortable."

"Why? Nobody's going to make a pass at you, not in an all-girl bar."

"I couldn't."

"You will." She pointed the wet end of her cigar at me. "I'm going to get you out enjoying yourself." She pocketed the book of matches. "Maybe I'll introduce you to Alice."


Of course she left me in a stew of insecurity. My mood now perfectly foul, I retired to the kitchen, to eat my sorrows away. It was a little before one in the morning; Dwight had long since retired to bed. L'Enfant was quiet. It was a little stuffy, so I opened the windows over the sink. There was a light breeze, which was very welcome, and I stood at the sink for a few moments to let it cool my face. Then I went to the refrigerator and began to prepare a glutton's sandwich: several slices of baked ham, slathered with mustard, some strips of braised aubergine, half a dozen sweet cherry tomatoes, sliced, and a dash of olive oil, all pressed between two slices of freshly cut rye bread.

Feeding my face put everything in context for me. What was I hanging on Marietta's opinion for? She was no great literary critic. This was my book, my ideas, my vision. And if she didn't like it, that was fine by me. Her opinion was a complete irrelevancy. I didn't just think all of this, I talked it through to myself, a mustardy mingling of words and ham.

"Whatever are you chattering about?"

I stopped talking, and looked over my shoulder. There, filling the doorway from side to side, was Zabrina. She was dressed in a tent of a nightgown, her face, upon which she usually puts a little paint and powder, ruddily raw. She had tiny eyes, and a wide thin-lipped mouth; Marietta called her a beady, fat frog once, in a moment of anger, and — cruel though the description may be — it fits. The only glamorous attribute she has is her hair, which is a deep, luxurious orange, and which she's grown to waist length. Tonight she had it untied, and it fell about her shoulders and upper body like a cape.

"I haven't seen you in a long while," I said to her.

"You've seen me," she said, in that odd, breathy voice of hers. "We just haven't spoken."

I was about to say — that's because you always rush away — but I held my tongue. She was a nervous creature. One wrong word and she'd be off. She went to the refrigerator and studied its contents. As usual, Dwight had left a selection of his pies and cakes for her delectation.

"Don't expect any help from me," she said out of the blue.

"Help for what?"

"You know what," she said, still studying the laden shelves. "I don't think it's right." She reached in and took out a pie with either hand, then, pirouetting with a grace surprising in one of her extreme bulk, turned and closed the refrigerator door with her backside. "So don't expect me to be unburdening myself."

She was talking about the book of course. Her antipathy was perfectly predictable, given that she knew it to be at least in part Marietta's idea. Even so, I wasn't in the mood to be harangued.

"Let's not talk about it," I said.

She set the pies — one cherry, one pecan — on the table side by side. Then she went back to the refrigerator, with a little sigh of irritation at her own forgetfulness, and took out a bowl of whipped cream. There was a fork already in the bowl. She lowered herself gently onto a chair and set to, loading up the fork with a little cherry pie, a little pecan, and a lot of whipped cream. She clearly had done this countless times before; watching the skillful way she created these little towers of excess, without ever seeming to drop a crumb of pastry into the cream, or a spot of cream onto the table, was an entertainment unto itself.

"So when did you last hear from Galilee?" she asked me.

"Not in a long while."

"Huh." She delivered a teetering mound between her lips, and her lids flickered with bliss as she worked it around her mouth.

"Does he ever write to you?"

She took her leisurely time to swallow before answering. "He used to drop me a note now and again. But not any more."

"Do you miss him?"

She frowned at me, her lower lip jutting out. "Don't start that," she said. "I told you already—"

I rolled my eyes. "In God's name, Zabrina, I just asked—"

"I don't want to be in your book."

"So you said."

"I don't want to be anybody's book. I don't want to . . . be *talked* about. I wish I was invisible."

I couldn't help myself: I smirked. The very idea that Zabrina, of all people, would dream of invisibility was sadly laughable. There she was, conspiring against her own hopes with every mouthful. I thought I'd wiped the smirk off my face by the time she looked up at me, but it lingered there, like the cream at the corners of her own mouth.

"What's so funny?" she said.

I shook my head. "Nothing."

"So I'm fat. And I wish I was dead. So what?"

The smirk had gone now. "You don't wish you were dead," I said. "Surely."

"What have I got to live for?" she replied. "I've got nothing. Nothing I want anyway." She put down her fork, and started on the cherry pie with her fingers, picking out the syrupy fruit. "Day in and day out, it's the same story. Serving Momma. Eating. Serving Momma. Eating. When I sleep I dream I'm up there with her, while she talks about the old days." With sudden vehemence she said: "I hate the old days! What about tomorrow? How about *doing something about tomorrow?*" Her face, which was as I mentioned, flushed to begin with, was now beet red. "We're all so passive," she said, the vehemence mellowing into a sadness. "You got your legs back but what did you do with them? Did you walk out of here? No. You sat exactly where you'd been sitting all these years, as though you were still a cripple. That's because you still are. I'm fat and you're a cripple, and we're going to go on, day after day after day living our useless lives, till somebody from out there—" she pointed out toward the world "—comes and does us the kindness of putting a bullet through our brains."

With that, she rose from the ruins of the pies, and made her exit. I didn't attempt to delay her. I just sat back in my chair and watched her go.

Then, I will admit, I sat for a while with my head in my hands and wept.

# VI

## i

Assaulted by both Marietta and Zabrina, feeling thoroughly uncertain of my talents, I returned to my room, and sat up through the rest of the night. I'd like to tell you that I did so because I was agonizing over the literary problems I had, but the truth was rather more prosaic: I had the squirts. I don't know whether it was the baked ham, the braised aubergine, or Zabrina's damn conversation that did it: I only know I spent the hours till dawn sitting on my porcelain throne in a private miasma. Somewhere around dawn, feeling weak, raw, and sorry for myself, I crawled into bed and snatched a couple of hours of sleep. By the time I woke my slumbering mind seemed to have decided that I'd be best writing about Rachel and Mitchell's wedding in a rather curter style than I'd been employing so far. After all, I reasoned, a wedding was a wedding was a wedding. No use belaboring the subject. People could fill in the pretty details for themselves.

So then: the bare facts. The wedding took place on the first week of September, in a little town in New York State called Caleb's Creek. I've already mentioned it in passing, I believe. It's not far from Rhinebeck, close to the Hudson. A pretty area, much beloved of earlier generations of American royalty. The Van Cortandts built a home up here; so did the Astors and the Roosevelts. Extravagant houses where they could bring two hundred guests for a cozy weekend retreat. By contrast, the property George Geary had purchased in Caleb's Creek was a modest place, five bedrooms, colonial style: described in one book about the

Gearys as "a farmhouse," though I doubt it was ever that. He'd loved the place; so had Deborah. After his death she'd many times remarked that the best times of her life had been spent in that house; easy, loving times when the rest of the world was made to wait at the threshold. It was actually Mitchell who had suggested opening the house up again—it had been left virtually unvisited since George's death—and holding the wedding celebrations there. His mother had warmed to the idea instantly. "George would like that," she'd said, as though she imagined the spirit of her beloved husband still wandering the place, enraptured by the echoes of happier times.

To clinch the deal, Mitchell drove Rachel up to Caleb's Creek in the middle of July, and they stayed over at the house for one night. A couple from the town, the Rylanders, who had been housekeeper and gardener during the halcyon days, and had kept the place clean and tidy during its years of neglect, had worked furiously to give the house a second chance at life. When Mitchell and Rachel arrived it looked like a dream retreat. Eric Rylander had planted hundreds of flowers and rose-bushes, and laid a new lawn; the windows, doors, and shutters had been painted, so had the white picket fence. The small apple orchard behind the house had been tidied up, the trees pruned; everything made orderly. Inside, Eric's wife Barbara had been no less diligent. The house had been thoroughly aired, the drapes and carpets cleaned, the wood-work and furniture polished until it shone.

Rachel was, of course, completely charmed. Not just by the beauty of the house and brightness of the garden, but by the evidence every-where of the man who'd fathered her husband-to-be. At Deborah's instruction the house had been left as George had liked it. His hun-dreds of jazz albums were still on their shelves, all alphabetically arranged. His writing desk, where according to Mitchell he'd been mak-ing notes for a kind of memoir about his mother Kitty, was just as he'd left it, arrayed with framed family photographs, which had lost most of their color by now.

The visit had not only served to confirm Mitchell's instincts that this was indeed the place to have the wedding; it had turned into a kind of tryst for the lovers. That night, after a splendid supper prepared by Barbara, they'd stayed up sitting out watching the midsummer sky darken, sipping whiskey and talking about their childhoods; and of their fathers. It had got so dark they couldn't even see one another's faces, but they kept talking while the breeze moved in the apple trees: about times they'd laughed, times they'd lost. When, finally, they'd retired to bed (Mitch would not sleep in the master bedroom, despite the fact that

Barbara had made up the old four-poster for them; they slept in the room he'd had as a child), they lay in each other's arms in the kind of blissful exhaustion that usually follows lovemaking, though they had not made love.

When they went back to New York the following morning, Rachel held Mitchell's hand the whole way. She'd never felt the kind of love she felt for him that day in her life; nothing even close to it.

## ii

On the Friday evening, with the whole place—house, garden, orchard, grounds—overrun with people (lantern-hangers, sign-posters, bandstand-erectors, table-carriers, chair-counters, glass-polishers; and on, and on) Barbara Rylander came to find her husband, who was standing at the front gate watching the trucks come and go, and having sworn him to · secrecy, said she'd just been out in the orchard, taking a break from the commotion, and she'd seen Mr. George standing there beneath the trees, watching the goings-on. He was smiling, she said.

"You're a silly old woman," Eric told his wife. "But I love you very much." And he gave her a great big kiss right there in front of all these strangers, which was completely out of character.

The day dawned, and it was spectacular. The sun was warm, but not hot. The breeze was constant, but never too strong. The air smelt of summer still, but with just enough poignancy to suggest the coming fall.

As for the bride: she outdid the day. She'd felt nauseous in the morning; but once she started to get dressed her nerves disappeared. She had a short relapse when Sherrie came in to see her daughter and promptly burst into happy tears, which threatened to get Rachel started. But Loretta wasn't having any of that. She firmly sent Sherrie away to get a brandy, then she sat with Rachel and talked to her. Simple, sensible talk.

"I couldn't lie to you," Loretta said solemnly. "I think you know me well enough by now to know that."

"Yes I do."

"So believe me when I tell you: everything's fine; nothing's going to go wrong; and you look . . . you look like a million dollars." She laughed, and kissed Rachel on the cheek. "I envy you. I really do. Your whole life ahead of you. I know that's a terrible cliché. But when you get to be old you see how true it is. You've got one life. One chance to be you. To have some joy. To have some love. When it's over, it's over." She stared intently at Rachel as she spoke, as though there was some deeper significance in this than the words alone could express. "Now, let's get you to the church," Loretta said brightly. "There's a lot of people waiting to see how beautiful you look."

Loretta's promise held. The service was performed in the little church in Caleb's Creek, with all its doors flung wide so that those members of the congregation who weren't able to be seated—fully half of them—could either stand along the walls or just outside, to hear the short ceremony. When it was over the whole assembly did as wedding parties had done in Caleb's Creek since the town's founding: they walked, with the bride and groom hand in hand at the head of the crowd, down Main Street, petals strewn underfoot "to sweeten their way" (as local tradition had it), the street lined on either side with local people and visitors, all smiling and cheering as the procession made its triumphant way through the town. The whole affair was wonderfully informal. At one point a child—one of the Creek kids, no more than four—slipped her mother's hand and ran to look at the bride and groom. Mitchell scooped the child up and carried her for a dozen yards or so, much to the delight of all the onlookers, and to the joy of the child herself, who only began to complain when her mother came to fetch her, and Mitchell handed her back.

Needless to say there were plenty of photographers on hand to record the incident, and it was invariably an image that editors chose when they were putting together their pieces on the wedding. Nor was its symbolism lost on the scribblers who wrote up the event. The anonymous girl-child from the crowd, lifted up into the strong safe arms of Mitchell Geary: it could have been Rachel.

# VII

## i

Once the pressures of preparation and the great solemnity of the service were over, the event became a party. The last of the formalities—the speeches and the toasts—were kept mercifully short, and then the fun began. The air remained warm, the breeze just strong enough to rock the lanterns in the trees; the sky turned golden as the sun sank away.

"Perfection, Loretta," Deborah said, when the two women chanced to be sitting alone for a moment.

"Thank you," Loretta said. "It just takes a little organization, really."

"Well it's wonderful," Deborah replied. "I only wish George were here to see it."

"Would he have liked her?"

"Rachel? Oh yes. He would have loved Rachel."

"Unpretentious," Loretta observed. She was watching Rachel even as she spoke: arm in arm with her beloved, laughing at something one of Mitchell's old Harvard chums had said. "An ordinary girl."

"I don't think she's ordinary at all," Deborah said. "I think she's very strong."

"She'll need to be," Loretta said.

"Mitchell adores her."

"I'm sure he does. At least for now."

Deborah's lips tightened. "Must we, Loretta . . . ?"

"Tell the truth? Not if you don't want to."

"We've had our happiness," Deborah said. "Now it's their turn." She started to get up from the table.

"Wait—" Loretta said. She reached out and lightly caught hold of Deborah's wrist. "I don't want us to argue."

"I never argue," Deborah said.

"No. You walk away, which is even worse. It's time we were friends, don't you think? I mean . . . there's things we're going to have to start planning for."

Deborah slipped her arm out of Loretta's grasp. "I don't know what you mean," she said, her tone making it perfectly clear that she did not wish the conversation to continue.

Loretta changed the subject. "Sit down a moment. Did I tell you about the astrologer?"

"No . . ." Deborah said, "Garrison mentioned you'd found someone you liked."

"He's wonderful. His name's Martin Yzerman; he lives out in Brooklyn Heights."

"Does Cadmus know you go to one of these people?"

"You should go to Yzerman yourself, Deborah."

"Why would I want to do that?"

"Advice like that's very useful if you're trying to make long-term plans."

"But I don't," she said. "I gave up trying. Things change too quickly."

"He could help you see the changes coming."

"I doubt it."

"Believe me."

"Could he have predicted what happened to George?" Deborah said sharply.

Loretta let a moment of silence fall between them before she said: "No question."

Deborah shook her head. "That's not the way things are," she said. "We don't know what's going to happen tomorrow. Nobody does." She rose from her chair. This time Loretta didn't try to stop her. "I'm astonished that a smart woman like you would put faith in that kind of thing. Really I am. It's nonsense, Loretta. It's just a way to make you feel as though you're in control of things." She looked down at Loretta almost pityingly. "But you're not. None of us are. We could all be dead this time tomorrow."

And with that, she walked away.

This odd little exchange wasn't the only crack in the bliss of the day. There were three other incidents which are probably worth remarking upon, though none of them were significant enough to spoil the celebrations.

The first of the three, perhaps inevitably, involved Margie. Champagne was not her preferred mode of transport, so she'd made sure that the bar was stocked with good whiskey, and once the first round of bubbly was drunk she switched to Scotch. She rapidly became a little testy, and took it into her head to tell Senator Bryson who, along with his family, had flown up from Washington, what she thought of his recent comments on welfare reform. She was by no means inarticulate and Senator Bryson was plainly quite happy to be chewing on a serious issue rather than nibbling small talk; he listened to Margie's remarks with suitable concern. Margie downed another Scotch and told him he was talking out of both sides of his mouth. The senator's wife attempted a little leavening here, remarking that the Gearys weren't likely to be needing welfare any time soon. To which Margie sharply replied that her father had worked in a steel mill most of his life, and died at the age of forty-five with twelve bucks in his bank account; and where the hell was the man with the whiskey anyway? Now it was Garrison who stepped in to try and bring the exchange to a halt, but the senator made it perfectly plain that he was enjoying the *contretemps* and wished to continue. The man with the whiskey duly arrived, and Margie got her glass refilled. Where were they, she said; oh yes, twelve bucks in his bank account. "So don't tell me I don't know what's going on out there. The trouble is none of you high and mighties gives a fuck. We've got problems in this country, and they're getting worse, and what are you doing about it? Besides sitting on your fat asses and pontificating."

"I don't think any caring human being would disagree with you," the senator said. "We need to work to make American lives better lives."

"And what does that all add up to?" Margie said. "A fat lot of nothin'. Is it any wonder nobody in this country believes a damn word any of you people say?"

"I think people are more interested in the democratic process—"

"Democratic, my ass!" Margie said. "It's all lobbies and paybacks and doing your friends favors. I know how it works. I wasn't born yesterday. You just want to make the rich richer."

"I think you're mistaking me for a Republican," Bryson chuckled.

"And I think you're mistaking me for someone who'd trust a fucking word any politician ever said," Margie spat back.

"That's enough now," Garrison said, taking hold of his wife's arm. She tried to shake him free, but he held on tight. "It's all right, Garrison," the senator said. "She's got a right to her opinion." He returned his gaze to Margie. "But I will say this. America's a free country. You don't have to live in the lap of luxury if it doesn't sit well with your political views." He smiled, though there was not a trace of warmth in his eyes. "I really wonder if it's entirely appropriate for a woman in your position to be talking about the agonies of the working man."

"I told you, my father—"

"Is part of the past. This administration is part of the future. We can't afford sentiment. We can't afford nostalgia. And most of all, we can't afford hypocrisy."

This little speech had the ring of an exit line, and Margie knew it. Too drunk by now to mount any coherent riposte, all she could say was: "What the fuck does that mean?"

The senator was already turning to leave, but he pivoted on his heel to reply to Margie's challenge. The smile, even in its humorless form, had gone.

"It means, Mrs. Geary, that you can't stand there in a fifty-thousand-dollar dress and tell me you understand the pain of ordinary people. If you want to do some good, maybe you should start off by auctioning the contents of your closet and giving away the profits, which I'm sure would be substantial."

That was his last word on the subject. He was gone the next moment, along with his wife and entourage. Garrison went to follow, but Margie clutched his arm.

"Don't you *dare*," she told him. "Or I'll quote what you said about him being a spineless little shit."

"You are contemptible," Garrison said.

"No. *You're* contemptible. I'm just a pathetic drunk who doesn't know any better. You want to take me inside before I start on somebody else?"

## ii

Rachel didn't hear about Margie's exchange with the man from Washington until after the honeymoon, when Margie herself confessed it. But she was very much a part of the second of the three notable exchanges of the afternoon.

What happened was this: toward dusk Loretta came to find her and asked if she'd mind bringing her mother and sister to meet Cadmus, who was going to be leaving very soon. The old man hadn't joined the celebration until the cake was about to be cut, at which point he'd been brought out to the big marquee in his wheelchair—to much applause—and made a short, eloquent toast to the bride and groom. He'd then been taken to a shady spot at the back of the house, where the flow of folks who wanted to pay their respects to him could be strictly controlled. Apparently he'd been anxious to meet Rachel's family earlier in the day, but only now, at nine in the evening, had the line of people eager to shake his hand diminished. He was very tired, Loretta warned; they should keep the conversation brief.

In fact, despite the demands of the day, Rachel thought he looked better than he had at his birthday party, certainly: positively robust for a ninety-six-year-old (sitting comfortably in a high-backed wicker chair generously packed with cushions in a backwater of the garden, nursing a brandy glass and the stub of a cigar). His face was still handsome, after its antique fashion; he'd aged beyond the gouges and furrows into a kind of skeletal grandeur, his skin so tanned it was like old wood, his eyes set in the cups of his sockets like bright stones. His speech was slow, and here and there a little slurred, but he still had more charisma than most men a quarter his age, and sufficient memory to know how to work it on the opposite sex. He was like some much beloved movie star, Rachel thought; so adored in his season that now, though he was well past his prime, he still believed in his own magic. And that was the most important part, belief. The rest was just window dressing.

Loretta made all the introductions, and then returned to the party, leaving Cadmus king of his own court.

"I wanted to tell you how proud I am," he told Rachel, "to have you, and your mother and your sister, as part of the Geary family. You are all so very lovely, if I may say so." He handed his glass to the woman (Rachel assumed it was a nurse) who stood close to his chair, and reached out to take the bride's hand. "Excuse my chilly fingers," he said. "I don't have the circulation I used to have. I know how strong the feeling is between you and Mitchell and I must tell you I think he is the luckiest man alive to have won your affections. So many people . . ." He stopped for a moment, and his eyelids fluttered. Then he drew a deep breath, as if pulling on some buried reserve of energy, and the moment of frailty passed. "I'm sorry," he said. "So many people, you know, never have in their lives anything like the kind of deep feeling you two have for one another. I had it in my life." He made a small wry smile. "Regrettably it wasn't for either of the women I married." Rachel heard Deanne suppress a guffaw behind her. She glanced back, frowning, but Cadmus was in on the joke. His smile had spread into a mischievous grin. "In fact, you my dear Rachel, bear more than a passing resemblance to the lady I idolized. So much so that when I first set eyes upon you, at that little party Loretta threw for me—as if I wanted to be reminded how antiquated I am—I thought to myself: Mitchell and I have the same taste in beauty."

"May I ask who this was?" Rachel asked him.

"I'd be pleased to tell you. In fact, I'll do better than that. Would you care to come to the house next week?"

"Of course."

"I'll show you the lady I loved," Cadmus told Rachel. "Up on the screen, where age can't touch her. And I'm afraid . . . neither can I."

"I'll look forward to that."

"So will I . . ." he said, his voice a little fainter now. "Well, I suppose I should let you ladies go back to the celebration."

"It's been wonderful to meet you," Sherrie said.

"The pleasure's all mine," Cadmus replied. "Believe me. All mine."

"They just don't make men like that any longer," Sherrie observed when they were out of the old man's presence.

"You sound quite smitten," Deanne said.

"I'll tell you this," Sherrie replied, directing her remarks to Rachel, "if Mitchell is half the man he is, you won't have a thing to complain about."

# VIII

### i

The third and final event I'm going to report took place long after dark, and it was the one that could have potentially spoiled the glory of the day.

Let me first set the scene for you. The evening, as I've said, was balmy, and though the number of guests slowly dwindled as the hour grew later a lot of people stayed longer than they'd planned, to drink and chat and dance. The time and trouble that had been taken to hang the lanterns in the trees around the house paid off handsomely. Though about nine-thirty or so clouds came in from the northeast, the lamps more than compensated for the lack of stars; it was as though every tree had luminous fruit swaying in its branches, lilac and lemon and lime. It was a time for whispered expressions of love, and among the older folks, a renewal of vows and the making of promises. *I'll be kinder; I'll be more attentive; I'll care for you the way I used to care when we were first married.*

Nobody gave any thought to being spied on. With so many luminaries in attendance the security had been fierce. But now, with many of the more important guests already departed and the party winding down, the vigilance of the guards was not what it had been, so nobody saw the two photographers who scrambled over the wall to the east of the house. They didn't find much that would please their editors. A few drunks passed out in their chairs, but nobody of any consequence. Disappointed, they moved on through the grounds, concealing their cameras beneath their jackets if they passed anyone who might question them, until they got to the edge of the dance floor. Here they decided to part.

One of them—a fellow called Buckminster—went to the largest of the tents, hoping he might at least find some overweight celebrity still pigging out. His partner Penaloza headed on past the dance floor, where there were still a few couples enjoying a moody waltz, toward the trees.

None of what Penaloza saw looked particularly promising. He knew the sordid laws of his profession by heart. The readers of the rags to whom he hoped to sell his pictures wanted to see somebody famous committing at least one—but hopefully several—deadly sins. Gluttony was good, avarice was okay; lust and rage were wonderful. But there was nothing significantly sinful going on under the lanterns, and Penaloza was about to turn back to see if he could talk his way into the house when he heard a woman, not far from him, laughing. There was a measure of unease in the sound which drew his experienced ear.

The laughter came again, and this time he made out its source. And, oh my Lord, did he believe what he was seeing? Was that Meredith Bryson, the daughter of Senator Bryson, swaying drunkenly under the tree, her blouse unbuttoned and another woman's face pressed between her breasts?

Penaloza fumbled for his camera. Now there was a picture! Perhaps if he could just get a little closer, so that no one was in doubt as to Meredith's identity. He took two cautious steps, ready to shoot and run if the need arose. But the women were completely enraptured with one another; if things got much more heated the picture would be unpublishable.

There was no doubting the identity of the Bryson girl now; not with her head thrown back that way. He held his breath, and got off a shot. Then another. He'd have liked a third, but Meredith's seducer had already seen him. She gallantly pushed the Bryson girl out of sight behind her, giving Penaloza one hell of a shot of her standing full on to him, shirt unbuttoned to the waist. He didn't wait for the bitch to start screaming.

"Gotta go," he grinned; then turned and ran.

What happened next confounded his every expectation. Instead of hearing one or both of the women set up a chorus of tearful hollering, there was silence, except for the din of his own feet as he ran. And then suddenly there was somebody catching hold of the collar of his shirt, and swinging him around, and it was he who let out the yelp of complaint as his attacker wrenched his camera out of his hands.

*"You fucking scum!"*

It was Meredith's lover, of course; though God knows she'd put on a supernatural turn of speed to catch up with him.

*"That's mine!"* he said, grabbing for his camera.

"No," she replied, very simply, and tossed it back over her shoulder.

"Don't touch it!" Penaloza yelled. "That camera is my property. If you so much as lay a finger on that camera I'll sue you—"

"Oh shut up," the woman said, and slapped him across the face. The blow stung so badly his eyes watered.

"You can't do this," he protested. "This is a Fifth Amendment issue."

The woman hit him again. "Amend that," she said.

Penaloza was a reasonably moral man. He didn't take pleasure in hitting women; but sometimes it was a necessity. Blinking the tears out of his eyes he feinted to the right, and then swung a left that caught the woman's jaw a solid crack. She let out a very satisfying yelp and stumbled backward, but to his surprise she was back at him before he recovered his own balance, throwing herself at him with such violence she brought them both to the ground.

"Jesus!" he heard somebody say, and from the corner of his eyes saw Buckminster standing a few yards away, photographing the fight.

Penaloza managed to pull one hand free and pointed toward his camera, which still lay on the grass a few yards from the senator's daughter. "Grab it!" he yelled. "Buck! You shit! *Pick up my camera!*"

But he was too late. The Bryson bitch was already there, snatching the camera up off the ground, and Buckminster—having decided he'd risked enough as it was—now turned on his heels and fled. Penaloza struggled to pull himself out of his attacker's grip, but she'd pinned him down, her knees clamped to either side of his head, and he had no energy left to throw her off. All he could do was squirm like a child while she casually beckoned Meredith Bryson over.

"Open the camera up, honey." Meredith did so. "Now pull out the film."

Penaloza started to shout again; there were people coming to see what all the commotion was about. If one of them could prevent Meredith from opening the camera, he might still have his evidence. Too late! The back of the camera snapped open, and the Bryson girl pulled the film out.

"Satisfied?" Penaloza growled.

The woman perched on him considered the question for a moment. "Did anybody tell you how lovely you are?" she said, reaching behind her. She took hold of his balls, clutching them tightly. "What a fine, wholesome specimen of manhood you are?" She twisted his scrotum. He sobbed, more with anticipation than fear. "No?" she said.

". . . no . . ."

"Good. Because you're not. You're a worthless piece of rat's doodoo." She twisted again. "What are you?" If he'd had a gun at that moment he'd have happily put a bullet through the bitch's brains.

"*What. Are. You?*" she said again, giving his balls a yank with every syllable.

"Rat's doo-doo," Penaloza said.

## ii

The woman who'd laid Penaloza low was of course none other than my darling Marietta. And you're probably sufficiently familiar with her by now to know that she was very proud of herself. When she got back here to L'Enfant she gave Zabrina and myself chapter and verse of the whole escapade.

"Why the hell did you go there in the first place?" I remember Zabrina asking her.

"I wanted to cause some trouble," she said. "But once I got there, and I'd had a few glasses of champagne, all I wanted to do was fuck. So I found this girl. I didn't know who she was." She smiled slyly. "And neither did she, poor sweetheart. But, I like to think I helped her find out."

There's one footnote to all of this, and it concerns the subsequent romantic career of the senator's daughter.

Maybe a year after the Geary wedding, who should appear on the cover of *People* magazine, there to announce her membership of the Sapphic tribe, but the radiant Meredith Bryson?

Inside, there was a five page interview, accompanied by a number of photographs of the newly uncloseted senator's daughter. One in the window seat of her house in Charleston; another in the back yard, with two cats; and a third of her and her family at the President's inauguration, with an inset blowup of Meredith herself, caught looking thoroughly bored.

"I've always been interested in politics," she averred in the body of the piece.

The interviewer hurried her on to something a little juicier. *When had she first realized she was a lesbian?*

"I know a lot of women say they've always known, somewhere deep down," she replied. "But honestly I didn't have a clue until I met the right person."

Could she tell the readers who this lucky lady was?

"No, I'd prefer not to do that right now," Meredith replied.

"Have you taken her to the White House?"

"Not yet. But I intend to, one of these days. The First Lady and I had a great conversation about it, and she said we'd be very welcome."

The article twittered on in the same substance-free manner for several pages; I don't think anything of any moment was said from beginning to end. But after the talk of White House visits I couldn't help but imagine Marietta and Meredith in Lincoln's bedroom, doing the deed beneath Abe's portrait. Now there was a picture the sleazehounds would have paid a nice price to own.

As to Marietta, she would not be drawn out any further on the subject of the senator's daughter. I can't help wondering, however, if at some point down the line the fate of L'Enfant and the secret lives of Capitol Hill won't again intersect. This is, after all, a house built by a president. I won't argue that it's his masterpiece—that's surely the Declaration of Independence—but L'Enfant's roots lie too close to the roots of democracy's tree for the two not to be intertwined. And if, as Zelim the Prophet once claimed, the process of all things is like the Wheel of the Stars, and what has seemed to pass away will come back again sooner or later, is it unreasonable to suppose that L'Enfant's demise may be caused or quickened by the order of power that brought it into being?

# IX

So now you know how Rachel Pallenberg and Mitchell Geary became husband and wife—from their first meeting to the vows at the altar. You know how powerful a family she had entered, and how possessive it was; you know she was in love with Mitchell, passionately so, and that her feelings were reciprocated.

How then, you ask, does such a romance fall from grace? How is it that, a little over two years later, at the end of a rainy October, Rachel was driving around the benighted streets of Dansky, Ohio, cursing the day she'd heard the name of Mitchell Geary?

If this were a work of fiction I could invent some dramatic scenario to explain all this. She'd step into the house one day and find her husband in bed with another woman, or they'd have an argument that would escalate into violence, or he'd reveal to her in the heat of an angry exchange that he'd married her for a bet with his brother. But there was nothing like that in their lives: no adulteries, no violence, and certainly no raised voices. It just wasn't the way Mitch dealt with things. He liked to be liked, even when being liked meant avoiding a confrontation that would be to everybody's good. That meant turning a blind eye to

Rachel's discomfort if there was the least risk of stirring up something unpleasant. His former empathy, which had been so much a part of what had enchanted her about him, disappeared. If she was unhappy, he simply looked the other way. There was always plenty of Geary family business to justify his inattention; and of course the inevitable seductions of luxury to soften Rachel's loneliness when he was gone.

It would be wrong to claim that she was not in some fashion complicit in all of this. It became apparent to her very quickly that her life as Mrs. Mitchell Geary was not going to be as emotionally fulfilling as she'd hoped. Mitchell was wholly devoted to the family business, and as she had no role in that business, nor wanted one, she found herself alone more often than she liked. Instead of sitting Mitch down and talking the problem through—telling him, in essence, that she wanted to be more than a public wife—she let his way of doing things carry the day, and that soon proved a self-fulfilling prophecy. The less she said the harder it became to say anything at all.

Anyway, how could she claim the marriage wasn't working when to the outside world she'd been given paradise on a platter? Was there anywhere she couldn't go if she wanted to? Any store she couldn't shop in until she was tired of saying *I'll take it?* They went to Aspen skiing, Vermont for a weekend in the autumn, to enjoy the turning of the leaves. She was in Los Angeles for the Oscar parties, in Paris to see the spring collections, in London for the theater, and Rio and Bali for spur-of-the-moment vacations. What did she have to complain about?

The only person in whom she could confide her growing unhappiness was Margie, who wasn't so much sympathetic as fatalistic.

"It's a trade-off," she said. "And it's been going on since the beginning of time. Or at least since the first rich man ever took himself a poor wife."

Rachel flinched at this. "I am not—"

"Oh *honey.*"

"That's not why I married Mitch."

"No, of course it isn't. You'd be with him if he was ugly and poor and I'd be with Garrison if he was tap-dancing on a street corner in Soho."

"I love Mitch."

"Right now?"

"What do you mean?"

"I mean, sitting here right now, having said all the things you've just said about how he's neglectful, and doesn't want to talk about feelings, and so on, sitting *right* here *right* now, you love him?"

"Oh Lord . . ."

"Is that a maybe?"

There was a pause while they thought about what she was feeling at that moment. "I don't know *what* I feel," she admitted. "It's just that he's not . . ."

"The man you married?" Rachel nodded. Margie refilled her whiskey glass and leaned forward as though to whisper something, though they were the only people in the room. "Sweetheart, he never *was* the man you married. He was just giving you the Mitch you wanted to see." She leaned back, waving her free hand in the air as though to swat a swarm of phantom Gearys out of her sight. "They're all the same. Christ knows." She sipped her whiskey. "Believe it or not, Garrison can be charm personified when it suits him. They must get it from their grandfather."

Rachel pictured Cadmus the way he'd been at the wedding; sitting in his high-backed chair dispensing charm like a benediction.

"If it's all a performance," she said, "where's the real Mitch?"

"He doesn't know any more. If he ever did, which I doubt. It's sort of pitiful when you think about it. All that power, all that money, and there's nobody home to use it."

"They use it all the time," Rachel said.

"No," Margie replied. "*It* uses *them*. They're not living. None of us Gearys are. We're all just going through the motions." She peered at her glass. "I know I drink too much. It's rotting my liver and it'll probably kill me. But at least when I've got a few whiskeys inside me I'm not stuck being *Mrs. Garrison Geary*. When I'm drunk I give up being his wife, I'm somebody he wishes he didn't know. I like that."

Rachel shook her head in despair. "If it's so bad," she said, "why don't you just leave?"

"I've tried. I've left him three times. Once I stayed away for five months. But . . . you get into a certain way of being. You get comfortable." Rachel looked uneasy. "It doesn't take long. Look, I don't like living in Garrison's shadow, but I like living without his credit cards even less."

"You could divorce him and get a very nice settlement, Margie. You could live anywhere you wanted, any*way* you wanted."

Now it was Margie who shook her head. "I know," she said softly. "I'm just making excuses." She picked up the whiskey bottle and poured herself another half tumbler. "The fact is, I'm not leaving because somewhere deep down I don't want to. I guess maybe what's left of my self-esteem's wrapped up in being part of the dynasty. Isn't that pathetic?" She sipped on her drink. "Don't look so appalled, honey. Just because I'm too screwed up to leave, doesn't mean you can't. How old are you now?"

"Twenty-seven."

"That's nothing. You've still got your life ahead of you. You know what you should do? Tell Mitch you want a trial separation. Get a few million in your pocket and go off to see the world."

"I don't think seeing the world's going to make me happy."

"All right. So what *is* going to make you happy?"

Rachel thought it over for a moment. "Being with Mitch the way he was before we got married," she finally replied.

"Oh Lord," Margie sighed. "Then you know what? You have a big problem."

Some of Mitchell's old charm returned, albeit briefly, when he talked with Rachel about their having children. More than once he rhapsodized about how blessed their kids were going to be: the girls beautiful, the boys all studs. He was keen to start a family as soon as possible, and he wanted the brood to be large. In fact, Rachel got the unwelcome impression that he wanted to make up for Garrison's relative lack of productivity (Margie having borne one child only: a girl, now eight, called Alexia).

But the act of love was welcome, even if it was in service of Geary productivity rather than pleasure. When Mitchell was close to her, his hands on her body, his lips against hers, she remembered how she'd felt when they'd first touched, first kissed. How special she'd felt; how rare.

He wasn't an inspired lover. In fact Rachel had been surprised at how gauche he was in bed; almost shy, in fact. He certainly didn't act like a man who'd reputedly bedded some of the most beautiful women of the day. She liked his lack of sexual sophistication. For one thing, it matched her own, and it was nice to be able to learn together how best to pleasure one another. But even at his best, he left her wanting more. He didn't seem to understand the rhythms of her body; how she wanted to be held tenderly sometimes, and sometimes fiercely. When she attempted to express those needs in words he made his discomfort clear.

"I don't like it when you talk dirty," he said to her after one of their lovemaking sessions had ended. "Maybe I'm just being old-fashioned, but I don't think women should talk that way. It's not . . ."

"Ladylike?" she said.

He was standing in the bathroom door, tying the belt of his robe. He made a little fussy business of it so as not to look at her. "Yeah," he said. "It's not ladylike."

"I just want to be able to say what I want, Mitch."

"You mean what you want when we're in bed?" he said.

"Isn't that allowed?"

He made an exasperated sigh. "Rachel . . ." he said, "I told you before. You can say whatever you want to say."

"No I can't," she replied. "You tell me that, but you don't mean it. You're ready to snap at me if I say anything critical."

"That's not true."

"You're doing it right now."

"I'm not. I'm just saying I've been brought up in a different way than you. When I'm in bed with somebody I don't want to be given orders."

Now he was beginning to annoy her, and she wasn't in the mood to keep her irritation out of sight. "If you think me asking you to fuck me a little harder—"

"There you go again."

"—is me giving you orders we've got a problem, because—"

"I don't want to hear this."

"—and that's part of the problem."

"No, the problem is you having a foul mouth."

She got up out of bed. She was still naked, still sweaty from their lovemaking (he was always the first to the shower, scrubbing himself clean). Her nakedness intimidated him. It was the same body he'd been coupling with ten minutes before; now he couldn't look at her below her neck. She'd not thought of him as absurd until that moment. Arrogant sometimes, childish sometimes. But never, until now, absurd. There he was, a grown man, averting his eyes from her body like a nervous schoolboy. She would have laughed had it not been so pitiful.

"Just so we understand one another, Mitchell," she said, her tone scarcely betraying the fury she felt. "I do not have a foul mouth. If you've got a problem with talking about sex—"

"Don't put it on me."

"Let me finish."

"I've heard all I need to hear."

"I haven't finished talking."

"Well I've finished listening," he said, crossing to the bedroom door.

She moved to intercept him, feeling bizarrely empowered by her own nakedness. She saw him cowed by her lack of shame and it aroused an exhibitionist streak in her. If he was going to treat her like a coarse woman, then damn it she'd behave like one, and take some pleasure in his discomfort.

"Is that all the baby-making we're going to be doing tonight?" she said to him.

"I'm not sleeping in this room with you tonight, if that's what you're asking."

"The more often we do it," Rachel pointed out, "the more chance I'll produce a little Geary. You do know that?"

"Right now, I don't care," he said, and walked out on her.


It wasn't until she'd showered, and was toweling herself dry, that the tears started to come. They were surprisingly inconsequential, given what had just taken place. She made swift work of them, then washed her face clean, and went to bed.

She'd slept alone for many years, and been none the worse for it, she told herself. If she had to do so again for the rest of her life, then so be it. She wasn't going to beg anyone for their company between the sheets; not even Mitchell Geary.

# XI

### i

Paradoxically, they'd made a baby the very night she'd ended up sleeping alone. Seven weeks later Rachel was sitting in the office of Dr. Lloyd Waxman, the Geary family physician, with Waxman telling her the glad news.

"You're in very good health, Mrs. Geary," he said. "I'm sure everything's going to proceed along just fine. Did your mother have easy pregnancies, by the way?"

"As far as I know."

"Well that's another good sign." He jotted the information in his notes. "Maybe you'd like to come in and see me again in, say, a month's time?"

"No instructions in the meantime?"

"Nothing to excess," Waxman replied, with a simple little shrug. "That's what I always tell people. You're a healthy woman, there's really no reason why this shouldn't be a breeze for you. Just don't go out on the town with Margie. Or if you go out, let her do all the drinking. She's very capable of that. Lord knows, it'll probably kill her one of these days."

Rachel had made a tentative peace with Mitchell about a week and a half after the argument in the bedroom, but things had not been fully repaired between them. She wasn't so much hurt by the exchange as she was insulted, and she wasn't about to kid herself that just because he was making an effort to be conciliatory the opinions he espoused weren't still lurking behind his smile. As he'd said at the time, they were part of the way he'd been brought up. Such deeply held feelings weren't going to disappear overnight.

But the news from Dr. Waxman was so rapturously greeted on all sides she forgot about the argument, for at least a few weeks. Everybody was so pleased, it was as though something miraculous had happened.

"It's only a baby," she remarked to Deborah one day.

"Rachel," Deborah said, with a faintly forbidding tone. "You know better than that."

"All right, it's a Geary baby," Rachel said. "But Lord, all this hoopla! And there's still seven months to go."

"When I was pregnant with Garrison," Deborah said, "Cadmus sent me flowers every day for the last two months of my pregnancy, with a little card attached, and the number of days left."

"Like a countdown?"

"Exactly."

"The more I know about this family, the stranger it seems."

Deborah smiled, her gaze sliding away.

"What does that mean?" Rachel said.

"What?"

"The smile."

Deborah shrugged. "Oh, just that the older I get the stranger *every-thing* seems." She was sitting on the sofa beside the window, and the sun was bright; it made her features hard to discern. "You know how you assume things'll come clear as you get older? But of course nothing does. Sometimes I find myself looking at the faces of people I've known for years and years and they're complete mysteries to me. Like something from another planet." She paused, sipped her peppermint tea, stared out of the window. "What were we talking about?"

"How strange all the Gearys are."

"Hm. I suppose you think I'm the oddest of the lot."

"No," Rachel protested. "I didn't mean to say—"

"Say whatever you feel like saying," Deborah said, her tone still distracted. "Take no notice of Mitchell." She looked in Rachel's direction, her gaze uncommitted. "He told me you were angry at him. I don't blame you, frankly. He can be very controlling. He doesn't get that from George, he gets it from Garrison. And Garrison gets it from Cadmus." Rachel didn't remark on any of this. "He said you had quite an argument."

"It's over with now," Rachel said.

"I had to pry it out of him. But he knows better than to try and conceal anything from his mother."

Several thoughts had come into Rachel's head at the same time and were competing for attention. One, that if Deborah didn't find it odd that her son was sharing bedroom conversation with her, then she was indeed just as strange as the rest of the family. Two, that Mitchell wasn't to be trusted to keep their intimate business to himself. And three, that she would hereafter take her mother-in-law at her word, and say whatever the hell came into her head, however unpalatable it sounded. They were stuck with her now. She was going to give the Geary clan a child. That conferred power upon her.

Margie put it best, in fact, when she remarked that "the kid's going to give you something to bargain with." This was a grim vision of things, to be sure, but by now all of Rachel's romantic delusions were in retreat. If the child she was carrying was a necessary part of getting her way, then so be it.


In late January, on one of those crystalline days that make even the most Arctic of New York winters bearable, Mitchell came to the apartment at noon and told Rachel he wanted to show her something; would she come with him? Right now? she asked him. Yes, he said, right now.

The traffic was abnormally snarled, even for New York. The leaden sky had begun to shed snow; a blizzard was promised within hours. It reminded her of that first afternoon, in Boston. Snow on the sidewalk, and a prince at the door. It seemed so very long ago.

Their destination was Fifth Avenue, at 81st: a tower of condominiums which she knew by reputation only.

"I bought you something," Mitchell said, as they stepped into the elevator. "I think you should have a place you can call your own. Somewhere you can shut out all the Gearys." He smiled. "Except me, of course."

His gift awaited them at the top of the tower: the penthouse duplex. It had been exquisitely appointed, the walls hung with modern masters, the furniture chic, but comfortable.

"There are four bedrooms, six bathrooms, and of course . . ." he led her to the window ". . . the best view in America."

"Oh my Lord," was all Rachel could say.

"Do you like it?"

How could she not? It was beautiful; perfection. She couldn't imagine what it had cost to create luxury on such a scale.

"It's all yours, honey," Mitchell said. "I mean, literally yours. The apartment, everything it contains, it's all in your name." He came over, and stood behind her, looking out over the snow-brightened rectangle of Central Park. "I know it's hard for you sometimes, living in the middle of this fucking dynasty. It's hard for me, so God knows what it's like for you." He put his arms around her from behind, his palms laid against her swelling belly. "I want you to have your own little queendom up here. If you don't like the pictures on the walls, sell 'em. I tried to choose things I thought you'd like, but if you don't, sell them and get something you do like. I put a couple of million dollars in a separate bank account for you, to change whatever you want to change. Put in a pool table. Or a screening room. Whatever you want. You call the shots here." He put his mouth close to her ear. "Of course, I hope you'll let me have a key, so I can come in and play sometimes." There was a gravely tone to his voice, and his hips were moving gently but insistently against her backside. "Hey, honey?"

"Yes?"

"Can I come in and play?"

"You need to ask?" she said, turning in his arms so that she faced him. "Of course you can play."

"Even in your delicate condition?"

"I'm not delicate," she said, pressing against him. "I'm feeling fine. Better than fine." She kissed him. "This is an amazing place."

"You're amazing," he said, returning her kiss. "The more I know you, the more I fall in love with you. I'm not very good at telling you that. You throw me off my stride. I'm supposed to be Mr. Cool, but when I'm with you, I get stupid, like a kid." He put his mouth against her face. "A very, very, very *horny* kid."

She didn't need to be told; he was so hard against her. And his pale face was flushed, and his neck blotchy. "Can I put it in you?" he said.

That was always his overture; *can I put it in you?* When she'd been angry with him, and thought of this phrase, it had struck her as perfectly ridiculous. But right now she was persuaded by its idiot simplicity. She *wanted* it inside her; that it which he couldn't bear to name.

"Which bedroom?" she said.


They made love without fully undressing, on a bed so big she could have thrown an orgy amid its countless pillows. He was more passionate than she could ever remember his being, his hands and mouth returning over and over to her silky belly. It was as if he was aroused by the evidence of his own fecundity; muttering words of adoration against her body. The session didn't last more than fifteen minutes; he couldn't hold back. And when he had finished, he was up and showering, and then away downstairs to make some calls. He was late for his meetings, he said; Garrison would be cursing him.

"I'll catch a cab and leave the limo downstairs for you," he told her, leaning over to kiss her forehead. His hair was still wet from the shower.

"Don't get a chill. There's a blizzard out there."

He glanced out. The snow was coming down so heavily it had almost obscured the park.

"I'll stay warm," he said softly. "I'll think of you two lying here, and I'll be toasty."


When he was gone her body remembered the motion of his erection inside her, as though there were a phantom phallus still sliding in and out of her. And she remembered too the way he spoke when he was aroused. Often, in the heat of the moment, he'd called her baby, and this afternoon had been no different. *Baby o baby o baby,* he'd said as he put it in. But now, when she conjured his voice, it was as if he were speaking to the child in her; calling to it in her womb. *Baby o baby o baby.*

She didn't know whether to be moved or disturbed, so she told herself to be neither. She pulled the sheets and quilt up around her, and slept, while the snow lay its own fat white quilt on the park below.

## ii

Since I wrote the foregoing passage—which was yesterday afternoon— I've had no less than three visits from Luman, which have so distracted me that I haven't been able to get back into the mood for continuing my story. So I've decided to tell you the matter of my distractions, and maybe that will put them out of my mind.

The more time I spend with Luman, the more troubling he seems to be. He'd decided from our last conversation—after all these years of estrangement—that I was now his best buddy: a smoking companion (he's been through half a dozen of my havanas), a confidante, and of course a fellow writer. As I told Zabrina, he's got the notion lodged in his head that I'm going to collaborate with him on the definitive tome about madhouses. I've agreed to no such thing, but I haven't got the heart to spoil his dream; it's plainly very important to him. He comes to my room with odd little scribblings he's made (actually, he doesn't barge in the way Marietta would; he waits on the veranda until I chance to look up, see him there, and invite him in) and gives me what he's written, telling me where he thinks it's going to fit in the grand scheme of his book. He's obviously thought the whole project through in great detail, because he'll say: *this belongs in Chapter Seven*; or: *this goes with the stories about Bedlam,* as though I shared his vision. I don't. I can't. For one thing, he hasn't communicated what this book of his is going to be (though he clearly assumes he has) and for another I've got a book of my own to think about. There isn't room in my head for two. In fact there's barely room for this.

I suppose it would have been better for all concerned if I'd just told him that I had no intention of collaborating with him. Then he'd have gone away and left me to get on with telling you what happened to Rachel. But he was so impassioned about it, I was afraid he'd be a wreck if I did that.

That's not the only reason that I didn't tell him the truth, I'll admit. Though it's a disruption having him come in and pick my brains the way he's been doing, he's also been strangely stimulating company. The more comfortable he becomes in my presence, the less effort he makes to keep his conversation on any coherent track. In the midst of telling me some lunatic detail of his book he'll veer off onto a completely different subject, then veer again, and again, almost as though there was more than one Luman in his head, and they were all vying for the use of his tongue. There's Luman the gossip, who has a chatty, faintly effeminate manner. There's Luman the metaphysician, who gazes at the ceiling while he pontificates. There's Luman the encyclopedia, who'll out of the blue talk about Roman law, or the finer points of topiary. (Some of the information he's provided in this latter mode has been fascinating. I didn't realize until he told me that in some species of hyena the female is indistinguishable from the male, her clitoris the size of a penis, her labia swollen and drooping like a scrotum. No wonder Marietta took to them. Nor did I know that the temples where Cesaria was worshipped were often also tombs; and that sacred marriages, the *heiros gamos*, were celebrated there, among the dead.)

And then there's Luman the impersonator, who can suddenly speak in a voice that is so unlike his own it's as though he were possessed. Last night, for instance, he impersonated Dwight so well if I'd closed my eyes I wouldn't have been able to tell it from the real thing. And then later, just as he was leaving, he spoke in Chiyojo's voice, quoting a piece of a poem my mother wrote:

> *"My Savior is most diligent;*
> *He has me in his book*
> *With all my faults enumerated,*
> *And I am certain there.*
> *It's only the Fallen One*
> *Who wants us perfect;*
> *For then we will not need an angel's care."*

You can imagine how strange that was to hear: my wife's voice, still distinctly Japanese, speaking a thought that came from my mother's heart. The two great women in my life, emerging from the throat of this raddled, wild-eyed man. Is it any wonder I've been distracted from the flow of my story?

But the strangest portions of these exchanges are those with a metaphysical cast; no question. He's evidently thought long and hard about the paradoxes of our state: a family of divinities (or in my case a semidivinity) hiding away from a world which no longer wants us or needs us.

"Godhood doesn't mean a damn thing," he said to me. "All it does is make us crazy."

I asked him why he thought it had done that. (I didn't argue with his basic assumption. I think he's right: all the Barbarossas are a little mad.) He said he thought it was because we were just minor gods.

"We're not that much better than them out there, when you come to think of it," he said. "Sure, we live longer. And we can do a few tricks. But it's not the deep stuff. We can't make stars. Or unmake 'em."

"Not even Nicodemus?" I said.

"Nah. Not even Nicodemus. And he was one of the First Created. Like her." He pointed up to Cesaria's chambers.

" 'Two souls as old as heaven . . . ' "

"Who said that?"

"I did," I replied. "It's from my book."

"Nice," he said.

"Thanks."

He fell silent for a few moments. I assumed he was mulling over the prettiness of my phrasing, but no, his grasshopper mind had already jumped to something else; or rather back, to our problematical god-hood.

"I think we're too farsighted for our own good," he said. "We can't seem to live in the moment. We're always looking off beyond the edge of things. But we're not powerful enough to be able to *see* anything there." He growled like an ill-tempered dog. "It's so fucking frustrating. Not to be one thing or the other."

"Meaning?"

"If we were *real* gods . . . I mean the way gods are supposed to be, we wouldn't be pissing around here. We'd be off—out there, where there's still things to do."

"You don't mean the world."

"No, I don't mean the world. Fuck the world. I mean out beyond anything anybody on this planet ever saw or dreamt of seeing."

I thought of Galilee while he was talking. Had the same hunger as Luman was describing—unarticulated, perhaps, but burning just as brightly—driven Galilee out across the ocean on his little boat, daring all he knew how to dare, but never feeling as though he was far enough from land; or indeed from home?

These ruminations had put Luman into a melancholy mood, and he told me he didn't want to talk any more, and left. But he was back at dawn, or a little thereafter, for his third visit. I don't think he'd slept. He'd been walking around since he'd departed my study, thinking.

"I jotted a few more notes down," he said, "for the chapter on Christ."

"Christ's in this book of yours?" I said.

"Has to be. Has to be," Luman said. "Big family connection."

"We're not in the same family as Jesus, Luman," I said. Then, doubting my own words: "Are we?"

"Nah. But he was a crazy man, just like us. He just cared more than we do."

"About what?"

"Them," he said; "Humanity. The fucking flock. Truth is, we were never shepherds. We were *hunters*. At least, she was. I guess Nicodemus had a taste for domesticity. Raising horses. He was a rancher at heart." I smiled at this piece of insight. It was true. Our Father, the fence-builder.

"Maybe we should have cared a little more," Luman went on. "Tried to love them, even though they never loved us."

"Nicodemus loved them," I pointed out. "Some of the women at least."

"I tried that," Luman said. "But they die on you, just as you're getting used to having them around."

"Do you have children out there?" I asked him.

"Oh sure, I've got bastards."

It had never occurred to me until this moment that our family tree might have undiscovered branches. I'd always assumed that I knew the extent of the Barbarossa clan. Apparently, I didn't.

"Do you know where they are?" I asked him.

"No."

"But you could find them?"

"I suppose so . . ."

"If they're like me, they're still alive. Growing old slowly, but—"

"Oh yeah, they're still alive."

"And you're not curious about them?"

"Of course I'm curious," he said, a little sharply. "But I can barely stay sane sitting out there in the Smoke House. If I went out looking for my kids, turning over the memories of the women I bedded, I'd lose what little fucking sanity I still possess." He shook his head violently, as though to get the temptation out from between his ears.

"Maybe . . . if I ever go out there . . ." I began. He stopped shaking his head, and looked up at me. His eyes were sparkling suddenly: tears in them, but also, I think, some little flame of hope. "Maybe I could look for them for you . . ." I went on.

"Look for my children?"

"Yes."

"You'd do that?"

"Yes. Of course. I'd . . . be honored."

The tears welled in his eyes now. "Oh *brother*," he said. "Imagine that. My children." His voice had dropped to a hoarse whisper. "My children." He caught hold of my hand; his palm was prickly against my skin, his agitation oozing from his pores. "When would you do this?" he said.

"Oh . . . well . . . I couldn't go until I'd finished the book."

"My book or yours?"

"Mine. Yours would have to wait."

"No problem. No problem. I could live with that. If I knew you were going to bring me . . ." He couldn't finish the thought; it was too overwhelming for him. He let go of me and put his hand over his eyes. The tears coursed down his cheeks, and he sobbed so loudly I swear everyone in the house must have heard him. At last, he recovered himself enough to say: "We'll talk about this again some other time."

"Whenever you like," I told him.

"I knew we'd become friends again for a reason," he said to me. "You're quite a man, Maddox. And I choose my words carefully. *Quite a man.*"

With that, he went out onto the veranda, stopping only to take another cigar from my humidor. Once outside, however, he turned back. "I don't know what this information is worth," he said, "but now that I trust you as I do, I think I ought to tell you . . ."

"What?"

He began feverishly scratching his beard, suddenly discomfited. "You're going to think I'm *really* crazy now," he said.

"Tell me."

"Well . . . I have a theory. About Nicodemus."

"Yes?"

"I don't believe his death was an accident. I think he orchestrated the whole thing."

"Why would he do that?"

"So that he could slip away from *her.* From his responsibilities. I know this may be hard to hear, brother—but I think the company of your wife gave him a hankerin' for the old days. He wanted human pussy. So he had to get away."

"But you buried him, Luman. And I saw him trampled, right there in front of me. I was lying on the ground, under the same hooves."

"A corpse ain't evidence of anything," Luman replied. "You know that. There are ways to get out, if you know 'em. And if *anyone* knew those ways—"

"—it was him."

"Tricky sonofabitch, that father of ours. Tricky and oversexed." He stopped scratching his beard and made me an apologetic little shrug. "I'm sorry if it hurts to have me bring it up, but—"

"No. It's all right."

"We have to start being honest around here, it seems to me. Stop pretending he was a saint."

"I don't. Believe me. He took my wife."

"There, you see," Luman said. "Lying to yourself. He didn't take Chiyojo. You gave her to him, Maddox." He saw the fierce look in my eyes, and faltered for a moment. But then decided to stay true to his own advice, and tell the truth, as he saw it, however unpalatable. "You could have taken her away, the moment you saw what was happening between them. You could have packed up in the middle of the night, and let him cool down. But you stayed. You saw he had his eyes on her, and you stayed, knowing she wouldn't be able to say no to him. You gave her to him, Maddox, 'cause you wanted him to love you." He stared at his feet. "I don't blame you for it. I probably would have done the same thing in your shoes. But don't be thinkin' you can stand back from any of this and pretend you're just observin' it all. You're not. You're just as deep in this shit as the rest of us."

"I think you'd better go," I said quietly.

"I'm going, I'm going. But you think on what I've said, and you'll see it's true."

"Don't come back for a while," I added. "Because you won't be welcome."

"Now, Maddox—"

"Go, will you?" I said. "Don't make it any worse than it is."

He gave me a pained expression. He was now obviously regretting what he'd said; he'd undone in a few sentences the trust we'd so recently forged. But he knew better than to try and explain himself further. He took his sad eyes off me, turned, and walked off across the lawn.


What can I tell you about this terrible accusation of his? It seems to me very little. I've recounted as honestly as I could the salient points of our exchanges, and I'll return to the subject later, when I have a better perspective on it all. It probably goes without saying that I wouldn't have been so distracted by all this, and felt the need to report it as I have, if I didn't think there was some merit in what he said. But as you can imagine it's not easy to admit to, however much I may wish to be honest with myself, and with you. If I believe Luman's interpretation of events, then I am to blame for Chiyojo's demise; and for my own injuries; and thus also for the years of loneliness and grief I've passed, sitting here. That's hard to accept. I'm not sure I'm even capable of it. But be assured that if I come to some peace with this suspicion, then these pages will be the first to know.


Enough. It's time to pick up the story of Rachel and Mitchell Geary. There's sorrow to come, very shortly. I promised early on that I'd give you enough of other people's despair to make you feel a little happier with your own lot. Well now it's me who needs the comfort of somebody else's tears.

# XII

### i

The Monday following Mitchell's gift of the apartment, Rachel woke with the worst headache of her life; so bad it made her vision blurred. She took some aspirin, and went back to bed; but even then the pain didn't pass, so she called Margie, who said she'd be over in a few minutes and take her to Dr. Waxman. By the time she reached Waxman's office she was shaking with pain: not just a headache now, but crippling spasms in her stomach. Waxman was very concerned.

"I'm going to put you into Mount Sinai right away," he said. "There's a Dr. Hendrick there, he's wonderful; I want him to take a look at you."

"What's wrong with me?" Rachel said.

"Let's hope nothing at all. But I want you to be examined properly."

Even through the haze of pain Rachel could read the anxiety in his voice.

"I'm not going to lose the baby, am I?" she said.

"We'll do everything we can—"

"*I can't lose the baby.*"

"Your health's what's important right now, Rachel," he said. "There's nobody better than Gary Hendrick, believe me. You're in good hands."

An hour later she was in a private room in Mount Sinai. Hendrick came to examine her, and told her, very calmly, that there were some troubling signs—her blood pressure was high, there was some minor bleeding—and that he would be monitoring her very closely. He had given her some medication for the pain, which was beginning to take effect. She should just rest, he said; there'd be a nurse in the room with her at all times, so if she should need anything all she had to do was ask.

Margie had been calling around looking for Mitchell during this period, and upon Hendrick's departure came back in to say that he hadn't yet been located, but his secretary thought he was probably between meetings, and would be calling in very soon.

"You're going to be just fine, honey," Margie said. "Waxman likes to be melodramatic once in a while. It makes him feel important."

Rachel smiled. The painkiller Hendrick had given her had induced a heaviness in her limbs and lids. She resisted the temptation to sleep however: she didn't trust her body to behave itself in her absence.

"God," Margie said, "this is a rare occurrence for me."

"What's that?"

"Cocktail hour and no cocktail."

Rachel grinned. "Waxman thinks you should give it up."

"He should try being married to Garrison sober," Margie quipped.

Rachel opened her mouth to reply, but as she did so she felt a strange sensation in her throat, as though she swallowed something hard. She put her hand up to touch the place, a squeak of panic escaping her.

"What's wrong, honey?" Margie said.

She didn't hear the last word; her head filled with a rush of sound, like a dam bursting between her ears. From the corner of her eye she saw the nurse rising from her chair, a look of alarm on her face. Then she felt her body convulse with such violence she was almost thrown from the bed. By the time the spasm had passed she was unconscious.


Mitchell arrived at Mount Sinai at a quarter to eight. Rachel had lost the baby fifteen minutes before.

## ii

Once Rachel was feeling well enough to sit up and talk—which took eight or nine days—Waxman came to visit, and in his kindly, avuncular manner explained what had happened. It was a rare condition, he said, called eclampsia; its causes were not clearly known, but it frequently proved fatal to both mother and child. She had been lucky. Of course it was a tragedy that she'd lost the child, and he was deeply sorry about that, but he'd been talking to Hendrick, who'd reported that she was getting stronger by the day, and would soon be up and around again. If she wanted any further details about what she'd endured he'd be happy to explain it more fully to her when she was ready. Meanwhile, she had one task and one only: to put this sorry business behind her.

So much for the medical explanation. It meant very little; and in truth she didn't entirely believe it. Whatever the doctors' reports said, Rachel had her own theory as to what had happened: her body had simply not wanted to produce a Geary. Her secret self had sent a message to her womb and her womb had sent a message to her heart, and between them they'd conspired to be rid of the child. In other words it was her fault that the infant had died before it had had a chance to live. If she'd only been able to love it, her body would have nurtured it better. Her fault; all her fault.

She shared this certainty with no one. When she got out of hospital after two weeks of convalescence Mitch suggested she see a counselor to talk it all through with.

"Waxman said you'll grieve for a time," he said. "It's like losing somebody, even though you didn't really know them. You should talk it all out. It'll be easier to deal with."

She couldn't help but notice that as far as Mitch was concerned it was *her* grief, *her* baby that had been lost, not his. All of which irrationally supported her thesis. He knew what she'd done; he probably hated her.

She refused to see a counselor however: this was her pain, and she was going to keep it for herself. Maybe it would fill up the emptiness in her where the child had been.

She had plenty of visitors. Sherrie came in from Ohio the day after the baby's death, and was a nearly constant presence at the hospital. Deborah came and went, as did Margie. Even Garrison visited, though he was so plainly uneasy Rachel finally told him he should leave, and he gladly took up the suggestion telling her he'd come back the next day when he had less on his mind. He didn't, and she was glad.

"Where do you want to stay when we get you out of here?" Mitchell asked after about ten days. "Do you want to go to the duplex or stay with Margie for a while?"

"You know where I'd really like to go?" she said.

"Tell me and it's done."

"George's house."

"Caleb's Creek?" He looked thoroughly perplexed that she'd choose such a place. "It's so far out from the city."

"That's what I want," she replied. "I don't want to have visitors right now. I want to just . . . hide away for a while. Think about things."

"Don't think too hard," Mitch said. "It's not going to do any good. The baby's gone and all the thinking in the world isn't going to bring him back."

"It was a boy . . . ?" she said softly. She'd kept herself from asking, though Waxman had told her he'd share any information she felt she needed to know in order to deal with the loss.

"Yes," Mitchell said, "it was a boy. I thought you knew."

"We had better names for the boy than the girl," she said, feeling the tears shaking in her. "You liked Laurence, right?"

"Rachel, don't do this . . ."

"I liked Mackenzie—"

"Please. God. Rachel."

"Trouble with Mackenzie . . . everybody would have . . ." and now the tears were too close to be held back ". . . called him Mac . . ."

She put her hand to her mouth to stop the sob that was coming. But it spilled from her anyway. "He wouldn't have liked Mac," she wept, reaching for a tissue to wipe her runny nose.

As she did so she looked up at Mitch. He had half turned from her, but even through the tears she could see that his face was crumpled up, his body wracked with sobs. She felt a sudden rush of love for him.

"Oh my poor honey," she said.

"I'm sorry. I shouldn't be—"

"No. Honey. No." She opened her arms to him. "Come here." He shook his head, still turned from her. "Don't be ashamed. It's good to cry."

"No," he said. "No, I don't want . . . I don't want to cry. I want to be strong for us both."

"Just come here," she said. "Please."

Reluctantly, he turned back toward her. His face was red and wet, his mouth turned down, his chin crumpled. "Oh God, oh God, oh God. Why did this have to happen? We didn't do anything to deserve this."

He was like a child who'd been punished, and didn't know why. Weeping as much for the injustice of his suffering as the suffering itself.

"Let me hold you," she said. "I need to hold you."

He went to her, and she put his arms around him. He smelled stale; his sweat had gone sour on a day-old shirt. Even his cologne had turned bitter.

"Why?" he asked her through his grief. "Why? Why?"

"I don't know why," she said. Her own sense of culpability seemed at that moment horribly self-indulgent. He'd been hurting quietly all along; she'd just chosen not to see it. But now, though she was looking at him through her own tears, she saw him more clearly than she'd seen him in weeks: the flecks of gray at his temples, the shadows around his eyes, the fever blister on his lip.

"Poor husband . . ." she murmured, and kissed his hair.

He put his face against her breast, and the sobbing went on, both of them crying, rocking one another.

*          *          *

Things got better after that. She wasn't alone with her pain after all. He felt it just as strongly in his way, and that was a comfort to her. It wasn't the last time they cried together—many times somebody would say something that would catch one of them amiss, and the other's eyes would fill with sympathetic tears. But there wasn't total darkness around her now; she could see the possibility that in a while her need to mourn would fade, and she'd be able to get on with her life.

There would be no further pregnancies; Dr. Waxman made that absolutely clear. If by some unlucky accident she were to become pregnant again they would need to terminate the pregnancy as quickly as possible so as to prevent any unnecessary stress upon her body.

"Am I frail?" she asked him when he told her this. "I don't feel frail."

"You're vulnerable, put it that way," Waxman replied. "In every other way but this, you can live a perfectly normal life. But as far as kids are concerned . . ." He shrugged. "Of course you can adopt."

"I don't know if the Gearys would approve."

He raised his eyebrow. "Perhaps you're being a little oversensitive," he said. "Which is perfectly understandable right now, by the way. But think if you were to ask Mitch or his mother or even the old man you'd be surprised how open they'd be to the idea of adoption. Anyway that's all for the future. What matters right now is that you take care of yourself. Mitch says you're going up to his father's house for a while."

"I'm hoping."

"That's a beautiful part of the state. I've been thinking of retiring up there. My wife didn't care for it, but now she's dead . . ."

"Oh, I'm sorry. Did you lose her recently?"

Waxman's easy smile had faded from his face. "Last Thanksgiving," he said. "She had cancer."

"I'm so sorry."

He sighed; such a sad sigh. "I don't suppose you want to hear platitudes from your old fart of a doctor, but if I may just say: you only get one life, Rachel, and nobody can live it for you. That means you have to take a long, hard look at what you want." He was taking just such a look at her as he spoke. "One door's just closed, and that's a terrible shock. But there's plenty of others, especially for a woman in your position." He leaned forward, his leather chair squeaking. "Just do one thing for me."

"What's that?"

"Don't end up like Margie. I've watched her for the last God knows how many years, drinking herself into an early grave." Again, that laden sigh escaped him. "I'm sorry," he said, "I'll shut my mouth now."

"No . . ." Rachel murmured. "It's good for me to hear this right now."

"I wasn't always such a melancholy old bird. But since Faith passed away I see things differently. I knew her for forty-nine years, you see. I met her when she was sixteen. So I saw almost a whole life come and go. That makes you think about things in a different way."

"Yes . . ."

"I said to one of my colleagues after Faith died that I felt like I'd been shot out into space, and I was looking back at everything that had seemed so permanent and what I saw was this fragile blue rock in all that . . . nothingness." His gaze had emptied as he spoke; now, when he looked up at Rachel again, she seemed to see right into him; into a loneliness that made her want to run from the room.

"You just be happy," he said to her softly. "You're a good person, Rachel. I see that. And you deserve happiness. So do what your instincts tell you, and if the Gearys don't like it then you just walk away." The words made her catch her breath. "Of course if you quote me," he went on, "I'll deny I ever said it. I'm hoping Cadmus is going to give me a little piece of land when I retire as a thank-you for putting up with his brood over the years."

"I'll put in a good word for you," Rachel told him.

# XIII

## i

There are occasions when the responsibilities of a storyteller and those of a simple witness contradict one another. For example: had I told you from the outset that the chief catalyst of Mitch and Rachel's separation was the loss of their child, I would have bled away what little suspense the previous chapters possessed. But I don't believe I misrepresented the facts. I began this portion of my account by telling you that there was no single calamitous event that began to undo the marriage, and I would still say that was the case. If the child had survived perhaps Rachel would have stayed with Mitchell a while longer, but she would have left him sooner or later. The marriage was in trouble long before the pregnancy; the most the death of the child did was hasten its collapse.

As Rachel had requested Mitchell took her up to the farmhouse in Caleb's Creek and stayed with her for almost ten days, going down to the city three or four times for meetings but returning in the evening to be with her. Though the Rylanders were there in his absence to attend to all Rachel's needs, Barbara told Mitch that Rachel had taken over most of her duties. It was true. The general homeliness of the house—its lack of expensive works of art, its modest scale—brought out the domestic side of Rachel's nature. She usurped the kitchen from Barbara and started to cook, remarking to Mitch one day that she hadn't so much as boiled a pot of water since they were married. She wasn't a particularly sophisticated cook, but she knew how to put a hearty meal together. There was a healing simplicity to the rituals of the kitchen: fresh vegetables from the garden, good wine from the cellar, the plates washed and neatly stacked when the meal was over.

After two weeks of this, Mitch asked her how she was doing, and she said: "I'll be fine on my own, if that's what you were wondering. Do you want to spend a few nights in the city?"

"I was just thinking about going until the weekend. I'll come back here on Friday night, and maybe if you're feeling better we can go home to New York on Sunday."

"Is somebody going to be using this house?"

"No," Mitch said. "Nobody uses this place any more."

"So why can't I stay?"

"Well you *can* stay, baby. I just thought you'd be wanting to get back with some of your friends."

"I don't have any friends in New York."

"Rachel, don't be silly. You've got plenty of—" He saw the unhappiness in her eyes, and raised his hands in surrender. "All right. If you say you've got no friends, you've got no friends. I only thought if you were making progress, it would be good for everybody to see you again."

"Oh, now I get it. You want to show me around so the family doesn't start thinking I've lost my mind."

"That's not it at all. Why do you have to be so paranoid?"

"Because I know the way you think. All of you. Always watching out for the family reputation. Well, right now I don't care about the family reputation, okay? I don't want to see anybody. I don't want to talk to anybody. And I certainly don't want to go back to New York."

"Calm down, will you?" Mitch said. "I just wanted to find out where we stand. Now I know." He left the kitchen without another word, but he came back in again ten minutes later. His anger hadn't dissipated, but he was doing his best to conceal it. "I haven't come back here for another argument," he said, "I only want to point out that you can't stay here forever. This is not a life I want my wife to be living, puttering around like an old woman, cutting roses and peeling potatoes."

"I like peeling potatoes."

"You're being perverse."

"I'm being honest."

"Well, that's all I wanted to say. I'm going to be staying with Garrison for the next few days, so we can work through all this Bangkok business." She didn't have a clue what he was talking about; nor did she care to inquire. "So if you need me . . ."

"I know where to find you," she replied, though she'd realized several seconds before that she wouldn't be coming to look.

## ii

Where would she go? That was the question that vexed her for the next few days. Even assuming she did what would once have been unthinkable, and actually left her husband, where would she go? She couldn't stay here at the farmhouse, though that would be blissful. It was Geary property. She could take up residence in the apartment, of course—that was hers—but she'd never feel comfortable there; certainly not without completely remodeling the place in line with her own tastes, and that was too large a scale of undertaking. Perhaps she'd be better off selling it, even if it didn't make a particularly good price, and finding a smaller place to purchase: perhaps somewhere off the beaten track like Caleb's Creek.

She slept on the thought, though not well. She passed the night in an uneasy state somewhere between sleep and wakefulness, and when she dreamed the dreams were of the room in which she was lying, only bleached of all color, like the photographs in George's study that had been left in the sun too long. There were people passing through the room, a few of them glancing down at her, their faces impassive. She knew none of them, though she had the suspicion that she'd known them once, and forgotten their names.

The next day she called Margie, and invited her to visit.

"I really can't bear the country," Margie protested. "But if you're not going to be coming back here for a while . . ."

"I'm not."

"Then I'll come."

She arrived the next day, her limo packed with boxes of her favorite indulgences—smoked bluefish pâté, the inevitable Beluga, Viennese coffee, a box of bitter chocolate florentines—plus, of course, a case of libations.

"This isn't the back of beyond," Rachel pointed out as she watched Samuel, Margie's driver, unload the supplies. "We have a very good market ten minutes' drive from here."

"I know, I know," Margie said, "but I like to come prepared." She pulled a bottle of single-malt Scotch out of one of the boxes. "Where's the ice?"

Margie had plenty of gossip. Loretta had become quite the harridan in the last few weeks, she reported. There'd been a very acrimonious exchange with Garrison a week ago, in which Loretta had inferred some misconduct in the way Garrison had disposed of several million dollars' worth of family holdings.

"I didn't think Loretta had any interest in the business side of things," Rachel said.

"Oh don't you believe it. She likes to pretend she's above it all. But she's watching her empire. In fact, the more I see her operate, the more I think she was always working behind the scenes. Even when George was alive. He did all the talking, but she was the one telling him what to say. And now she's seeing things she doesn't approve of, so she's showing her hand."

"So what happened with Garrison?"

"Oh it was a mess. He told her she didn't know what she was talking about, which was exactly the wrong thing to say. Apparently she went into the boardroom the next day and dismissed five of the board members on the spot."

"She can do that?"

"She did it," Margie replied. "Told them all to pack their bags and go. Then she gave an interview to *The Wall Street Journal* saying they were incompetent. They're all suing of course. I'm surprised Mitchell didn't say anything about any of this."

"He doesn't talk about the business. He never has."

"This isn't business. This is civil war. Garrison was madder than I've seen him in a long time. It was all very satisfying." They exchanged smiles; co-conspirators in their pleasure at all this unrest. "The way he was talking," Margie went on, "I wouldn't be surprised if he doesn't come up with some kind of ultimatum. You know: either she goes or I go."

"And who's going to make that decision?"

"I don't know," Margie laughed. "Especially now Loretta's put half the board out of a job. I suppose in the end it'll come down to whether Mitchell sides with Garrison or his grandmother."

"It all seems so old-fashioned."

"Oh, it's positively *feudal*," Margie said. "But that's the way the old man set it up when he retired. He kept all the power in the family."

"Does Cadmus have any kind of vote?"

"Oh sure. He still sends memos to Garrison, believe it or not."

"Do they make any sense?"

"I think it depends how much medication he's had that day. Last time I went to see him he was *flying*. Talking about something that happened fifty years ago. I don't think he even knew who I was. Then there's days when he's really sharp, according to Garrison." She grew a little pensive. "I think it's pretty sad, personally. To be so old and not be able to let go of his little empire."

"Isn't that what keeps him alive?" Rachel said.

"Well it's pitiful," Margie said. "But it's the way they are. Control freaks."

"Including Loretta?"

"Especially Loretta. She's got nothing better to do."

"She's not too old to marry again, once Cadmus dies."

"She'd be better off taking a lover," Margie said. She had a sly expression on her face. "It's a nice feeling."

"Are you telling me—?" The slyness became a smile. "You have a lover?"

"Doesn't everyone?" Margie laughed. "His name's Danny. I wouldn't trust him as far as I could throw him, but he's a wonderful distraction in the middle of a dreary afternoon."

"Does Garrison know about him?"

"Well we haven't had a nice chat about it, if that's what you mean, but he knows. I mean Garrison and I haven't slept together for six years, except for a rather wretched night after that damned birthday party for Cadmus, when both of us got a little mawkish. Otherwise he goes his way and I go mine. It's better that way."

"I see."

"Are you shocked? Oh, please tell me you're shocked."

"No. I'm just thinking . . ."

"About?"

"Well . . . the reason I asked you to come here's because I'm going to leave Mitchell." It took a lot to silence Margie, but this did the trick. "It's for the best," Rachel added.

"Does Mitchell agree?"

"He doesn't know."

"Well when exactly were you intending to tell him, honey?"

"When I've got everything sorted out in my head."

"Are you sure you wouldn't be wiser doing what I've done? There's a lot of cute bartenders in New York."

"I don't want a bartender," Rachel said. "With the greatest respect to . . . what's his name?"

"Daniel." She grinned. "Actually it's Dan Dan the Fuck Fuck Man."

"With the greatest respect to the Fuck Fuck Man it's not what I'm looking for."

"Was Mitchell any good in bed?"

"I don't have that much to compare him with."

"Put it this way: it wasn't a once-in-a-lifetime experience?"

"No."

"So you don't want a bartender. What do you want?"

"Good question," Rachel said.

She closed her eyes so as not to be distracted by the quizzical look on Margie's face. "I guess . . . I just want to feel more passionate."

"About Mitchell?"

"About . . . getting up in the morning." She opened her eyes again. Margie was perusing her, as though trying to decide something.

"What are you thinking?" Rachel asked her.

"Just that it's all very fine talking about passion, honey. But if it ever came along—I'm talking about real passion, not some soap-opera baloney—it'd change everything in your life. You do know that? *Every-thing.*"

"I'm ready for that."

"So you've given up on Mitchell completely?"

"Yes."

"He's not going to let you divorce him without a fight."

"Probably not. But I'm sure he doesn't want us all over the tabloids either. Neither do I. I just want to live my life as far away from the Gearys as I can get."

"What if you could have both?"

"I don't follow."

"What if you could have all the passion you could take, and still keep your share of the Geary lifestyle? No divorce proceeding; no judge going through the dirty linen."

"I don't see how that's possible."

"The only way it's going to happen is if you promise to stay with Mitchell. He's got his eye on a place in Congress, and he wants his private life to be as squeaky clean as possible. If you help him look like a saint, maybe he'll look the other way when you go have an adventure."

"You make it sound all very civilized."

"Why shouldn't it be?" Margie said. "Unless he decides to get jealous. Then . . . well, then you might have to talk some reason into him. But you're smart enough to do that."

"And where am I going to find this adventure?"

"We'll talk about that later," Margie said with a little smile. "Right now, you've got some deciding to do, honey. But let me remind you of something. I tried leaving. And I tried and I tried. And, believe me, it's a hard world out there."

## iii

Perversely enough it was this last remark that finally convinced Rachel that she had to leave. So what if it *was* a hard world? She'd survived out there for the first twenty-four years of her life, without the Gearys. She could do so again.

When Margie finally rose, sometime after noon, and was downing her first Bloody Mary of the day (complete with a stick of celery, for the roughage) Rachel explained that she'd thought everything over and decided to take a long drive, back to Ohio. It would give her time to think, she said; time to make up her mind about what she really wanted.

"Do you want Mitchell to know where you've gone?" Margie asked her.

"Preferably not."

"Then I won't tell him," Margie said, very simply. "When are you planning to go?"

"I'm already packed. I just wanted to say goodbye to you."

"Oh Lord. You don't waste any time. Still, maybe it's for the best." Margie opened her arms. "You know you're very dear to me, don't you?"

"Yes I know," Rachel said, hugging her hard.

"So you be careful," Margie said. "No picking up hitchhikers because they've got pretty asses. And don't stay in any sleazy motels. There's a lot of strange folks out there."

*          *          *

So she began the homeward journey. It took her four days and three nights, stopping off, despite Margie's warnings, at a couple of less than salubrious motels along the way. Though she'd thought the journey would give her plenty of time to think, her mind didn't want to be bothered with problems. Instead it idled, concerning itself only with the practical problems of finding places to eat, and choosing between routes. Whenever there was a choice between a bland highway and something more picturesque (but inevitably longer), she picked the latter. It was nice to be in the driving seat again, after two years of being chauffeured around; turning up the radio and singing along with old favorites.

But once she crossed into Ohio, with Dansky only a couple of hours away, her high spirits faded. She had some difficult times ahead. What would she say when people asked her how her life in the lap of luxury was going? What would she tell them when they enquired about Mitchell, her handsome husband, who had given up his eligible bachelorhood to be with her? Oh Lord, what would she say? That it had all gone to hell, and she was running home to escape? That she didn't love him after all? That he was a sham, he and his whole damn world, a hollow spectacle that wasn't worth a damn. They wouldn't believe her. How could she complain, they'd say, when she had so much? When she was rolling in wealth, and they were still living in their one-bedroom tract homes worrying about the mortgage and the cost of a new pair of sneakers for the kids?

Well, it was too late to turn back now. She was crossing the railroad tracks that had always been in her childhood the limits of the town; the place where the world she knew ended and the greater world began. She was back in streets that she still dreamed about some nights; wandered the way she'd wandered in the troubled years before puberty, when she didn't know what to make of herself (doubted, indeed, that she would ever amount to anything). There was the drugstore, owned by Albert McNealy, and now by his son Lance, with whom Rachel had had a brief but innocent affair in her fifteenth year. There was the school where she'd learned something of everything and nothing in particular, its yard still fenced with the same chain-link, like a shabby prison. There was the little park (or so the city fathers dubbed it; in fact the term was pure flattery). There was the birdshit-bespattered statue of Irwin Heckler, called the founding father of the town, who had in 1903 started a little business manufacturing hard, tartly flavored candies which had proved uncommonly popular. There was the town hall and the church (the only building that still possessed some of its remembered grandeur) and the little mall that contained the hairdresser's and the offices of the town lawyer, Marion Klaus, and the dog groomer's, and half a dozen other establishments that served the community.

All of them were closed at this hour; it was well past nine o'clock in the evening. The only place that would still be open would be the bar on McCloskey Road, close to the funeral home. She was tempted to drive over there and get herself a glass of whiskey before she called on her mother, but she knew the chances of getting in and out of the bar without meeting somebody who knew her were exactly zero, so she drove straight to the house on Sullivan Street. She wasn't arriving unannounced; she'd called her mother from somewhere outside Youngstown and told her she was on her way. The porch light was on and the front door stood an inch or two ajar.

There was a sublime little moment on the front step, when—after she'd called out to Sherrie and before the answering call came—she stood there and listened to the sounds of the night around her. There was no traffic: just the gentle hiss of the leaves of the holly tree that had grown unchecked to the side of the house, and the rattle of a piece of loose guttering, and the tinkle of the wind chime that hung from the eaves. All familiar sounds; all reassuring. She took a deep breath. Everything was going to be fine. She was loved here; loved and understood. Maybe there'd be some people in town who'd look at her askance and spread rumors about what had happened, but here she was safe. Here was home, where things were as they had always been.

And now here was Sherrie looking a little fretful, but smiling to see her daughter on the step.

"Well this *is* a surprise," she said.

# XIV

## i

The night after Rachel started her drive to Ohio, Garrison invited Mitchell out for dinner. It was a long time since they'd had a heart-to-heart, he said, and there was no better time than the present.

When Ralph brought him to the restaurant Garrison had chosen, Mitchell was certain there'd been a mix-up. It was a dingy little Chinese place on Canal Street and Mott; not the most welcoming of neighborhoods. But Ralph hadn't made an error. Garrison was there, sitting toward the back of the narrow room at a table that could have seated six but was set for two. He had a bottle of white wine in front of him, and was drawing on an havana. He offered Mitchell a glass of wine, and a cigar, but all Mitchell wanted was a glass of milk, to settle his stomach.

"Does that really work for you?" Garrison said. "Milk just gives me gas."

"Everything gives you gas."

"That's true," Garrison said.

"Remember that kid Mario, used to call you Stinky Geary?"

"Mario Giovannini."

"That's right, Giovannini. I wonder what the fuck happened to him?"

"Who cares?" Garrison said, sitting back in his chair. "Hey, Mr. Ko?" The manager, a rather dapper fellow with his hair plastered to his pate so carefully it looked as though it had been painted on strand by strand, appeared. "Can we get some milk over here for my brother? And some menus."

"I'm not hungry," Mitchell said.

"You will be. We've got to get your energies up. We've got a long night ahead of us."

"I can't do that, Gar. I've got two breakfast meetings tomorrow."

"I took the liberty of canceling them."

"What for?"

"Because we need to talk." He took out a box of matches and carefully rekindled his cigar. "Chiefly about the women in our lives." He drew on the cigar. "So . . . tell me about Rachel."

"There isn't a lot to tell. She was up at the farmhouse—"

"—with Margie."

"Right. Then she decided to take a road trip. Nobody knows where."

"Margie knows," Garrison said. "The bitch probably suggested it."

"I don't know why she'd do that."

"To cause trouble. That's her favorite thing. You know what she's like."

"Will you see if you can get some answers out of her?"

"You'd be better off trying instead of me," Garrison replied. "If I ask for something we're guaranteed not to get it."

"Where's Margie tonight?"

Garrison shrugged. "I don't ask 'cause I don't care. She's probably out drinking somewhere. There's three or four of them just go out and get plastered together. That bitch who was married to Lenny Bryant—"

"Marilyn."

"Yeah. She's one of them. And the woman who ran the restaurants."

"I don't know who you mean."

"Thin woman. Big teeth, no tits."

"Lucy Cheever."

"You see you've got a good memory for these women."

"I had an affair with Lucy Cheever, that's why."

"You're kidding. You did Lucy Cheever?"

"I took her down to New Orleans and fucked her brains out for a week."

"Big teeth. Small tits."

"She's got nice tits!"

"They're fucking minuscule. And she's never sober."

"She was sober in New Orleans. At least some of the time."

Garrison shook his head. "I don't get it with you. I mean, she's got to be fifty."

"This was five or six years ago."

"Even so. You could have any piece of ass you want and you go spend a week with a woman who's ten, fifteen years older than you are? What the fuck for?"

"I liked her."

"You liked her." Mr. Ko had returned with the menus and the milk. "Get me a brandy will you?" Garrison said to him, "We'll order later." Ko withdrew, and Garrison returned to the mystery of his brother's liaison with Lucy Cheever. "Was she good?"

"Will you just let it alone? I've got more important things to think about than Lucy fucking Cheever." He drank half of his glass of milk. "I want to know where Rachel is."

"She'll come back. Don't worry."

"What if she doesn't?"

"She will. She's got no choice."

"Of course she's got a fucking choice. She could decide she wants a separation."

"She could, I suppose. She'd be stupid, but she could." He drew on his cigar. "Does she know anything she shouldn't?"

"Not from me she doesn't."

"Meaning what?"

"Meaning she talks with Margie. Who knows what the hell they've discussed."

"Margie knows better."

"Maybe when she's sober."

"You've had Rachel sign some kind of prenuptial agreement, right?"

"No."

"Why the fuck not?"

"Don't raise your voice."

"I told Cecil to have her sign it."

"I convinced him it wasn't necessary," Mitchell said. Garrison snorted at the absurdity of this. "I didn't want her thinking she was entering a business arrangement. I was in love with her, for fuck's sake. I still am."

"Then you'd better make sure she keeps her mouth shut."

"I know," Mitch said.

"Well if you know why the fuck didn't you have her sign the prenuptial?" He leaned across the table, catching hold of Mitchell's arm. "Let me put this really simply. If she tries to say anything about our business, family business, to anyone, I'm going to slap a gag order on her."

"There's no need for that."

"How do you know? You don't even know where she is right now. She could be sitting down talking to some dickhead journalist." Mitchell shook his head. "I mean what I say about the gag order," Garrison reiterated. "I don't mind being the heavy if you think you've got a chance of patching things up."

"It's not a question of patching things up. We've had a bad time, but it's nothing permanent."

"Sure, sure . . ." Garrison said, his tone wearied, as though he'd heard this kind of self-deception countless times before. "You tell yourself whatever the fuck you need to hear."

"I married her because I feel something for her. That feeling hasn't gone away."

"It will," Garrison replied, waving Mr. Ko over, "Trust me, it will."

## ii

Mitchell discovered he had a better appetite than he'd expected. The food was good, though Garrison was able to tolerate far spicier versions of the dishes than Mitchell. Twice during the meal he exhorted Mitchell to try a forkful of something he was eating, and Mitchell was left gasping, much to Garrison's amusement.

"I'm going to have to start educating your palate," he said.

"It's a little late for that." Garrison glanced up from his plate, his spectacles slightly fogged.

"It's never too late," he said.

"And what's that supposed to mean?"

"You've always had a more delicate stomach than me. But that's got to change. For all our sakes." Garrison set down his fork and picked up his glass of wine. "Did you know Loretta goes to an astrologer?"

"Yes, Cadmus let it drop one day. What's that got to do with anything?"

"Last Sunday I got a call from Loretta. She wanted me to come over to the house. Urgently. She'd just been to see this astrologer, and he was full of bad news."

"About what, for God's sake?"

"About us. The family."

"What did he say?"

"That our lives were going to change, and we weren't going to like it very much." Garrison was cradling his wine glass in his hands, staring out past his brother with middle distance. "In fact, we're not going to like it at all."

Mitchell rolled his eyes. "Why the hell does Loretta waste money on this bullshit—"

"Wait. There's more. The first sign of this . . ." Garrison paused, searching for the word ". . . big *change,* is that one of us is going to lose our wife." His gaze finally came back to Mitchell. "Which you have."

"She'll be back."

"So you keep insisting. But whether she comes back or she doesn't, the point is she left."

"Are you telling me you *believe* what this guy was saying?"

"I haven't finished. He said the other sign was going to have something to do with a man from the sea."

Mitchell sighed: "That's so lame," he said. "She probably told him something about the situation . . . and he just fed it back to her."

"Maybe," Garrison said.

"Well what's the alternative?" Mitchell said, a little irritably, "That this dickhead's right, and we're all heading for disaster?"

"Yeah," Garrison said. "That's the alternative."

"I prefer my version."

Garrison sipped his wine. "Like I said . . ." he murmured, "you've always had a weak stomach."

"What's that supposed to mean?"

Garrison gave a rare smile. "That you don't want to even contemplate the possibility that there's something going on here we should be taking seriously. That maybe things *are* falling apart?"

Mitchell threw up his hands. "I can't believe I'm having this conversation," he said. "With you, of all people. You're supposed to be the rational one in the family."

"And look where it got me," Garrison growled.

"You look just fine to me."

"*Jesus.*" Garrison shook his head. "That goes to show how much we understand one another, doesn't it? I'm chewing antidepressants like fucking candies, Mitch. I go to analysis four times a week. The sight of my wife naked makes me want to puke. Does that help paint the picture for you?" He eyed his wine. "I shouldn't really be drinking alcohol. Not with antidepressants. But right now I don't give a fuck." He paused, then said, "You want something more to eat?"

"No thanks."

"You've got room for ice cream. Allow yourself some childish pleasures once in a while. They're very therapeutic."

"I'm putting on love handles."

"No woman on the fucking planet's going to throw you out of bed because you've got a fat ass. Eat some ice cream."

"Don't change the subject. We were talking about you mixing drink and pills."

"No we weren't. We were talking about me getting a little crazy, because it's done me no fucking good staying sane."

"So get crazy," Mitchell said. "I don't give a shit. Take the next board meeting naked. Fire everyone. Hire deaf-mutes. Do whatever the fuck you want, but don't start listening to some crap from a fucking astrologer."

"He was talking about Galilee, Mitch."

"A *man from the sea!?* That could be anybody."

"But it wasn't *anybody.* It was him. It was Galilee."

"You know what," Mitchell said, raising his hands, "Let's stop talking about this."

"Why?"

"Because the conversation's going round in circles. And I'm bored."

Garrison stared at him, then expelled a long, strangely contented breath. "So what are you doing with the rest of the night?" he said.

Mitch glanced at his watch. "Going home to bed."

"Alone?"

"Yes. Alone."

"No sex. No ice cream. You're going to die a miserable man, you know that? I could arrange some company for you if you like."

"No thanks."

"Are you sure?"

Mitchell laughed. "I'm sure."

"What's so funny?"

"You. Trying to get me laid, like I was still seventeen. Remember that whore you brought back to the house for me?"

"Juanita."

"Juanita! Right. Jesus, what a memory!"

"All she wanted to do—"

"Don't remind me—"

"—was sit on your face! You should have married her," Garrison said, pushing his chair back and getting up. "You'd have twenty kids by now." Mitchell looked sour. "Don't get mad. You know it's true. We both fucked up. We should have married dumb bitches with childbearing hips. But no. I choose a drunk and you choose a shopgirl." He picked up his glass and drained the last of his wine. "Well . . . have a nice night."

"Where are you off to?"

"I've got an assignation."

"Anyone I know?"

"*I* don't even know her," Garrison said as he headed away from the table. "You'll see. It's much easier that way."

# XV

### i

There was a time in my life—many, many years ago; more years than I care to count—when nothing gave me more pleasure than to listen to songs of love. I could even sing a few, if I was drunk enough. On occasion, before I lost the use of my legs, we'd venture out together, my wife Chiyojo, Marietta and myself, to see traveling players in Raleigh, and there'd always been a spot or two in the show when the mood would become sweetly melancholy, and a crooner, or a quartet of crooners, or the leading lady with a handkerchief clutched to her bosom, would offer up something to tug at our hearts. "I'll Remember You, Love, In My Prayers," or "White Wings"; the more grotesquely sentimental the better as far as I was concerned. But I lost my appetite for such entertainments when Chiyojo died. A plaintive ballad about love irrevocably lost was a fine thing to indulge in when the idol of your affections was sitting beside you, her hand clutching yours. But when she was taken from me—under circumstances so tragic they beggared anything a songwriter might dream up—I would start to weep as soon as a minor chord was played.

And yet, in spite of my resistance to the subject, it creeps closer to these pages with every passing moment. Sentence by sentence, paragraph by paragraph, this account draws nearer and nearer to a time when love must appear, transforming the lives of the characters I've set before you. Few will be untouched by its consequences, however immune they may believe themselves.

And that, of course, includes myself. I've wondered more than once if fear of my own vulnerability was not the reason I didn't attempt to put pen to paper earlier. The passion for words was always in me, from my mother, and I've certainly had plenty of spare time in the last century or so. But I could never do it. I was afraid—I am still afraid— that once I begin to write about love I will find myself consumed by the very fire I am building to burn other hearts.

Of course in the end I have no choice. The romance approaches, as inevitable as the apocalypse Garrison was telling his brother about in the restaurant: because, of course, they are one and the same.

Garrison parted from Mitchell outside the restaurant, dismissed his driver and went uptown to an apartment which he had purchased, unknown to anyone else in the family, for exactly the purpose he intended to use it tonight. He let himself in, pleased to find that the temperature of the place was far lower than would usually be thought to be comfortable, which fact meant the erotic rituals of the evening had already begun. He didn't go directly to the bedroom, though he was now in a state of excitement. In the living room he poured himself a drink, and stood by the window to sip it and savor the moments of anticipation. Oh, if only all life were as rich and real to him as these moments; as charged with meaning and emotion. Tomorrow, of course, he would despise himself a little, and behave like a perfect sonofabitch to any and all who crossed his path. But tonight? Tonight, marinating in the knowledge of what lay before him, he was as close as he knew how to being a happy man. At last he set down the glass, without really drinking much at all, and loosening his tie wandered through to the elegantly appointed bedroom. The door was ajar. There was a light burning inside. He entered.

The woman was lying on the bed. Her name was Melodie, he'd been told (though he doubted any woman who sold her body for this kind of purpose used the name they'd been brought with to God). There she lay, under a sheet, perfectly still, her eyes closed. There were a dozen white and yellow lilies on the pillow around her head; a nice funereal touch, courtesy of the man who arranged these scenarios for Garrison, Fred Platt. The smell of the flowers was not strong enough to compete with the other scent in the room however: that of disinfectant. Again, one of Platt's felicities, this piney scent; one which Garrison had been a little unsettled by at first, pressing his fantasies as it did still closer to grim reality. But Platt knew Garrison's psyche well: that first time with the disinfectant stinging the sinuses had been an erotic revelation. Now the scent was an indispensable part of the fantasy.

He approached the bed, and stood at the end of it, looking down at the woman, studying her body for some sign of a shudder. But he could see only the very slightest tremor, which clearly the woman was doing her best to suppress. Good for her, he thought; she was a professional. He admired professionalism in all matters: in the trading of stocks, in the cooking of food, in the imitation of death. If it was worth doing, as Loretta was fond of saying, then it was worth doing properly.

He reached down and plucked at the sheet, sliding it out from beneath Melodie's hands, which were crossed on her breasts. She was naked beneath the sheet, her body made up with a pale pancake, then dusted down, to lend her a cadaverous hue.

"Lovely," he said, without a trace of irony.

She was indeed a pretty sight: her breasts small, her nipples alert with cold, and long. Her pubic hair was neatly trimmed, so as to offer him a glimpse of her intricately-made labia. He would lick there soon.

But first, the feet. He pulled the sheet off her completely, and let it drop to the floor. Then he went down on his knees at the end of the bed and applied his lips to the woman's flesh. She was cold: the consequence of lying on a bed of ice sealed in plastic. He kissed her toes, and then the soles of her feet, slipping his hands around her slim ankles while he did so. Now that he had his skin against hers he could feel the tremors deep in her tissue, but they weren't violent enough to distract him from the illusion. He could believe she was dead with very little difficulty. Dead and cold and unresisting.

I won't go on with the description; there's no need. For those of you who wish to picture Garrison Geary pleasuring himself with a woman playing dead, you have all the information you need to conjure it; go to it if you wish. For the rest of us, enough to know that this was his special pleasure, his most-anticipated bliss. I can't tell you why. I don't know what strange twist his psyche took that made this ritual so arousing to him: or who put it there. But there it was; and there I'll leave him, covering the pseudo-corpse with kisses in preparation for the so-called act of love.


For his part, Mitchell had decided to go back to the apartment to sleep. Rachel would come back there, tonight, he thought, and all would be forgiven. He'd hear a sound in the bedroom, and open his eyes to see her silhouette against the starry sky (he hated to sleep with the drapes closed; it made him dream smothering dreams), and she'd shed her clothes, and say she was *sorry, so sorry*, then slip into bed beside him. Perhaps they'd make love, but probably not. Probably she'd just put her head in the crook of his arm, and lay her hand on his chest, and they'd fall asleep that way, as they had when they'd first shared a bed.

But his romantic expectations were dashed. She didn't come home that night. He slept alone in the huge bed; at least he slept for the first hour or so, before waking with a stabbing ache in his lower abdomen, so sharp it made him want to cry like a baby. Cursing Garrison and his damnable Mr. Ko, he staggered, bent nearly double, into the bathroom, and dug through the medications there for something to soothe the pain. His sight was blurred with agony, and his hands shaking. It took him fully two or three minutes to locate the appropriate bottle of tablets and he'd no sooner fingered a couple of them onto his tongue than he felt a crippling spasm in his bowels, and only just reached the toilet in time before expelling a watery stream of foul-smelling feces. When the expulsion came to an end he stayed put, knowing the respite was only temporary. The ache in his belly had not been mellowed at all; he still felt as though his bowels were being pierced with needles.

He began to cry while he sat there, the tears coming haltingly at first, then as a flow he could not halt. He put his hands over his face, which was burning hot, sobbing behind his palms. It seemed he could not imagine misery profounder than the misery he felt now: abandoned, sick, confused. What had he done to deserve this? Nothing. He'd lived the best life he knew how to live. So why was he sitting here like a damned soul, smelling his own stench rising all around him, tormented by the predictions Garrison had whispered in his ear? And why didn't he know where his wife was tonight? Why wasn't she here to comfort him, waiting in the bed to hold him in her arms once the spasms had passed; her touch cool, her voice full of love? Why was he alone?

*Oh Lord, why was he alone?*

\*         \*         \*

Across town, Garrison returned from the bedroom where he had lately shot his seed. The icy recipient of his love had been admirably inert throughout his plugging of her body; not once had she grunted or cried out, even when his ministrations had become less than gentlemanly. Sometimes, not satisfied with his vaginal explorations, he liked to roll the "corpses" over and take them anally. Tonight had been one of those times, and once again Mr. Platt had planned for the eventuality. When Garrison had rolled the girl over and parted her fesses, he'd found the back passage already lubricated for him. In he'd gone, eschewing the protection that most would think advisable when screwing with this class of woman, and had discharged inside her.

Then he'd got up, wiped himself on the sheet, and zipping up his pants (which he had not even dropped to mid-thigh during this whole business), left the room. As he exited he said: "It's over. You can get up," and was curiously comforted to see that the woman made a move to rise from the bed before he departed the room. It was all just a game, wasn't it? There was no harm in it. Look, she was resurrected! Stretching, yawning, looking for her envelope of cash, which Garrison had placed on the bedside table, as always. She would go on her way without even knowing who her violator was (or so Garrison liked to imagine. The women were instructed to keep their eyes closed throughout the game. If they peeped, Platt could be cruel).

Garrison went straight down into the street, to his car, and drove away. Anyone catching sight of him in the driver's seat would have thought: there goes a man happy with his lot in life.

As I said earlier, it wouldn't last. He would get up tomorrow feeling thoroughly disgusted with himself; but the self-disgust would last twenty-four hours—forty-eight at most—and then the desire he'd quenched tonight would flicker into life again, and grow in strength over a period of a week or two, until at last he couldn't resist it any longer, and he'd be on the phone to Platt in a kind of trance, saying that he needed one of his "special nights," just as soon as possible. And the whole ritual would be repeated.

What a strange thing it was, he thought, to be Garrison Geary. To possess as much power as he possessed, and yet feel in his troubled soul such a lack of self-regard that he was only able to make love with a woman who passed for dead. What a peculiar specimen of humanity he was! And yet he could not feel entirely ashamed of this peculiarity. There was a part of him that was perversely proud tonight; proud that he was capable of doing what he'd just done; proud that even in this city, which was a magnet for men and women who lived unusual lives, the fantasy he'd enacted would be thought disgraceful. What might he not do with this perversity of his, he wondered, if he once unleashed it outside the bounds of his sexual life? What changes might he work upon the world if he put his darker energies to better purpose than fucking an icy cunt?

But what, what? If there was some greater purpose to his life, why couldn't he see it? If there was a path that he was intended to follow, why hadn't he stumbled onto by now? Sometimes he felt like an athlete who'd sweated himself into a frenzy in preparation for a race that nobody had summoned him to run. And with every day he failed to compete his chances of winning that race—when he finally knew what course it would follow—became more remote.

*Soon,* he thought to himself; I have to know what my purpose is soon, or I'll be too old to do anything about it. I'll die without having really lived, and the moment I'm in the ground I'll be forgotten.

It has to be soon.

# XVI

The night Rachel had come home she'd told her mother that she wanted as few people as possible to know that she was here, but in a community as small and as well-knit as Dansky no secret so large could be kept for very long. The following morning she'd gone out to put some letters in the postbox for her mother, and had been seen doing so by Mrs. Bedrosian, the widow who lived next door.

"Well, well," Mrs. Bedrosian had said, "Is that you Rachel?"

"Yes. It's me."

That was the full extent of the exchange. But it was all that was needed. Half an hour later the telephone started to ring—people from around town making apparently casual calls to see how Rachel's mother was doing, then lightly dropping into conversation the fact that they'd heard Rachel was home for the weekend; and—just by the way—had she brought her husband home with her?

Sherrie simply lied. She hadn't been feeling very well, she told everyone, and Rachel had come to spend a few days with her. "And no," she invariably added, "Mitchell isn't with her. So you can stop sniffing after an invitation to meet him, if that's why you're asking."

The lie worked well. After half a dozen such calls word spread that even if there *was* something worth gossiping about here, Sherrie Pallenberg wasn't going to be providing any fuel.

"Of course that won't stop them talking," Sherrie remarked. "They've got nothing better to do, you see. This damn town."

"I thought you liked it here," Rachel said to her.

They were sitting in the kitchen at lunchtime, eating peach cobbler.

"If your father was still alive, it might be different. But I'm on my own. And what do I have for company? Other widows." She rolled her eyes. "We get together for brunches and bridge, and you know they're all sweet souls, they really are, and I don't want to sound ungrateful, but, Lord, after a while I get so bored talking about drapes and soap operas and how little they see their children."

"Is that one of *your* complaints?"

"No, no. You've got your own life to live. I don't expect you to be on my doorstep every five minutes checking up on me."

"You might be seeing rather more of me in future," Rachel said.

Her mother shook her head. "It's just a bad patch you and Mitch are going through. You'll come out the other side of it, you'll see."

"I don't think it's as simple as that," Rachel said. "We're not suited to one another."

"Nobody ever is," her mother replied nonchalantly.

"You don't mean that."

"I certainly do. Honey, listen to me. Nobody, and I mean nobody, is ever deep in their hearts perfectly suited to anybody else. You have to make compromises. Great big compromises. I know I did with Hank and I'm sure if Hank were alive he'd say exactly the same thing about me. We *decided* to make it work. I suppose . . ." she allowed herself a sad little smile. ". . . I suppose we realized that we weren't going to do any better than what we had right there and then. I know it doesn't sound very romantic, but it's the way it was. And you know, once I got over that silly feeling that this wasn't Prince Charming—that he was just an ordinary man who farted in bed and couldn't keep his eyes off a pretty waitress—I was quite happy."

"The thing is Mitch *doesn't* look at waitresses."

"Well . . . lucky you. So what's the problem?"

Rachel set down her fork and stared at her half-eaten cobbler. "I've got so much to be grateful for," she said, as though she were saying her prayers. "I know that. Lord, when I think of how much Mitch has given me . . ."

"Are you talking about *things?*"

"Yes, of course."

Sherrie waved them away. "Irrelevant. He could have given you half of New York and still be a bad husband."

"I don't think he's a bad husband. I just think he's never going to belong to me the way Daddy belonged to you."

"Because of his family?"

Rachel nodded. "God knows, I don't want to feel like I'm in a competition with them for his attention, but that's how it feels." She sighed. "It's not even as though I could point to something they do that proves it. I just feel excluded."

"From what, honey?"

"You know, I don't really know," Rachel said. "It's just a feeling . . ." She exhaled; puffing out her cheeks. "Maybe the problem's all in here." She tapped her fingers to her breast. "In me. I don't have any right not to be happy." She looked up at her mother, her eyes brimming. "Do I? I mean, really and truly, what right in all the world do I have to be unhappy? When I think of Mrs. Bedrosian losing her family . . ."

Judith Bedrosian had lost her husband and three kids in an automobile accident when Rachel was fourteen. Everything the woman lived for—all the meaning in her life—taken away from her in one terrible moment. Yet she'd gone on, hadn't she?

"Everybody's different," Sherrie said. "I don't know how poor Judith made peace with what happened to her, and you know what? Maybe she never has. The way people are on the outside and the way they feel deep down are never the same. Never. I *do* know she still has very bad times, after all these years. Days on end when I don't see her; and when I do she's obviously been crying for hours. And at Christmas I know she goes to her sister's in Wisconsin, even though she doesn't like the woman, because she can't bear to be alone. The memories are too much. So . . ." She sighed, as though the weight of Judith's grief was heavy on her too. "Who knows? All you can do is just get on with things the best way you know how. Personally, I'm a great proponent of Valium, in reasonable moderation. But each to their own."

Rachel chuckled. She'd always known her mother to be an entertaining woman, after her odd fashion. But as the years went by Sherrie's sophistication became more apparent. Under the veneer of small town pieties lay a self-made mind, capable of a willfulness and a waywardness Rachel hoped she had inherited.

"So now what?" Sherrie said. "Are you going to ask him for a divorce?"

"No, of course not," Rachel replied.

"Why's that such a surprising idea? If you don't love him—"

"I didn't say that."

"—if you can't live with him then—"

"I didn't say that either. Oh God, I don't know. Margie said I *should* get a divorce. And a nice big settlement. But I don't want to be on my own."

"You wouldn't be."

"Mom, it sounds like you think I *should* leave him."

"No, I'm just saying you wouldn't be on your own. Not for very long. So that's not a reason to stay in a marriage that's not giving you what you want."

"You amaze me," Rachel said. "You really do. I was absolutely certain you were going to sit me down and tell me I had to go back and give it another chance."

"Life's too short," Sherrie said. "That's not what I would have said a few years ago, but your viewpoint changes as time goes on." She reached up and touched Rachel's cheek. "I don't want my beautiful Rachel to be unhappy for one more moment."

"Oh, Mom . . ."

"So if you want to leave the man, leave him. There are plenty more handsome millionaires where he came from."

# XVII

That night Deanne had invited them both to a church barbecue, assuring Rachel the guests were all people she knew and liked, and she'd already passed the word around that nobody was to ply Rachel with questions about life in the fast lane. Even so, Rachel wasn't keen to go. Deanne, however, made it plain that she'd take it as personal affront if she declined. Once they got to the barbecue, however, Rachel lost her protection. The kids went off to play, and her sister—despite promising to stay close by—was off after five minutes to have a heart-to-heart with the hostess. Rachel was left in the midst of people she didn't know but who were all too familiar with her.

"I saw you and your husband on television just a few weeks ago," one of the women, who introduced herself as Kimberly, Deanne's second-best friend, whatever that meant, remarked. "It was one of those gala nights. You all looked to be having such a wonderful time. I said to Frankie—that's my husband, Frankie, over there, with the hotdog; he used to work with your sister's husband—I said to Frankie don't they look as though they're having a wonderful time? You know, everything so polished."

"Polished?"

"Everything," Kimberly repeated, "so polished. You know, everything sparkling." Her eyes gleamed as she recalled the sight; Rachel didn't have the heart to tell her what a drab affair the gala had been; the food sickly, the speeches interminable, the company wretched. She just let the woman blather on for a few minutes, nodding or smiling when it seemed appropriate to do so. She was saved from this depressing exchange by a man with a napkin tucked in his shirt, a sizable sparerib in his hand and his face liberally basted in barbecue sauce.

"You don't mind me barging in," he said to Rachel's captor, "but it's a long time since I saw this little lady."

"You're a mess, Neil Wilkens," the woman declared.

"I am?"

"All round your mouth."

The man plucked his napkin from his shirt and wiped his mouth, giving Rachel time to realize who this was: Neil Wilkens, the first boy who'd had her heart (and broken it) all grown up. He had a gingery beard, a receding hairline, and the beginnings of a beer belly. But his smile, when it emerged from behind the napkin, was as bright as ever.

"You do know who I am?" he said.

"Neil."

"The same."

"It's wonderful to see you. I think Deanne told me you'd gone to Chicago."

"He came back with his tail between his legs," Kimberly remarked, somewhat uncharitably.

Neil's brightness was undimmed. "I didn't like living in a big city," he said, "I guess I'm a small-town boy at heart. So I came back home and started up a business with Frankie—"

"That's my husband," Kimberly put in, in case Rachel had missed this fact.

"We do general house repairs. A little bit of plumbing, a little bit of roof work."

"They argue all the time," Kimberly said.

"We do not," Neil said.

"Fighting like dogs one minute. Best friends the next."

"Frankie's a Communist," Neil said.

"He is *not*," Kimberly protested.

"Jack was a card-carrying Commie, Kimberly," Neil replied.

"Who's Jack?" Rachel asked him.

"Frankie's Dad. He died a while back."

"Prostate cancer," Kimberly put in.

"And when Frankie was going through the old man's papers he found a Communist Party card. So now he carries it around with him, and he's talking about how we should all rise up against the forces of capitalism."

"He doesn't mean it," Kimberly said.

"How do you know?"

"It's just his stupid sense of humor," she said. Neil caught Rachel's eye, and gave her a tiny smile. He was obviously stirring Kimberly up.

"Well you can say whatever you like," he remarked, "but if a guy's carrying a Commie card, he's a Commie."

"Oh you are *so* infuriating sometimes," Kimberly said, and without another word, stalked away.

"It's too easy," Neil chuckled. "She gets so hot under the collar if you say anything about her Frankie, but she gives the poor man hell day and night. He had a good head of hair when he married her. Not that I have much to boast about." He ran his palm over his semi-naked pate.

"I think it rather suits you," Rachel said.

Neil beamed. "Do you? Really? Lisa hated it."

"Lisa's your wife?"

"The mother of my children," Neil said, with ironic precision.

"You're not married."

"We were. Actually technically we still are. But she's in Chicago, with the kids, and I'm . . . well, I'm here. They were going to come back and join me when I was all set up, but that's not going to happen. She's got someone else now, and the kids are happy. At least, she says they are."

"I'm sorry."

"Yeah," he said, the word one long sigh. "I suppose it's happening all the time, but it's hard when you want to make something work but you just can't." He stared down at his paint-stained boots, as if embarrassed by this confession.

"Did I know Lisa?" Rachel asked.

"Yeah, you knew her," he said, still studying his boots. "Her name was Froman. Lisa Angela Froman. She's the same age as your sister. In fact, they were in Sunday school for a year or so."

"I remember her," Rachel said, picturing a pretty, bespectacled blonde girl of sixteen or so. "She was very quiet."

"She still is. She's very smart and the kids got her brains, which is great for them, 'cause God knows I'm not the brightest guy on the block."

"So you miss them?"

"Like crazy. All the time. All the time." He said it as though it was still hard for him to believe. "I mean, you'd think after a while it'd become easier, but . . ." He shook his head. ". . . you want a beer or something?" He made a halfhearted little laugh. "I got a joint."

"You still smoke?"

"Not like I used to. But, you know, when things are boring I like to tune out. Then I don't think about things too much. I mean, it could break your heart . . ."


They wandered down to the bottom of the yard. There, at Neil's instigation they clambered over the low wall onto a strip of land which had been used as a dumping ground for vehicles, including an old school bus. It was all delightfully furtive, which made the mild high Rachel got when she took a hit of Neil's joint all the more fun.

"*Ah*, that's better," Neil said. "I should have done this before I came. I don't like these shindigs any more. Not on my own." He took his third drag on the reefer and passed it back to Rachel. "In fact, you know what?"

"What?"

"I don't like much any more. I'm going to end up like my Dad. Did you meet my Dad?"

"Everrett."

"You remember."

"Of course I remember," Rachel said, with a little laugh.

"Everrett Hancock Wilkens."

"Hancock?"

"Hey, don't knock it. Hancock's my middle name too."

She repeated the name, through mounting laughter. The syllables suddenly seemed funny as hell. "Does anybody ever call you Hancock?" she giggled.

"Only my Mom," he said, dissolving into laughter himself. "I always knew I was in trouble when I was a kid 'cause I'd hear her yelling—"

They yelled together—"*Hancock!*"—then in perfect synchronicity glanced guiltily back toward the yard, where several heads had turned in their direction.

"We're making fools of ourselves," Rachel said, attempting to suppress her laughter.

"That's the story of my life," Neil said. There was hurt behind the remark, despite his offhand manner. "But I'm past caring."

By sheer force of will Rachel wiped the smirk off her face. "I'm sorry things turned out the way they did," she said; then lost her composure completely, and began laughing so hard she was doubled up.

"What's so funny?" Neil wanted to know.

"Hancock," she said again. "It's such a silly name." She wiped the tears away from her eyes. "Oh Lord," she said, "I'm sorry. You were saying . . ."

"Never mind," Neil said. "It wasn't anything important." He was still grinning; but there was something else in his look.

"What's wrong?" she said.

"Nothing's wrong," he replied. "I was only thinking . . ."

She suddenly knew what he was going to say, and willed him not to spoil the moment by doing so. But she failed.

". . . what an idiot I was . . ."

"Neil."

". . . giving you up . . ."

"Neil, let's not . . ."

". . . no, please let me. I might never get another chance to tell you what's in my head . . ."

"Are you sure we shouldn't just have another smoke?"

"I've thought about you such a lot over the years."

"That's nice of you to say."

"It's true," he said. "I've had so many regrets in my life. So many things I wished I'd done differently; wished I'd done *right*. And you're at the top of the list, Rachel. The number of times I've seen you in a magazine, or on the television, and thought: she could have been with me. I could have made her so happy." He looked directly into her eyes. "You know that, don't you?" he said. "I could have made you so happy."

"We took different paths, Neil," she said.

"Not just different. Wrong."

"I don't think—"

"Not you. I'm not talking about you. God knows, you made a smart move marrying Geary. No. I'm talking about my screwups." He shook his head, and she realized that there were sudden tears in his eyes.

"Oh, Neil—"

"Don't mind me. It's just the fucking pot."

"Do you want to go back to the party?"

"Not particularly."

"I think we should. They'll be wondering where we got to."

"I don't care. I don't even fucking like 'em. Any of 'em."

"I thought you said you were a small-town boy at heart," Rachel countered.

"I don't know what I am," Neil confessed. "I used to know . . ." His gaze lost its focus; he stared off between the rusted vehicles into the darkness. "I had such dreams, Rachel . . ."

"You can still have them."

"No," he said. "It's too late. You have to seize the moment. If you don't seize the moment suddenly it's passed, and it doesn't come again. You get one chance. And I missed mine." He returned his gaze to her. "You were that chance," he said.

"That's sweet, but—"

"You don't have to tell me, I know. You never loved me, so it wouldn't have worked anyway. But I still think about you, Rachel. Never stopped thinking about you. And I swear I could have made you love me. And if I had . . ." He smiled, so sadly. "If I had everything would have been different."


She got a little lecture from Deanne the morning after the barbecue. What was she thinking, going off like that, with Neil Wilkens, of all people, Neil *Wilkens?* That kind of thing might be all right in New York, but this was a small community, and you just didn't behave like that. Rachel felt as though she were being chastised like an errant child, and told Deanne to keep her opinions to herself. Besides, what the hell was wrong with Neil Wilkens?

"He's practically an alcoholic," Deanne said. "And he got violent with his wife."

"I don't believe that."

"Well it's true," Deanne said. "So really, Rachel, you'd be better off staying away from him."

"I wasn't intending to—"

"You can't just waltz in here—"

"Wait—"

"—as if you owned the place—"

"What are you talking about?"

Deanne looked up from her cleaning, her face flushed. "Oh you know damn well."

"I'm sorry, I don't."

"Embarrassing me."

"What? When was this?"

"Last night! Leaving me with all these people asking where you'd gone. What was I supposed to say? Oh she's off somewhere flirting with Neil Wilkens like a fifteen-year-old—"

"I was not."

"I saw you! We *all* saw you, giggling like a schoolgirl. It was very embarrassing."

"Well I'm sorry," Rachel said coolly. "I won't embarrass you any longer."


She went back to her mother's house, and packed. She wept while she packed. A little out of anger at the way Deanne had talked to her; but more out of a strange confusion of feelings. Maybe Neil Wilkens *had* beaten his wife. But, Lord, she'd liked him, in a way she couldn't entirely explain. Was it that she half-believed she belonged here? That the girl who'd been enamored of Neil all those years ago had not entirely disappeared, but was still inside her, trembling in expectation of a first kiss, her hopes for perfect love still intact? And now she was weeping, that girl, out of sorrow that her Neil and she had taken separate roads?

How perfectly ridiculous all this was; and how predictable. She went to the bathroom, washed her tearstained face, and gave herself a talking to. This whole trip had been a mistake. She should have stayed in New York and faced what was going on between herself and Mitch head-on.

On the other hand, perhaps it was healthy to have been reminded that she was now an exile. She would no longer be able to entertain sentimental thoughts of returning to her roots; she had to be ready to move on down the road she'd chosen. She would go back, she decided, and talk everything out with Mitch. She had nothing to lose from being honest. And if they decided they were mismatched, then she'd explain that she wanted a divorce, and they'd begin proceedings. Maybe she'd get some advice from Margie about what she was worth on the ex-wife market. After that? Well, she'd have to see. The only thing she knew for certain was that she wouldn't be coming back to live in Dansky. Whatever she was at heart (and right now she didn't have a clue) she was absolutely certain she was no longer a small-town girl.


She left that day, despite her mother's protests. "Stay another night or two at least," Sherrie said. "You've come all this way."

"I really need to get back."

"It's Neil Wilkens, isn't it?"

"It's nothing to do with Neil Wilkens."

"Did he make a pass at you?"

"No, Mom."

"Because if he did—"

"Mom, he was a perfect gentleman."

"That man doesn't know the meaning of the word gentleman." She stared at Rachel fiercely. "A hundred Neil Wilkens aren't worth one Mitchell Geary."

The observation stayed with her, and on the long drive back to New York she found herself idly musing on the two men, like a princess in a storybook weighing the relative merits of her suitors. One handsome and rich and boring; one balding and beer-bellied but still capable of making her laugh. They were in every way different, except in this: they were both sad men. When she brought their faces to mind they were sad faces, defeated faces. She knew where the source of Neil's defeat lay: he'd told her himself. But why was Mitch, with all the gifts history and genetics had showered upon him, ultimately just as sorrowful? It was a mystery to her; and the more she thought about the mystery the more it seemed there could be no healing the wound between them until she'd solved it.

# PART FOUR

# The Prodigal's Tide

# I

Last night I had a visit from Marietta. She brought me some cocaine, which she said she'd acquired in Miami and was of the very best quality. She also brought me a bottle of Benedictine, along with instructions on how to dissolve the drug in the liquor, so as to make, she promised, a potent concoction. It was time we went out adventuring together, she said; and this would put me in the perfect mood. I told her I couldn't go anywhere. There were too many ideas in my head; threads of my story which I had to keep from becoming knotted up.

"You'll work better after a little play," she pointed out.

"I'm sure you're right, but I'm still going to say no."

"What's the *real* reason?" she demanded.

"Well," I said, "the fact is . . . I'm about to start writing about Galilee. And I'm afraid if I stop now—before I face the challenge—I may not want to start again."

"I don't understand why," Marietta remarked. "I would have thought it would be something wonderful to write about him."

"Well I find the prospect intimidating."

"Why?"

"He's been so many people in his life. He's done so much. I'm afraid I won't capture him. He'll just become a cluster of contradictions."

"Then maybe that's what he is," she remarked, sensibly enough.

"People will still think the error's mine," I protested.

"Oh Eddie, it's only a book."

"It is not . . . *only a book*. It's my book. And it's a chance to tell something nobody else has ever told."

"All right, all right," she said, showing her palms in surrender, "don't get yourself stirred up. I'm sure it's going to be brilliant. There."

"I don't want to hear that. You'll make me self-conscious."

"Oh Lord. Well then what *can* I say?"

"Absolutely nothing. You can just leave me to get on with it."

✳    ✳    ✳

Even then I had not told her everything. Yes, I was fearful of the subject
that lay before me—of *Galilee*—and was nervous that if I once lost the
flow of my story I would not find it easy to return to it with the prospect
of his appearance looming. But I was more fearful still of accompanying
Marietta out beyond the perimeters of the house; of going back into the
world after so many years. I was afraid, I suppose, of finding whatever lay
out there now so overwhelming that I'd be like a lost child. I'd weep, I'd
shake, I'd wet my pants. God knows, ridiculous as all these thoughts
must seem to you, who live out there in the midst of things and presumably take all you see and experience for granted, they were very real
concerns to me. I had been, you must remember, a kind of willing pris-
oner of L'Enfant for so long that I had become like a man who has
passed the bulk of his life in a tiny cell, and when he is released—
though he has dreamed of the open sky for decades—cowers at the sight
of it, in terror of being unconcealed by his prison walls.

In short, Marietta left me in a foul mood, feeling as though there
was no comfort anywhere tonight. If I stayed, I faced Galilee. If I went,
I faced the world. (Which implies, now I read it back, that Galilee is all
the world is not, and vice versa. Unintentionally, I may have said something true about him there.)

As much to put off the moment when I had to return to the text I
decided to experiment with the makings of the aphrodisiac Marietta
had left me. Just as she had instructed, I poured out a measure of Benedictine into a cordial glass, and then, opening the little bag of cocaine,
some of which was powdery, some of which was lumpen, I selected a
sizeable nugget and dropped it into the liquor, stirring it around with
my pen. It didn't entirely dissolve; the result was a slightly cloudy liquor.
I toasted my text, there on the desk before me, and downed the mixture.
It burned my throat, and I instantly thought I'd made an error. I sat
down, my eyes watering. I could feel the track of the liquor all the way
down my esophagus, or so I imagined, then seeping over the wall of my
stomach, still burning.

"*Marietta . . .*" I growled. Why did I ever listen to a word that damn
dyke said? She was a liability. But I'd no sooner uttered her name than
the drug began to take its effect. I felt a welcome enlivening of my
limbs; and a kind of brightening of my thoughts, a quickening.

I got up from my desk, feeling a rush of strength in my lower limbs.
I needed to get out of my room for a while, out into the balmy evening.
I needed to stride awhile beneath the chestnut trees; fill my head with
the scents of dusk. Then I could come back to my desk refreshed, ready
to tackle the task of Galilee.

# II

Before I went I mixed myself another cordial glass to brimming, with a somewhat larger pebble of cocaine dissolved therein. Rather than drink it down then and there I took it with me, down the stairs and out, via a side door, onto the lawn. It was a beautiful evening—calm and sweet. The mosquitoes were out in force, but the coke and brandy had rendered me indifferent to their assaults. I wandered through the trees to the place where the cultivation of the grounds is relinquished to the glorious disorder of the swamp. The honeyed smells of garden flowers give way here to ranker scents: to the mingled fragrances of rot and stagnancy.

My eyes gradually became better accustomed to the starlight and by the glitter of those distant suns I was able to see some considerable distance between the trees. I watched the alligators on the banks, or moving through the laval waters; I watched the bats passing overhead, weaving their way between the branches in great multitudes.

Please realize that the pleasure I took in all this—the night animals, the rotted trees, the general miasma—had nothing to do with the cocaine. I have always enjoyed sights and species that the common throng would think of as unsavory, even signs of evil. Some of this enjoyment is aesthetic; but part comes out of the kinship I feel with unprettified nature, being as I am, a good example of same. I smell more rank than sweet, I look more degenerate than newly budded.

So, anyway; there I was, wandering at the edge of the lawn, surveying the swamp before me, and taking no little pleasure in the sight. I had carried my cordial glass down thus far without sipping a drop from it (sometimes the best of a drug—as with so much else—lies not in the consumption, but in the anticipation of the consumption). Now I took a mouthful, and swallowed it down. It was quite considerably stronger than the first draught. Even as it slid down my throat I seemed to feel my body responding to its presence: the same agitation in my limbs as I'd felt before, the same quickening of my thoughts. I've heard it said that this quickening is purely an illusion; that all the cocaine is doing is tricking the mind into believing it's performing mental gymnastics, when all it's doing is tripping over itself. I beg to differ. I've enjoyed some fine intellectual sport riding the white powder, and I've come away from the exercise with ruminations that stood the test of straight study.

But tonight I could not have had an intellectual exchange with someone if my life had depended upon it. Perhaps it was the potent mixture of cocaine and Benedictine; perhaps it was the fact of being out here in the wilderness alone; perhaps it was simply a *readiness* in me, but I found myself aroused. My head throbbed pleasantly, my heart beat hard in my breast, as though preparing itself for something, and my cock, which, excepting the visit from Cesaria, had been quiescent for several months, had risen up in my baggy pants, and was nuzzling at my fly in the hope of release.

My desire had no object, let me say; real or imagined. Marietta's concoction had simply given my body a wake-up call, and its first thoughts, now that it was awake, were sexual. I laughed out loud, perfectly happy with my lot at that moment; not desiring anything more than what I had: the stars, the swamp, the glass in my hand; my heart, and a hard-on. All lovely; and laughable.

Maybe I should return to the desk now, I thought, while I was still in such a positive frame of mind. If I was brave, and wrote on through my doubts, I could perhaps get the beginnings of Galilee on the page— his skeleton, so to speak—before the confidence the cocaine bestowed passed. I could flesh it out later. What mattered was to begin. And of course if I needed a little more courage along the way, I could always mix another glass of the concoction.

The plan pleased me. I decided to drain the cordial glass there and then, which I did, (tossing the empty glass into the brackish water) and then starting back toward the house. Or so I thought. What became apparent after fifty yards or so was that my mind, enamored of its own aroused state, had misled me, and instead of walking the safe, solid ground of the lawn I was getting deeper into the swamp. This was probably not a wise thing to do, some cautious corner of my mind muttered; but the greater part, being under the influence of powder and brandy, declared that if this was the way my instincts were taking me, then I should obey those instincts, and take pleasure in the journey. The earth was sodden beneath my feet, and relinquished my feet only with a comical sucking sound; the canopy had so thickened overhead that only a fraction of the starlight still made its way through to illuminate the path. And still my instincts took me on, deeper into the thicket. Even in my rush-headed state I knew very well I was daring disaster. This terrain was unsuitable for trekking through in broad daylight, much less at such an hour as this. At any moment the glaucous mud underfoot might give way and I'd be up to my neck in wicked waters, foul and full of alligators.

But what the hell? I had a hard-on to comfort me *in extremis*; and I would take my death as God's way of telling me I was not the writer I imagined myself to be.

Then, a strange thing. A certainty rose in me that I was not alone here. There was another human presence nearby; I could feel a curious gaze brushing the back of my neck. I stopped walking, and glanced back over my shoulder.

"Who's there?" I said, speaking softly.

I didn't expect a reply (one who comes after a traveler in near total darkness does not usually reply to an inquiry); but to my surprise I got one. It was not in the form of speech however, at least not at first. It came as a kind of fluttering in the murk, as though my unseen companion carried birds in his coat, like a magician. I stared at the motion, trying to make sense of it, and as I was staring I became unaccountably certain that I knew who this was. After decades of exile L'Enfant's sorrowful son, Galilee the wanderer, had come home.

# III

I said his name, barely raising my voice to audibility this time. Again, there came the fluttering, and because my gaze knew where to look I seemed to see him there. He was shaped out of shadow rather than starlight; shadow on shadow. But it was him, no doubt. There are not two faces as beautiful as his on the planet. I wish there were. I wish he were not without equal. But he is, damn him. He's an order of nature unto himself, and the rest of us have to take what little comfort we can from the fact of his unhappiness.

"Are you really here?" I said to him. It would be a strange question, I realize, to ask most people; but Galilee inherited from his mother the ability to send his image where he wishes and having for a moment believed he was here in the flesh I now suspected this agitated form was not the man himself, but a message that he'd willed my way.

This time, I comprehended words in the midst of the flutterings. "No," he said. "I'm a long way off."

"Still at sea?"

"Still at sea."

"So to what do I owe the honor? Are you thinking of coming back home?"

The fluttering became laughter; laughter, but bitter.

"Home?" he said. "Why would I come home? I'm not welcome there."

"I'd welcome you," I said. "So would Marietta." Galilee grunted. He was plainly unconvinced. "I wish I could see you better," I said to him.

"That's your fault, not mine," the shadow-in-shadow replied.

"What do you mean by that?" I replied, a little testily.

"Brother, I appear to you as clearly as you can bear me to be," Galilee replied. "No more, no less." I assumed he was telling the truth. There was no purpose in his lying to me. "But this is as close to home I will be getting anytime soon."

"Where are you?"

"Somewhere off the coast of Madagascar. The sea's calm; not a breath of wind. And there are flying fish all around the boat. I put my frying pan over the side and they just jump on into it . . ." His eyes shone in the murk, as though reflecting back at me some portion of the sunlit sea upon which he was gazing.

"Is it strange?" I asked him.

"Is what strange?"

"Being in two places at one time?"

"I do it all the time," he said. "I let my mind slip away and I go walking round the world."

"What if something were to happen to your boat while your thoughts were off walking?"

"I'd know," he said. "Me and my *Samarkand*, we understand one another. But there isn't any danger of that happening tonight. It's as calm as a baby's bath. You'd like it out here, Maddox. Once you get out here you have a different perspective on things. You start to let your dreams take over, start to forget the hurts you were done, start not to care about life and death and the riddles of the universe . . ."

"You missed out love," I said.

"Ah, well, yes . . . love's another matter." He looked away from me, into the darkness. "It doesn't matter how far you sail, there's always going to be love isn't there? It comes after you, wherever you go."

"You don't sound very happy about that."

"Well, brother, the truth is it doesn't matter whether I'm happy or not. There's no escape for me and that's all there is to it." He reached out his hand. "Do you have a cigarette?"

"No, I don't."

"Damn. Talking about love always makes me want to smoke."

"I'm a little confused," I said. "Suppose I *had* been in possession of a cigarette . . ."

"Could I have taken it from you and smoked it? Is that the question?"

"Yes."

"No. I couldn't. But I could have watched you smoke it, and been *almost* as satisfied. You know how much I enjoy experiences by proxy." He laughed again. This time there was no bitterness, just amusement. "In fact, the older I get—and I feel old, brother, I feel very, very old—the more it seems to me all the best experiences are second-hand, third-hand even. I'd prefer to tell a story about love, or hear one, than be in love myself."

"And you prefer to watch a cigarette being smoked than actually to smoke it?"

"Well . . . not quite," he sighed. "But I'm almost there. So, to business, brother of mine. Why did you call me?"

"I didn't call you."

"I beg to differ."

"No, truly. I didn't call you. I wouldn't even know *how* to."

"Maddox," he said, with just a touch of condescension. "You're not listening to me—"

"I'm listening, damn it—"

"Don't raise your voice."

"I'm not raising—"

"Yes you are. You're shouting at me."

"You accused me of not listening," I replied, attempting to keep my tone reasonable even though I wasn't feeling particularly reasonable. I never did in Galilee's presence; that was the simple truth of the matter. Even in the balmy days before the war, before Galilee ran off to seek his fortune in the world, before the calamities of his return, and the death of my wife, and the undoing of Nicodemus, even then—when we'd lived in a place that comes to look paradisiacal in hindsight—we had fought often, and bitterly, over the most insignificant things. All I would have to do was hear a certain tone in his voice—or he hear some unwelcome nuance in mine—and we'd be at one another's throats. The subject at hand was usually an irrelevance. We fought because we were at some profound level antithetical to one another. The passage of years had not, it seemed, mellowed that antipathy. We had only to exchange a few sentences and the old defenses were up, the old anger escalating.

"Let's change the subject," I suggested.

"Fine. How's Luman?"

"As crazy as ever."

"And Marietta? Is she well?"

"Better than well."

"In love?"

"Not at the moment."

"Tell her I asked after her."

"Of course."

"I was always fond of Marietta. I see her face in dreams all the time."

"She'll be flattered."

"And yours," Galilee said. "I see yours too."

"And you curse me."

"No, brother, I don't. I dream we're all back together again, before all the foolishness."

This seemed a particularly inappropriate word for him to use—almost insulting in its lack of gravity. I couldn't help but comment.

"It may have seemed foolishness to you," I said, "but it was a lot more to the rest of us."

"I didn't mean—"

"You went away to have your adventures, Galilee. And I'm sure that's given you a lot of joy."

"Less than you'd imagine."

"You had responsibilities," I pointed out. "You were the eldest. You should have been setting an example, instead of pleasuring yourself."

"Since when was that a crime?" Galilee countered. "It's in the blood, brother. We're a hedonistic family."

(There was no gainsaying this. Our father had been a sensualist of heroic proportions from his earliest childhood. I myself had found in a book of anthropology a story about his first sexual exploits recanted by Kurdish horsemen. They claim proudly that all seventeen of their tribe's founding fathers were sired by *my* father while he was still too young to walk. Make what you will of that.)

Galilee, meanwhile, had moved onto another matter.

"My mother . . ."

"What about her?"

"Is she well?"

"It's hard to tell," I said. "I see very little of her."

"Was it she who healed you?" Galilee said, looking down at my legs. Last time he'd seen me I had been an invalid, raging at him.

"I think she'd probably say it was both of us did the work together."

"That's unlike her."

"She's mellowed."

"Enough to forgive me?" I said nothing to this. "Do I take that to mean no?"

"Perhaps you should ask her yourself," I suggested. "If you like I could talk to her for you. Tell her we've spoken. Prepare her."

For the first time in this exchange I saw something more than Galilee's shadow-self. A luminescence seemed to move up through his flesh, casting a cool brightness out toward me, and delineating his form as it did so. I seemed to see the curve of his torso lit from within; up through his throbbing neck to the cave of his mouth.

"You'd help me?" he said.

"Of course."

"I thought you hated me. You had reason enough."

"I never hated you, Galilee. I swear."

The light was in his eyes now; and spilling down his cheeks.

"Lord, brother . . ." he said softly ". . . it's a long time since I cried."

"Does it mean so much to you to come home?"

"To have her forgive me," he said. "That's what I want, more than anything. Just to be forgiven."

"I can't intercede for you there," I said.

"I know."

"All I can do is tell her you'd like to see her, and then bring you her answer."

"That's more than I could have expected," Galilee said, wiping away his tears with the back of his hand. "And don't think I don't know that I have to ask your forgiveness too. Your sweet lady Chiyojo—"

I raised my hand to ward off whatever he was going to say next. "I'd prefer we didn't . . ."

"I'm sorry."

"Anyway, it isn't a question of forgiveness," I replied. "Both of us made errors. Believe me, I made as many as you did."

"I doubt that," Galilee replied, the sourness that had first marked his speech returning. He hates himself, I thought. Lord, this man hates himself. "What are you thinking?" he said to me.

I was too confounded to admit the truth. "Oh . . ." I said. "Nothing important."

"You think I'm ridiculous."

"What?"

"You heard me. You think I'm ridiculous. You imagine I've been strutting around the world for the last God knows how many years fucking like a barnyard cock. What else? Oh yes, you think I never grew up.

That I'm heartless. Stupid probably." He stared at me with those sealit eyes. "Go on. I've said it for you now. You may as well admit it."

"All right. Some of that's true. I thought you didn't care. That's what I was going to write: that you were heartless and—"

"*Write?*" he said, breaking in. "Where?"

"In a book."

"What book?"

"*My* book," I said, feeling a little shiver of pride.

"Is this a book about me?"

"It's about us all," I said. "You and me and Marietta, and Luman and Zabrina—"

"Mother and Father?"

"Of course."

"Do they all know you're writing about them?" I nodded. "And are you telling the truth?"

"It's not a novel, if that's what you mean. I'm telling the truth as best I can."

He mused on this for a moment. The news of my work had clearly unsettled him. Perhaps he feared what I would uncover; or already had.

"Before you ask," I said, "it's not just *our* family I'm writing about."

By the expression on his face it was clear that this went to the heart of his anxiety. "Oh Christ," he murmured. "So that's why I'm here."

"I suppose it must be," I said. "I was thinking about you and—"

"What's it called?" he said to me. I looked at him blankly. "Your book, dummy. What's it called?"

"Oh . . . well, I'm toying with a number of titles," I said, pretending my best literary tone. "There's nothing definite yet."

"You realize I know a lot of details that you could use."

"I'm sure you do."

"Stuff you really can't do without. Not if it's to be a true account."

"Such as?"

He gave me a sly smile. "What's it worth?" he said. It was the first time in this meeting I'd seen a glimpse of the Galilee I remembered; the creature whose confidence in his own charms had once been inviolate.

"I'm going to Mama for you, remember?"

"And you think that's worth all the information I could give you?" he countered. "Oh no, brother. You have to do better than that."

"So what do you want?"

"First, you have to agree."

I just said, "To what?"

"Just agree, will you?"

"This is going round in circles."

Galilee shrugged. "All right," he said. "If you don't want to know what I know, then don't. But your book's going to be the poorer for it, I'm warning you."

"I think we'd better stop this conversation here and now," I said. "Before it goes bad on us."

Galilee regarded me with great gravity, a frown biting into his brow. "You're right. I'm sorry."

"So am I," I said.

"We were doing so well, and I got carried away."

"So did I."

"No, no, it was entirely my fault. I've lost a lot of social graces over the years. I spend too much time on my own. That's my problem. It's no excuse but . . ." The sentence trailed away. "Well, shall we agree to talk again?"

"I'd like that."

"Maybe around this time tomorrow? Will that give you sufficient opportunity to talk to Mama?"

"I'll do what I can," I said.

"Thank you," Galilee said softly. "I do think of her, you know. Of late, I've thought of her all the time. And the house. I think of the house."

"Have you visited?"

"Visited?"

"I mean, you could come looking and nobody would know."

"*She'd* know," he said. Of course she would, I thought. "So no," he went on. "I haven't dared."

"I don't think you'll find it's changed."

"That's good," he said, with a tentative smile. "So much else . . . almost everything, in fact . . . everywhere I go . . . things change. And *never* for the better. Places I used to love. Secret places, you know? Corners of the world where nobody ever went. Now there's pink hotels and pleasure cruises. Once in a while I've tried to scare people off." His shape shuddered as he spoke, and in the midst of his beauty I saw another form, far less attractive. Silver slits for eyes, and leathery lips drawn back from teeth like needles. Even knowing that he meant me no harm, the sight distressed me. I looked away. "See, it works," he said, not without pride. "But then as soon as my back's turned the rot creeps in again." I glanced up at him; his rabidity was in retreat. "And before you know it . . ."

"Pink hotels—"

"—and pleasure cruises." He sighed. "And everything's spoiled." He glanced up at the sky. "Well I should let you go. It won't be long till morning, and you've got a day's work ahead of you."

"And you?"

"Oh I don't sleep that much," he replied. "I'm not sure that divinities ever do."

"Is that what you are?"

He shrugged, as though the issue of his godhood were neither here nor there. "I suppose so. Ma and Pa are as pure a form of deity as this world will ever see, don't you think? Which makes you a demigod, if that makes you feel any better." I laughed out loud. "Goodnight then, brother," he said. "I'll see you tomorrow."

He started to turn from me, and in so doing seemed to eclipse himself. "Wait," I said. He glanced back at me.

"What?"

"I know what you were going to ask for," I said.

"Oh do you?" he said with a little smile. "And what was that?"

"If you gave me information for the book you were going to demand some kind of control over what I wrote."

"*Wrong*, brother," he said, pivoting back on his heel and eclipsing himself again. "I was only going to ask you to call the book *Galilee*." His eyes glittered. "But you'll do that anyway," he said. "Won't you?"

And then he was gone, back to whatever sea glittered in his eyes.

# IV

Need I tell you that Galilee did not come back the following night as he'd promised? This despite the fact that I spent most of the day seeking an audience with Cesaria in order to plead his case. In fact, I failed to find her (I suspect she knew my purpose, and was deliberately avoiding me). But anyway, he didn't turn up, which I suppose I shouldn't be surprised at. He always had an unreliable nature, except in matters of the heart, where everyone else is unreliable. There he was divinely constant.

I told Marietta what had transpired, but she already knew. From Luman, who had happened to see me there by the swamp, apparently having a conversation with a shadow, and passing through so many moods, he said, that he knew I could only be talking to one person.

"He guessed it was Galilee?" I said.

"No, he didn't guess," Marietta said. "He knew because he had conversations like that himself."

"You mean Galilee's been here before?" I said.

"So it seems," she said. "Many times, in fact."

"At Luman's invitation?"

"I assume so. He wouldn't confirm it either way. You know how he gets when he thinks he's being interrogated. Anyway it doesn't really matter whether Luman invited him or not, does it? The point is, he was here."

"Not in the house though," I said. "He was too afraid of mother to go near the house."

"He told you that?"

"You don't believe it?"

"I think it's perfectly possible he's been spying on us all for years without our knowing it. The little shit."

"I think he prefers the word *divinity*."

"How about divine little shit?" Marietta said.

"Do you really dislike him so much?"

"I don't dislike him at all. It's nothing so simple. But we both know our lives would have been a damn sight happier if he'd never come home that night."

That night. I must tell you about that night, sometime soon. I'm not being deliberately coy, you understand. But it's not easy. I'm not entirely certain I *know* what happened the night Galilee came home. There were more visions and fevers and acts of delirium at work that night than had been unleashed on this continent since the arrival of the Pilgrims. I could not tell you with any certainty what was real and what was illusion.

No, that's a lie. There are some things I'm certain of. I know who died that night, for one thing: the desperate men who made the mistake of accompanying Galilee onto this sacred ground, and paid the price of trespass. I could take you to their graves right now, though I haven't ventured near them in a hundred and thirty years. (Even as I write this the face of one of these men, a man called Captain Holt, comes into my mind's eye. I can see him in his grave, his form in such disarray it seemed every bone in his body, even to the littlest, had been shattered.)

What else am I certain of? That I lost the love of my life that night. That I saw her in my father's arms—oh Lord, that's a sight that I've prayed to have removed from me; but who listens to the prayers of a man sinned against by God?—and that she looked at me in her last moments and I knew she'd loved me, and I would never be loved with such ferocity again. All this I know is incontestably true. If you like, it's history.

But the rest? I couldn't tell you whether it was real or not. There was so much high emotion unleashed that night, and in a place such as this rage and love and sorrow do not remain invisible. They exist here as they existed at the beginning of the world, as those primal forces from which we lesser things take our purpose and our shape.

That night—with senses raw and skins stripped—we moved in a flood of visible feeling, which made itself into a thousand fantastic forms. I don't expect to see such a spectacle ever again; nor do I particularly want to. For every part of my being that comes from my father, and takes pleasure in chaos for its own sake, there is a part that makes me my mother's child, and wants tranquillity; a place to write and think and dream of heaven. (Did I tell you that my mother was a poet? No, I don't believe I did. I must quote you some of her work, later.)

So, after all my claiming I could not find the courage to describe that night, I just gave you a taste of it. There's so much more to tell, of course, and I'll tell it as time goes by. But not just yet. These things have to be done by degrees.

Trust me; when you know all there is to know, you'll wonder that I was even able to begin.

# V

## i

Where did I last leave Rachel? On the road, was it?, heading back into Manhattan contemplating the relative merits of Neil Wilkens and her husband?

Oh yes, and then thinking that they were both in their secret hearts sad men, and wondering why. (My own theory is that Neil and Mitch were in no way unusual; that they were unhappy in their souls because many men, perhaps even most, are unhappy in their souls. We burn so hard, but we shed so little light; it makes us crazy and sad.)

Anyway, she came back into Manhattan determined to tell her husband that she could not bear to live as his wife a moment longer, and it was time for them to part. She hadn't worked out the exact words she'd use; she preferred to trust to the moment.

That moment was delayed by a day. Mitchell had left for Boston the night before, she was told by Ellen, one of Mitchell's phalanx of secretaries. Rachel felt a twinge of anger that he'd departed this way; wholly irrational, of course, given that she'd done precisely the same thing a few days earlier. She called the Ritz-Carlton in Boston, where he always stayed. Yes, he was a guest there, she was informed; but no, he wasn't in. She left a short message, telling him she was back at the apartment. He was obsessive about messages, she knew, usually picking them up on the hour, every hour. The fact that he didn't call back could only mean that he was choosing not to speak to her; punishing her, in other words. She resisted the temptation to call him again. She didn't want to give him the satisfaction of imagining her doing exactly what she was doing, sitting by the phone waiting for him to call her back.

About two in the morning, just as she'd finally fallen asleep, he returned the call. His manner was suspiciously convivial.

"Have you been partying?" she asked him.

"Just a few friends," he replied. "Nobody you'd know. Harvard guys."

"When are you coming home?"

"I'm not quite sure yet. Thursday or Friday."

"Is Garrison with you?"

"No. Why?"

"I just wondered."

"I'm having some fun if that's what you're getting at," Mitch said, his tone losing its warmth, "I'm sick of being a workhorse, just so that everybody stays rich."

"Don't do it for me," she said.

"Oh don't start that—"

"I mean it. I—"

"—was quite happy with nothing," he said, doing a squeaky imitation of her voice.

"Well I was."

"Oh for Christ's sake, Rachel. All I said was, I was working too hard . . ."

"So that we could all stay rich, you said."

"Don't be so fucking sensitive."

"Don't swear at me."

"Oh Jesus."

"You're drunk, aren't you?"

"I told you, I've been partying. I don't have to apologize for that. Look, I don't want to have this conversation any more. We'll talk when I get back."

"Come back tomorrow."

"I said I'd come Thursday or Friday."

"We've got to have a proper conversation, Mitch, and we've got to have it sooner rather than later."

"A conversation about what?"

"About us. About what we do. We can't go on like this."

There was a long, long silence. "I'll come back tomorrow," he said finally.

## ii

While Rachel and Mitchell played out their melancholy domestic drama, there were other events occurring, none of them so superficially noteworthy as the separation of lovers, which would in the long term prove to have far more tragic consequences.

You'll remember, perhaps, that I made mention in passing of Loretta's astrologer? I don't know whether the fellow was a fake or not (though I have to think that any man who sells his services as a prophet to rich women is not driven by any visionary ambition). I do know, however, that his predictions proved—after a labyrinthine fashion that will become apparent over the course of the next several chapters—to *become true.* Would they have done so had he kept them to himself? Or was his very speaking of them part of the great plot fate was laying against the Gearys? Again, I cannot say. All I can do is tell you what happened, and leave the rest to your good judgment.

Let me begin with Cadmus. The week Rachel returned from Dansky was good for the old man. He managed a short car trip out to Long Island, and had spent a couple of hours sitting on the beach there, looking out at the ocean. Two days later one of his old enemies, a congressman by the name of Ashfield who had attempted to start an investigation into the Gearys' business practices in the forties, had died of pneumonia, which had quite brightened Cadmus's day. The illness had been painful, sources reported, and Ashfield's final hours excruciating. Hearing this, Cadmus had laughed out loud. The next day he announced to Loretta that he intended to make a list of all the people who'd attempted to get in his way over the years whom he'd now outlived. Then he wanted her to send it into *The Times,* for the obituary column: a collective *in memoriam* for those who would never cross his path again. The conceit had gone out of his head an hour later, but his lively mood remained. He stayed up well past his usual bedtime of ten, and demanded a vodka martini as a nightcap. It was as he sipped it, sitting in his wheelchair looking out on the city, that he said:

"I heard a rumor . . ."

"What about?" Loretta said.

"You saw that astrologer of yours."

"Yes."

"What did he have to say?"

"Are you sure you should finish that martini, Cadmus? You're not supposed to drink on your medications."

"Actually, it's rather a pleasant feeling," he said, his voice a little slurred. "You were telling me about the astrologer. He told you something grim, I gather."

"You don't believe any of that stuff anyway," Loretta said. "So why the hell does it matter?"

"Was it *that* terrible?" Cadmus inquired. He studied his wife's face woozily. "What in God's name did he say, Loretta?"

She sighed. "I don't think—"

"*Tell me!*" he roared.

Loretta stared at him, amazed that a sound so solid could emanate from a body so frail.

"He said something was about to change all our lives," Loretta replied. "And that I should be ready for the worst."

"The worst being what exactly?"

"I suppose death."

"Mine?"

"He didn't say."

"Because if it's mine . . ." he reached out and took her hand ". . . that's not the end of the world. I feel quite ready to be off somewhere restful." His hand went up to her face. "My only concern is you. I know how you hate to be alone."

"I won't be long following you," Loretta said softly.

"Oh now hush. I won't hear that. You've got a good long life ahead of you."

"Not without you I don't."

"There's nothing to be afraid of. I've made very good financial arrangements for you. You'll never want for anything."

"It's not money I'm worried about."

"What then?"

She reached for her cigarettes, fumbling with the packet a moment. "Is there something about this family you've never told me?" she said.

"Oh I'm sure there's a thousand things," Cadmus remarked blithely.

"I'm not talking about a thousand things, Cadmus," Loretta said. "I'm talking about something important. Something you've kept from me. And don't lie to me, Cadmus. It's too late for lies."

"I'm not lying to you," he said. "I meant what I said: there are a thousand things I haven't told you about this family, but none of them, sweet, I swear, none of them is very terrible." Loretta looked somewhat placated. Smiling and stroking her hand, Cadmus quickly capitalized on his success. "Every family has a few unfortunates in its midst. We've got those. My own mother died miserably. But you know that. There was some business done in the Depression that doesn't reflect well on me, but—" he shrugged "—the Good Lord seems to have forgiven me. He granted me beautiful children and grandchildren, and a longer, healthier life than I ever dared hope I'd have. And most of all, He gave me you." He tenderly kissed Loretta's hand. "And believe me, darling, when I tell you there's not a day goes by without my thanking Him for His generosity."

That was more or less the end of the conversation. But it was only the beginning of the consequences of the astrologer's prediction.

The following day, when Loretta was out at her monthly lunch with several philanthropic widows of Manhattan, the old man wheeled himself into the library, locked the door, and took from a certain hiding place behind the rows of leather-bound tomes, all undisturbed by any curious reader, a small metal box, bound with a thin leather thong. His fingers were too weak to untie the knot, so he took a pair of scissors to it, and then lifted the lid. If anyone had witnessed him doing this they would have assumed the box contained some priceless treasure, his manner was so reverential. They would have been disappointed. There was nothing glorious in the box. Just a small book that smelled brown with age, its cover stained, its pages stained, the handwritten lines upon those stained pages faded with the years. And between the pages, here and there, loose sheets of paper, a small fragment of blue cloth, a skeletal leaf that went to motes of grey dust when he tried to pick it up.

He roved back and forth through the book perhaps half a dozen times, pausing for a moment to study the contents of a page, then moving on.

Only when he'd examined it this way did he return to one of the pieces of loose paper and remove it, unfolding it with such delicacy it might have been a living thing—a butterfly perhaps, whose wings he wanted to admire without doing the creature harm.

It was a letter. The hand it was written in was elegant, but the mind shaping the words more eloquent still, the thoughts so compressed it read less like prose than poetry.

*My dearest brother,* it said. *The great griefs of the day have passed, and through the twilight, all pink and gold, I hear the tender music of sleep.*

*The philosophers are misled, I have come to believe, when they teach us that sleep is death's similitude. It is rather a nightward journey back into our mother's arms, where we may be blessed to hear the lovely rhythm of a slumber song.*

*I hear it now, even as I write these words to you. And though our mother has been dead a decade, I am returned to her, and she to me, and the world is good again.*

*Tomorrow, we do battle at Bentonville, and are so greatly outnumbered there is no hope of victory. So forgive me if I do not tell you I long to embrace you, for I entertain no such hope, at least in this world.*

*Pray for me, brother, for the worst is yet to come. And if your prayers are answered, perhaps also the best.*

*I have ever loved thee.*

The letter was signed *Charles.*

Cadmus studied it for more than a little time; especially the penultimate paragraph. The words made him shake. *Pray for me, brother, for the worst is yet to come.* There was nothing in this library, in all the great, grim masterworks of the world, that had the power to distress him that these words possessed. He'd not known the letter-writer personally, of course—the battle of Bentonville had been fought in 1865—but he felt a powerful empathy with him nonetheless. When he read the page it was as though he was sitting beside the man as he sat in his tent before that calamitous battle, listening to the rain beating on the canvas, and the forlorn songs of the infantrymen as they huddled about their smoky fires, knowing that the following day a vastly superior force would be upon them.

Earlier in his life, when he'd first become familiar with the journal, and particularly with this letter, Cadmus had made it his business to discover as best he could the circumstances in which it had been written. What he discovered was this: that in March of 1865 the depleted forces of the Rebel States, led by Generals Johnston and Bragg, had been driven across North Carolina, and at a place called Bentonville, exhausted, hungry and despairing, they had dug in to face the might of the North. Sherman had the scent of victory; he knew his opponents would not last much longer. The previous November, he had overseen the burning of Atlanta, and Charleston—brave, besieged Charleston—

would very soon fall beneath his assault. There was no hope of victory for the South, and surely every man who made up the forces at Bentonville knew it.

The battle would last three days; and by the standards of that war there was not a great loss of life. A thousand and some soldiers of the Union perished, two thousand and some Confederates. But such numbers mean nothing to a soldier in battle, for he need only die one death.

Cadmus had often thought about going to visit the battleground, which had been left, he'd been told, relatively untouched by time. The Harper house, a modest domicile that stood close by the field, and had been turned into a makeshift surgery during the conflict, still stood; the trenches where the Confederate soldiers had waited for the army of the North could still be lain in. With a little research he could probably have discovered where the officers' tents had been pitched; and sat himself down close to the place where the letter he held in his hand had been penned.

Why had he never gone? Had he simply been afraid that the threads binding his destiny to that of the melancholy Captain Charles Holt would have been strengthened by such a visit? If so, then he'd denied himself in vain: those threads were getting stronger by the moment. He could feel them wrapped around him now—tightening, tightening—as if to draw his fate and that of the captain into some final embrace. He might not have been so troubled had it only been his life which was affected, but of course that wasn't the case. Loretta's damned astrologer knew more than he realized, with his insinuations of Geary family secrets and predictions of apocalypse. The intervention of almost a hundred and forty years could not provide asylum from what was in the wind; its message carried like a contagion from that distant battlefield.

*Pray for me, brother*, the captain had written, *for the worst is yet to come.*

No doubt those words had been true enough when they were written, Cadmus thought, but the passage of time had made them truer still. Crime had mounted upon crime over the generations, sin mounted on sin, and God help them all—every Geary, and child of a Geary, and wife and mistress and servant of a Geary—it was time for the sinners to come to judgment.

# VI

The conversation between Rachel and Mitch was surprisingly civilized. There were no raised voices; no tears on either side; no accusations. They simply exchanged disappointments in hushed voices, and agreed, after an hour or so, that they were failing to give one another joy, and that it would be best to part. Their only difference of opinion lay in this: Rachel had come to believe that there was no chance of reviving the marriage, and it would be best to start divorce proceedings immediately, while Mitch begged that they give one another a grace period of a few weeks to turn the decision over and be certain they were doing the right thing. After a little discussion, she said she'd go along with this. What was a few weeks? In the meantime they agreed to keep any discussion of the matter to a very small circle, and not consult lawyers. The moment a lawyer was brought into the picture, Mitch argued, any hope of reconciliation would be at an end. As to living arrangements, they would keep it very simple. Rachel would stay in the Central Park apartment; Mitch would either go back to the mansion or take a suite at a hotel.

They parted with a tentative embrace, like two people made of glass.


The following day, Rachel got a call from Margie. How about lunch, she said; somewhere grotesquely expensive, where they could linger so long over dessert that they could go straight on to cocktails?

"Just as long as we don't talk about Mitch," Rachel said.

"Oh no," Margie said, with a faint air of mystery in her voice, "I've got something much more interesting than *him* to talk about."

The restaurant Margie had chosen had been open only a few months, but it had already won a spate of four-star reviews, so it was packed, with a line of people all vainly hoping they'd get themselves a table. Inevitably, Margie knew the maître d' (in a much earlier incarnation, she later explained, he'd been a barman at a little dive she'd frequented in Soho). He treated them both royally, taking them to a table which offered a full view of the room.

"Plenty of people to gossip about," Margie said, surveying the faces before them. Rachel knew a few of them by sight; a couple by name.

"Something for you to drink?" the waiter wanted to know.

"How many martinis do you have?"

"We have sixteen on our list," the waiter replied, proffering the document, "but if you have some particular request . . ."

"Bring us two very dry martinis to start. Straight up. No olives. And we'll look at the list while you're bringing them."

"I didn't know you could mix so many martinis," Rachel said.

"Well I'm quite sure after the third or fourth you can't tell the difference," Margie said. "Oh look . . . the table by the window . . . isn't that Cecil?"

"Yes it is."

The Gearys' lawyer, who was a man in his early sixties, was leaning across the table gazing at a blonde, decorative woman a third his age.

"That's not his wife, I presume?" Rachel said.

"Absolutely not. His wife—what's her name? Phyllis, I believe— looks like our maître d' in bad drag. No, *that's* one of his mistresses."

"He has more than one?"

Margie rolled her eyes. "When Cecil shuffles off to heaven, there will be more women at the graveside than are walking Fifth Avenue right now."

"Why?" said Rachel. "I mean, he's so unattractive."

Margie cocked her head a little. "Is he?" she said. "I think he's quite well preserved for his age. And he's fabulously wealthy, which is all a woman like that cares about. She's going to get a little sparkly something before lunch is over. You just watch. She's counting the minutes. Every time his hand gets near his pocket she salivates."

"If he's so rich, why does he go on working? Couldn't he just retire?"

"He only has the family as clients now. And I think he does that out of loyalty to the old man. Garrison says he's very smart. Could have been the best of the best, Garrison says."

"So what happened?"

"The same thing that happened to you and me. He got dragged into the Geary family. And once you're in there's really no way out."

"You promised, Margie. No talking about Mitchell."

"I'm not going to talk about Mitchell. You asked me what happened to Cecil. I'm telling you."

The waiter was back at the table with the martinis. Margie was intrigued to know what a Cajun Martini—number thirteen on the list—was like. The waiter began to describe the recipe, but she stopped him after half a florid phrase.

"Just bring us two," she said.

"You'll have me drunk," Rachel said.

"I need you a little tipsy," Margie said, "for what I'm going to tell you about."

"Oh my Lord."

"What?"

"You were right," Rachel said, nodding across the room in the direction of Cecil's table. Just as Margie had predicted the lawyer had taken out a slim box from his pocket, and was opening it to let the blonde see her reward.

"Didn't I say?" Margie murmured. "Sparkly."

"It used to happen all the time in Boston," Rachel said.

"Oh that's right, you worked in a jewelry store."

"These men would come in and they'd ask me to choose something for their wives. At least they'd *say* wives, but I got the picture after a few weeks. These were older men, you know—forties, fifties—and they'd always want something for a younger woman. That's why they'd ask me. It was like they were saying: if you were my mistress, what would you like? That's how I met Mitchell."

"Now who's talking about Mitchell? I thought he was verboten."

Rachel drained her martini. "I don't mind. In a way I'd sort of like to talk about him."

"You would?"

"Don't sound so surprised."

"What's to talk about?" Margie said, "He's your husband. If you love him, that's fine. If you don't, that's fine too. Just don't depend on him for anything. Get your own life. That way he hasn't got any power over you. Oh, look, that's a pretty sight." The waiter, who'd appeared with the next round of martinis, thought she meant him, and smiled dazzlingly. "I meant the drinks, honey," Margie said. The smile decayed somewhat. "But you're sweet. What's your name?"

"Stefano."

"Stefano. What do you recommend? Rachel's very hungry, and I'm on a diet."

"The chef's specialty is the sea bass. It's lightly sautéed in pure olive oil with a little cilantro—"

"I think that sounds fine for me. Rachel?"

"I'm in the mood for meat."

"Oh," Margie said, with a cocked eyebrow. "Stefano. The lady wants meat. Any suggestions?"

The waiter momentarily lost his cool. "Um . . . well we have . . ."

"Maybe just a steak?" Margie suggested to Rachel.

Stefano looked flustered. "We don't actually serve a straightforward steak. We don't have it on the menu."

"Good Lord," Margie said, thoroughly relishing the young man's discomfort. "This is New York and you don't serve a simple steak?"

"I don't really want steak," Rachel said.

"Well that's not the point," Margie said, perversely. "It's the principle of the thing. Well . . . do you have anything that can be served rare?"

"We have lamb cutlets which the chef offers with almonds and ginger."

"That's fine," Rachel told him. Grateful to have the problem resolved, Stefano beat a hasty retreat.

"You're mean," Rachel said to Margie once he'd gone.

"Oh, he enjoyed it. Men secretly love to be humiliated. As long as it isn't *too* public."

"Have you ever thought of writing all this down?"

"All what?"

"Your pithy observations."

"They don't stand up to close scrutiny, honey," she said. "Like me, really. I'm very impressive as long as you don't look too closely." She guffawed at this. "So now, drink up. Number thirteen's really rather good."

Rachel declined. "My head's already spinning," she said. "Will you stop teasing me and tell me what all this is about?"

"Well . . . it's very simple, really. You need to take a vacation, honey."

"I just came back from—"

"I don't mean a trip *home*, for God's sake. That's not a vacation, it's a sentence. You need to go somewhere you can be yourself, and you can't be yourself with family."

"Why do I think you've already got something planned?"

"Have you ever been to Hawaii?"

"I stopped over in Honolulu with Mitch, on our way to Australia."

"Horrible," Margie said.

"Australia or Honolulu?"

"Well, actually both. But I'm not talking about Honolulu. I'm talking about Kaua'i. The Garden Island."

"I've never heard of it."

"Oh honey, it's simply the most beautiful place on earth. It's paradise. I swear. Paradise." She sipped her martini. "And it so happens that

I know a little house in a little bay on the North Shore which is fifty yards from the water, if that. It's so perfect. Oh you can't imagine. Truly, you can't imagine. I mean I could tell you about it and it'd sound idyllic, but . . . it's more than that."

"How so?"

Margie's voice had become sultry as she talked about the house; now it was so quiet Rachel had to lean in to catch what she was saying. "I know this is going to sound silly, but it's a place where there's still just a chance that something . . . oh shit, I don't know . . . something *magical* might happen."

"It sounds wonderful," Rachel said. She'd never seen Margie this way before, and found it strangely moving. Margie the cynic, Margie the lush, talking like a little girl who'd thought she'd seen wonderland. It almost made Rachel believe she had.

"Who does the house belong to?"

"Ah," she said, raising her index finger over the rim of her glass, and giving Rachel a narrow-eyed smile. "That's the thing. It belongs to us."

"Us."

"The Geary women."

"Really?"

"The men are forbidden to go anywhere near the place. It's an ancient Geary tradition."

"Who started it?"

"Cadmus's mother I believe. She was quite the feminist, in her time. Or it may have been a generation earlier, I don't know. The point is, the house isn't used very much any longer. There's a couple of local people who go every other month and mow the lawn and trim the palm trees, dust a little, but basically the place is left empty."

"Loretta doesn't go?"

"She went just after she and Cadmus first got married. So she said. But now she just stays right here with him, night and day. I think she's afraid he's going to start changing the will behind her back. Oh . . . speaking of legal matters . . ." She nodded across the restaurant. Cecil and the blonde were rising from the table. "He's going to have a busy afternoon. She looks like the acrobatic type."

"Maybe she'll just lay back and let him get it over with," Rachel said.

"I know how that feels," Margie replied.

"I hope he doesn't look in our direction," Rachel said as Cecil headed for the door.

"I rather hope he does," Margie said, and as luck would have it at that very instant Cecil glanced back across the restaurant and laid eyes on them. Rachel froze, still hoping Cecil wouldn't recognize them. But Margie, murmuring *oh good* under her breath, raised her arm, replete with empty martini glass, above her head.

"Now look what you've done," Rachel said. "He's coming over to talk to us."

"Just don't mention Kaua'i," Margie said. "That's our little secret."

"Ladies," Cecil was saying. He'd left the blonde at the door. "I almost missed you, tucked away in the corner."

"Oh you know us," Margie said. "We're the shy, retiring types. Unlike . . ." she glanced back toward Cecil's girlfriend ". . . what's her name?"

"Ambrosina."

"Well that's a bit of a mouthful for such a precious little thing," Margie said.

Cecil glanced back at his conquest. "She is precious," he said, with surprising sincerity.

"And extremely blonde," Margie replied, without any apparent irony. "Actress, is she?"

"Model."

"Of course she is. You're helping her get started. How sweet you are."

Cecil's smile had faded. "I must get back to her," he said. He looked over at Rachel. "I heard from Mitchell this morning . . ." he said. "I'm sorry things aren't going well." He reached up and oh-so-lightly wrapped his hand around Rachel's wrist. "But we'll sort it all out, eh?" Rachel glanced down at his encircling fingers. He removed his hand, his manner effortlessly shifting into the paternal mode. "If there's anything you need, Rachel. Anything at all, to make things easier."

"I'll be fine."

"Oh I know," he said, as though he were a doctor reassuring a dying patient. "You'll be just dandy. But if you need anything . . ."

"I think she gets the message, Cecil," Margie remarked.

"Yes . . . well, it's lovely to see you, Rachel . . . and Margie, always wonderful . . ."

"Really?"

"Really," Cecil replied, and headed back to his girlfriend, who was looking decidedly pouty.

"I think the drinking's finally catching up with me," Margie said, staring after the lawyer as he put his arm around the blonde and escorted her out.

"Why?"

"I was just looking at Cecil's face, and I thought: I wonder what he's going to look like when he's dead?"

"Oh, that's not very nice."

"Then I thought: well I just hope I'm there to find out."

# VII

### i

Rachel called Mitch that evening and told him she'd seen Cecil, pointing out that he'd broken the terms of their agreement by talking to a lawyer. Mitch protested that he hadn't been seeking legal advice. He thought of Cecil as a surrogate father, he said. They'd talked about love, not about the law; to which Rachel couldn't help but observe that she doubted Cecil knew a damn thing about love.

"Don't be mad at me," Mitchell begged. "It was a genuine mistake. I'm sorry. I know it must look like I was going behind your back, but I wasn't. I swear I wasn't."

His whining apology only irritated her further. She wanted to tell him he could take his apology and his lawyer and his whole damn family and go to hell. Instead, she found herself saying something she hadn't planned to say.

"I'm going away for a while," she told him.

The statement surprised her almost as much as it surprised Mitchell; she'd not been aware of making a decision either way about going to Kaua'i.

Mitchell asked her if she was going back home. She said no. Where then? he asked her. Just away, she said. Away from me, you mean, he said. No, she replied, I'm not running away from you.

"Well where the hell *are* you running?" he demanded.

There was an answer, right there on her tongue, ready to be spoken, but this time she governed herself and said nothing. It was only when the exchange with Mitchell was over, and she was sitting on the balcony, looking over the park and thinking about nothing in particular that the unspoken reply came onto her lips.

"I'm not running away," she murmured to herself, "I'm running *toward* something . . ."

\*        \*        \*

She shared this thought with no one, not even Margie. It was silly, on the face of it. She was going off to an island she'd never heard of before, on the suggestion of a woman whose blood was seventy percent alcohol. There was no reason for her to be going, much less to sense any purpose in the journey. And yet she felt it, indisputably, and the feeling made her happy. So what did it matter if the source of the feeling was a mystery? She was grateful to have some measure of lightness back in her heart, and content to take the pleasure in it while it lasted. She knew from experience it could be gone without warning, like love.

Margie made all the arrangements for the trip. All Rachel had to do was be ready to leave the following Thursday, with all her business in New York done and dusted. Once she got to the island, Margie predicted, she wouldn't want to be talking on the telephone. She wouldn't even want to think about the city, or even her friends. There was a different rhythm there; a different perspective.

"I almost feel as though I have to say goodbye to the old Rachel," Margie said, "because believe me, she's not coming back."

"Now you're exaggerating," Rachel said.

"I am not," Margie said. "You'll see. The first couple of days, you'll be restless, and thinking there's nothing to do, there's nobody to gossip about. And then it'll slowly dawn on you that you don't need any of that. You'll be sitting watching the clouds on the mountains, or a whale out at sea, or just listening to the rain on the roof—oh my Lord, Rachel, it's so beautiful when it rains—and you'll think: I don't need anything I haven't got right now."

It seemed to Rachel each time Margie talked about the place she spoke more lovingly of it.

"How many times have you been there?" she asked.

"Just twice," Margie replied. "But I should never have gone back the second time. That was a mistake. I went for the wrong reasons the second time."

"What do you mean?"

"Oh, it's a long story," Margie said. "And it's not important. You've got the first time ahead of you, and that's all that matters."

"So I get to be a virgin again," Rachel said.

"You know, honey, that's exactly right. You're going to be a virgin again."

## ii

If Rachel had entertained any last doubts about taking the trip, they evaporated once she got on the plane, settled back in her seat in the first class cabin and took a sip of champagne. Even if the island wasn't all that Margie had advertised it as being—and in truth nothing short of Eden would match up to the promises—it was still good to be going away where she wasn't known; where she could quietly and quirkily be *herself.*

The first leg of the journey, to Los Angeles, was unremarkable. A couple of glasses of alcohol and she began to feel pleasantly sleepy, and dozed through most of the flight. There was a two-hour stopover in Los Angeles, and she got off the plane to stretch her legs and get herself a cup of coffee. The airport was frenetic, and she watched the parade of people—rushing, sweating, tearful, frustrated—like a visitor from another world, interested but unmoved. When she got back on the plane there was a delay. A minor mechanical problem, the captain explained; nothing that would keep them on the ground for long. For once, the prediction from the flight deck was correct. After twenty, perhaps twenty-five minutes, the captain duly announced that the flight was now ready for departure. Rachel stayed awake for the second flight. A little tick of anticipation had begun in her. She found herself turning over in her head things that Margie had said about the island and the house. What was it she'd said at the lunch table? Something about it being a place where magic still happened, miracles still happened?

If only, Rachel thought; if only she could get back to the beginning again; back to the Rachel she'd been before the hurt, before the disappointment. But when had that been, exactly? The careless Rachel, who'd had some faith in the essential goodness of things; where was she? It was years since she'd seen that brazen, happy creature in the mirror. Life in Dansky—especially after the death of her father—had knocked that girl to the ground and kept her from getting up again. She'd lost hope by and by; hope that she'd ever be unburdened again, ever be blithe, ever be wild. Even when Mitchell had come into her life, and turned her into a princess, she'd not been able to shake her doubts. In fact for the first two or three months, even after he'd confessed his love for her, she'd been expecting him to tell her she needed to brighten her outlook a little. But he seemed not to notice what a quietly despairing partner he had. Or perhaps he *had* noticed, he'd just assumed he could rescue her from her doubts with a touch of Geary largesse.

Thinking about him, she became sad. Poor Mitchell; poor optimistic Mitchell. In parting from him, she had done both of them a kindness.

Honolulu Airport was much as she remembered it. Stores selling hula-hula girls crudely carved from coconuts, and bars advertising tropical cocktails, parties of lei-draped travelers being led about by escorts carrying notices on sticks. And everywhere that preeminent symbol of the crass American tourist: the Hawaiian print shirt. Was it possible that the paradise Margie had described lay just a twenty-minute flight from this? It was hard to believe.

But her doubts started to fall away once she stepped outside to catch the charmingly dubbed Wikki-Wikki Shuttle that ferried her to the terminal from which her flight would depart. The air was balmy and fragrant. Though it came off the sea, it came with the scent of blossom.

The plane was small, but it was still less than half full. A good sign, she thought. She was leaving the Hawaiian-shirted vacationers behind. The plane rose more suddenly and more steeply than its bulkier brethren, and in what seemed seconds she was looking down on the turquoise ocean, and the high-rises of Honolulu were gone from sight.

# VIII

The flight that carries the traveler from the high-rises of Honolulu to the Garden Island is short; less than twenty-five minutes. But while Rachel's in the air let me describe to you a scene that occurred almost two weeks before.

The place is a small, raffish town called Puerto Bueno, a community which probably takes the prize as the most unfrequented in this book. It is located on one of the outlying islands of the province of Magallanes, which lies in Chile, at the tip of South America. Not a place people go to take relaxing vacations; the islands are wind-scoured and charmless, many of them so desolate they are completely uninhabited. In such a region, a town like Puerto Bueno, which boasts seven hundred citizens, represents a sizable community, but nobody on the neighboring islands talks about the place much. It is a town where the rule of law is only loosely observed, which fact has over the years attracted a motley collection of men and women who have lived their lives at, or sometimes beyond, the limits of permissible behavior. People who have escaped justice or revenge in their own countries, who have gone from one place to another looking for a place of refuge. A few have even enjoyed a certain notoriety in the outside world. There was a man who'd laundered fortunes for the Vatican; and a woman who'd murdered her husband in Adelaide, and who still kept a snapshot of the body in her purse. But most of the citizens are unimportant felons—abusers of substances and forgers of banknotes—whose capture is not of great significance to their pursuers.

Strange to say, given its populace, Puerto Bueno is a curiously civilized little place. There is no crime, nor is the subject of crime ever raised in conversation. The townspeople have turned their backs on their pasts, and want only to live out their remaining years in peace. Puerto Bueno isn't the most comfortable of places to retire (it has only two stores, and the electricity supply is tetchy) but it is preferable to a prison cell or the grave. And on certain days it is possible to sit on the crumbling harbor wall and—viewing a sky unmarked by the trails of aircraft—think that even this charmless spot is proof of God's charity.

Very few boats come to drop anchor here. Occasionally a fishing vessel, plying its way up and down the coast, takes shelter from a squall, and even more occasionally a pleasure boat, its captain hopelessly lost, will appear, only to disappear again just as soon as its passengers get a glimpse of the town. Other than these, the harbor is a hospice for a handful of small boats, none of which look healthy enough to put out to sea again. In the winter, at least one of them will sink there in the harbor, and rot.

But there was one vessel that fell into none of these categories: a vessel, called *The Samarkand*, more practical than any of the fishing boats and yet more beautiful than any of the pleasure boats. It was a yacht, of sorts, the timbers of its hull not painted but stained and varnished. Its cabin, wheel and two masts were likewise deeply stained, so that in certain lights the grain of the wood was uncannily clear, as though the vessel had been etched by a master draughtsman. As for the sails, they were of course white, but they'd been repaired many times over the years, and the patches were apparent; irregular shapes of canvas that were slightly paler or darker.

Perhaps to most eyes it was not as remarkable a vessel as I'm making it out to be. In one of the fancier marinas of the world, in Florida or San Diego, it would have not looked particularly fine a thing, I suppose. But here in Puerto Bueno, its arrival on a gray, cold day seemed like the visitation of something from a realm of dreams. Even though its captain (who was also its first mate and bosun and sole passenger) had been bringing the vessel to Puerto Bueno for far longer than any citizen could remember, its appearance on the horizon always brought folks down to the quay to watch its approach. There was a certain rightness to its coming—like the return of spring birds after a season of ice—that made even these hard hearts a little more pliant.

Once the vessel was safely within the arms of the harbor, however, the spectators would hurry away. They knew better than to watch the actual docking, or worse still spy on the solitary black man who captained this boat as he disembarked. Indeed something very like a superstition had occurred over the years that anyone watching the captain of *The Samarkand* set foot on *terra firma* would die before a year or so had passed and the vessel came back again. All eyes were therefore averted when the man known by just one name made his way up the hill to the house he kept high above the harbor. The name, of course, you already know. It was Galilee.

How, you may well ask, did my half brother come to be keeping a residence in a criminal community somewhere in the back of beyond? Chance, is the answer. He had been sailing down the coast when—like one of those fishing boats I made mention of earlier—he was driven to seek refuge from a storm or be drowned. Believe it or not, this was not an easy decision at the time. He had been passing through a period of profound depression, and when the storm came he was of half a mind to let *The Samarkand* be driven before it and turned to timberwood. He had decided against this course not for his own sake but for that of his vessel, which he considered his only true friend. It was no decent fate for a boat as noble as his to have its entrails washed up on the shores of this coast and picked over by peasants. He had promised *The Samarkand* that when the time came he'd make certain it died a good death, somewhere far, far from land.

So he took shelter in Puerto Bueno—which at that time was a quarter of its present size, or less, its harbor newly built, and almost entirely unused. The man who'd founded the construction was one Arturo Higgins, a man of English descent who had lost all his money in the endeavor, and had taken his own life the year before. His house stood unoccupied at the top of the hill, and Galilee, out of some perverse desire to see the place of suicide, had gone up the hill and entered. Nobody had visited the house since the body had been removed: gulls had come to roost in its bedrooms, and there were rats' nests in the fireplace, but its desolation suited the trespasser mightily. He purchased the house the next day, from Higgins's daughter, and moved a few belongings in. The view, on clear days, was peaceful, and he came to think of it as his second home; his first, of course, being the vessel moored in the harbor.

After a couple of weeks he'd departed, locking the house up behind him and making it quietly known that anyone who ventured over the threshold would regret it.

He'd not come back for thirteen months, but come back he did, sometimes three or four times in a single year, sometimes with several years intervening. He became a mystery of some note, and there's force to the argument that the felons and the fugitives who came to the town thereafter did so because they'd heard of him. If this is so, you may ask, then why did the tale of the voyager, a man with divine blood running in his veins, not also attract a few finer spirits? It's a reasonable question. Why didn't saints come to Puerto Bueno, and Galilee's presence turn it into a town where the lame skipped and the dumb sang patter songs?

I have only this answer: he was too crippled. How could his legend inspire healing saints when he was incapable of healing himself?

So there you have the way things were, until a week or so before Rachel departed for Hawaii.

It happened that Galilee was not out at sea at that time, but resident in the house on the hill. He'd brought *The Samarkand* into Puerto Bueno because it was in need of repairs, and for the last few weeks he'd been back and forth between the harbor and the house daily, laboring from dawn to dusk on repairing the boat, and spending the hours of darkness sitting at the window of the Higgins house looking out over the Pacific. He would not let anybody set foot on *The Samarkand* to help him. He was a perfectionist: no other hand but his could be put to the tasks of nailing and planing and staining. Occasionally some inquisitive soul would idle along the quayside and watch him at work, but his glare was enough to drive them away after a little while. Only once did he engage in any social activity in the town, and that was one windy night—just a few days before his departure—when he appeared at the little bar on the hill where it seemed half of Puerto Bueno's citizens came to drink on any given evening, and downed enough brandy to have poleaxed any man in the bar. All it did was make Galilee a little merry, and he became quite loquacious—at least by previous standards. Those who talked with him came away with the flattering impression that he'd opened up to them: shared a few intimacies. The following morning, however, when they came to repeat what he'd said, they could recall very little that had pertained to

Galilee himself. His conversation, it seemed, had been a form of listening; and when he had chimed in with something it had invariably been a fragment of somebody else's life he'd been recounting.

Two days later, his work on *The Samarkand* seemed suddenly to become much more intensive. He worked the next seventy-two hours without a break, his nightly labors lit by hurricane lamps set all about the boat. It was as though he'd suddenly been given sailing orders, and was obliged to depart sooner than he'd expected.

Sure enough, he was at the general store in the late afternoon of the third day of his labors, ordering supplies. His manner was brusque, his expression thunderous: nobody dared ask him where he was headed this time. The supplies were delivered to the boat by Hernandez, the son of the owner of the store; Galilee paid him extravagantly for his efforts, and asked the young man if he'd apologize to Hernandez Sr. on Galilee's behalf; that he knew he'd been less than civil earlier in the day, and he'd meant to cause no offense by it.

That was the last conversation anyone in Puerto Bueno had with their fellow citizen during his visit. Galilee weighed anchor as the night fell, and *The Samarkand* slipped out of the tiny harbor on the evening tide, to destinations much speculated upon, but unknown.

# IX

### i

Nicodemus, as I've already indicated, was a man of prodigious sexual energies. He loved all things erotic (except books, of course): I doubt more than two consecutive minutes ever passed without his thinking some sexual thought. Nor was his interest limited to human, or superhuman, congress. He enjoyed the spectacle of an unleashed libido in whatever skin it showed itself. His horses especially, of course. He loved to watch his horses fuck. Many times he'd be right there with them, in a fine old sweat himself, whispering now to the stallion, now to the mare, encouraging them in the act. And if things weren't going well, he'd have his hands in the heat of things, helping it all along. Masturbating the stallion if need be, and guiding him home if he was clumsy; touching the mare with such tenderness she'd be calmed and accepting.

I remember one such incident with particular clarity; it happened perhaps two years before his death. He had a horse called Dumuzzi, of

which he was particularly proud. And with reason. This was a stallion in
the genes of which I'm certain my father had divinely meddled, for I
never saw, nor expect to ever see again, so remarkable a horse. Forget all
you've heard of Arabian stallions, or of the warrior steeds of the Kazak.
Dumuzzi was another order of animal, preternaturally intelligent,
exquisitely proportioned and magnificently formed. His bloodline, if it
had survived, would have redefined what we understand by the word
"horse." I've sometimes wondered if my father hadn't been sculpting
this splendor as a kind of inspiration to the human world; a species of
such perfection it would make all who witnessed its strength and beauty
meditate on the sublimity of creation. (Then again: perhaps it was
merely a selfish indulgence and he intended to keep Dumuzzi's son
and daughters at L'Enfant; I will probably never know.)

The point is: the night of which I speak there was a thunderstorm
of majestic scale, which had been moving in since the late afternoon.
Darkness had fallen prematurely, as great bruise-and-iron clouds covered the last of the sun. Even at several miles distance the thunder was
so deep it made the ground shake.

The horses were panicky, of course; in no mood to be fucking.
Especially Dumuzzi, whose only real frailty was temperamental: he
seemed to know he was a special creature and was wont to behave oper-
atically. That night he was feeling particularly difficult: when my father
came to the stable to prepare him Dumuzzi stamped and kicked and
refused every calming word. I remember suggesting to Nicodemus that
we try again the following morning, when the storm had passed, but
there was a battle of wills here that no suggestion of mine was going to
pacify. Nicodemus addressed Dumuzzi as he might have spoken to an
inebriated and volatile friend; told him that he was in no mood for this
drama, and the sooner Dumuzzi calmed down and began to behave
sensibly, the better for all concerned. Dumuzzi ignored the warning; if
anything his shenanigans escalated. He kicked his trough to splinters,
and then kicked a hole in the stable wall—just punched out a dozen
bricks as though they were so much papier-mâché. I wasn't afraid for
my father—at that time I believed him immune from harm—but I was
certainly anxious for my own safety. In my various travels on behalf of
Nicodemus, in search of great horses, I'd seen what harm they could do.
I'd visited the grave of a breeder in Limoges who'd had his brain kicked
to mush two days before I arrived (by the very horse I'd come to view);
I'd seen another fellow, in the Tian Shan mountains, who'd lost his
hands to an irate mare, just had them bitten off: one! two! And I'd seen
horses fight among themselves until there was more blood on their

flanks and the ground beneath their hooves than in their veins. So there I was, afraid for my limbs and my life, but unable to take my eyes off the spectacle before me. The storm was almost overhead by now, and Dumuzzi was in an eye-rolling frenzy. Sparks of static electricity ran up and down his mane, and leapt between his hooves and the ground; his complaints were so loud they cut through the thunder.

Nicodemus was undismayed. He'd dealt with countless fractious animals in his time; for all Dumuzzi's heroic strength and size, he was just one more. After some struggle, my father bridled the beast and dragged him out of the stable to the open ground where he had the mare tethered. As I describe this now my heart has quickened, the scene is so vivid in my mind's eye: the lightning erupting in the clouds overhead, the horses shrieking in their hysteria, foamy lips curled back from lethal teeth; Nicodemus yelling at his beauties against the din of the storm, the front of his trousers showing plainly how much this scene aroused him.

I swear he looked half-bestial himself, by the glare of the lightning; his hair, which hung to his waist when he was standing still, roiling around him, his face cracked in half by a rabid smile, his skin iridescent. If he'd lost all trace of his human form then and there—convulsed and stretched and cracked his spine to become some other thing (a horse, a storm; a little of both)—I wouldn't have been surprised. I was more astonished that his humanity held in the midst of this; that he didn't unleash himself. Perhaps it excited him better to be confined by his anatomy in such circumstances; to have to sweat and fight.

There he was—divinity made flesh, and that flesh halfway to becoming animal—hauling the protesting Dumuzzi into the presence of the mare. I thought the last thing the stallion would want to do was fuck, but I was wrong. Nicodemus insinuated himself between the two horses and proceeded to arouse them: rubbing their flanks, their bellies, their heads, and all the while talking to them. Despite his agitation, Dumuzzi became hot for the mare. His massive phallus was unsheathed, and he promptly threw himself up on her. Still talking, still patting and rubbing, my father took hold of the stallion's rod and put it at the mare's opening. Dumuzzi needed no help with the rest. He covered the mare with the efficiency of one born to the task.

My father stood back and let them couple. His entire body seemed to be bristling: I swear to have touched him then would have proved fatal to my common heart. He was no longer laughing. His head had drooped, his shoulders were hunched: he seemed like a stalking predator, ready to tear out the throats of these creatures should they fail him.

They didn't. Though the storm continued to rage around—the lightning so frequent it visited a ghastly vivid day upon this midnight, the thunder so loud its reverberations shook down several trees and cracked a dozen windows in the house—the animals fucked and fucked and fucked, their panic subsumed into the frenzy of their mating.

The foal that came of this coupling was a male. Nicodemus called him Temujin, the birth name of Genghis Khan. As for Dumuzzi, he seemed to dote on my father thereafter; as though that night they'd become brothers. I say *seemed* because I suspect the animal's devotion was a sham. Why do I think that? Because the night my father died the panicked charge that trampled him to death was led by Dumuzzi, whose eyes carried in them—I swear—a flicker of revenge.


I've told you all this in part to give you a better picture of my father, whose presence in this story must necessarily be anecdotal, and in part because it serves as a reminder to me of the capacities that lie dormant in my nature.

As I said at the opening of the chapter, my own libido is a pitiful echo of Nicodemus's sexual appetites. My erotic life has never been particularly complex or interesting, except for a short period in Japan, when I was courting, in the most formal fashion, Chiyojo, the woman who would become my wife, while nightly sharing the bed of her brother Takeda, who was a Kabuki actor of some renown (an *onagatta*, to be precise; that is to say, he only played women). Otherwise, the scandals of my sexual life would not fill a small pamphlet.

And yet—as I prepare to enter the portion of this story dedicated to the act of love, I can't help wondering where my father's fire went to when it flowed into me. Is there a lover in me somewhere, waiting for his moment to show his skills? Or has that energy been turned to less frenetic purpose? Is it what fuels my laying these very words on the page? Have the juices of Nicodemus' desire become the ink in my pen?

I've taken the analogy too far. Ah well. It's written, and I'm not going to abort it now, after so much effort.

I have to move on. Leave the memories of my father, and the storm, and the horses. I only hope that if the passion which drives me to my desk (obsessively now; every waking moment I'm thinking about what I've written, or about to write) isn't as blind and confused as love can be. I need clarity. Oh Lord, how I need clarity!

You see there are times now, often, when I think to myself: I've lost my way. I've got all these tantalizing pieces laid out, but I don't know how to put them together. They seem so utterly disparate: the fishermen at Atva, the hanged monks, Zelim in Samarkand; a letter from a man facing death on a Civil War battlefield; a silent movie star pursued to Germany, loved by a man too rich to know his true worth; George Geary dead in a car on a Long Island shore, and Loretta's astrologer predicting catastrophe; Rachel Pallenberg, out of love with love, and Galilee Barbarossa, out of love with life itself. How the hell do all these pieces belong in one coherent pattern?

Perhaps (this thought nauseates me, but I have to entertain it) they *don't* belong together. Perhaps I lost my bearings some while ago, and I've simply been gathering up pieces that for all their individual prettiness can never be made to fit together.

Well, it's too late to do anything about it now. I can't stop writing; I've got too much momentum. I have to forge on, using whatever little part of my father's genius I've inherited to interpret the scenes of human need which are about to come before me, and hope that in their interpreting I'll discover some way to make sense of all that I've described hitherto.

## ii

One last thing. I can't let another chapter go by without making mention of the conversation I had with Luman.

I don't want you to think I'm a coward; I'm not. I fully realize that at some point I have to address the accusations my half brother flung at me; both face to face with him, and face to face with myself (which is to say: here, in this book). He said my devotion to Nicodemus was in some measure the reason for my wife's death; that if I'd been the loving husband I claimed I would not have turned a blind eye to Chiyojo's seduction. I would have told Nicodemus she was mine, and he was to keep his hands off her. I didn't. I let him work his wiles upon her, and she paid the price.

I'm guilty as charged.

There; I've admitted it. Now what? It's too late to make amends to Chiyojo. At least I can't do so here; if her ghost still walks the mundane realm—which I suspect it does—then she's at home in the hills above Ichinoseki, waiting for the cherry trees to blossom.

The only peace I can make here in L'Enfant is with Luman, who I don't doubt stirred up this trouble between us out of perfectly innocent motives. He's not a man who knows how to conceal his thoughts. He had an opinion and he spat it out. Not only that, but what he said was right, though it agonizes me to admit the fact. I should go down to the

Smoke House (with a conciliatory offering of cigars) and tell him that I'm sorry for my outburst; that I want us to start talking again.

But I fear the thought of venturing down that overgrown path to the Smoke House door makes my head ache: I can't do it. At least not yet. The time will come, I'm sure, when I have no excuses left—when I haven't got a character suspended in the air—and I'll go make my apologies.

Maybe I'll go tomorrow, or the day after. When I've written about the island, that's when I'll go. Yes, that's it. Once I've cleared my head of all that I have to tell you about the island, and what happened to Rachel there, I'll be in a better state to sit and talk with him. He deserves my full attention, after all, and I can't possibly give it to him when I'm so distracted.

I feel a little better now. I've confessed my guilt, and that's oddly comforting. I won't undermine that confession by attempting to justify what I did. I was weak, and too eager to please. But I can't leave this passage without returning to the image of Nicodemus, the night of the storm. He was a rare creature, no question of that; I think many sons would have put their service to such a father before their duties as a husband. The irony is this: that if I hoped to be like him, as I did, and that in letting him have Chiyojo I would gain his approbation, and come closer to him, I worked against my own interests with heroic thoroughness. In one night I lost my idol, I lost my wife, and—let this be said, once and for all—I lost myself. What little there was of me—a self separate from my desire to please my father—was trampled under the same hooves that took his life. It's only been in the last few weeks, as I've been writing this history, that my sense of a soul called Maddox, alive in my flesh and worthy of preservation, has appeared. I suppose the moment of my rebirth was the moment I walked out of the skyroom, leaving the wheelchair behind me.

Another irony, of course: the strength to do that was ignited in me by my stepmother; she's the architect of my resurrection. Even if she doesn't want payment for that service—beyond the words I'm writing—I know there's a debt to be paid; and with every sentence, every paragraph, the Maddox who will make that payment comes into clearer focus.

This is what I see: a man who has just confessed his guilt, and will make amends, in time. A man who loves telling stories, and will find a way to understand what he's telling, in time. And a man who is capable of love, and who will find somebody to love again—oh please God yes; in time, in time.

R achel's first view of Kaua'i was tantalizingly brief; just enough to glimpse a series of bright scalloped beaches, and lush, rolling hills. Then the plane was making its steep descent into the airport at Lihu'e, and moments later a bumpy landing. The airport was small and quiet. She wandered through to pick up her bags, keeping her eyes open for the manager of the house where she'd be staying. And there he was, dutifully standing by the tiny baggage carousel, with a cart for her luggage. They recognized one another at the same moment.

"Mrs. Geary . . ." he said, forsaking his cart to come and present himself before her. "I'm Jimmy Hornbeck."

"Yes. I thought it must be you. Margie told me to look out for the best-pressed clothes on Kaua'i."

Jimmy laughed. "So that's my reputation," he said. "Well, I suppose it could be worse."

They exchanged a few pleasantries about the flights until the baggage arrived, then he led the way out into the sunshine.

"If you'd like to wait here," he said, "I'll go and fetch the car and bring it round for you. It saves you the walk to the parking lot."

She didn't protest this; she was perfectly happy to stand on the sidewalk and feel the ocean breeze on her face. It seemed as she stood there she could feel the grime and anxiety of New York ooze out of her pores. Soon, she'd wash it all away.

Hornbeck was back with the vehicle—which looked robust enough for jungle exploration—in two or three minutes. Another minute to load Rachel's bags, and then they were out of the little maze of roads around the airport and onto the closest thing the island had to a highway.

"I'm sorry about the transport, by the way," he said. "I had intended to pick you up in something a bit more civilized, but the road to the house has deteriorated so badly in the last couple of months—"

"Oh, really?"

"We've had a lot of rain recently, which is why the island looks particularly lush at the moment."

Lush was an understatement. Off to the left of the highway, toward the island's interior, were fields of rich red earth and green sugar cane. Beyond them, velvety hills, rising in ambition as they receded, until they became steep peaks whose heights were draped with sumptuous cloud.

"The problem is that the little backroads just aren't being taken care of the way they should be," Hornbeck was saying. "And there's a little tussle going on right now about who's actually responsible for the road to the house. The local council says it's really part of the property, and so I should be getting money from your people to get it fixed. But that's nonsense. It's public property. The council should be filling in the holes, not a private contractor."

Rachel was only half-attending to this. The beauty of the fields and mountains—and on the other side of the highway, the blue, pounding ocean—had claimed her attentions.

"So this argument has been going on for two years," Hornbeck went on. "Two years! And of course nothing's going to be done about the road until it's resolved. Which means it just deteriorates whenever there's rain. It's very frustrating so I apologize—"

"There's really no need . . ." Rachel said dreamily.

"—for the vehicle."

"Really," she said, "it's fine."

"Well just as long as you understand. I don't want you thinking I'm neglecting my duties."

"Hm?"

"When you see the road."

She glanced at the man, and saw by his fretful demeanor, and the whiteness of his knuckles, that he was genuinely concerned that his job was in jeopardy. As far as he was concerned she was a visiting potentate; he was afraid of making a mistake.

"Don't worry, James. Do people call you James or Jim?"

"Usually Jimmy," he said.

"You're English, yes?"

"I was born and raised in London. But then I came here. It'll be thirty years ago next November. And I said to myself: this is perfect. So I never went back."

"And you still think it's perfect?"

"Sometimes I get a little stir-crazy," Jimmy admitted. "But then you get a day like today and you think: where else would I want to be? I mean, look at it."

Rachel looked back toward the mountains. The clouds had parted on the heights, and the sun was breaking through.

"Can you see the waterfalls?" Jimmy said. She could. Silvery threads of water plummeting down from cracks in the mountainside. "Up there's the wettest place on earth," Jimmy informed her. "Mount Waialeale gets about forty feet of rain a year. It's raining right now."

"Have you been up?"

"I've taken a helicopter trip once or twice. It's spectacular. If you like I'll organize a flight for you. One of my best friends runs a little operation down in Po'ipu. He and his brother-in-law pilot these little choppers."

"I don't know that I trust helicopters."

"It's really the best way to see the island. And if you ask Tom he'll take you out over the ocean whale-spotting."

"Oh that I'd like to see."

"You like whales?"

"I've never seen any up close."

"I can arrange that too," Jimmy said. "I can have a boat organized for you at a day's notice."

"That's kind, Jimmy. Thank you."

"No problem. That's what I'm here for. If there's anything you need, just ask."

They were coming into a little town—Kapa'a, Jimmy informed her—where there were some regrettable signs of mainland influence. Beside the small stores of well-weathered clapboard stood the ubiquitous hamburger franchise, its gaud somewhat suppressed by island ordinance or corporate shame, but still ugly.

"There's a wonderful restaurant here in Kapa'a which is always booked up, but—"

"Let me guess. You have a friend—"

Jimmy laughed. "I do indeed. They always keep a prime table open each night, for special guests. Actually, I think your husband's stepmother invested some money in the place."

"Loretta?"

"That's right."

"When was she last here?"

"Oh . . . it must be ten years, maybe more."

"Did she come with Cadmus?"

"No, no. On her own. She's quite a lady."

"She is indeed."

He looked over at Rachel. Clearly he had more to say on the subject, but was afraid to say anything out of place.

"Go on . . ." Rachel said.

"I was just thinking that . . . well, you're different from the other ladies I've met. I mean, the other members of the family."

"How so?"

"Well, you're just less . . . how should I put it?"

"Imperious."

He chuckled. "Yes. That's good. Imperious. That's perfect."

They had emerged from Kapa'a by now, and the road, which still hugged the coastline, became narrower and more serpentine. There was very little traffic. A few of the locals passed by in rusted trucks, there was a small group of bicyclists sweating on one of the inclines, and now and then they were overtaken by a slicker vehicle—tourists, Jimmy remarked, a little contemptuously. There were however several long stretches when they were the only travelers on the road.

Nor was there much evidence of a human presence beyond the highway. Occasionally there'd be a house visible between the trees, sometimes a church (most so small they could only have served a tiny congregation), and on the beaches a handful of fishermen.

"Is it always this quiet?" Rachel asked.

"No, it's off-season right now," Jimmy said. "And we're only slowly recovering from the last hurricane. It closed a lot of the hotels and some of them still haven't reopened."

"But they will?"

"Of course. You can't hold back the rule of Mammon for ever."

"The rule of what?"

"Mammon. The demon of acquisitiveness? I mean commerce. People exploiting the island for profit."

She looked back at the mountain, which in the ten minutes since she'd last glanced toward the interior had transformed yet again. "It seems such a pity," she said, picturing the Hawaiian-shirted tourists she'd seen in Honolulu traipsing through this Eden, leaving trails of Coke cans and half-eaten hamburgers.

"Of course he wasn't always a demon," Jimmy went on. "I think originally *he* was a *she*: Mammetun, the mother of desires. She's Sumer-Babylonian. And with a name like that she probably had a lot of breasts. It's the same root as mammary. And Mama, of course." All this he said in an uninflected voice, almost as though he were talking to himself. "Don't mind me," he said.

"No, it's interesting," she said.

"I was a student of comparative religion in my younger days."

"What made you study that?"

"Oh . . . I don't know. Mysteries, I suppose. Things I couldn't explain. There's a lot of that here."

Rachel glanced again at the clouded mountains. "Maybe that's why it's so beautiful," she said.

"Oh, I like that," Jimmy murmured. "No beauty without mystery. I hadn't really thought about it that way before, but that's nice. Elegant."

"I'm sorry?"

"The thought," he said. "It's elegant."

They drove on in silence for a time, while Rachel pondered the notion that a thought, of all things, could be elegant. It was a new idea for her. People were sometimes elegant, clothes could of course be elegant, even an age; but a thought? Her musings were interrupted by Jimmy.

"You see the cliff straight ahead of us? The house is half a mile from there."

"Margie said it was right on the beach."

"Fifty yards from the ocean, if that. You can practically fish from your bedroom window."

Despite this promise the road now took them out of sight of the water, descending by a winding route to a bridge. They were now in the shadow of the crag which Jimmy had pointed out earlier, the origins of the river which the bridge spanned, a torrent of water that cascaded down the rock face above.

"Hang on," Jimmy said, once they were over the bridge, "we're going on to that lousy road I was telling you about."

Moments later they made a hard right, and just as Jimmy had warned, the road deteriorated rapidly, the hard asphalt of the highway replaced by a pitted, puddled track that wound back and forth between trees that had obviously not been trimmed for many years, their lower branches, heavy with blossom and foliage, brushing the top of Jimmy's vehicle.

"Watch out for the dog!" Rachel yelled over the din of the revved engine.

"I see him," Jimmy said, and leaning out of the window, yelled at the yellow mutt, who continued to sit in the middle of the track until the last possible moment, when it lazily raised its flea-bitten rump and sauntered to safety.

There was other animal traffic on the track: a fine-looking cockerel strutted about while his wives pecked in the ruts of the road. This time

Jimmy didn't need to yell. They were up in a flurry of aborted little flights, and into the dense foliage of what had once perhaps been hedgerows. Here and there, when there was a break in the greenery, she saw signs of habitation. A small house, in an advanced state of disrepair; a piece of farm machinery, rusted beyond reclamation, in a field that had mutinied many seasons before.

"Are there people living around here?"

"Very few," he said. "There was a flood about four years ago. Terrible rains; disastrous. In maybe two or three hours the river washed out the bridge we crossed, and washed a lot of houses away at the same time. A few people came back to rebuild. But a lot more decided to go somewhere less risky."

"Was anybody hurt?"

"Three people drowned, including a little kiddie. But the waters never came as far as the Geary house. So you're quite safe."

During this conversation the track had deteriorated yet further, if that were possible, the thicket to the left and right so fecund it threatened to obliterate the track completely. Now the birds that rose before the vehicle were not wild chickens but species Rachel had never seen before, winged flashes of scarlet and iridescent blue.

"Almost there," Jimmy promised, as the track threw the vehicle back and forth. "I hope you didn't pack any fine china." There was one last kink in the rutted track, which Jimmy took a little too fast. The vehicle tipped sideways, and for a few moments it seemed they'd overturn. Rachel let out a little shout of alarm.

"Sorry," Jimmy said. The vehicle righted itself with a thump and a squeak. He applied the brakes, and brought them to a halt perhaps ten or twelve yards from a pair of large wooden gates. "We're here," he announced.

He turned off the engine, and there was a sudden flood of music from the birds in the trees and thicket, and from somewhere out of sight, the thump and draw of the ocean.

"Do you want to go in alone, or shall I show you around?"

"I wouldn't mind just a couple of minutes on my own," she said.

"Of course," he said. "Take your time. I'll just unload the baggage, and have a cigarette."

She got out of the vehicle.

"I wouldn't mind one of those," she said, as Jimmy lit up.

He proffered the packet. "I'm sorry, I should have offered. So few folks smoke these days."

"I don't usually. But it's a special occasion."

She took a cigarette. He lit it for her. She drew a lungful of tobacco smoke. It was the first cigarette she'd had in a while, and the rush made her feel pleasantly light-headed: a perfect state, in fact, to enter the house.

She went to the gate, stepping gingerly between the frogs squatting in the long, damp grass, and lifted the latch. The gate opened without her needing to push it. She glanced back at Hornbeck. He was sitting with his back to her, staring up at the sky. Comforted that he was as good as his word, and would not be interrupting her, she stepped through the gate and into the presence of the house.

# XI

## i

It was not magnificent; not by any stretch of the imagination. It was a modest structure, built in the plantation style, a veranda running around it, shuttered windows and pale pink walls. For perhaps two-thirds of its length it was a single story, but at one end a second floor had been added, giving the whole structure a lopsided look. The tiles on this portion of the roof were ocher rather than reddish brown, as they were elsewhere, and the windows were mismatched, but none of this robbed the place of its charm. Quite the reverse. She was so used to environments that had been designed by protofascists, polished and grandiose, that it was a relief to discover the house was so quirky.

All of this would have been beguiling enough had it stood in isolation, but it did not. The house was entirely swathed in greenery and blossom. Giddy palms swayed languidly over its roof and vines crept over its veranda and along the eaves.

She lingered at the gate for a minute or so to take all this in. Then she took a last drag of the cigarette, put it out beneath her heel, and wandered up the front path to the door. Vivid green geckos darted ahead of her like a nervous welcoming committee, ushering her to the threshold.

She opened the front door. Before her was an extraordinary sight. The interior doors stood open, and by some conceit of the architect were so aligned that standing on the doorstep a visitor might see through the house and out the other side, as far as the glittering ocean. The rooms themselves were dark—especially by contrast with the sunny pathway—

so for a few enchanted moments it seemed she was staring into a dark maze in which a sliver of sky and sea had been caught.

She paused there on the threshold to admire the illusion, then stepped inside. The impression she'd had from the exterior—that this was by no means as luxurious a property as the rest the Gearys owned—was quickly confirmed. The place smelt pleasantly musty; not the must of neglect, perhaps, but rather of walls dampened by the sea air, or by the humidity of the island. She wandered from room to room to get some general sense of the layout of the place. The house was furnished eclectically, almost as though it had been at some time a repository of items that had some sentimental attachment. None of it matched. Around the dining table—which was itself scored and nicked and stained—were five distinctively different wooden chairs, and one pair. In the sizable kitchen the pots and pans that hung overhead were refugees from a dozen mismatched sets. The cushions that were heaped in hedonistic excess on the sofa were similarly unlike. Only the pictures on the walls showed any sign of homogeny. By contrast with the austere modernist pieces Mitchell had chosen for Rachel's apartment, or the vast American West paintings Cadmus collected (he owned a Bierstadt the size of a wall), there were modest little watercolors and pencil sketches hung everywhere—all renderings of the island: bays and boats; studies of blossoms or of butterflies. On the stairs was a series of drawings of the house, which though unsigned and undated had obviously been made many years before: the paper was yellowed, the pencil marks fading.

The furniture upstairs was every bit as odd as that below. One of the beds looked spartan enough for a barracks, but shared its room with a chaise lounge that would not have shamed a boudoir, while the master bedroom contained furniture which had been carved and painted with bowers of strange flora, in the midst of which naked men and women lay in blissful sleep. The paint had been worn to flecks of color over the years, and the carving itself was crude, but the presence of these pieces rendered the room strangely magical.

She thought again of what Margie had said about the place. It was proving to be true. She'd been on the island perhaps two hours and already she had felt its enchantment at work.

She went to the window. From it she had a view across the small unkempt lawn to a patch of low-lying scrub, on the other side of which lay the beach, its sand bright in the sunlight; and a little way beyond that the glittering turquoise water.

There was no doubt which bedroom she was going to use, she thought, throwing herself back on the bed like a ten-year old. "Oh

God—" she said, throwing her eyes up to the ceiling, "—thank you for this. Thank you so much."

## ii

By the time she came back downstairs Jimmy had her bags on the doorstep, and was dutifully standing among them, lighting up another cigarette.

"Bring them in," she told him. He went to toss the cigarette aside. "No, you can smoke inside the house, Jimmy."

"Are you sure?"

"I will be," she said. "I'll be smoking and drinking and—" She halted there: what else would she be doing? "And eating everything I shouldn't."

"Speaking of which . . . ," Jimmy said, "the cook's name is Heidi, and she lives a couple of miles from here. Her sister comes in to clean four times a week, but you can have her come in every day if you'd prefer, to change the bed—"

"No, that's fine."

"I took the liberty of stocking up the fridge and the freezer with food. Oh, and there's a few bottles of wine and so forth in one of the kitchen cabinets. Just send Heidi into Kapa'a for whatever else you need. I presume you're taking the larger bedroom?"

"Yes, please."

"I'll take the luggage up."

He went to his task, leaving Rachel to finish her exploration of the house. She wandered to the French windows through which she'd first glimpsed the beach, unlocked them and stepped out into the veranda. There were some weather-beaten chairs and a small wrought iron table out here; along with more vines, more blossoms, more geckos and butterflies. The wind had deposited an enormous desiccated palm frond on the stairs. She stepped over it and went down to the lawn, her sights set on the beach itself. The water looked wonderfully inviting, the waves breaking like soft, creamy thunder.

"Mrs. Geary?"

Jimmy was calling, but it wasn't until he'd done so three times that she snapped out of her mesmerized state and remembered that she was the Mrs. Geary he was calling to. She turned back toward the house. It was even more beautiful from this direction than from the front. The wind and rain coming off the sea had battered it a little more fiercely on this side; and the vegetation, as though to compensate for its wounds, cradled it more lushly. I could live here forever, she thought.

"I'm sorry to interrupt you, Mrs. Geary—"

"Please call me Rachel."

"Thank you. Rachel it'll be. I put your bags up in your room, and I've left a list with my telephone number and Heidi's number, on the kitchen counter. Oh by the way—I almost forgot—there's a jeep in the garage. If you want something fancier I'll rent something for you. I'm sorry I've got to rush away, but I have a church meeting . . ."

"No, that's fine," Rachel said. "You've done more than enough."

"I'll be off then," he said, heading back into the house. "If there's anything you need . . . anything at all."

"Thank you. I'm sure I'll be fine."

"Then I'll see you soon," he said, waving as he departed for the front door.

She heard it slam, then listened for the sound of the vehicle as he drove away. At last, it faded completely, leaving her with birdsong and sea.

"Perfect," she said to herself, imitating Jimmy's slightly clipped English pronunciation. It wasn't a word she would have thought of using until she'd heard it on Jimmy's lips; but was there any place on earth, or any time in her life, when it had seemed more appropriate?

No; this was perfect, perfect.

# XII

### i

She decided, now that Jimmy was gone and she had the house to herself, to delay her visit to the beach and instead shower and make herself a drink. He'd stocked the kitchen with wonderful thoroughness. When she'd cleaned up and changed out of her traveling clothes into a light summer dress, she went in search of the makings of a Bloody Mary and to her delight found all she needed. A bottle of vodka, tomato juice, Tabasco sauce, a little horseradish; even celery. Drink in hand she made one telephone call to Margie, to tell her that she'd arrived safely. Margie wasn't home, so she left a message, and then headed out to the beach.

The balmy afternoon had mellowed into a lovely evening; the last of the sun catching the heads of the palms, and gilding the clouds as they sailed on south. A couple of hundred yards from her a trio of local boys were surfing, shouting to one another as they plowed up and over the waves to catch a ride. Otherwise, the vast crescent of the beach was deserted. She set her glass in the sand and walked down to the water, venturing in until she was calf-deep. The shallows were warm, passing over sand heated by a day of sun. She let the waves break against her legs, the spray splashing her torso, her neck, her face.

The trio of surfers had meanwhile given up their sport for the night and had built a small fire at the top of the beach, which they were feeding with driftwood. Rachel was starting to feel somewhat chilly, so she left the water and went back up the sand to fetch her drink. It was less than twenty minutes since she'd stepped out of the house, but the short, tropical dusk was already almost over. The clouds and palms had lost their gold, and there were eager stars overhead.

She drained the spicy dregs of her Bloody Mary, and went back to the house. In her haste to be out on the beach she'd neglected to turn any lights on, and once she got onto the path that wound through the scrub she was stumbling in near darkness. But the house, even in this murk, looked beautiful, its pale walls and white paintwork all bluish in the deepening night. She'd forgotten what it was like to be in a place where there were no street lights nor car lights; not even a distant city glow to taint the sky. It made her aware of the world in a new way; or rather, a very old way that she was suddenly rediscovering. She heard nuances in the air around her she would normally have missed, in the voices of frogs and nightbirds, in the subtle shifting of palm and bough; smelled a dozen different scents: up out of the dewy earth beneath her feet, and from blooms the night was hiding.

Eventually she got back to the house, and after some fumbling around switched on a couple of lamps. Then she went upstairs to change out of her damp clothes. As she did so she caught sight of herself in the long dressing mirror in the bedroom. What she saw made her laugh out loud: in the space of a few minutes the combined effects of wind and sea-spray had made a wild woman of her: tangled her hair and reddened her cheeks; undone any pretensions to chicness she might have entertained. No matter; she liked what she saw. Perhaps she hadn't been entirely tamed by sorrow and the Gearys. Perhaps the Rachel she'd been in the easy years before Daddy's death, before the disappointment of Cincinnati and all that came after, was still alive in her. Yes, there! There! Smiling at her out of the mirror: the unrepentant wildling of her youth, the scourge of schoolmistress and sheriffs, the girl who'd loved nothing more than to make mischief; there she was.

"Where the hell have you been?" she said to herself.

*I never left*, that smile seemed to say. *I was just waiting until the time was right to show myself again.*

## ii

She made herself a light supper of cold cuts and cheese, and opened a bottle of wine — red, not white, for a change; something with a bit of body to it. Then she curled up on the sofa, and ate. There was a small television in the living room, but she had no desire to watch it. If the stock market had crashed, or the White House gone up in flames, so what? The rest of the world and its problems could go to hell, at least for now.

Halfway through her leisurely meal, the phone rang. She was sorely tempted to let it ring out, but thinking it was probably Jimmy Hornbeck checking to see that she was comfortable she picked up. It wasn't Hornbeck, it was Margie, returning her call. She sounded weary.

"What time is it in New York?"

"I don't know: two, two-thirty," Margie said. "Are you all settled in?"

"I'm perfect," Rachel said. "It's even better than you said it would be."

"It's just beginning, honey," Margie said. "You'll be amazed what happens when you get into the rhythm of the place. Did you take the big bedroom?"

"With all of the carved furniture . . ."

"Isn't that place amazing?"

"The whole house is amazing," Rachel replied. "I felt right at home as soon as I stepped inside."

"You'll never guess where I've been," Margie said.

"Where?"

"With Cadmus."

"Loretta had a dinner party?"

"No, just the two of us."

"What did he want?"

"It was weird. He swore me to secrecy. But I'll tell you when you get back." She laughed. "I don't know," she said. "This family."

"What about it?"

"All the men are crazy," Margie said. "And I think we must be even crazier, because we fell in love with the bastards." Her voice dropped to a whisper. "I've got to go, honey. I hear Garrison. Love you."

Without waiting for a reply, she put down the phone.

The call unsettled Rachel slightly, putting back into her head a notion she didn't want there: that until she divorced Mitchell she was a part of the Geary story.

She was too tired for the uneasiness to keep her from sleep, however. The bed was a joy to lie in, when she got there; the pillows deep, the sheets fragrant. She had scarcely pulled the cover up over her body then she was gone into a place where the Gearys—their crazy men, their sad women, their secrets and all—could not come after her.

# XIII

### i

She woke at first light, got up, went to the window, admired the way the world was looking, and went straight back to bed for another three blissful hours. Only then did she clamber out of bed and go down to brew herself some coffee. The feeling of rediscovery she'd experienced the night before—dead senses awakened, the wildling Rachel in the mirror—had not deserted her; nor did the morning light diminish the charms of the house. She was as happy wandering around as she'd been the afternoon before; every shelf and nook carried some new interesting item. She'd even missed a couple of rooms in her previous explorations: one a little writing room facing out to a side yard, with a desk, some old, comfortable chairs and several shelves of well-thumbed books, the other a much smaller room, which seemed to have been used as a depository for items found on the beach: pieces of sea-smoothed timber, shells, fragments of coral, lengths of unraveling rope, even a cardboard box filled with stones that had caught some beachcomber's eye. The most promising discovery however was in a cupboard in the living room: a collection of old phonograph records, still neatly sleeved; and on the shelf above a player. The last time she'd seen either was at the house in Caleb's Creek, although these recordings looked to be much older than anything in George's treasured collection. Later, she promised herself, she'd select a few tunes and see if she could get the phonograph up and running. That would be her one and only project for the day.

Toward noon, having made herself some brunch (and devoured it; she was surprised at how hungry she was, given how little she'd done) she went back down to the beach, this time intending to take a walk along its entire length. Halfway along the path a brown hen suddenly darted in front of her, panicking to join her three chicks, who were waiting for her on the other side. Clucking to them, the mother led them away through the debris of dead palm fronds and rotting coconut husks.

This time the beach was completely deserted. The waves were smaller than they'd been the night before; too small to tempt even the

most cautious surfer. She wandered down the beach as she'd planned—
wishing after a few minutes she'd had the forethought to look for a wider-
brimmed hat in the house; the sun was fierce—until she came to the
place where the waters that cascaded from the crag emptied themselves
into the sea. Red-brown with the freight of silt they had picked up on
their way, they spread once they reached the beach, and though the
waters didn't look treacherous, she didn't want to risk wading the fifty
yards to get to the other side, so she turned back. On the return journey
she kept her eyes on the horizon. Jimmy had said this was whale-spotting
season; if she was lucky perhaps she'd see one of the humpbacks breaching. She was out of luck however; there were no whales to be seen. Just
a couple of small fishing boats bobbing around not far from the shore,
and much, much further off, a white sail. She paused to watch it for a
minute or two as it flickered there at the limit of her gaze, bright against
the sky one moment, gone the next. At last she tired of watching and
headed back to the house, parched and a little sunburned.

There was a visitor waiting at the front door. A dark-skinned, broad-
shouldered man of perhaps thirty-five, who introduced himself as
Niolopua.

"I'm here to take care of some stuff around the house," he said.

"Like what?" Rachel said. She didn't remember Jimmy mention-
ing this man, and despite his open expression and his easy manner,
she'd brought her New York suspicion of strangers with her.

"The lawn," he said, nodding towards the back of the house. "The
plants."

"Oh . . . you mean outside the house?"

"Yeah."

"No problem," she said, stepping aside to let him in.

"I'll go around the side," he said, looking at her more intensely
now. "I just wanted to introduce myself."

"Well thank you," she said. There was something about the way he
looked at her that made Rachel think maybe there was some subtext to
this; but then his body language contradicted the suspicion. He stood a
respectful distance from her, his hands behind his back, simply looking.
She returned his gaze, fully expecting him to look away, but he didn't.
He kept staring, with almost childlike frankness until she said:

"Is there anything else?"

"No," he said. "It's fine. Everything's fine." He spoke as though to
reassure her.

"Good," she said. "Then I'll let you go." With that she turned from
him and closed the door.

Later, she heard the drone of the lawnmower, and went to the living room window to glance out at him. He was shirtless now, his back the color of the silted river. If this were one of the trashy novels Margie so adored, Rachel thought, then all she'd have to do was invite him in for a glass of ice water and a minute later she'd be backed up against the door with his tongue down her throat. She smiled to herself, feeling wicked. Maybe she'd try it, in a couple of days; see how reality matched up to the fantasy.

A little later, as she was attempting to get the phonograph to work, she realized the sound of the mower had ceased, and glanced up to see that Niolopua had left off his labors and had wandered down to the bottom of the lawn. There he was standing, staring out to sea, one hand shading his eyes from the blaze of the sky.

There was no doubt as to what he was watching. The boat with the white sail had come closer to shore, close enough for her to see that it had not one sail, but at least two. She watched for a little time as the vessel rose and fell against the dark blue waters. It was mesmeric; like watching the hands of a clock, the motion so subtle it was impossible to catch. Yet there was no doubt that even as she watched the boat, it had come a little closer to the shore.

There was a sudden eruption of squawking in the palms off to the right of the house, which drew her gaze. Several house finches were involved in a bitter dispute among the fronds; feathers drifted down. By the time the argument had been settled, and she again looked toward the lawn, Niolopua had forsaken his watch and returned to his lawnmower. The boat had meanwhile passed out of sight, the wind or the currents or both carrying it down the coast, and she felt mildly disappointed. She'd been looking forward to watching the boat's progress while she sipped her cocktail. No matter, she said to herself. There'd surely be plenty of other vessels plying their way between the islands in the next few days.

## ii

The wind rose in strength as the day progressed, shaking the palms around the house and whipping the ocean, which had looked so benign at daybreak, into a white-headed frenzy. It made her uneasy; it always had. Even as a child she'd become fractious when the wind blew; heard voices in it, sometimes, crying and sobbing. *Lost souls*, her grandmother had explained, which had of course done nothing to soothe her unease.

She decided not to stay in the house but to take the jeep and drive along the coast. It turned out to be a fine idea. After driving around for a while she found herself on a narrow spit of land, at the end of which sat a tiny white church, with thirty or so graves around it. The building itself was only partially intact: a victim, perhaps, of the hurricane Jimmy Hornbeck had mentioned. Its roof tiles had been entirely stripped away, as had many of the ceiling timbers. Only three of the four walls were still standing; the seaward wall was missing. So was the altar. All that remained inside were a few plain wooden chairs, which for some reason nobody had claimed.

She wandered among the graves, most of which were at least thirty or forty years old, and some, to judge by their eroded and sunken state, considerably older. A few of those buried here had names she could pronounce — a Robertson, a Montgomery, even a Schmutz — but several were beyond her. How was Kaohelaulii said aloud she wondered; or Hokunohoaupuni?

After spending maybe ten minutes examining the names she started to realize she'd come out underdressed for the elements. Though the sun still appeared now and then between the speeding clouds, the wind was chilling her to the bone. She was reluctant to get back into the jeep and drive home, however, so she took refuge in what remained of the church. The wooden walls creaked whenever a strong gust of wind came along. It would only take one more heavy storm, she thought, and the whole structure would come crashing down. In the meantime it provided her with exactly what she needed; protection from the worst of the bluster, while still offering her a clear view of both sky and sea.

She sat in one of the battered chairs and listened to the changing notes of the wind as it whistled between the boards. Perhaps her grandmother had been right after all. It certainly wasn't hard to imagine, in such a place as this, that the departed were indeed voicing their grief in the wind. Perhaps the souls of men and women buried on this headland — Montgomerys and Kaohelauliis — came back off the sea to the spot where their bones lay. It was a melancholy thought; but it didn't unsettle her. Perhaps they'd see her sitting calmly here, unafraid of their voices, and when they returned to the wastes be comforted by the memory.

She felt a spatter of rain on her face. Getting up out of her chair she stepped back out onto the headland and saw that a great mass of dark cloud was moving toward the island, its gloomy offspring driven ahead to sprinkle a warning shower or two. It was time to go. She pulled up the collar of her blouse and started to pick her way through the graves back to the jeep. The rain was coming quickly; before she was halfway to the vehicle it was coming down hard, and getting harder. It was cold; cold enough to take her breath away.

She got into the car, fumbling for the ignition key. The rain was beating hard on the roof, its din drowning out the noise of the wind. As she put the car into reverse she glanced back at the ocean, and through the rain-smeared windshield saw a white shape in the dark sea. She turned on the windshield wipers, clearing the glass.

There, out in the bay, was the boat she'd seen earlier in the day; the two-masted vessel which had been the object of Niolopua's scrutiny. It was foolish to get back out of the car to look, but for some reason she felt the need to do so.

Out she got, the rain so heavy it soaked her to the skin in five seconds. But she didn't care. It was worth the soaking to see her boat braving the swell, its sails fat with wind, its bows cutting a white swath through the gray-green water. Satisfied that this was without a doubt the vessel she'd seen earlier, and that its master and crew were in no danger, she ducked back into the car, slammed the door, and started the homeward journey.

# XIV

O f late when I write I find myself gripping my pen so tightly that I can feel the tick of my pulse in my thumb and forefinger. My grip is more and more an obsessive's grip. I swear if I were to die at this moment, writing these very words, it would take several strong men to part me from my pen.

You'll remember I confessed a few chapters back that I was lost; that I didn't know how all the pieces of the story I have fitted together. In the last few nights of writing that unease is beginning to lift. Perhaps it's self-deception, but it seems to me I can see the connections more clearly than before: the grand scheme of what I'm telling is slowly becoming apparent to me. And as it comes clear I feel myself drawn deeper into the tale I'm telling, the way a worshipper is drawn to the altar steps, and—dare I venture this?—for much the same reason. I am hoping to ascend to a place of revelation.

Meanwhile, I keep the company of my characters as though they were dear friends. I have only to close my eyes, and there they are.

Rachel, for instance? I can see her in my mind's eye right now, sipping her evening's Bloody Mary before she goes to bed; not remotely suspecting that the night of her life lies before her. I can picture Cadmus just as clearly. There he is, sitting in his wheelchair in front of his sixty-inch television, his eyes glazed as he contemplates a scene remote from him in years yet closer than the liver spots on the back of his hand. I can bring Garrison before me—poor, sick Garrison, who has such harm in his heart, and knows it—and Margie, in her cups; and Loretta, plotting successions; and my father's wife, busy with plots of her own; and Luman and Marietta and Galilee.

Oh, my Galilee. I see him more clearly tonight than ever I've seen him in my life, even when he was standing before me in the flesh. Does that sound absurd, that he should appear in my imagination more completely than he ever did before my eyes? However it sounds, it's true. Dreaming of Galilee as I do, conjuring him not as a thing of flesh and personality, but as a creature half gone into myth, I believe I am in the presence of a truer soul than that phantom man whom I lately met.

You may say: what nonsense. We live in flesh and blood, you may say. To which I reply: yes, but we die into spirit. Even divinities like Galilee give up the limitations of the flesh eventually, and unbounded swell into legend. So imagining him in his mythic form—as a wanderer, as a lover, as a brute—am I not closer to the Galilee with whom my soul will spend eternity?

I just made the mistake of proudly reading the preceding paragraphs to Marietta. She snorted at them; called them "pretentious claptrap" (that was the mildest epithet); told me I should strike all such ruminations from my text and get on with doing my job, which is—as far as she's concerned—simply to report what I know about the history of the Barbarossas and the Gearys in as clear and concise a fashion as I can.

So I've decided I'm not going to share any more of what I'm writing with Marietta. If she wants a book about the rise and fall of the Geary dynasty, then she can damn well write it herself. I'm making something entirely different. It'll be a ragtag thing, no question, sewn together from mismatched parts, but I find that just as beautiful in its way as a small, nicely formed tale. And, by the way, more like life.

Oh, there was two other things Marietta said that day which bear reporting here, if only because they both contain more than a measure of truth. One, she accused me of liking words because of their music. I pleaded guilty to this, which infuriated her. "You put music before meaning!" she said. (This was just spiteful; I don't. But I think meaning is always a latecomer. Beauty and music seduce us first; later, ashamed of our own sensuality, we insist on meaning.)

Which brings me to her second remark: something to the effect that I was no better than a village storyteller. I smiled from ear to ear at this, and told her that nothing would give me more pleasure than to have my book by heart, and to tell it aloud. Then she'd see how much pleasure there was to be had from my bag of tales. You don't like what I'm telling you, sir? Don't worry. It'll change in two minutes. You don't like scandal? I'll tell you something about God. You hate God? I'll recite you a love scene. You're a puritan? Have patience; the lovers will suffer. Lovers always suffer.

Marietta's response to all this was inevitably sour.

"You're no better than a crowd-pleaser then, are you?" Marietta replied. "Pandering to whatever people want to hear. Why don't you just slather the thing in sex and have done with it?"

"Have you quite finished?"

"No."

"Well I'd really like you to leave. You just came in here to have an argument, and I've got better things to be doing."

"Ha!" she said, snatching one of the sheets I'd been reading from off my desk. "This is one of your better things? *We live in flesh and blood, you may say—*" I retrieved the page from her hand before she could go any further. "Just . . . *go away*," I said, very firmly. "You're being a philistine."

"Oh so now I'm too stupid to appreciate your artistic ambitions, is that it?"

I contemplated this for a moment. "Well, as you put it that way . . ." I said. "Yes."

"Fine. Then we both know where we stand don't we? I think this work is wretched *crap* and you think I'm stupid."

"That seems to be a fair summary."

"No," she said, as though I was about to change my mind (which I wasn't). "You've said it now. And that's the end of it."

"I'm agreeing with you, Marietta."

"I won't be coming back in here," she warned.

"Good," I said.

"You'll get no more support from me."

"I just said: *good.*"

She was red-faced with rage by now. "I mean it, Maddox," she said.

"I know you mean it, Marietta," I said, quietly. "And believe me, it's tearing me apart. It may not appear that way, but I am in agonies at the prospect." I pointed to the door. "That's the way out."

"*God*, Maddox," she said. "Sometimes you can be such a *dickhead*."

That was, as best I remember it, the entire exchange. I haven't seen her since. Of course, she'll come crawling back sooner or later, probably pretending that the conversation never happened. Meanwhile, I'm undisturbed, which suits me fine. I have to write what may be the most important passages of my story so far. The less distraction I have the better I can focus upon it.

There's only one portion of the conversation that I have returned to muse over: and that's the part about being a village storyteller. I realize she meant it as a form of condemnation, but in truth I can see nothing undesirable about being thus employed. Indeed I have imagined myself many, many times sitting beneath an ancient tree in some dusty square—in Samarkand, perhaps; yes! in Samarkand—telling my epic in pieces, for the price of bread and opium. I would have had a fine time doing that: get myself fat and flying by parceling my tale out, day after day. I would have had my audience wrapped around my little finger; coming back every afternoon to visit me in the blue shadows, and asking me to sell them another piece of the family saga.

My father was a great improviser of stories. In fact, it's one of the few truly fond memories I have of him. My sitting at his feet when I was a child, while he wove wonderful fictions for me. There were often malevolent stories, by the way: violent, blood-thirsty tales about the way the world was in some uncalendered time. When he was young, perhaps; if indeed he ever was.

A lot later, when I was approaching adulthood and about ready to go out looking for female company, he told me that I shouldn't underestimate the potency of stories in the art of seduction. He had not seduced my mother with kisses or compliments, he said (and he certainly hadn't got her drunk and raped her, as Cesaria had told me); he'd brought her to his lap, and thence to his bed, with a story.

Which brings us back (though you do not yet see why, you will) to that night on Kaua'i, and to Rachel.

# PART FIVE

# The Act of Love

# I

The wind had carried the rain clouds off toward Mount Waialeale by early evening, where they'd shed the bulk of their freight. The skies cleared over the North Shore, and about seven-fifteen the gusts died to nothing with uncanny suddenness. Rachel was eating at the time—a plate of baked chicken, prepared by Heidi, who'd come in, cooked, and departed. She looked up from her meal to see that the palms were no longer churning, and the sea was quite placid.

The silence unnerved her a little, so she put on some music: a big-band melody. It was a mistake; it reminded her of a night early in her courtship with Mitchell when they'd gone out dancing, and he'd chosen a very exclusive place uptown where a small band played forties tunes, and everyone danced cheek to cheek. Oh but she'd been in love that night; like a fifteen-year-old infatuated with the school quarterback. He'd plied her with champagne, and told her that he was devoted to her, and always would be.

"Liar . . ." she murmured as she stared out at the sea. Sometimes, when she remembered things he'd said—sweet things that he'd betrayed, hard things that he'd known he would hurt her by saying—she wanted him right there in front of her, to point an accusing finger and say: why did you say that? God Mitchell, you were such a liar, such a miserable *liar* . . .

Rather than turn the music off, however, she sat it out, determined to endure every last, melancholy note. The only way to get past the hurt was to face it. If this trip to Eden did nothing else, she thought, it would at least give her an opportunity to leaf through her memories, and look at them clearly. Then, and only then, could she move on. Put Mitchell and all he'd been to her in the past, where he belonged, and start a new life.

A new life. There was a daunting thought. It wasn't the first time she'd wondered what would become of her now, but the question had a new pertinence on this island, where she knew others had come before her, and begun again. Jimmy Hornbeck, for one. And what of the Montgomerys and the Robertsons and Schmutzes buried on the cliff? They too had been emigrants, presumably. Fugitives perhaps, like her: running from lives that had hurt and disappointed them. It wouldn't be so bad at that, she thought, to disappear from the world and live and die in this paradise; to be buried on a cliff where nobody came, nobody mourned, nobody remembered.

She went to bed at ten, or thereabouts, and fell asleep as quickly as she had the night before. But this time she didn't sleep through till daybreak. Instead she stirred from a dream some while after midnight. She had the impression that she'd been woken by something, but she wasn't sure what it was. All she could hear was the rhythmic rasp of crickets, and the soft croaking of frogs. There was a little moonlight coming between the drapes, but there was nothing disturbing enough to have roused her.

Then she realized: it was a smell that had woken her. The sharp-sweet scent of something burning. Her mind reluctantly formed the thought that she'd better get up and check that the source of the smell wasn't somewhere in the house. Her body still heavy with sleep she pulled back the sheet and climbed out of bed. Then she slipped into a T-shirt and knickers and went downstairs to investigate. As soon as she reached the living room she spotted the fire: it was burning brightly at the top of the beach. Had the three surfers she'd seen the first day come back in the middle of the night to make a bonfire, and maybe smoke a little pot? If so, they'd built a much bigger fire than last time. It was a steep pyramid of timbers, from the flanks and apex of which bright yellow flames sprang. The smell however, wasn't just that of burning wood. There was an aromatic pungency about it, which lent it a pleasing exoticism.

She slid open the French doors and stepped outside, thinking she would see the fire-tenders better. But she could see nobody. There were stars, a great array of them bright overhead, but no moon. She went back into the house, located a pack of cigarettes she'd bought in Honolulu Airport, lit one, and wandered back out again, this time stepping off the veranda onto the chilly grass, and on down the lawn to the path.

Though she was now no more than ten or twelve yards from the fire, she could still see no sign of its architects. But she could smell the fragrance more strongly than ever, rising out of the pyramid like incense from a mountainous censer. The smell pleased her even more than it had at first. It was sweet yet sharp, like the honey from ancient hives.

She wandered through the shrubs and over the sand toward the fire, enjoying its warmth on her face and bare legs. Obviously the fire-makers had departed, leaving their handiwork to blaze away through the night. Not the cleverest thing to do, she thought. If the wind were to rise again it could easily blow splinters of fiery wood into the bushes, and, worse still, toward the house.

What should she do, she wondered? Wait here until the fire burned itself out or attempt to smother the flames with sand? The second option was beyond her, she decided. The fire was simply too big, and too well made. And as to waiting here; well, it would be a long, long wait.

Perhaps for once she was just going to have to have a little faith that the worst would not happen.

She should just go back to bed and sleep. By morning the fire would be a blackened, smoky pit in the sand, and her fears of cataclysm would seem ridiculous. Still, she might tell the surfers next time she saw them not to build their fires so big, or so close to the tree line. So thinking, she walked once around the fire, and started back to the house.

The scent came with her. It was in her clothes, in her hair, on her skin, in her mouth even. And it seemed—though this was plainly non-sensical—that the further she got from its source the more powerful it became, as though cooler air was refining it. By the time she got into the house it was so strong it might have been oozing out of her pores.

She was of half a mind to shower before she climbed back into bed, but she decided against it, persuaded less by fatigue as by the subtle sense of intoxication the fragrance had induced. Her head felt feathery, her perceptions a little awry (when she reached to turn off the bedside lamp she missed it by a couple of inches, which amused her). When she'd finally found the switch, and lay her head down in darkness, there were colors billowing behind her lids, intense as the hues crawling on a soap bubble. She watched them entranced, vaguely wondering if they'd been burned onto her retina from staring at the fire. The thought came into her head that they were with her for ever now—the colors, the aroma—and that she was therefore their captive: bounded by them, shaped by them. She would never see the world without it being colored for her; never draw breath but that she'd smell the fragrance of the fire.

She opened her eyes again, just to be certain the world she'd left out there, beyond her lids, was still in existence. There was a nice, mellow sense of dislocation in all this: no paranoia, no fear; simply suspicion that things outside her head were not to be taken too seriously tonight.

The room was still there: the ring of lamplight on the ceiling, the open window, the drapes lifted and let go by the breeze; the carved bed in which she lay, with its lovers lying in their ripe bowers; the door at the end of the bed, leading out onto the hallway, down the stairs—

Her gaze seemed to go with her thoughts, out onto the darkened landing—floating up to the ceiling one moment, grazing the footworn weave of the rug the next.

By the time she got to the top of the stairs an unbidden thought had formed in her head: she wasn't alone in the house. Somebody had come in. As silent as smoke, and just as harmless—surely, on a night like this nobody meant harm—somebody had entered the house and was there at the bottom of the stairs.

The realization didn't trouble her in the slightest. She felt absurdly inviolate, as though she had not simply watched the fire on the beach but stood in its midst and walked through it unscorched.

She looked down the flight in the hope of seeing him, and thought she caught the vaguest impression of his form, there in the darkness: a big, broad man; a black man, she thought. He started to climb the stairs. She could feel the air at the top of the flight become agitated at his approach, excited at the prospect of being drawn into his lungs. Her gaze retreated along the landing, back toward the bedroom; back into her head. She would pretend she was asleep, perhaps. Let him come to her bedside and touch her awake. Put his hand to her lips, to her breast; or if he wanted to, press his fingers against her belly; then down, between her legs. She'd let him do that. None of this was quite real anyway, so why the hell not? He could do whatever he wanted, and no harm would come to her. Not here, in her carved bower-bed. Only joy here; only bliss.

For all these fearless thoughts there was still a corner of her intellect that was counseling caution.

"*You're not being rational,*" this fretful self said to her. "*The smoke's got into your head. The smoke and this island. They've got you all turned about.*"

Probably true, the dreamy wildling in her said. So what?

"*But you don't know who he is,*" the cautious one pointed out. "*And he's black. There aren't any blacks in Dansky, Ohio. Or if there are, you don't know any. They're different.*"

So am I, the wildling replied. I'm not who I was, and I'm all the better for it. So what if the island's working magic on me? I need a little magic. I'm ready. Oh Lord, I'm more than ready.

She'd closed her eyes, still thinking she would pretend to be sleeping when he came in. But as soon as she felt the stirring of the air against her face, announcing his presence at the threshold, she opened them again, and asked him, very quietly, who he was.

By way of reply, he spoke one word only.

"Galilee," he said.

# II

At that moment, on the cloud-obscured summit of Mount Waialeale, the rain was falling at the rate of an inch and a half an hour. In gorges too inaccessible for exploration, plants that had never been named were drinking down the deluge; insects that would never venture where a human heel could crush them were sheltering their brittle heads. These were secret places, secret species; rare phenomena on a planet where little was deemed sacred enough, exquisite enough, tremulous enough, to be preserved from the prod, the scalpel, the exhibition.

Out in the benighted sea, whales were passing between the islands, mothers and their children flank to flank, playful adolescents breaching in the dark, rising up in frenzied coats of foam and twisting so as to spy the stars before they came crashing down again. In the coral reef below them, its caves and gullies as untainted as Waileale's heights, other secret lives proceeded: the warm currents carrying myriad tiny forms, transparent flecks of purpose which for all their insignificant size nourished the great whales above.

And in between the summit and the reef? There was mystery there too. No less an order of life than the flower or the plankton, though it belonged to no class or hierarchy. It lived, this life, in the human head, the human heart. It moved only when touched, which was rarely, but when it did—when it shifted itself, showed itself to the creature in which it lived—there was revelation. The prospect of love could stir it, the prospect of death could stir it; even, on occasion a simpler thing: a song, a fine thought. Most of all it was moved by the prospect of its own apotheosis. If it felt its moment was near, then it would rise into the face of its host like a light, and blaze and blaze —

"*Whoever you are* . . ." Rachel said softly, ". . . *come and show me your face.*"

The man stepped into the doorway. She couldn't see his face, as she'd requested, but she could see his form, and it was, as she'd guessed, a fine form: tall and broad.

"Who are you?" she said. Then, when he didn't reply: "Did you make the fire?"

"Yes." His voice was soft.

"The smoke . . ."

". . . followed you."

"Yes."

"I asked it to."

"You asked the smoke," she said. It made an unlikely kind of sense to her.

"I wanted it to introduce you to me," he said. There was a hint of humor in his voice, as though he only half-expected her to believe this. But the half that *did* believe it believed it utterly.

"Why?" she said.

"Why did I want to meet you?"

"Yes . . ."

"I was curious," he said. "And so were you."

"I didn't even know you were here," she said. "How could I be curious?"

"You came out to see the fire," he reminded her.

"I was afraid . . ." she began; but the rest of the thought eluded her. What had she been afraid of?

"You were afraid the wind would blow the sparks . . ."

"Yes . . ." she murmured, vaguely remembering her anxiety.

"I wouldn't have let that happen," Galilee reassured her. "Didn't Niolopua tell you why?"

"No . . ."

"He will," Galilee replied. Then, more softly. "My poor Niolopua. Do you like him?"

She mused on this for a moment; it hadn't been something she'd given much thought to. "He seems very gentle," she said. "But I don't think he is. I think he's angry."

"He has reason," Galilee replied.

"Everybody hates the Gearys."

"We all do what we have to do," he replied.

"And what does Niolopua do? Besides cutting the grass?"

"He brings me here, when I'm needed."

"How does he do that?"

"We have ways of communicating that aren't easy to explain," Galilee said. "But here I am."

"Okay," she said. "So now you're here. Now what?"

There was more than enquiry in her voice. Though her tongue was lazy, the words slow, she knew what she was inviting; she knew what answer she wanted to hear. That he'd come to share her bed, whoever he was; come to exploit the dreamy ease she'd inhaled, and make love to her. Come to kiss her back to life, after an age of thorns and sorrow.

He didn't give her the answer she expected. At least, not in so many words.

"I want to tell you a story," he said.

She laughed lightly. "Aren't I a bit too old for that?"

"No," he said softly. "Never."

He was right of course. She was perfectly ready to have him weave a story for her; to let the deep music of his voice shape the colors in her head: give them lives, give them destinies.

"First," she said, "will you come into the light where I can see you?"

"That's part of the story," he said. "That's always part of it."

"Oh . . ." she said, not understanding the principle of this, but accepting that at least for tonight it was true. "Then tell me."

"It would be my pleasure," he said. "Where should I start?" There was a little pause while he considered this. When he spoke again his voice had changed subtly; there was a lilting rhythm in it, as though there was a melody to these words, that he was close to singing.

"*Imagine please,*" he began, "*a country far from here, in a time of plenty, when the rich were kind and the poor had God. In that country there lived a girl called Jerusha, whom this story concerns. She was fifteen at the time when what I'm about to tell you happened, and there was no happier girl in the world. Why? Because she was loved. Her father owned a great house, filled with treasures from the furthest reaches of the empire, but he loved his Jerusha more than anything he owned or anything he ever dreamed of owning. And not a day went by without his telling her so. Now on this particular day, a day in late summer, Jerusha had gone out taking a winding path through the woods to a favorite place of hers: a spot on the banks of the River Zun, which marked the southern perimeter of her father's land.*"

"*Sometimes in the morning when she visited the river bank the local women would be there washing their clothes, then spreading them out on the rocks to dry, but the later in the day she went the more likely she was to be there alone. Today, however, though it was late afternoon, she saw—as she wound between the trees—that there was somebody sitting in the water. It was not one of the women. It was a man, or nearly a man, and he was staring down at his own reflection in the river. I say he was nearly a man, because although this creature had a man's shape, and a pretty shape at that, his form glistened strangely in the sunlight, silvery one moment, dark the next.*

"*Now Lord Laurent, who was Jerusha's father, had taught her to be afraid of nothing. He was a rational man. He didn't believe in the Devil, and he had over the years punished any man who committed a crime on his land so quickly and severely that no felon ventured there. And he had also taught his daughter that there were far stranger things in the world than she'd seen in her schoolbooks. Perfectly rational things, he'd told her, that one day science would explain, though they might at first glance seem unusual.*

"*So Jerusha didn't run away when she saw this stranger. She just marched down to the river's edge and said hello. The fellow looked up from his reflection. He had no hair on his head; nor did he have lashes or brows; but there was an uncanny beauty to him, which awoke feelings in Jerusha that had not stirred until this moment. He looked at her with his flickering eyes, and smiled. But he said nothing.*

"  '*Who are you?*' *she asked him.*

"  '*I don't have a name,*' *he told her.*

"  '*Of course you do,*' *she said.*

"  '*No I don't. I swear,*' *the stranger said.*

"  '*Were you not baptized?*' *she asked him.*

"  '*Not that I remember,*' *he told her.* '*Were you?*'

"  '*Of course.*'

"  '*In the river?*'

"  '*No. In a church. My mother wanted it. She's dead now—*'

"  '*If it was in a church then it wasn't a true baptism,*' *the stranger replied.* '*You should come into the river with me. I would give you a new name.*'

"  '*I like the one I have.*'

"  '*Which is what?*'

"  '*Jerusha.*'

"  '*So, Jerusha. Please come into the river with me.*' *As he spoke he stood up, and she saw that at his groin, where a normal man would have a penis, there was instead a column of water, running from him the way water pours from a pipe, all corded and glittering, and seeming almost solid in the sunlight . . ."*

Rachel had been completely still until this moment; enraptured by the pictures these simple words were conjuring: of the girl, of the summer's day and the riverbank. But now she sat up a little in the bed and began to scrutinize the shadowy man in the doorway. What kind of story was he telling here? It was certainly no fairy story.

He read her unease. "Don't worry," he said. "It's not going to get obscene."

"Are you sure?"

"Why? Would you prefer that it did?"

"I just want to be ready."

" *'Don't be afraid.'*

"I'm not afraid," she said.

" *'Come into the river.' "*

Oh, she thought; he's started again.

" *'What is that?' Jerusha said, pointing to the stranger's groin.*

" *'Do you have no brothers?'*

" *'They went away to war,' Jerusha said. 'And they're supposed to come back, but every time I ask my father when that will be he kisses me and tells me to be patient.'*

" *'So what do you think?'*

" *'I think maybe they're dead,' Jerusha said.*

*"The fellow in the water laughed. 'I meant of this,' he said, looking down at the water flowing out of him. 'What do you think of this?'*

*"Jerusha just shrugged. She wasn't very impressed, but she didn't want to say so."*

Rachel smiled. "Polite girl," she remarked.

"You wouldn't be so polite?" Galilee said.

"No. I'd be the same. You don't want to break his heart with the truth."

"And what's the truth?"

"That it's not as pretty as . . ."

"As?"

". . . you'd like to believe?"

"That's not what you were going to say, is it?" Rachel kept her silence. "Please. Tell me what you were going to say."

"I want to see your face first."

There followed a moment in which neither of them moved, neither of them spoke. At last Galilee made a soft sigh, as though of resignation, and took half a step toward the bed. The moonlight grazed his face, but so lightly she had only the most rudimentary sense of his features. His flesh was a burnished umber, and he had several days' growth of beard, which was even darker than his skin. His head was shaved clean. She could not see his eyes: they were set too deeply for the light to discover them. His mouth seemed to be beautiful, his cheekbones high and fine; perhaps there were some scars on his brow, she couldn't be sure.

As to the rest of him: he was dressed in a heavily stained white T-shirt and loosely belted jeans and sandals. His frame was, as she'd already guessed, impressive; a wide, solid chest, a slight swell of a belly, massive arms, massive hands.

But here was what she hadn't guessed: that he'd lingered in the shadows not to tease her but because he was unhappy being looked at. His discomfort was plain in the way he held himself; in the way he shuffled his feet, ready to retreat once she'd seen all she needed to see. She almost expected him to say *can I go now?* Instead he said: "Please finish your thought."

She'd forgotten what she was talking about; the sight of him, in all its contrary sweetness—his effortless authority and his desire to be invisible, his beauty, and his strange inelegance—had taken all thought of anything but his presence out of her head.

"You were telling me," he prompted her, "how what he has isn't as pretty as . . ."

Now she remembered. "As what *we* have down there," she said softly.

"Oh . . ." he replied. "I couldn't agree more." Then, so quietly she would not have caught the words had she not seen the shape his mouth made: "There's nothing more perfect."

He raised his head a fraction as he spoke, and the moonlight found his eyes. For all the depth of their setting, they were huge; filling the sockets with feeling; so much feeling she could not hold his gaze for more than a few seconds.

"Shall I go on with the story?" he asked her.

"Please," she said.

He kindly averted his stare, as though he knew its effect from experience, and didn't want to discomfort her. "I was telling you how the man had asked Jerusha how she felt about his cock." The word startled her. "And Jerusha had not answered."

*"But she wanted to go into the river to join him; she wanted to know what it would feel like to have his face close to hers, his body close to hers, his fingers on her breasts and belly, and down between her legs.*

"He seemed to know what she was thinking, because he said:

" 'Will you show me what's under your petticoats?'

"Jerusha pretended to be shocked. No, that's not fair. She was shocked, though not as much as she pretended. You have to remember this was a time when women wore clothes that smothered them from neck to ankle, and here was this man asking—as though it were just a casual question—to show him her most private place."

"What did she say?" Rachel asked.

"Nothing at first. But as I told you at the beginning, she was fearless, thanks to her father. He would have been appalled, of course, if he'd seen what his lessons and his kisses had created, but he wasn't there to tell her no. She had only her instincts to go by, and her instincts said: why not do it? why not show him? So she said:

" 'I'm going to lie down on the grass where it's comfortable. You can come and look if you like.'

" 'Don't go into the trees,' he said to her.

" 'Why not?' she asked him.

" 'Because there are poisonous things there,' he replied. 'Things that have fed on the flesh of dead men.'

"Jerusha didn't believe him. 'That's where I'm going,' she said. 'If you want to come, then come. If you're afraid, stay where you are.' And she got up to leave.

"The man called after her, telling her to wait. 'There's another reason,' he said.

" 'What's that?' she said.

" 'I can't go very far from the water. Every step I take is dangerous to me.'

"Jerusha just laughed at this. It was a silly excuse she thought. 'Then you're just weak,' she said.

" 'No. I—'

" 'Yes you are! You're weak! A man who can't climb out of a river without complaining? I never heard anything so ridiculous!'

"She didn't wait for him to reply. She could tell by the expression on his face that she stirred him up. She just turned around and traipsed off into the trees, wandering until she found a small grove where the grass looked soft and inviting. There she lay down on her back, with her feet towards the river, so that when the stranger found her the first thing he'd see was what lay between her legs."

Rachel had not missed the fact that her own position, lying there on the bed in front of Galilee, was not so unlike that of Jerusha.

"What are you thinking?" he said to her.

"I want to know what happens next."

"You could make it up for yourself if you'd prefer," he replied.

"*No,*" she said. "I want you to tell me."

"Your version might be better," he said to her. "Less sad."

"Is this going to end sadly?"

He turned his head toward the window, and for the first time the moonlight showed her his full face. She hadn't been mistaken before: his forehead *was* scarred, deeply scarred, from the middle of his left eyebrow to his hairline, and his mouth was indeed wide and full: a sensualist's mouth, if ever there was one. But it was the foundation upon which these details rode that were the true astonishment. She had never seen a face, in a photograph or a painting or the flesh, that so exquisitely wed the curves and gullies of its bones with the filigree of tissue and nerve covering them. It was as though his flesh, instead of masking his skull, expressed it. And his skull—which had been made long before the sorrow in his eyes—had known in the womb that sorrow was coming, and had shaped itself accordingly.

"Of course it's going to end sadly," he said. "It has to."

"Why?"

"Let me tell how it goes," he said, glancing down at her. "And if you know a better way to finish it, please God tell me."


So he began again, revisiting the scene that he'd been describing, to be sure she remembered where the story stood.

"*Jerusha was lying down on the grass, a little distance from the river. She was certain he'd come, and she wanted to be ready for him when he did, so she pulled off her shoes and her stockings, then lifted her hips off the ground to pull her underwear down. Then she drew up her petticoats and her skirt until they were over her knees. She didn't need to touch herself to be aroused. A warm breeze came along just as she opened her legs and moved like a breath against her sweet pink pussy; spears of grass sprang up and gently pricked the insides of her thighs. She started to moan; she couldn't help herself. If her life had depended on her silence at that moment then she would have perished, she was so utterly overwhelmed.*

"*Then she heard him . . .*"

"The river god," Rachel said.

"You've heard this before."

Rachel laughed. "That's what he is, isn't he?"

"A *god,* no. But something like that."

"Is he old?"

"Ancient."

"But not very clever."

"What makes you say that?"

"If he was smart he'd know to stay in the river. That's where he belongs."

Galilee sighed. "It's not always possible to stay where you belong. You know that."

She stared at him in silence for several seconds. "You know who I am," she said.

"You're my Jerusha," he replied, conferring the name upon her with the greatest gentility. "My child bride."

At this, Rachel reached up and took hold of the sheet that concealed her lower body. "Then I should let you see me," she said, and pulled the sheet off. Her knees were a little raised; the space between them was shadowy. But Galilee's eyes lingered there nonetheless, as though his gaze was piercing the darkness and seeing her clearly; piercing her too, maybe: insinuating himself between her labia to see what he would find.

The thought did not distress her; quite the reverse. She wanted him to look at her, and keep looking. She was his Jerusha, his child bride lying on a bed of soft grass, excited as she'd never been excited before. She was trembling with pleasure, and the prospect of pleasure, as aroused by him as he was by her; by his face, by his words, by his very presence. Most of all, by the sight of his watching her. She'd never experienced anything remotely like this before. She'd had sex with seven men in her life, including her fumblings with Neil Wilkens. She was no great sexual sophisticate, to be sure; but nor was she a complete novice. She'd had wild times. But nothing so *intense* as this; nothing so naked.

They hadn't even touched one another, for God's sake, and she was shaking. The bed between her legs was soaked. Her breaths were shallow and fast.

"You were telling me . . ." she said.

"*Jerusha . . .*"

". . . lying on her back, waiting for the river god . . ."

"*She looked up—*"

"Yes."

"*—it was strange to see him coming between the trees the way he did, with every step an effort, a terrible effort, that made his head sink lower and lower.*"

"Did she wish she'd never asked him?" Rachel whispered.

"No," Galilee replied. "*She was too excited for regrets. She wanted him to see her more than she'd wanted anything in her life.*"

"*And as he came toward her, there were times when he passed through a shaft of sunlight, and rainbows sprang from him, rising up into the trees.*

"*She was about to ask him if he liked what he saw when she heard the whirring of wings, and a beetle—about as big as a hummingbird, but dark and ugly—came circling over her. She remembered what the man in the river had said—*"

"Poisonous things," Rachel said. "Things that have been eating corpses."

"*This beetle was the worst of the worst. It ate only the bodies of people who'd died of disease. It carried every kind of contagion.*"

Rachel made a disgusted sound. "Can't you make it fly away?" she said.

"I told you before: you can finish it if you like."

She shook her head. "No," she said. "I want to hear it from you."

"Then the beetle has to circle . . . *and suddenly it dropped down onto her body.*"

"Where?"

"Shall I show you?" Galilee said, and without waiting for a reply he went to the bottom of the bed and reached between her legs. She wanted him to touch her labia, but instead his fingers nipped the inside of her thigh between finger and thumb. "*It bit her,*" he said. "*Hard.*"

She cried out.

"*She cried out, more with surprise than pain, and killed the beetle with one blow, squashing its body against her white skin.*"

He withdrew his hand. Rachel could feel the beetle's ooze running down her leg; she reached up as if to wipe it away, and then reached further, to catch hold of Galilee's fingers.

"Don't go yet," she said.

"I have not finished telling you what happened," he murmured, and eased his fingers from her grip. Instinctively she pulled the sheet back over her nakedness. The story was souring. If Galilee noticed what she'd done, he made no sign of it. He simply kept talking.

"*It was as if the beetle's bite had broken a trance,*" he said. "*Jerusha looked down at herself in horror. What was she doing lying here this way? She started to get up, tears stinging her eyes.*"

"*'Where are you going?' she heard somebody ask her, and looked round to see that the man from the river was standing just a few yards from her.*

"He looked wasted. His body, which had been shiny and strong when he was sitting in the water, was thinner now. His teeth were chattering. His eyes were rolling in their sockets. How could she ever have thought he was beautiful, she wondered?

"Then she turned her back on him and started to make her way home."

"Did he follow her?"

"No. He was too confused. He hadn't seen the beetle, you see. He just assumed she'd changed her mind; decided he was too strange for her after all. It wasn't the first time a woman had rejected him. He went back to the river, and sank from sight."

"What happened to Jerusha?"

"Terrible things."

"Almost as soon as she got back into her father's house she started to sicken. The beetle had put so much poison into her she was barely conscious by sunset. Of course her father sent for his doctors but none of them looked between her legs, because they didn't dare, not with their patron standing over them, telling them what a good, pure child she was. They did what they could to bring down her fever—cold compresses, leeches, the usual rigmarole—but none of it worked. Hour by hour through the night she grew hotter and sicker, until blisters started to appear on her neck and face and breasts as the poisons showed themselves."

"Finally, Jerusha's father lost patience with the doctors and sent them away. Then, once he was alone with her, lying on the bed, he started to talk to her, whispering close to her ear.

" 'Can you hear me, child?' he asked her. 'Please, my sweet Jerusha, if you can hear me, tell me what happened to you, so I can find somebody to heal you.'

"At first she said nothing. He wasn't even sure she'd even heard him. But he was persistent. He kept talking to her as daylight approached. And finally, just as dawn was breaking, she said one word . . ."

"River," Rachel whispered.

"Yes. She said river."

"Her father instantly sent for his majordomo, and told him to take all the maids and footmen and cooks and to comb the banks of the river until they discovered what had happened to his beloved Jerusha.

"The majordomo immediately roused the whole house, even to the smallest boy who dusted the ashes from the hearth, and they all went down through the woods to the river. Jerusha and her father were the only ones left in the great house, as the light crept through it room by room.

"He wept, and he waited, holding his daughter's hand all the while, rocking her in his arms sometimes, telling her how much he loved her, then—forgetting all his rational principles, going down on his knees and praying to God for a miracle. It was the first prayer he'd spoken since he was a little boy and he'd been made to pray over his mother's casket, and thought to himself: if you don't wake her up God, then I'm never going to believe in you ever again. Of course his mother had remained dead in her casket, and the boy had become a rationalist.

"But now all his faith in reason failed him, and he prayed with more passion than the Pope, begging God to bring a miracle.

"Down by the river, the servants were praying too, sobbing as they searched the bank.

"It was the smallest boy, the one who brushed away the ashes from the hearth, who saw the man in the river first. He started yelling for everyone to come and see, come and see.

"By the time the majordomo got to where the boy was standing a figure had risen out of the river, and the morning sun, striking him crossways, pierced him, and emerged again as beams of pure color. Nobody knew whether to be terrified or ecstatic, so they simply stood rooted to the spot while the creature emerged from the water. Some of the women averted their eyes when they saw his naked state, but most just stared, the tears they'd been shedding forgotten.

" 'I heard somebody praying for my Jerusha,' the riverman said. 'Is she sick?'

" 'To the death,' said the boy.

" 'Will you lead me to her?' the riverman asked the child.

"The boy simply took the creature's hand, and off they went between the trees."

"Nobody tried to stop them?" Rachel said.

"It crossed the majordomo's mind. But he wasn't a superstitious man. He shared his lord's belief that there was nothing in this world that was not finally natural, that one day science would explain. So he followed the boy and the riverman at a little distance, without interfering.

"Meanwhile, in the house, Jerusha was very close to death. The fever was so high it was as though she would catch fire in the bed and burn away to nothing.

"Then her father heard a sound like somebody mopping the stairs outside the bedroom; slapping a wet mop down on the marble, then dragging it up a step and slapping it down again. He let go of his daughter's hand for a moment and opened the door. There was a flickering light filling the hallway, like sunlight off water. And there on the stairs, mounting one torturous step after another, was the riverman. His watery body was diminished with every stair he climbed. The further from his home he strayed, the more of his life-essence he spent.

"Of course Jerusha's father demanded to know who he was, and what he was doing in the house. But the riverman had no strength to waste answering questions. It was the boy who spoke.

" 'He's come to help her,' he said.

"Jerusha's father didn't know what to make of this. The rational part of him said: don't be afraid, just because you've never seen anything like this before. While the part that had prayed to God for intercession now whispered: this is what heaven has sent. And that part was very much afraid, for if this was an angel—this silvery form, swaying in front of him—then what kind of God sent it? And what kind of salvation had it brought his daughter?

"He was still puzzling over this, and blocking the riverman's way to the door, when he heard Jerusha say:

'Please, Papa . . . let . . . him . . . in . . .'

"Amazed to hear his daughter speaking, he pushed open the door, and with a sudden rush, like a broken dam, the riverman pushed through it and went to stand at the end of Jerusha's bed.

"Her eyes were still closed, but she knew her saviour was there. She started to pull at the clothes she was wearing, which were horribly dirtied with pus and blood and all the rest. She tore them with such ferocity she was lying there naked in half a minute, every inch of her wounded body exposed to her father and to the riverman.

"Then she raised her arms, like a woman welcoming her love into her bed . . ." Galilee halted here; then began again more softly: ". . . which of course was what she was doing.

"The room was suddenly completely still. Jerusha's arms raised, the riverman waiting at the bottom of the bed, the father staring at him, still not certain what he'd done, letting this thing into his daughter's presence.

"Then, without a word, the riverman threw himself down onto the girl. And as he touched her he broke like a wave, splashing against her face and arms and breasts and belly and thighs. In that instant all trace of his human shape disappeared. Jerusha cried out in pain and shock, as the water seethed and hissed on her body like water thrown onto a fire. Steam rose off the bed, and a foul stench filled the room.

"But when it cleared . . ."

"She was healed?" Rachel said.

"She was healed."

"Completely?"

"*Every wound she'd had was gone. Every sore, every blister. She was healed from head to foot. Even the first bite, on her thigh, had been washed away.*"

"And the riverman?"

"Well of course he'd gone too," Galilee said lightly, as though that part of the story wasn't very important to him.

But it was to Rachel. "So he sacrificed himself," she said.

"I suppose he did," Galilee replied. Then, as though he were more comfortable addressing this question in the body of his story, he said:

"*Jerusha's father believed that the whole thing had been brought about by his own lack of faith; that God had visited these torments on his Jerusha in order to make him realize that he needed divine help sometimes.*"

"To make him pray, in other words."

"That's right."

"*And if it was indeed the work of God, then it was effective work, because Jerusha's father became a very religious man. He spent all his money building a cathedral right beside the river, where the creature had first been seen. It was a magnificent place. Vast. An eighth wonder. Or it would have been if it had ever been finished.*"

"Why wasn't it finished?"

"Well . . . this part of the story's very strange," Galilee warned.

"Stranger than the rest?"

"I think so. *You see it was the old man's idea that the water from the river should supply the font in the cathedral. This met with some opposition from the local bishops who insisted that the water could not be used to baptize babies because it wasn't holy water. To which Jerusha's father said . . . well, you can imagine what he said. These were already sacred waters, he told the bishops. They'd healed his Jerusha. They didn't need somebody mumbling Latin over them to make them holy. The bishops complained to Rome. The Pope said he'd look into it.*

"*Meanwhile, work went on laying the pipes from the river into the nave, where a beautiful font, carved in Florence, had been set.*

"*I should explain that this was very early spring. The snows in the mountains had been heavy that winter, and now that they were melting the river was high and white; more violent than it had been in living memory. People working on the cathedral could barely hear one another, even when they were shouting; the din was so great. All of which may explain what happened next . . .*"

"Which was what?"

"*Jerusha's father was taking a tour around the cathedral, and happened to be approaching the font when somebody—perhaps misunderstanding some instruction—let the water flow through the pipes for the first time.*

"*There was a noise like an earthquake. The cathedral shook, to its highest spire. The stone flags laid over the pipes—each one of them weighing a ton or a ton and a half—were thrown up into the air like playing cards as the waters washed down the pipe toward the font—*"

Rachel could see all this quite clearly: her head was filled with noise and chaos. She felt the walls shaking, heard people screaming and praying, watched them running in all directions, hoping to escape the cataclysm. She knew they wouldn't make it; even before Galilee had said so. They were all going to die.

"*—and when the water came up through the font it came with such force, such power, the font simply shattered. A thousand pieces of stone flew—*"

Oh this she hadn't seen—

"*—like bullets, some of them. Others big as cannonballs.*"

—she'd imagined the roof collapsing on everyone, the walls caving in. But it was the font that was going to do the most damage—

"*—splitting open skulls, piercing people's hearts, slicing off their arms, their legs. All in a matter of seconds.*

"*Jerusha's father was the closest to the font, so he was the luckiest, because he was the first to die. A huge slab of stone, decorated with a cherub, slammed into him and carried his body out into the river. He was never found.*"

"And the rest?"

"*It's as you imagine.*"

"They all died."

"*Every single one. Nobody working in the cathedral that day survived.*"

"Where was Jerusha?"

"*Back at her father's house, which had fallen into terrible disrepair since he'd begun to build the cathedral.*"

"So she survived."

"*She, and a few of the servants. Including, by the way, the boy who'd swept the ashes from the hearth.*

"*The one who'd let the riverman to her bed.*"

There he stopped, much to her astonishment.

"Is that it?" she said.

"That's it," he replied. "What more could there be?"

"I don't know . . . something more . . ." She pondered the question. "Some closure . . ."

Galilee shrugged. "I'm sorry," he said. "If there's more to tell I don't have it."

She felt faintly annoyed; as though he'd led her on, tempting her with clues as to what all this meant, but now that she was at the end—or at least as far as he claimed to be able to take her—it wasn't clear at all.

"It's a simple little story," he said.

"But it hasn't got a proper ending."

"It's as I said before: you could make it up for yourself."

"I said I wanted you to tell me."

"I've told all I know," Galilee replied. He glanced toward the window. "I think it's about time I was going."

"Where?"

"Just back to my boat. It's called *The Samarkand*. It's anchored off-shore."

She didn't ask him why he had to go, in part because of her irritation at the way he'd finished his story, in part because she didn't want him to think her needy. Still she couldn't help asking:

"Will you be coming back?"

"That depends on you," he said. "If you want me to come back, I will."

This was said so simply, so sweetly, that her irritation evaporated.

"Of course I want you to come back," she said.

"Then I will," he replied, and then he was gone. She listened for him moving away through the house, but she heard nothing—not a breath, not a footfall. She slipped out of bed and went to the window. Clouds had come in to cover the moon and stars; there was very little light on the lawn. But her eyes found him nevertheless, moving quickly down toward the beach. She watched him until he disappeared. Then she went back to her bed, and lay awake in the darkness for an hour, listening to the double rhythm of her heart and the waves, wondering idly if she'd lost her mind.

# III

### i

She woke at first light and headed straight down to the beach. She'd hoped to find *The Samarkand* moored close to the shore—perhaps even see Galilee on deck—but the bay was deserted. She scoured the horizon, looking for a sail, but there was no boat in sight. Where the hell had he gone? Just a few hours before he'd asked if she wanted him to come back, and she'd told him unequivocally that she did. Had that just been a sop to her feelings; a way to extricate himself from her presence without having to say goodbye? If so, then he was a coward.

She turned her back on the water and started up the sand toward the house. A few yards from the path she came upon the remains of the fire Galilee had made the night before: a black circle of burned timber and ash, the latter being slowly spread across the beach by the breeze. She went down on her haunches beside the pit, still quietly cursing the fire-maker for his inconstancy. A bittersweet smell rose up from the embers: the acrid smell of dead fire mingled with a hint of the fragrance she'd carried into the house with her the night before: the aroma which had set her head spinning and put such strange pictures behind her eyes.

Was it possible, she wondered, that her first instincts had been correct and Galilee had been some kind of hallucination, a waking dream induced by an inhalation of smoke?

She got to her feet, and looked out toward the empty bay. Her memory of his presence was perfect: the way he'd appeared, the sound of his voice, the intricacies of the story he'd told her: Jerusha at the water, the river god in all his glory, the beetle carrying contagion. If there was any certain proof that he'd been there in the flesh, it was the story. She hadn't invented it, she hadn't told it to herself; somebody had been there to put those images and ideas in her head.

Galilee was no figment of her imagination. He was just another unreliable male.

She brewed herself a very strong pot of coffee, which she drank sickly-sweet, showered, ate a miserable breakfast, made some more coffee, and then called Margie.

"Is this a good time to talk?" she asked.

"I've got about ten minutes," Margie said. "Then I'm out of the house. I've got to be on time today."

Rachel was surprised at this; punctuality wasn't Margie's strong suit. "What's the occasion?"

"You mean: *who's* the occasion?" Margie said.

"Oh . . . the Fuck Fuck Man."

"Danny," Margie reminded her. "He's really good for me, honey. I mean *really* good. He told me last week he wouldn't make love with me if I was drunk, so the last couple of nights I didn't drink. We fucked instead. Oh Lord, we fucked! Then I didn't *want* to drink. I just wanted to go to sleep in his arms. Oh God, listen to me."

"It sounds wonderful, Margie."

"It is. So wonderful it's scary. Anyway . . . I've got to dash off, so just give me the highlights. How is it all?"

"It's as you said: it's magical." She wanted to start talking to Margie about her visitor, but with so little time to do it in, she was afraid she'd end up trivializing the event, so she said nothing. Instead she said: "When were you last here?"

"Oh . . . sixteen or seventeen years ago. I was very happy there for a little while. I was very *consoled.*" The strangeness of the word was not lost on Rachel. "It was one of those times when I saw my life clearly for once. Do you know what I mean?"

"Not really . . ."

"Well that's what happened to me. I saw my life. And instead of doing something about what I saw, I just took the path of less resistance. Oh Lord, honey, I really have to go. I don't want to leave my lover-boy waiting."

"I understand."

"Let's talk again tomorrow."

"Before you go—"

"Yes?"

"—did anything really strange happen to you while you were here?" There was a long silence.

At last Margie said: "When I've got more time we have to talk, honey. Yes, of course strange stuff happened."

"And what did you do?"

"I told you. I took the path of least resistance. And I've always regretted it. Believe me, there'll never be another time in your life like this, hon. It comes round once, and if you're ready, then you don't look back, you don't worry about what other people are going to think, you don't even wonder what the consequences are going to be. You just go." Her voice dropped to a near-whisper. "We'll all be jealous as hell, of course. We'll all curse you for doing what we didn't do, maybe what we couldn't do. But deep down we'll be happy for you."

"Who's *we?*" Rachel said.

"The Geary women, honey," Margie replied. "All of us sad, sorry and utterly fucked-up Geary women."

## ii

After lunch, Rachel went walking, not along the beach this time, but inland. There'd been a light breeze in the morning, but it had dropped away completely at noon, and the air now felt hot and stale. The atmosphere suited Rachel's mood. She felt stagnated; unable to move very far from the house in case she missed Galilee's return, and unable to think of very much other than him; him or his story.

There were some sizable bugs out today. Whenever one of them rose up from the shrubbery she thought of the beetle on Jerusha's thigh; and of how Galilee had imitated its bite. That had been his only touch, hadn't it? A cruel nip at her skin. So much for tenderness. But then as he'd retreated from her she'd caught hold of his hand, and felt the hard skin of his wide fingers, and the heat of his flesh.

She would have that again, and next time they wouldn't just be holding hands. She'd make him put his mouth to the place he'd pinched; make him kiss her hurt better. Kiss her and keep kissing, lower and deeper, and deeper, until he'd made amends. He'd do it too. She knew he'd do it. The story had been a game; a way of deliciously postponing the inevitable moment when they made love.

She sat down at the side of the road, fanning herself with a plate-sized leaf she'd plucked, and thought about him, standing there in her doorway. The way his T-shirt had clung to his body; the way his eyes had glinted when he looked at her; the tentative smile that had come into his face now and then. These few details, and his name, were all she really knew about him. Why then, she asked herself, did she feel such a sense of loneliness, thinking she might never see him again? If she was so desperate for the physical comfort of a man then she could find it readily enough; either here on the island or back in New York. It wasn't about the presence of another body, it was about him, about Galilee. But that was nonsensical. Yes, he was handsome, but she'd met more beautiful men. And she knew too little about him to be enchanted by his spirit. So why was she sitting here moping over him like a lovelorn fifteen-year-old?

She cast her makeshift fan aside, and got to her feet. Whatever the reasons for her feelings, she had them, and they weren't about to evaporate just because she couldn't get to their root. She wanted Galilee; it was as simple as that. And the possibility that he'd sailed away without telling her where she could find him made her sick with sorrow.


Niolopua was sitting on the front step when she got back to the house, drinking a can of beer. There was a ladder leaning against the eaves of the house, and a great litter of pruned vines on the lawn. He'd been hard at work, for a while at least. Now he was simply sitting in the sun, drinking his beer. He made no attempt to conceal what he was doing when Rachel appeared. He didn't even stand. He simply squinted up at her, his face pouring sweat, and said:

"There you are . . ."

"Were you looking for me?"

He shook his head. "I was just surprised you'd gone, that's all."

He set his beer can down at his side. It was not the first he'd had, she saw. There were three more empty cans sitting there. No wonder the shyness he'd evidenced at their first meeting had disappeared. "You look like you didn't sleep very well," he said.

"As it happens, I didn't."

He reached into his bag and pulled out another beer. "Want one?" he said.

"No. Thank you."

"I don't always drink on duty," he said, "but today's a special occasion."

"Oh?" Rachel said. "What's that?"

"Guess."

She could no longer keep up a pretense of bonhomie: his tone was irritating her. "Look, I think you should just pack up your tools and go home," she said.

"Oh do you now?" he said, popping the beer can. "And what if I said to you: this *is* home."

"I don't know what you're talking about," she replied, and went to open the front door.

"My mother worked here all her life. I've been coming here since I was a baby."

"I see."

"I know this house better than you'll ever know it." He turned away from her, now that he was certain he had her attention. "I love this house. You come, one after the other, and you act like the place belongs to you—"

"It doesn't belong to me. It belongs to the Geary family."

"No, it doesn't," Niolopua said, "it belongs to the Geary *women*. There's never been any men come here. Just women." A look of contempt crossed his face. "Why can't you have your husbands service you? Why'd you have to come here and . . ." the contempt deepened ". . . and . . . defile everything?"

"What the hell are you talking about?" Rachel said, turning back from the door and going to stand right beside him. Niolopua didn't avert his gaze. He stared right up at her with something very close to hatred on his face.

"You don't think about what you do to him, do you?"

"Him?"

"It's not like there's ever any love."

"Him."

"Yes. Him."

"Galilee?"

"Yes! Of course!" Niolopua said, as though she was an imbecile for asking the question. "Who the hell else would it be?" There were tears in his eyes now: of rage, of frustration. "My mother was the only one who ever loved him. The *only* one!" He looked away from Rachel, and tears dropped from his eyes onto the wooden steps. "He built this house for her."

"Galilee built this house?" Niolopua nodded, still not looking up. "When?"

"I don't know exactly. A long time ago. It was the first house to be built on this shore."

"That can't be right," Rachel said. "He's not that old. I mean he's what, forty? If that."

"You don't know what he is," Niolopua said. There was a measure of pity in the remark, as though Rachel's ignorance was more profound than a lack of information.

"So tell me," she said. "Help me understand."

Niolopua took a mouthful of beer. Stared at the ground. Said nothing.

"Please," she said softly.

"All you want to do is use him," came the reply.

"You've got me wrong," she said. He didn't respond to this. At last she said: "I'm not like all the rest, Niolopua. I'm not a Geary. Well . . . no that's not true . . . I married a man I thought I loved and his name happened to be Geary. I didn't realize what that meant."

"Well, my father hates you all. In his heart, he *hates* you."

"Your father being?" She paused, realizing the answer. "Oh Lord. You're Galilee's son."

"Yes. I'm his son."

Rachel put her hands over her face and sighed into her palms. There was so much here she didn't comprehend: secrets and anger and sorrow. The only thing she grasped with any certainty was this: that even here, even in paradise, the Gearys had done their spoiling. No wonder Galilee hated them. She hated them too. At that moment she wished every one of them dead. A little part of her even wished herself dead. There seemed to be no other way out of the trap she'd married into.

"Is he coming back?" she said after a time.

"Oh yes," Niolopua replied, his voice monotonal. "He knows his responsibilities."

"To whom?"

"To you. You're a Geary woman, whether you like it or not. That's why he's with you. He wouldn't come otherwise." He glanced up at her. "You've got nothing he needs."

He was being cruel for the satisfaction of it, she knew, but the words stung her nevertheless.

"I don't need to listen to this," she said, and leaving him on the steps to drink his warm beer, she went back into the house.

# IV

## i

It's no accident that events of great significance, when they happen, do so in clusters; it's the nature of things. Having been a gambling man in my youth, I know from experience how this principle works, for instance, in a casino. The roulette table suddenly becomes "hot"; there's win after win after win. And if you happen to be at the right table at the right time then the odds are suddenly tipped spectacularly in your favor. (The trick, of course, is to sense the moment when the table cools, and not to keep betting beyond that point, or you'll lose your shirt.) Observers of natural phenomena large and small, astronomers or entomologists, will tell you the same thing. For long periods—millions of years in the life of a star, minutes in the life of a butterfly—nothing of moment seems to happen. And then, suddenly, a plethora of events: convulsions, transformations, cataclysms.

Of course it's the apparently tranquil periods that deceive us. Though our instruments or our senses or our wits may not be able to see the processes that are leading toward these clusters of events, they're happening. The star, the wheel, the butterfly—all are in a subtle state of unrest, waiting for the moment when some invisible mechanism signals that the time has come. Then the star explodes; the wheel makes poor men rich; the butterfly mates and dies.

If we think of the Geary family as a single entity, then the first of the events that would transform it had already taken place: Rachel and Galilee had met. Though much of what happened in the next few days had, at least superficially, nothing to do with that meeting, it seems from a little distance that everything else was somehow precipitated by their liaison.

I don't entirely discount the possibility. Any feeling as profound (and as profoundly irrational) as the passion which moved these two has consequences: vibrations, which may begin processes utterly remote from it.

In this sense love is of different order to any other phenomenon, for it may be both an event and a sign of that invisible mechanism I spoke of before; perhaps the finest sign, the most certain. In its throes we need neither luck nor science. We are the wheel, and the man who profits by it. We are the star, and the darkness it pierces. We are the butterfly, brief and beautiful.

All of this was by way of preparing you for how things proceeded with the Gearys in a short space of time following Galilee's encounter with Rachel: how all at once a system that had survived and prospered for a hundred and forty years came apart at the seams in forty-eight hours.

## ii

For those who knew Cadmus Geary well the most certain sign of his sudden deterioration was sartorial. Even though he'd had bad, and sometimes extended, periods of ill health from his early eighties on, he had continued to pride himself on the way he looked. This had been a preoccupation since childhood. There's a photograph taken of him when he was barely four years old in which he presents himself like a little dandy, clearly proud of his perfectly pressed shirt and his immaculately polished shoes. He'd more than once been mistaken for a homosexual, which never troubled him. He'd laid more women that way.

Today, however, he refused his freshly laundered clothes; he wanted to stay in his pajamas, he declared. When his nurse, Celeste, gently pointed out that he'd soiled them in the night he replied that it was his shit and he liked its company. Then he demanded to be taken downstairs and put in front of the television. The nurse complied, and called in the doctor. Cadmus would have nothing to do with being examined however. He told Waxman to go away and leave him alone. Noncompliance, he warned, would result in a withdrawal of all funds made by the Geary family or any of its trusts to medical research, along with Waxman's retirement bonus.

"He still sounds like the Cadmus we all know and love," the doctor told Loretta. "Do you want me to try again?"

Loretta told him not to bother. If there was some worsening of her husband's condition she'd call. Much relieved the good doctor duly did as Cadmus had demanded and went away, leaving the old man to sit on the sofa and watch baseball. After an hour or so Loretta brought some food in: soup, half a toasted bagel and some cream cheese. He told her to set it down on the table, and he'd get to it later. Right now, he said, he wanted to watch the game.

"Are you feeling all right?" she asked him.

He didn't take his eyes off the screen, though his features showed not a flicker of interest in what was going on. "Never better," he said.

She set the tray down on the table. "Could I get you something different . . . maybe some fruit?"

"I've already got the shits, thank you," he said politely.

"Some chocolate pudding?"

"I'm not a child, Loretta," he said. "Though I realize it's a very long time since I proved it to you. I'm sure you're getting a good fucking from somebody—"

"*Cadmus—*"

"—I just hope he appreciates how much of my money you've spent getting your tits tucked and your ass tucked and that belly of yours all stapled up—"

"Stop that!"

"Did you get a pussy tuck while you were at it?" he remarked, his tone not once wavering from the lightly conversational. "You must be sloppy down there after all these years."

"Don't be disgusting," Loretta said.

"Do I take that as a yes?"

"If you don't stop this—"

"What will you do?" he said, a tiny smile coming onto his parchment lips. "Throw me over your lap and spank me? Remember how I used to do that to you, love? Remember that lacquered hairbrush you used to present me with when you were in need of a little discipline?" Loretta was having no more of this. She walked smartly to the door, her heels clicking on the hardwood floor. "Don't you ever wonder how much of it I told people about?" he said.

She stopped a yard short of the door. "You didn't," she said.

"Don't be ridiculous," he said. "Of course I told people. Just a select little group. Cecil of course. Some members of your family."

"Oh you are a *filthy, disgusting* old man—"

"That's it, sweet pea. Let it out. It may be your last chance."

"You never had any shame—"

"If I had I daresay I wouldn't have married you."

"What's that supposed to mean?"

"Nobody else would have had you. Not with your reputation. I thought when I first got you naked: there isn't anywhere on this body that's still virgin territory. Every inch of it's been licked and pinched and screwed and smacked. I found that quite arousing at the time. And when people said, why *her*, she's a whore, she's slept with half of Washington, I used to tell them, I can still show her a few tricks she hasn't seen." He paused for a moment. Loretta was quietly weeping. "What the fuck are you crying for?" Cadmus said. "When I'm dead you can tell everyone what a brute I was. You can write a book about what a dirty-minded, decadent old goat I was. I don't care. I won't be listening. I'll be too busy paying for my sins." At last, having not taken his eyes off the screen throughout this exchange, he slowly, painfully, turned his head to look back at her. "There's a special hell for people who die as rich as us," he said. "So say a few prayers for me, will you?" She looked at him blankly. "What are you thinking?"

"I was wondering . . . if you ever loved me."

"Oh sweet pea," he said. "Isn't it a little late to be sentimental?"

She left without another word. There was no purpose arguing with him; clearly his medication was disordering his thoughts. She'd have to talk to Waxman; perhaps the doses were too strong. She went upstairs and put on a dress she'd had made for her the previous season, but had then never been in the mood to wear. It was white, and rather plain, and when she'd first tried it on she'd thought it made her look pallid. But now, seeing herself in the mirror, she approved of its severity; and of the somewhat frigid quality it conferred.

He'd called her whore, and that wasn't just. She'd had her high times, to be sure: what he'd said about there not being a piece of her body untouched was true. But so what? She'd made the best of what God had given her; taken her pleasures where, when and with whom she could. There was nothing shameful in that. Indeed, Cadmus had been perversely proud of her wild reputation at the beginning. He'd liked nothing better than to know that their courtship was the subject of gossip and tittle-tattle. And yes, she'd succumbed to the demands of vanity several times, and gone under the knife. But again: so what? She looked ten years her own junior; fifteen in a flattering light. But she had no wish to use her beauty the way Cadmus had implied. Once she'd taken his name, she'd had one lover only besides Cadmus, and even that had barely lasted a week. It would have been nice to think she'd broken his heart, but she harbored no such illusions. He'd been immune to love, that other one. He'd sailed away when he had finished with her, and nearly broken her heart.

So out she went, dressed in white, leaving Cadmus sitting on the sofa in front of his beloved baseball. Of course, he saw none of it. He hadn't actually watched a game in months. There was something about sitting there that helped him remove his thoughts from his present condition—from its pain and humiliation—and talk himself into the past. He had work to do there; things to put in order before death took him and he found himself removed into that special hell made for the rich.

Catholic atheist that he was, he half-believed in that hell; half believed he would suffer—if not eternally at least for a long, long time—in a barren spot where every comfort wealth and power could bestow was denied him. He'd never really cared about luxury so he wouldn't miss the silk pajamas and the Italian shoes and the thousand-bucks-a-bottle champagne. He'd miss control. He'd miss knowing he could get any politician, to the very highest, on the phone in five minutes, whatever their affiliations. He'd miss knowing every word he uttered was scrutinized for a clue to his desires. He'd miss being idolized. He'd miss being hated. He'd miss having a purpose. That was the real hell waiting for him: the wasteland where his will meant nothing, because he had nothing to work it upon.

Yesterday he'd cried quietly to himself at the prospect. Today, he had no tears left. His head was just a cesspool, filled with dirty little words that he had no use for now that his bitch-wife had gone. Gone to get herself fucked, no doubt; gone to spread her cunt for some stinking donkey-dick—

He was saying the words aloud, he vaguely realized; talking filth to himself while he sat in his own caked shit. And in his head there were pictures to accompany the monologue; too blurred for him to know if they were excremental or erotic.

Somewhere in the midst of all this confusion there were other concerns he knew he should address. Business unfinished, good-byes unsaid. But he couldn't pin his thoughts down long enough to name them; the dirt kept distracting him.

At one point the nurse came in and asked him how he was doing. It took the greatest effort of will not to let out a flood of filth, but he used the last remnants of his self-control to order her out of the room. She told him she'd be back in ten minutes with his noon medication, and then left.

As he listened to her footsteps receding across the hall he heard a whirring sound in his head. It seemed to be coming from the back of his skull; an irritating little din that rose in volume by degrees. He tried to shake it out—like a dog with a flea in its ear—but it wouldn't go. It simply got louder, and more shrill. He grabbed hold of the arm of the sofa so as to pull himself to his feet. He needed help. A head awash with dirty words was one thing, but this was too vile to be endured. He got to his feet, but his legs weren't strong enough to support him. His hand slipped out from under him and he fell sideways. He cried out as he went down, but he heard no sound. The whine had become so loud it overwhelmed everything else: the crack of his brittle bones as he hit the floor, the din of the table lamp as it came smashing down, caught by his outflung hand.

For a few moments, when he hit the ground, he lost consciousness, and in a kinder world than this he might never have found it again. But fate hadn't finished with him yet. After a period of blissful darkness his eyes flickered open again. He was lying on his side where he'd fallen, the whine now so loud he felt certain it would shake his skull apart.

No; not even that excruciating luxury was granted him. He lay there alive, and deafened, until somebody came and found him.

His thoughts, if such they could be called, were chaotic. There were still fragments of filth in the stew, but they were no longer complete words. They were just syllables, thrown against the wall of his skull by the relentless whine.

When Celeste came back in, she was a model of proficiency. She cleared her patient's throat of some vestiges of vomit, ascertained that he was breathing properly, and then called for an ambulance. That done, she went back out into the hallway, alerted a member of the household staff to the crisis, and told them to find Loretta, and have her go to Mount Sinai where Cadmus would be taken. When she returned to Cadmus she found that he'd opened his eyes, just a fraction, and that his head had turned away from the door.

"Can you hear me, Mr. Geary?" she asked him gently.

He made no reply, but his eyes opened a little wider. He was trying to focus, she saw, the object of his attempted scrutiny the painting that was hung on the far wall of the room. The nurse knew nothing about art whatsoever, but this mammoth picture had slowly exercised a fascination over her, so much so that she'd asked the old man about it. He'd told her it was painted by an artist called Albert Bierstadt and that it represented his conception of a limitless American wilderness. Looking at it, he'd said, was supposed to be like taking a journey: your eye traveled from one part of the panorama to the next, always finding something new. He'd even shown her how to look at it through a rolled-up sheet of paper, as if viewing the scene through a telescope. On the left was a waterfall feeding a pool where buffalo drank; behind them, stretching across the canvas, was a rolling plain, with patches of bright sunlight and shadow, and beyond the grasslands a range of snow-capped mountains, the grandest of which had its heights wreathed in creamy cloud, except for its topmost crag, which was set against a pocket of deep blue sky. The only human presence in the picture was a solitary pioneer on a dappled horse, who was perched on a ridge to the right of the scene, studying the terrain before him.

"That man's a Geary," Cadmus had once told the nurse. She hadn't known whether the old man was joking or not, and she hadn't wanted to risk his ire by asking. But now, watching his face as he struggled to focus on the painting, she somehow knew that the pioneer was what Cadmus' eyes were straining to see. Not the buffalo, not the mountains, but the man who was surveying all of this, in readiness for conquest. At last, he gave up: the effort was too much for him. He made a tiny, frustrated sigh, and his top lip curled a little, as if in contempt at his own incapacity. "It's all right . . ." she said to him, smoothing a stray strand of silver-white hair back from his brow. "I can hear them coming."

This was no lie. She could indeed hear the medics outside in the hallway. A moment later, and they were tending to him, lifting Cadmus up off the floor and onto the stretcher, covering him with blankets, their gentle reassurances echoing her own.

At the last, as they picked the stretcher up to carry him out, his gaze went back in the direction of the canvas. She hoped his exhausted eyes had caught a glimpse this time, though she doubted it. The chances of his ever coming back to study the painted pioneer again were, she knew, remote.

# V

For Rachel the house was a different place now that she knew that Galilee had built it. What a labor it must have been for a man on his own; digging and laying the foundations, raising the walls, fashioning windows and doors, roofing it, tiling it, painting it. No doubt his sweat was in its timbers, and his curses, and a kind of genius, to make a house that felt so comforting. It was no wonder Niolopua's mother had wanted to possess it. If she couldn't have its builder, then it was the next best thing.

Following the conversation on the veranda Rachel no longer doubted that Galilee would come back, but as the afternoon went on, and she turned over all she knew about the man her mood grew steadily darker. Perhaps she was deceiving herself, thinking that something rare and tender had passed between them the previous night; perhaps when he returned he'd be doing so out of some bizarre obligation. After all she was just another Geary wife as far as he was concerned; another bored bitch getting her little fix of paradise. He didn't know how much of a captive she felt: how could he? And how could he be blamed if he thought her despicable, taking up residence in his dream house, lying in the cool like some planter's wife while Niolopua trimmed the grass?

And then, as if that weren't enough, the things she'd done last night! She grew sick with embarrassment thinking about it. The way she'd displayed herself to him; what the hell had she been thinking? If she'd seen any other woman behave that way she'd have called them a slut; and she'd have had reason. She should have protested the instant she'd realized where his story was going. She should have said: I can't listen to this, and firmly told him to leave. Then maybe he would have come back because he wanted to; instead of—

"Oh my Lord . . ." she said softly.

There he was, on the beach.

There he was, and her heart was suddenly beating so loudly she could hear it in her head, and her hands were clammy and her stomach was churning. There he was, and it was all she could do not to just go to him; tell him she wasn't a Geary, not in her heart; she wasn't even a wife, not really; it had all been a stupid mistake, and would he please forgive her, would he please pretend he'd never laid eyes on her before, so that they could start again as though they'd just met, walking on the beach?

She did none of this, of course. She simply watched him as he made his way toward the house. He saw her now; waved at her, and smiled. She went to the French window, slid it open and stepped out onto the veranda. He was halfway up the lawn, still smiling. His pants were soaked to the knee, the rest of him wet with spray, his grubby T-shirt clinging to his belly and chest. He extended his hand to her.

"Will you come with me?" he said.

"Where are we going?"

"I want to show you something."

"Let me get my shoes."

"You won't need shoes. We're just going along the beach."

She closed the screen door to keep out the mosquitoes and went down onto the lawn to join him. He took her hand, the gesture so casual it was as though this was a daily ritual for them, and he'd come to the lawn a hundred times, and called to her, and smiled at her, and taken her hand in his.

"I want to show you my boat," he explained as they took the short path to the sand. "It's moored in the next bay."

"Wonderful," she said. "Oh . . . by the way . . . I really think I should apologize for last night. I wasn't . . . behaving . . . the way I normally behave."

"No?" he said.

She couldn't tell whether he was being sarcastic or not. All she could see was the smile on his face, and it seemed perfectly genuine.

"Well I had a wonderful time last night," he said, "so if you want to behave that way again, go for it." She offered an awkward grin. "Do you want to walk in the water?" he said, moving on from her apology as though the whole subject was over and done with. "It's not cold."

"I don't mind cold water," she said. "We have hard winters where I come from."

"Which is where?"

"Dansky, Ohio."

"Dansky, Ohio," he said, turning the words over on his tongue as he spoke them, as though savoring the syllables. "I went to Ohio once. This is before I took to the sea. A place called Bellefontaine. I wasn't there long."

"What do you mean when you say you 'took to the sea?' "

"Just that. I gave up the land. And the people on it. Actually it was the people I gave up on, not the land."

"You don't like people?"

"A few," he said, throwing her a sideways glance. "But not many."

"You don't like the Gearys, for instance."

The smile that had been at play on his face dropped away. "Who told you that?"

"Niolopua."

"Huh. Well he should keep his mouth shut."

"Don't blame him. He was upset. And from what he was telling me it sounds like the family gave everybody a raw deal."

Galilee shook his head. "I'm not complaining," he said. "This is a hard world to get by in. It makes people cruel sometimes. There's a lot worse than the Gearys. Anyway . . . you're a Geary." The smile crept back. "And you're not so bad."

"I'm getting a divorce," she said.

"Oh? Don't you love him then?"

"No."

"Did you ever?"

"I don't know. It's hard to be sure of what you feel when you meet somebody like Mitchell. Especially when you're just a Midwestern girl, and you're lost and you're not sure what you want. And there he is, telling you not to worry about that anymore. He'll take care of everything."

"But he didn't?" Galilee said.

She thought about this for a moment. "He did his best," she admitted. "But as time went by . . ."

"The things you wanted changed," Galilee said.

"That's right."

"And eventually, the things you end up wanting are the things they can't give you." He wasn't talking about her any longer, she realized. He was talking about himself; of his own relationship with the Gearys, the nature of which she did not yet comprehend.

"You're doing the right thing," he said. "Leaving before you start to hate yourself."

Again he was talking autobiographically, she knew, and she took comfort from the fact. He seemed to see some parallel between their lives. The fears that had threatened her that afternoon were toothless. If he understood her situation as he seemed to—if he saw some sense in which his pain and hers overlapped—then they had some common ground upon which to build.

Of course now she wanted to know more, but having made the remark about hating yourself he fell silent, and she couldn't think of a way to raise the subject again without seeming pushy. No matter, she thought. Why waste time talking about the Gearys, when there was so much to enjoy: the sky turning pink as the sun slid away, the sea calmer than she'd seen it, the motion of the water around her legs, the heat of Galilee's palm against hers.

Apparently much the same thoughts were passing through her companion's head.

"Sometimes I talk myself into such foul moods," he said, "and then I think: what the hell do I have to complain about?" He looked up at the reef of coral clouds that was accruing high, high above them. "So what if I don't understand the world?" he went on. "I'm a free man. At least most of the time. I go where I want when I want. And wherever I go . . ." his gaze went from the clouds to Rachel ". . . I see beautiful things." He leaned toward her and kissed her lightly. "Things to be grateful for." They stopped walking now. "Things that I can't quite believe I'm see-ing." Again he put his lips against hers, but this time there was no chaste-ness. This time they wrapped their arms around one another and kissed deeply, like the lovers they'd been bound to be from the beginning.

It passed through Rachel's head that she wasn't living this but dreaming it: that every detail of this moment was in such a perfect place there was no improving it. Sky, sea, clouds, lips. His eyes, meeting hers. His hands on her back, at her neck, in her hair.

"I'm sorry . . ." he murmured to her.

"For what?"

"For not coming to find you," he said. "I should have come to find you."

"I don't understand."

"I was looking away. I was staring at the sea when I should have been watching for you. Then you wouldn't have married him."

"If I hadn't married him we'd never have met."

"Oh yes we would," he said. "If I'd not been watching the sea, I would have known you were out there. And I would have come looking for you."

They walked on after a time, but now they walked with their arms around one another. He took her to the end of the beach, then led the way over the spit of rocks that marked the divide between the two bays. On the other side was a stretch of sand perhaps half the length of the beach behind them, in the middle of which was a small, and plainly very antiquated, wooden jetty, its timbers weathered to a pale gray, its legs shaggy with vivid green weed. There was only one vessel moored there: *The Samarkand.* Its sails were furled, and it rode gently on the incoming tide, the very picture of tranquillity.

"Did you build it?" she asked him.

"Not from scratch. I bought her in Mauritius, stripped her down to the bare essentials and fashioned her the way I wanted her. It took two years, because I was working on my own."

"Like the house."

"Yeah, well, I prefer it that way. I'm not very comfortable with other people. I used to be . . ."

"But?"

"I got tired of pretending."

"Pretending what?"

"That I liked them," he said. "That I enjoyed talking about . . ." he shrugged ". . . whatever people talk about."

"Themselves," Rachel said.

"Is that what people talk about?" he said quizzically. It was as though he'd been out of human company so long he'd forgotten. "I mustn't have been paying attention." Rachel laughed at this. "No seriously," he said, "I wouldn't have minded if they'd really want to talk about what was going on in their souls. I'd have welcomed that. But that's not what you hear. You hear about pretty stuff. How fat their wives are getting and how stupid their husbands are and why they hate their children. Who could bear that for very long? I'd prefer to hear nothing at all."

"Or tell a story?"

"Oh yes," he said, luxuriating in the thought, "that's even better. But it can't be just any story. It has to be something true."

"What about the story you told me last night?"

"That was true," he protested. "I swear, I never told a truer story in all my life." She looked at him quizzically. "You'll see," he said, "if it isn't true yet, it will be."

"Anybody could say that," she replied.

"Yes, but anybody didn't. I did. And I wouldn't waste my time with things that weren't true." He put his hand to her face. "You have to tell me a story sometime soon. And it has to be just as true."

"I don't know any stories like that."

"Like what?"

"You know," she said. "Stories that could stir you up the way that story stirred me up."

"Oh it stirred you up did it?"

"You know it did."

"You see. Then it must have been true."

She had no answer to this. Not because it made no sense but because after some fashion that she couldn't articulate, it did. Obviously his definition of *true* wasn't the standard definition, but there was a kind of cockeyed logic to it nevertheless.

"Shall we go?" he said, "I think the boat's getting lonely."

# VI

## i

As they walked along the creaking jetty Rachel asked him why he had dubbed his boat *The Samarkand*. Galilee explained that Samarkand was the name of a city.

"I've never heard of it," she told him.

"There's no reason why you should. It's a long way from Ohio."

"Did you live there?"

"No. I just passed through. I've done a lot of passing through in my life."

"You've traveled a lot?"

"More than I'd like."

"Why don't you just find a place you like and settle down?"

"That's a long story. I suppose the simple answer is that I've never really felt I belonged anywhere. Except out there." He glanced seaward. "And even there . . ."

For the first time since they'd begun this conversation, she sensed his attention wandering, as though this talk of things far off was making him yearn for them. Perhaps not for the specific of Samarkand; simply for something remote from the here and now. She touched his arm.

"Come back to me," she said.

"Sorry," he replied. "I'm here."

They'd reached the end of the jetty. The boat was before them, rocking gently in the arms of the tide.

"Are we going aboard then?" she asked him.

"We surely are."

He stepped aside, and she climbed the narrow plank laid between the jetty and the deck. He followed her. "Welcome," he said with no little pride. "To my *Samarkand*."

The tour of the boat didn't take long; it was in most regards an unremarkable vessel. There were a few details of its crafting he pointed out to her as having been difficult to fashion or pretty in the result, but it wasn't until they got below deck that she really saw his handiwork. The walls of the narrow cabin were inlaid with wood; the colors, the grain and even the knotholes in the timber so chosen and arranged that they almost suggested images.

"Is it my imagination," Rachel said, "or am I seeing things in the walls?"

"Anything in particular?"

"Well . . . over there I can see a kind of landscape, with some ruins, and maybe some trees. And there's something that could be a tree, but might be a person . . ."

"I think it's a person."

"So you put it there?"

"No. I did all of this work thinking I was just making patterns. It wasn't until I was a week into my next voyage I started to see things."

"It's like looking at inkblots—" Rachel said.

"—or clouds—"

"—or clouds. The more you look the more you see."

"It's useful on long voyages," Galilee said, "when I'm sick of looking at the waves and the fish I come down here, smoke a little, get a buzz going, and look at the walls. There's always something I hadn't seen." He put his hands on her shoulders and gently turned her round. "See that?" he said, pointing to the door at the far end of the cabin, which was constructed in the same way as the walls.

"The design on the door?"

"Yes."

"Does it remind you of anything?"

She walked toward it. Galilee followed, his hands still laid on her shoulders. "I'll give you a clue," he said, his voice dropping to a whisper. "The grass looks very comfortable . . ."

"The grass?"

She stopped a yard or so from the door, and looked at the patterns in the wood. There were arrangements of dark shapes towards the top of the door; and a sliver of pale wood running horizontally, broken in places, and some more forms she could make no sense of arbitrarily laid here and there. But where was the grass? And why was it so comfortable?

"I'm not getting it," she said.

"Just look for the virgin," Galilee said.

"The virgin?" she said. "What virgin?" He drew breath to give her another clue, but before he could speak she said: "You mean Jerusha?"

He put his smiling lips against the nape of her neck and kept his silence.

She kept looking, and piece by piece the picture began to emerge. The grass—that comfortable bed on which Jerusha had lain down—was there in the middle of the door, a patch of lightly speckled wood. Above it were those dark, massy shapes she'd first puzzled over: the heavy summer foliage of ancient trees. And that bright horizontal sliver running across the door? It was the river, glimpsed from a distance.

Now it was she who smiled, as the mystery came clear in front of her. She had only one question: "Where are the people?"

"You have to put those in for yourself," he said. "Unless . . ." He stepped past her and put his finger on a narrow, almost spindly shape in the grain of one of the pieces of wood. "Could this be the riverman?"

"No. He was better looking than that."

Galilee laughed. "So maybe it isn't Jerusha's forest after all," he said. "I'll have to invent a new story."

"You like telling stories?"

"I like what it does to people," he said, smiling a little guiltily. "It makes them feel safe."

"Going to your country? *Where the rich were kind and the poor had God—*"

"I suppose that *is* my country. I hadn't thought about it that way before." The notion seemed to trouble him somewhat. He grew pensive for a moment; just a moment. Then he looked up from his thoughts and said: "Are you hungry?"

"Yes, I am a little."

"Good. Then I'll cook," he said. "It'll take a couple of hours. Can you wait that long?"

"A couple of hours?" she said, "What are you going to cook?"

"Oh it's not the cooking that takes the time," he said. "It's the catching."

## ii

There was no trace of the day remaining when *The Samarkand* left the jetty; nor was there a moon. Only the stars, in brilliant array. Rachel sat on deck while the boat glided away from the island. The heavens got brighter the further they sailed, or such was her impression. She'd never seen so many stars, nor seen the Milky Way so clearly; a wide, irregular band of studded sky.

"What are you thinking about?" Galilee asked her.

"I used to work in a jewelry store in Boston," she said. "And we had this necklace that was called the Milky Way. It was supposed to look like *that*." She pointed to the sky. "I think it was eight hundred and fifty thousand dollars. You never saw so many diamonds."

"Did you want to steal it?" Galilee said.

"I'm not a thief."

"But did you?"

She grinned sheepishly. "I did try it on when nobody was looking. And it was *very* pretty. But the real thing's prettier."

"I would have stolen it for you," Galilee said. "No problem. All you needed to say was—*I want that*—and it would have been yours."

"Suppose you'd got caught?"

"I never get caught."

"So what have you stolen?"

"Oh my Lord . . ." he said. "Where do I start?"

"Is that a joke?"

"No. I take theft very seriously."

"It *is* a joke."

"I stole this boat."

"You did not."

"How else was I going to get it?"

"Buy it?"

"You know how much vessels like this cost?" he said reasonably. She still wasn't sure whether he was joking or not. "I either stole the money to buy the boat, or stole the boat itself. It seemed simpler to steal the boat. That cut out the middle man." Rachel laughed. "Besides, the guy who had the boat didn't care about her. He left her tied up most of the time. I took her out, showed her the world."

"You make it sound like you married her."

"I'm not that crazy," Galilee replied. "I like sailing, but I like fucking better." An expression of surprise must have crossed her face, because he hurriedly said: "Sorry. That was crude. I mean—"

"No, if that's what you meant you should say it."

He looked sideways at her, his eyes gleaming by the light of the lamp. Despite his claim not to be crazy, that was exactly how he looked at that moment: sublimely, exquisitely crazy.

"You realize what you're inviting?" he said.

"No."

"Giving me permission to say what I mean? That's a dangerous invitation."

"I'll take the risk."

"All right," he said with a shrug. "But you remember . . ."

". . . I invited it."

He kept looking at her: that same gleaming gaze.

"I brought you on this boat because I want to make love to you."

"Make love is it now?"

"No, *fuck*. I want to fuck you."

"Is that your usual method?" she asked him. "Get the girl out to the sea where she hasn't got any choice?"

"You could swim," he said. He wasn't smiling.

"I suppose I could."

"But as they say on the islands: *Uliuli kai holo ka mano.*"

"Which means what?"

*"Where the sea is dark, sharks swim."*

"Oh that's very reassuring," she said, glancing down at the waters slopping against the hull of *The Samarkand*. They were indeed dark.

"So that may not be the wisest option. You're safer here. With me. Getting what you want."

"I haven't said—"

"You don't need to tell me. You just need to be near me. I can smell what you want."

If Mitchell had ever said anything like that as a sexual overture he would have killed his chances stone dead. But she'd invited this man to say what was in his head. It was too late to play the Puritan. Besides, coming from him, right now, the idea was curiously beguiling. *He could smell her.* Her breath, her sweat; God knows what else. She was near him and he could smell her; she was wasting his time and hers protesting and denying . . .

So she said: "I thought we were going to fish?"

He grinned at her. "You want a lover who keeps his promises, huh?"

"Absolutely."

"I'll get a fish," he said, and standing up he stripped off his T-shirt, unbuckled his belt and stepped out of his pants; all this so swiftly she didn't comprehend what he was intending to do until he threw himself overboard. It wasn't an elegant dive, it was a ragged plunge, and the splash soaked her. But that wasn't what got her up and shouting at him. It was what he'd said about sharks and dark water.

"Don't do this!" she yelled. She could barely see him. "Come out of there!"

"I'm not going to be long."

*"Galilee.* You said there were sharks."

"And the longer I talk to you the more likely they'll come and eat my ass, so can I please go fish?"

"I'm not hungry any more."

"You will be," he said. She could hear the smile in his voice, then saw him throw his arms above his head and dive out of sight.

"You sonofabitch," she said to herself, her mind filling with unwelcome questions. How long could he hold his breath for? When should she start to be concerned for his safety? And what if she saw a shark: what was she to do then? Lean over the side and beat on the hull of the boat to divert its attention? Not a very pleasant idea, with the water so concealing. The thing would be on her before she knew it; taking off her hand, her arm, dragging her overboard.

There was no doubt in her mind: when he got back on board she was going to tell him to take her straight back to the jetty; the sonofabitch, *the sonofabitch*, leaving her here staring down into the darkness with her heart in her mouth—

She heard a splashing sound on the other side of the boat.

"Is that you?" she called out. There was no reply. She crossed the deck, stumbling over something in the dark. *"Galilee, damn you! Answer me!"*

The splashing came again. She scanned the water, looking for some sign of life. Praying it was a man not a fin.

"Oh God, don't let anything happen to him," she found herself saying, "Please God, please, don't hurt him."

"You sound like a native."

She looked in the direction of the voice. There was something that looked like a black ball bobbing in the water. And around it, fish were leaping, their backs silvery in the starlight.

"Okay," she said, determined not to sound concerned for fear she encouraged his cavortings. "You got the fish? That's great."

"There was a shark god at Puhi, called Kaholia-Kane—"

"I don't want to hear it!" she yelled.

"But I heard you praying—"

"No—"

*"Please God,* you were saying."

"I wasn't praying to the fucking shark!" she yelled, her fury and fear getting the better of her.

"Well you should. They listen. At least this one did. The women used to call to him, whenever somebody was lost at sea—"

"Galilee?"

"Yes?"

"It's not funny anymore. I want you back on board."

"I'm coming," he said. "Let me just—" She saw his arm shoot out of the water and catch one of the leaping fish. "Gotcha! Okay. I'm on my way." He began to plow through the water toward the boat. She scanned the surface in every direction, superstitiously fearful that the fin would appear just as Galilee came in striking distance of the boat. But he made it to the side without incident.

"Here," he said, passing the fish up to her. It was large, and still very much intending to return to its native element, thrashing so violently that she had to use both hands to keep hold of it.

By the time she'd set the fish down where it couldn't dance its way back over the side Galilee had hoisted himself up out of the water and was standing, dripping wet, just a step or two behind her.

"I'm sorry," he said, before she could start to tell him how angry she was. "I didn't realize I was upsetting you. I thought you knew it was all a joke."

"You mean there aren't any sharks?"

"Oh no. There are sharks out there. And the islanders do say *Uliuli kai holo ka mano*. But I don't think they're talking about real sharks when they say that."

"What are they talking about?"

"Men."

"Oh I see," Rachel said. "When it gets dark, the men come out—"

"—looking for something to eat." He nodded.

"But you could still have got attacked," she said, "if there *are* real sharks out there."

"They wouldn't have touched me."

"And why's that? Too tough?"

He reached out and took hold of her hand, escorting it back toward him, and laying her palm against the middle of his massive chest. His heart was thumping furiously. He felt as though there was just a single layer of skin between hand and heart; as though if she wanted to she could have reached into his chest and taken hold of it. And now it was she who could smell *him*. His skin like smoke and burnt coffee; his breath salty.

"There's a lot of tales about sharks, men and gods," he said.

"More of your true stories?"

"Absolutely true," he replied. "I swear."

"Such as?"

"Well, they come in four varieties. Legends about men who are really shape-changing sharks; that's the first. These creatures walk the beaches at night, taking souls; sometimes taking children."

Rachel made a face. "Doesn't sound like a lot of fun."

"Then there are stories about men who decided to go into the sea and become sharks."

"Why would they do that?"

"For the same reason I got myself a boat and sailed away: they were fed up with pretending. They wanted to be in the water, always moving. Sharks die if they don't keep moving, did you know that?"

"No . . ."

"Well they do."

"So that's number two."

"Then there's the one you already know. Kaholia-Kane and his brothers and sisters."

"Shark gods."

"Protectors of sailors and ships. There's one in Pearl Harbor, watching over the dead. Her name's Ka'ahupahau. And the greatest of them is called Kuhaimuana. He's thirty fathoms long . . ."

Rachel shook her head. "Sorry. I don't like any of these stories," she said.

"That leaves us with just one category."

"Men who are gods?" Rachel said. Galilee nodded. "No, I'm not buying that either," she told him.

"Don't be so quick to judge," Galilee said. "Maybe you just haven't met the right man."

She laughed. "And maybe it's all just stories," she replied. "Look, I'm quite happy to talk about sharks and religion tomorrow. But tonight let's just be ordinary people."

"You make it sound easy," he said.

"It is," she told him. She moved closer to him, her hand still pressed against his chest. His heart seemed to beat more powerfully still. "I don't understand what's going on between us," she said, their faces so close she could feel the heat of his breath. "And to be honest I don't really care any more." She kissed him. He was staring at her, unblinking, and continued to stare as he returned her kiss.

"What do you want to do?" he said, very quietly.

She slid her other hand down over the hard shallow dome of his stomach, to his sex. "Whatever you want," she said, unhooding him. He shuddered.

"There's so much I need to tell you," he said.

"Later."

"Things you have to know about me."

"Later."

"Don't say I didn't try," he said, staring at her with no little severity.

"I won't."

"Then let's go downstairs and be ordinary for a while."

She led the way. But before he followed her he walked back across the deck to where the fish lay, and going down on his haunches, picked it up. She watched his body by the lamplight; the muscles of his back and buttocks, the bunching of his thighs as he squatted down, the dark, laden sac hanging between his legs. He was glorious, she thought; perhaps the most glorious man she'd ever seen.

He stood up again—apparently unaware that she was watching him—and seemed to murmur a few words to the dead fish before tossing it overboard.

"What was that about?" she asked him.

"An offering," he explained. "To the shark god."

# VII

## i

My half brother Galilee was always impatient with other people; it doesn't surprise me that he became "tired of pretending," as he explained to Rachel. What *does* surprise me is that he didn't assume that sooner or later he'd find himself playing that same game with her, and tire of her too.

Then again, perhaps he did. Perhaps even at the beginning, now I look at what he said to her more closely, there were contradictions there. On the one hand he seemed to be infatuated with her—all that sentimental talk about staring at the sea when he should have been watching for her—on the other quite capable of condescension. Samarkand, he dryly explains, is a long way from Ohio, as though she were too parochial to have any knowledge of what lay beyond her immediate experience. It's a wonder she didn't kick him off the jetty.

But then I think that from the beginning she understood him—contradictions and all—better than I ever have. And of course she was susceptible to his charms in a way that I'll never be, and perhaps therefore more forgiving of his flaws. I'm doing my best to evoke a measure of his allure for you. I think I caught his voice, and the physical details are right. But it's difficult to go into the sexual business. Describing an act of *coitus* involving your own sibling feels like a form of literary incest, though I'm certain that my reticence does him an injustice. I haven't, for instance, told you how finely he was made between the legs. But for the record, very finely indeed.

So on. For the sake of my blushes, on.

## ii

There is, as I promised, much more calamity within the Geary family to report, but before I start into that I want to tell you about a little drama here in the Barbarossa household.

It happened last night, just as I was midway through describing Rachel and Galilee's encounter on *The Samarkand*. There was a great din at the other end of the house (and I really mean a cacophony: shouting and thundering enough to shake down a few of the smaller books off my shelves). I couldn't work, of course. I was far too curious. I ventured out into the hallway, and tried to make some sense of the noise. It wasn't difficult. Marietta was one portion of it: when she gets angry she becomes so *shrill* it makes your head ring, and she was shouting up a storm. Accompanying her complaints—which I could make no real sense of—was the sound of slamming doors, as she apparently raged her way from room to room. But these weren't the only elements in the noise. There was something far more disturbing: a clamor that was like the din of some benighted jungle; a lunatic mingling of chatters and howls.

My mother, of course. I'm sorry, my father's wife. (It's strange, and probably significant, that I think of her as my mother whenever I picture her more peaceful aspects. The warrior Cesaria Yaos is my father's wife.) Anyway, it was she, no doubt. Who else had a voice that could express the rage of a baboon, a leopard and a hippopotamus in one rise and fell swoop?

But what was she so furious about? I wasn't entirely certain I wanted to find out. There was some merit in retreat, I thought. But before I could about turn and creep back to my room I saw Marietta running down the hallway, with what appeared to be an armful of garments. You'll recall that the last time we two had spoken we'd parted furious with one another, she having commented less than favorably on my work. But I think even if we'd been bosom buddies she would not have halted at that moment. Cesaria's menagerie noises were escalating by the second.

As Marietta ducked out of sight, I did what I'd been planning to do ten seconds before, and turned around so as to head back to my room. Too late. I'd barely taken a step when the noises ceased all at once, every last howl, only to leave room for Cesaria's other voice; her human voice, which is—I'm sure I've told you—nothing short of mellifluous.

"Maddox," she said.

Shit, I thought.

"Where are you going?"

(Isn't it strange, by the way, that we're never too old to feel like errant children? There I was, old by any human standards, frozen in my tracks and guilty as any infant caught with sticky fingers.)

"I was going back to my work," I said. Then added, "Mama," as a sop.

It may have mellowed her. "Is it going well?" she asked me, quite conversationally. I was sufficiently reassured to turn round and look at her, but she wasn't visible to me. There was just a busy darkness at the far end of the hallway where moments before there'd been a well-lit lobby. I was frankly grateful. I've never actually witnessed the form my mother takes in these legendary furies of hers, but I'm quite sure it's sufficient to drop a saint in his tracks.

"It's going okay," I replied. "I have days when—"

Cesaria broke in before I got any further. "Did Marietta go outside?" she said.

"I . . . yes . . . yes, I believe she did."

"Fetch her back."

"I'm sorry?"

"You're not deaf, Maddox. Go find your sister and bring her back inside."

"What happened?"

"Just fetch her."

(There's another second strangeness here, worth remarking on. Just as there's a guilty child lurking in everyone, there's also a rebellious self that prickles at the idea of being ordered about, and is not easily silenced. It was this voice that answered Cesaria back, foolish though it was to do so.)

"Why can't you go and fetch her yourself?" I heard myself saying.

I knew I was going to regret the words even as I spoke them. But it was already too late to recant: Cesaria's shadow self was in motion. She was moving—not quickly, but steadily, *inevitably*—down the hallway toward me. Though the ceiling is not especially high, there was something vast about her manifestation; she seemed like a thunderhead at that moment. And I diminished to a fraction of myself before her; I was a mote, a sliver—

She began to speak as she approached, but every word she uttered seemed about to collapse back into that terrible cacophony of hers; as though she was only keeping anarchy at bay with the greatest effort.

"You," she said "remind me" I knew what was coming "of your father."

I don't believe I said anything by way of reply. I was frankly too intimidated. Besides, if I'd tried to speak I doubt my tongue would have worked. I simply stood there as she roiled before me, and the animal din erupted out of her with fresh ferocity.

This time, however, there was a vision to go with the din, not uncovered by the cloud but seemingly sculpted from it. I had a mercifully short glimpse of it, though I'm certain that had Cesaria not wanted me to be her errand boy she might have given me more. That wasn't to her present purpose, however, so she showed me just enough to make me lose control of my bladder; perhaps three or four seconds' worth, if that. What did I see? It's no use telling you there are no words. Of course there are words; there are *always* words. The question is: can I wield them well enough to evoke the power of what I witnessed? That I doubt. But let me do my best.

I saw, I think, a woman erupting at every pore and orifice; spewing unfinished forms. Giving birth, I suppose you'd say, expelling not one, nor even ten, but a thousand creatures; ten thousand. And yet here's the problem with that description. It doesn't take account of the fact that at the same time she was becoming—how do I express this?—*denser*; like certain stars I've read about, which as they collapse upon themselves draw light and matter into them. So was she. How did my mind deal with the fact that she was doing two contrary things? Not well. In fact the vision did such violence to my system I fell down as though she'd struck me, and covered my head with my hands as though she might get the sight into me again through the top of my skull.

She chose to spare me. Just left me lying on the ground in my wet pants, sobbing. It took me a little time to recover my composure, but when I finally raised my head and chanced a look in her direction, I found that the thunderhead was no longer looming over me. She'd covered that furious face of hers and was waiting some little distance from me.

"I'm sorry . . ." were the first words out of my mouth.

"No," she said, her voice suddenly drained of either music or strength. "It was my fault. You're not a child to be ordered around. It was just that in that moment I saw your father so clearly."

"May . . . I . . . ask you a question?"

"Ask anything," she said, sighing.

"That face I just saw . . ."

"What about it?"

"Did Nicodemus ever see it?"

Despite her fatigue she was amused by this. There was a hint of a smile in her voice when she replied. "Are you asking me if I scared him off?" I nodded. "Then I'll tell you: that face, as you call it, is what he chiefly loved me for."

"Really?" I must have sounded astonished—as indeed I was—because she replied somewhat defensively:

"He had aspects that were just as terrible."

"Yes I know."

"Of course you know. You saw some of what he could do."

"But that wasn't all he was," I said.

"Just as what you saw a moment ago isn't all of me."

"But it's the truest part, isn't it?" I said. Under other circumstances I surely wouldn't have pressed her on this business so closely, but I knew the chances of my having the freedom to interrogate her like this again were nil. If I was to know who Cesaria Yaos was before the house of Barbarossa came crashing down, it was now or never.

"The truest part?" she said. "No. I don't think I have one face that's truer than any other. I used to be worshipped in dozens of temples, you know."

"I know."

"They're all heaps of rubble now. Nobody remembers how I was loved . . ." Her voice trailed off. She'd apparently lost her point. "What was I saying?"

"Nobody remembering."

"Before that."

"All the temples—"

"Oh yes. So many temples, with statues and embroideries, all depicting me. But not one of them resembled any other."

"How do you know?"

"Because I visited them," she said. "When your father and I had a spat we'd go our separate ways for a while. He'd go find himself some poor woman to seduce, and I'd go touring my holy sites. It's comforting when you're feeling a little woebegone."

"Hard to imagine."

"What? Me, woebegone? Oh I can be self-pitying, just like anybody else."

"No. I meant it's hard to imagine how it must feel, going into a temple where you're being worshipped."

"Oh it can be wonderful. Wandering among your devotees."

"Were you ever tempted to tell them who you were?"

"I did it many, many times. I usually picked somebody who wasn't a particularly reliable witness. The very old. The very young. Somebody with a sanity problem, or a saint, which is often one and the same."

"Why do that? Why not show yourself to somebody literate, intelligent? Somebody who could spread your gospel?"

"Somebody like you?"

"If you like."

"Is that what your book's going to be: one last desperate attempt to put your father and me back up on our pedestals?" What did she want to hear from me? I wondered. And if I chose incorrectly, would I be subjected to her fury again? "Is that what you're up to, Maddox?"

I decided on the truth. "No," I said, "I'm simply telling the story as best I can."

"And this conversation? Will it be in your book?"

"I'll put it in if it seems relevant."

There was a silence. Finally, she said: "Well, I suppose it doesn't matter whether you do or you don't. Stories; temples. Who cares nowadays? You're going to have fewer readers than I have worshippers, Maddox."

"I don't have to be read to be a writer," I pointed out.

"And I don't have to be worshipped to be a goddess. But it helps. Believe me, it helps." She made a phantom smile, and I—to my great surprise—returned it. We understood one another better at that moment than we ever had. "So, now . . . Marietta."

"One more question," I begged.

"No, enough."

"Please, Mama. Just one. For the book."

"One then. And only one."

"Did my father have temples?"

"He certainly did."

"Where were they?"

"That's another question, Maddox. But, as you're so curious . . . The finest of his temples to my way of thinking was in Paris."

"Really? Paris. I thought Nicodemus hated Paris."

"Later, he did. It's where I met Mr. Jefferson, you see."

"I didn't know that."

"There's a great deal about that man you don't know; that the world doesn't know. I could tell you enough about him to fill five books. He was such a charmer. But quiet . . . so quiet when he talked that you had to strain to hear him. I remember the first time I met him he'd just been given an apricot, which he'd never tasted before. And oh, the blissful look on that pinched face of his! I wanted him to make love to me on the spot."

"Did he?"

"Oh no. He played very hard to get. He was in love with an English actress at the time. What a wretched combination that was: English *and* an actress. The worst of all possible worlds. Anyway, Thomas toyed with my affections for weeks. There was a revolution going on around us, but I swear I was so besotted with him I barely noticed. Heads being lopped off every hour and I was wandering around in an adolescent daze trying to find a way to make this scrawny little American diplomat love me."

"How did you do it?"

"I'm not sure I ever did. If I were to raise him up now, out of his grave at Monticello, and say to him: did you love me? I think he'd say, at best, for a day or two, an hour or two, that afternoon you showed me the temple."

"You took him to my father's temple?"

"Every woman knows if you fail to get the man you want with words, you show him a sacred place." She laughed. "Usually it's the one between your legs. Don't look so shocked, Maddox. It's a fact of life. If a woman's going to get a man on his knees, she has to give him something to worship. But I knew raising my skirts for Jefferson wasn't going to be enough. He'd had that from his tarty little actress, Miss Cosway. I had to show him something that she could never supply. So I took him to your father's temple."

"What happened?"

"He was very impressed. He asked me how I knew about the place. It was a very secret cult your father had at that time. Noble families, mostly. And of course they'd either fled or lost their heads. So the temple was deserted. We wandered around while the mobs raged on the streets outside, and I think—just for that little while—he was quite in love.

"I remember he asked me who'd designed the place, and I took him to the altar, where there was a statue of your father. It had a red velvet cloth draped over it. And I said to Jefferson: before I show you this, will you promise me something? He said yes, of course, if it was in his power. So I said to him: design me a house, where I can live happily, because it'll remind me of you."

"So that's how you got him to design you this place?"

"I made him swear. On his wife. On his dreams of Monticello. On his dearest hopes for democracy. I made him swear on them all."

"You didn't trust him?"

"Not remotely."

"So he swore—"

"—and I uncovered your father's statue. There he was in all his tumescent glory!" Again she laughed. "Oh, Thomas was the very picture of discomfort. But to be fair to him, he kept his aplomb and asked me, with great seriousness, if the representation was a true and proportionate likeness. I reassured him that it was an exaggeration, though not much of one. I remember exactly what he said to that. 'Then I am certain, ma'am, you are a very contented wife.' Ha! 'A very contented wife.'

"I showed him how contented I was, there and then. With your father's painted eyes looking down at us, I showed Jefferson how little I cared for marriage.

"We never did it again. I didn't really want to, and I'm quite certain he didn't. His affair with the actress ended in tears, and he went back to his wife."

"But he built you your house, just as he promised he would."

"Oh he did more than that," she said. "He also built a perfect copy of the temple. Perfect down to the last detail."

"Why?"

"That's another question for his ghost. I don't know. He was a strange man. Beautiful things obsessed him. And the temple was beautiful."

"Did he put an altar in it?"

"Do you mean did he have a statue of your father? I wouldn't be surprised."

"Where was this place?"

"Where is it, you mean."

"It's still standing?"

"I believe so. It's one of the best kept secrets in Washington."

"Washington . . ." The thought that there was a place of ritual sacred to my perpetually priapic father laid in the heart of the nation's capitol astonished me. "I want to see it," I said.

"I'll write a letter of introduction," Cesaria said.

"To whom?"

She smiled. "To the highest in the land. I'm not entirely forgotten," she said. "Jefferson made certain I would never want for influence."

"So he knew you'd outlive him?"

"Oh yes, he understood perfectly, though he never put what he knew into words. I think that would have been too much for him."

"Mother . . . you astonish me."

"Do I really?" she said, with something approximating fondness in her voice. "Well I'm pleased to hear it." She shook her head. "Enough of this," she said. "I'm quite talked out." She pointed at me. "And you be careful how you quote me," she said. "I won't have my past misrepresented, even if it is in a book that nobody's going to read."

So saying, she turned her back on me, and calling her porcupines to follow, she headed off down the passageway. I called after her:

"What do you want me to do about Marietta?"

"Nothing," she growled. "Let her play. She'll regret what she's done. Maybe not tonight, but soon."

While I was pleased to be relieved of the duty of going after Marietta, I was left somewhat curious as to the felony my half sister had committed. Indeed I was tempted to seek her out and ask her for myself. But I had such a wonderful freight of information from Cesaria, and I didn't want to risk forgetting a word of it. So I went straight back to my room, lit the lamps, poured myself some gin, and started to set it down. I paused only once, to reflect on what it might mean that Thomas Jefferson, the principal architect of the Declaration, the father of democracy in America, should have built a replica of my father's temple. To have gone to all that trouble in pursuit of beauty seemed to me unlikely. Which begged two questions: one, why had he done it? And two, if there was some other purpose, did anybody on Capitol Hill know what it was?

# VIII

## i

I will revisit Marietta's theft in due course; be assured of that. There are several threads of this tapestry woven together in her crime as you'll see. And—just as Cesaria predicted—there would be consequences.

But first, I must return to *The Samarkand*, and the pair who'd passed the night upon it.

When Rachel woke, dawn was creeping into the tiny cabin, and by its virtuous light she saw Galilee asleep at her side, one arm thrown over his face, the other across her body. Comforted by the sight, she closed her eyes and went back to sleep. When she stirred again, he was gently stroking her breasts, kissing her face. Still only half-awake she slid her hand down between their bodies and raised her leg a little to guide him into her. He murmured something against her cheek that she didn't catch, but she was in too dreamy a state to ask him to repeat it. All she wanted was the fullness of him inside her; his gentle motion, his touch.

She didn't even need to see him: he was there in her mind's eye when she closed her lids; her perfect lover, who'd brought her more sexual pleasure in one night than she'd experienced in all the years preceding it. She reached out and touched his chest, his nipples, then to his armpit and the mass of his shoulder, luxuriating in the polished muscle beneath her fingertips. One of his huge hands was at her face, stroking her with the back of his fingers, the other down between her legs, parting her, easing the passage of his sex by spreading her fluids down its length.

She made a little sob of pleasure when he was fully housed; begged him to stay there. He didn't move. Just kept his place, her body enclosing him so tightly she could feel the tick of his blood. At last, she began to move; just a tiny motion at first, but enough to send a shudder through him.

"You like that?" she whispered.

He replied with short expulsion of air, almost a grunt, as he pressed his sex back into her, and the next instant withdrew it almost entirely. She let him do so without protest; the emptiness was delicious, as long as she knew it was only temporary.

She reached up and put her arms around his neck, knotting her fingers at the base of his skull. Then, oh so slowly, she preempted his return stroke by raising her hips toward his.

He spoke again. This time she heard what he said.

"Oh Lord in heaven . . ."

Slowly, slowly, she took him into her, both of them tender from a night of excesses; the line between bliss and discomfort perilously fine. As she rose he started down to meet her motion, and the image of him she'd had in her mind's eye lost its particularity, his substance dissolved in the wash of pleasure. The gleaming darkness of his limbs spread behind her lids, filling her thoughts completely. He was quickening now. She urged him on, her urges incoherent. No matter; he understood. She didn't need to tell him when to redirect his pressure, she'd no sooner formed the thought than he was doing so. And before he lost control of his body and came, she was distracting him from his crisis, slowing her own motion so as not to have their pleasure end too quickly.

So it went on, for two hours, almost three: sometimes a contest— jabs and sobbing; sometimes so quiet, so still, they might almost have been asleep in one another's arms. They made no declarations of love; at least nothing audible. They didn't even speak, not even to call out one another's name. There was no failure of feeling in this; just the reverse. They were so entirely immersed in one another, so entirely joined in their bliss, that for a short, sacred time they imagined themselves indivisible.

## ii

Not so, of course.

The illusion passed when their bodies had been wracked to exhaustion. They lay beside one another shivering in their sweat, gloriously satisfied, but returned into their own skins.

"I'm hungry," Rachel said.

They hadn't gone entirely without sustenance since boarding *The Samarkand*. Though Galilee had returned the fish to the sea as an offering to Kuhaimuana—all thirty fathoms of him—he'd opened cans of shucked oysters and brandied peaches in the middle of the night, which they'd eaten off and out of one another's bodies, so that the satisfying of one appetite didn't interrupt the satisfying of the other.

Still, it was now midmorning, and her stomach was complaining.

"We can be back on land in an hour," Galilee said.

"I don't want to go," Rachel replied. "I never want to go. I want to stay out here, just the two of us . . ."

"People would come looking," he said. "You're still a Geary."

"We'd find somewhere to hide," she said. "People disappear all the time, and they're never found."

"I have a house . . ."

"You do?"

"In a tiny village in Chile, called Puerto Bueno. It's right at the top of the hill. A view of the harbor. Parakeets in the trees."

"Let's go there," she said. Galilee laughed. "I'm serious," she said.

"I know you are."

"We could have children . . ."

The amusement left his face. "I don't think that'd be wise," he said.

"Why not?"

"Because I'd be no use as a father."

"How do you know?" she said, putting her hand over his. "You might find out you really liked it."

"Bad fathers run in our family," Galilee said. "Or rather, one does."

"One bad father out of how many?"

"One out of one," he said.

She thought he'd misunderstood what she was saying. "No, I mean, what about your grandfathers?"

"There aren't any."

"You mean they're dead."

"No, I mean there aren't any. There never were."

She laughed. "Don't be silly. Your mother and father had parents. They might have been dead before you were born, but—"

"They had no parents," Galilee said, taking his eyes off her. "Believe me."

There was something faintly intimidating about the way he said *believe me*. It wasn't an invitation, it was a command. He didn't wait to see if she'd obey it or not; he just got up and started to dress. "It's time we went back," he said. "People'll be looking for you."

"Let them look," she said, sliding her arms around him from behind, and pressing her body against him. "We don't have to go yet. I want to talk; I want to get to know you better."

"There'll be other times," he said, moving away from her to pick up his shirt.

"Will there?" she said.

"Of course," he replied, not turning back to look at her.

"What was it I said that offended you?"

"You haven't said anything," he replied. "I just think we should get back, that's all."

"Last night—"

He stopped buttoning his shirt. "Was wonderful," he said.

"So stop being like this," she said, irritation creeping into her voice. "I'm sorry if I talked out of turn. It was just a joke."

He sighed. "No it wasn't. You meant it or you wouldn't have said it. You'd like to have children . . ."

"Yes," she said, "I would. And I'd like to have them with you."

"We scarcely know one another," he replied, and started up the stairs to the deck.

She went after him, angry now. "What about what you said on the beach?" she demanded. "About watching for me? Was that just a way to get me here?" She followed him up the stairs. By the time she got on deck he was sitting on the narrow bench beside the wheel, his face in his hands. "Is that all this was about?" she said to him. "And now we've had the night together you're just going to move on?"

He kept his face buried. From the sound of his voice, he might have been dead. "I meant nothing by any of this," he said. "I just got caught up in the moment, and that wasn't fair to you. It wasn't fair. I thought you understood . . ."

"Understood what?"

"That this was just another story," he replied.

"Look at me," she said. He didn't move; his face remained hidden from her. "Look at me and say that!" she demanded.

With great reluctance he looked up at her. His face was gray; so was the expression in his eyes. "I meant nothing by any of this," he said steadily. "I thought you understood this was just another story."

Her eyes pricked, she heard the whine of the blood in her ears. How could he be saying this? Her vision began to blur as the tears came. How could he sit there and tell her it was all just a game, when they both knew, they both knew, surely, *surely*, that something wonderful had happened?

"You're a liar," she said.

"That may be."

"You know it's not true!"

"It's as true as any story I ever told you," he said, looking down at the deck. She wanted to quote him back at himself on the subject of what was true and what was not, but she couldn't remember the argument he'd made. All she could think was: he's running away from me. I'm never going to see him again. It was unbearable. Ten minutes ago, they'd been talking about his house on the hilltop. Now he was telling her nothing he'd said was worth a damn.

"Liar," she said again. "Liar, liar, liar."

He got up and went into the wheelhouse, not looking at her once. He switched on the engine, and then flipped the switch to haul up the anchor. Between engine and anchor-raising there was quite a noise; any further conversation was out of the question. Frustrated, Rachel went below to dress.

The cabin was in total disarray, the pillows and sheets cast in every direction about the bed, her clothes scattered. She focused her emotions on a missing shoe for a minute or two, which kept the tears from coming again. By the time she'd found the shoe and got herself dressed, the weepy feeling had passed, and she was almost ready to have a rational conversation.

Shoes on, she went back up on deck. The boat was ploughing through the placid waters at quite a clip, the wind cold and bracing.

"Look!" Galilee yelled to her, pointing toward the bow. She could see nothing. "Go see!" he urged her.

She climbed up past the wheelhouse and onto the forward deck to see what he was so anxious she see. There was a pod of dolphins keeping pace with *The Samarkand*, three or four of them racing to stay so close to the bow they were practically touching it, their bodies like velvet torpedoes as they sped along. Now and then a smaller individual—a juvenile, she supposed—leaped out of the water to one side of the boat or the other, the leaps decorated with a fillip of the tail or a half-twist of the body.

She glanced back at Galilee to show her appreciation, but he had his eyes on the island. There were rain clouds obscuring the heights of Mount Waialeale, as there had been the first day she'd arrived. It was just a short time since she'd been driving with Jimmy Hornbeck and they'd had their conversation about Mammon, the demon of acquisitiveness; but it seemed like weeks. No; more than weeks: another life. She'd been a different Rachel then; she'd been a Rachel who hadn't known Galilee was in the world. For better or worse, that changed everything.

# IX

The jetty had an occupant when they came in sight of it: a solitary figure sitting staring out at the sea. Rachel assumed the man was fishing, and paid him little attention. It wasn't until *The Samarkand* was within a few boatlengths of its destination that she studied the figure more closely and realized that it was Niolopua. He'd risen now and was waiting at the end of the jetty, plainly agitated. Before the boat had even come alongside the jetty he leapt aboard. He took no notice of his father; it was Rachel he needed to talk to; and urgently.

"There have been messages for you," he said, "from New York."

"About what?"

"The woman wouldn't say. She just told me to find you. Very important, she said. I've been looking for you since dawn."

"Who was it you were talking to?"

"Mrs. Geary."

"Yes, but *which* Mrs. Geary? Was it Margaret?" The man shook his head. "Loretta? It was Loretta?"

"The old one?" Niolopua said.

Before Rachel could confirm that yes, Loretta was the old one, Galilee had done it for her. "And she didn't tell you what it was about?"

"No. Just that . . . this Mrs. Geary had to call as soon as possible, because there was something she had to know."

"Cadmus," Rachel said. The old man was dead, more than likely. "Come with me," she said to Galilee.

"Niolopua can go with you. I'll follow."

"You promise me?" she said.

"Of course."

"We need to talk."

"I know. I understand. I'll come in a while. Let me just take care of the boat."

It was hard not to look back as she and Niolopua returned to the house; hard not to fear that Galilee was lying to her, and that the moment she was out of sight he'd cast off and sail away. But she had to have some faith, she told herself. If she didn't believe the promise he'd made her, then there was no hope for them. And if he broke that promise, then there'd been no hope anyway.

Still, it was hard. The closer they came to the ridge of rocks which divided one bay from the other, on the far side of which she would be out of sight of the jetty, the more the temptation grew to cast just one glance over her shoulder and confirm that he was still there. She resisted successfully, but the effort of doing so must have been visible to Niolopua because once they were down on the sand again, with the house almost in view, he said:

"Don't worry. He'll come."

She glanced sideways at him. "Is it that obvious?"

Niolopua shrugged. "He's who he is. You're who you are."

"What's that supposed to mean?"

"That he won't break his promise."

It was only once she reached the house, and stood still for a few moments, that she realized how she'd lost some of her equilibrium from being on board *The Samarkand*. The floor felt unreliable beneath her bare soles, and she felt oddly queasy: a strange reversal of seasickness. She went into the bathroom and splashed some cold water on her face, then asked Niolopua if he'd mind making her some hot, sweet tea while she called New York. He was happy to oblige. She retired to the relative privacy of the dining room and dialed the mansion, wondering as she did so how to best express her condolences. Would Loretta expect her to be tearful at the news? Surely not.

The voice at the other end of the telephone was not one she recognized: a man with a Bronx accent and what sounded like a heavy cold. She asked for Loretta.

"Mrs. Geary can't come to the phone right now. Who is this?" Rachel told him. There followed some muffled sounds as the receiver was passed over to somebody else. This time she recognized the voice. It was Mitchell. She felt a sudden spasm of panic—the way she felt when an elevator lurched between floors, and she feared it was going to stop. The prospect of entrapment loomed.

"I had a message from Loretta," Rachel said.

"Yes. I know."

"Who was that I was talking to?"

"A detective."

"What's going on?"

"It's Margie . . ."

"What about her?"

There was a short silence. Then Mitchell said: "She's dead, Rachel. Somebody shot her dead."

The elevator lurched a second time. "Oh God, Mitch . . ."

"They're saying Garrison did it," Mitchell went on. "But that's just bullshit. He was set up. It's just bullshit."

"When did it happen?"

"Late last night. Somebody must have broken into the house. Somebody with a grudge against her. God knows, Margie could piss people off."

"Poor Margie. Oh Lord, poor Margie."

"You have to come back, Rachel. The police need to talk to you."

"I don't know anything."

"You talked to Margie a lot lately. Maybe she told you something—"

"I don't want to come back, Mitchell."

"What are you talking about?" For the first time in the exchange there was some emotion in his voice; a mingling of rage and disbelief. "You've got to come back. Where the hell are you anyway?"

"It's none of your business."

"You're out on that fucking island, aren't you?" he said, his tone all anger now. "You think we don't know about that place? You think it's some big secret? I know what goes on out there."

"You don't have the first clue," she said, hoping he heard the certainty in her voice.

"If you don't come back, the police are going to come looking for you. Is that what you want?"

"Don't try bullying me. It won't work any more."

"*Rachel.*"

"I'll call you back."

*"Don't hang up."*

She hung up. "You bastard," she said quietly. Then, more quietly still: "Poor Margie."

"Something bad?" Niolopua said. He was at the door with her cup of hot tea.

"Very bad," she said. He brought the tea to her table and set it down. "My sister-in-law was murdered last night."

"How?"

"She was shot. By . . . her own husband." She was laying all this out more for her own benefit than for Niolopua's; putting what was nearly beyond belief into words.

"Do you want me to go tell my father?"

"Yes," Rachel said, "if you don't mind. Would you ask him to hurry up? Tell him I need him here."

"Is there anything else before I go?"

"No, thank you."

"I'm sorry," he said. "She was a nice woman." So saying, he left her alone.

She took a few sips of tea, which Niolopua had sweetened with honey, then got up and went to the cabinet. If her memory served she'd seen a half-emptied carton of cigarettes in one of the drawers. That's what she needed right now: a bitter lungful of carcinogenic smoke inhaled in memory of her Margie. Several lungfuls, in fact, and fuck the consequences.

The carton was where she'd hoped it was, but there were no matches. Taking her tea and the cigarettes, she went through to the kitchen. The vestiges of her land-sickness remained; not the queasiness, but the unsettling sense that the ground beneath her was rocking. She found some matches and went out to sit in the veranda, where she could watch for Galilee.

The cigarette tasted stale, but she smoked it anyway, thinking of the countless times she'd sat happily immersed in the cloud of smoke that hung about Margie, talking with happy purposelessness. If the victim had been somebody else, Margie would have been thoroughly entranced, she knew; eager to talk over every possible scenario of how the murder had come about. She'd had no sense of tragedy, she'd told Rachel once. Tragedy only happened to people who gave a damn, and she'd never met anybody who did. Rachel had said this was nonsense. Amongst all the important people Margie had rubbed shoulders with there'd been some who genuinely wanted to make a difference. Not a one, Margie had replied; cheats, liars and thieves, every last one. Rachel remembered the conversation not for Margie's cynicism, but because there had been such disappointment in her voice as she spoke. Somewhere behind the veil there'd been a woman who'd wanted nothing more than to be proved wrong about what wretched bastards the movers and shakers of the world were.

Which thought led on, inevitably, to Garrison, about whom Margie had never said one good word. According to her he'd been— among other things—selfish, pompous and inept in bed. But these were minor felonies beside the crime of which he was now accused; and it was difficult for Rachel to imagine any circumstances in which he would pick up a gun and shoot his own wife. Yes, it seemed they'd despised one another; but they'd lived in a state of mutual contempt for years. It didn't make him a murderer. If he'd wanted an end to the marriage, there were easier resolutions.

She turned over what Mitchell had said, about coming home of her own volition, or having the police come and fetch her. It was nonsense, surely. She plainly wasn't a suspect, so any information she could supply would be purely anecdotal. If they needed to talk to her, they could do it by phone. She didn't have to go back if she didn't want to; and she didn't want to. Especially now, with so much to work out between Galilee and herself.

She'd finished her cigarette by now, and had almost finished her tea. Rather than sit on the veranda she decided to go back inside and change into fresh clothes. She picked up some cookies on her way through the kitchen, and went into the bathroom to shower.

It was only when she caught sight of herself in the mirror—her skin flushed from wind and sun—that she realized how strangely calm she felt. Was she simply too stunned by all that had happened in the last few hours to respond to it? Why wasn't she weeping? Her best friend was dead, for God's sake, and here she was staring at herself out of the mirror without a tear shed. She looked hard at her reflection, as though it might speak back to her and solve this mystery; but her face showed her nothing.

She went to the shower, and turned it on, shedding her clothes where she stood. The flow of water was weak, but she luxuriated in it nevertheless, remembering Galilee's touches as she sluiced off her salted skin. His hands on her face, her breasts, her belly, his tongue at play between her legs. She wanted him again, now. Wanted him to be whispering to her the way he'd whispered that first night: a story of water and love. She'd even take a tale of sharks if that was what he felt like telling. She was in the mood to be devoured.

Taking her leisurely time, she washed her hair and then rinsed the remaining soap from her body. She'd neglected to bring a towel from the rack, so she stepped out of the shower soaking wet, and there he was, standing in the doorway, looking at her.

Her first instinct was to cover her nakedness, but the way he was looking at her made the idea nonsensical. There was nothing salacious in his stare; the expression he wore was almost childlike in its simplicity. His eyes were wide, his face almost slack.

"So now they're killing their own," he murmured. "I suppose it had to happen sooner or later." He shook his head. "This is the beginning of the end, Rachel."

"What do you mean?"

"My brother Luman predicted all this."

"He knew there was going to be a murder?"

"Murder's the least of it. Margie was a sad creature, and she's probably better off—"

"Don't say that."

"It's true. We both know it's true."

"I loved Margie."

"I'm sure you did."

"So don't say she's better off dead, because that's not right, that's not true."

"Nobody could have healed her. She'd been swimming in that poison for too long."

"So I shouldn't care that she's dead?"

"Oh no, I'm not saying that. Of course you should care. Of course you should mourn. But don't expect any justice to be done."

"The police already have her husband."

"They won't have him for long."

"Another of your brother's predictions?"

"No, that one's mine," he said. "Garrison'll walk away from what he did. He's a Geary. They always find someone else to blame."

"How do you know so much about them?"

"They're the enemy," he said simply.

"So what makes me any different?" Rachel said. "I've been swimming in the poison too."

He nodded. "I know," he said. "I tasted it."

She was reminded of her nakedness as he spoke. It was no accident; as he spoke of tasting the poison his eyes had left her face. Gone to her breasts; to her sex.

"Will you pass me a towel?" she said to him.

He dutifully took the largest of the towels off the rack. She reached out to take it from him, but rather than pass it over he said, *"Please, let me . . ."* and, opening the towel, he pressed it against her body and began to dry her. Despite the prickly exchanges they'd had of late—first in the boat, now here—she was instantly comforted by his attentions; the intimacy of his touch muted by the plushness of the towel, but all the more teasing for the fact. When he dried her breasts she couldn't keep herself from sighing appreciatively.

"That feels nice," she said.

"Yes?"

"Yes . . ."

He drew her a little closer, carefully drying beneath her breasts, then making his way down towards her groin.

"When will you go back to New York?" he asked her.

She had some trouble concentrating on the question; even more formulating an answer. "I don't see . . . any reason why I should."

"I thought she was a friend of yours."

"She was. But I'm no use to her now. I'm better off here, with you. I know that's what Margie would tell me. She'd say: you've got something that gives you pleasure, hold on to it."

"And I've given you pleasure?"

"You know you have," she purred.

"Good," he said, with a kind of forced brightness, as though the idea was in equal measure pleasing and troubling to him.

His hands were between her legs now. She took hold of the towel and pulled it away. "Let's go to the bedroom," she said.

"No," he said. "Here," and suddenly his fingers were inside her, and he was pressing her against the wall, his mouth on hers. He tasted strange, almost acidic; and the way he stroked her was far from tender. There was suddenly something ungainly about all of this. She wanted to call a halt, but she was afraid of driving him away.

He was unbuckling his pants now, pressing himself so hard against her she could barely draw breath.

"Wait . . ." she said to him. "Please. Slow down."

He didn't heed her. If anything his behavior became more frenzied. He pushed her legs open. She felt his erection jabbing at her, like something blind, poking around for its bed. She told herself to relax; to trust him. He'd made the most extraordinary love to her last night; he understood the signals her body was putting out better than any man she'd ever been with.

So why did she want to push him away now? Why did it hurt when he got inside her? What had seemed like a wonderful fullness a few hours before now made her want to cry out. There was no pleasure in this; none.

She couldn't govern her instincts any longer. She closed her mouth against his kisses, and put her hands on his chest to push him away.

"I don't like this," she said.

He ignored her. He was buried deep in her, to the root, his cock brutally rigid, his hips grinding against hers.

"No," she said. "No! Will you please get *off me!*"

Now she pushed him as hard as she could, but his body was too strong, his erection was too implacable: she was pinned against the wall.

"Galilee," she said, trying to look into his eyes. "You're hurting me. *Listen to me! You're hurting me.*"

Was it the fact that she was shouting now, her words echoing around the tiled walls, that roused him out of his stupor? Or was he simply bored with his own cruelty, as his body language seemed to suggest? He pushed himself off and out of her like someone leaving a dining table because the food didn't suit them, his expression one of mild distaste.

"Get out of here," she told him.

He retreated a step or two, still not looking at her, then turned and crossed to the door. She hated everything about him at that moment— his idling gait, the way he glanced down at his erection, the little smile she caught in the mirror as he slipped through the door. She closed it after him, then listened as he made his way through the house. Only when she heard the sound of the French window opened, and then being slammed as he exited, did she go to her clothes and start to dress. By the time she ventured out into the house he'd disappeared.

Niolopua was sitting on the lawn watching the ocean. She went out onto the veranda, and called to him.

"You had an argument?" he said.

She nodded.

"He didn't even speak to me. He just went down onto the beach, looking like thunder."

"Will you stay here for a little while? I don't want him coming back."

"I'll stay, if it makes you feel more comfortable, but I'm sure he's not coming back."

"Thank you," she said.

"He'll set sail now," Niolopua said. "You'll see."

"I don't care what he does as long as he stays the hell away from me," she said.

Just as Niolopua had predicted, Galilee didn't come back. The day waned, and Rachel stayed in the house, feeling drained of any energy or desire, eating a little, drinking a little, but getting pleasure from nothing. As she'd requested Niolopua kept his watch on the lawn, coming to the veranda once to ask for a beer, otherwise leaving her alone. The telephone rang several times, but she didn't pick up. It was probably Mitch, or perhaps Loretta, trying to persuade her to go back home. In fact, since Galilee's leaving, she'd started to think that returning to New York was not such a bad idea. Certainly staying here in the house would not be wise; she'd only brood on things. Better to go back to the family, where at least she understood her feelings. After the emotional chaos of the last few days there would be something bracingly plain about being among the Gearys. They were hateful, it was as simple as that. No confusion, no ambiguity, no kisses one moment and brutality the next. Maybe she'd just get drunk and stay that way, like Margie; pronounce against the world from behind her funeral veil. It wasn't a very pretty prospect, but what did she have left? This island had been a last resort: a place to heal herself; to watch the miraculous at play. But it had failed her. She was left empty-handed.

As the last of the light was going out of the sky she heard Niolopua calling her name, and went out onto the veranda to find him standing at the bottom of the lawn pointing out to sea.

There was *The Samarkand*. Even though its sails were little more than white specks against the darkening blue, Rachel knew without a doubt it was Galilee's vessel. For an aching moment she imagined herself on deck with him, looking back at the island from the sea. The stars coming out overhead; the bed below, waiting for them. She indulged the romance for a moment only, then told herself to stop it.

Even so, she couldn't turn her back on the ocean; not until he'd gone. She watched the boat get smaller and smaller, until at last it was utterly eroded by distance and darkness. Only then did she look away.

So that's the end of it, she thought. The man she'd fleetingly imagined might be her prince had gone. And what a perfect departure he'd made, carried away by the tide; who knew where?

Still she didn't weep. Her prince was gone, and she didn't weep. Yes, there was regret. Of course there was regret. However long she lived, she'd never stop wondering what would have happened if she'd better navigated the shoals of his nature; wonder what kind of life they might have had together in his house on the hill.

But there was something else besides regret: there was anger. That, she finally decided, was what kept the tears from coming: her fury at the way life piled hurt on hurt. It dried her eyes the moment they moistened.

Margie's methodology had been much the same, hadn't it? By turning spite into an art form, by pronouncing loudly on the meaninglessness of life, Margie kept herself functioning.

That's how things would have to be for Rachel from now on. She'd have to learn to be just like Margie.

God help them both.

# PART SIX

# Ink and Water

# I

## i

So Galilee sailed away; I cannot tell you where. If this were a different kind of book I might well invent the details of his route, culled from books and maps. But in doing so I would be trading on your ignorance; assuming you wouldn't notice if I failed to get the details right.

It's better I admit the truth: Galilee sailed away, and I don't know where he went. When I close my eyes, and wait for an image of him to come I usually find him sitting on the rolling deck of *The Samarkand* looking less than happy with his lot. But though I've searched the horizon for some clue as to his whereabouts I see only the wastes of the ocean. To an eye more canny than mine perhaps there are clues even here, but I'm no sailor. To me, one seascape looks much like the next.

I will confess that I tried to apply what I thought would be simple logic to the question. I took down from the shelves several maps I'd been given over the years (the older ones may even have belonged to Galilee himself; long before he left to wander the world, he loved to trace imaginary journeys) and having spread them out on the floor of my study I walked among them with a book on celestial navigation in one hand and a volume on tides and currents in the other, trying to plot the likeliest course for *The Samarkand* to have taken. But the challenge defeated me. I set his course north past the island (that much I remember seeing, through Rachel's eyes); I began to calculate the prevailing winds at that time, and set *The Samarkand* before them, but I became hopelessly distracted by the very charts that were supposed to be anchoring my imagination. They were, as I said, old charts; made at a time when knowledge was not so vigorously (some would say calamitously) divided from the pleasures of fancy. The makers of these maps had seen nothing wrong with adding a few decorative touches here and there: filigreed beasts that rose out of the painted ocean to foam at passing ships; flights of windy angels poised at every quarter, with streaming hair and trumpeters' cheeks; even a great squid on one of the maps with eyes like twin furnaces and tentacles (so the note informed me) the length of six clippers.

In the midst of such wonders, my pathetic attempts at rational projections went south. I left off my calculations and sat in the midst of the maps like a man trading in such things, waiting for a buyer.

## ii

Galilee had been in love before, of course, and survived to tell the tale. But he'd only once been in love with a Geary, and that made all the difference in the world. Loving a woman who belonged in the family of your enemy wasn't wise; there were plenty of tragedies that testified to that. And in his experience love always ended up a bitter business. Sweet for a time yes, but never for long enough to justify the consequences: the weeks of self-recrimination, the months of lost sleep, the years of loneliness. Every time a romance ended, he'd tell himself that he'd never fall again. He'd stay out at sea, where he was safe from his own appetites.

What did he want from love anyway? A mate or a hiding place? Both perhaps. And yet hadn't he raged again and again against the witless contentment of his animal self, smug in its nest, in its ease, in the comfort of its own dirt? He hated that part of himself: the part that wanted to be wrapped in the arms of some beloved; that asked to be hushed and sung to and forgiven. What stupidity! But even as he railed against it, fled it, out to sea, he shuddered at the thought of what lay ahead, now that love was gone again. Not just the loneliness and the sleepless nights, but the horror of being out in the fierce, hard light that burned over him, set there by his own divinity.

As he guided *The Samarkand* out into the ocean currents, he wondered how many more times he'd be able to sail away before the toll of partings became intolerable. Perhaps this was the last. That wouldn't be such a terrible oath to take: to swear that after Rachel there'd be no more seductions, no more breaking of hearts. It would be his mark of respect to her, though she'd never know he'd made it: to say that after her there would only be the sea.

That said, he couldn't readily put the woman from his mind. He sat out on deck through the night, while *The Samarkand* was carried further and further from land, thinking about what had passed between them. How she'd looked, lying in the carved bed that first night; how she'd talked to him as he told the story of Jerusha and the riverman, asking questions, prodding him to make the story better, finer, deeper. How she'd imitated the child bride while she lay there, pulling the sheet off her body to show herself to him; and how exquisite that sight had been. How they'd touched; how he thought of her all the time they were parted, wondering whether to risk bringing her on board the boat. He'd never let a woman set foot on *The Samarkand* before, holding to ancient superstition on the matter. But her presence made such fears seem nonsensical. What boat would not be blessed to have such a creature tread its boards?

Nor did he now regret the decision. Sitting under the stars he seemed to see her, turning to smile at him. There she was, with her arms open to welcome him in. There she was, saying she loved him. Whatever wonders he saw after this—and he'd seen wonders: the sea turned silver with squid, storms of gold and vermilion—there would be no vision out of sea or sky that would command his devotion as she had.

If only she hadn't been a Geary.

# II

So, Galilee sailed away, and—as I said—I don't know where he wandered. I do know where he ended up, however. After three weeks *The Samarkand* put into the little harbor at Puerto Bueno. There had been storms all along that coast earlier in the month, and the town had taken a severe battering. Several houses close to the quay, repeatedly assaulted by waves breaking over the harbor wall, had been damaged; and one had collapsed entirely, killing the widow who'd lived there. But Galilee's house at the top of the hill was virtually unharmed, and it was here he returned, climbing the steep streets of the town without speaking to anyone he encountered, though he knew them all, and they all knew him.

The roof of the Higgins house had leaked during the storms, and the place smelled damp. There was mildew everywhere; and much of the furniture in the upper rooms had begun to rot. He didn't care. There was nothing here that mattered to him. Any vague dreams he might have once entertained of bringing a companion here, and living a kind of ordinary life, now seemed foolish; laughable. What a perfect waste of time, to indulge dreams of domesticity.

By chance the weather brightened the day after he appeared—which fact did nothing to harm his reputation as a man of power among the townspeople—but the scene from the windows of his house—the clouds steadily sculpted to nothingness by the wind, the sea glittering in the sun—gave him no pleasure. He'd seen it all before. This, and every other glory. There was nothing new to watch for; no surprises left in earth or heaven. He could close his eyes forever, and pass away without regret, knowing he'd seen the best of things.

Oh, and the worst. He'd seen the worst, over and over again.

He wandered from one stagnant room to the next, and up the stairs and down; and everywhere he went, he saw visions of things he wished he'd never witnessed. Some of them had seemed like brave sights at the time. In his youth, bloody business had excited him; why did its echoes now come to bruise him the way they did?

Why when he lay down on the mildewed bed did he remember a whorehouse in Chicago, where he'd chased down two men and slaughtered them like the cattle they made such profit from? Why, after all these years, did he remember how one of them had made a little speech as he lay dying, and thanked his murderer for the ease of it all?

Why when he sat down to empty his bowels did his mind conjure up a yellow dog, which had shit itself in terror, seeing its master with his throat cut on the stairs, and Galilee sitting at the bottom of the flight, drinking the dead man's champagne?

And why, when he tried to sleep—not in the bed but on the threadbare sofa in the living room—did he remember a rainy February night and a man who had no better reason to die than that he'd crossed the will of one mightier, and he, Galilee, no better reason to commit murder than that he served that same will? Oh that was a terrible memory. In some ways—though it was not the bloodiest of his recollections—it was the most distressing because it had been such an intimate encounter. He remembered it so clearly: the car rocking as gusts of wind came off the ocean; the rain rattling on the car roof; the stale heat of the interior, and the still staler heat that came off the man who died in his arms.

Poor George; poor, innocent George. He'd looked up at Galilee with such confusion on his face; his lips trying to form some last coherent question. He'd been too far gone to shape the words; but Galilee had supplied the answer anyway.

"I was sent by your father," he'd said.

The confounded look had slipped away and George's face had

become oddly placid, hearing that he was dying at the behest of his father; as though this were some last, wretched service he could render the old man, after which he was finally free of Cadmus's jurisdiction.

Any ambition Galilee might have entertained of fathering a child had gone at that moment: to be the father's agent in the murder of a son had killed all appetite in him. Not simply the appetite for parenthood — though that had been the saddest casualty of the night at Smith Point Beach; the very desire to live had lost its piquancy at that moment. Destroying a man because he stood between your family and its ascendance was one thing (all kings did it, sooner or later); but to order the death of your own child because he disappointed you: that was another order of deed entirely, and to have been obliged to perform it had broken Galilee's heart.

And still, after all this time, he couldn't get the scene out of his head. The hours of the whorehouse in Chicago, and his memories of the yellow dog shitting on the stairs, were bad enough; but they were nothing by comparison with the memory of the look on George Geary's face that rainy night.

And so it went on for a week and a half: memories by day and dreams by night, and nothing to do but endure them. He ventured out of the house at evening, and went down to check that all was well with *The Samarkand*, but even that journey became harder as time passed; he was so exhausted.

This could not go on. The time had come to make a decision. There was no great heroism in suffering, unless perhaps it was for a cause. But he had no causes, nor ever had; not to live for, not to die for. All he had was himself.

No, that wasn't true. If he'd just had himself he wouldn't have been haunted this way.

She'd done this to him. The Geary woman; the wretched, gentle Geary woman, whom he'd wanted so badly to put out of his heart, but could not. It was she who'd reminded him of his capacity for feeling, and in so doing had opened him up as surely as if she'd wielded a knife, letting these unwelcome things have access to his heart. It was she who'd reminded him of his humanity, and of all that he'd done in defiance of his better self. She who'd stirred the voice of the man on the whorehouse floor, and roused the yellow dog, and put the sight of George Geary before him.

His Rachel. His beautiful Rachel, whom he tried not to conjure but who was there all the time, holding his hand, touching his arm, telling him she loved him.

Damn her to hell for tormenting him this way! Nothing was worth this pain, this constant gnawing pain. He no longer felt safe in his own skin. She'd invaded him, somehow; possessed him. Sleeplessness made him irrational. He began to hear her voice, as though she were in the next room, and calling to him. Twice he came into the dining room and found the table set for two.

There was no happy end to this, he knew. There would be no escaping her, however patiently he waited. She had too strong a hold on his soul for him to hope for deliverance.

It was as though he were suddenly old—as though the decades in which time had left him untouched had suddenly caught up with him—and all he could look forward to now was certain decline; an inevitable descent into obsessive lunacy. He would become the madman on the hill, locked away in a world of rotted visions; seeing her, hearing her, and tormented day and night by the shameful memories that came with love: the knowledge of his cruelties, his innumerable cruelties.

Better to die soon, he thought. Kinder to himself, though he probably didn't deserve the kindness.


On the sixth evening, climbing the hill to the house, he conceived his plan. He'd known several suicides in his life, and none of them had made a good job of it. They'd left other people with a mess to clear up, for one thing, which was not his style at all. He wanted to go, as far as it were possible, invisibly.

That night, he made fires in all the hearths in the house, and burned everything that might be used to construe some story about him. The few books he'd gathered over the years, an assortment of bric-a-brac from the shelves and windowsills, some carvings he'd made in an idle hour (nothing fancy, but who knew what people would read into what they found here?). There wasn't a lot to burn, but it took time nevertheless, what with his state of mind so dreamy and his limbs aching from want of rest.

When he had finished, he opened all the doors and windows, every one, and just before dawn headed down the hill to the harbor. His neighbors would get the message, seeing the house left open. After a couple of days some brave soul would venture inside, and once word spread that he'd made a permanent departure the place would be stripped of anything useful. At least so he hoped. Better somebody was using the chairs and tables and clocks and lamps than that they all rot away.

The wind was strong. Once *The Samarkand* was clear of the harbor, its sails filled; and long before the people of Puerto Bueno were up and brewing their morning coffee or pouring their breakfast whiskies their sometime neighbor was gone.

His plan was very simple. He would sail *The Samarkand* a good distance from land, and then—once he was certain neither wind nor current would not bear him back the way he'd come—he'd surrender his captaincy over both vessels, his body and his boat, and let nature take its course. He would not trim his sails if a storm arose. He would not steer the boat from reef or rocks. He would simply let the sea have him, whenever and however she chose to take him. If she chose to overturn *The Samarkand* and drown him, so be it. If she chose to dash the boat to pieces, and him along with it, then that was fine too. Or if she chose to match his passivity with her own, and let him linger becalmed until he perished on deck, and was withered by the sun, then that lay in her power too, and he wouldn't lift a hand to contradict her will.

He had only one fear: that if hunger and thirst made him delirious he might lose the certainty that moved him now, and in a moment of weakness attempt to take control of the vessel again, so he scoured the boat for anything that might be put to practical use, and threw it all overboard. His mariner's charts, his life jackets, his compass, his flares, his inflatable life raft: all of it went. He left only a few luxuries to sweeten these last days, reasoning that suicide didn't have to be an uncivilized business. He kept his cigars, his brandy, a book or two. Thus supplied, he gave himself over to fate and the tides.

# III

## i

Most murder, as you're probably aware, is domestic. The conventions of popular fiction tell an untruth: the person most likely to take your life by violence is not some anonymous maniac but the man or woman with whom you breakfasted this morning. So I doubt that I'm spoiling any great mystery if I confirm here that the man who murdered Margie was Garrison Geary.

He didn't do it because he despised her, though he did. He didn't do it because she had a lover, though she had. He did it because she refused him knowledge, which may seem like an obscure reason for slaughtering your spouse, but will probably be one of the lesser strangenesses ahead.


By the time Rachel got back to New York, Garrison had confessed. Not to cold-blooded murder, of course, but rather to an act of self-defense in the face of his wife's crazed attempt on his life. According to his testimony it had happened like this: he'd come home to find Margie in a drunken state, wielding a Colt .38. She was sick of their life together, she'd told him, and wanted an end to it all. He'd tried to reason with her, but she'd been in far too inflamed a state to be talked down. Instead she'd fired at him. The bullet had missed, however, and before she could fire a second time Garrison had attempted to disarm her. In the struggle the gun had gone off, wounding Margie. He'd called the police instantly, but by the time medical help arrived it was too late. Her body—weakened by years of abuse—had given up.

There was a good deal of evidence in support of Garrison's account. The first and most potent piece was this: the gun was Margie's. She'd bought it six years ago, after one of her drinking circle had been attacked on the street, and died in the resulting coma. Margie hadn't concealed her pleasure in the weapon; it was a "pretty gun," she'd said, and she'd have not the least hesitation in using it should the occasion arise.

According to Garrison, she had. She'd intended to kill him, and he'd done what anybody would have done under the circumstances. He didn't make any false show of grief. His marriage to Margie had been little more than a duty for years, he freely admitted. But if he'd wanted her out of his life, he pointed out, there were less foolhardy ways to engineer that than to shoot her in his own bathroom. Divorce, for instance. It didn't make any sense for him to murder her. It only jeopardized his liberty.

Portions of his testimony appeared on the front pages of *The New York Times* and *The Wall Street Journal*, along with quotes from a number of sources that suggested his arguments carried weight. Nor could most of the commentators refrain from reporting some unflattering anecdote about Margie's alcoholism, which had been public knowledge (and on occasion a public spectacle) for a decade or more. Of course there was also no scarcity of gossip pieces, both in magazines and on television, raking up some of the less savory stories from Garrison's past. Two of his former mistresses consented to be interviewed, as did a number of sometime employees. The portraits they drew weren't particularly flattering. Even if only half of what they were remembering was true Garrison still emerged as self-centered, autocratic and on occasion sexually compulsive. But when each of them was asked the important question— *in your opinion, was this self-defense or murder?*—they were all of the opinion that the man they'd known would not have shot his wife in cold blood. One of the mistresses even added that *"Garrison was very sentimental about Margie. He'd always be telling me how it had been when they were first in love. I used to tell him I didn't want to hear about all that, but sometimes I think he couldn't help talking about her. It used to make me a little jealous, but looking back I think it's sort of sweet."*

The other subject that came under close scrutiny during this period was the family itself. The Garrison Geary Murder Case gave the press across the country, from the most high-minded journals to the lowliest gutter rags, a perfect excuse to dust off all their old stories about the Gearys. *"As rich as the Rockefellers and as influential as the Kennedys,"* the piece in *Newsweek* began, *"the Geary family has been an American institution since the end of the Civil War, when its founding fathers came to a sudden and impressive prominence which has not diminished since that time. Whatever the demands of the age, the Gearys have been their equal. Warmongers and peacemakers, traditionalists and radicals, hedonists and Puritans; it has sometimes seemed that within the ranks of the Geary clan an example of every American extreme could be found. With the police investigations into the murder of Margaret Geary ongoing, a cloud of doubt hangs over the family's reputation; but however those investigations are concluded one thing may be reliably predicted: the family will survive, as will the American public's endless fascination with its affairs."*

## ii

Rachel had not told anybody she was on her way back, but she didn't doubt that word would precede her, courtesy of Jimmy Hornbeck. She was right. The Central Park apartment was adorned with fresh flowers, and there was a note on the table from Mitchell, welcoming her home, and thanking her for coming. It was a curiously detached little missive, not that far removed from a hotel manager's note of thanks to a returning guest. But nothing about Mitchell surprised her any more. She was perfectly sanguine about what lay before her. Whatever new grotesqueries she was about to witness she was determined to view them with the same amused detachment that she'd seen in Margie.

She called Mitchell in the early evening to announce her arrival. He suggested she come to the mansion for some supper. Loretta would like to see her, he said; and so would he. She agreed to come. Good, he said, he'd send Ralphie to pick her up.

"There are reporters outside the home all the time," he warned.

"Yes, they were waiting for me when I came back here."

"What did you tell them?"

"Absolutely nothing."

"Who the hell's telling them our business, that's what I want to know. When all this is over, I'm going to find out who the fuck these people are—"

"And do what?"

"Fire their asses! I'm so sick of having cameras everywhere and people asking stupid fucking questions." She'd never heard Mitch exasperated this way before; he'd always accepted scrutiny as the price of living the high life. "You know some sonofabitch got a photograph of Garrison in jail, sitting on the can. And some fucking rag printed it! A picture of my brother taking a dump in a cell. Can you believe that?"

The outburst shocked her; not because somebody had taken a picture of Garrison relieving himself, but because until this moment she hadn't imagined his being behind bars. She'd just assumed that Cecil, or the phalanx of lawyers the family had hired to defend Garrison, had secured his release on bail.

"When does he get out?" she asked him.

"We're pressing for that right now," Mitch said. "I mean, he's innocent. We all know that. It was a horrible accident and we all wish it hadn't happened, but it's ridiculous keeping him locked up like he was a common criminal."

A common criminal: that went to the heart of it. Whatever else Garrison might have been, Mitchell seemed to be saying, he was American royalty, and deserved to be treated with appropriate respect. It was an impression Rachel had reinforced when she went over to the mansion: the atmosphere was one of besiegement; the drapes closed against the curious eyes of the hoi polloi, while the noble Gearys debated their response to the crisis. Loretta set the tone for these exchanges. The imperiousness was intact, but it was shaded now with a certain bruised melancholy, as though some martyrdom had been visited upon her which she was bearing with fortitude. She welcomed Rachel back with a dry kiss.

They gathered for supper around the dining room table, with Loretta at one end and—rather pointedly positioned, Rachel thought—Cecil at the other. Besides Deborah, Rachel and Mitch three other members of the clan were present. Norah was there, tanned and brittle; George's brother Richard had come up from Miami, where he'd just successfully defended a man who'd cut up a hooker with an electric carving knife, and Karen, flown in from Europe. She was the one member of the group Rachel had not met; she'd been out of the country during the wedding. She was a contained woman, her body, her gestures and her voice neat and unassuming. Rachel had the impression that she'd not come back out of love for either Garrison or the family, but because an edict had gone out, demanding her presence. She certainly had little to contribute to the debate. In fact she said scarcely a word throughout the supper, seldom even looking up from her plate.

There was no doubt as to the star of the evening: it was Loretta. She made a statement of intent the moment they all sat down.

"We're going to start acting like a family again," she said to everyone. "This business with Garrison is a wake-up call, to us all. It's time to put our differences aside. Whatever problems we have with one another—and they're bound to come along in the best of circumstances—this is the time to forget about them and show people what we're made of. Cadmus, as I'm sure you know, is now bedridden, and I'm afraid he's very weak. In fact, some of the time he doesn't even know who I am, which is of course very painful. But he has periods when his mind's suddenly very lucid, and then he can be astonishingly acute. Earlier this evening he started talking about hearing voices in the house. And I told him that yes, we were having a little family gathering. I didn't tell him why, of course. He doesn't know about . . . what happened . . . and I don't intend to tell him. But he did say to me, when I explained to him that we were all gathering together, that he was going to be here with us. And I think in a very real sense he is. He should be our inspiration right now." There were murmurs of assent around the table, the loudest coming from Richard. "We all know what Cadmus would say if he knew what was going on," Loretta said.

"Fuck 'em all," said Mitch. Norah laughed into her wine glass.

Loretta moved on without glancing in her stepson's direction. "He'd say: business as usual. We have to demonstrate our strength as a family. Our solidarity. Which is why I'm particularly grateful to you, Rachel, for coming back at such short notice. I know things between you and Mitchell aren't very easy at the moment, so it means a lot to me personally that you're here. Now, Cecil, why don't you tell us all the situation as far as Garrison's bail is concerned?"

The next hour was dedicated to legal issues: the history of the judge who would be presiding over the hearing, supplied by Richard; brief assessments of the prosecutors from Cecil, then onto the business problems arising from Garrison's temporary indisposal. Rachel didn't understand many of the issues under discussion, but there was no doubt that despite Loretta's talk of business as usual family affairs were hard to keep on track without Garrison to give the orders. A dozen times, maybe more, a question had to be left unanswered because it fell into Garrison's area of expertise.

Finally, the conversation returned to Rachel.

"Has Mitchell told you about the fund-raiser on Friday night?" Loretta asked her.

"No, I . . ."

Loretta threw Mitchell a weary look. "It's for the hospital. The pediatric ward. It was about the only charity Margaret had the slightest interest in, and I think it's important we have a presence there."

"I was going to talk to Rachel about it later," Mitchell put in.

"Later's no good, Mitchell," Loretta said. "We've had too much 'later' in this household. Things being put off and put off . . ." What the hell was she talking about, Rachel wondered. "We've got to get on and do what we need to do. Even if it makes us uncomfortable or—"

"All right, Loretta," Mitchell said. "Calm down."

"Don't you condescend to me," Loretta replied, her voice monotonal. "You're going to listen to me for once in your pampered little life. We're in a mess here. Do you understand me?" Mitchell just stared, which inflamed Loretta all the more. "DO YOU UNDERSTAND ME?" she yelled, slamming her palm down on the table. All the silverware jumped.

"Loretta—" Cecil said softly.

"Don't you start pouring oil, Cecil. This isn't any time to be making nice. We're in terrible trouble. All of us. The whole family. Terrible, terrible trouble."

"He'll be out in a week," Mitchell said.

"Is this willful or are you just too stupid to see what's right in front of your nose?" Loretta said, her voice not quite so loud, but still several notches above the conversational. "There's more to all this than what happened to poor Margie . . ."

"Oh don't start your Cassandra act, for God's sake," Mitchell said, his voice thick with contempt.

"Mitchell," Cecil said, "a little respect . . ."

"If she wants some respect she should start being practical, and not telling us it's all in the fucking stars."

"That's not what I'm saying," Loretta said.

"Oh I'm sorry. What is it today? Tarot cards?"

"If your father could hear you—"

"My father thought you were as crazy as a coot," Mitchell said, getting up from the table. "And I'm not going to waste my time sitting here listening to you chatter on like you understand a damn thing about the way the business life of this family works."

"You're the one who's out of his depth," Loretta said.

"There you go again with your inane little threats!" Mitchell yelled. "I know what you're doing! You think I don't see you trying to get Rachel over to your side?"

"Oh for God's sake—"

"Sending her off to that stinking little island, thinking it's some kind of secret."

Rachel caught hold of his hand. "Mitch," she said. "You're making a fool of yourself. Shut up."

He looked as though she'd just slapped him, hard. He pulled his hand out of her grip. "Are you in with her then?" he said, looking at Rachel but pointing at Loretta. "Is this some fucking conspiracy? Cecil? Help me out here. I want to know what's going on."

"*Nothing's* going on," Cecil said, wearily. "We're just all tired and stressed out. And sad."

"*She* isn't sad," Mitchell said, looking back at Loretta, who was wearing an expression of regal inviolability. "She's fucking glad Margie's dead and my brother's in a jail cell."

"I think you should apologize for that," Cecil said.

"It's the truth!" Mitchell protested. "Look at her!"

Now it was Cecil who rose. "I'm sorry, Mitchell, I can't permit you to talk to Loretta that way."

"*Sit the fuck down!*" Mitchell yelled. "Who the hell do you think you are?" Cecil did and said nothing. "You know what happens when the old man goes? It's Garrison and me. We're in charge. And if Garrison stays in jail, then it's just me." He made a tight little smile. "So you'd better watch yourself, Cecil. I'm going to be looking very hard at the kind of support I'm getting. And if I see a lack of loyalty, I'm not going to think twice." Cecil glanced down at his plate. Then he sat down. "Better," Mitchell said. "Rachel. We're leaving."

"So go," Rachel said, "I'll talk to you tomorrow." Mitchell hesitated. "I'm not coming with you," Rachel said.

"It's up to you," Mitchell replied, with an unconvincing show of indifference.

"I know," Rachel said. "And I'm staying here."

Mitchell made no further attempt to convince her. He left the room without another word.

"Brat," Loretta remarked quietly.

"I'd better go and calm him down," Richard said.

"Why don't we all just go home to bed?" Norah suggested.

"I think that's probably a very good idea," Loretta said. "Rachel . . . would you stay just a couple of minutes? I need to have a word with you."

The rest of the company departed. When the last of them had gone, and the door was closed Loretta said: "I noticed you didn't eat."

"I wasn't hungry."

"Lovesick?" Rachel said nothing. "It'll pass," Loretta went on. "You'll have plenty to distract you in the next few days." She sipped on her white wine. "You've got nothing to hide," she said. "We've all felt what you're feeling now."

"I don't know what you're talking about."

"Him," Loretta said quietly. "Galilee. I'm talking about Galilee." Rachel looked up, and found Loretta's eyes there, ready to read her. "Was he all you wanted him to be?" she asked.

"I told you. I don't . . . know . . ."

Loretta looked pained. "There's no need for deceit," she said. "Lie to Mitchell, by all means. But not to me." She kept looking at Rachel; as if waiting for her to spill her pain. Greedy for it, in fact.

"Why should I lie to Mitchell?" Rachel said, determined to deflect this interrogation by gaze.

"Because it's all he deserves," Loretta said flatly. "He was born with too many blessings for his own good. It's made him stupid. If he'd had a harelip he'd have been twice the man he is."

"So I take it you think I'm rather stupid too."

"Why would I think that?"

"I married him."

"Brilliant women marry perfect clods every day of the week. Sometimes you have to do that to get on in the world. If you're a shoe-girl in a shoestore and if you don't get out all you'll ever do is sell shoes then by God you do everything in your power to change your circumstances. There's no shame in that. You did what you had to do. And now you're finished with him. And there's no shame in that either." She paused for a moment, as if to allow time for Rachel to respond; but this little speech had left Rachel dumbstruck. "Is it really so hard to admit to?" Loretta went on. "If I were you I'd be proud of myself. I really would."

"Proud of what?"

"Now you're being obtuse," Loretta said, "and it's not worthy of you. What are you afraid of?"

"I just don't know . . . I don't know why you're talking this way to me when we scarcely know one another and . . . well, to be honest I thought you didn't really like me."

"Oh I like you well enough," Loretta said. "But liking isn't really the point any more, is it? We need one another, Rachel."

"For what?"

"For self-protection. Whatever your dense husband thinks, he's not going to be running the Geary empire."

"Why not?"

"Because he's inheriting a lot more than he'll be able to deal with. He'll crack. He's already cracking because he doesn't have Garrison to hold his hand."

"What if Garrison gets off?"

"I don't think there's any 'what if?' about it. He'll get off. But there's other stuff, just waiting to be uncovered. His women, for one thing."

"So he has a mistress. Nobody's going to care."

"You know what he likes to do?" Loretta said. "He likes to hire women to play dead. Doll themselves up to look like corpses and lie there and be violated. That's one of his milder obsessions."

"Oh my God . . ."

"He's been getting more indiscreet over the last year or so. In fact, I think he wants to get caught. There are some photographs . . ."

"Of what?"

"You don't need to know," Loretta said. "Just take it from me that if the least disgusting of them was to be made public Garrison's little circle of influence would disappear overnight."

"And who has these pictures?" Loretta smiled. "You?" Rachel said. "You've got them?"

Loretta smoothed out a wrinkle in the tablecloth, her tone completely detached. "I'm not going to sit back and watch a necrophile and his idiot brother take charge of all this family owns. All this family stands for." She looked up from the smoothed linen. "The point is: we all have to take sides. You can either work with me to make sure we don't lose everything when Cadmus dies, or you can run to Mitchell and tell him I'm conspiring against the two of them, and take your chances with them. It's up to you."

"Why are you trusting me now?" Rachel said. "Because Margie's dead?"

"God, no. She was no use to me. She was too far gone. Garrison again. God knows what he put Margie through, behind locked doors."

"She'd never have put up with—"

"With playing dead on a Saturday night? I think a lot of women do that and a lot worse to keep their husbands happy."

"So you still haven't answered my question. Why are you telling me all this now?"

"Because now there's something you want and I can help you get it."

There was a long silence. Then Rachel said: "Galilee?"

Loretta nodded. "Who else?" she said. "In the end, everything comes back to Galilee."

# IV

## i

Under normal circumstances Rachel would have hated the Hospital Benefit Gala. It was exactly the kind of grand, glittering event which had come to seem like an unpleasant duty after a few months of marriage: all glassy gazes and frigid smiles. But circumstances had changed. For one thing, Mitchell was wary of her, which she liked. Several times during the evening when she strayed from his side for some innocent reason he came to join her and quietly told her to stay close by. When she asked him why he told her he didn't want her cornered by some inquisitive sonofabitch who'd pump her for information about Garrison, to which she replied that she was quite capable of talking her way out of a difficult situation, and anyway what did she know that was worth gossiping about?

"You're making a fool of me," he said when he caught up with her for the fourth time. There was fury in his eyes, but he had to perfection the trick of maintaining a benign expression despite his true feelings; the accusations emerged through an opulent smile. "I don't want you talking to anybody—do you understand me: *anybody*—without me right there with you. I'm perfectly serious, Rachel."

"I'm going to go where the hell I like and say whatever I feel like saying, Mitchell, and neither you nor your brother nor Cecil nor Cadmus nor any other damn Geary is going to stop me."

"Garrison'll destroy you, you know that," Mitchell said. He wasn't even attempting to smile any longer.

Rachel was incredulous. "You sound like a bad imitation of a gangster."

"But he will. He's not going to let you get away with anything."

"God, you are so infantile. Now you're going to set your big brother on me?"

"I'm just trying to warn you."

"No. You're trying to frighten me. And it's not going to work."

He looked away for a moment, to see that nobody was close enough to hear him. "Who do you think's going to be there to help you if you get into trouble?" he said. "We're the only real family you've got, baby. The only people you could turn to if things got nasty."

Rachel was beginning to feel faintly sick. There was no mistaking what Mitch was saying.

"I think I need to go home," she told him.

"You know, you do look a little flushed," he said, his hand going up to her cheek. "What's wrong?"

"I'm just tired," she said.

"I'll take you down to the street."

"I'll be all right."

"No," he said, linking his arm through hers, and drawing her close to him. "I'll go with you."

Together they made their way through the crowd, pausing a couple of times so that Mitchell could exchange a few words with someone he knew. Rachel made little attempt to play the attentive wife; she slipped his hold and moved on toward the door after a few seconds, leaving him to follow her.

"We should talk some more," he said once they reached the street.

"About what? I have nothing to say to you."

"Just because we'd had some hard times—hear me out, Rachel *please*—that doesn't mean we have to throw up our hands and let everything we ever had, everything we ever felt for one another, go to hell. We should talk. We really should." He kissed her lightly on the cheek. "I want the best for you."

"Is that why you threatened me in there?" Rachel said.

"If it came out that way then I'm sorry, I'm truly sorry, it's not what I meant at all. I just want you to see things the way I see them." She stared at him, hoping he felt her contempt. "I've got a much better picture of the situation right now," he said. "I have more . . . information about the way things are. And I know—trust me, Rachel, I *know*—that you're not in a safe place."

"I'll take the risk."

"Rachel—"

"Go to hell," she told him very calmly.

The chauffeur was out of the car, opening the door for her.

"Call me tomorrow," Mitchell said. She ignored him. "We're not done yet, Rachel."

"You can close the door," she told the driver, who obliged her, leaving a muted Mitchell standing on the sidewalk, looking both irritated and faintly forlorn.

## ii

As she stepped out of the car at the other end of her journey, a young bespectacled man—who'd been out of sight behind the potted cypress at the door—stepped into view.

"Mrs. Geary?" he said. "I have to talk to you."

He was dressed in what her mother would have called his Sunday best: a powder-blue suit; a thin black tie; polished shoes. His blond hair was trimmed close to his scalp, but the severity of the cut didn't spoil the amiability of his features. His face was round, his nose and mouth small; his eyes soft and anxious.

"Please hear me out," he begged, though Rachel had done nothing to indicate that she would ignore him. "It's very important." He glanced nervously toward the security guard who kept twenty-four-hour vigilance at the door of her building. "I'm not crazy. And I'm not begging. It's—"

"Is he causing a problem here, Mrs. Geary?" the guard wanted to know.

"—it's about Margie," the young man said hurriedly. His voice had dropped to a whisper.

"What about her?"

"We *knew* one another," the young man said. "My name's Danny."

"The barman?"

"Yeah. The barman."

"Do you want to just go inside, Mrs. Geary?" the guard went on. "I can deal with this guy for you."

"No, he's okay," Rachel said. Then, to Danny: "You'd better come on in."

"No, I think I'd feel safer if we just walked."

"All right, we'll walk."

At Danny's request they crossed to the other side of the street, and walked under the trees around the park.

"Why all the secrecy?" she asked him. "You're not in any danger."

"I don't trust the family. Margie said they were like the Mafia."

"Margie exaggerated."

"She also said you were the only one worth a damn."

"That's nice to hear."

"She loved you so much, you know?"

"I loved her," Rachel said. "She was a wonderful lady."

"So she told you about me?"

"A little. She said she had a younger man in her life. Boasted, really."

"We got on great. She liked my martinis and I . . . I thought she was like somebody you'd see in a movie, you know?"

"Larger than life."

"Right. Larger than life."

"She never did anything by halves, that's for sure."

"I know that," he said, with a little smile. "She was, you know, really . . . passionate. I never met any woman like her. Not that I've been around that many older women—I mean, I wouldn't want you to think I was some kind of gigolo or something."

"What a nice, old-fashioned word."

"Well, that's not me."

"I understand, Danny," Rachel said gently. "You genuinely felt something for Margie."

"And she felt something for me," Danny replied. "I know she did. But she didn't want everybody gossiping. She knew people would think she was being sleazy. You know, with me being younger; and a barman, for Chrissakes."

"So is all this about making sure I don't say anything? Because you needn't worry. I'm not going to blab about it."

"Oh, I know that," he said. "Really. She trusted you and so do I."

"So, what do you want?"

He studied the sidewalk for a few yards. Then he said: "I wrote her some letters, talking about things we'd done together. Physical things." He put his hand to his face and plucked at his moustache. "It was a stupid thing to do; but there were days when I was so full of feelings I had to write it down."

"And where are these letters?"

"Somewhere in her apartment, I guess."

"And you want me to get them back?"

"Yes. If possible. And . . . there's some photographs too."

"How much stuff are we talking about?"

"Only five or six photographs. There's more letters. Maybe ten or twelve. I wasn't keeping track. I mean, I never expected . . ." For the first time in the conversation she thought he was going to start crying. His voice cracked; he reached into his pocket and dug out a handkerchief. "God," he said. "I'm a wreck."

"You're doing really well," Rachel said.

"I know you probably think I was in it for what she could give me, and right at the beginning that's what it was about. I'm not going to lie about that. I liked that she had plenty of money, and I liked that she gave me things. But in the end, I didn't care any more. I just wanted her." Without warning, the tears became a rant. "And that bastard sonofabitch husband of hers! Jesus! *Jesus!* How could anybody believe a word he says? He should be fried! Fucking fried!"

"He's going to get off," Rachel said quietly.

"Then there's no justice. Because he killed her in cold blood."

"You seem very sure about that," Rachel said. Danny didn't reply. "Is that because you were with her that night?"

"I don't know that we should get into this," Danny said.

"It seems to me we're already there."

"Suppose you have to testify under oath."

"Then I'll lie," Rachel said flatly.

Danny cast her a sideways glance. "How come you're like this?"

"Like what?"

"Just . . . not all pissy with me, you know? I'm just a barman."

"And I'm a girl who sold jewelry."

"But you're a Geary now."

"That's a mistake I'm going to fix."

"So you're not afraid of them?"

"I don't want Margie's name dragged in the dirt any more than you do. I'm not guaranteeing I'll find this stuff, but I'll do what I can."

Danny gave her his telephone number, and they parted. If he didn't hear from her, he said, he'd just assume she'd changed her mind, which he'd perfectly understand, given the circumstances.

But Rachel had no intention of changing her mind. As she walked home she was already laying plans for how best to get into Margie and Garrison's apartment in the Trump Tower and search it without being discovered. There were risks involved, no doubt of that; she was consorting with somebody who the police would surely want to interrogate, if they knew of his existence. Her silence in the matter was probably a crime; and searching a murder site, then removing (if she was successful) evidence of the affair was certainly interfering with the processes of the law. But she didn't care. There was more at stake in this endeavor than finding Danny's love letters and a few indiscreet photographs.

She was all but lost in a labyrinth of potential alliances: Loretta wanted her on her side, Danny needed her help, Mitchell had effectively threatened her if she didn't stay close by. Suddenly she was important to the balance of power; but she didn't entirely know why. Nor did she know what the consequences of choosing the wrong allegiance would be. What fell to the victor in this battle between sons and stepmother? Simply the incalculable wealth of the Gearys? Prize enough to murder for, without question; but only if those involved were not already rich beyond dreams of avarice.

Something else moved these people, and it wasn't money. Nor was it love; nor did she think it was power. Until she knew what it was she would not be safe, of that she was certain. Perhaps if she went to the place where Margie had died—Margie, who had been a victim of this thing she could not grasp or understand—its nature would come clear. It was a primitive hope, she realized; close to a kind of superstition. But what else was she to do? Her analytical powers had failed her. It was time to trust to her instincts, and her instincts told her to go and look where the harm had already been done; to look, as it were, back along the path of the bullet that had taken poor Margie's life. Back into the dark heart of Garrison Geary, and to whatever hopes or fears had moved him to murder.

V

i

Glancing back over the last several chapters, I realize that I've left a thread of my story dangling (actually, I'm certain I've left a good many more than one, but the rest will be sewn into the design in due course). I'm speaking of my sister's adventures. You'll recall that the last time I saw her she was in flight from Cesaria, who was furious with her for some unspecified crime. If you'll allow me a moment here I'll tell you what all that was about. My fear is that if I don't tell you now the urgency of what is about to happen in the lives of the Gearys will prevent me from breaking in at a later point. In short, this may be the last real breath I can take. After this, the deluge.

So; Marietta. She appeared in my chambers three or four days after my encounter with Cesaria, wearing a dreamy smile.

"What are you on?" I asked her.

"I've had a couple of mushrooms," she replied.

I was irritated with her, and I said so. She had too little sense of responsibility, I said: always in pursuit of some altered state or other.

"Oh, listen to you. So you didn't take the cocaine and Benedictine?"

I admitted that I had, but that I'd had a legitimate reason: it was helping me stay alert through the long hours of writing. It was quite a different situation, I said, to indulging day after day, the way she did.

"You're exaggerating," she said.

In my fine self-righteousness I made a list for her. There was nothing she wouldn't try. She smoked opium and chewed coca leaves; she ate pharmaceutical painkillers like candies and washed them down with tequila and rum; she liked heroin and cherries in brandy and hashish brownies.

"Lord, Maddox, you can be so tiresome sometimes. If I play music and the music's worth a damn, I'm altering my state. If I touch myself, and I give myself pleasure, I'm altering my state."

"They're not comparable."

"Why not?" I drew a breath before replying. "See? You don't have an answer."

"Wait, wait, wait—" I protested.

"Anyway," she went on, "I don't see that it's your business what I do with my head."

"It becomes my business if I have to deal with your mother."

Marietta rolled her eyes. "Oh Lord, I knew we'd get round to that eventually."

"I think I deserve an explanation."

"She found me going through some old clothes, that's all," Marietta replied.

"Old clothes?"

"Yes, . . . it was ridiculous. I mean, who cares after all this time?"

Despite her cavalier attitude she was plainly concealing something she felt guilty about. "Whose clothes were they?" I asked her.

"His," she said with a little shrug.

"Galilee's?"

"No . . . *his*." Another shrug. "Father's."

"You found clothes that belonged to our father—"

"—who art in Heaven . . . yes."

"And you were touching them?"

"Oh for God's sake, Maddox, don't you start. They were clothes. Old clothes. I don't think he'd even worn them. You know what a peacock he was."

"That's not what I remember."

"Well maybe he only did it for my benefit," she said with a sly smirk. "I had the pleasure of sitting in his dressing room with him many times—"

"I've heard enough, thank you," I told her. I didn't like the direction the conversation was taking; nor the gleam in Marietta's eye. But I was too late. The rebel in her was roused, and she wasn't about to be quelled.

"You started this," she said. "So you can damn well hear me out. It's all true; every word of it."

"I still—"

"*Listen to me*," she insisted. "You should know what he got up to when nobody else was looking. He was a priapic old bastard. Have you used that word yet by the way? *Priapic?*"

"No."

"Well now you can, quoting me."

"This isn't going in the book."

"Christ, you can be an old woman sometimes, Maddox. It's part of the story."

"It's got nothing to do with what I'm writing."

"The fact that the founding father of our family was so oversexed he used to parade around in front of his six-year-old daughter with a hardon? Oh, I think that's got *everything* to do with what you're writing." She grinned at me, and I swear any God-fearing individual would have said the Devil was in that face. The beautiful exuberance of her features; the naked pleasure she took in shocking me.

"Of course I was fascinated. You know the origin of the word fascinated? It's Latin. *Fascinare* means to put under a spell. It was particularly attributed to serpents—"

"Why do you insist on doing this?"

"He had that power. No question. He waved his snake and I was . . . enchanted." She smiled at the memory. "I couldn't take my eyes off it. I would have followed it anywhere. Of course I wanted to touch it, but he told me no. When you're a little older, he said, then I'll show what it can do."

She stopped talking; stared out the window at the passing sky. I was ashamed of my curiosity, but I couldn't help myself."

"And did he?" I said.

She kept staring. "No, he never did. He wanted to—I could see it in his eyes sometimes—but he didn't dare. You see I told Galilee all about it. That was my big mistake. I told him I'd seen Papa's snake and it was wonderful. I swore him to secrecy of course but I'm damn sure he told Cesaria, and she probably gave Papa hell. She was always jealous of me."

"That's ridiculous."

"She was. She still is. She threw a fit when she found me in the dressing room. After all these years she didn't want me near his belongings." She finally pulled her gaze from the clouds and looked back at me. "I love women more than life itself," she said. "I love everything about them. Their feel, their smell, the way they move when you stroke them . . . And I really can't bear men. Not in that way. They're so lumpen. But I'd have made an exception for Papa."

"You're grotesque, you know that?"

"Why?" I just made a pained face. "We don't have to live by the same rules as everybody else," she said. "Because we're not *like* everybody else."

"Maybe we'd all be a little happier if we were."

"Happy? I'm ecstatic. I'm in love. And I really mean it this time. I'm in love. With a farmgirl no less."

"A farmgirl."

"I know it doesn't sound very promising but she's extraordinary, Maddox. Her name's Alice Pennstrom, and I met her at a barn dance in Raleigh."

"They have lesbian barn dances these days?"

"It wasn't a dyke thing. It was men and women. You know me. I've always liked helping straight girls discover themselves. Anyway, Alice is wonderful. And I wanted to dress up in something special for our three-week anniversary."

"That's why you were looking through the clothes?"

"Yeah. I thought maybe I'd find something special. Something that would really get Alice going," Marietta said. "Which I did, by the way. So anyway thank you for taking the heat from Cesaria. I'll do the same for you one of these days."

"I'm going to hold you to that," I said.

"No problem," Marietta said. "If I make a promise, I'm good for it." She glanced at her watch. "Hey, I gotta go. I'm meeting Alice in half an hour. What I came in here for was a book of poems."

"Poems?"

"Something I can recite to her. Something sexy and romantic, to get her in the mood."

"You're welcome to look around," I said. "I presume, by the way, that all this means you think we've made peace?"

"Were we ever at war?" Marietta said, as though a little puzzled at my remark. "Where's the poetry section?"

"There isn't one. They're scattered all over."

"You need some organization in here."

"Thank you, but it suits me just the way it is."

"So point me to a poet."

"You want a lesbian poet? There's some Sappho up there, and a book of Marina Tsvetaeva."

"Is any of that going to make Alice moist?"

"Lord, you can be crude sometimes."

"Well is it or isn't it?"

"I don't know," I snapped. "Anyway, I thought you'd already seduced this woman."

"I have," Marietta said, scanning the shelves. "And it was amazing sex. So amazing that I've decided to propose to her."

"Is this a joke?"

"No. I want to marry my Alice. I want to set up house and adopt children. Dozens of children. But first I need a poem, to make her feel . . . you know what I mean . . . no, come to think of it, you probably don't . . . I want her to be so in love with me it hurts."

I pointed. "To your left—"

"What?"

"—the little dark turquoise book. Try that." Marietta took it down.

"It's a book of poems by a nun."

"A nun?" Marietta went to put the book back.

"Wait," I said to her, "give it a chance. Here—" I went over to Marietta, and took the book—which she hadn't yet opened—from her hand. "Let me find something for you, then you can leave me alone." I flicked through the musty pages. It was years since I'd perused these lyrics, but I remembered one that had moved me.

"Who is she?" Marietta said.

"I told you: a nun. Her name was Mary-Elizabeth Bowen. She died in the forties, at the age of a hundred and one."

"A virgin?"

"Is that relevant?"

"Well it is if I'm trying to find something sexy."

"Try this," I said, and passed the book back to her.

"Which one?"

"*I was a very narrow creature.*"

Marietta read it aloud:

> *"I was a very narrow creature at my heart,*
> *Until you came.*
> *None got in and out of me with ease;*
> *Yet when you spoke my name*
> *I was unbounded, like the world—"*

She looked up at me. "Oh I like this," she said. "Are you sure she was a nun?"

"Just read it . . ."

> *"I was unbounded, like the world.*
> *I never felt such fear as then, being so limitless,*
> *When I'd known only walls and whisperings.*
> *I fled you foolishly;*
> *Looked in every quarter for a place to hide.*
> *Went into a bud, it blossomed.*
> *Went into a cloud, it rained.*
> *Went into a man, who died,*
> *And bore me out again,*
> *Into your arms."*

"Oh my Lord," she said.

"You like that?"

"Who did she write it for?"

"Christ, I assume. But you needn't tell Alice that."

## ii

She went away happy, and despite my protests at her disturbing me, I felt curiously refreshed by her conversation. The idea of her marrying Alice Pennstrom still seemed absurd, but who am I to judge? It's so long since I felt the kind of sensual love Marietta obviously felt; and I suppose I was slightly envious of it.

There's nothing more personal, I think, than the shape that emptiness takes inside you; nor more particular than the means by which you fill it. This book has become that means for me: when I'm writing about other people's loss, and the imminence of disaster, I feel comforted. Thank God this isn't happening to me, I think, and lick my lips as I relate the next catastrophe.

But before I get to that next catastrophe, I want to add a coda to my account of Marietta's visit. The very next day, at noon or thereabouts, she returned to my study. She'd obviously not slept since the previous meeting—there were bruisy rings around her eyes, and her voice was a growl—but she was in a fine mood. The poem had worked, she said. Alice had accepted her proposal of marriage.

"She didn't hesitate. She just told me she loved me more than anybody she'd ever met, and she wanted to be with me for the rest of our lives."

"And did you tell her that *your* life's going to be a hell of a lot longer than hers?"

"I don't care."

"She's going to have to know sooner or later."

"And I'll tell her, when I think she's ready for it. In fact, I'm going to bring her here after we're married. I'm going to show her everything. And you know what, brother o' mine?"

"What?"

Marietta's voice dropped to a raspy whisper. "I'm going to find a way to keep her with me. The years aren't going to take Alice away from me. I won't let it happen."

"It's a natural process, Marietta. And how do you propose to stop it?"

"Papa knew a way. He told me."

"Was this one of your dressing room conversations?"

"No, this was a lot later. Just before Galilee came home."

I was fascinated now. Clearly this was no joke. "What did he tell you?"

"That he'd contemplated keeping your mother with him, but Cesaria had forbidden it."

"Did he tell you how he'd intended to do it?"

"No. But I'm going to find out," Marietta said nonchalantly. Then, dropping her voice to something less than a whisper: "If I have to break into his tomb and shake it out of him," she said, "I'll do it. Whatever it takes, I'm marrying my Alice till the end of the world."

*          *          *

What do I make of all this? To be truthful, I try my best not to think too hard about all that she said. It unsettles me. Besides, I've got tales to tell: Garrison's in jail and Margie's in the morgue; Loretta's plotting an insurrection. I have more than enough to occupy my thoughts without having Marietta's obsessions to puzzle over.

All that said, I'm certain there's some truth in what she told me. My father was undoubtedly capable of extraordinary deeds. He was divine, after his own peculiar fashion, and divinity brings capacities and ambitions that don't trouble the rest of us. So it seems quite plausible that at some point in his relationship with my mother, whom I think he loved, he contemplated a gift of life to her.

But if my sister believes she can get his bones to tell her how that gift might have been given, she's in for a disappointment. My father is beyond interrogation, even by his own daughter, and however much Marietta may strut and boast, she wouldn't dare go where his soul has gone.

If you think I'm tempting fate with these assertions, then so be it. I don't have the will to explain to you where Nicodemus has gone; and I fervently hope—hope more passionately than I could imagine hoping for anything—that I never have cause to try and find that will. Not because I would fail in that pursuit (though I surely would) but because it would mean the unknowable was attempting to make itself known, and the laws by which this world lives would be littered at our feet.

On such a day, I would not want to be sitting writing a book. On such a day I'm not certain I would want to be alive.

# VI

### i

The day after Rachel's encounter with Danny was the day of the funeral. Margie had told her lawyers some years before how she wanted to be buried: alongside her brother Sam—who'd died in a motorcycle accident at the age of twenty-two—and her mother and father, in a small churchyard in Wilmington, Pennsylvania. The significance of this wasn't lost on anybody. It was Margie's last act of rejection. Whatever choices she'd made in her life, she knew exactly where she wanted to be in death: and it wasn't entombed with the Gearys.

Rachel got an early morning call from Mitchell suggesting they travel together, but she declined, and drove to Wilmington alone. It was an ill-tempered day, blustery and bleak, and only the most hardy of celebrity-spotters had trekked through the rain to ogle the mourners. The press were present in force, however, and they had a rare assortment of luminaries to report on. Gossip though she was, Margie had never been much of a name-dropper (she was almost as gleeful discussing the intricacies of a favorite waiter's adulteries as those of a congressman), and it wasn't until now that Rachel realized just how many famous and influential people Margie had known. Not simply known, but impressed herself so favorably upon that they'd left the comfort of their fancy houses and their congressional offices, their weekend homes by the shore and in the mountains, to pay their respects. Rachel found herself wondering if Margie's spirit was here, mingling with the mighty. If so, she was probably remarking uncharitably on this one's facelift and that one's waistline; but in her heart she'd surely be proud that the life she'd lived—despite its excesses—had earned this show of sorrow and gratitude.

Mitchell had not yet arrived, but Loretta was already sitting on the front row of the pews, staring fixedly at the flower-bedecked casket. Rachel didn't particularly want to share the woman's company, but then nor did she want to be seen to be making any statement by sitting apart, so she made her way down the aisle, pausing in front of the casket for a few moments, then went to sit at Loretta's side.

There were tears on Loretta's immaculately painted face; in her trembling hands a sodden handkerchief. This was not the calculating woman who'd presided over the family table at the mansion a few evenings before. Her sadness was too unflattering to be faked: her eyes puffy, her nose running. Rachel put her hand over Loretta's hand, and gripped it. Loretta sniffed.

"I wondered if you'd come," she said quietly.

"I'm not going anywhere," Rachel said.

"I wouldn't blame you if you did," Loretta said. "This is all such a mess." She kept staring at the casket. "At least she's out of it. It's just us now." There was a long silence. Then Loretta murmured: "She hated me."

Rachel was about to mouth some platitude; then thought better of it. Instead she said: "I know."

"Do you know why?"

"No."

"Because of Galilee."

It was the last name Rachel had expected to hear in these circumstances. Galilee belonged in another world; a warm, enchanted world where the air smelled of the sea. She closed her eyes for a moment and brought that place into her mind's eye. The deck of *The Samarkand* at evening: the sleepy ocean rolling against the hull, the creaking ropes calling out the stars, and Galilee encircling her. She longed to be there as she'd longed for nothing in her life. Longed to hear his promises, even knowing he'd break them.

Her thoughts were interrupted by murmurings from the pews behind her. She opened her eyes, in time to follow Loretta's gaze toward the back of the church. There was a small group of dark-suited mourners there. The first one she recognized was Cecil; then the tallest of them turned to look toward the altar, and she heard Loretta murmur *oh Lord, that's all we need* and realized she was looking at Garrison. He'd changed since Rachel had seen him last: his hair was short, his face pinched and pale. He looked almost frail.

The murmurs quickly subsided, and eyes were averted, but a subtle change had passed through the assembly. The man responsible for the death of the woman they'd come to mourn was here, walking down the aisle to pay his respects before her casket. Mitchell accompanied him, his arm lightly holding Garrison's elbow, as if to guide him.

"When did he get out?" Rachel whispered to Loretta.

"This morning," she replied. "I told Cecil to keep him away." She shook her head. "It's grotesque."

Garrison was standing in front of Margie's casket now. He leaned over to his brother, and whispered something. Mitchell stepped back. Then Garrison reached over and put both his hands on the casket. There was nothing theatrical about the gesture; indeed he seemed oblivious to the presence of those around him. He simply stood there with his head bowed, as if attempting to commune with the body. Rachel glanced over her shoulder. Everyone—even those members of the congregation who'd earlier averted their eyes—were now watching the mourning man. How many of them, she wondered, believed his version of events? Probably most. Lord knows it was hard enough for her to believe that Garrison was capable of mourning at the casket of a woman he'd murdered.

As she turned back she found Mitchell staring at her. He looked exhausted. For the first time in the years she'd known him she saw the resemblance to Garrison: in the fierceness of his stare and the weary shape of his shoulders. In other circumstances she might have said a couple of weeks in the Caribbean would have cured his ills, but she knew better: he was sliding away from himself—or at least from the polished illusion of himself he'd presented to the world; away into the sad, shadowy place where Garrison had skulked all these years.

What had Loretta called them? The idiot and the necrophile? A little excessive perhaps, but it probably wasn't so very far from the truth. They certainly belonged together, the tainted fruit of a tainted tree.

Mitchell had taken his gaze off her by now, and was gently tugging on his brother's arm. Garrison looked back at him. Rachel saw Mitchell say *come along*, and lamblike Garrison went with him. They sat together at the far end of the same row as Rachel and Loretta. Again, Mitchell glanced Rachel's way. This time she too averted her gaze.

The service was conducted with considerable decorum by a very elderly preacher who during his eulogy told the gathering that he'd baptized Margie in this very church, forty-eight years before. He had followed the life of "this remarkable woman," as he called her, with the same mixture of astonishment and sadness he was certain they all felt. She had been troubled, he said, and had perhaps not always made the best of choices in her life's journey, but now she stood on the Golden Floor, where the vicissitudes of her life were lifted from her, and she could go lightly on her way. Rachel had never heard anybody refer to heaven as the Golden Floor before. She liked the phrase immensely, though she suspected that if Margie had been one of the mourners rather than the mourned she would have slipped away at the first mention of paradise, and gone to sit among the gravestones and smoke a cigarette.

With the service over, the casket was carried out to the graveside. This was the part Rachel had been dreading; but by the time the moment of descent came, and she was standing there in the drizzle watching the casket go from view, she'd been anticipating the horror of it for so long the actuality was something of an anticlimax. There were more prayers; flowers thrown down into the grave; then it was over.

## ii

The rain came on heavily as she drove back to the city. A few miles short of the bridge she was overtaken by a white Mercedes being driven at suicidal speed, which was pursued through the deluge by two police cars. Another two miles and she saw red lights flashing through the downpour, and flames burning on the highway. The pursued car had plowed into the back of a large truck; and two other vehicles had then struck it, spinning across the slick asphalt. One was burning, its lucky occupants standing in the rain watching the conflagration. The other had turned over and sat in the rain like a tortured tortoise, while the officers attempted to free the family inside. As for whoever had been driving the Mercedes, he or she had presumably been given up for dead, along with any passengers: it had concertinaed against the rear of the truck and was virtually unrecognizable. Needless to say, the entire highway was blocked. She waited for half an hour before the flow was reestablished, during which time she saw a whole melancholy scenario played out before her like a piece of rain-sodden theater. The arrival of firetrucks and ambulances; the freeing of the family (one of whom, a child, was delivered from the wreckage dead); grief and accusations; and finally the prying apart of the truck and the Mercedes, the contents of which were thankfully concealed from her view.

It was only when she was off on her way again that she turned her thoughts to the business of the following day: the search for Danny's letters. If she was lucky Garrison would go to Mass in the morning, as he sometimes did. He had his liberty to give thanks for. And while he was being a good Catholic boy she'd go up to the apartment in the Trump Tower and start her search. If she failed to find anything in the first attempt, she'd either have to wait for the following Sunday, when she could guarantee his absence, or else somehow monitor his whereabouts during the week. It would be hard to spy on the Tower without being noticed. There'd be journalists cruising around for a little while yet; and there had of course been some staff in residence, though she'd heard from somebody that two of them had left after Margie's murder and the third had been telling all kinds of tales to the gutter-press, so she'd presumably been fired.

In the end she'd just have to trust to luck, and have a good, solid excuse for her presence in the apartment if she was discovered. The fact was she felt perversely exhilarated at the thought of going into the Tower. For too long she'd been a passive object; part of the grand Geary scheme. Even her trip to Kaua'i had been initiated by somebody within the family. By helping Danny—or attempting to do so—she was defying her allotted role; and her only regret was that she'd taken so long to do it. Such were the seductions of luxury.

Now, as she began to see the path before her more clearly, she found herself wondering whether Galilee, the prince of her heart, was also one of those seductions. Was he the ultimate luxury? Dropped in her path to distract her from looking where she was not supposed to look? How she longed to have Margie at the other end of a telephone, to share these ruminations with her. Margie had always been able to go unerringly to the heart of a subject; to strip away all the high-minded stuff and focus on the real meat of a thing. What would she have said about Rachel's theorizing? That it was irrelevant, probably, to the business of getting through the day. That attempting to understand the big picture was to partake of a peculiarly male delusion: the belief that events could be shaped and dictated, forced to reflect the will of an individual. Margie had never had much time for that kind of thinking. The only things in life that could truly be controlled were the little things: the number of olives in your martini, the height of your heel. And the men who believed otherwise—the potentates and the plutocrats—were setting themselves up for terrible disappointment sooner or later; which fact, of course, gave her no little pleasure.

Perhaps, Rachel thought, these things worked differently on the Golden Floor. Perhaps up there the Grand Design was the subject of daily chitchat, and the spirits of the dead took pleasure in working out the vast patterns of human endeavor. But she doubted it. Certainly she couldn't imagine Margie having much time for that kind of business. Matters of destiny might be the subject of debate in other quarters, but where Margie held court there would be a happy throng of gossipers, rolling their eyes at the theorists.

The thought made Rachel smile; the first smile of that long, unhappy day. Margie had earned her freedom. Whether her suffering had been self-inflicted (or at least self-perpetuated) the point was surely that she'd endured it without losing sight of the sweet soul she'd been before the Gearys had found her. She'd made the trick look simple, but, as Rachel had found, it was hard to pull off. This world was like a labyrinth; it was easy to get lost in, to become a stranger to yourself. Rachel had been lucky. She'd rediscovered herself back on the island; found the wildling Rachel, the woman of flesh and blood and appetite. She would not lose that woman again. However dark the maze became, however threatening its occupants, she would never again let go of the creature she was; not now that Galilee loved her.

# VII

Sunday morning, and the rain was heavier than ever, so heavy at times you couldn't see more than a block in any direction. If there'd been any photographers outside the Tower they'd taken refuge until their subject came back from Mass; or else they'd followed him there.

Margie had given Rachel a key to the apartment when the first difficulties with Mitchell had begun, telling her to use the place whenever she wanted to escape.

"Garrison's scarcely ever here," she'd said, "so you needn't worry about meeting him in his underwear. Which is quite a sight, believe me. He looks like a stick of dough with a paunch."

Rachel had never liked the Tower, or the apartment. It had always seemed, despite its glitz, a rather depressing place, even on bright days. And on a day like today, with the sky gray, it was murky and melancholy. The fact that the rooms were furnished with antiques, and the halls hung with huge, futile paintings which Garrison had collected as investments in the early eighties, only added to the charmlessness of the place.

She waited in the hallway for a few moments listening for any sound of occupancy. The only noise she heard came from outside; rain beating against the windows; the distant wail of a siren. She was alone. Time to begin.

She started up the stairs, her ascent taking her into still darker territory. There was a grandfather clock at the top of the flight and her heart jumped when she saw it looming there, imagining for a moment it was Garrison, waiting for her.

She paused while the hammering in her heart subsided. I'm afraid of him, she thought. It was the first time she'd admitted the fact to herself: she was afraid of what he might do if he found her trespassing where she had no business going. It was one thing to hear Loretta talk about his perversions, or to see him, weak and pale, standing before Margie's casket. It was quite another to imagine encountering him here, in the place where he'd slaughtered his own wife. What would she say to him if he did suddenly appear? Did she have a single lie in her head that he'd believe? Probably not. Her only defense against his malice was the fact that she had once been his brother's bride, and how secure a lien against assault was that? The bond between the brothers was far stronger than any claim she might have. At that moment, standing on the stairs, she believed he would probably kill her if the occasion called for it.

She thought of what Mitchell had said two days before; that remark about how dangerous her life would become if he weren't there to protect her. It wasn't an empty threat; it had carried weight. She was forfeitable, just like Margie.

"Get a grip," she murmured to herself. This was neither the place nor time to contemplate her vulnerability.

She had to do what she'd come here to do and then get out. Daring the pale face of the clock (which had not worked, Margie had once told her, since the last years of the Civil War) she climbed the rest of the stairs to the second floor. Margie's private sitting room was on this floor; so was her bedroom, and the bathroom where she'd died. Rachel had intended not to go into the bathroom unless she ran out of places to search, but now, marooned on the landing, she knew the proximity of the place would haunt her unless she confronted it. Flipping on the landing light she went to the bedroom door. It was open a few inches. The room was bright: the investigating officers had left all the drapes wide. They'd also left the room in a state of complete disarray; the whole place had clearly been picked over for evidence. This was the only room in the house hung with pictures that reflected Margie's eclectic taste: a cloyingly sweet Chagall, a small Pissarro depicting a little French village, two Kandinskys. And in bizarre contrast to all this color, two Motherwell Elegies, stark black forms against dirty white, which hung like *memento mori* to either side of her bed.

Rachel picked her way through the numerous drawers which had been pulled out and lain on the floor to be searched, and went to the bathroom door. Her heart began to hammer again as she reached for the handle. She disregarded its din, and opened the door.

It was a big room, all pink marble and gold; the tub—which Margie had loved to lounge in—enormous. "I feel like a million-dollar hooker when I'm in that tub," Margie had liked to boast.

There were still countless reminders of her presence littered about. Perfume bottles and ashtrays, a photograph of her brother Sam tucked into the frame of the Venetian mirror, another photograph (this one of Margie in lacy underwear, taken by a society photographer who'd specialized in aesthetically sleazy portraits), hanging beside the door to the shower. Again, there was also ample evidence that the police had been here. In several places the black marble surface had been dusted for fingerprints, and a layer of dust remained. The congealed remains of a pizza—presumably consumed while the investigators were at work—sat in a greasy box beside the bath. And the contents of the drawers had been sorted through; a selection of questionable items set on the counter. A plethora of pill bottles; a small square mirror, along with a razor (kept for sentiment's sake, presumably; Margie had stopped using recreational cocaine years ago) and a collection of sexual items: a small pink vibrator, a jar of cherry-flavored body lubricant, some condoms.

The sight of all this distressed Rachel. She couldn't help but imagine the officers smirking as they dug through the drawers; making tasteless jokes at Margie's expense. Not that she would have given a damn.

Rachel had seen enough. She wasn't going to be haunted by this place; any power it might have had over her had been trampled away. At least so she thought until she went to switch off the light. There on the wall was a dark spatter. She told herself to look away, but her eye went no further than the next dried drop, which was larger. She touched it. The drop came away on her fingertip, like cracked paint. It was Margie's blood. And there was more of it, a lot more of it, invisible on the speckled marble until now.

Suddenly it didn't matter that the police had defiled the room with their pizza and their sticky fingers. Margie had died here. Oh, God in Heaven, *Margie had died here*. This was her lifeblood, spilled on the wall: a smear close to Rachel's shoulder, where she'd fallen back or reached out in the hope of keeping herself from falling, a larger clot on the floor between Rachel's feet, almost as dark as the marble.

She looked away, revolted, but the defenses she'd put up to keep herself from picturing what had happened here had collapsed. Suddenly she had the scene before her, in horrid detail. The sound of the shots echoing off the marble, off the mirrors; the look of disbelief on Margie's face as she retreated from her husband; the blood running out between her fingers, slapping on the floor.

What had Garrison done when the shots were fired? Dropped the gun and fallen to his knees beside her? Or stumbled to the phone to call for an ambulance? More likely he'd called Mitchell, or a lawyer; put off the moment when help could come for as long as possible, to be certain that the life had gone from Margie. Every last breath.

Rachel covered her face with her hands, but the image refused to be banished so easily. It pulsed before her: Margie's face, openmouthed; her hands, fluttering, her body, robbed of motion, or the prospect of motion, darkening as the blood spread over it.

"Stop this," Rachel said to herself.

She wanted to get out of the bathroom without looking at it again, but she knew that was the worst thing she could do. She had to uncover her eyes and confront what she'd seen. There was nothing here that could hurt her, except for her own superstition.

She reluctantly let her hands drop from her face and forced herself to study the scene afresh. First the sink and its surrounds; then the mirror and the tub. Finally, the blood on the floor. Only when she'd taken it all in did she turn to leave the bathroom.

Where now? The bedroom lay before her, with all the drawers laid out. She could waste an hour going through the room, but it was a fool's errand. If the letters were here, then they were so well hidden the police had failed to find them, and so, more than likely, would she.

Instead she picked her way back across the littered floor to the landing and crossed to Margie's sitting room. She glanced at her watch as she did so. She'd been in the house twelve minutes already. There was no time for further delay.

She opened the sitting room door, and immediately retreated, pursued out onto the landing by Didi, Margie's pug, who yapped with all the ferocity of a dog three times his size.

"Hush, hush—." She dropped down to her knees so he could sniff her hands. "It's only me."

He ceased his din on the instant, and instead began a round of grateful mewlings, dancing around in circles before her. She'd never much cared for the animal, but her heart went out to it now. It was doubtless wondering where its mistress had disappeared to, and took Rachel's presence as a sign of her return.

"You come with me," she said to the animal. It duly trotted after her into the sitting room, where a plate of uneaten food and an excrement-caked newspaper testified to its sorry state. The rest of the room was in a far tidier condition than either the bedroom or the bathroom. Either the police had neglected to examine it thoroughly, or else the officer who'd done so was a woman.

Rachel didn't linger. She immediately started to go round the room, opening every cupboard and drawer. There were plenty of plausible hiding places—rows of books (mostly airport romances), heaps of Broadway playbills, even a collection of letters (all of them from charitable organizations begging Margie's support)—but there was no sign of anything vaguely incriminating. Didi stayed close by throughout the search, plainly determined not to lose his companion now he had her. Once only did he leave her side, waddling to the door as though he'd heard somebody in the house. Rachel paused and ventured out onto the landing, listening as intently as the dog, but it seemed to be a false alarm. Back to her search she went, checking on the time as she did so. She'd spent almost half an hour in the sitting room; she couldn't afford to stay in the house much longer. But if she left empty-handed, would she have the courage to return? Certainly she'd used up every cent of enthusiasm she had for the venture. It wouldn't be easy to persuade herself to repeat the process; not now that she had specifics to dwell on: the blood, the murk, the disarray.

When she returned into the sitting room Didi was not at her heel.

She called to him, but he didn't come. She called again, and this time heard a lapping sound from the far side of the room. There was another door, which led into a small bathroom, with room for only a sink and a toilet. Didi had somehow scrambled up onto the toilet seat and was drinking from the bowl, the sight both sad and absurd. She told him to get down. He looked up, water dripping from his chops, and gave her a quizzical look. She told him again to get down, this time coming to pluck him off his perch. He was off the seat before she could get to him however, and scampered off between her legs.

She glanced around the tiny room: there was nowhere here to hide anything, except for the plain cabinet that boxed the sink. She bent down and opened it up. It smelt of disinfectant. There was a small store of bathroom cleansers and spare toilet tissue. She pulled them out and peered into the shadows. The pipes coming from the sink were wet; when she reached up to touch them her fingers came away covered in mold. She peered in again. There was something else in beneath the sink beside pipes; something wrapped up in paper. She reached a second time, and this time took hold of the object, which was wedged between the pipe and the damp-sodden plaster. It wouldn't move. She cursed, which sent Didi, who'd returned to see what was going on, scurrying from her side. Suddenly, the object shifted, and her cold fingers weren't quick enough to catch it before it dropped to the ground. There was the muffled sound of a breaking bottle, and then the smell of brandy wafted up out of the cabinet. Clearly what she'd found was liquor Margie had stashed away during some long-surrendered attempt at drying out. Didi was back again, sniffing after the brandy, the smell of which was giddying.

"Get out of there!" Rachel said, catching hold of him to haul him from the muck. He squealed like a piglet. She told him to stop complaining and unceremoniously threw him in the direction of the door. Then she proceeded to put the bleach and disinfectant and toilet tissue back. Hopefully if she closed the cabinet door tight nobody would catch the smell of liquor. And even if they did, she reasoned, what were they going to find? Just a broken bottle. As she slid the last of the disinfectants into the cabinet she caught sight of something else, lying beside the brandy. Not one but two envelopes, both bulky. Either Danny wrote very long letters, she thought, or else he'd miscalculated the number of photographs he'd taken. She pulled the envelopes out into the light. They had both been in contact with the wall; there were flecks of decayed plaster adhering to them. Otherwise, they'd survived their hiding place intact. One of them was considerably heavier than the other however. It didn't contain letters or photographs, she thought; more like a small, thick book.

This wasn't the place to examine the contents; she could do that at home. She finished putting the disinfectants into the cabinet, firmly closed the door, and bidding Didi a quick farewell headed out of the sitting room onto the landing.

If Garrison came in now, she thought, she wouldn't be able to tell a lie worth a damn. The pleasure at her discovery was written all over her face. She tucked the envelopes into her coat and hurried down the stairs, keeping her eye on the front door as she descended; but the good fortune which had delivered the envelopes into her hands held. She opened the door a few inches, checking to see if there were any photographers out there, and finding that the rain was still pelting down and the sidewalk deserted, slipped out and down the steps, thoroughly pleased with herself.

# VIII

## i

I have to make room here for the briefest of digressions on the inevitable and probably inexhaustible subject of my invert sister. The last I wrote of her she'd come into my room flushed with success, having read Sister Mary-Elizabeth's poem to her beloved, and had her proposal of marriage accepted. A few hours ago she came back with details of the arrangements.

"No excuses," she said to me. "You have to be there."

"I've never been to a lesbian wedding," I said, "I wouldn't know what to do."

"Be happy for me."

"I am."

"I want you to dance and get drunk and make a sentimental speech about our childhood."

"Oh what? You and Daddy in the dressing room?"

She gave me a fierce look. Maybe it's some remnant of an atavistic power lodged in her, but when she gets fierce she looks rabid.

"Has Alice ever seen you angry?" I asked her.

"Once or twice."

"No. I mean really angry. Crazy-angry. I-could-tear-your-heart-out-and-eat-it angry."

"Hm . . . no."

"Shouldn't she be warned, before you tie the knot? I mean, you can be a terror."

"So can she. She's the only girl in a family of eight."

"She has seven brothers?"

"Seven brothers. And they treat her very respectfully."

"Rich family?"

"White trash. Two of the brothers are in jail. The father's an alcoholic. Beer for breakfast."

"Are you sure she's not just after you for your money?" I said. Marietta glowered. "Jesus, I'm just asking. I don't want to see you hurt."

"If you're so suspicious, then you come and meet her. Meet them all."

"You know I can't do that."

"Why not? And don't tell me you're working."

"But that's the truth. I am. Morning, noon and night."

"This is a damn sight more important than your book. This is the woman I love and adore and idolize."

"Hm. Love, adore and idolize, huh? She *must* be good in bed."

"She's the best, Eddie. I mean, *the very best.* She eats me out like she'd just invented it. I scream so loud the trailer shakes."

"She lives in a trailer? Are you *sure* you're doing the right thing?"

Marietta picked at her front tooth, which she always does when she's uneasy. "Most of the time," she replied.

"But . . . ?"

"But what?"

"No. You tell me. Most of the time's enough?"

"Okay, smartass. When you met Chiyojo were you *absolutely* certain—not even a breath of doubt—that she was the one?"

"Absolutely."

"You had an affair with her brother," she reminded me lightly.

"So?"

"So how certain could you be about marrying a woman when you were screwing her brother?"

"That was different. He was . . ."

"A transvestite."

"No. He was an actor." She rolled her eyes. "How did we get into this?" I said.

"You were trying to talk me out of marrying Alice."

"No I wasn't. I really wasn't. I was observing that . . . I don't know what I was observing. Never mind."

Marietta came over to me and took hold of my hand. "You know, you're very good for me," she said.

"I am?"

"You make me question things. You make me think twice."

"I don't know if that's such a good thing. Sometimes I wish I hadn't thought twice so many times, if you see what I mean. I might have done more with my life."

"I think Alice is the one, Eddie."

"Then marry her, for God's sake."

She squeezed my hand hard. "I *really* want you to meet her first. I want your opinion. It means a lot to me."

"So maybe you should bring her here," I said. Marietta looked doubtful. "She's going to see this place eventually. And I think we'd both have a better idea of whether it was going to work out once we saw how she responded."

"You mean: tell her everything?"

"Not everything. Nobody could handle *everything*. Just enough to see whether she's ready for the truth."

"Hm. Would you help me?"

"Like how?"

"Keep Cesaria from scaring her."

"I can't stop her if she wants to do something. Nobody could. Not even Dad."

"But you'd do your best."

"Yes. I'll be the voice of reason, if that makes any difference."

"You'd tell Cesaria you suggested it?"

I sighed. "If I must," I said.

"Then that's settled. I'll go talk to Alice now."

"Just give me a little warning. So I can organize myself."

"I'm excited."

"Oh Lord. I don't like the sound of that."


Of course I'm regretting it. Who wouldn't? The best it can be is a fiasco. But what else was I going to do? This obviously isn't some overnight romance. Marietta feels something profound for this woman. I can see it in her eyes. I can hear it in her voice. And it would be hypocritical of me to be writing with such enthusiasm about the grand—if stymied—passion between Rachel and Galilee and at the same time turn a blind eye to something that's happening right in front of me.

Anyway, I've agreed. The woman will come to us and we'll see what we'll see.

Meanwhile, I have a story to tell.

## ii

The Central Park apartment was deserted when Rachel got back from her expedition to the Trump Tower. Even so, she didn't sit down at the dining room table and open the two envelopes she'd found, just in case somebody were to walk in on her. She went to her bedroom, where she locked the door and drew the drapes. Only then did she sit cross-legged on the bed to examine her booty.

In the less bulky of the two envelopes she found the letters and the photographs. Danny was quite the eroticist, to judge by what he'd written. His concern that if these letters had fallen into the wrong hands they might be used to besmirch Margie were well founded. There were dates and times and locations here; there were heated reminiscences of deeds done and boastful promises of how much more intricate it was going to get next time. Nor was any of this put in a roundabout way. "*We're going to have to start fucking in a soundproof room,*" he said in one of the letters, "*the way you like to shout. I'm sitting here hard as a rock thinking about you yelling your head off, and me just sliding in and out, long strokes, the way you like. There isn't a thing I wouldn't do for you, you know that? When we're together I feel as though the rest of the world can just go to hell—we don't need anybody but each other. I wish I could have been a baby, sometimes, and drunk the milk from your beautiful tits. Or been born out of you. Fuck, I know that sounds twisted, but you said we shouldn't be afraid of any of the things we feel, right? I'd like to fuck you so deep I get lost inside you, and you'd carry me around for a while, like I was your baby. Then when you wanted me out and giving you the nasty you'd just open your legs and out I'd come, all ready to service you.*"

The photographs were not as graphic as the letters, by any means, but they were still notably perverse. Danny was obviously proud of his endowment, and quite happy to have it recorded for posterity, while Margie's sense of humor was evident in the way she toyed with him. In one photograph she had drawn on his lower belly and upper thighs with lipstick; flames perhaps, as though his groin was on fire. In another, he was coupling with her while wearing her pantyhose, through which his dick stuck, ripe cherry red. All good old-fashioned fun.

Rachel called Danny at home and told him the good news. He was just about to go down to the bar to start his shift, but he was happy to call in sick and come and pick the letters and photographs up immediately if that suited Rachel best. She told him not to do anything that would make people even faintly suspicious. The stuff was quite safe in her possession, she said. They could meet when Danny's shift was over, at midnight or so, and she could give everything to him then. They agreed on a meeting place, two blocks north of the bar where Danny worked.

That duty done, she turned her attention to the contents of the other envelope. She was expecting to find further evidence of Margie's philanderings; but what she found was something else entirely. It was a journal, clothbound and in an advanced state of disrepair, its cover stained and torn, its spine cracked, its pages loosened from their stitching. A thin brown leather strap had been tied around it to keep its contents together: when she untied it she discovered that several separate sheets of paper had been interleaved with the journal's pages. Their condition varied wildly. There were a few neatly folded, and well preserved, there were others that were little more than scraps. What was written on the sheets similarly ran the gamut: from perfect copperplate to a chaotic scrawl. Some were letters, some seemed to be fragments of a sermon (at least there was much talk of God and redemption there); some were crudely illustrated, their subjects always the same: soldiers, in what looked to be Civil War garb. There was no form of identification at the beginning of the book—indeed it seemed to start in midsentence—but when she flipped on through it she found that the first four or five pages had come loose at some point, and the owner had slipped them into the middle of the book. On the first page was an inscription written in an elegant, feminine hand.

> *This is for your thoughts, my darling Charles.*
> *Bring it back to me when this horrid war is over, and we'll put it away, and put all the suffering away with it.*
> *I love you more than life, and will show my love a thousand ways when you are here again.*
> *Your adoring wife,*
> *Adina*

Below this, the date:

*September the Second, 1863*

So they *were* Civil War soldiers in the sketches, Rachel thought. This journal had belonged to some military man who'd used it to record experiences as he went to battle. She knew little about the war between the states; history had never been a subject she'd warmed to. Especially when it was brutal; and what little she did remember of her lessons about the period concerned the cruelties that had brought the war about and the cruelties that had ended it. There had been nothing to engage her sympathies, so whatever dates and names she'd learned had quickly fled from her head.

But a history book and a journal such as this were very different things. One was filled with facts, to be learned parrot-fashion. The other had a voice, a drama, a sense of the specific. In a short time, she found herself entranced, not by the details of what was being described—much of it was a forlorn catalog of woes and privations: inedible food, dying animals, long, exhausting marches, foot rot and gut rot and lice—but the tangible presence of the man who was doing the describing, his self-portrait becoming more detailed, line by line. He loved his wife, he had faith in God and in the cause of the South, he hated Lincoln (a "damned hypocrite") and almost all Northerners ("they pretend righteousness because it suits them"); he liked his horse better than most of the men he commanded, and yet seemed to feel their hardship more than his own.

> *Isn't there a better way to settle our differences,* he wrote, *than to put before the bullet and the bayonet common men such as these, who have no true comprehension of what is at issue here, nor in truth care to, but only want to have this bloody business done so that they can return to doing what the Lord made them to do: to plow and drink and die surrounded by their children and their children's children.*
>
> *When I hear them talking among themselves they don't talk of politics and the greatness of our cause: they talk about clean water and strawberry pie. What is the use of putting such simple souls to death? Better that we chose ten princes of the South, and ten gentleman of the North, if they could find that number, and set them in a field with swords, to fight until there was only one remaining. Let the victory go to that side then, and spill only the blood of nineteen men, instead of this wholesale slaughter, which so grievously wounds the body of the nation.*

Just a few pages later, in a passage dated August 22nd, 1864 ("*a filthy, clammy night*") he returned to the subject of how the men suffer, but from a different point of view.

*I find myself losing patience with the idea that this war is the Lord's work. We were given free will; and we have chosen what? To make one another suffer.*

*Yesterday we came upon a hill which had apparently been, for a week or a month, who knows now, a place of some strategic importance. There were dead men, or what the foul heat of this season makes of dead men, everywhere. Blue and gray, in what seemed to me equal numbers. Why had they not been given Christian burials? I can only assume because there were not enough infantrymen of either side left alive to perform that duty, nor enough compassion left in their commanders to bring in a brigade and put the dead in the ground. The battle moves on to another hill—which will for a week or a month seem of vital strategic importance—and these hundreds of men, all somebody's sons, left for flies to breed in.*

*I'm ashamed of myself tonight. I wish I were not a man, if this is what men are.*

The more Rachel read, the more questions she had. Who was this fellow, who had poured his feelings onto the page so eloquently she felt as though she could hear him, speaking to her? How had he learned to express himself so powerfully, and what purpose had he turned that power to when the fighting was finished? A preacher? A pacifist politician? Or had he done as his wife intended, and taken the book, with all its rage and its disappointment, back home to be sealed up and never spoken of again?

Then there was another series of questions, that were nothing to do with Charles and Adina. How had Margie come by the book? And why had she wrapped it up and hidden it alongside the letters from Danny? This was scarcely scandalous material. Perhaps at the time Charles's views would have been thought radical, but almost a century and a half later, what did it matter what he'd written?

She read on. Every now and then she'd unfold one of the loose notes tucked between the pages, some of which had nothing to do with anything she'd so far read, some of which looked to be thoughts he'd jotted down when he couldn't get to his journal, some of which were letters. There were two, side by side, from Adina, both sad and curiously abrupt. The first said:

*Dearest husband,*
*I write with the worst of news, and know of no way to sweeten it. Two days ago the Lord took our darling Nathaniel from us, in a*

*fever which came so suddenly that he was gone before Henrietta could bring Dr. Sarris to the house.*

*He would be four the first Tuesday of next month, and I had promised him you would take him up on your horse as a birthday treat when you came home. He spoke of this at the last.*

*I do not think he much suffered.*

The second was shorter still.

*I must go to Georgia, if I can,* Adina wrote. *I have word from Hamilton that the plantation has been brought to ruin, and that our father is in such despair he has twice attempted to end his own life. I will bring him back to Charleston with me, and tend to him there.*

The hand that had written these letters was still just recognizably the same that had penned the inscription, but it had deteriorated into a spiky scrawl. Rachel could scarcely imagine what state the woman must have been reduced to: her husband gone, one of her children dead, her family fortune lost; it was a wonder she'd kept her sanity. But then, perhaps she hadn't.

Again, Rachel moved on. In an hour or so she'd have to set out for her meeting with Danny, but she didn't want to leave the journal. It fascinated her; these tragic lives, unraveling before her, like the lives of people in a novel. Except that this book gave her none of the familiar comforts of fiction. No authorial voice to put these events in a larger context; no certainty, even, that she would be shown how their troubles were resolved.

A few pages on, however, about halfway through the journal, she chanced upon a page which would significantly change the direction of all that followed.

*Tonight I do not know if I am a sane man,* Charles wrote. *I have had such a strange experience today, and want to write it down before I go to sleep so that I do not dismiss it tomorrow as something my exhausted mind invented. It was not. I'm certain, it was not. I know how the visions that arise from fatigue appear—I've seen some of them—and this was of a different order.*

*We are marching southeast, through North Carolina. It rains constantly, and the ground has turned to mud; the men are so tired they neither sing nor complain, barely having the energy left to put*

*one boot in front of another. I wonder how long it will be before I
have to join them; my horse is sick, and I believe he only continues
to walk out of love of me. Poor thing! I've seen the cook, Nickelberry, eyeing him now and then, wondering if there's any way in
the world he can turn such a carcass into edible fare.*

*So, that was what the day brought, and it was horrible
enough. But then, as dusk came, and it was that hour when nothing
in the world seems solid and certain, I looked down and saw—oh
God in Heaven, my pen does not want to make these words—I saw
my boy, my golden-haired Nathaniel, sitting on the saddle in front
of me.*

*I thought of Adina's letter: of how she had promised that ride
upon the horse, and my heart quickened, for today was Nathaniel's
birthday.*

*I expected the presence to disappear after a time, but it did
not. As the night drew on he stayed there, as though to comfort me.
Once, in the darkness, I sensed him look round and back at me,
and saw his pale face and his dark eyes there before me.*

*I spoke then. I said: I love you, my son.*

*He replied to me! As if all this weren't extraordinary enough,
he replied. Papa, he said, the horse is tired, and wants me to ride
her away.*

*It was unbearable, to hear that little voice in the darkness
telling me that my horse was not long for this world.*

*I told him: then you must take her. And I had no sooner spo-
ken than I felt my horse shudder beneath me, and the life went out
of her, and she fell to the ground. I fell with her, of course, into the
mud. There were lamps brought, and some fuss made of me, but I
had fallen, I think, in a kind of swoon, which had perhaps kept me
from any serious harm.*

*Of Nathaniel, of course, there was no sign. He had gone, rid-
ing the spirit of my horse away, wherever the souls of the loyal and
the loving go.*

There was a small space on the page now. When Charles took up
his account again, he was plainly in an even more agitated state.

*I cannot sleep. I wonder if I will ever sleep again. I think of the child
all the time. Why did he come to me? What was he telling me?*

*Nickelberry is a better man than I took him to be. Most cooks
are vile men in my experience. He is not. The men call him Nub.*

*He saw me writing in this book earlier, and came to me and asked me if I would write a letter for him, to send back to his mother. I told him I would. Then he said he was sorry my horse had died but I should take comfort that it had nourished many men who were so sick if they had not eaten tonight they would have perished. I thanked him for the thought, but I could see that he wanted to say more, and couldn't find a way to begin. So I told him simply to spit it out. And out it came. He said he'd heard that there was now no hope that we could win this war. I told him that was probably true. To which he said, plain as day: then why are we still fighting?*

   *Such a simple question. And I listened to the rain beating on the tent, and heard the wounded sobbing somewhere near, and thought of Nathaniel, come to ride with me, and I wanted to weep, but I did not dare. Not because I was ashamed. I like this man Nickelberry; I wouldn't care that I wept in front of him. I didn't dare begin to weep because I was afraid I would never stop.*

   *I told him truthfully: "Once I would have said we should fight to the death to prove the righteousness of our cause. But now I think nothing is pure in this world, nor ever was, and we will die uselessly, as we have lived."*

   *Did I say that he was a little drunk? I think he was. But he seemed quickly sobered by this, and said he would visit me again tomorrow, so that I could write the letter to his mother. Then he left me to sleep.*

   *But I cannot. I think of what he said, and what I replied, and I wonder if tomorrow I should not forsake my uniform, and the cause I was ready to die for, and act as a man not as a soldier; and go my own way.*

   *I can scarcely believe I wrote those words. But I believe that's why Nathaniel came to take the horse: it was his way of shaking me out of my stupor; of stopping me marching to my death. What would I have died for? For nothing. All of this for nothing.*

Rachel looked at the clock. It was time to go, but she didn't want to stop reading, so she slipped the letters and the photographs back into one envelope, and the book back into the other, and took them both with her. As so often happened in this city the weather had changed suddenly: a warm wind had blown the rain clouds upstate, and for once the streets smelled sweet. As the cab bounced and rattled its way toward Soho she took out the journal again, and began to read.

# IX

## i

The battle of Bentonville began on Monday, the twenty-first day of March, in the year of our Lord eighteen hundred and sixty-four. It was not, by the standards of the war between the states, a great, decisive or even particularly bloody battle: but it has this distinction: it is the last hurrah of the Southern Confederacy. Thirty-six days later General Joseph E. Johnston would meet William T. Sherman at the Bennett farmhouse and surrender his men. The war would be over.

Captain Charles Rainwill Holt did not desert on the night before the battle, as he had intended to; he thought better of it. The weather, which had been inclement during the march, became fouler still, and he judged his chances of getting away in the darkness without some harm or other coming to him less than good.

On the following day the battle began, and from the beginning it was a mess. The terrain was in places forested with pine, and in others swamp and briar. The men on both sides were exhausted, and there was scarcely an encounter through that first day and night that did not end chaotically. Men lost in smoke and rain and darkness firing back upon their own comrades. Charges led upon lines that did not exist. Earthworks abandoned before they were half dug. The wounded left in the woods (which had been set alight by cannon fire despite the rain) and burned alive within earshot of their fellows.

There was worse to come, and the captain knew it, but as the hours passed that stupor from which his son had come to stir him fell upon him again. More than once he saw an opportunity, and could not bring himself to take it. It was not fear of a stray bullet that kept him from moving. There was something leaden in him, like a weight that war had poured into his bowels, and it kept him from his escape.

It was Nickelberry the cook who finally persuaded him to leave. Not with words, but with his own departure.

It was just after dusk on the second day, and Charles had gone out from the encampment a little way, to try and put his thoughts in order. Behind him the men gathered round their cautious fires, trying by whatever means they could to keep their spirits up. Somebody was plucking a banjo; one or two exhausted voices were raised to sing along. The sound came strangely between the trees, like the sound of phantoms. Charles tried to bring to mind the garden in Charleston where he'd proposed to Adina; he'd calmed his troubled spirits many times thinking of that spot. Of the fragrance of its air; of the nightbirds that made such melody in the trees. But tonight he could not remember to perfume of that place, or its music. It was as if that Eden had never existed.

As he stared off into the darkness, lost in these melancholy thoughts, he saw a figure moving between the trees not ten yards from him. He was about to challenge the man, when he realized who it was.

"Nickelberry . . . ?" he whispered.

The figure froze, so still the captain could barely distinguish him from the trees amongst which he stood.

"Is that you, Nickelberry?"

There was no reply, but he was certain that it was indeed the cook, so he began to walk in the man's direction. "Nickelberry? It's Captain Holt."

Nickelberry responded by moving off again, away from the camp.

"Where are you going?" the captain demanded, picking up his pace to catch up with the cook. The briars slowed the advance of both men, but Nickelberry in particular. He had walked into a very thorny patch, and flailed at them, cursing in his frustration.

The captain was almost upon him now.

"Don't get any closer!" Nickelberry said. "I don't want to hurt you none, but I ain't staying and you ain't gonna make me stay. No sir."

"It's all right, Nub. Calm down."

"I'm done with this damn war."

"Keep your voice down, will you? They'll hear us."

"You ain't gonna try and turn me in?"

"No I'm not."

"If you try—" The captain saw one of Nub's meat carving knives, pale silver, between them. "I'll kill you before they take me."

"I'm sure you would."

"I don't care no more. You hear me? I'd prefer to take my chances out there than stay and be killed."

The captain studied the man before him. He could barely see Nub's expression in the darkness, but he could bring the man's broad, expressive face into his mind's eye readily enough. There was cunning in that face; and tenacity. He wouldn't make a bad companion, Charles thought, if a man had to be living by his wits out there.

"You want to go on your own?" Holt said.

"Huh?"

"Or we could go together."

"Together?"

"Why not?"

"A captain and a cook?"

"Makes no difference what we were back there. Once we run we're both deserters."

"You're not trying to trick me?"

"No. I'm going. If you want to come with me, then come. If you don't—"

"I'm coming," Nickelberry said.

"Then put away the knife." Holt could feel Nickelberry's gaze on him, still doubtful. "Put it away, Nub." There was a further moment of vacillation; then Nickelberry slid the knife back into his belt. "Good," Charles said. "Now . . . did you know you were headed toward enemy lines?"

"I thought they were east of here."

"No. They're right there," Holt said, pointing off between the trees. "If you look carefully, you can see their fires."

Nickelberry looked. The fires were indeed visible; flickers of yellow in the enveloping night.

"Lord, look at that. I would have walked straight into their arms." Any lingering reservations he might have had about the captain's allegiances were plainly allayed. "So which way we goin'?" he said.

"The way I've reckoned it," the Captain said, "our best hope is to head south toward the Goldsboro Road, and then make our way from there. I want to head home to Charleston."

"Then I'll come with you," Nickelberry said. "I ain't got no better place to go."

## ii

None of what I've just recounted found its way into the pages of Holt's journal. He did not write in it again for almost two weeks, by which time the battle of Bentonville was long since over.

This is what Rachel read, as the cab carried her down Madison Avenue:

*We came into Charleston last night. I can barely recognize the city, such is the violence that has been done to it by the Yankees. Nickelberry kept asking me questions as we went, but I had not the life in me to answer. When I think of how this noble city stood*

*before the war, and the way it is laid waste now, such despair rises
in me, for truly all that was good seems to me to have passed away.
This city, which was so fine, is now a kind of hell: blackened by fire
and haunted by the dead. Entire streets I knew have disappeared.
People wander the rubble, their faces blank, their hands bloody
after turning over brick upon brick upon brick, looking for something by which to remember the life they had.*

*We went straight way to Tradd Street, expecting the worst, but
found a strange thing. Though much around in the street lay in
ruins, my house was almost whole. Some damage to the roof, windows blown in, and the gardens all withered of course, but otherwise intact.*

*But, oh, when I went inside, I almost wished a volley had
blown it to smithereens. My house, my precious house, had been
used as a place for the dying and the dead. I do not know why it
was so chosen—I cannot believe Adina would have allowed this; I
must assume it was done after she had departed for Georgia. I only
know that every room seemed to contain some sight more sickening
than the one before.*

*The living room had been stripped of furniture, but for the
mahogany table which had been fetched from the dining room and
used for a surgeon to work upon. The floor around it was black with
old blood, the table the same. And all around the room, the remnants of the surgeon's craft: saws and hammers and knives. The
kitchen had been used to make poultices and the like, and stank so
badly that Nickelberry, who I may say has a stronger stomach than
most, vomited. I did the same, but I went on from room to room
despite Nub telling me I should not.*

*Upstairs, in what used to be the bedroom in which Adina and
I slept—the bedroom where Nathaniel was conceived, and Evan-
geline and Miles—I found an empty coffin. The bed had gone;
looted, I presume, or used for firewood. And in the other bedrooms
filthy mattresses, blankets, bowls and all the accoutrements of the
sickroom. I cannot bring myself to write further what vile signs I
found of the souls who had passed their last there.*

*Nickelberry kept urging me away, and finally I went with
him. But before I left I said I wanted to go out into the garden. He
begged me not to; said he had come to like my company on the
road and was fearful for my sanity. But I would not be persuaded
to depart until I had seen the place where I had sat in the years
before the war, and taken such joy. Somehow I knew that the worst*

would be there; and I would not be finished with this business until I had laid eyes upon that worst, whatever it was.

I know of no place that proffered such fragrances as that little plot of ground: jasmine and magnolia, tea olive and banana shrub; all lent the air a sweetness that could make my head swim on summer nights. And now, despite the harms all around, nature was still doing its best to grace the air. Some of the smaller trees and shrubs had survived the destruction, and their branches were budding. There were even a few flowers underfoot.

But these little victories could not compete with the terrible sight that lay in the middle of the garden. The surgeons' accomplices had dug holes there, to bury the gangrenous parts hacked from the wounded. They had done their job poorly. Upon their departure dogs had come and dug up this horrid meat, and picked it clean. Here, where my children had played, and my darling Adina walked in love, were human bones in their many dozens. I think my coming out had disturbed some of the animals, because in places the dirt was freshly turned, and as yet undevoured trophies lay. A leg, its foot still booted. An arm, severed at midbicep. Much else I could not make sense of, nor wanted to.

I have seen every kind of misery in these three years, and endured everything as best a man may be expected to endure such horrors. But to find sights that rank with the worst I have witnessed in this place, where my children played, where I spoke words of devotion to my wife, where—in short—I made my heaven, is nearly more than I can bear.

Were it not for Nub, I should now surely be dead by my own hand.

He says we should leave the city tomorrow. I have agreed. For tonight, we are sleeping on the steps of St. Michael's Church, where I am presently writing this. Nub has gone off to beg or steal some food (which he's very good at doing) but the thought of what I saw this evening makes me so sick to my stomach I doubt I shall eat.

### iii

The little club where Danny had arranged to meet Rachel was thronged with the late-night crowd, and she had to search it for several minutes before she located him. She felt strangely dislocated, as though she'd left some part of herself behind her in the pages of Captain Holt's journal. There was nothing in her experience that remotely approached the horrors he had described, but the fact that she was holding in her hands the book which he'd had in his pocket when he'd walked into his house on Tradd Street made the vision he was evoking all the more immediate. It was the crowd before her which seemed unreal; their alcohol-flushed features smeared in the murk.

Even Danny, when she finally located him, seemed remote from her, viewed through smoke-thickened gloom.

"I was beginning to think you weren't going to come," he said. His voice was a little slurred with drink. "You want one?"

"I'll have a brandy," Rachel said. "Make it a double, will you?"

"Why don't you go sit down? I'm sorry about the crowd. I guess somebody's having a birthday party. Do you want to go somewhere else?"

"No, I'll just have a drink, and give you the stuff, then—"

"—you don't have to lay eyes on me again," Danny said. "That's a promise." He didn't wait for Rachel to protest, which she would have done out of politeness, but headed off into the midst of the birthday celebrants.

Rachel went to an empty table at the back of the room, and sat down. She was sorely tempted to take out the journal again, though this was scarcely an ideal place to be reading it. The lights were so dim she probably wouldn't be able to make sense of it, she told herself. To distract herself she looked for Danny. He was still at the bar, waving a bill to attract somebody's attention.

Without consciously planning to do so, she reached into the envelope and pulled out the journal again. At a nearby table a group of drunken partiers had started to sing a birthday song. Several of them attempting vainly to harmonize. The cacophony troubled her as far as the end of the first sentence. Then she was back with the deserters, in the silent city.

> *I am writing this two days after we came into Charleston, and I am not certain I know how to describe what has taken place since my last entry.*
>
> *Best to keep it plain, I think. Nub came back to St. Michael's a little before dawn, and he not only brought food, good food, the best I'd seen in many months, he also came with news of a strange encounter he'd had.*
>
> *It seemed he'd met a woman whom he'd first taken to be some kind of apparition, she was, he said, so perfect in this ghostly place, so beautiful, so graceful. Her name was Olivia, and she was apparently so charmed by Nickelberry, and he so enamored of her, that*

*when she invited him halfway across the city to meet a friend of
hers, he went.*

*By the time he came back to see me he had not only met this
friend, who goes by the strange name of Galilee—*

Rachel stopped reading, as though struck. She looked up. The
crowd was wild around her. The singers were up from their table, reel-
ing around, the unlucky focus of their attentions still sitting, dumb-
founded by drink. Danny had secured a glass of brandy, along with
something for himself, and was working his way back towards Rachel's
table, but he was having difficulty weaving between the partiers. Before
he could catch Rachel's eye, she looked back at the journal, half expecting the words she'd seen there to have disappeared.

But no. They were there:

*—this friend, who goes by the strange name of Galilee—*

It couldn't be the same man, of course. This Galilee had lived and
died in an earlier age; long before the Galilee she knew had been born.

She had a few seconds before Danny reached her. Long enough to
quickly scan the next few lines:

*—but had tasted some generosity of his which had changed him in
a fashion I cannot quite describe. He said to me that we had to go
together to meet this man, and that when we'd met I would feel to
some measure the hurts I had suffered in this city undone—*

"What are you reading?"

Danny was setting the drinks down on the table. Holt's words were
still in Rachel's eyes—

*—the hurts I had suffered in this city—*

"Oh it's just an old diary."

"Family heirloom?"

"No."

*—undone—*

Danny sat down. "Your brandy," he said, pushing the glass in
Rachel's direction.

"Thank you." She picked up the brandy and sipped. It burned a little against her lips and on her tongue. "Are you all right?" Danny said.

"Yes, I'm fine."

"You look a little shaken up."

"No . . . I'm just . . . these last few days . . ." She could barely put a
coherent sentence together, she was so distracted by what she'd just read.

"I don't want to seem rude—" she said, making a concerted effort to be articulate. The sooner this conversation was over, the sooner she'd be back with the journal, finding out what awaited the captain. "I've just got a lot on my mind right now. This is what I found at the apartment." She handed Danny the envelope containing letters and the photographs. He glanced around to see if anybody was looking his way, and then, a little tentatively, reached into the envelope and slid out the contents.

"I didn't count them," Rachel said, "but I assume it's everything."

"I'm sure it is," Danny said, staring down at the evidence of his romance. "Thank you so much."

"What are you going to do with it all?"

"Keep it."

"Just be careful, Danny." He glanced up at her. "Don't talk to anybody about Margie. I wouldn't want . . . you know . . ."

"You wouldn't want me to be found in the East River."

"I'm not saying—"

"I know what you're saying," he replied. "And thank you. But you don't have to worry about me. Really you don't. I'm going to be fine."

"Good," she said, draining the last of her brandy. "Thank you for the drink."

"You're going already?"

"Stuff to do."

Danny got up, and somewhat awkwardly took her hand. "I know it's a cliché," he said, "but I don't know what I would have done without you." He looked, suddenly, like a lost twelve-year-old. "You took some risks, I know."

"For Margie . . ." she said.

"Yes," he replied, with a sad little smile, "for Margie."

"You keep well, Danny," Rachel said, hugging him. "I know there's good things ahead for you."

"Oh?" he said doubtfully. "I think the best times went with Margie." He kissed her on the cheek. "She loved us both, huh? So that's something."

"That's a lot, Danny."

"Yeah," he said, trying to put on a little brightness. "You're right. That's a lot."

# X

About the time Rachel caught her cab back uptown, and opened the journal to pick up Captain Holt's story where she'd left off, Garrison was pouring his fourth Scotch of the night, slipping the bottle down beside the high-backed armchair set before his dining room window. He wasn't alone in his liquored state. Mitchell was sitting in front of the fire, which he'd insisted be lit, in a worse state of intoxication than he'd been in since law school. Two maudlin drunks, talking of how their women had betrayed them. They'd poured out their hearts tonight, as liberally as they'd poured the Scotch: confessed their indifference to the labors of the marital bed, and their weariness with their adulteries; promised that their only loyalties lay with one another, and that whatever betrayals there might have been, they were a thing of the past; and most significantly, debated in detail how their dealings had to be handled from now on, now that they knew how isolated they were.

"I know it's no good looking back . . ." Mitchell slurred.

"No it isn't . . ."

"But I can't help it. When I think of the way things were."

"They weren't as wonderful as you remember. Memories are lies. Especially the good ones."

"Were you never happy?" Mitch said. "Not once? Not for an afternoon?"

Garrison grunted as he thought about this. "Well now you mention it," he said finally. "I do remember that day I dumped you in the yard with the fire ants, and you got bit all over your ass. I was pretty damn happy that day. Do you remember that?"

"Do I remember—"

"I got beaten black and blue for that."

"By Poppa?"

"No, by mother. She never left it to George when it came to something important, because she knew we weren't scared of him. She beat me within an inch of my life."

"You deserved it," Mitchell said, "I was sick for a week. And you didn't give a shit."

"I didn't like that you got all the attention. But you know what? When I was moping around, pissed off that you were being pampered,

Cadmus said to me: *see what happens if you make people sorry for some-one?* I remember him saying that, plain as day. He wasn't angry with me. He just wanted me to understand that I'd done a stupid thing: I'd made everybody lovey-dovey with you. So I didn't try and hurt you after that, in case you got the attention."

Mitchell got up and went to fetch the bottle from Garrison.

"Speaking of the old man—" Mitchell said, "Jocelyn told me you kept him company last night."

"I sure did. I sat by his bed for a few hours when they brought him back from the hospital. I tell you, he's tough. The doctors didn't think he was going to come home."

"Did he tell you anything?"

Garrison shook his head. "He was raving most of the time. It's the painkillers they've got him on. They make him delirious." Garrison fell silent for a long moment. "You know what I started to wonder."

"What?"

"If we took him off the medication . . ."

"We can't—"

"I mean just took his pills away."

"Waxman wouldn't allow that."

"We wouldn't tell Waxman. We'd just do it."

"He'd be in agony."

A tiny smile appeared on Garrison's face. "But we'd get some straight answers from him, if we had the pills." He shook his fist, as though it contained the means to Cadmus's comfort.

"Fuck . . ." Mitchell said softly.

"I know it's not a very pretty idea," Garrison said, "but we don't have a lot of options left. He's not going to hang on forever. And when he's gone . . ."

"There's got to be some other way," Mitch said. "Let me try talking to him."

"You can't get anything out of him. He doesn't trust either of us any more. I don't think he ever did. He didn't trust anybody but himself." Garrison thought on this for a moment. "Smart man."

"So how do you know all this stuff exists?"

"Because Kitty told me about it. She was the only one who ever talked to me about the Barbarossas. She'd seen the journal."

"So at least the old man trusted her."

"I guess he did. At the beginning. I guess we all start out trusting our wives . . ."

"Wait," Mitch said. "I just had a thought—"

"Margie."

"Yeah."

"I'm there before you, brother."

"Cadmus liked her."

"So maybe he gave her the journal? Yeah. Like I say, I'm there before you." He slid deeper into his seat, cocooned in shadow. "But if she had it, she certainly wasn't going to tell me about it. Even with a gun waved in her face."

"Have you searched your apartment?"

"The police already went through it, top to bottom."

"So maybe they took it."

"Yeah, maybe . . ." Garrison said, without much confidence. "Cecil's trying to find out what they lifted from the place while I was locked up. But I can't see why they'd remove something like that. It's no use to them."

Mitchell sighed. "I'm so sick of this," he said.

"Sick of what?"

"All this shit about the Barbarossas. I don't know why we don't just forget about 'em. If they were such a fucking problem, the old man would have done something about them years ago."

"He couldn't," Garrison said, sipping on his whisky. "They're too powerful."

"If they're so powerful why have I never heard of them?"

"Because they don't want you to know. They're secretive."

"So what have they got to hide? Maybe it's something we can use against them."

"I don't think so," Garrison said, very quietly. Mitchell looked at him, expecting him to say more, but he kept his silence. Several seconds passed. Then Garrison murmured, "The women know more than we do."

"Because they get serviced by that sonofabitch?"

"I think they get more than that," Garrison said.

"I want to kill the fuck," Mitchell replied.

"I don't want you trying anything," Garrison said calmly. "Do you understand me, Mitch?"

"He fucked my wife."

"You knew you'd have to let her go to him sooner or later."

"It's bullshit . . ."

"It won't happen again," Garrison said, his voice colorless. "She was the last." He looked out at his brother from the cleft of the chair. "We're going to bring them down, Mitch. Him and all his family. That's why I don't want any personal vendettas from you. I don't want them getting twitchy. I want to know everything there is to know about them before we move against them."

"Which brings us back to the journal," Mitchell said. He set his glass on the sill. "You know maybe *I* should talk to Cadmus."

Garrison didn't reply to the suggestion. He didn't even acknowledge it. Instead he drained his whisky glass, and then—his voice no more than a bruised whisper—he said: "You know what Kitty told me?"

"What?"

"That they're not human."

Mitchell laughed; the sound hard and ragged.

Garrison waited until it died away, then he said: "I think she was telling the truth,"

"That's fucking stupid." Mitchell said. "I don't want to hear about it." He bared his teeth in disgust. "How could you fucking believe a thing like that?"

"I think she even took me to the Barbarossa house, when I was a baby."

"Fuck the house," Mitchell said, swatting all this irritating talk away. "I don't want to hear any more! Okay?"

"We've got to face it sooner or later."

"No," Mitchell said, with absolute resolution. "If you're going to start talking like this, I'm going home."

"It's not something we can hide from," Garrison said mildly. "It's a fact of our lives, Mitch. It always has been. We just didn't know it."

Mitchell paused at the door. Sluggish and befuddled with drink, he couldn't raise any coherent counter to what Garrison was saying. All he could say was: "Bull. Shit."

Garrison went on, as though Mitch hadn't spoken. "You know what?" he said. "Maybe it's for the best. We've run our course the way we are. It's time for something new." He was talking to an empty room now; Mitch had already left. Still, he finished his thought. "Something new," he said again, "or maybe something very old."

# XI

Garrison didn't sleep that night. He'd never needed more than three and a half hours' rest a night, and since Margie's death that number had gone down to two hours, sometimes just one. He was running on fumes, of course, and he knew it. He couldn't go on denying his body the rest it needed without paying a price. But with his fatigue came a strange clarity. The conversation he'd had with his brother tonight, for instance, would have been unthinkable a few weeks before: his mind would have rejected the ideas he'd espoused as surely as Mitchell had done. But now he knew better. He was living in a world of mysteries, and out of fear he'd chosen to ignore their presence. Now it seemed to him the only way forward was to reach out and touch those mysteries; know what they were, know what they meant; let them work whatever changes they wished upon him.

Mitchell would come to share his point of view in time. He'd have no choice. The old empire was receding into oblivion: the old powers dying, the old certainties going with them. Something had to replace those powers, and it wouldn't be a democracy of love and truth; of that Garrison was certain. The new age, when it came, would be just as élite as the one passing away. A chosen few—those with the will to live superior lives—would have the wherewithal to do so. The rest, as ever, would live and die in futility. The difference lay only in the coinage of power. The age of railroads and stockyards and timber and oil would give way to a time in which power was measured by some other means; a means which he as yet had no language to describe. He felt its imminence as he sometimes felt things in dreams; a knowledge beyond the scope of his five senses; beyond measurement or even materiality. He did not know where his appetite for such possibilities came from, but he knew it had always been in him. The day Grandma Kitty had told him of the Barbarossas he'd felt some sleeping part of his nature awaken. He could remember everything about that conversation still. How she'd stared at him as she spoke, watching every nuance of his response; how she'd touched his face, her touch kindlier than he'd ever had from her before; how she'd promised to tell him secrets that would change his life forever, when the time was right. Of course she'd been the one to tell him about the journal, though he'd pretended to Mitchell he wasn't certain this was so. There was a book, she'd said, in which the way to get into the heart of the Barbarossas' land was described; along with all that had to be endured on that road. Terrible things, she'd implied; horrors that would drive a soul to insanity if they weren't prepared. That was why it was essential to have this book: the information it contained was vital to any endeavor concerning the Barbarossas.

Oh, the nights he'd lain awake, wondering about that book! Trying to imagine how it might look, how it might feel in his hands. Was it large or small; were its pages thick or thin? Would he know the moment he read it what wisdom it was imparting, or would it be written in a code which he had to crack? Then there was the most important question of the lot: where did his Cadmus keep this book? He would sometimes steal into his grandfather's study—which was a room he was strictly forbid to enter—and stare at the shelves and cupboards (he didn't dare touch anything) wondering where it might be hidden. Was there a safe behind the books, or a secret compartment under the floor? Or was it hidden away in one of the drawers of Cadmus's antique desk, which had seemed so intimidating to him as a child that he'd had an almost superstitious fear of it, as though it had a life of its own and might come after him, snorting like a bull, if he stared at it for too long?

He was never once caught in the study. He was far too clever for that. He knew how to wait and watch and plan; he knew how to lie. The one thing he couldn't do was charm; not even his own grandmother. When, after Cadmus's recovery, he'd asked Kitty to talk about what she'd intimated to him, she bluntly refused to do so, to the point of denying that they'd ever had the conversation. He'd grown sullen, realizing that there was nothing he could say or do that would persuade her to open the subject again, and his sullenness had become thereafter his chief defining feature. In any family photograph he was the one without the smile; the glowering adolescent whom everybody treated gingerly for fear he snap like an ill-tempered dog. He didn't much like the pose, or the response it elicited, but he couldn't compete with Mitchell's effortless charm. If he was patient, he knew, the time would come when he'd have the power to seek these secrets out for himself. Meanwhile he'd work, and play the loving grandson, watching for any clues that might inadvertently fall from Cadmus's lips; about where he might find the journal, and what it contained.

But Cadmus had let nothing slip. Though he'd encouraged Garrison in his rise to power, and countless times made it clear how much he trusted Garrison's judgment, that trust had never extended to talking about the Barbarossas. Nor had Garrison been able to draw Loretta into his confidence. She'd made her suspicion of him, mingled with a mild distaste, plain from the outset, and nothing he'd said or done had made her warm to him. More irksome still was the knowledge that she, though new to the Geary dynasty, had access to information that he was denied. More than information, of course. She, like Kitty and Margie and Mitchell's wife, had taken herself off to Kaua'i more than once, to be with one of the Barbarossa clan. Why this ritual was sanctioned Garrison had never understood; he only knew that it was a tradition that went back a long way. He'd raised some objections to it when he'd first heard it mooted, but Cadmus had made it unequivocally clear that the matter was not up for debate. There were some things, he'd said to Garrison, that had to be accepted without challenge, however unpalatable. They were part of the way the world worked.

"Not my world," Garrison had said, working himself up into a fine fury. "I'm not allowing my wife to go off to some island and play around with a total stranger."

"Just be quiet," Cadmus had said. Then, in hushed, even tones he'd explained that Garrison would do exactly as he was told on this matter, or suffer the consequences. "If you can't behave as I wish you to behave, then you have no place in this family," he'd said.

"You wouldn't throw me out," Garrison had replied. "Not now."

"You watch me," his grandfather had said. "If you argue with me about this, you go. It's as simple as that. It's not as though you're devoted to your wife, after all. You cheat on her, don't you?" Garrison had sulked. "Well don't you?"

"Yes."

"So let her cheat on you, if it helps the family."

"I don't see how—"

"It doesn't matter whether you see or not."

That had been the end of the conversation, and Garrison had left with not the slightest doubt as to his grandfather's sincerity. Cadmus was not a man to make idle threats. Duly warned, Garrison had kept his objections to himself thereafter. And what little faith he'd had in his grandfather's love for him died.


Now, as the first light of dawn crept into the sky, he thought of the old man, sick to death but unwilling to die, and wondered if he should have one more try at getting the truth out of him. No doubt, as Mitchell had said, taking Cadmus's pills off him for half a day would be a torment;

but it might make him talk. And even if it didn't, there'd be some satisfaction to be had from making the bastard beg for his painkillers. Picturing the scene, Cadmus yellow-white with agony, sobbing to have his opiates back, brought a smile to Garrison's face. But first he would see how well Mitchell did getting the truth out of Cadmus. If his brother failed, then he'd have no choice but to play the torturer, and be thankful for the chance.

# XII

### i

*Ink and water; water and ink.*

Last night, I dreamt about Galilee. It wasn't one of the waking dreams—the visions, if you will—in which I witness the matter of these pages. It was a dream that came to me while I was asleep, but which so forcibly impressed itself upon my mind that it was still there when I woke.

This is what I dreamed. I was hovering like a bird above a churning sea, and adrift in that sea, bound to a wretched raft, and naked, was Galilee. He was covered in wounds, and his blood was running off into the water. I couldn't see any sharks, but that's not to say they weren't all around him. The sea was *black*, however, like the ink in my pen; it concealed its inhabitants.

As I watched, wave after dark wave struck the raft, and one by one its pieces were disengaged and swept away, so that soon Galilee's body was draped over the three or four planks that remained, his head and lower limbs submerged in the water. Now, for the first time, he seemed to realize that he was about to die, and began to struggle to work the knots free. His body glistened with sweat, and sometimes, as the scene grew more frenzied, I couldn't decide what I was seeing. Was that black, shining form broken on the planks still my brother, or was it the breaking wave that had swept him away?

I wanted to wake now; the whole scene distressed me. I had no desire to watch my brother drown. I told myself to *wake up. You don't have to endure this*, I said, *just open your eyes.*

I started to feel the dream receding from me. But even as it did so my brother's writhings became more desperate—the wounds on his body gaping as he thrashed—and he pulled a hand free of the ropes. He hauled his head up out of the waves. When he did so the water seemed to cling around his skull, as though it had knitted a spumy crown there; his eyes were wild, his mouth was letting out a soundless scream. He tore at the binding around his other wrist, and then, sitting up on what was left of the raft, reached down into the water to free his legs.

He wasn't quick enough. The planks beneath him were sundered, and swept away. He fell backward into the water, his wounds pouring blood as he did so, and the waterlogged boards to which his feet were still tied dragged him down, down beneath waves.

And now came the most curious event in the sequence. As his dark body sank from sight, the waters into which he was disappearing forsook their negritude, as though in reverence to the flesh they'd claimed. It was not that they became translucent, like any common sea. Rather their concealing darkness become a revelatory light, which blazed so brightly it outshone the sky.

I could see my brother's body, sinking into the bright depths. I could see every living form that swam in the sea around him, all silhouetted against the brightness of the water. Shoals of tiny fish, moving as a single entity; vast squid—vaster than any such creature I'd seen before—watching Galilee descend toward their realm; and of course innumerable sharks, circling him as he sank, describing protective spirals around his body.

And then, as they say in books of cowardly fancy, I woke, and it was all a dream.


I don't discount the possibility that though the images I saw were not real, as I believe my visions are, they were true. That Galilee, if not already drowned, is about to be drowned.

What does that do to the story I thought I was telling? Well, to put it crudely, it pinches it off before it was fully shit out. (I'm sorry, that's not the prettiest of metaphors, but I'm not in the prettiest of moods; and it expresses indecently well how I feel today about what I'm doing. That this whole wretched business has simply been one long, problematic excretion. One day I'm constipated, the next it runs out of me like foul water.)

But now I revolt you. I'll stop.

Back to Rachel for a while. I'll let the dream sit, and revisit it in a few hours. Maybe it'll make a different kind of sense later.

## ii

The last we heard of Rachel she was in a cab returning to the apartment on Central Park. In her hands, the journal which Garrison had spent so many hours in his youth wondering about; imagining its size, and its weight; puzzling over what it might contain. And there in its pages she'd discovered a mystery: that there had been a man called Galilee in Charleston, in the spring of 1864. Now Nickelberry was taking Holt to meet him, promising that the encounter would help the captain heal the pain he'd endured here.

*I had not witnessed such excess I was about to see,* the captain wrote, *since the early days of the war, when I had occasion to come into a bordello where one of my men had been murdered in a brawl. To be truthful luxury, especially in excess, has never pleased me; only in nature do I find an overabundance delightful; evidence of creation's limitless cup. It was my darling Adina who was the one who liked to have fine things in the house—vases and silks and pretty pictures. For me, as I think for most of my sex, fineries are acceptable in moderation, but can quickly come to seem smothering.*

*So then, imagine this: two houses in the East Battery, facing the water, and so damaged by enemy fire as to seem from the outside little more than the husks of dwellings, but which, upon entering, are revealed to contain the gleanings from fifty of Charleston's finest houses, every article chosen because it speaks precociously to the senses.*

*This was the place into which Nickelberry took me; the place he'd been brought by his guide and advocate Olivia, who was but one of a dozen or so people who occupied this unlikely palace.*

*It seems Nub had accepted the bounty of the place without questioning it (such is a cook's nature, perhaps; especially during times of scarcity). I, on the other hand, began to interrogate Olivia immediately. How had all this sickly magnificence been accrued, I demanded to know. The woman was black, and ill-educated (she'd been a slave, though she was now dressed in a gown, and draped in jewelry, that would have been the envy of any fine woman on Meeting Street): she could not answer me coherently. I became frustrated with her, but before my agitation grew too great a white woman, much older than Olivia, appeared at my side. She introduced herself as the widow of General Walter Harris, a man under whose command I had fought in Virginia. She seemed quite happy*

*to answer my questions. None of the luxuries in the midst of which
we stood had been pirated or looted, she explained, but given freely
to the man who lived here, the aforementioned Galilee. I expressed
surprise at this, for besides the great treasure-house of valuables
here there was also food and drink in an abundance I think no
Charlestonian has seen since the beginning of the siege. I was
invited by the ladies to sit and eat, and after so many months in
which the best fare available was fried biscuits in bacon fat could
not restrain myself. I was not alone at the table. There was a Negro
boy, no more than twelve, and a young man from Alabama by the
name of Maybank and a fourth woman, very pale and elegant,
whom this fellow Maybank fed with his fingers, as though he were
enslaved to her. I ate gingerly at first, overwhelmed by what was
before me, but my appetite grew rather than diminishing, and I ate
enough for ten men; was then sick to my stomach; and, having
vomited, came back to the table quite refreshed, and partook
again. Sweetbreads with sherry, thick slices of a baked calf's head,
oysters and mushrooms, a fine she-crab soup and a brown oyster
stew with benne seeds. There was a wine soufflé for dessert, and
huckleberry pie and conserved peaches—what we used to call
peach leather when I was young—and fruit candy such as we
would have for Christmas. Nickelberry, Olivia and the general's
widow ate with me, while the younger woman, one Katherine Morrow, made herself very drunk with brandy, and at last took herself
off in search of our host, then promptly passed out on the floor next
door. The young man Maybank, declared suddenly that he wished
to have congress with the woman while she was in this state, and
called for the Negro boy Thaddeus to help him undress the woman.*

*I protested, but Nickelberry advised me to hold my tongue.
They had a perfect right to pleasure themselves with the drunken
Miss Morrow if they so chose, he said; such was the law of this
place. Olivia confirmed the fact. If I was to intervene, she warned
me, and Galilee chanced to hear of it, he would kill me . . .*

Rachel had not noticed the journey back to the apartment; nor the trip
in the elevator. Now she was sitting at the window, with the glory of
New York before her, and she didn't see it. All she saw was the house in
the East Battery, its rooms a catalog of excesses; and the captain, sitting
at the table, gorging himself—

I asked what manner of man this Galilee was, and Olivia smiled at me. You'll see, she said. And you'll understand, when he starts to speak to you, what kind of king he is.

King? I said, of what country? Of every country, Olivia replied; of every city, of every stone.

He's black, the widow Harris said, but he was never a slave. I asked her how she knew this, and she answered, simply, that there was not a man on earth who could put Galilee in chains.

All, needless to say, strange talk; and while it was going on the sounds from the adjacent room growing louder, as Maybank and the boy violated Miss Morrow.

Nickelberry left the table, and went to watch. He called me presently to join him, and to my shame I picked up the bottle of wine I had all but emptied and went to see.

Miss Morrow was no longer incapacitated, but responding to her violations with vigor. The boy was naked by now, and straddled her, rubbing his little rod between her breasts, while Maybank took the route between her legs, which he had made available by tearing her fine silk dress apart.

The scene was entirely bestial, but I will not lie: I was aroused. Fiery, in fact.

After years of sickness and corpses, I was glad to see healthy flesh sweating healthy sweat. The din of their mutual pleasuring filled the room, echoing back and forth between the bare walls so that it was as though there were not three but ten lovers before me. I began to feel giddy, my head pounding, and I turned away to find that Nickelberry was back at the table with Olivia, who had bared herself for his perusal. He looked like a greedy child, his hands plunged into plates of creamy dessert, which he then smeared upon the woman's handsome bosom. She seemed quite happy at this, and pressed his face against her, so he might lick the cream off her body.

The widow Harris now came to me, and offered her own flesh for my pleasure. I declined. She promptly told me I could not. If I was capable of giving her the pleasure of love, then I was obliged to do so. This too was the law.

I told her that I was a married man, at which she laughed, saying that in this place it mattered not at all what a man or woman had been before they entered; that all histories were forgotten here, and a person became what suited them.

Then I do not belong here, I told her. Are you so proud of what

*you were out there? she said to me, her face all flushed. You fled
your duty; you lost your family and your house. You're less than me,
out there. Imagine that! You who were so fine, less than an ugly old
widow.*

*She angered me, and I struck her, drunk as I was, I struck her
hard across her painted face. She fell back against the wall, shrieking at me now—obscenities I would not have believed she knew,
except that she was spitting them at me in a vile stream. I threw
down the bottle I'd been drinking from, and for a moment, thinking perhaps I meant to do her more serious harm, she ceased to
shriek. But then I turned from her, and she began again, following
me like a fury, berating me.*

*In my drunken desire to get away from the woman I became
lost. The route I had supposed would take me out into the street
brought me instead to a darkened flight of stairs. I ascended them
stumbling, and crouched in the gloom halfway up. The widow had
not seen me ascend; she passed below, cursing me.*

*I waited there in the darkness, shuddering. Not from fear of
the widow, but from grief at what she'd said. The woman was right,
I knew. I'm nothing now. Less than nothing.*

*And then, as if my sorrow had been spoken, a man appeared
at the top of the stairs and looked down at me. No, not at me; into
me. I never felt such a gaze as this. I was in fear of it at first. I felt
he might kill me with it, as readily as a man who reached into
another's body and took hold of his heart.*

*But then he came down the stairs a little way, and sat there,
and quietly said: "A man who is nothing has nothing to lose. I am
Galilee. Welcome," and I felt as though I had a reason to live.*

# XIII

### i

A reason to live.
  Rachel put the journal down and stared out across the darkened
park. It was impossible that this Galilee be the same man as she'd met,
but it was so easy to imagine him there on the stairs, imagine him speak-

ing those words of welcome, imagine him being the man who'd given the captain reason to live.

Hadn't he done that for her, in a way? Hadn't he reawakened her sense of her own significance, her own power?

She set the journal down on the table, glancing at the opening of the next paragraph.

*How shall I say what happened to me then?*

She looked away from it. She couldn't bear to read any more, not tonight. Her head was too filled up, sickened almost the way the captain had been sickened, by the sheer excess of what she'd read. There was a change in the prose too, which was not lost on her. The earlier entries had been nicely written, but their eloquence had been that of a man striving for some distance from the horrors in which he was immersed. But now he had begun to write like a storyteller, creating the scene and his place in it with terrible immediacy. The visions his words had put in Rachel's head still swarmed before her: the house, the food, the sexual couplings.

The last time she'd felt so consumed by a story, Galilee had been the man telling it—

She looked at the journal again, without touching it; at the way the words were neatly laid on the page. Too neatly perhaps. Was this the diary of a man who was living out these experiences, and hours later setting them down? Or had this all been constructed after the fact, by a man who'd been tutored in the art of telling a tale? Tutored by a man who loved stories; who told them as seductions.

"No . . ." she said to herself. No, *this was not the same man*; once and for all, there were two Galilees: one in the journal, the other in her memory. She looked at the teasing words again:

*How shall I say what happened to me then?*

It was a clever bluff, that sentence. The writer knew *exactly* how he was going to say what happened to him; he had the words ready. But it made those words seem more true, didn't it, if they appeared to come from a man uncertain of his own skills? She felt a spasm of revulsion for the story, and for her own complicity in its deceits. She'd gorged on it, hadn't she? Lapped up every decadent detail, as though this other life could give her clues to her own.

So far, it had shown her nothing of any real value. Yes, it had titillated her with its Gothic nonsenses; its tales of ghost children and unearthed limbs, but these scenes in the house had gone too far. She didn't believe it any longer. It might pass itself off as history, but it was a fabrication; its excesses made it absurd.

\*     \*     \*

She was still angry with herself when she went to bed, and she couldn't sleep. After an hour and a half lying in an unease doze she got up, popped a sleeping pill, and went back to bed to try again. The pill turned out to be a bad idea. Something in her simply didn't want to rest, and her body fought the soporific. When she finally succeeded in falling asleep for a few minutes her head was filled with a chaotic rush of fragments, from which she woke in an aching sweat, with such a dread upon her, such a profound, wrenching dread, that she had to get up again, turn on the light and talk herself back into a semblance of calm.

She padded down to the kitchen, made herself a cup of Earl Grey tea and returned to the journal. What was the use of trying to resist it, she thought as she sat down in the circle of lamplight and turned her eyes to the page. Nonsense or not, it had her in its grip, and she couldn't be free of it until it had finished with her.

## ii

Halfway across town, lying awake in his bed, Cadmus Geary thought of his beloved Louise, and of those days of dalliance that sometimes seemed so far off they'd happened in another life and at others, as tonight, seemed to have taken place just a few days ago, the memory was so clear. What a beauty she had been! Entirely deserving of his devotion. Of course she was playing hard to get tonight, but that was one of the prerogatives of beauty; all he could do was stay close to her, and hope she saw his sincerity.

"Louise . . ." he murmured.

A man's voice answered. "There's nobody called Louise here," it said quietly.

His faint condescension irritated Cadmus. "I know that," he snapped. He reached for his spectacles which were on the bedside table.

"You want some water?" the man said.

"No, I want to see who the hell I'm talking to."

"It's Mitchell."

"Mitchell?" His fumbling fingers had found his spectacles, and he put them on, peering at his grandson through the thumbed glass. "What time is it?"

"It's the middle of the night."

"So what are you doing here?"

"We've been talking, on and off."

"Have I been making any sense?"

"Of course," Mitchell reassured him. This was not strictly true. Though the old man had been more coherent than Garrison had reported, he was still in a semidelirious state much of the time. "You've been sleeping, on and off."

"Talking in my sleep?"

"Yes," Mitchell said. "Nothing scandalous. You've just been calling for this woman Louise."

Cadmus sank back into the pillow. "My lovely Louise," he sighed. "She was the best thing that ever happened to me." He closed his eyes. "What are you waiting for?" he said. "You've got to have something better to be doing than sitting here. I'm not planning to die just yet."

"I didn't think you were."

"So go have a party. Get drunk. Fuck your wife, if she'll let you."

"She won't."

"Then fuck somebody else's wife." He opened his eyes again and laughed, the sound like the hiss of escaping air. "That's more fun anyway."

"I'd prefer to be here with you."

"Would you really?" the old man said incredulously. "Either I'm more interesting than I thought or you're even duller." He raised his head an inch or so and peered at his grandson. "You got the looks didn't you, Mitch? I mean, you really are a handsome fellow. But . . . you're not as bright as your mother and you're not as honest as your father, and that's a pity, because I had some hopes for you."

"Help me then."

"Help you?"

"Tell me how you want me to be, and I'll work at it."

"You can't work at it," Cadmus said, his tone close to contempt. "Just get on with what you've got. Nobody blames you. It's the luck of the draw." He settled his head back on his pillow, delicately, as though his skull was cracked. "Are you here alone?" he said.

"There's a nurse . . ."

"No. I mean your brother."

"Garrison's not here."

"Good. I don't want him here." He closed his eyes. "We've all done things we regret, but . . . but . . . oh Lord, oh Lord . . ." He shivered a little.

"Should I get another blanket for you?"

"It doesn't help. I'm just cold and there's nothing to be done about it. What I want is my Louise . . ." He made a puckish little smile. "She'd warm me up."

"I don't know who you're talking about."

"Your wife . . . resembles my Louise . . . did you know that?"

"Really?"

"We have that much in common, at least. A taste in beauty."

"Where is she now?" Mitchell said.

"Your wife?" Cadmus said. "You don't know where your wife is?" He made another laugh. "That was a joke, Mitchell."

"Oh."

"I don't remember you being so humorless."

"Things have changed. *I've* changed."

"Well, don't lose your sense of humor. In the end it may be all you've got. Christ knows, it's all I've got." Mitchell started to protest, but the old man hushed him. "Don't tell me how deeply loved I am because I know better. I'm an inconvenience. I'm standing between you and your inheritance."

"We just want to do our best for the family," Mitchell said.

"*We* meaning . . . ?"

"Garrison and myself."

"Since when was murder a smart thing to do?" Cadmus said, with agonizing sloth. "All your brother has brought this family is shame. *Shame*. I'm ashamed of my own grandchildren."

"Wait—" Mitchell protested. "That was all Garrison. I had nothing to do with what happened to Margie."

"No?"

"Absolutely not. I loved Margie."

"She was like a sister to you."

"She was."

"You don't understand how it could have happened. It's a tragedy. Poor Margie, poor drunken Margie. What did she ever do to deserve it?" He bared his brown teeth. "You want to know what she did? I'll tell you what she did. She gave birth to a nigger, and your big brother never forgave her that."

"What?"

"You didn't know? She had Galilee's kid. At least, that's what Garrison thought. How could it be his? I mean, he's a Geary. So how could it be his, a little black fuck of a thing?"

"I don't understand."

"I think that's the first honest thing you've said tonight. No, I'm sure you don't understand. I'm sure it's all completely beyond you." He shook his head. "What did you *really* come here for?" he said.

"Wait. Back up. I want to know about Margie."

"You've heard all you're going to hear from me. I want to know what you came here for."

"I just wanted to talk."

"About what?"

"Anything you wanted to talk about. We used to be so close and—"

"Stop. Stop," Cadmus said. "I'm squirming, listening to this crap. I'll ask you one more time: what did you come here for? You answer me truthfully or get the hell out of here and don't ever come back." He leaned up out of the pillow. "And when I say that, I mean it. *Don't ever come back.*"

Mitchell nodded. "Okay," he said quietly. "So . . . it's simple. I want to find the Barbarossas."

"Now we get to it," Cadmus said. For the first time in the conversation he looked genuinely pleased. "Go on."

"Garrison says there's a book—"

"Does he indeed?"

"—some kind of journal, which your first wife told him about."

"Kitty didn't know how to keep her mouth shut."

"So this book exists?"

"Oh yes. It exists."

"I came here to get it."

"I don't have it, son."

Mitchell leaned closer to his grandfather. "Where is it?" he said again. "Come on. Tell me. I've been honest with you."

"And I'm returning the compliment. I don't have it. And even if I did, I wouldn't give it to you."

"Why the hell not? What do you care what we do to those people?"

"By *we* you mean this family?" He narrowed his watery eyes. "Are you planning a war, Mitch? Because if you are, don't. You don't know what you're taking on."

"I know the Barbarossas have got some kind of hold over us."

"They have more than a hold," Cadmus said, his voice emotionless. "They own us. And let me tell you, we're lucky, we are *very lucky*, to have been left alone all these years. Because if they took it into their heads to come after us, we wouldn't stand a chance."

"Are they Mafia?"

"Oh Lord, wouldn't that be nice? If they were just men with guns."

"So who are they?"

"I don't know," the old man replied. "But I'm afraid I'm going to find out, the moment my heart stops beating."

"Don't say that."

"Does it make you nervous?" Cadmus said. "It should." His eyes were shiny with tears. "There's more to this than you'll ever get your head round, son, so for your own sake, let it go. Don't let Garrison pull you into this mess. He's got no other option, you see. He was born into it. But you . . . you can walk away if you want to. Save yourself. God knows it's too late for me. And for your brother. And of course your wife—"

"She hasn't a clue about any of this."

"She's theirs," Cadmus said flatly. "All the women are. I sometimes think that's what's saved us from being wiped out. Galilee likes the Geary women. The Geary women like Galilee." He pressed his fingers to his pale lips, and wiped away some spittle. "I lost Kitty to him. Long before the cancer got her, she was gone from me. Then I lost Loretta. That's hard to take. I loved them both, but it wasn't enough."

Mitchell put his head in his hands. "Garrison said they weren't like us," he murmured.

"He's right and he's wrong. I think they're more like us than not. But they're also more than we could ever be." The tears began to tumble down his cheeks. "I suppose I should be comforted by that. I didn't stand a chance against the likes of him. Nothing I could have done for my wives would ever have been enough. He had them the moment he laid eyes on them."

"Don't cry, Pops," Mitchell said. "Please."

"I cry all the time, take no notice."

Mitchell moved closer to the bed. "Let me be a part of this," he said, his voice soft and full. "*Please.* I know you think I'm a fuckup . . . but . . . it's just because nothing's ever been clear to me. Nobody ever took the time to explain. So I just looked the other way. I pretended I didn't care. But I do. Pops, *I do.* I want to know who these people are; I want to make them suffer the way you've suffered."

"No."

"Why not?"

"Because you're my grandson and I won't be responsible for sending you to your death."

"Why are you so afraid of them?"

"Because I'm almost dead, son. And if I've got an eternal soul, it's in a lot of trouble. I don't want you on my conscience. It's already heavy enough."

Mitchell drew a deep breath. "All right," he said, rising from the chair. "I don't know what else to say. You've got your agenda, I've got mine."

"Christ, son, listen to yourself," Cadmus said softly. "This isn't a business deal that's going sour. This is our lives."

"You made us that way, Pops," Mitchell said. "You taught Dad, and Dad taught us: business before pleasure. Business before anything."

"I was wrong," Cadmus said. "You won't hear me admit that ever again, but I was wrong." Mitchell stood at the door for a moment, and stared at the stick figure in the bed.

"Goodnight, Pops."

"Wait," the old man said.

"What?"

"Do this for me," Cadmus said. "Wait until I'm in the ground. You won't have to wait long, believe me. Just . . . wait until I'm gone. Please."

"If I agree to that—"

"More business?"

"If I agree to that, you have to tell me where the journal is."

Cadmus closed his eyes again, and for several seconds Mitchell was marooned at the door, not knowing whether to leave or stay. At last, the old man drew a creaking breath, and said:

"All right. Have it your way. I gave the journal to Margie."

"That's what Garrison thought. But he couldn't find it."

"Then ask Loretta. Or your wife. Maybe Margie passed it on. But just you remember . . . I told you to walk away. I warned you, and you didn't want to hear."

"I'm sure that's got you a place in heaven, Pops," Mitchell said. "Goodnight."

The stick man didn't answer. He was weeping again, quietly. Mitchell didn't offer any further words of consolation. As his grandfather had said, old men weep; there was nothing to be done about it.

# XIV

### i

One by one, all the secrets are coming out, like stars at twilight. Just for the record, Cadmus's claim about Garrison's wife having borne him a black child is at least partially true. She indeed became pregnant, but the child didn't live. She miscarried in the fifth month, and the few people who knew that the infant brought dead from her body was black were paid off handsomely for their silence. Garrison, as Cadmus said, assumed it was Galilee's child. That was perhaps the profoundest error he ever made; one which goes to the heart of all that he is; and more pertinently, all he must in time become.

As for Margie, I can't tell you with any certainty what information she was given when she recovered; though I think it's more than likely that she was never told that her womb had produced such a heresy. Cadmus certainly didn't want any disruptions in the equilibrium of the family; he surely kept the knowledge to the smallest possible circle of people. And Garrison had no reason to tell a single soul: all the sight of that dead child did—yes, he saw the corpse; he made a point of going to the morgue and looking at it, all wrapped in its tiny shroud—all that sight did was deepen the divide between himself and his wife. The first stone on the road that led to Margie's death was laid that day.

There's more to tell of this matter, of course; but some stars take longer to show themselves than others. The paradox is this: that the darker it gets, the more of these secrets we can see. Eventually, they're arrayed in all their glory; and it's the very things we hid from sight, the things we're most ashamed of, that we use to steer our course.

## ii

Three, four, five days went by, and Galilee let *The Samarkand* go where the tides took it. For thirty-six hours the boat scarcely moved at all, becalmed in silken water. He sat on deck most of the time, sucking his cigar, looking down into the cool depths. A great white shark came by for a while, and circled the vessel several times, but most of the time the sky and sea were deserted, and the only sound came from some part of *The Samarkand*, a board creaking, a knot grinding, as though the boat, like its owner, was starting to doubt its own existence, and was making a noise to remind itself that it was still real.

It might have been forgiven its doubts, when there was so much that was illusory walking its deck. The emptier Galilee's belly became, the more his delirium grew, and the more his delirium grew, the more visions he saw. He saw his family, in various groupings. I appeared to him more than once, I'm sure, and at one point we entered into a long and convoluted exchange inspired by a quote from Heraclitus which had lodged in his mind—something about *rubble making the fairest of worlds*. He had an even longer conversation with a vision of Luman, and for a time sat in the company of Marietta and Zabrina singing a filthy sailors' ballad, tears pouring down his cheeks.

"Why didn't you come home?" the hallucination of Zabrina asked him.

"I couldn't. Not after what happened. Everybody hated me."

"We got over it," Zabrina said. "At least I did."

Marietta said nothing. She was rather less solid than Zabrina and for some reason Galilee felt faintly guilty around her.

"It seems to me," Zabrina said, rather formally, "that you've played just about every role in the repertoire except the Prodigal. You've been a lover. You've been a fool. You've been a murderer."

"Your point?" he said.

"You could still go home if you wanted to. All you have to do is take command of the boat again."

"I have no compass. I have no maps."

"You could steer by the stars," Zabrina said.

Galilee smiled at his own delusion. "I've played this role too," he said. "The Tempter. I've played it over and over again. I know how it works. Don't waste your breath."

"That's a pity," Zabrina purred. "I would have liked to have seen you, one last time. We could have gone to the stables together, and said hello to father."

"Do you think it's just a coincidence?" Galilee said. "Christ born in a stable. Dad dying in one."

"Pure accident," Marietta said. "Christ and father have absolutely nothing in common. For one thing, father was quite the cockmeister."

"I've never heard that before," Zabrina said.

"About Dad?"

"No, the phrase. *Cockmeister.* I never heard it before."

So the hallucinatory conversations went on, seldom elevated above this chatty level, and when they were, only fleetingly so. Others besides family members came and went. Margie lingered for a little time one night, her voice slurred with drink as she told him how much she loved him. Kitty, the exquisite Kitty, drifted in a little later, but would not speak: she only stared at him for a while, with a look of incredulity on her face, as though she couldn't believe his stupidity. She'd always berated him for his self-pity, and this last time was no exception; she simply chose to do it in silence.

There were many others who didn't make it as far as the deck: haunting presences whom he glimpsed beneath the water, looking up at him as they drifted by. Victims of his, mostly; men and women whose lives he'd taken, always as quickly as he could; but what violent death was ever quick enough? Oh, some pitiable creatures there. Many he could not lay name to, thankfully; a few whose accusing looks made him want to hide his head. He didn't succumb to his cowardice; but met their gazes as best his tears would allow, until at length they drifted out of sight.

There was one further class of visitation, which did not make itself known until the afternoon of the fifth day. The becalming had long since passed; *The Samarkand*, now in the grip of a powerful current, was moving through a mounting swell, her bows on occasion dipping so deep into the spumy water it seemed she would not rise again; but each time emerging. Galilee had lashed himself to the mainmast so as not to be swept overboard. Lack of nourishment had made him weak; his legs would scarcely bear him up, and his arms would not have had the strength to prevent a wave from taking him. There he sat, the very image of a beleaguered mariner, while the boat rocked and pitched, and his teeth chattered with the cold, and his eyes rolled in their sockets.

But then, it seemed to him he glimpsed—down a valley between the steep steel waves—a stand of golden trees. For a grim instant he thought the currents had played some wretched trick, and carried him back to Kaua'i, but when the sight came again he saw this was not an island. It was instead the most beautiful and torturous vision of them all. It was home.

There down an alley of oaks swathed in Spanish moss he saw the house that Jefferson had built; his mother's house; the place from which he had fled and fled, and never escaped. Cesaria was there, behind one of those windows. She saw him, in his exile. Perhaps she'd always seen him, always had him in the corner of her eye, as a mother will; never let him go entirely, despite all that he'd done to be free of her.

He watched as the scene came and went—eclipsed by the mounting waves, then revealed again—thinking he might glimpse her there. But the vision contained nothing that breathed: not so much as a squirrel in the grass. Or at least nothing that cared to show itself to him.

And after a time, this too passed away. Another darkness fell and he remained where he was, tied to the mast, while the sky swung back and forth above him.

# XV

i

Rachel had returned into Holt's journal with the utmost cynicism, determined that this time it would not catch her up in its manipulations. But she failed. After just a few paragraphs she was back in the world the words conjured: the house in the East Battery, filled with the smells of food and sex. And Galilee on the stairs, welcoming Holt into his world. Whether this was a true account or not, she couldn't resist turning the pages.

The passages that followed were filled with descriptions of how Holt and Nickelberry lived for the next week or so: an almost obsessive listing of how their palates and their groins were titillated. Holt now seemed to have little trouble confessing his own excesses. Despite the fact that he had once been a devoted family man, he was almost boastful of them, recounting without embarrassment his liaisons with several of the women of the house. It made astonishing reading, especially as all this salacious detail was set down in a journal which he'd been given by his own wife (and whose dedication—*I love you more than life, and will show my love a thousand ways when you are here again*—was there on the opening page). Poor Adina; she'd been forgotten, at least for now. Her husband had entered a world whose laws did not allow for sentimental attachments. They were all living too desperately, too hungrily, to care what they'd been before they'd stepped into the house. All reserve, all shame, all common decencies had evaporated. According to the journal they ate, drank and coupled morning, noon and night, inspired to this behavior by three things. One, the fact that everybody in the house was engaged in the same headlong pursuit of pleasure, all spurring one another to new experiments. Two, a steady supply of erotic stimulants from Galilee, most of which Holt (and Rachel) had never heard of. And thirdly, the presence of the lawmaker himself. There was nobody in the house, male or female, young or old, who had not been bedded by Galilee. That fact emerged first in a conversation Holt reportedly had with Nickelberry; a man who'd seemed until now assuredly heterosexual. Not so. He had, in Holt's words, *played the wife to our host, and told me without a blush that he had seldom felt so loved as when he had lain in Galilee's embrace.*

Rachel was surprised that she could still be shocked after the exhaustive sexual litany that the preceding pages had contained, but shocked she was. Though she believed it preposterous to think that this Galilee was the same man she'd known, her mind's eye conjured him whenever the name appeared on the page. Then it was her Galilee, in all his beauty, she saw holding Nickelberry in his arms; kissing him, seducing him, making a wife of him.

She should have anticipated what would come next, but she didn't. While she was still struggling with her repugnance at what Holt had described, he began a confession much closer to his heart, and no doubt the hardest thing he had written in the book.

*I went to Galilee last night,* he wrote, *as Nickelberry had. I don't know why I went particularly; I felt no desire to be with him. At least not the same kind of desire that I feel when I go with a woman. Nor did he ask me for my company; though once I was with him he confessed that he'd wanted my arms about him, and my lips on his. I should not be ashamed, he said, to take pleasure this way. It was a wasted hope in most men; only the bravest rose to the challenge.*

*I told him I did not feel brave. I was afraid of the act before us, I said; afraid of its consequences for my soul; and most of all, afraid of him.*

*He didn't laugh off this confession. Instead he wrapped me up tenderly, as though he held something more precious than flesh and bone. He told me to listen to him, and would tell me a story to calm my fears—*

A story? What was this? Another Galilee who told stories?

*—I felt like a child there in his embrace, and part of me wanted to be free of it. But his presence was so calming to my troubled spirit, that this child in me, which had not spoken in so many years, said: lie still. I want to hear the story. And I lay still, obedient to this child, and presently all the horrors I had seen, every one, all the death, all the pain, became a kind of dream I'd had from which I was waking into this embrace.*

*The story he told began like a nursery tale, but by degrees it grew stranger, calling forth all manner of feelings in me. It was a tale of two princes who lived, he said, in a country far from here, where the rich were kind—*

—And the poor had God. Rachel knew that country. The child bride Jerusha had lived there. It was Galilee's invented land.

She sat absolutely still, the whine of her blood loud in her ears, while her eyes passed stupidly over the line, as if by study they might change it.

*It was a tale of two princes . . .*

But no; the words remained the same, however many times she read them. She could not avoid the truth, though it was hard—oh more than hard; nearly impossible—to contemplate. But she had no choice, besides willful self-deception. The sum of evidence was now too persuasive.

This Galilee, here on the page before her—this man who'd lived a hundred and forty years ago, and more; this man was the same Galilee she loved. Not his father or his grandfather: *him.* The same flesh and blood and bone; the same spirit in that flesh and blood and bone; the same soul.

She accepted it, though it made chaos of all she'd understood about the world. She wouldn't squirm around any longer, hoping that something easier to believe was true if she could only find it. She was only tormenting herself if she did that; putting off the moment when she accepted the facts and tried to make sense of them.

It wasn't as though he'd lied to her. Quite the reverse, in fact. He'd intimated several times that he was not quite the same order of being as she was. He'd talked of being a man without grandparents, for instance. But she hadn't wanted to know. She'd been too deeply infatuated with him to want to countenance anything that might spoil the romance.

So much for denial. It was time to accept the truth, in all its strangeness. Two human lifetimes ago he'd been up to the same seductive tricks he'd worked on her, with Captain Holt as the object of his affections. The image of the two men entwined was lodged in her mind's eye: Holt like a child in his lover's arms, lulled into a state of passivity by the story Galilee was telling.

*In a country far from here, there lived two princes . . .*

She didn't care what happened next, neither to the princes nor to the men they represented. Her hunger for the journal had suddenly passed; her eyes were no longer drawn to the page. It had told her all that she needed to know. More, in fact.

She wiped the tears from her cheeks with the heel of her hand and got up from the table, flipping the journal closed. She felt light-headed and hot, as though she was catching the flu. She went through to the kitchen, got herself a glass of water, sipped it for a moment, then decided she'd go back to bed. Maybe she'd feel better after a few more hours of sleep. And now, with the journal's hold on her finally broken, she'd have a better chance of getting the rest she needed.

Glass in hand, she padded back to the bedroom. It was a little after five o'clock. She set the glass down, and lay down thinking that if she needed to take half of another sleeping pill she would. But as she was in the process of shaping the thought, exhaustion overtook her.

## ii

I settled down to sleep a couple of hours ago believing I'd brought Part Six to an adequate conclusion. But here I am, appending these paragraphs, and effectively spoiling the neatness of my conclusion by so doing. Ah well; this was never fated to be a book distinguished by its tidiness. I'm sure it's going to get a damn sight less orderly before we get to the final pages.

What was so urgent that I had to get up out of bed and write about it? Only another dream. I offer it here not because I think it's prophetic, like my dream of Galilee on the raft, but because it moved me so strangely.

It was a dream about Luman's children.

That's odd in itself, because I hadn't given any conscious thought to the conversation I'd had about his bastards for several weeks. My unconscious mind was apparently turning the subject over however, and its investigations produced this bizarrity: I dreamed I was a piece of paper; a sheet of tattered paper. And the wind had me. It was blowing me across an immense landscape, flipping me over and over. As so often happens in dreams, I saw more than I could possibly describe, all concentrated into a few seconds of dream time. Sometimes I was lifted high into the air, and I was looking down at towns that were so far below me their inhabitants were tiny dots; sometimes I was skimming a dusty road with all the other windborne trash. I saw canyons and cities; I clung to picket fences and telegraph poles; I was becalmed in the heat of a Louisiana summer, and forked up with the leaves in Vermont; I was frozen to a fence in Nebraska, while the wire whined in the wind; I was in the meltwaters when the spring warmed the rivers of Wisconsin. By degrees a sense of imminence crept upon me. The landscapes continued to roll on—the peaks of the High Country, a palmy beach, a field of poppies and wild violets—but I knew my journey was moving toward resolution.

My destination was an unpromising place. A grimy neighborhood in a minor city somewhere in Idaho; a wasteland of gutted buildings and rubble and gray grass. But there a man sat in the remnants of a broken-down truck, and when I came to his feet he reached down and picked me up. It was a strange sensation, to be held in those tobacco-stained fingers, but I knew, looking at the man's face, that he was one of Luman's children. There was something of my half-brother's satiric fever there, and something of his piercing curiosity, though both had been dulled by hardship.

He seemed to sense that he had found more than a piece of trash in me, because he tossed his cigarette away, and getting up from his seat in the crippled vehicle he shouted:

"Hey! Hey! Lookee what I got here!"

He didn't wait for those he'd summoned to come to him, but strode with a quickening step to the remains of a garage, its pumps like rusted sentinels guarding a half-demolished building. A black woman in early middle age—her bones marking her indisputably as Cesaria's grand-child—appeared.

"What is it, Tru?" she asked him.

He handed his prize over to her, and the woman studied me.

"That's a sign," Tru drawled.

"Could be," the woman said.

"I *told* you, Jessamine."

The woman called over her shoulder, back into the garage. "Hey, Kenny. Look what Tru's found. Where'd you find it?"

"It just blew my way. And you was saying I was crazy."

"I didn't say you was crazy," Jessamine replied.

"No, *I* did," said a third voice, and a man who was in age and color somewhere between his companions came and snatched me out of Jessamine's hands. His skull was as bald as an egg, but the rest of his face was covered with a thick growth of beard. Again, there was no doubt of his ancestry. He didn't even look at what he had in his hand.

"Ain't nothing but a piece of trash," Kenny said, and before the other two could protest he'd turned his back on them and was stalking away.

They didn't follow him. At a guess, he intimidated them. But once his back was turned on them, I saw him cast a forlorn look at what he held. His eyes were wet with tears.

"Don't want to hope no more," he murmured to himself.

Then he turned my face to the flames of a small fire burning among the bricks. There was a moment of sheer panic, as the heat caught hold of me. I felt my body curl up in the flames, and blacken,

blacken until I was the color of Galilee. Then I woke, bathed in enough sweat that had I indeed been burning I would have surely extinguished myself.

There; that's the dream, as best I remember it. One of the stranger night visions I've had, I must say. I don't know what to make of it. But now that I've written it down, I withdraw what I said earlier, about it not being prophetic. Perhaps it is. Perhaps somewhere out in the middle of the country three of Luman's bastards are waiting for an omen, even now; knowing that they're more than the world has let them be, but not knowing what. Waiting for someone to come and tell them who they are. Waiting for me.

# PART SEVEN

# The Wheel of
# the Stars

# I

Today I made my peace with Luman. It wasn't an easy thing to do, but I knew that I was going to have to do it sooner or later. Just a few hours ago, sitting back from my desk to muse on something, I realized suddenly how sad I'd be if events were somehow to quicken, and L'Enfant fell, and I was to have reconciled with Luman. So I got up, fetched my umbrella (a pleasant drizzle has been falling for most of the day; perhaps it will clear the air a little) and took myself off to the Smoke House.

Luman was waiting for me, sitting on the threshold, picking his nose and staring down the path along which I approached.

"You took your time," was his first remark to me.

"I did what?"

"You heard me. Taking all this time to come an' tell me you're sorry."

"What makes you think I'm going to do that?" I replied.

"You *look* sorry," Luman replied, flicking something he'd mined from his nostrils into the vegetation.

"Do I indeed?"

"Yes, Mr.-High-and-Mighty-I'm-a-Writer-Maddox, you look very sorry indeed." He grabbed the rotted doorjamb and pulled himself to his feet. "In fact I wouldn't be surprised if you didn't jus' throw that sorry carcass down on the ground an' beg me to forgive you." He grinned. "But you don't have to do that, brother o' mine. I forgive you your trespasses."

"That's generous of you. And what about yours?"

"I don't have none."

"Luman, you virtually accused me of killing my own wife."

"I was just telling the simple truth," he said. Then added: "As I saw it. You didn't have to believe me." His goaty face became sly. "Though somethin' tells me you do." He regarded me in silence for a time. "Tell me I'm wrong."

What I really wanted to do was beat that smug smile off his face, but I resisted the temptation. I'd come here to make peace, and peace I was going to make. Besides, as I've admitted in these pages, the guilt for Chiyojo's death does in some measure lie with me. I'd confessed it on paper; now it was time to do the same thing staring my accuser in the face. That shouldn't be so difficult, should it? I knew the words; why was it so much more difficult to speak them than to write them?

I put my umbrella down and turned my face up to the rain. It was warm but it still refreshed me. I stood there for perhaps a minute, while the raindrops broke against my face, and my hair became flattened to my scalp. At last, without looking back at Luman, I said:

"You were right. I'm responsible for what happened to Chiyojo. I let Nicodemus have her, just as you said. I wanted . . ." I began to feel tears rising up in me. They thickened my voice; but I went on with my confession. "I wanted to have his favor. To have him love me." I put my hand up to my face, and wiped the rainwater off. Then, finally, I looked back at Luman. "The thing is, I never really felt as though I was his son. Not the way you were. Or Galilee. I was always the half-breed. So I scampered around the world trying to please him. But it didn't work. He just took me for granted. I didn't know what else to give him. I'd given myself and that wasn't enough . . ." Somewhere in the midst of saying all this I'd started to tremble; my hands, my legs, my heart. But nothing short of death would have now stopped me finishing what I'd begun. "When he set eyes on Chiyojo I felt angry at first. I was going to leave. I should have left. I should have taken her—just the way you said—taken her away from L'Enfant so we could have had a life of our own. An ordinary life, maybe—a human life. But that wouldn't have been so bad, would it?"

"Compared to this?" Luman said softly. "It would have been paradise."

"But I was afraid to go. I was afraid that after a while I'd regret going but that there'd be no way back."

"Like Galilee?"

"Yes . . . like poor Galilee. So I ignored my instincts. And when he came after Chiyojo I looked the other way. I suppose, deep down, I hoped she'd love me enough to say no to him."

"Don't blame her," Luman said. "The Virgin Mary would have given up her pussy for Nicodemus."

"I don't blame her. I never blamed her. But I still hoped."

"You poor idiot," Luman said, not without tenderness. "You must have been a mess."

"The worst, Luman. I was torn in half. Part of me wanted her to reject him. To come running to me and tell me he'd tried to violate her.

And part of me wanted him to take her from me. Make her his mistress if that made him pay more attention to me."

"How was that going to happen?"

"I don't know. He was going to feel guilty so he was going to be kinder to me. Or we'd simply have shared her. Him at one end and me at the other."

"You'd have done that?"

"I think so."

"Wait. Let me be certain I understand this. You would have had a *ménage à trois* with your wife and your own father?" I didn't answer, but I suppose my silence was reply enough. Luman slapped his hand over his eyes with comic gusto. "I thought I was twisted," he said. Then he grinned.

For myself I didn't know whether to laugh or cry. This was more than I'd confessed with pen and paper; this was the dirtiest truth; the most wretched, sickening truth.

"Anyway, it never happened," I said.

"Well that's something," Luman replied. "You're still a pervert, mind."

"He took her and fucked her and gave her feelings I guess I never gave her."

"He could do that," Luman said. "He had the gift."

"Was it . . . physical?" I asked him, voicing a question that had haunted me for years. Luman looked at me blankly. "His gift," I said. "Oh come on, Luman, you know what I'm talking about. Was that how he made women love him?" I glanced down between my legs. "With that?"

"Are you asking me how big his dick was?" Luman said. I nodded. "Well, judging by my own attributes, sizeable. But I think that's only half the story. If you don't know how to wield it . . ." He sighed. "I never have, you see. That's always been my problem. Plenty of substance, but no style. I'm hung like a stallion but I fuck like a one-legged mule." Finally, I laughed, which plainly pleased Luman no end, because he beamed. "Well we certainly know more about one another than we knew five minutes ago," he said. Then, more quietly:

"Pervert."

We talked a little longer before I returned here to the study, with him standing in the shelter of his door, and me out in the rain. Only a couple of significant things were said. Luman suggested that in the near future the two of us go down to the stables and visit Nicodemus's grave. I agreed that we should do so, adding that I didn't think we should delay going, in case events overtook us and we were denied the opportunity. Luman's response to this was interesting.

"Are we at war then?" he said. "Should we expect an invasion any day?"

I told him I didn't know, but that the House of Geary had become unstable of late, which was certainly reason for nervousness.

"If you're nervous then I'm nervous," Luman said. "I'm going to get out my knives tonight. Start polishing. Have you got yourself a gun?"

"No."

He ducked back inside the house and reemerged a few moments later with an antiquated pistol. "Take it," he said.

"Where did you get it?" I asked him.

"It belonged to Nub Nickelberry," he said. "He gave it to me when he left. In fact Galilee made him give it to me. He told Nickelberry he wouldn't have any use for it. He had all the protection he'd ever need."

"Meaning himself?"

"I guess so." He proffered the weapon again. "Go on, Eddie, take it. Even if you don't think you'll ever use it. I'll feel better knowing you've got something to wave around 'sides your pen, which will do you no damn good when things get nasty."

I took the weapon from his hand. It was a Griswold and Gunnison revolver, my researches later discovered; plain and heavy.

"It's fully loaded," Luman said. "But that's all the bullets I got for it, so you're going to have to choose your targets. Hey! Point it away from me. How long is it since you handled a revolver?"

"A long time," I admitted. "It feels strange."

"Well don't be afraid of it. Accidents happen when people pussyfoot around a gun. You're in charge of it, not the other way about. Got it?"

"I got it. Thanks, Luman."

"My pleasure. I'll see what else I can dig up. I've got a nice saber in there somewhere, made in Nashville. They had a factory there in the war, turned plowshares into swords."

"How very Biblical."

"You know what else I got?" He was smiling from ear to ear now. "I got a Confederate snare drum."

"From Nickelberry?"

"No . . . Marietta brought it back, just after the war ended. She found it out there in a ditch somewhere. Along with the drummer. He wasn't going to be beating it no more so she pried it out of his hands and brought it back for me. I'm going to have to learn to beat it again. Nice and loud. Sound the alarm . . ." His smile had gone again; he was staring at the revolver in my hand. "Strange," he said. "After all these years, things you never thought you'd need again."

"Maybe we won't."

"Who are you kidding?" he said. "It's just a matter of time."

# II

## i

I returned to my study thoroughly soaked, but curiously revivified by my conversation with Luman. While I was stripping out of my sodden clothes I looked around the room, and realized that it had deteriorated into chaos: piles of notes everywhere, books and newspapers heaped on every side. It was time to clear the mess away, I thought; time to put things in better order; to gird myself for whatever battles lay ahead. I began right there and then, without even putting on a dry pair of socks. Naked as a babe I set to work, sorting through the stuff I'd accrued over the months I'd been writing. The books were easily collected up and returned to the shelves, the newspapers and magazines I bundled up and set outside the study door for Dwight to collect. The real challenge was my notes, of which there were many hundreds of pages. Some were midnight inspirations, jotted down in darkness when I woke from a dream; some were doodlings I made to break my own silence on a day when the pen refused to move. Some read like the jottings of a dyslexic poet, some like a paranoid's stab at metaphysics; the worst are beyond comprehension.

I've been afraid to throw any of them out, in case there was something here that I was going to need. Even in the foulest of this shit I thought there might be something that illuminated a murky corner of my intentions; offering a glimpse of grandeur where my text was squalid.

Enough of that, I told myself. It all had to go. I need to proceed from here less encumbered than I've been. I need to travel lightly to keep up with events. Things are getting desperate for everyone, and I need to be right there at their shoulders as they make love, at their lips as they whisper their dying words, in their heads as their sanity curdles. So it all goes. My potted history of the warlord Timur-i-leng, for instance, whose bones lie in Samarkand: I'll never make use of it. Out it goes. My notes on the genital configurations of the hyena; all very interesting, but wholly irrelevant. Out they go. My pages of meditations on the nature of my endeavor—pretentious stuff most of it, written while I was high—they have to go too. There's no room for that kind of stuff now; not if we're preparing for war.

It took me about seven hours to finish all this tidying, including a thorough scouring of the drawers of my desk. By the time I had finished it was dark, and I was exhausted. It was a pleasant exhaustion, however; I'd achieved something: I could see the rug again. And my desk was clear, except for my single copy of the book, which I'd set in the upper left corner; a pile of paper, along with my pen and ink, set in the middle, and the revolver Luman had given me, which was set on my right, where I could quickly snatch it up if occasion demanded.

There remained only one thing to do. The redundant notes I'd collected up needed to be destroyed. I didn't want anyone sifting through them at some later date, finding my sentimental ramblings or my spelling mistakes; nor did I want to be tempted back to them myself, at some moment of weakness. I gathered them all up in my arms and took them out onto the lawn. I was still stark naked, but what the hell? Nobody was going to waste their time spying on my nakedness; it's a singularly unedifying sight. So out I went, and dumped the papers in the grass. Then I struck a match, and set fire to them. There was no wind to blow the burning sheets around; they simply blackened and curled where they lay, one after the other. I sat down on the grass, which was still damp from the rain, and toasted the disappearing words with a glass of gin. Every now and again I'd catch a phrase as it was burned away, and once—watching something I rather liked eaten up before my eyes—a wave of regret broke over me. I tried to comfort myself by thinking that if these thoughts had flown through my head once then they'd always be there to be recaptured, but I don't entirely believe that. Suppose the mind that's making this book is steadily winding down—the heat-death of its creator reported on its pages in a hundred subtle ways? Then there's no recovering what I've burned; none of the meditations anyway. The facts, yes; the facts I can find again. But the feelings I set down? They've gone, and they've gone forever.

Oh Lord! A few minutes ago I was in a fine old mood about what I did, and now I'm sickened. What's wrong with me? This bloody book, that's what's wrong. It's wearing me out. I'm tired of listening to the bloody voices in my head. I'm tired of feeling as though I'm responsible to them. My father wouldn't have wasted a day of his life, long though it was, writing about Galilee and the Gearys. And the idea that anyone, let alone his son, could sit down day upon day to report the voices that chatter in his head would have struck him as ludicrous.

My only defense would have been to convince him that my book keeps at bay a creeping madness that I owe entirely to him. Though even as I say that I can well imagine what his response would be.

"*I was never mad.*"

How would I reply? "But Poppa," I'd say. "There were months on end when you wouldn't speak to anybody. You let your beard grow to your navel, and you wouldn't wash. You'd go out into the swamp and eat rotted alligator carcasses. Do you remember doing that?"

"*Your point?*"

"That's the act of a madman."

"*By your definition.*"

"By *anybody's* definition, father."

"*I was not mad. I knew exactly why I was doing what I was doing.*"

"Tell me, then. Help me understand why half the time you were a loving father, and the rest of the time you were covered in lice and excrement—"

"*I made a pair of boots out of excrement. Do you remember those?*"

"Yes, I remember."

"*And one time I brought back a skull I'd found in the swamp—a human skull—and I told my bitch-wife that I'd been away in Virginia and I'd dug up you know who.*"

"You told her you had Jefferson's skull?"

"*Oh yes.*" He gives me a sly smile here, remembering with pleasure the pain he caused. "*And I reminded her how his narrow lips had looked, and put my fingers in his sockets where his watery eyes had been. I said to her: did you kiss his eyes? Because this is where they lay . . .*"

"Why did you do something so cruel?"

"*She did a lot worse to me. Anyway it was good to see her weep and wail once in a while. It reminded me she still had a heart, because sometimes I doubted it. And oh Lord, how she carried on! Screaming at me to give her the skull. It wasn't dignified, she said. Dignified! Ha! As if she ever gave a damn about being dignified! She could behave like the filthiest gutter whore when she was in heat. But she came after me, telling me about dignity!*" He shook his head, laughing now. "*The hypocritical slut.*"

I remembered this now. The walls of L'Enfant literally shaking as husband and wife raged at one another. I hadn't known what was at issue at the time; but in hindsight it's little wonder Cesaria was so distressed.

"*Eventually she snatched the thing from me — or tried to — and somehow in the mêlée it dropped to the ground and smashed. Pieces flew in every direction and she let out such a shriek and went down on her knees to gather these pieces up so fucking tenderly you'd have thought he was still in there somewhere . . .*"

"So did you tell her it wasn't Jefferson's skull?"

"*Not right then. I watched her for a while, sobbing and moaning. I'd never been completely certain of what went on between them until that minute. I mean I'd had my suspicions —*"

"He built L'Enfant for her."

"*Ah, that proved nothing. She could make men do anything, if she put her mind to it. The question wasn't: what did he feel for her? The question was: what did she feel for him? And now I had my answer. Watching her picking up the pieces of what she thought was his bones, I saw how — oh how — she loved him.*" He paused and regarded me with black and turquoise eyes. "*How did we get to this?*"

"You being mad."

"*Oh yes . . .*" He smiled. "*My madness . . . my wonderful madness . . .*" He drew a deep breath; a vast breath. "*I was never mad,*" he said again. "*Because the mad don't know what they're doing or why. And I always knew. Always.*" He exhaled. "*Whereas you . . .*" he growled.

"Me?"

"*Yes, my son. You. Sitting there day after day, night after night, listening to voices which may or may not be real. That's not the behavior of a sane man. Look at you. You're even writing this down. Just take a moment and think about how preposterous that is: setting down something as if it were the truth, though you know you're inventing it.*"

"I don't know that for certain."

"*But I've been dead and gone a hundred and forty years, son. I'm as dusty as Jefferson.*"

I fumbled for an answer to this. The thing is, he was right. It was strange — no, it *is* strange — to be exchanging words with a dead man the way I am now, not knowing how much of what I'm writing is reportage and how much of it invention; not knowing if my father is speaking to me through my genes, through my pen, through my imagination, or whether this dialogue is just evidence of some profound insanity in me. Sometimes I hope it's the latter. For if it's the former — if the man is here in me now — then that prospect he said I feared so much is close; that time when he comes back from his journey into death, leaving the door through which he passed open wide.

"Father?"

Writing the word on the page is a kind of summons, sometimes.

"Where are you?"

He was here moments ago, filling my head with his voice. (That story of the skull he showed to Cesaria; I'd never heard it before. When I see her next I'm going to ask her if it's true. If it is, then I'm not inventing his voice, am I? He's here with me.) Or at least he was.

"Father?"

Now he doesn't answer.

"We didn't finish our conversation about madness."

Still silence. Ah well; another time perhaps.

## ii

I began this passage talking about clearing my desk, and I end up with a visitation from my deceased father. That's how it's been from the beginning: the strange, the grotesque, even the apocalyptic, has constantly intersected with the domestic, the familial, the inconsequential. While I sat sipping tea I dreamed I was on the Silk Road to Samarkand. While I listened to the crickets I saw Garrison Geary playing the horny mortician. While I was plucking the hairs from my ears one evening I saw Rachel looking back at me from the mirror in my bathroom, and I knew she had fallen in love.

It's perhaps not surprising that I choose the Silk Road as an example of the strange and Garrison's cold coupling as an image of the grotesque. But why do I think of Rachel and Galilee when I picture the apocalyptic?

I don't exactly know, to be honest. I have some uneasy suspicions, but I'm afraid to voice them in case doing so turns a possibility into a likelihood.

I can only say this with any certainty: that as the visions continue to come, it's Rachel I feel closest to. So close in fact that sometimes when I get up from a period of writing about her—especially if I've been recording something that happened to her in private (just the two of us, in other words)—I feel as though I *am* her. My body's heavy and hers is light, my skin is Italianate, hers is pale, I move like a man who has only just regained his mobility (I'm lumpen; I stumble), she moves as though she were a silk sail. And yet, I feel I am her.

Many, many pages ago—having somewhat awkwardly described the first liaison between Rachel and Galilee—I remember writing that I was faintly sickened by the pall of incestuous feeling that attended such description. I can honestly say now that all such concerns have disappeared, and for that I must thank the presence of my Rachel. She's made me shameless. Taking this journey with her, listening to her

weep, listening to her rage, listening to her express her longings for
Galilee, I have become braver.

Had I to tell that scene again, I wouldn't be so puritanical. If you
doubt me, wait a while. If they meet again I'll prove the boast. Maddox
will have vanished from the equation: I will be Rachel, lying in the arms
of her beloved.

# III

Rachel opened her eyes, just a slit, and looked at the clock. It was just
a little after six; only an hour since she'd given up on the journal
and retired to bed. Her head was throbbing, and her mouth tasted stale.
She contemplated getting up to take some aspirin, but she didn't have
the will to move.

As her eyes fluttered closed, however, she heard a noise on the floor
below. Her heart jumped. There was somebody in the apartment. She
held her breath, raising her head from the pillow half an inch so as to
hear better. There was another sound now; not a footfall this time, but
a voice, a man's voice. Was it Mitchell? If so, what the hell was he doing
letting himself into her apartment at this hour of the morning; and who
the hell was he talking to? She strained to hear the words. She recognized the cadence of voice, though she could make no sense of what he
was saying. It was indeed Mitchell; the bastard! Walking in as though
he still had the right to come and go.

There was a short pause, then he began to speak again. He was on
the telephone to somebody, she realized, and to judge by the speed of
his speech, he was excited.

She was almost as curious as she was enraged: what had got him
into such a state? She got up, quickly slipped on her underwear and a
sweatshirt, and went to the door.

Once she got there she could hear him more clearly. He was talking to Garrison. Even if she hadn't heard him say his brother's name,
which she did, she would have known from the tone of his voice: that
mingling of respect and familiarity which he reserved for Garrison
alone.

"I'm coming over right now, . . ." Mitchell was saying, "just let me
grab some coffee and—"

She opened the door and went out onto the landing. He was still out of sight, but he obviously heard her coming because he truncated his conversation. "I'll see you in an hour," he said, and put the phone down.

She was at the top of the stairs now, and she could hear him getting up from the table and crossing the room, though she still couldn't see him. "Mitchell?"

Finally he stepped into view, a sunny smile already fixed on his face, though his pallor was gray and his eyes bloodshot.

"I thought I heard you up there. I didn't want to wake you, so—"

"What the hell are you doing here?"

"Just dropped by to say hi," he replied, the smile still in place. "You look like you had a rough night. Are you okay?"

Rachel started down the stairs. "It's six in the morning, Mitchell."

"There's a lot of flu going around, you know. Maybe you should see—"

"Are you listening?"

"Don't be mad, baby," he said, the smile finally making its exit. "You don't have to yell and scream every time we see one another."

"I'm not screaming," Rachel said calmly. "I'm just telling you I don't want you in my apartment."

She was three steps from the bottom of the flight. He stepped back, hands raised in surrender. "I'm going," he said, and turning on his heel walked back toward the table. "I should have known she'd pass it on to you," he said as he went. He was talking about the journal. It was there on the table where Rachel had left it. "Garrison said you were all bitches, and I didn't want to believe it. Not my Rachel. Not my sweet, innocent Rachel." He reached for the journal.

"Don't touch that," she said.

"I'll do what the fuck I like," Mitchell said. He picked up the journal, and turned back to look at her. "I gave you a chance—" he said, waving his prize in front of him as he spoke. "I warned you at the gala: don't mess with things you don't understand because you'll end up having nobody to protect you. Didn't I say that?"

"It's not yours, Mitch," Rachel said, doing her best to preserve her equilibrium. "Put it down and leave."

"Or what?" Mitchell said. "Huh? What can you do? You're on your own." His manner softened abruptly, as though he was genuinely distressed at her vulnerability. "Why didn't you just come to me and tell me she'd given you this?"

"She didn't give it to me. I found it."

"You *found* it?" The softness was gone as quickly as it had appeared. "You went digging around in Garrison's place?"

"Yes."

He shook his head in disbelief. "You are a piece of work," he said. "Do you have any idea what you're playing around with?"

"I'm beginning to."

"And you thought your lover-boy Galilee was going to come and save you if you got in too deep?"

"No," she said, slowly walking toward him. "I know that's not what happens. I have to look after myself. I'm not afraid of you. I know how your mind works."

"Not any longer you don't," he said. The look in his bloodshot eyes gave credence to the claim; there was something she hadn't see there before; something unstable. "You know what you should do, baby? You should go back to Dansky and be thankful you got out alive. I really mean that, baby. Go and don't look back . . ."

At the gala his threatening talk had seemed faintly ludicrous; now it carried weight. He frightened her. She was weak with sadness and confusion and lack of sleep; if he chose to harm her now, she wouldn't be able to put up much of a defense.

"You know you may be right," she said, doing her best to conceal her unease. "I should go home."

He was clearly pleased that he'd made some impression on her. "Now you're being smart," he said.

"I hadn't realized . . ."

"No, how could you?"

". . . things are more serious . . ."

"Than you thought. I did try and warn you."

"Yes. You did. And I wasn't ready to listen."

"But now you see . . ."

She nodded; he seemed to have bought her performance. "Yes, I see. I was wrong and you were right."

Oh, he liked that; that made him smile from ear to ear. "You know, you are so sweet when you want to be," he said. Without warning, he approached her, his free hand reaching out and catching hold of her chin. She smelled sour sweat and stale cologne. "If I had the time . . ." he said, that volatile gleam clearer still now he was a foot from her, "I'd take you upstairs and remind you what you're missing."

She wanted to tell him to go fuck himself, but there was nothing to be gained from escalating things again when she'd just worked to turn down the heat. Instead she kept her silence, and let him plant a dry kiss on her lips, in that proprietorial manner that had once made her feel like a princess. He hadn't finished with her, however. His hand dropped from her chin and lightly touched her breast. "Say something," he murmured.

"What do you want me to say?"

"You know," he said.

"You want me to ask you to come upstairs?"

He gave her a crooked-eye grin. "It might be nice," he said.

She swore to herself she'd make him suffer for this one day; she'd have her foot on his neck. But until then: "Well, will you?"

"Will I what?" he said.

"Take me upstairs—"

"And?"

"—fuck me."

"Oh, baby, I thought you'd never ask." His hand made one final descent, from her breast to her groin. He slipped his fingers beneath the waistband of her panties. "You're not wet, baby," he said. He pushed in a little. "Feels like a fucking grave." He pulled his hand out, as though he'd been stung. "Sorry, baby. Gotta go."

He turned away from her and started in the direction of the door. It was all she could do not to go after him, telling him what a worthless piece of shit he was. But she resisted the temptation. He was leaving, and that was all that mattered right now.

"One thing—" he said when he reached the door.

"Yes?"

"Do you want me to put this place back on the market for you? You're not going to stay here are you?"

"You can do what the hell you want with it."

"Whatever I get for it, I'll put in your account." He glanced over his shoulder, though not far enough to lay eyes on her. "Of course, if you don't trust me . . ."

"Sell it, Mitch. I'll be out of here in two weeks."

"Where will you go?"

"I don't know yet. I've got plenty of friends. Maybe back to Boston. I'll keep Cecil informed."

"Yeah. Do that, will you?"

That was his departure line: a remote echo of a man who'd once cared for her, and whom she'd been ready to call her husband to the end of her days.

What had happened to him? What was happening to them all? It was as though everybody was shedding their skin, and revealing somebody new—or perhaps somebody they'd always been—to the world. The question that lay before Rachel was simple: who was she? She was no longer Mitchell's wife, that much was certain. But then nor was she Galilee's lover. Was she doomed to be one of the melancholy women she saw around town noted only for the brevity of their moment—a failed marriage to a public man, or a taste of celebrity, then eclipse? Growing old as gracefully as they knew how: preserving their place at the table with minor good works though half the time people couldn't quite remember who they were.

She'd go back to Dansky before she'd live a life like that. She'd propose to Neil Wilkens and if he'd take her, settle down to a life of total anonymity. Anything, rather than be pointed out as the woman who'd loved and lost Mitchell Geary.

But she was getting ahead of herself. Her first concern was to preserve her life and sanity in the midst of a situation that was far from safe. She could still see the subtle gleam of lunacy in Mitchell's eyes, and the curl of his lips as he took his fingers out of her.

*Feels like a fucking grave . . .*

She shuddered, thinking of what he'd said. Not just of its easy cruelty—though that was horrible enough—but the fact that it seemed to taint her with death. Was that what Mitch really believed? Did he look at her and see a woman who was already halfway to joining Margie on the Golden Floor? It would be nice and convenient for him if she died, wouldn't it? He could play the grieving soulmate for a little while, and then move on to find himself a more accommodating wife—one who'd pop out little Gearys on a regular basis and who wouldn't be too critical of her husband's lack of passion.

This was probably all paranoia, she told herself, but that didn't make her any less fretful. And to add to her sum of anxieties, there was the fact that Mitchell now had the journal. It was plainly important to him; and to Margie too apparently, or else why had she gone to so much trouble to hide it? What was the significance of its contents, that Mitchell had been so happy to have it in his hands?

Well, there was no use sitting and stewing over it all; what was done was done. The best thing to do, she decided, was to get the hell out of the apartment and walk.

She quickly got dressed, and headed down to the street. The day was fine and bright, and she knew as soon as she started walking that she'd made a smart decision. Her spirits lifted, especially once she got into the crowds on Fifth Avenue. There was a pleasant sense of anonymity there; she was just one of thousands striding the sidewalks, enjoying the day.

The subject of Mitch and his vile talk didn't come back into her head, but thoughts of Galilee did. The mysteries that attended him didn't trouble her as they had previously. In the open air, with the bustle of people all around her, they seemed simply intriguing: inexplicable, even magical, elements in her personal landscape. What *was* he, this man who spoke of shark gods as though they were his bosom buddies? Who had lived several lifetimes, wandering the oceans of the world? Who was so lonely, and yet took no comfort in the presence of other living beings?

She wished she'd quizzed him more closely when they'd been together, particularly about his family. Assuming that he'd been telling the truth when he'd said he had no grandparents, what did that imply about his mother and father? That they were somehow *original souls*, the Adam and Eve of their species? If so, then what did that make Galilee? Cain or Abel? The first murderer? The first victim?

Biblical parallels wouldn't have seemed so pertinent but for the fact of the man's name. He was called Galilee, after all; somebody in his family knew their Gospels.

Well, whatever he was, whatever the nature of his mystery, she didn't expect to be solving it any time soon. The journal's contents had only served to confirm the suspicion that his path and hers went in very different directions. She would not be sitting down to talk about his name or his childhood anytime soon. He was gone from her life, perhaps forever; and she had no way back to him. No means of tracing him except through the coils of Geary family history, where she was now effectively forbidden to go. She was an exile, like him. He on the water, she on Fifth Avenue; he alone, she surrounded by people: but still, in the end, outcasts.

Walking gave her a hunger, so she dropped into Alfredo's—a little Italian place she'd gone more than once with Mitchell—for lunch. She arrived thinking she'd have a salad, but when she scanned the menu her appetite sharpened, and she ended up with a plate of spaghetti followed by profiteroles. What now? she wondered as she ate. She couldn't walk the streets of New York forever; sooner or later she was going to have to decide where her best hope of safety lay.

Her espresso was not brought by her waiter but by the owner of the establishment, Alfredo himself: a round, pink, cherubic man who had never lost his thick Italian accent. Indeed he probably nurtured it, as part of his charm.

"Mrs. Geary . . ." he said, with great gravity, ". . . we are all so very, very sad when we hear about your sister-in-law. She came in once, with the older Mrs. Geary—Loretta—and we all just fell in love with her."

Loretta and Margie, sharing a bottle of wine and reminiscences? It was hard to picture.

"Does Loretta come in here often?"

"Now and again," Alfredo said.

"And what do you make of *her?* Does everybody love Loretta too?"

The plainness of the question defeated Alfredo's considerable powers of diplomacy. He opened his mouth, but no answer came.

"No instant love for Loretta, huh?"

"She is very powerful lady," Alfredo finally replied. "Back home in Italy we have such women. Very strong, in their hearts. They are the real power in the family. All the men, they make the noise, they make the violence sometimes, but the women just go on in their way, you know, being strong."

That certainly described Loretta: hard to love, but impossible to ignore. Perhaps it was time Rachel paid her a visit; followed up on the conversation they'd had just after Margie's death, when Loretta had so very clearly laid out her vision of the way things would be, and had asked Rachel to side with her. Was it too late to say yes? She didn't particularly like the prospect of asking for Loretta's help; but the woman had known whereof she spoke that night. *We need each other,* she'd said; *for self-protection. Whatever your dense husband thinks, he's not going to be running the Geary empire.*

*Why not?* Rachel had asked her.

And the answer? Oh, Rachel remembered it well, and with the passage of time it began to look like an astonishing prophecy.

"*. . . he's inheriting a lot more than he'll be able to deal with,*" Loretta had said. "*He'll crack. He's already cracking . . .*"

She thanked Alfredo for a delightful lunch, and went out into the busy street. The espresso had given her a fair buzz, but it wasn't just coffee that quickened her step as she headed north; it was the sudden realization that she had, after all, a place of refuge, if it wasn't too late to request it.

# IV

Given how little warmth there is in my relationship with Zabrina (I think my last reported exchange with her was in the kitchen, while she juggled the devouring of pies) you can imagine how surprised I was when she appeared in my room yesterday evening. She had tears pouring down her face, and all the usual ruddiness had gone out of her skin.

"You have to come with me!" she said.

I asked her why, but she insisted that she had no time for explanations. I was simply to come; right now.

"At least tell me where we're going," I said.

"It's Mama," she said, her sobs coming on with new vigor. "Something's happened to Mama! I think maybe she's dying."

This was enough to make me get up out of my chair and follow Zabrina, though as we went I was quite certain she'd made a mistake. Nothing was ever going to happen to Cesaria: she was an eternal force. A creature born out of the primal fire of the world does not pass away quietly in her bed.

And yet the closer we got to Cesaria's chambers the more I began to suspect there might be real reason for Zabrina's panic. There had always been a subtle agitation in the passageways close to Cesaria's rooms, as though her presence excited motion at a molecular level. To be there was to feel, in some unaccountable way, more *alive*. The light seemed clearer, the colors brighter; when you inhaled you seemed to feel the shape of your lungs as they expanded. But not today; today the passageways were like mausoleums. I began to feel a prickling dread creep over me. What if she was dead? Cesaria Yaos, the mother of mothers, dead? What would that mean for us who were left behind? The Gearys were about to mount an assault against us, I had no doubt of that. Holt's journal, containing a detailed description of how to get to this very house, was in the hands of Garrison Geary himself. And Mama Cesaria was dead? Oh God.

Zabrina had halted a few yards from the door of Cesaria's chambers.

"I can't go in again . . ." she said, a new flood of tears coming.

"Where is she?"

"In her bedroom."

"I've never been in her bedroom."

"Just . . . go straight in, make the second right, and it's at the end of the passageway."

I was more than a little nervous now. "Come with me," I said to Zabrina.

"I can't," she said. I don't think I've ever seen anyone look so scared.

I left her to her trembling, and entered, my dread growing with every step I took. No doubt Cesaria had intended that anyone coming into these chambers should feel they were entering the temple of her body;

certainly that was how I felt. The walls and ceiling were painted a purplish red, the bare boards underfoot were darkly stained. There was no furniture in the passageways; the rooms that lay to right and left were too gloomy for me to see into very clearly, but they also appeared to be bare.

I made the second right as Zabrina had instructed. For the first time since my healing at Cesaria's hands I felt a stab of the old pain in my legs, and had a paranoid vision of my muscles atrophying in this dead air.

"Stop it," I murmured to myself.

I might have uttered the words in a vacuum. Though I could feel my palate shape the syllables, and my breath expel them, the passageway refused to hear them uttered. They were snatched away and smothered.

I didn't say anything more; I didn't dare. I simply walked on to the door of Cesaria's bedroom, and stepped inside.

It was as gloomy as all the other rooms, the heavy drapes closed against the sky, against the world. I waited for a few moments to let my eyes accommodate themselves to the murk, and by degrees they did just that.

There was a massive bed in the room. That was all, a massive bed, upon which my father's wife lay like a body on a catafalque. None of her splendor was removed by her supine position. Even in death—if indeed she was dead—the physical fact of her demanded reverence. There was an uncanny precision about her; she seemed perfect, even in this state: like a great funereal work sculpted by her own genius.

I approached the bed, glad now that Zabrina hadn't come with me. I didn't want to share this moment with anybody. Though I was afraid, it was a glorious fear, a fear that surely you could only feel in the presence of a dead or dying goddess: a fear mingled with great swelling gratitude that I was allowed this sight.

Her face! Oh her face. The great black mane of her hair swept back from her wide brow, her dark skin gleaming, her mouth open, her lids open a little way too, but showing only the whites of her eyes.

Finally, I found the courage to speak. I said her name.

This time, the air consented to bear my word; it went from me lightly. But there was no response from Cesaria Yaos. Not that I expected there to be. I was increasingly certain that Zabrina was right. Mama was dead.

What now, I thought. Did I dare approach the bed and actually touch the body? Look for vital signs as if the woman before me were just a common cadaver? I couldn't face that possibility. Better to go to the window, I thought, and open the drape a little way, so that I could see the body more clearly. That way I could make an assessment of her condition from a respectful distance.

Moving with due reverence I crossed the room to the window, thinking as I went what a life of sad confinement Cesaria had lived since my father's passing. What had she done to fill the years, I wondered? Had the memories been enough to give her a taste of happiness? Or had she stewed in her sorrow up here, cursing her longevity, and the children who'd failed to give her joy?

I caught hold of one of the drapes, and started to pull it open. But as I did so, I felt something brush the back of my neck — just a feather touch, but it was enough to make me freeze. I glanced back over my shoulder, my hand still gripping the fabric. Had some subtle change come over Cesaria's face? Were her eyes open a fraction wider? Her head was turned a little in my direction? I stared at her for fully a minute, studying her face for some evidence of life. But I was imagining it: there was nothing.

Mastering my courage, I once again began to draw back the drape, and had opened it perhaps an inch when whatever had brushed my neck a little while before came against my face, not lightly this time, but like a blow. I heard a cracking sound in my head, and the next moment blood began to run from my nose. Needless to say, I let go of the drape instantly. If I hadn't had to pass the bed to get to the door I might have run for it there and then, but I decided passivity was the wisest response. Whatever was here in the room with me, I didn't doubt it could do me some serious damage if it set its mind to the task. I wanted to prove that I was no threat to it; or, perhaps more pertinently, to the sanctity of the body on the bed.

I didn't even tend to my bleeding nose while I waited. I just let it run, and after a while the flow slowed and stopped. As for my attacker, wherever he was, he seemed satisfied of my innocence, because he made no further assault upon me.

And then, the strangest thing. Without moving her lips, Cesaria spoke.

*Maddox*, she said, *what are you doing here?*

The question wasn't presented as a challenge. There was a gentle musicality in her voice. She almost sounded dreamy, in fact; as though she were speaking in her sleep.

"I thought — that is, Zabrina thought — something had happened to you," I said.

*It has*, Cesaria replied.

"Are you sick? We thought perhaps you were dying?"

*I'm not dying. I'm just traveling.*

"Traveling? Where?"

*There's somebody I need to see, before he passes out of this life.*

"Cadmus Geary," I said.

She murmured her assent. *Of course you've been telling his story,* she said.

"Some of it."

*He lived a troubled life,* Cesaria said, *and he's going to die a troubled death. I'm going to make certain of that.* She spoke without vehemence, but the observation made me glad I was nowhere near the dying man. If Cesaria wanted to give him grief, then grief she would give, and let anyone in his vicinity beware.

*You're hurt,* she said.

"No, just—"

*You're bleeding. Was that Zelim's doing?*

"I don't know who it was. I was trying to open the drape, to get a better look at you."

*—and you were struck.*

"Yes."

*It was Zelim,* Cesaria said. *He knows I don't like the light. But he was being overzealous. Zelim? Where are you?*

There was a sound off in the far corner of the room like buzzing of bees, and it seemed to my somewhat befuddled eyes that the murky air knotted itself up, and something that resembled a human form appeared in front of me. It was only rudimentary; a slim, androgynous creature with large dark eyes.

*Make your peace,* Cesaria said. I assumed the instruction was for me, and I proceeded to apologize but she broke in: *Not you, Maddox. Zelim.*

The servant bowed his head. "I'm sorry," he said. "The error was mine. I should have spoken to you before I struck you."

*Now both of you can leave me,* Cesaria said. *Zelim, take Maddox into Mr. Jefferson's study and make him a little more presentable. He looks like a schoolboy who's just been in a brawl.*

"Come with me," said Zelim, who by now had reached such a level of corporeality that his nakedness was somewhat discomforting to me, despite the naïve form of his genitals.

I followed him to the door, and was just about to step out when I heard Cesaria call my name again. I looked back. Nothing had changed. She lay as she had, completely inert. But from the direction of her body there came—how can I describe this without stooping to sentimentality—there came a wave of love (there, I've stooped) which broke invisibly but touched me more profoundly than any visible force could have done. Tears of pleasure ran from my eyes.

"Thank you, Mama," I murmured.

*You're very welcome child*, she said, *now go and be tended to. Where's Zabrina by the way?*

"She's outside."

*Tell her not to be a ninny. If I were truly dead I'd have every creature in the county weeping and wailing.*

I smiled at this. "I think you would," I said.

*And tell her to be patient. I'll be home soon.*

# V

$M$r. Jefferson's study, as Cesaria had referred to it, was one of the small rooms I had passed by on my way to the bedroom. I was ushered into it by Zelim, whose newfound politeness did nothing to sooth my unease at his presence. His voice, like his appearance, was wholly nondescript. It was as though he were holding on to the last vestiges of his humanity (I say *holding on*, but perhaps it was the other way about; perhaps I was simply witness to the final and happy sloughing off of the man he'd once been). Whichever it was, the sight of him, and the sound of a voice that barely sounded human, distressed me. I didn't want to spend any time in his company. I told him there was nothing he need do for me; I'd quite happily mend myself once I got back downstairs. But he ignored my protestations. His mistress had told him to make good the damage he'd done, and he plainly intended to do so, whether I considered myself an injured party or not.

"Can I get you a glass of brandy?" he said. "I understand you're not a great imbiber of brandy—"

"How do you know that?"

"I listen," he said. So the rumors were true, I thought. The house was indeed a listening machine, delivering news from its various chambers up to Cesaria's suite. "But this is a bottle we seldom touch. It's potent. And it will take away the sting."

"Then thank you," I said. "I will have a little."

He inclined his head to me, as though I'd done him great service by accepting the offer, and retired to the next room, allowing me the freedom to get up and wander around the study. There was plenty to see. Unlike the rest of the rooms, which were empty, it was filled with furniture. Two chairs and a small table, a writing desk set in front of the window, with its own comfortable leather chair tucked in beneath it, a bookcase, weighed down with sober tomes. On the walls were a variety of decorations. On one hung a crude map, painted on the dried pelt of some unlucky animal: the territory it charted unfamiliar to me. On another a modestly framed drawing, in a very academic style, of Cesaria reclining on a chaise longue. She was dressed prettily, in a high-waisted gown much decorated with small bows. An unfamiliar Cesaria; at least to me. Was this the way she'd looked when she'd been the glory of Paris society? I assumed so. The rest of the pictures were small, undistinguished landscapes, and I passed over them quickly, saving the chief focus of my attention for the strange object which sat on Jefferson's desk. It looked like a large, carpentered spider.

"It's a copying machine," Zelim explained when he came back in. "Jefferson invented it." He pulled out the chair. "Sit please." I sat down. "By all means try it," he said. There was paper on the desk, and the pen already fitted into the device. Now that I knew its purpose it wasn't hard to fathom how it worked. I raised and dipped my pen—which, courtesy of a system of struts, automatically raised and dipped the second pen, and proceeded to scratch out my name on a second sheet. Glancing over to my right I found my signature replicated almost perfectly.

"Clever," I remarked. "Did he ever use it?"

"There's one at Monticello he used all the time," Zelim explained. "This device he used only once or twice."

"But he definitely used it?" I said. "I mean . . . Jefferson had his fingers around this very pen?"

"Indeed he did. I saw him with my own eyes. He wrote a letter to John Adams, as I remember."

I couldn't prevent a little shudder of delight, which you might think strange given the divine company I've kept. After all, Jefferson was only human. But that was perhaps the reason I felt the *frisson*. He was mortal stuff, reaching for a vision that was grander than most of us dare contemplate.

Zelim handed me my glass of brandy. "Again, I apologize for my violence. May I wash the blood off your face?"

"No need," I said.

"It's no trouble."

"I'm fine," I told him. "If you want to make amends—"

"Yes?"

"Talk to me."

"About what?"

"About what it's been like for you, over the centuries."

"Ah . . ."

"You're Zelim the fisherman, aren't you?"

The pale face before me, despite its lack of specificities, seemed to grow troubled. "I don't ever think of that any longer," he said. "It doesn't seem to be my life."

"More like a story?" I ventured.

"More like a dream. A very distant dream. Why do you ask?"

"I want to be able to describe everything in my book. *Only everything*, that was my promise to myself. And you're a unique individual. I'd like to be sure I tell it all truthfully."

"There's nothing much to tell," Zelim said. "I was a fisherman, and I was called into service. That's an old story."

"But look what you became."

"Oh this . . ." he said, glancing down at his body. "Does my nakedness trouble you?"

"No."

"The longer I live with her the more I tend to androgyny, and the less important clothing comes to seem. I can't remember how I looked any longer, when I was a man."

"I've got a picture of you in my head," I said. "On the shore with Cesaria and Nicodemus and the baby. Dark hair, dark eyes."

"My teeth were good, I do know that," he said. "The widow Passak used to love to watch me tear at my bread."

"So you remember her?"

"Better than most things," Zelim replied. "Better than my philosophies, certainly." He gazed toward the window, and in the wash of light I saw that he was virtually translucent, his eyes iridescent. I wondered to myself if he had bones in his body, and supposed that he must, given the blow he'd delivered. Yet he seemed so very delicate now; like a frail invertebrate visitor from some deep-sea trench.

"I forgot her for a while . . ." he said, his voice gossamer.

"You mean the widow Passak?"

"Yes," he murmured. "I moved on through my life, and the love I felt for her . . ." The sentence trailed away; his face fluttered. I didn't prompt him—though I badly wanted to hear what more he had to say on the subject. He was in a deeply emotional state, for all the colorlessness of his voice. I didn't want to disturb his equilibrium. So I waited. At last, he picked up the thread of his ruminations: ". . . the love I felt seemed to pass away from me. I thought it had gone forever. But I was wrong . . . the feelings I had toward her come back to me now, as though I was feeling them for the first time. The way she looked at me, when the wind came off the desert. The sweet mischief in her eyes."

"Things come around," I said. "Didn't you teach that to your students?"

"I did. I used the stars as a metaphor, I believe."

"The Wheel of the Stars," I prompted.

Zelim made the faintest of smiles, remembering this. "The Wheel of the Stars," he murmured. "It was a pretty idea."

"More than an idea," I said. "It's the truth."

"I wouldn't make that claim for it," Zelim said.

"But the proof of it's right here. You said yourself that your feelings for Passak have come back."

"I think it may be for the last time," Zelim replied. "I've run my course, and I won't be rising again after this."

"What do you mean?"

"When L'Enfant falls—as it will, as it must—and everybody goes out into the world, I'm going to ask Cesaria to put an end to me. I've lived as a man, and I've lived as a spirit, and now I want an end to it all."

"No more resurrections?"

"Not for me. I think it's what comes naturally, after androgyny. Out of sexlessness into selflessness. I'm looking forward to it."

"Looking forward to oblivion?"

"It's not the end of the world," he said with a little laugh. "It's just one man's light going out. And if it's no great loss to me than why should anybody else be upset?"

"I'm not upset, I'm just a little confused," I said.

"By what?"

I thought about the question for a moment before I replied. "I suppose living here I've got used to the idea of things going on."

"Or rising again, like your father."

"I beg your pardon?"

Zelim's features fluttered again, as they had when he'd first begun to talk. His Socratic calm disappeared; he was suddenly anxious. "I'm sorry," he said. "I shouldn't have—"

"Don't apologize," I told him. "Just explain."

"I can't. I'm sorry. It was inappropriate."

"*Zelim*. Explain."

He glanced back toward Cesaria's chambers. Was he fearful that she'd come to punish him for his indiscretion? If so, his glance reassured him that he was not being overheard. When he looked back at me, his agitation had almost gone. Apparently Cesaria was off on her way to meet with Cadmus Geary.

"I'm not sure I could explain anything where your father's concerned," he said. "Explanations and gods are mutually exclusive, aren't they? All I can do is tell you what I *feel*."

"And what's that?"

He took a deep breath. His body seemed to grow a little more substantial with the inhalation. "Cesaria's life is empty here. Completely empty. I know because I've shared it with her, day after day after day for the last God knows how many years. It's an empty life. She simply sits at the window, or feeds the porcupines. The only time she steps outside is when one of the animals dies and we have to go out to bury it."

"I have something of that life myself," I said. "I know how wretched it is."

"At least you had your books. She doesn't like to read any longer. And she can't abide television or even recorded music. Remember this is a woman who has been the toast of every great city in the world at some point in her life. I saw her in her glory days, and they were beyond anything you could imagine. She was the very essence of sophistication; the most courted, the most adored, the most emulated woman in the world. When she left a room, they used to say, it was like a kind of death . . ."

"I don't see what this has got to do with Nicodemus."

"Don't you think it's strange that she stays?" Zelim replied. "Why hasn't she pulled this house down? She could do that. She could raise a storm and trash it in a heartbeat. You know she raises storms."

"I've never seen her do it, but—"

"Yes you have. It was one of her storms that came in the night your father mated Dumuzzi."

"That I didn't know."

"She was angry because Nicodemus was showing more interest in his horses than he was in her, so she conjured a storm that laid waste to half the county. I think she was hoping the animals would be struck dead. Anyway, my point is this: if she wanted to bring this house down she could. But she won't. She just stays. She watches. She *waits*."

"Maybe she's preserving the house for Jefferson's sake," I suggested. "It's his masterpiece."

Zelim shook his head. "She's waiting for your father. That's what I believe. She thinks he's coming back."

"Well he'd better be quick about it," I said. "Because if the Gearys get here there'll be no more miracles—"

"I realize that. And I think so does she. After all these years of idling, suddenly things are urgent. This business with Cadmus Geary, for instance. She would never have stooped to meddle with one of the Geary family before this."

"What's she going to do to him?"

Zelim shrugged. "I don't know." His gaze left me; he looked off toward the window again. "But she can be very unforgiving."

If he had more to say on the subject of her lack of compassion, he didn't get a chance to say it. There was light rapping on the study door and Zabrina appeared. She'd sought out, and found, some comfort for her anxieties about Cesaria. She carried not one but two slices of pie in between the fingers of her right hand, and like a cardsharp manipulating aces at a poker table, delivered first one then the other to her mouth.

"All's well," I told her.

"So I gathered," she said.

"I'm sorry. I should have come to tell you earlier."

"I'm used to being ignored," she replied, and made her departure, pausing only to maneuver the last remaining pieces of pie crust into her mouth.

# VI

## i

As I headed back downstairs I found myself in a mingled state of exhaustion and agitation. What I needed was a little entertainment. A conversation with Marietta would have been the perfect thing, but she was off making wedding plans with her beloved Alice, so I decided to smoke a little hashish and let my mind wander over the contents of my conversation with Zelim—the talk of his love for the widow Passak, his hopes for oblivion, his reflections on the loneliness of Cesaria's life, and what her patience really meant—and wondered, in that nonchalant, noncommittal way you wonder when you're smoking good hashish, if I shouldn't have spent less time with the Gearys in my book, and more time here at home. Had I trivialized what might have been a mightier work by following the story of Rachel Pallenberg so closely; been seduced by that most populist of idioms, the rags-to-riches story, when the real meat of what I should have told lay in the troubled body of the Barbarossa clan?

Back in my study I picked up the manuscript and flicked through it, deliberately letting my eye go where it would, to see how the thing sounded when sampled arbitrarily. There were plenty of stylistic infelicities which I promised myself I'd fix later; but the matter seemed to walk the line I'd intended it walk, between this world and that other, out there beyond the perimeters of L'Enfant. Perhaps I could have been less gossipy in my accounts of the daily business of this house, but there's honesty in that gossip. Whatever the mythic roots of this family may be, we've dwindled into pettiness and domesticity. We're not the first gods to have done so, of course. The occupants of Olympus bickered and bed-hopped; we're no better nor worse. But they were inventions, we're not. (I suspect, by the way, that in the creation of divinities we see the most revealing work of the human imagination. And of course in the life of that imagination, the most compelling evidence of the divine in man. Each is the other's most illuminating labor.)

Where does that leave me? I, who sit in the middle of a house of divinities talking about invented gods. It leaves me in confusion, as always; set against myself, as though my heart were divided, and each half beat to a different drummer.

The hashish put an appetite on me, and after a couple of hours of skipping through my text I went to the kitchen and made myself a sandwich of rare roast beef on black bread, which I ate sitting on the back door step, feeding the crumbs to the peacocks.

Then I slept for a while, thinking I would get up in the middle of the evening and continue to tinker with the text. Those few blissful hours of sleep were, I suspect, the last easy slumbers I will enjoy; for when I woke (or rather, was woken) it was not only with visions of the Geary house in New York filling my head, and my right hand twitching as if it were warming up for the challenge of setting down all I was about to see, but also with the uncanny sense that any last vestige of calm had gone from the places I was witnessing.

The final sequence of cataclysms was about to begin. I drew breath and ink; waited, watched, and then began to write.

## ii

When Rachel got to the mansion to see Cadmus she was told by one of the staff, a pleasant woman called Jocelyn, that she couldn't see Loretta tonight. The old man had been very sick since noon, and

Loretta had sent the nurse away, saying she wanted to look after Cadmus herself, which she was doing. Her instructions were that they were not to be disturbed.

Rachel was insistent: this wasn't business that could be put off until tomorrow. If Jocelyn wouldn't go up and get Loretta, Rachel said, then she'd be obliged to do so herself. Reluctantly, Jocelyn went up; and after ten minutes or so Loretta came downstairs. It was the first time Rachel had ever seen her look less than perfect. She looked like a painting that had been slightly smeared; her hair, which was usually immaculate, a little out of place, one of her drawn brows a little smudged.

She instructed Jocelyn to make some tea, and took Rachel into the dining room.

"This is a bad time, Rachel," she said.

"Yes, I know."

"Cadmus is very weak, and I may need to go up to him, so please, say whatever you have to say."

"We had a conversation in this room, just after Margie's death."

"I remember it, of course."

"Well, you were right. Mitch was at my apartment a little while ago, and I don't think he's entirely sane."

"What did he do?"

"You want the short version and I'm not sure there is one," Rachel explained. "Margie had a book—I don't know the full story, but it was a kind of journal—and it came into my hands. It doesn't matter how. The point is, it did; and contains information about the Barbarossas."

Loretta showed no sign of response to any of this, until she spoke. When she did, her voice betrayed her. It trembled.

"You have Holt's journal?" she said.

"No. Mitchell does."

"Oh Jesus," she said quietly. "Why didn't you come to me with it?"

"I didn't know it was so important."

"Why do you think I've been sitting upstairs with Cadmus, listening to him ramble for hours on end?"

"*You* wanted the journal?"

"Of course. I knew he had it because he'd told me, years ago. Never let me see it—"

"Why not?"

"I guess he didn't want me to know anything more about Galilee than I already knew."

"It's not very flattering. What Holt says about him."

"So you've read it?"

"Not all of it. But a lot. And the way Holt describes him . . . oh Lord, how's it even possible?"

"How's *what* possible?"

"How could Galilee have been alive in 1865?"

"You're asking the wrong person," Loretta said. "Because I'm just as much in the dark as you about how and why. And I gave up asking a long time ago."

"If you gave up asking, why do you want the journal so badly?"

"Don't come here looking for my help and then start needling me, girl," Loretta replied. She looked away from Rachel for a moment, expelling a long, soft sigh. "Would you fetch me a cigarette?" she said finally. "They're on the sideboard over there."

Rachel got up and brought the silver cigarette case, along with the lighter, back to the table. While Loretta was lighting up Jocelyn came in with the tea. "Just set it down," Loretta said. "We'll serve ourselves. Oh, and Jocelyn? Would you go upstairs and check on Mr. Geary?"

"I just did," Jocelyn said. "He's sleeping."

"Keep looking in on him will you?"

"Of course."

"She's been a godsend," Loretta observed when Jocelyn had gone. "Never a complaint. What were we talking about?"

"Galilee."

"Forget about Galilee."

"You once told me that he was at the heart of everything."

"Did I now?" Loretta said. She drew deeply on her cigarette. "Well I was probably feeling sorry for myself." She exhaled the blue-gray smoke. Then she said: "You're not the only one who's been in love with him, you know. If you really want to understand what's happening to us you have to stop thinking from a selfish point of view. Everybody's had their disappointments, Rachel. Everybody's had their lost loves and their broken hearts. Even the old man."

"Louise Brooks."

"Yes. The exquisite Louise. That was in Kitty's time, of course. I didn't have to endure his mooning over the woman. Though she *was* lovely. I will say that. She was lovely." She poured herself a cup of tea as she spoke. "Do you want some tea?"

"No. Thank you."

"He's going to die in the next twenty-four hours," Loretta went on, matter-of-factly. "And when he's gone, I intend to take charge of this family and its assets. That's what's in his will."

"You've seen the will?"

"No. But he's promised me. If the will says what he swears it says then I'll be in a position to make some kind of deal with Garrison and Mitchell."

"And if it doesn't?"

"If it doesn't?" Loretta sipped her tea before replying. "Then maybe we'll need Galilee after all," she said quietly. "Both of us."

# VII

In his bedroom on the floor above, Cadmus woke. He was cold, and there was an emptiness at the pit of his stomach which was not hunger. He turned his face toward the dimmed lamp on the bedside table, hoping its light would drive from his head the shadowy forms that had accompanied him from sleep. He didn't want them with him in the real world. They'd have him soon enough.

The door opened. He raised his head from the pillow.

"Loretta?"

"No, sir. It's Jocelyn."

"Where's Loretta? She said she was going to stay with me."

"She's just downstairs, sir. Mitchell's wife came by to see her. Do you want something to eat, sir? Maybe some soup?"

"Send Rachel up."

"Sir?"

"You heard me. Send Rachel up. And have her bring me a snifter of brandy. Go on, woman."

Jocelyn went on her way, and Cadmus let his head sink back into the pillow. Lord, he was so, so cold! But the thought that Rachel was downstairs, and that he'd be laying eyes on her in a few moments, made him a little happier with his lot. She was a sweet girl; he'd always liked her. No doubt some of her innocence had been sullied by Mitchell; she'd lost some of her faith in the goodness of things. But she was a strong creature; she'd survive. He reached out, opened the drawer of the bedside cabinet, and reached around for a roll of peppermints. He could no longer chew gum—his jaws didn't have the power—and his mouth was so filled with cankers that brushing his teeth was an ordeal, but he wanted to be sure his breath was reasonably sweet when Rachel came to sit with him. With palsied fingers he fumbled a peppermint on to his dry tongue, and began, as best he could, to suck.

Somebody was shouting in the street outside, and he longed to be there; out from this cold bed, where he could see the sky. Just once more; was that too much to ask?

In finer times he'd liked to walk. He didn't care if it was fair weather or foul; he'd just get out of his limo wherever and whenever the urge struck him and walk. Arctic winter mornings, he remembered, and blistering August afternoons; days in spring when he'd felt like a happy truant, meandering his way home; evenings in midsummer, with half a dozen martinis in him, high as a king, singing as he went.

Never again. Never the street, never the sky, never a song. Only silence soon; and judgment. Much as he'd tried to ready himself, he was prepared for neither.

The window rattled. There was quite a wind getting up. The rattling came again, and this time the heavy drapes shook. No wonder he was cold! That silly bitch of a nurse had left one of the windows open. Another gust, and the drapes filled like sails. This time he felt the wind across the room; it was strong enough to shake the lampshade.

He felt a fluttering in his empty belly, and pushed himself up against the headboard to get a better look at the billowing drapes. What the hell was going on?

He needed his spectacles; but as he reached to pluck them up from amid the bottles of pills he heard somebody say his name.

A woman. There was a woman in the room with him.

"Loretta?"

The woman's voice plunged into a deeper register, and this time there were no words, just a sound, like a kind of roar, that shook the bed.

He fumbled to get his spectacles on, but before he could do so the lamp was thrown off the cabinet, and smashed, leaving him and the trespasser together in the darkness.


"What in God's name was that?" Loretta said. She got up from the table, yelling for Jocelyn, but Rachel was ahead of her, out into the hallway.

There was a shout now: a shrill shout. Ignoring Loretta's instructions to *wait, girl, wait!* Rachel headed for the stairs. She had a momentary flash of *déjà vu*: ascending the flight two or three steps at a time, hearing the din of panic above, and the howling of wind. This was a scene she'd played out before, and for some reason she had kept the memory in her soul.

At the landing, she glanced back down the flight. Loretta was coming after her, clinging to the banister for support, Jocelyn at the bottom of the stairs, asking to know what the noise was.

"It's Cadmus, you damn fool!" Loretta yelled back at her. "I thought I told you to look in on him!"

"I did!" Jocelyn said. "He asked for brandy. And for Rachel."

Loretta didn't respond to this. It was Rachel she called after.

"Stay away from that door!"

"Why?" Rachel demanded.

"It's not your business! Just go back downstairs."

The door was rattling, violently, and there was no small part of Rachel that wanted to do exactly as Loretta had instructed. Perhaps after all this wasn't her business—it was Geary lunacy, Geary grief. But how could she ignore the sobs of panic that were coming from the bedroom? Somebody was terrorizing the old man, and it had to be stopped, right now. She turned the handle of the door—which rattled in her palm—and pushed. There was a force pressing on the door from the other side; she had to lay her whole body against the door to get it to open. When it did, it flew wide, and she pitched forward, so that appropriately enough she didn't step but stumbled into the midst of the tragedy waiting for her on the other side.

# VIII

Cadmus's room was chaos. The enormous bed was empty, the covers thrown off, the pillows scattered around. All but one of the lights had gone out, the exception being his bedside lamp, which lay on the floor, flickering nervously. The cabinet it had stood upon had been overturned, as had the chairs and the small dressing table. All the appurtenances of the sickroom—the pill bottles and their contents, the medicines and the measuring spoons, the IV stand, the vomit bowl and the oxygen machine—were littered about, smashed, pounded, rendered useless.

Rachel looked for Cadmus, but she couldn't see him. Nor could she see any sign of whoever had caused this mess. She advanced into the room a little way. The drapes fluttered. The window, she saw, was open wide. Oh Lord! Had he tried to escape and fallen? Or been thrown out?

As she started across the room, pills and glass crunching under her feet, she heard a soft sobbing. She looked in the direction of the sound, and there, crouched in the deep shadows in the corner of the room, she saw Cadmus. He was naked, his hands cupping his genitals, his face like that of a terrified monkey: lips curled back from his teeth, brow deeply furrowed. His eyes were upon her, but he made no sign of recognition. He simply stared, and shook.

"You're going to be all right," she said to him.

He said nothing. Just kept staring at her as she approached. The closer she got to him, the more she saw the harm that had been visited upon him. There were raised welts on his shoulders and chest, fiercely red against his sallow skin; and there was blood coming between his fingers, and pooling between his legs. She was appalled. Who would come into a dying man's room and cause such suffering? It was inhuman.

He had begun to sob loudly now. She hushed him gently, as a mother might hush a frightened child, but his eyes grew more panicky the closer to him she came.

"Don't . . ." he said, "Don't touch me . . ."

"I have to get you out of here," she told him.

He shook his head, drawing his limbs still closer to his body. The motion caused him pain, she saw; he closed his eyes for a moment, and a little cry escaped him.

From the landing now, the sound of Loretta yelling at Jocelyn, telling her to go back downstairs. Rachel glanced up at the door. She had time to catch a glimpse of Loretta, then the door slammed hard, locking Loretta out. The noise started Cadmus wailing, the frail knot of his body shaking violently.

She didn't attempt to soothe him. He was too traumatized to be comforted; she'd be wasting her breath. Besides, she had another concern. Whatever force had slammed the door in Loretta's face, and was holding it closed, it was here in the room with her. She could feel its power, grazing the back of her neck.

Very slowly, she turned round. She wanted to be face to face with it if it decided to move against her: to see it plainly, if it was the last thing she did.

She scanned the room again. Her eyes had grown accustomed to the light from the flickering lamp, but they were still unable to find the cause of the maelstrom. She decided to simply call it forth.

"Where are you?" she said. Behind her, the old man's wails abruptly died away. He seemed to hold his breath, as if anticipating the worst. "My name's Rachel," she went on, "and he—" she pointed back toward Cadmus "—is my father-in-law. I'd like you to let me take him out of this room and get him some help. He's bleeding."

There was a silence. Then, a voice, across the room: a place between the windows which her gaze had twice passed over and found empty. Now she saw her error. There was somebody sitting there, formally, like a statue, every drape of her dress, every hair on her head, immaculate.

*I didn't touch him*, the woman said.

Even now, though Rachel's eyes had found her, the woman was hard to keep in focus. Her black, silken skin seemed to deflect Rachel's gaze. But she persevered. When her eyes slid left or right, she returned them to the woman, back and back and back again, refusing to be put off.

*He tried to unman himself*, the woman was explaining, *thinking it'd placate me*.

Rachel didn't know whether to believe what she was being told or not. The idea that Cadmus had done the damage between his legs to himself was grotesque.

"May I take him then?" Rachel said.

*No you may not*, the woman replied. *I came here to watch him die, and that's what I'm going to do.*

Rachel glanced back over her shoulders. Cadmus was watching his tormentor, the terror on his face replaced with a blank look, as though he was too used up by what he'd endured to even weep.

*You may stay with him if you wish*, the woman went on. *You won't have to wait very long. He's only got a few more breaths left in him.*

"I don't want to watch him die," Rachel protested.

*Where's your sense of history?* the woman replied. She rose as she spoke, and dropped the last defenses she'd put up against Rachel's gaze. She was perhaps the most beautiful woman Rachel had ever seen; her glorious face had about it the same nakedness that Rachel had seen in Galilee's face, that first night. Skin and nerve and muscle and bone all extolling one another.

Now she understood what the woman meant when she talked about a sense of history. She was a Barbarossa, attending the death of a Geary.

"Are you his sister?" Rachel said.

*Sister?*

"Galilee's sister?"

The woman made a tiny smile. *No. I'm his mother: Cesaria Yaos Barbarossa. And you . . . who were you before you were a Geary?*

"My name was Pallenberg."

*Rachel Pallenberg.*

"Right."

*Tell me . . . do you regret it? Marrying into this wretched family?*

Rachel contemplated the question before replying. Perhaps it would be politic to tell the woman that she regretted it heart and soul, but she couldn't bring herself to do so. It wasn't true. There were losses and gains, as in everything.

"I thought I loved my husband, and I thought he loved me," Rachel said. "But I was in love with a lie."

*And what was that?*

"That I'd be happy once I had everything—"

*—even though you lost yourself?*

"Almost," Rachel said. "Almost lost."

*Tell me: is your husband here in the house?*

"No."

*Just the women out there?* Cesaria said, glancing toward the door.

"Don't hurt them," Rachel said. "They're good people."

*I told you, I didn't come here to hurt anybody. I came to bear witness.*

Rachel glanced at the destruction on all sides. "So why do this?"

*He annoyed me,* Cesaria said, *trying to bargain with me.* "Leave me alone and I'll give you whatever I've got." Her eyes flickered in Cadmus's direction. *You've got nothing I want, old man,* she said. *Besides, this house needs to be cleansed from top to bottom. He knows why. He understands. It's time to strip away all the pretense. All the comforting things he collected to make him feel like a king. It all has to go.* She began to walk back in Cadmus's direction. *In the end, it'll be easier for him to move on, when there's nothing to keep him here.*

"If you want to wreck the house," Rachel said, "that's one thing. But he's just a sick old man, and sitting here watching him bleed to death is cruel." Cesaria stared at her. "You don't think it's cruel?"

*I didn't ask myself,* Cesaria said. *But yes, probably. And let me tell you, he deserves a lot worse, for the things he's done.*

"To you?"

*No, to my son. To Atva. Or as he prefers it: Galilee.*

"What did Cadmus ever do to Galilee?"

*Tell her,* Cesaria said. *Go on. Tell her. You'll never have another chance, so say it!* Rachel looked back at Cadmus, but there was no answer forthcoming. He'd hung his head, whether out of exhaustion or shame Rachel didn't know. *Did you think you were so secret that nobody saw?* Cesaria went on. *I saw. When you made my child murder your own flesh and blood. I saw.* There was a barely audible sob out of Cadmus. *Tell her it's true,* Cesaria said. *Don't be such a coward.*

"It's true . . ." Cadmus murmured.

*Does your wife know, by the way?* Cesaria said.

Very slowly, Cadmus raised his head. If he'd looked sick before, he looked a dozen times sicker now. There was no blood left in his face; his lips were bluish, his eyes and teeth yellow. "No," he said.

*Let her in,* Cesaria told Rachel. *I want her to know what he hid from her. And tell the servant to leave. This is family business.*

Though Rachel didn't much like being treated like a servant herself, she didn't argue with the instruction. She dutifully went to the door, which opened without effort. Both Loretta and Jocelyn were waiting there, Jocelyn sobbing uncontrollably.

"Why did you lock the door?" Loretta demanded.

"I didn't," Rachel told her. "Cesaria Barbarossa's in there with Cadmus. She wants you to come in. And she wants Jocelyn out of the house."

"Cesaria . . . ?" Loretta said, her strident tone dropping to a murmur. "How did she get in?"

"I don't know," Rachel said, moving aside to allow Loretta a glimpse into the sickroom. "She says she's come to watch Cadmus die."

"Well she's not going to have the pleasure," Loretta said, and pushing past Rachel stepped through the door.

"What should I do?" Jocelyn wanted to know.

"Just leave."

"Shall I call Garrison?"

"No. Just get out of the house. You've done what you can."

It was clear from the fearful expression on Jocelyn's face that she wanted to go; but deep-seated loyalty was preventing her from doing so.

"If you don't go now," Rachel warned, "you may not get another chance. You've got your own family to think of. *Go.*"

A look of relief crossed Jocelyn's face; here were the words that let her go with a clear conscience. "Thank you," she said, and slipped away.

Rachel closed the door after her, and turned back to face the events of the room. Loretta had already decided on her method of dealing with Cesaria: head-on attack.

"You don't have any business being here," she was saying. "You're trespassing in my house and I want you out."

*This isn't your house,* Cesaria said, her eyes fixed not on Loretta but on the man still squatting against the wall. *And it isn't his either.* Loretta started to protest but Cesaria waved her words away. *My son built this house, as he*—she pointed at Cadmus—*well knows. He built it with the blood he spilled to make you your fortune. And the seed he spilled.*

"What are you talking about?" Loretta said. Her tone, though still assertive, was tinged with unease, as though she knew there was truth in what she was hearing.

*Tell her*, Cesaria said to Cadmus. The figure crouched in the shadows shook its heavy head. Cesaria took a step toward Cadmus. *Old man*, she said. *Get yourself up off the floor.*

"He can't—" Loretta said.

*Shut up*, Cesaria snapped. *You heard me, old man. I want you up.*

As the instruction left her lips Cadmus's head rolled backward, so that now he was looking straight up at Cesaria. Then, inch by quivering inch, he started to rise, his back pressed against the wall; but not of his own volition. His legs were too wasted to bear him up this way. This was Cesaria's doing. She was raising him by sheer force of will.

It seemed he was not entirely unhappy to be puppeteered this way. A tight-lipped smile had crept onto his face, as though in some perverse way he was taking pleasure in being handled this way; in feeling the woman's power upon him.

As fascinated as she was appalled, Rachel crossed the room and went to stand at Loretta's side. "Please, don't do this," she said to Cesaria. "Let him die in peace."

*He doesn't want to die in peace*, Cesaria replied. Then, to Cadmus: *Do you? It's better to suffer now, because that way you think you will have paid your debts. Isn't that what you hope?*

Cadmus made the tiniest of nods.

*You may be right, by the way*, Cesaria said. *I don't have any better idea of what waits for you than you do. Maybe your soul's free after this. Maybe it's the ones you leave behind who'll pay the real price.* She took another step toward him. *Your children. Your grandchildren. Your wife.* She was so close to him now she could have touched him. But she didn't need to make physical contact; she had a profound hold on him: that of her will and her words.

His eyes were filled with tears. His mouth opened a little way, and he started to speak. It was the ghost of a whisper.

"Can't we . . . make peace?" he murmured.

*Peace?*

"Your family . . . and mine."

*It's too late for that.*

"No . . ."

*You had your own flesh and blood murdered by my son,* Cesaria said. *You drove Atva to madness for your ambition. You sowed terrible seeds when you did that. Terrible, terrible seeds.*

The tears were pouring down Cadmus's face now. The perverse smile had gone; he looked like a mask of tragedy: his mouth turned down, his cheeks gouged, his brow furrowed.

"Don't punish them for what I did," he sobbed. "You can stop this . . . war . . . if you want to."

*I'm too tired,* Cesaria said, *and too old. And my children are as willful as yours are. There's nothing I can do. If you'd come to me fifty years ago, and repented, maybe I could have done something. But now it's too late, for all of us.*

She drew a little breath, and it seemed that as she did so the last of Cadmus's life went from him. His body ceased to shake, his face, that tragic mask, was abruptly wiped clean. There was a long moment of absolute stillness. Then Cesaria turned to Loretta and said: *He's all yours,* and turned her back on wife and corpse. The moment she withdrew her patronage, Cadmus slid back down the wall like a sack of bones. Loretta let out a tiny cry and went down on her knees beside him.

Cesaria wasn't interested in the drama, now that Cadmus had left the stage. She didn't turn to look back at Loretta keening over the body; she simply strode to the door and out onto the landing. Rachel went after her.

"Wait!" she called.

She could feel the air in Cesaria's wake becoming agitated. An aura rose off her, like heat off a stove. The air shook and melted. But Rachel wasn't about to let the woman go without at least attempting to question her. Too much had been said that needed explanation.

"Help me understand," she said.

*There's nothing you need concern yourself with. It's over now.*

"No, it's not! I need to know what happened to Galilee."

*Why?* Cesaria said, still descending. The emanations were beginning to cause some major disturbances now. The ceiling was making a peculiar grinding sound, as though the beams were shaking behind the plaster; the banister was rocking, as if buffeted by gusts of wind.

"I love him," Rachel said.

*Of course you do,* Cesaria replied. *I'd expect nothing less.*

"So I want to help him," Rachel said. She'd hesitated at the top of the stairs, but now—realizing that nothing she could say was going to halt Cesaria—she went down after her. A wave of sickly air struck her, smelling of camphor and dirt. She plunged through it, though it stung her eyes until they watered.

*Do you know how many men and women have wanted to heal my Atva over the years?* Cesaria said. *None of them succeeded. None of them could.*

She was at the bottom of the stairs now, and there hesitated for a moment, as if making up her mind where she would start her blitzkrieg. If Rachel had entertained any doubt that Cesaria intended to take up the offer made in Cadmus's room, and wreck the mansion, she had it silenced now, as the great Venetian mirror hanging in the hallway shook itself loose and came crashing down, followed in quick succession by every item on the walls, even to the smallest picture.

Rachel halted, shaken by the sudden violence. Cesaria, meanwhile, moved off down the passageway toward Cadmus's sitting room. "You should go," said a voice above.

Rachel looked up. Loretta had come out onto the landing, and was now standing at the top of the stairs.

"She won't hurt us," Rachel said; brave talk, though she wasn't entirely certain it was true. The noise of vandalism had erupted again; clearly Cesaria was demolishing the sitting room. The woman might not intend to do any harm, but when such chaotic forces as these were loosed, was anybody safe?

"Are you leaving?" Rachel said to Loretta.

"No."

"Then neither am I."

"Don't go near her, Rachel. What's going on here is beyond you. It's beyond us both. We're just little people."

"So what? We just give up?"

"We never had a prayer," Loretta said, the expression on her face bereft. "I see that now. We never had a prayer."

Rachel had watched events transform a lot of people of late: Mitchell, Cadmus, Galilee. But none of those changes distressed her quite as much as the one before her now. She'd looked to Loretta as a place of solidity in a shifting terrain. She'd seemed so certain of her path, and what measures she had to take to clear the way ahead. Now, suddenly, all that certainty had drained out of her. Though she'd known Cadmus was not long for this world, and though she'd certainly known the Barbarossas were something other than human stock, the proof of those facts had undone her.

*I'm more alone than ever,* Rachel thought. *I don't even have Loretta now.*

The din from the sitting room had died away during this exchange, and had now ceased entirely. What now? Had Cesaria tired of her furies already, and decided to leave? Or was she just catching her breath between assaults?

"Don't worry about me," Rachel said to Loretta. "I know what I'm doing."

And with that hopeful boast she headed on down the stairs and into the passage that led to the sitting room.

# IX

## i

A bizarre sight awaited her. The room which Cadmus Geary had used as his sanctum had been as comprehensively trashed as the sickroom and the lobby, but two items had been left untouched by the assault: the landscape painting on the wall and a large leather armchair. Cesaria sat in the latter looking at the former, surrounded by a brittle sea of shards and splinters. Bierstadt's masterpiece seemed to have her entranced. But she was not so focused upon the canvas that she missed the fact of Rachel's presence. Without turning to look at her visitor, she started to speak.

*I went out west . . .* she said *. . . many, many years ago.*

"Oh?"

*I wanted to find somewhere to settle. Somewhere to build my house.*

"And did you?"

*No. Most of it was too barren.*

"How far west did you go?"

*All the way to California,* Cesaria replied. *I liked California. But I couldn't persuade Jefferson to join me.*

"Who was Jefferson?"

*My architect. A better architect than he was a president, I may say. Or indeed a lover.*

The conversation was rapidly straying into the surreal, but Rachel did her best to keep her amazement to herself. "Thomas Jefferson was your lover?"

*For a short while.*

"Is he Galilee's father?"

*No, I never had a child by him. But I got my house.*

"Where did you end up building it?"

Cesaria didn't reply. Instead she got up from the armchair and wandered over to the painting, apparently indifferent to the shards of ceramic and glass beneath her bare feet.

*Do you like this picture?* she asked Rachel.

"Not particularly."

*What's wrong with it?*

"I just don't like it."

Cesaria glanced back over her shoulder. *You can do better than that,* she said.

"It tries too hard," Rachel said. "It wants to be really impressive and it ends up just . . . being . . . big."

*You're right,* Cesaria said, looking back at the Bierstadt. *It does try too hard. But I like that about it. It moves me. It's very male.*

"Too male," Rachel said.

*There's no such thing,* Cesaria replied. *A man can't be too much a man. And a woman can't be too much a woman.*

"You don't seem to try very hard," Rachel replied.

Cesaria turned to face Rachel again, a look of almost comical surprise on her exquisite features. *Are you doubting my femininity?* she said.

Challenged, Rachel lost a little of her confidence. She faltered before beginning to say: "Upstairs—"

*You think womanhood should be all sighs and compassion?* The expression on Cesaria's face had lost its comic excess; her eyes were heavy and hooded. *You think I should have sat by that bastard's bed and comforted him? That's not womanhood. It's trained servitude. If you wanted to be a bedtender you should have stayed with the Gearys. There's going to be plenty of deathbeds to tend there.*

"Does it have to end this way?"

*Yes. I'm afraid it does. I meant what I said to the old man: I'm too old and I'm too weary to stop war breaking out.* She returned her gaze to the canvas, and studied it for a little time. *We finally built the house in North Carolina,* she went on. *Thomas would go back and forth to Monticello, which he was building for himself. Forty years that house of his took to build, and I don't think he was ever satisfied. But he liked L'Enfant because he knew how much pleasure it gave me. I wanted to make it a glorious place. I wanted to fill it with fine things, fine dreams . . .* Hearing this, Rachel couldn't help but wonder if Cadmus and Kitty, and later Loretta, hadn't felt something of the same ambition for this house, which Cesaria had just waged her own war against. *Now of course the Gearys are going to come, and walk into that house of mine and see some of those dreams for themselves. And it's going to be very interesting to see which of them is the stronger.*

"You seem quite fatalistic about it."

*That's because I've known it was coming for a very long time. Ever since Galilee left, I suppose, somewhere in my heart I've known there'd come a time when the human world would come looking for us.*

"Do you know where Galilee is?"

*Where he always is: out at sea.* She looked back at Rachel. *Is he all you care about? Answer me honestly.*

"Yes. He's all I care about."

*You know that he can't protect you? He's never been good at that.*

"I don't need protecting."

*We all need protecting sometimes,* Cesaria said, with a hint of wistfulness.

"Then let *me* help *him*," Rachel said. Cesaria looked at her with a strange gentility. "Let me be with him," Rachel went on, "And take care of him. Let me love him."

*The way I should have done, you mean,* Cesaria said. Rachel had no opportunity to deny the accusation. Cesaria was up and out of the chair, coming at her. *There aren't many people I've met who'd talk to me the way you talk. Not after having seen all that's gone on here tonight.*

"I'm not afraid of you," Rachel said.

*I see that. But don't imagine being a woman's any protection. If I wanted to harm you—*

"But you don't. If you hurt me then you hurt Galilee, and that's the last thing you want."

*You don't know what that child did to me,* Cesaria said. *You don't know the hurt he caused. I'd still have a husband if he'd not gone off into the world . . .* She trailed off, despairing.

"I'm sorry he gave you so much pain," Rachel said. "But I know he's never forgiven himself."

Cesaria's stare was like light in ice. *He told you that?* she said.

"Yes he did."

*Then why didn't he come back home and tell me?* Cesaria said. *Why didn't he just come home and say he was sorry?*

"Because he was certain you wouldn't forgive him."

*I'd have forgiven him. All he had to do was ask and I'd have forgiven him.* The light and ice were melting, and running down her cheeks. *Damn you, woman,* she said. *Making me weep after all these years.* She sniffed hard. *So what is it you're asking me to do?* she said.

"Find him for me," Rachel replied. "I'll do the rest. I'll bring him home to you. I swear I will. If I have to drag him myself, I'll bring him home to you."

Cesaria's tears kept coming, but she didn't bother to wipe them away. She just stood there, while they fell, her face as naked as Galilee's had been that first night on the island; all capacity for deception scoured from it. Her unhappiness was there, plain to see; and the rage she'd nurtured against him all these years. But so too was her love for him; her tender love, planted among these griefs.

*You should go back to the Garden Island,* she said. *And wait for him.*

Rachel scarcely dared believe what she was hearing. "You'll find him for me?" she said.

*If he'll let me,* Cesaria said. *But you make sure he comes home to me, woman, you understand? That's our bargain.*

"I understand."

*Bring him back to L'Enfant, where he belongs. Somebody's going to have to bury me, when all this is over. And I want it to be him.*

## ii

"Are we at war then?"

That was the question Luman had asked me, the day I went down to the Smoke House to make my peace with him. I didn't have an answer for him at the time. Now I do. Yes, we're at war with the Gearys, though I would still be hard-pressed to tell him when that war actually began.

Perhaps, in reflection, that's true of all wars. The war between the states for instance, from the furnace of which the Gearys rose to such wealth and power—when did that begin? Was it the moment that the first shot was fired at Fort Sumter? That's certainly a convenient choice for historians: they can pinpoint the day, the date and even the man—a trigger-happy civilian called Edmund Ruffin—who did the firing. But of course by the time this even takes place the grinding work of war had been under way for many years. The enmities which fueled that work in fact go back generations, nurtured and mythologized in the hearts of the people who will bankrupt their economies and sacrifice their sons for that enmity.

So it is with the war between the Gearys and the Barbarossas: though its first casualty, Margie, may only just be in the ground and the knives have only lately been sharpened, the plots and counterplots that have brought us to this moment go back a long, long way. Back to Charleston, in the early spring of 1865: Charles Holt and Nub Nickelberry stepping into Galilee's strange boudoir in the ruins of the East Battery, and giving themselves over to pleasure. Had they known what they were initiating would they have done otherwise? I suspect not. They were living in the moment of their hunger and their despair; if they'd been told, as they consoled themselves with cake and meat and the comfort of kisses, that the consequences of their sensuality would be very terrible, a hundred and some years hence, they would have said: so what? And who would have blamed them? I would have done the same, in their boots. You can't go through life worrying about what the echoes of the echoes of the echoes of your deeds will be; you have to do what you can with the moment, and let others take care of their moment when it comes.

So I lay no blame with Charles and Nub. They lived their lives, and moved on into the hereafter. Now we have our lives to live, and they will be marked by a period of war that may undo us all. It will be, I suspect, a subtle war, at least at the beginning, its significance calculated not in the number of coffins it fills, but in the scale of the structures it finally brings to ruin. I don't simply speak of physical structures (though those too will inevitably come down); I speak of the elaborate edifices of influence and power and ambition that both our families have constructed over the years. When this war is over, I doubt any of them will still be standing. There will be no victor: that's my prediction. The two clans will simply cancel one another out.

No great loss, you may say, knowing what you now know about us. There's a certain pettiness in the best of us, and such malice in the worst that their passing will probably be something to be celebrated.

My only hope as we move into these darker times is that the war will uncover some quality in one or other of us (I dare not hope all) that will disprove my pessimism. I don't wish to say that war is ennobling, you understand; I don't believe that for a moment. But I do believe it may strip us of some of the pretensions that are the dubious profits of peace — the airs and graces that we've all put on — and return us to our truer selves. To our humanity or our divinity; or both.

So, I'm ready. The pistol lies on one side of my desk, and my pen lies beside it. I intend to sit here and go on writing until the very last, but I can no longer promise you that I'll finish this story before I have to put my pen aside and arm myself. That *only everything* of mine now seems like the remotest of dreams: one of those pretensions of peace that I was talking about a few paragraphs back.

I will promise you this: that in the chapters to come I won't toy with your affections, as though we had a lifetime together. I'll be as plain as I know how, doing what I can to furnish you with the means to finish this history in your own head should I be stopped by a bullet.

And—while I'm thinking of that—maybe this isn't an inappropriate place to beg mercy from those I've neglected or misrepresented here. You've been reading the work of a man learning his craft word by word, sentence by sentence; I've often stumbled, I've often failed.

Forgive me my frailties. And if I am deserving of that forgiveness, let it be because I am not my father's son, but only human. And let the future be such a time as this is reason enough to be loved.

# PART EIGHT

# A House of Women

# I

I was in a fine, maudlin mood when I wrote the last portion of the preceding chapter; with hindsight it seems somewhat premature. The barbarians aren't here yet, after all. Not even a whiff of their cologne. Perhaps I'll never need the gun Luman gave me. Wouldn't that be a fine old ending to my epic? After hundreds of pages of expectation, nothing. The Gearys decide they've had enough; Galilee stays out at sea; Rachel waits on the beach but never sees him again. The din of war drums dwindles, and they finally fall silent.

Clearly Luman doesn't believe there's much likelihood of this happening. A little while ago he brought me two more weapons; one of them a fine cavalry saber, which he'd polished up until it gleamed, the other a short stabbing sword which was owned, and presumably used, by a Confederate artilleryman. He'd worked to polish this also, he told me, but it hadn't been a very rewarding labor: the metal refused to gleam. That said, the weapon possesses a brutal simplicity. Unlike the sword, which has a patrician elegance, this is a gutting weapon; you can feel its purpose in its heft. It fairly begs to be used.

He stayed an hour or two, chatting about things, and by the time I got back to writing it was dark. I was making notes toward the scene in which Garrison Geary visits the room where Cadmus died—and was thoroughly immersed in the details—when there was a knock on the door and Zabrina presented herself. She had a summons for me, from Cesaria.

"So Mama's home?" I said.

"Are you being sarcastic?" she said.

"No," I protested. "It was a simple observation. Mama's home. That's good. You should be happy."

"I am," she said, still suspicious that I was mocking her earlier dramas.

"Well I'm happy that you're happy. There. Happy?"

"Not really," she said.

"Why the hell not?"

"She's different, Maddox. She's not the woman she was before she left."

"Maybe that's all to the good," I said. Zabrina didn't remark on this; she just tightened her lips. "Anyway, why are you so surprised? Of course she's different. She's lost one of her enemies." Zabrina looked at me blankly. "She didn't tell you?"

"No."

"She killed Cadmus Geary. Or at least she was there when he died. It's hard to know which is true."

"So what does that mean for us?" Zabrina said.

"I've been trying to figure that out myself."

She eyed the three weapons on my desk. "You're ready for the worst," she said.

"They were a gift from Luman. Do you want one?"

"No thank you," she said. "I've got my own ways of dealing with these people if they come here. Is it going to be Garrison Geary, or the good-looking brother?"

"I didn't realize you were following all this," I said. "It could be both."

"I hope it's the good-looking one," Zabrina said. "I could put him to good use."

"Doing what?"

"You know very well," she said. I was astonished that she was being so forthright, but then why shouldn't she be? Everybody else was showing their true colors. Why not Zabrina?

"I could happily have that man in my bed," she went on. "He has a wonderful head of hair."

"Unlike your Dwight."

"Dwight and I still enjoy one another when the mood takes us," she said.

"So it's true," I said, "you did seduce him when he first came here."

"Of course I seduced him, Maddox," she said. "You think I kept him in my room all that time because I was teaching him the alphabet? Marietta's not the only one in the family with a sex drive, you know." She crossed to the desk and picked up the saber. "Are you really going to use this?"

"If I have to."

"When was the last time you killed a man?"

"I never have."

"Really?" she said. "Not even when you were out gallivantir Papa?"

"Never."

"Oh it's fun," she said, with a gleam in her eye. This was turning into a most revelatory conversation, I thought.

"When did you ever kill anyone?" I asked her.

"I don't know if I want to tell you," she said.

"Zabrina, don't be so silly. I'm not going to write about it." I watched her expression as I said this, and saw a flicker of disappointment there. "Unless you want me to," I added.

A tiny smile appeared on her lips. The woman who'd once told me — in no uncertain terms — that she despised the notion of appearing in this book had been overtaken by somebody who found the idea tantalizing. "I suppose if I don't tell you and you don't write it down nobody's ever going to know . . ."

"Know what?" She frowned, nibbling at her lip. I wished I'd had a box of bonbons to offer her, or a slice of pecan pie. But the only seduction I had to hand was my pen. "I'll tell it exactly as you tell it to me," I said to her. "Whatever it is. I swear."

"Hm . . ."

Still she stood there, biting her lip. "Now you're just playing with me," I told her. "If you don't want to tell me then don't."

"No, no, no," she said hurriedly. "I want to tell you. It's just strange, after all these years . . ."

"If you knew the number of times I've thought that very thing, while I was writing. This book's going to be full of things that have never been told but should be. And you're right. It's a strange feeling, admitting to things."

"Have you admitted to things?"

"Ohhhh yes," I said, sitting back in my chair. "Hard things sometimes. Things that make me look pretty bad."

"Well this doesn't make me look bad, exactly . . ." I waited, hoping my silence would encourage her to spit it out. The trick worked. "About a year after Dwight came to live with me," she said, "I went out to Sampson County to find his family. He'd told me what they'd done to him, and it was . . . so horrible. The cruelty of these people. I knew he wasn't lying about it because he had the scars. He had cigarette burns all over his back and on his butt. His older brother used to torture him. And from his father, different kinds of scars." She seemed genuinely moved at her recollections of the harm he'd been done. Her tiny eyes glistened. "So I thought I'd pay them a visit. Which I did. I made friends with his mother, which wasn't very difficult. She obviously didn't have anyone to talk to. The family were pariahs. Nobody wanted anything to do with them. Anyway, she invited me over one night. I offered to bring over some steak for the menfolk. She said they'd like that. There were five brothers and the father, so I brought six steaks and I fried 'em up, while they all sat in the backyard and drank.

"The mother knew what I was doing, I swear. She could sense it. She kept looking at me while I cooked up the steaks. I was adding a little of this, a little of that. It was a special recipe for the men in her life, I told her. And she looked at me dead in the eye and she said: *Good. They deserve it.* So she knew what I was going to do.

"She even helped me serve them. We put the steaks out on the plates—big steaks they were, and I'd cooked them so rare and tender, swimming in blood and grease the way she'd said her boys liked them—we put them on the plates and she said: I had another boy, but he ran away. And I told her: *I know.* And she said: *I know you know.*

"Then we gave them their steaks. The poison didn't take long. They were dead after half a dozen bites. Terrible waste of good meat, but it did the job. There they were, sitting in the backyard with the stars coming out, their faces black, and their lips curled back from their teeth. It was quite a night . . ."

She fell silent. The possibility of tears had passed.

"What happened to the mother?"

"She packed up and left there and then."

"And the bodies?"

"I left them in the yard. I didn't want to bring them back here. Godless sons of bitches. I hope they rotted where they sat, though I doubt they did. Somebody probably smelled them the next day, once the sun got up."

A hundred thousand words ago, I thought, I'd wondered in these pages if the family of Dwight Huddie ever wondered about their missing son. Now I had the answer.

"Did you tell Dwight what you did?"

"No," Zabrina said. "I never did. I never told anybody until now."

"And did you *really* enjoy it?" I asked her.

She thought on this a moment. Finally, she said: "Yes I did. I suppose I got that from Mama. But I remember distinctly looking at those bastards dead, and thinking: I have a talent for this. And you know there's nothing in the world more fun than doing something you're good at."

She seemed to realize that she wasn't going to be able to improve on this as a departure line, because she gave me a crooked little smile, and without another word, she headed for the door, and was gone.

# II

Astonishment upon astonishment. I would never have believed Zabrina would be capable of such a thing. And the way it just came out like that, in the most matter-of-fact way; amazing. The truth is, it gives me hope. It makes me think I've maybe underestimated our ability as a family to oppose the powers that are going to come our way. At the very least we'll take a few of the bastards with us when we go. Zabrina can get Mitchell Geary into bed, and when she's had her wicked way, poison him.

Anyway, I went to see Cesaria.

It wasn't as oppressive up there as it had been the last time I'd entered her chambers, nor was Cesaria lying inert on her bed. She was sitting in the Jefferson room, which Zabrina told me was an extremely rare thing for her to do. It was a little before dawn; there were candles lit around the room, which flattered it considerably. Their light mellowed Cesaria too. She sat at the table, sipping hot tea and looking resplendent. There was no trace of the vengeful creature I'd seen unleashed in the Geary house. She invited me to sit down, and offered me some tea, which Zelim brought and set before me. Zabrina had already gone. There was just the two of us; and I will admit I was a little nervous. Not that I feared she was going to fly into an uncontrollable fury and tear the house apart. It simply made me anxious to be in the company of someone who contained such power, but who was displaying not a mote of it. It was like taking tea with a man-eating tiger; I couldn't help but wonder when she was going to show her claws.

"I'm leaving again, very soon," she explained. "And this time—just so you know—I may not come back. If I don't return, then the control of this house falls to you." I asked her where she was off to. "To find Galilee," she said.

"I see."

"And if I can, to save him from himself."

"You know he's out at sea?" I said.

"Yes, I know."

"I wish I could tell you where. But you probably already know."

"No. I don't. That's one of the reasons why I'm putting you on notice that I may not return. There was a time when I'd have visions of him almost every day, but I put them out of my head—I didn't want to deal with him—and now he's invisible to me. I'm sure he worked to make it so."

"So why do you want to find him now?"

"To persuade him that he's loved."

"So you want him to come home?"

Cesaria shook her head. "It's not me who loves him . . ." she said. "It's Rachel."

"Yes. It's Rachel." Cesaria set down her teacup and took out one of her little Egyptian cigarettes. She passed the packet over to me. I took one, and lit up. It was the foulest tasting thing I've ever smoked.

"I never thought I'd hear myself say this but what that woman feels for Galilee may be the saving of us all. Do you not like the cigarette?"

"No, it's fine."

"I think they taste like camel dung personally, but they have sentimental associations."

"Yes?"

"Your father and I spent some blissful weeks in Cairo together, just before he met your mother . . ."

"So when you smoke them you remember him?"

"No, when I smoke them I remember an Egyptian boy called Muhammed, who fucked me among the crocodiles on the banks of the Nile."

I coughed so hard tears came to my eyes, which amused her mightily.

"Oh poor Maddox," she said when I'd recovered myself somewhat, "you've never really known what to make of me, have you?"

"Frankly, no."

"I suppose I've kept you a distance because you're not mine. I look at you and you remind me of what a philanderer your father was. That hurts. After all these years, that still hurts. You know, you look very like your mother. Around the mouth, especially."

"How can you say that it hurts you to be reminded that he was a philanderer when you were just telling me about fucking with some Egyptian?"

"I did it to spite your father. My heart was never really in it. No, I take that back. There were occasions when I was in love. Jefferson of course. I was completely besotted with Jefferson. But doing the deed among the crocodiles? That was for spite. I did a lot of things for spite."

"And he did the same?"

"Of course. Spite begets spite. He used to have women morning, noon and night."

"And he loved none of them?"

"Are you asking me whether he truly loved your mother?"

I drew a bitter lungful of the cigarette. Of course that was what I wanted to know. But now it came time to ask the question, I was tongue-tied, even a little emotional. And even as I felt the tears pricking my eyes another part of me—the part that's dispassionately setting this account on the page—was thinking: what's all the drama about? Why the hell should it matter, after all these years, what your father felt for your mother the day they conceived you? Would you really feel better about yourself if you knew they'd been in love?

"Listen carefully," Cesaria said. "I'm going to tell you something that may make you a little happier. Or at least, let you understand better how it was between your parents.

"Your mother was illiterate when Nicodemus met her. She was really a sweet woman, I have to say, a very sweet woman, but she couldn't even write her name. I think your father rather liked her that way, frankly, but she was ambitious for herself, and who can blame her? They were hard times for men and women, but for a woman like her, her beauty was her only advantage, and she knew that wasn't going to last forever.

"She wanted to be able to read and write—more than anything in the world—and she begged your father to teach her. Over and over she begged him. It was like an obsession with her—"

"So you knew her?"

"I met her a few times only. At the beginning, when he was showing her off to me, and at the very end, I'll come to that in a moment.

"Anyway, she tormented your father night and day about teaching her to read—teach me, teach me, teach me—until eventually he consented. Of course he didn't have the patience to do it the way ordinary folks would do it. He didn't want to waste his precious time with A B Cs. He just put his will into her and the knowledge flowed. She learned to read and write overnight. Not just English. Greek, Hebrew, Italian, French, Sanskrit—"

"What a gift."

"So she believed.

"You were about three weeks old when this happened. Such a quiet little baby; with that same frown you have on your face right now. One day you had a mother who couldn't read a word, and the next day the woman could have made intelligent conversation with Socrates. Let me tell you, it was quite a transformation. And of course she wanted to use what she'd learned. She started to read, anything your father could bring her. She'd be sitting there with you suckling, and a dozen books open on the table, going from one to the other, holding all these ideas in her head at the same time. She kept demanding books and he kept bringing them. Plutarch, St. Augustine, Thomas Aquinas, Ptolemy, Virgil, Herodotus—there was no end to her appetite.

"Nicodemus was proud as a peacock. 'Look at my genius girlfriend. She talks dirty in Greek!' He didn't know what he'd done. He didn't have the first clue. Her poor brain, it was cooking in her skull. And all the while she was suckling you . . ."

It was quite an image. My mother, surrounded by books, with me pressed against her breast, and her head so filled with words and ideas her brain was frying in its pan.

"That's horrible . . ." I murmured.

"It gets worse, so prepare yourself. Word started to spread, and in a couple of weeks she'd become a celebrity. Do you have any recollection of this? Of the crowds?" I shook my head. "People started to come from all over England, eventually all over Europe, to see your mother."

"And what did father do?"

"Oh he got tired of the hoopla very quickly. I'm sure he regretted what he'd done, because he asked me if maybe he should take back what he'd given. I told him I didn't care what he did. She was his problem, not mine. I regret that now. I should have said something. I could have saved her life. And when I think back, I knew . . ."

"You knew what—?"

"—what it was doing to her. I could see it in her eyes. It was more than her poor, human brain could take.

"Then, one night, she apparently asked your father to bring her pen and paper. He refused her. He said he wasn't going to let her waste time writing while she should be tending to you. Your mother threw a fit, and she just took herself off, leaving you behind.

"Of course, your father had no idea how to deal with a tiny child, so he handed you over to me."

"You looked after me?"

"For a little while."

"And he went to find my mother?"

"That's right. It took him a few days, but he found her. She'd gone to the house of a man in Blackheath, and exchanged her sexual favors for an endless supply of what Nicodemus had refused her: pen and paper."

"What did she write?"

"I don't know. Your father never showed it to me. He said it was incomprehensible. Whatever it was, it must have been very important to your mother, because she'd worked night and day on it, scarcely stopping to eat or sleep. When he brought her back to the house she was a shadow of herself: thin as a stick, her hands and face all stained with ink. She didn't make any sense when she talked. It was a crazy mixture of all the languages she knew, and all the things she'd read. Listening to her was enough to make you crazy yourself: the way she spewed out all these bits and pieces that had nothing to do with one another, all the time looking at you as if to say: please understand me, please, please —

"I thought maybe she'd feel better if she had you back in her arms, so I brought her to the crib, and I gently told her you needed to be fed. She seemed to know what I was saying to her. She picked you up and rocked you for a little while, then she went to sit down by the fire where she always fed you. And she'd no sooner sat down than she gave a little sigh, and died."

"Oh my God . . ."

"You rolled out of her arms and fell to the floor. And you began to cry. For the first time, you began to cry, and from then on — having been the quietest, most gentle little baby — from then on you were a monster. You wept and you screamed and I don't think I saw you smile again, oh for years."

"What did my father do?"

"About you or her?"

"Her."

"He took her body and he buried her somewhere in Kent. Dug the grave himself, and stayed with her, mourning her for weeks on end. Leaving me to take care of you, I may add, which I didn't thank him for."

"But you didn't stay with me," I said. "Gisela . . ."

"Yes, Gisela came to take care of you. She looked after you for the next six or seven years. So now you know," Cesaria said. "I don't know what good it does. It's all so long ago . . ."

A long silence hung between us; each of us, I suppose, in our own thoughts. I was remembering Gisela, or at least the Gisela I imagine in my dreams. First I hear her voice — she had a thin, reedy voice — singing some lilting song. Then I see the sky; small white clouds passing over. And finally her face comes into view, smiling as she sings, and I realize

I'm lying on the grass—it must be the first summer of my life; I'm too little to do anything but lie there—and she lifts me up into her arms and puts me to her breast.

Perhaps I bawled and complained when I was with Cesaria, but I think I was happy with Gisela. At least I remember it that way. I don't know what Cesaria was remembering, but I think it was probably my father. Quietly cursing him, most likely. And who could blame her?

"I'd like you to go now," she said.

I got up from the table, and thanked her again, but it seemed to me I'd already lost her attention. She was gazing into middle distance, remote from me. Was it the past or the future that had her attention? The husband who'd been lost to her, or the son she was going to find? I didn't have the courage to ask.

Very quietly, I made my exit, a little part of me hoping she'd call after me, tell me to take care of myself; but a greater part preferring to go unnoticed.

# III

## i

Rachel needed help to get out of the city. The death of Cadmus Geary—and the bizarre circumstances of that death—were headline news the following morning, and the journalists who'd appeared after Margie's murder were back in force, gathered around the entrance of her apartment building, photographing just about everyone who came and went. Determined to slip away quickly, without being quizzed by the police (what was she going to tell them anyway?) or worse still detained by Mitchell and Garrison, Rachel turned to Danny, who was happy to return a favor and assist in her escape. He went to her apartment, packed a suitcase for her, picked up some money, credit cards and the like, and met her at Kennedy Airport, where he bought her a ticket to Honolulu. By noon, she was off on her way back to Kaua'i.

As she and Danny parted, he said:

"You're not planning to come back are you?"

"Is it that obvious?"

"Something about the way you were looking at things as we drove. As if you thought you'd never see them again."

"Well, if I'm lucky I won't."

"Can I ask . . . ?"

"What's going on? I can't tell you, Danny. It's not that I don't trust you. It would just take too long to explain. And even if I had all the time in the world I'm not certain I could make sense of it all."

"Just tell me one thing: is it Garrison? Are you running away from that bastard. Because if you are—"

"No, I'm not running away from anything," Rachel said. "I'm going to go meet the man I love."

By a curious coincidence she'd been allocated the same seat in first class as she'd had on her first flight out to Kaua'i, so there was an odd moment of *déjà vu* as she accepted a glass of champagne and settled back. Only once it had passed did she allow herself the luxury of indulging her memories of the island. The conversations she'd had with Jimmy Hornbeck as they drove to Anahola, talking about mystery and Mammon; then the house, and the lawn and the beach, and Niolopua; later, the church on the bluff the day she'd been caught in the rainstorm; her first sighting of the sails of what she'd later know to be *The Samarkand*, and the fire on the beach, and finally Galilee's appearance at the house. It was just a few weeks since all this had taken place, but so much had happened to her since then—so many things she wanted to put out of her head forever—that it felt like a memory of a dream. She would only believe it all completely when she was back there, in the house. No, when she saw the sails of *The Samarkand*, that's when she'd believe it; when she saw the sails.

## ii

Out in the unforgiving waters of the South Pacific, the boat Rachel longed to see was a pitiful sight. It had been uncaptained for eleven days now, its sole occupant allowing it to take the brunt of whatever the waves and the wind brought along. Most of the equipment on deck, which in normal circumstances Galilee would have stowed or lashed down, had been washed away; the main mast was cracked, and the sails tattered. The wheelhouse was chaotic; and the scene below deck was even less pretty.

*The Samarkand* knew she was doomed. Galilee could hear the sound in her boards; the way they moaned and shuddered when she was struck on broadside by a wave. She'd never made noises quite like this before. Sometimes he thought he could almost hear her speaking to him; begging him to stir himself from his stupor and take charge of her again. But the last four days had seen such a vertiginous descent into frailty that he had no reserves of energy left. Even if he'd wanted to save himself and his vessel now, it was too late. He'd let go of his desire to live, and his body—which had survived so many excesses—quickly fell into a state of decay. He wasn't even visited by deliriums now, though he was still drinking two bottles of brandy a day. His mind was too exhausted to hallucinate; just as his limbs were too weary to bear him up. He lay on the pitching deck, staring up at the sky, and waited.

Toward dusk, he thought the moment had come; the moment of his death that is. He'd been watching the sun drop into the ocean, the clouds it burned through as molten as the water below, when *The Samarkand* suddenly fell absolutely silent around him. The boards gave up their complaints, the tattered canvas was stilled.

He raised his head off the deck a few inches. The sun was still falling, but its descent had slowed. So had his pulse, as though his body—knowing it was close to the end—had become covetous of every sensation, and was turning down its flame so that it could burn just a little longer. Just until the sun disappeared; until the sky lost the last of its color; until he could see the Southern Cross, bright above.

What a mess his life had been, what an ungainly performance. There was scarcely a part of it he didn't have reason to regret. Nor did he have any excuses for what he'd done. He'd come into the world with all the blessings of divinity, and he was leaving it empty-handed, every gift he'd been given wasted. Worse than wasted: turned to cruel purposes. He'd hurt so many people (few of them true innocents, of course, but that was no comfort now); he'd allowed himself to be reduced to a common assassin, in service of mere ambition. Human ambition; Geary ambition; the hunger to own stockyards and railroads and plains and forests, to govern people and states; to be little kings.

They'd almost all of them passed away, of course, and many times he'd been there to witness their last moments: their tears, their pathetic prayers, their desperate hope for redemption. Why hadn't he learned the lessons of those departures? Why hadn't he changed his life, seeing what death was like? Defied his masters, and dared go home to look for forgiveness?

Why, in the end, was he alone, and frightened, when he'd been born into certainties the faiths of the world would have given all their dogmas and their holy books to taste?

There was only one face he could bring to mind without agony; only one soul he hadn't betrayed. He said her name as the disc of the sun touched the sea, and the last phase of its descent, and his, began.

"Rachel," he murmured. "Wherever you are . . . I love you . . ."

Then he closed his eyes.

# IV

Garrison Geary stood in his grandfather's bedroom and surveyed the scene before him with a tic of exhilaration in his belly. It was hard to suppress his happiness, but he was doing his best. He'd made a brief, somber statement to the press, explaining that nobody yet knew the precise circumstances of Cadmus Geary's passing, but that it hadn't come as any great surprise to anyone. He'd then gone on to spend a frustrating hour with Loretta, in which he'd attempted to get her to tell him what had taken place in the house. There were plenty of rumors flying, he told her; the din of destruction had been audible a block away. Wouldn't it be better if she told him the truth, so that he could present the facts to the authorities and the press in a suitably doctored form, rather than their being reduced to speculation like everyone else? She couldn't help him, she said; she simply didn't remember. Whatever the nature of the cataclysm, it had driven all recollection out of her head. Maybe it would all come back, given time. But right now, he and the police and the press would have to invent their own answers to whatever questions they had.

All this was fabrication, of course; she didn't even attempt to make it sound particularly plausible. She just mouthed the words, and defied him to contradict her. He chose not to challenge her, at least for now. He could afford to wait. Lord knows, he'd learned patience, playing the supplicant grandchild while Cadmus held on to his life and his power. Now the old bastard was gone, and Loretta was almost out of cards to play. The only thing she had left in her hand was the truth; and being the cool player she was she'd hold on to it for as long as she could. It would avail her nothing. Events would move quickly now, and before she knew it the card she held would be valueless. He'd pluck it out of her fingers, for curiosity's sake, when she was out of the game completely.

Mitchell came to join him in the bedroom.

"I had a few words with Jocelyn," he said. "She always liked me."

"So?"

"So I got her to tell me what happened." Mitchell wandered over to the old man's bed, milking the moment for all it was worth. "For one thing, Rachel was here."

"So what?" Garrison said, with a shrug. "She's an irrelevance, Mitchell. For God's sake start treating her like one."

"Don't you think it's suspicious that she was here?"

"Suspicious how?"

"Maybe she's working with whoever did this. Maybe she let them in. Then helped them get away."

Garrison stared at his brother with that waxwork look of his. "Whoever did this," he said slowly, "does not need help from your fucking wife, Mitchell. Do you understand me?"

"*Don't talk to me that way,*" Mitchell said, jabbing his finger in his brother's direction. "I'm not an imbecile and neither's Rachel. She got hold of the journal, remember that."

Garrison ignored the remark.

"What else did Jocelyn tell you?" he said.

"Nothing."

"That's all you got out of her?"

"That's more than you got out of Loretta."

"Fuck Loretta."

"Has it ever occurred to you that we might be underestimating these people—"

"Let it go."

"No, you listen to me. They could be conspiring behind our backs."

"Let 'em. What the fuck can a couple of women do?"

"You don't know Rachel."

"Yes I do," Garrison said wearily. "I've seen her type over and over. She's nobody. Anything she has, you gave her, this family gave her. She's not worth *one minute* of our time." With this he turned his back on his brother, and walked away. He was almost at the door when very quietly Mitchell said:

"I can't get her out of my mind. I want to. I know what you say is right. But I can't stop thinking about her."

Garrison stopped and, after a moment, pivoted on his heel to face Mitchell again. "Oh," he said, very slowly. He regarded his brother with a new sympathy. "What do you want to hear?" he said. "Do you want me to tell you it's okay to get her back? If that's what you really want. Go get her."

"I don't know how," Mitchell said. His anger had drained away completely; suddenly he was Garrison's little brother, desperate for guidance. "I don't even know why I want her. I mean, you're right: She's a nobody. She's *nothing*. But when I think of her with that . . . animal . . ."

Garrison smiled, comforted. "Oh I see. It's Galilee."

"I don't want her near him. I don't even want her *thinking* about him."

"You can't stop her thinking." He paused for a moment, the smile still on his lips. "Well . . . you can, but you probably don't want to go that far."

"I've thought about it," Mitchell said. "Believe me. I've thought about it."

"That's how it starts," Garrison said. "You think about it and you think about it and one day the opportunity presents itself. And you do it." Mitchell stared at the littered carpet. Garrison stared at Mitchell. There was a long silence. Finally Garrison said: "Is that what you want?"

"I don't know."

"So think about it some more."

"Yes."

"Good."

"No. I mean: *yes, that's what I want.*" He was shaking. Still staring at the ground, and shaking. "I want to know nobody is ever going to have her but me. I married her; I made her into something." He looked up now, his eyes wet. "Didn't I? Didn't I make her into something?"

"You don't have to convince me, Mitch," Garrison said, oh-so-gently. "It's like I said: just a question of the right opportunity."

"I made her into something and she turned her fucking back on me as though I was nothing."

"You want to punish her for that. Of course. It's natural."

"What do I do?"

"Well for one thing, you find out where she is. Make nice to her."

"What the hell for?"

"So she doesn't suspect anything."

"Okay."

"And then we'll sit down after the old man's buried and we'll work out how to get this sorted out for you."

"I'd like that."

Garrison opened his arms. "Come here," he said. Mitchell went to him. Garrison hugged him tight. "I'm glad you told me," he said, his mouth against his brother's cheek. "I didn't realize how much you were hurting."

"She just treated me like shit."

Garrison patted his back. "It's okay," he said. "I understand. It's okay. We've got a long way to go, you and me. And I want you happy."

"I know you do."

"So whatever it takes to make it better, that's what we'll do. You've got my word on that, okay? Whatever it takes."

# V

Later, Garrison went to see a lady whose company he hadn't kept in several weeks: his lovely and ever-accommodating Melodie. It was thoroughly relaxing to keep such quiet company after the stresses of the day. He watched her lying there for fully half an hour, touching her chilly feet now and again; her thighs, her belly; slipping his fingers into her pussy. Lord, she was good at her job. Not once did she flinch, even when he rolled her over and roughly fucked her ass.

When he'd shot his load into her he didn't leave, as he would normally have done. He went into the narrow lime-green bathroom and washed his dick and his reddened neck, then returned to sit and look at her for a while longer. In rolling her over he'd crushed the flowers around her body, and their perfume seemed to quicken all his senses. Her skin looked almost luminous to him, the brandy he sipped contained nuances of flavor he could not remember tasting before; even the glass was silky against his fingertips.

What was happening to him? It was as though there was some kind of transformation about to take place; as though the Garrison he'd been—the dogged, nose-to-the-grindstone Garrison whose presence had never truly inspired anybody, least of all himself—was about to be sloughed off like a dead skin, and something else show itself: something brighter, stronger, stranger.

It was surely no coincidence that this other self was only coming out of hiding now that Cadmus was dead. The old regime was finished. Its rules, its hypocrisies, its limitations were a thing of the past. It was time for something new to make itself known; to impress its visions upon the world. And that something was moving in him—deep, deep in him—tantalizing his senses with the bliss that would come when it made itself known.

Yes, of course a corner of him was afraid of the prospect. Any transfiguration was a kind of death; a passing away of what had been in order
to make room for what was to come. But he wouldn't be losing anything
he'd much cared for. The man known as Garrison Geary had been a
construct; he'd learned by example—much of it Cadmus's—how to
present a bland, civil face to people so as to distract their attention from
his real motives. Naively enough, he'd assumed those motives were
identical to those of his mentor: the advancement of the family, the
accrual of wealth and power and influence.

Now he knew better; and what more perfect place to come to that
realization than here, where he'd showed a truer face than he'd ever
shown his family? Shown it, but been unseen, because its only witness
had never opened her eyes.

Perhaps it was time. He set down his brandy glass, got up off the
chair, and went over to the bed. The woman remained as still as stone.
He reached across her body, hooked his hands beneath her, and rolled
her over onto her back. She rolled most convincingly. He went down on
his haunches, and lay his hand, palm down, on her stomach.

"The game's over . . ." he said.

She didn't move. He lifted his hand off her belly and laid it against
her breast.

"I can feel your heart," he said. "You're good at what you do, but I
can always feel your heart." He leaned close to her. "Open your eyes."
He tweaked her nipple. "No more playing dead. I'm resurrecting you."

A tiny frown nicked her brow.

"You've been wonderful," he went on, "really. Very convincing.
But I don't want to play any more."

She opened her eyes.

"Brown," he said. "Your eyes are brown. I always thought they'd be
blue."

"You're done with me?" the woman said. Her voice was slightly
slurred. Perhaps she played the corpse so well because she was in a
drugged state.

"I'll be done with you when I tell you I'm done with you," Garrison
said, "not before."

"You said you didn't want to play any more."

"Not that game," he said. "Another."

"What?"

"I haven't decided yet."

"I'm not letting you mess with me—"

Garrison laughed, so hard and loud the whore gaped. Then he reached out and took hold of her breast. "I can do what the fuck I like to you. I'm paying for your company. And you're very expensive."

She visibly brightened at the mention of her commercial value. "What do you want?" she said, looking down at his hand, the fingers of which were digging deep into her breast.

"Look at me."

"What?"

"Just look at me. At my eyes. Look into my eyes."

She let out a halfhearted giggle, like a little girl playing a naughty game. The incongruity of it made Garrison smile. "What's your name?" he said. "Your real name."

"Melodie's my real name," she replied. "My mother says it's because I was singing to myself even before I was baptized."

"Your mother's still alive?"

"Oh sure. She moved to Kentucky. I'm going to move there too, as soon as I get enough money. I want to get out of New York. I hate it."

With his newly sharpened sight Garrison seemed to be able to see right into her as she spoke. She was bruised to the marrow, poor bitch; whatever hopes she'd ever had for herself gone to hell.

"What would you do in Kentucky?" he said.

"Oh . . . I'd like to have a little hairdressing place. I'm good at fixing people's hair."

"Really?"

"But . . . I don't . . ." The words slid away.

"Listen to me," Garrison said, his hand going up to her face. "If you want something you have to have faith. And patience. Things come when you least expect them."

"That's what I used to think. But it's not true. It's a waste of time hoping for things."

Garrison suddenly stood up, his motion so abrupt Melodie flinched. He gave her reason: a blow across the face so hard she fell back onto the bed. A sob escaped her, but she didn't try to move out of his range.

"I shoulda known," she said. She raised her head off the bed. Tears of shock ran from the corners of her eyes, but she didn't otherwise seem concerned. She'd been struck before, many times. It had its price, like everything. "You leave marks, and it'll cost you," she said. She sat up again, presenting her face to him. "It'll cost you big time," she said.

"Then I'd better make sure I get my money's worth, hadn't I?" he said, and struck her again so hard spatters of blood hit the wall.

*              *              *

He got her to beg him to stop eventually, but it took time. She let him strike her over and over—mainly her face, but on occasion her breasts and thighs. Only when she was so sick from his assault that she fell, and found that she was too weak to get up again, did she tell him she'd had enough. He didn't listen, of course. The more he hurt her, the more he felt that bright, strange self rising up in him; and the more it rose the more he wanted to hurt her.

Only once did he pause, catching his reflection in the mirror, his face shiny with sweat and exhilaration. He'd never been a narcissist, unlike Mitchell; never enjoyed the sight of himself. But now he liked the way he looked, more than a little. There was a magnificence about him, no question. He began to beat the woman with renewed vigor, deaf to her protests, her sobs, her pathetic attempts at negotiation. She would do this, she would do that, if only he would leave her alone. He ignored her, and beat on, blow after blow after blow, driving her into that corner where she attempted to rise, and finding that she couldn't, began to panic.

She was afraid for her life, he saw; afraid that in his new state he would casually dispatch her. As soon as he saw that look, he stopped striking her, and without another word returned to the bathroom to piss and wash his hands. There had been nothing faintly arousing about what he'd just done. He suspected he was beyond arousal now (it was too human: a thing of the past). With his hands clean and his bladder emptied he went back into the bedroom.

"I need your full name," he said to the woman, who had made an attempt to crawl to the door (which he had locked anyway, pocketing the key).

The woman mumbled something he didn't comprehend. He pulled the chair out from the table, and sat down.

"Try again," he said. "It's very important." He reached into his jacket and pulled out his wallet and his checkbook. "I'm going to give you some money," he said. "Enough money for you to go to join your mother in Kentucky and buy yourself a little business, and start over."

Even in her confused and semiconscious state Melodie understood what she was being told. "This is a filthy, perverted city," Garrison went on, "and I want you to promise me that if I give you this money—" he was writing the check now "—let's say a million dollars—that you will never come back. Never. Your full name."

The woman had begun to sob quietly. "Melodie Lara Hubbard," she said.

"I'm not paying you this for what I just did to you," Garrison said as he wrote, "I did that because I wanted to, not because you were offering me a service. And I'm not paying you to stop you going to some supermarket gossip rag. I couldn't give a fuck who you tell. Do you understand? I couldn't care less. I'm giving you this because I want you to have some faith." He signed the check, then took a card from his wallet and scrawled a short sentence on the back of it. "You take this to my lawyer, Cecil Curry, tomorrow, and he'll make sure the funds get transferred." He got up from the table and put the check and the card on the bed, among the crushed flowers. Melodie squinted at the row of noughts Garrison had set down. Yes, there were six, preceded by a dollar sign and a one.

"I'll leave you to clean up then," Garrison said, fishing the key from his pocket. "Be clever with what you've been given. People like me don't come along very often." He inserted the key, turned it, and opened the door. "In fact, they never come along twice. So you count yourself lucky." He smiled at her. "And you name one of your kids after me, huh? The one you love the most."

# VI

Garrison didn't sleep for most of the rest of the night. He went back to the apartment in the Trump Tower, and took a long ice-cold shower, which left him feeling pleasantly tender. Then he sat in the big armchair where he'd sat talking with Mitchell about Margie's death. He'd felt inviolate that night, but the feeling was nothing beside the sense of power that suffused him now.

He sat through the rest of the night, thinking what his next move should be. Plainly he had first to make good on his promise to Mitchell, which prospect pleased him. The Pallenberg woman posed no threat to him whatsoever, but if she was such a thorn in his brother's side, then it was better for all concerned that she be summarily dealt with, as Margie had been dealt with. Once that was done he'd have Mitchell's full attention, and they could begin their real work. He didn't doubt that whatever the nature of the other self he'd discovered rising in him, it was also in Mitchell. Dormant, but there to be awoken, and called out into glory. What a revelation they'd make together!

At dawn, with a pleasant weariness finally coming over him, he retired to bed. He slept for no more than two hours, and dreamed a species of dream his head had never before entertained.

He dreamed he was floating through a great forest. The canopy was thick overhead, but not so thick that sunlight didn't pierce it, falling warm on his upturned face. Somebody was taking to him—a woman, her voice light and happy. He couldn't understand anything that she was saying, but he knew there was love in the words, and that the love was for him.

He wanted to see her face; he wanted to know what kind of beauty he had accompanying him. But though he tried to make his dream-gaze obey his will, and shift in the direction of her voice, he was not sufficiently master of himself. All he could do was float, and listen, and feel the sweetness in the woman's voice bathing him, caressing him.

Finally, his motion slowed, and then stopped. For a moment he hovered there, and then he was slowly lowered to the ground. Only now, when he was laid in grass that was tall enough to partially obscure his view, did he realize that he had not been traveling independently, as he'd thought, but been carried: that in this dream he was a babe in arms. And now, majestically, the woman who'd carried him walked into view. Her back was turned to him, her focus fixed upon a house, a magnificent house, which was situated some distance from them.

He started to cry. He wanted the woman to come and pick him up again. But she just kept looking at the house, and though he couldn't see her face something about the way she stood, her arms hanging at her sides, convinced him that all the happiness he'd heard in her voice had deserted her, and that now she was consumed with yearning. She wanted to be there, in that splendid, white-pillared place, but she was forbidden.

And still he bawled, doing his best to get her to attend to him, his sobs echoing around the glade of moss-draped trees with such violence birds rose in panic from the branches and fled away. Finally, she gave up watching the house, and looked back at him.

It was his mother.

Why was he so astonished by that? Why did the sight of her face so startle him that the dream-scene fluttered and threatened to be extinguished? It was his mother; mothers were supposed to carry their babies in their arms, weren't they?

And yet he was shocked to see her; distressed even. It wasn't the fact that her face was tear-streaked and pale (that was his preferred state for a woman's face) it was the fact of her very presence here, where he sensed the uncanny. She belonged to a more mundane existence, whose minor enchantments could be bought and sold like any other commodity; not here, not here.

She went down on her knees beside him, as if she intended to pick him up. Tears fell from her eyes, and splashed on him. Then she said the only word in the entire dream he understood. She said:

"Goodbye."

Those syllables said—and without kissing him, without laying so much as a finger upon him—she stood up again, and walked away, leaving him there in the grass.

He started to cry again, his voice shrill and pathetic. But now his lips could form words—

"Don't leave me!" he sobbed. "Mama! Mama! Don't leave me!"

He woke to the din of his own voice, crying out in his sleep. He sat up in bed, his heart beating furiously. He waited for the inevitable retreat of the images that his mind had conjured up, but they didn't go. Even with his eyes wide open, feeding on a hundred concrete details of his bedroom, the sights he'd just seen and the feelings he'd felt insisted upon him.

Perhaps this was part of his transfiguration: his mind revisiting old anxieties so that they could be dealt with and sloughed off. It wasn't a particularly pleasant experience, but any change—especially one as powerful as that which had seized him—brought with it some measure of discomfort.

He got out of bed, and went to the window to open the drapes. As he did so—as his hand caught hold of the heavy fabric—he was suddenly seized by a sickening suspicion. He put on his robe, and went across the landing to his study, where he'd left Holt's journal. He'd begun reading it as soon as his brother had brought it to him, but events had overtaken his analysis, and he'd not returned to it. Now he began to search through its dog-eared pages, scanning the text. He passed over the passages about Bentonville, and the section dealing with Holt's return to his house; on through the portions dealing with the events in the East Battery, on through Holt and Nickelberry's departure from Charleston. The deserters were moving north, in Galilee's company, heading back to the Barbarossas' territory. There were four or five pages devoted to the precise methodology of entrance: several small diagrams that almost looked like brands, and paragraphs speaking of the mysteries of L'Enfant, which if unsolved would prove fatal to any who attempted to gain access to the Barbarossa residence. He lingered long enough on this passage to confirm that the solutions had indeed all been set down on the page, then he moved on to look for a description of the house itself.

And there, just a few pages from the end of the journal, he found the passage he was afraid he'd find.

*I have never seen such a house as was presented before us as we came between the trees,* Holt wrote, *nor felt so strongly the sense that we were walking in the presence of things unseen, forces that would have done us calamitous harm had we not been Samaritans carrying a prodigal back onto his native soil. That's two Biblical stories in one, but that's probably appropriate, for I believe that here, gathered in this place, were enough mysteries to be the subject of a dozen Testaments.*

*So the house. It was painted white, with a classical façade, such as you might see in many great plantation houses; but there rose above these familiar forms a dome of such beauty and magnitude, shining white in the sunlight—*

Garrison put the book down. He'd read all that he needed to read. The house in his dream was the same which Holt had written about: the Barbarossas' great mansion. He'd be going there soon enough. But did the dream mean that he'd already been there? If not, how had he imagined the house so well?

Mystery upon mystery. First the death of the old man, and all the destruction that had accompanied it. Then his transfiguration: the force he'd seen in the mirror, blazing back at him. Now this enigma: dreaming of his mother abandoning him on the grounds of the Barbarossa home.

He'd always been a man who trusted his intellect: in matters of money and in the management of human beings it didn't do to be too emotional. But a wise intellect knew its limitations. It didn't go where analytical power had no jurisdiction. It fell silent, and left the mind find other ways to comprehend whatever troubled it.

Here was such a border, where intellect retreated. To go on, into the place of sloughings and furies and abandonments that lay ahead, he would need to look to his instincts, and hope they were sharp enough to protect him.

Others had taken similar journeys and lived to tell the tale. One such traveler had written the very journal that sat there on Garrison's desk: the captain whose life and seed lay fatally close to the root of the Geary family tree.

Perhaps that same prospect lay ahead for him; perhaps he was on this journey so as to found a dynasty of his own. The idea had never occurred to him before, but why would it? He'd been sweating in service of the Gearys all his life; a sterile preoccupation at best. Now he was free both of his servitude and his skin. It was time to think things over from the beginning. To find wombs; to make children. And to take them—in his own arms if need be—and lay them down in the grass where he'd been lain, where they might see the pillars and the dome of the palace that the Barbarossas had dreamed into being, but which he would steal from them, by and by, to house his own sons and daughters.

# VII

This time, Rachel didn't come to the island as the pampered Mrs. Mitchell Geary. The deferential Jimmy Hornbeck wasn't there to meet her, eager to cater to her every whim. She rented a car at the airport, loaded in her bags, and with the help of a map she'd been given at the rental office drove to Anahola. The sky was overcast, the heavy, rain-bearing clouds that had previously masked the heights of Mount Waialeale now lowering over the entire island. It was still hot, however; humid, in fact. She decided against sealing the car windows and turning up the air-conditioning. She wanted to smell the air: the fragrance of the flowers, the sharpness of the sea. She wanted to be reminded of what it had felt like to be here before, not knowing what lay in wait for her.

It was impossible, of course, to return to a state of innocence, especially when its loss had brought with it such far-reaching consequences. But as she turned off the main road and wound her way down the rutted track that led to the house, she was surprised to discover how readily she could make believe the agonies of the recent past belonged to somebody else, and that she was coming here unburdened.

The trees and shrubs had swelled and thickened since her last visit, and had largely gone untrimmed. The vines had grown up over the eaves and were creeping across the roof; large rotted blossoms littered the front veranda, and the geckos that scurried there seemed less alarmed by her presence than previously, as though they had assumed possession of the place, and were not about to be intimidated by her trespass.

The front door was locked, which didn't surprise her. She walked around the back, remembering that the lock on the sliding door had been faulty, and hoping (not unreasonably given the general neglect) that it had not been mended.

She was right. The door slid open, and she stepped into the house. It smelled musty, though not unpleasantly so. And it was nicely cool after the oppressive heat of the air outside. She closed the door behind her, and went straight to the kitchen, where she filled a glass with cold water, and drank. Glass in hand she made a quick tour of the rooms to reacquaint herself with the place. She hadn't anticipated how much pleasure she'd take in simply being back here; that pleasure sharpened by the illicitness of her presence.

The big bed had been stripped after her departure and not remade. She went to the linen closet, found some fresh sheets and pillowcases and made it up again. She was sorely tempted just to lie down and sleep, but she resisted. Instead she had a shower, made herself some sweet, hot tea and went outside to smoke a cigarette and watch the last of the day's light. She had no sooner brushed the leaves off the antiquated furniture and sat down than the gloomy heavens unleashed a torrent. Geckos zigzagged for cover, a panicked hen was blown across the lawn like a feathered balloon. For some reason, the rain's percussion made her want to laugh; so laugh she did. Sat there on the veranda laughing like some crazy woman who'd lost her mind waiting for her lover, laughing, laughing while the rain beat down and obscured from sight the ocean that had failed to give him up.

# VIII

Galilee had not expected to ever wake again—at least not into this world—but wake he did.

His eyes, which were encrusted, opened painfully, and he raised his head to look at the water.

Somebody had called his name. It wasn't the first time he'd heard somebody speak to him in his solitude, of course; there'd been plenty of talkative delusions. But this was something different; this was a voice that made his heart shake itself like a wet animal, and roused him with its motion. He looked up. The sky was the color of heated iron.

*Sit up, child.*

Child? Who called him child? Only one woman in all the world.

*Sit up and attend to me.*

He opened his mouth to speak. The sound that emerged was pitiful. But she understood.

*Yes you can,* she told him.

Again, he complained. He was too weak, too close to death.

*I'm just as tired as you are, child,* his mother said, *and just as ready to die. Believe me. Perfectly ready. But if I take the trouble to come and search for you, the least you can do it sit up and look at me.*

There was no doubting the authenticity of this voice. Somehow, she was here. The woman who'd warmed him in the oven of her womb; who'd fed him off her body, and shaped his soul; the woman who'd raged against him for his folly, and told him—in what was surely the defining moment of his youth—that he was flawed beyond fixing; a thing that would only ever bring harm and hurt—that woman had found him, and he had no place to hide, except to throw himself into the sea. And who was to say she wouldn't follow him there, elemental that she was? She had no fear of death, whatever she might claim about her readiness.

*I don't come here on my own account,* she went on.

"Why are you here then?"

*Because I met your woman. Your Rachel.*

Now, finally, he raised his head. His mother, or rather her projection, stood at the stern of *The Samarkand.* Despite all her demands that he look at her, now that he had done so he found her own gaze averted. She was looking at the setting sun; at that molten sky. A day had passed, he vaguely thought, since he'd counted off the last moments of his life against the decaying light. He and the boat had survived another twenty-four hours.

"Where did you see her? She didn't come to—"

*L'Enfant? No, no. I saw her in New York.*

"You went to New York. Why?"

*To see Old Man Geary. He was dying, and I promised myself I'd be there when his last moments were upon him.*

"You went to kill him?"

Cesaria shook her head. *No. I simply went to bear witness to the passing of an enemy. Of course once I got there it was difficult not to cause a little trouble.*

"What did you do?"

Cesaria shook her head. *Nothing of consequence.*

"But he's dead?"

*Yes, he's dead.* She looked up, directly above her head. The first stars were appearing. *But I didn't come here to talk about him. I came for Rachel's sake.*

Galilee laughed; or did his best, given how dry his throat was.

*What's so funny?* Cesaria demanded.

Galilee reached for his brandy bottle, which had rolled into the gunnel, and drank from it. "The thought of you doing anything for any-body's sake but your own," he replied.

Cesaria ignored the barb. *This is shameful behavior,* she said. *Turning your back on a woman who feels something for you, the way Rachel does.*

"Since when have you given a damn what a human being felt?"

*Maybe I'm getting sentimental in my old age. You've found an extraordinary woman. And what do you do? You try to kill yourself. I despair of you.* Her voice dropped as she spoke these last words, and the boards of *The Samarkand* trembled at their timbre. *I truly despair of you.*

"So despair," Galilee replied. "I don't give a shit. Leave me alone and let me die." He waved her away as he spoke, his head sinking down so that his face was pressed to the boards of the deck. He was no longer looking at her, but he knew of course that she hadn't departed. He felt the emanations of her power coming against him, subtle and rhythmi-cal. Though she was just a vision here, she'd carried with her a measure of her physical authority.

"What are you waiting for?" he said to her, without raising his head.

*I don't exactly know,* she replied. *I suppose I keep hoping you'll remember who you are.*

"I know who I am . . ." he growled.

*THEN RAISE YOUR HEAD.* The boat shook from bow to stern when she uttered these words; fish in the deeps below convulsed. But Galilee was unimpressed; at least, he didn't obey the instruction. He stayed put, face down.

*You're a wretch,* she told him.

"No doubt," he murmured.

*A selfish, willful—*

"No doubt," he said again. "I'm the worst piece of shit that ever floated on the ocean. So now will you *please leave me the fuck alone?*"

The boat shook again when he spoke, though not as violently. There was a few moments of silence between them. Finally he glanced sideways at her. "You've got plenty of other children," Galilee said. "Why don't you torment them?"

*They don't mean what you mean to me,* Cesaria said. *You know that. Maddox is a half-breed, Luman's crazy, and the women . . .* She shook her head. *Well, they're not what I had in mind when I raised them.*

Galilee lifted his head a little. "Poor mother. What a disappoint-ment we are. You wanted perfection and look what you got." He raised himself up now, into a kneeling position. "Of course none of it's your fault is it? You're never to blame for anything."

*If I were guiltless I wouldn't be here,* she said. *I made my mistakes, especially with you. You were the first, so I spoiled you. I indulged you. I loved you too much.*

"You loved me *too much?*"

*Yes! Too much! I couldn't see what a monster you were.*

"Now I'm a monster?"

*I know what you've done all these years—*

"You don't know the half. I've got more innocent blood on my hands—"

*I don't care about that! It's the squandering that appalls me. The time you've wasted.*

"And what should I have been doing instead? Raising horses?"

*Don't bring your father into this. This has nothing to do—*

"It has everything to do with him." He reached out and caught hold of the toppled mast, hauling himself to his feet. "He's the one who really disappointed you. We're just getting the aftermath."

Now it was Cesaria who averted her eyes, staring off across the water.

"Did I touch a nerve?" Galilee said. Cesaria didn't reply. "I did, didn't I?"

*Whatever happened between your father and me is over and done with. Lord knows I loved him. And I worked to make him happy.*

"Well you failed."

She narrowed her eyes. He was certain another boat-shaking assault was on its way, but no: when she replied she did so softly, the sound of her voice almost drowned out by the slop of the waves against the hull.

*Yes I failed . . .* she said. *. . . . and I've paid for my failure with years of loneliness. Years when I might have expected my firstborn to be some comfort to me.*

"You drove me out, mother. You told me if I set foot in L'Enfant ever again you'd kill me."

*I never said that.*

"Oh yes you did. You ask Marietta."

*I don't trust her opinion on anything. She's as willful as you. I should have torn you both out of my womb with my own hands.*

"Oh Christ, mother, not the womb speech! I've heard it all before! You regret having me and I regret being born. So where does that leave us?"

*Where it always leaves us,* Cesaria said after a moment, *at each other's throats.* She sighed, and the sea shuddered. *I can see this is a waste of time. You're never going to understand. And maybe it's better this way. You've done enough damage for a hundred men—*

"I thought you didn't care about the blood I'd spilled?"

*It's not spilled blood I'm talking about. It's the broken hearts.* She paused, touching her fingers to her lips, stroking them. *She deserves someone who'll care for her. Stay with her. Right to the end. You don't have what it takes to do that. You're all talk. Just like your father.*

Galilee had no reply to this. Just as his earlier remark about "the aftermath" had struck a nerve, this little stab found its place. She saw what she'd done too; and made it her cue to depart.

*I'll leave you to your martyrdom,* she said, turning from him. Her image, which had appeared quite solid until now seemed to shake like a torn sail. In a few gusts it would be carried away.

"Wait," Galilee said.

Cesaria's image continued to flutter, but her eyes fixed upon her son like driven nails. The moment she looked away, he knew, she'd be gone. Only her scrutiny was keeping her here.

*What now?* she said.

"Even if I wanted to go back to her . . ."

*Yes?*

". . . I don't have the means. I destroyed everything on board."

*You didn't leave yourself so much as a raft?*

"I didn't plan to change my mind."

Cesaria raised her chin two or three inches, regarding him imperiously down her nose. *But now you have?*

Galilee couldn't stand the piercing stare any longer. He looked down at the deck. "I suppose . . . if I could . . ." he said quietly, "I'd like to see Rachel again . . ."

*She's waiting for you, not six hundred miles from here.*

"Six hundred?"

*On the island.*

"What's she doing there?"

*I sent her there. I told her I'd do my best to send you to her.*

"And how do you intend to do that?"

*I'm not certain I can. But I can try. If I fail, you'll drown. But you were ready for that anyway.* Galilee gave her a troubled glance. *You're not so ready now, are you?*

"No," he confessed. "I'm not so ready."

*You'd like to live.*

"Yes . . . I suppose I would . . ."

*But, Atva—*

This was the first time in the exchange she'd used the name he'd been baptized with; it made what followed ring like an edict.

*If I do this and you grow bored with her and desert her—*

"I won't."

*I'm saying: if you do, Atva, and I hear about it, I swear I'll find you and I'll drag you back to the shore where we baptized you and I will make it my business to drown you. Do you understand me?* She said none of this with great drama; it was simply a statement of fact.

"I understand you," he replied.

*I won't do this because I bear Rachel any great affection, I don't. She's a damn fool for feeling what she feels for you. But I will not have you leave another soul dying for love of you. I know how it feels, and I'd rather slaughter my own child than have him visit that hurt on one more heart.*

Galilee opened his arms, palms up, like a saint surrendering. "What do I need to do?" he said.

*Prepare yourself . . .* Cesaria replied.

"For what?"

*I'm calling up a storm,* she said, *which will drive what's left of this little boat of yours back toward the islands.*

"It won't survive a storm," Galilee warned her.

*Do you have a better idea?*

"No," he replied.

*Then shut up and be thankful you're getting another chance.*

"You don't know your own strength when you do these things, Mama."

*Well it's too late to stop it now,* Cesaria said. Even as she spoke Galilee felt the wind come with fresh power against his face. It was veering, south-southeast.

He looked up. The clouds above *The Samarkand* were in uncanny motion, as though they were being stirred up by an invisible hand. The newly shown stars were abruptly eclipsed.

He felt a distinct quickening in his own veins; plainly whatever force of divine will Cesaria was using to stir the elements had some casual government over his blood.

*The Samarkand* bucked, broadsided by a wave; he felt its timbers shudder beneath his feet. The short, wiry hairs at the nape of his neck prickled; his stomach began to churn. He knew what feeling this was, though it was many, many years since he'd last experienced it. He was afraid.

The irony of this was not lost on him. Half an hour ago he'd been resigned to his demise. Not simply resigned; happy at its imminence. But Cesaria had changed all that. She'd given him hope, damn her. Despite her bullying and her threats (or perhaps in some part because of them) he wanted a chance to be back with his Rachel, and the prospect of death, which had seemed so comforting just minutes before, now made him afraid.

Cesaria was not indifferent to his unease. She beckoned to him. *Come here*, she said. *Partake of me.*

"What?"

*You'll need all the strength you can get in the next few hours. Take some of mine.*

She made quite a sight there at the bow, her arm extended to him, her body—lit by the flickering lamps—gleaming against the murderous sky.

*Make it quick, Atva!* she said, her voice raised now against the wind, which was whipping up spume off the waves. *I can't stay here much longer.*

He didn't need another invitation. He stumbled towards her along the pitching deck, reaching out to catch hold of her hand.

She'd promised him strength, and strength he got, but in a fashion that made him wonder if his mother had not changed her mind and decided instead upon infanticide. His marrow seemed to catch fire—a profound and agonizing heat that rose from the core of his limbs and spread out, through sinew and nerve, to his skin. He didn't simply feel it, he saw it; at least his eyes reported a brightness in his flesh, blue and yellow, which spread out through his body from his stomach; coursing through his wasted limbs, and revivifying them with its passage. This was not the only sight he saw, however. The blaze climbed into his head, running around his skull like wine swilled in a cup, and as it brightened there he saw his mother in a different place: in her room in the house Jefferson had built for her, lying on her temple-door bed with her eyes closed. Zelim was at the foot of the bed—loyal Zelim, who'd hated Galilee with a fine, fierce hate—his shaved head bared as if in prayer or meditation. The windows were open, and moths had fluttered in. Not a few: thousands, tens of thousands. They were on the walls and on the bed, on Cesaria's clothes and hands and face. They were even on Zelim's pate, crawling around.

This domestic vision was short, supplanted in a couple of heartbeats by something entirely stranger. The moths grew more agitated, and the flickering darkness of their wings unsealed the scene from ceiling to floor. The only form that remained was that of Cesaria, who now, instead of lying on the bed, hung suspended in a limitless darkness.

Galilee experienced a sudden, piercing loneliness: whatever void this was—real or invented—he had no wish to be there.

"Mother . . ." he murmured.

The vision remained, his gaze hovering uncertainly above Cesaria's body as though at any moment it, and he, might lose their powers of suspension and fall away into the darkness.

He called to his mother again, this time by name. As he called to her, the form before him shimmered and the third and final vision appeared. The darkness didn't alter, but Cesaria did. The robes in which she was wrapped darkened, rotted, and fell away. She was not naked beneath; or at least his eyes had no chance to witness her in that state. She was molten, laval; her humanity, or the guise of that human-ity, flowing out of her into the void, trailing brightness as it went. He glimpsed her face as it melted into light; saw her eyes open and full of bliss; saw her burning heart fall like a star, brightening the abyss as it went.

The insufferable loneliness was burned away in the same ecstatic moment. The fear he'd felt hanging in this nowhere seemed suddenly laughable. How could he ever be alone in a place shared with so mirac-ulous a soul? Look, *she was light!* And the darkness was her foil, her other, her immaculate companion; they were lovers, she and it, partners in a marriage of absolutes.

And with that revelation, the vision went out of him, and he was back on the deck of *The Samarkand*.

Cesaria had gone. Whether in the process of tending him her strength had exhausted her, and she'd withdrawn her spirit to a place of rest—the bedroom where he'd seen her lying, perhaps—or she'd simply made her departure because she was done with him and had nothing more to say (which was perfectly in keeping with her nature) he didn't know. Nor did he have time to ponder the question. The storm she'd stirred up was upon him, in all its ferocity. The waves would have been high enough to match the mast, if he'd had a mast, and the wind enough to tatter his sails, if he'd had sails. As it was—and by his own choosing—he had nothing. Just his limbs, no longer wasted by denial, and his wits, and the creaking hull of his boat.

It would be enough. He threw back his head, filled with a fierce exhilaration, and yelled up at the roiling clouds.

"RACHEL! WAIT FOR ME!"

Then he fell down on his knees and prayed to his father in heaven to deliver him safely from the storm his mother had made.

# IX

## i

There was a great commotion in the house a few hours ago; laughter, for once. L'Enfant hasn't heard a lot of laughter in the last few decades. I got up from my desk and went to see what the cause was, and encountered Marietta—holding the hand of a woman in jeans and a T-shirt—ambling down the hallway toward my study. The laughter I'd heard were still on their faces.

"Eddie!" she said brightly. "We were just coming to say hello."

"This must be Alice," I said.

"Yes," she replied, beaming with pride.

She had reason. The girl, for all her simple garb, was slim and pretty; small-boned and small-breasted. Unlike Marietta, who enjoys painting herself up with kohl and lip gloss, Alice wore not a scrap of makeup. Her eyelashes were blonde, like her hair, and her face, which was milky white, dusted with pale, pale freckles. The impression such coloring sometimes lends is insipid, but such was not the case with this woman. There was a ferocity in her gray eyes, which made her, I suspected, a perfect foil for Marietta. This was not a woman who was going to take orders from anybody. She might look like buttermilk, but she most likely had an iron soul. When she took my hand to shake it, I had further proof. Her grip was viselike.

"Eddie's the writer in the family," Marietta said proudly.

"I like the sound of that," I said, extricating the hand that did the writing before my fingers were crushed.

"What do you write?" Alice asked.

"I'm writing a history of the Barbarossa family."

"And now you'll be in it," Marietta said.

"I will?"

"Of course," Marietta said. Then to me: "She'll be in the book, won't she?"

"I guess so," I responded. "If you really intend to bring her into the family."

"Oh we're going to marry," Alice said, laying her head fondly on Marietta's shoulders. "I ain't lettin' this one out of my sight. Not ever."

"I'm going to take her upstairs," Marietta said. "I want to introduce her to Mama."

"I don't think that's a good idea right now," I told her. "She's been traveling a lot, and she's exhausted."

"It don't matter, honey," Alice said to Marietta. "I'm goin' to be here all the time soon enough."

"So you two are going to live here at L'Enfant?"

"Sure are," Marietta said, her hand going up to her beloved's face. She stroked Alice's smooth cheek with the outer edge of her forefinger. Alice was in bliss. She closed her eyes languidly, snuggling her face deeper into the curve of Marietta's neck. "I told you, Eddie," Marietta said. "I'm in this for keeps. She's the one . . . no question."

I couldn't help hearing an echo of Galilee's conversation with Cesaria on the deck of *The Samarkand*; how he'd promised that Rachel would be the idol of his heart hereafter; that there would be no other. Was it just a coincidence, or was there some pattern in this? Just as the war begins, and the future of our family is in doubt, two of its members (both notably promiscuous in their time) put their wild ways behind them and declare that they have found their soulmates.

Anyway, the conversation with Marietta and Alice meandered on for a little while, pleasantly enough, before Marietta announced that she was taking Alice outside to look at the stables. Did I want to come? she asked me. I declined. I was tempted to ask if Marietta thought a visit to the stables was wise, but I kept my opinion to myself. If Alice was indeed going to be a resident here, then she was going to have to know about the history of the house—and the souls who've lived and died here—sooner or later. A visit to the stables would be bound to elicit questions: why was the place so magnificent and yet deserted? Why was there a tomb in their midst? But perhaps that was Marietta's purpose. She might reasonably judge by Alice's response to the atmosphere of palpable dread which clings about the stables how ready her girlfriend is for the darkest of our secrets. If she seems untroubled by the place, which well she might, then perhaps Marietta would sit her down for a couple of days and tell her everything. If on the other hand Alice seemed fearful, Marietta might decide to dole the information out in easy portions, so as not to drive her away. We'll see.

The point is they departed to go walk about, and I went back to my study to begin the chapter which will follow this, dealing with the arrangements for the funeral of Cadmus Geary, but the words refused to flow. Something was distracting me from the business at hand. I set down the pen, sat back in my chair and tried to work out what the problem was. I didn't have to puzzle over it for very long. I was fretting about Marietta and Alice. I looked at the clock. It was by now almost an hour since they'd left the house to visit the stables. Should they not be back by now? Perhaps they were, and I hadn't heard them. I decided to go and find out; plainly I wasn't going to get a stroke of work done until I laid my unease to rest.

## ii

It was by now the middle of the evening, and I found Dwight in the kitchen, sitting watching the little black-and-white television. Had he seen Marietta lately? I asked him. He told me no; then—obviously seeing my anxiety—asked if there was a problem. I explained that she had a guest and that the two of them had gone to visit the stables. He's a smart man; he didn't need any further information. He rose, picked up his jacket and said:

"You want me to go and see that everything's okay?"

"They may have come back already," I said. He went to check. Two minutes later he was back, having picked up a flashlight, reporting that there was no sign of Marietta about the house. She and Alice were presumably still outside.

We set off; and we needed the flashlight. The night was dismal; the air cold and clammy.

"This is probably a complete waste of time," I said to Dwight as we made our way toward the dense screen of magnolia trees and azalea bushes which conceals the stables from the house. I very much hoped this was the case, but nothing about the journey so far had given me any reason for optimism. The unease which had got me up from my desk in the first place had escalated. My breathing was quick and jittery; I was ready for the worst, though I couldn't imagine what the worst could be.

"Are you armed?" I asked Dwight.

"I always carry a gun," he replied. "What about you?"

I brought out the Griswold and Gunnison revolver. He trained the flashlight upon it.

"Lordie," he said. "That's an antique. Is it safe to use?"

"Luman told me it was fine."

"I hope to God he knows what he's talking about."

I could see the expression on Dwight's face from the light splashing up from our pale hands, and it was plain he was just as unnerved by the atmosphere as I was. I felt more than a little guilty. I'd instigated this adventure, after all.

"Why don't you give me the flashlight?" I said. "I'll lead on."

He made no objection to this. I took the flashlight off him, trained it on the bushes ahead, and we began our trek afresh.

We didn't have much farther to go. Ten yards on and we cleared the shrubbery: the stables were fifty yards from us, their pale stone visible even in the murk. As I've pointed out before, the place is remarkable; an elegant building of some two thousand square feet, which might be mistaken for a classical temple, with its modest pillows and portico (which is decorated, though we couldn't see it in the gloom, with a frieze of riders and wild horses). In its glory days it was an airy, sunlit place, filled with the happy din of animals. Now, as we came into its shadow, it seemed like one immense tomb.

We halted in front of it. I splashed the flashlight beam over the enormous doors, which were open. The light barely penetrated beyond the threshold.

"Marietta?" I said. (I wanted to shout, but I was a little afraid of what forces I might disturb if I did so.)

There was no answer at first; I called again, thinking if she didn't answer on the third summons we could reasonably assume she wasn't there, and retreat. But I got my answer. There was the sound of somebody moving inside the temple, followed by a bleary *who is it?* Reassured by the sound of Marietta's voice, I stepped over the threshold.

Even after all these years, the stables still smelled of their tremendous occupants: the ripe scent of horse sweat and horseflesh and horse dung. There had been such life here; such energies contained in stamping vessels of muscle and mane.

I could see Marietta now. She was coming toward me, buttoning up her vest as she approached. There was no doubting what she and Alice had been up to here. Her face was flushed; her mouth seemed swelled with kissing.

"Where's Alice?" I asked her.

"Asleep," she said. "She's exhausted, poor baby. What are you doing here?"

I was a little embarrassed now; I'm certain Marietta knew I had indulged my voyeuristic instincts where she was concerned, and probably suspected I was here doing the same thing. I didn't protest my innocence; I simply said: "You're both okay?"

"Fine," Marietta said, plainly puzzled. "Who's out there with you?"

"Dwight," came the reply from the darkness behind me.

"Hey, what's up?" Marietta called back to him.

"Nothin' much," Dwight said.

"I'm sorry we disturbed you," I said.

"No problem," Marietta replied. "It's time we were going back to the house anyhow . . ."

As she spoke, my gaze moved past her into the darkness. Despite the ease of the exchanges going on, there was still something troubling me; drawing my eye into the murk.

"What is it, Eddie?" Marietta said.

I shook my head. "I don't know. Maybe just memories."

"Go on in if you want to," she said, stepping aside. "Alice is quite decent—" I stepped past her "—you'll be disappointed to hear." I threw back an irritated glance, then ventured into the stables, leaving Marietta and Dwight behind me. My sense that there was a presence here was growing apace. I let the beam of the flashlight rove back and forth: over the marble floor, with its gullies and drains; across the stalls, with their intricately inlaid doors; up to the shallow vaults of the ceiling. Nothing moved. I couldn't even find Alice. I advanced cautiously, resisting the urge to glance back at Marietta and Dwight for the comfort of it.

The place where we'd laid the body of Nicodemus, along with all the belongings he'd wanted buried with him (his jade phalli; the white gold mask and codpiece he'd worn in his ecstasies; the mandolin he'd played like an angel)—was in the center of the stables, perhaps twenty yards from where I now stood. The marble floor had been lifted there, and not replaced after the burial. Mushrooms had grown from that dirt, in supernatural profusion. I could see their pale heads in the gloom; hundreds of them. More phalli, of course. His last joke.

A motion off to my right; I halted, and looked round. It was Marietta's lady love, rising from the spot where she'd been sleeping.

"What's going on?" she said. "Why's it so cold, honey?"

I hadn't noticed until now, but she was right: my breath was visible before me.

"It's not Marietta, it's Maddox," I told her.

"What are you doin' here?"

"It's okay," I said. "I just came to—"

I didn't finish the sentence. What halted me was a sound from the darkness beyond my father's grave. A clattering on the marble floor.

"Oh my Lord . . ." Alice said.

Emerging from the shadow, its hooves making a din this place had not heard for almost a century and a half, was a horse. Nor was it any horse. It was Dumuzzi. Even at this distance, even in this gloom, I knew him. There had never been an animal so splendid, nor so certain of his splendor. The way he pranced as he came, striking sparks off the marble, which flashes lit his gleaming anatomy, and made his eyes blaze. Whatever wounds had been visited upon the animal by Cesaria—and though I wasn't conscious to witness her slaughter, I'm certain she reserved her greatest cruelties for Dumuzzi, the ringleader—all of them had been healed. He was perfection again.

Somehow, he had been revivified, lifted up out of the pit into which his body had been dispatched, and returned to glorious life.

I had no doubt who had performed this handiwork. Just as it had been the hand of Cesaria Yaos which had slaughtered Dumuzzi so it had been the hand of her husband, my father, who had resurrected him again. Nothing was more certain.

Never in my life was I seized with such a boundless supply of contrary feelings as at that moment. Dumuzzi's living presence before me—indisputable, irresistible—was proof of a greater presence in this melancholy place. Nicodemus was here: at least some portion of him, piercing the veil between this world and the kingdom to come. What was I to feel about that? Fear? Yes, in some measure; the primal fear that the living inevitably feel when the spirits of the dead return. Awe? Absolutely; I'd never had more certain proof of my father's divinity than I did at that moment. Gratitude? Yes, that too. For all the trembling in my belly, and in my legs, I was thankful that my instincts had brought me here: that I was able to witness this omen of Nicodemus's return.

I glanced back toward Alice, intending to tell her to retreat, but Marietta had come to join her, and wrapped her arms around her. Alice was looking at Dumuzzi, but Marietta was looking at me. There were tears in her eyes.

Dumuzzi, meanwhile, had pranced to the edge of my father's grave, and now, suddenly, advanced upon it, hooves high, and proceeded to stamp on the earth which covered Nicodemus's corpse. The mushrooms were pounded to pulp, pieces flying off in all directions.

After perhaps half a minute, he grew calmer, at last simply standing in the mess of earth and pulped mushrooms, his head a little turned so that he could watch us.

"Dumuzzi?" I said.

At the sound of his name he snorted.

"You know this animal?" Marietta said.

"He was father's favorite."

"Where the hell did he come from?"

"Back from the dead."

"He's so beautiful," Alice murmured, her voice filled with wonder. It seemed she hadn't heard the exchange between Marietta and myself, she was so engrossed in the sight before us. Marietta took hold of her arm.

"Alice," she said firmly. "We have to go. *Now.*"

She started to pull Alice back toward the door. But as she did so, Dumuzzi rose up again, higher than he had before, and loosing a sound that struck the eardrums so hard we all gasped, charged in our direction. The sight of his sudden approach—mane flying, hooves high—glued me to the spot. This was the last sight I'd seen before I'd fallen beneath him and his comrades all those years ago: the memory made my limbs stupid. If it hadn't been for Dwight catching hold of me and dragging me out of the way history might well have repeated itself. I don't believe Dumuzzi meant any harm this time—as he most assuredly had on the first occasion—he was simply making for the door by the most direct route. But nor do I doubt that he would have knocked me down and broken my bones if I'd remained in his path.

I didn't see him leave the building; I was too busy being hauled out of his path. By the time I'd picked myself up again, he was gone. I heard the sound of his hooves as he pounded away; then silence, broken only by the breathing of four exhilarated people.

"I think we should get back to the house," Marietta said. "That's about as much excitement as I can take for one night."

How things have changed! Didn't I write once that the prospect of being around if Nicodemus were to show himself was so terrifying I'd rather be dead? Now, with the evidence for his presence indisputable, I'm perversely excited. This family has been riven for too long; it's time we were together again. There are wounds to be healed, peace to be made, questions to be answered.

I want to know, for instance, what Chiyojo said to my father just before she died. Something passed between them, I know. The last sight I saw before I lost consciousness was Nicodemus—horribly wounded himself, of course—leaning close to my wife, listening to her final words. What did she tell him? That she loved him? That she would wait for him? I've wondered about that so many times over the years. Now, perhaps, I might be able to get an answer from the only man who knows the truth.

And the other question I want to ask? Well, it's perhaps less easily answered. I want Nicodemus to tell me what he had in mind when he created me. Was I an accident? A casual by-product of his lust? Or did he knowingly create a half-breed—a union of divine father and mortal

mother—because there was some function that such an unhappy creature was uniquely equipped to serve?

   If I could have an answer to that question would I not be the happiest man alive? That's what makes the prospect of Nicodemus's return
more inspiring than fearful. The chance to stand before the man who
caused my soul to be made and ask that most ancient of questions:
*Father, father, what was I born for?*

   Loretta had begun an informal list of guests for Cadmus's funeral a
   year before, jotting down names in the back of her diary when they
occurred to her. There was a certain morbidity to this, she realized, but
she'd always been a practical creature. The list would be useful, sooner
or later, and there was no harm in being prepared for the event when it
came, even if he lived to be a hundred and five.

   Of course the events of the night he'd died had shocked her. But
she'd always known in her heart that the truth about the Barbarossas, if
she ever discovered it, would astonish her; and so it had. Not that she
imagined she'd learned everything that there was to know that night. All
she'd witnessed was a tiny piece of a puzzle which she suspected she
would never entirely understand. Perhaps it was better that way. The
same New England pragmatism which allowed her to start a funeral list
before the death of her spouse, and to plan for her own empowerment,
also made her brittle in matters that defied easy categorization. The life
of the spirit was one matter, and the life of the flesh another entirely.
When the two became muddied—when the invisible aspired to solidity,
and the drama of the soul was played out before her eyes—she was
deeply discomfited. It did not reassure her one jot that there were such
forces as she'd witnessed at the mansion operating in the world. She
took no metaphysical comfort from the fact. But a fact it was, and that
very same pragmatism kept her from lying to herself. She'd seen what
she'd seen, and in the fullness of time she'd have to deal with it. In the
meanwhile, she'd make her list.


Mitchell came to see her in the late afternoon. He wanted to know
whether she'd seen or heard from Rachel.

"Not since she left the house after Cadmus passed away," Loretta said.

"She hasn't called you?"

"No."

"You're absolutely sure? Maybe Jocelyn took a message and forgot to give it to you."

"Do I gather from this that she's gone missing?"

"Have you got any cigarettes?"

"No. Mitchell—will you stop pacing for a moment and answer the question."

"*Yes*, she's gone missing. I need to talk to her. I haven't . . . finished . . . with her."

"Well. This may be hard to hear, but perhaps she's finished with you. Forget about her. You've got other things to be occupying your time right now. We've got a lot of press to deal with; a lot of rumors—"

"To hell with that! I don't care what people think. I've spent all my life trying to be Mr. Perfect. I'm over it. I just want my wife back! *Right now!*" He came to Loretta suddenly, and it was hard to believe the face he wore had ever smiled. "If you know where she is," he said, "you'd be better off telling me."

"Or what, Mitchell?"

"Just tell me."

"No, Mitchell. Finish the thought. If I know where she is and I don't tell you, *what?*" She stared hard at him as she spoke and he averted his eyes. "Don't go the same way your brother's gone, Mitchell. It's not the way to do things. You don't threaten people if they don't give you what you want. You persuade them. You get them on your side."

"So suppose I wanted to do that . . ." Mitchell said, softening his tone. "How would I get you on my side?"

"Well you could start by promising me you're going to go shower. Right now. You smell rank. And you look terrible."

"I'll do that," Mitchell said. "Is that all? You're right, I've been letting myself go. But right now it's hard for me to think about anything but her."

"If you find her, what then?" Loretta said. "She isn't going to want to start over, Mitch."

"I know that. I fucked up. It can't ever be the way it was. But . . . she's still my wife. I still have feelings for her. I want to know that she's okay. If she doesn't want to see me, I can deal with that."

"Are you sure?"

Mitchell put on a dazzling smile. "Sure I'm sure. I'm not saying it won't be difficult, but I can deal with it."

"Here's what we should do. You go upstairs and take a shower. Let me make a couple of telephone calls."

"Thank you."

"If you want to put on some clean clothes ask Jocelyn to fetch one of Cadmus's shirts for you. Maybe she can find a pair of pants that'll fit you too."

"Thank you."

"Stop saying thank you, Mitch. It makes me suspicious."


She poured herself a brandy when he'd gone. Then she sat by the fire and thought over what he'd said to her. She didn't believe for a moment the little performance he'd put on for her at the end: all that forced brightness was grotesque. But nor did she believe that he was a lost cause; that she couldn't, with some manipulation, win him to her side. She was going to lose Rachel, if she hadn't already. The woman was too obsessed with Galilee Barbarossa to be a reliable ally. If or when she found him, then they'd efficiently form a faction of their own. And if she failed to find him, or was rejected, she would be so crippled she'd be more of a burden than a help.

She needed somebody to work with her, and maybe—despite her doubts about his intelligence—Mitchell was the likeliest candidate. In truth, she didn't have much choice. Cecil had always been loyal, of course, but he'd change his allegiance if it was fiscally advantageous to him; and Garrison could make it so. The other members of the family—Richard and the rest—were too remote from the heart of things to be able to step into the breach at short notice. And she had no doubt that time was of the essence here. Her only advantage at present was her knowledge of Cadmus's private methodologies: how he'd computed and predicted, right up until a month before his death, the flow of his fortunes; where he'd planned to invest, and where he'd planned to sell; secrets and predictions he had kept from everyone, even Garrison, but which toward the end he'd shared with her. To that advantage she could perhaps now add Mitchell: if, and only if, she could deliver to him the woman with whom he was still so very plainly obsessed.

She felt only the tiniest twinge of guilt at this. Though she'd warmed to Rachel somewhat of late (there was certainly no denying her courage), the woman was no sophisticate, nor ever would be. She'd done well, for someone from such unpromising roots, but she'd never be the kind of presence Margie might have been under other circumstances: it simply wasn't in her blood. And when all the fine sentiments about democracy had been voiced, that's what it always came down to: the blood in the veins.

So she would sacrifice Rachel in a bid to gain Mitchell: it was a chance worth taking. And she knew exactly where to begin with her investigations. She called Jocelyn in, and told her to go and fetch her address book. Jocelyn returned five minutes later, apologizing that it had taken her so long. Though she was putting on a brave, loyal face, she was in a deeply distressed state; her hands had a constant tremor, and she looked as though she might burst into tears at the slightest provocation.

"Will there be anything more?" she asked Loretta as she handed over the book.

"Only Mitchell . . ." Loretta said.

"I've already found him a shirt," Jocelyn said, "and I was just going to look for some trousers. Then I thought I might go for a little walk, if you don't need me."

"No, no. Of course. Take your time."

Once she'd gone Loretta flipped through the book and found the number she needed. Then she called it.

Niolopua was there to answer.

# XI

Rachel woke with the dawn, the birds making fine music all around the house. It was surprisingly chilly once she was out from under the covers. She wrapped herself up in the faded quilt and walked, bleary-eyed, into the kitchen to put on the kettle for tea. Then she went out onto the veranda to watch the unveiling of the day. Prospects looked good. The rain clouds had moved off to the northeast, and the sky was clear, at least for the present. There were signs of a storm on the horizon, however, clouds that looked still darker than those that had brought yesterday's rain, and quite a mass of them too. She went back in, brewed her tea, sweetened it decadently, and returned to the veranda, where she sat for twenty minutes or so while the scene before her came to life. Several birds flew down onto the lawn, and pecked around for worms coaxed up by the dew; a piebald dog wandered up from the beach, and had advanced as far as the veranda steps before she realized he was blind, or nearly so. She called to him softly, and he came to her hand, staying to be muzzled for a little time then taking himself about his dog's business, sniffing his way.

When she had finished her tea she went back inside again, showered and got dressed. She would drive into Hanalei this morning, she'd decided, and buy herself some fresh food from the little market there; along with some cigarettes.

It was an easy and picturesque journey, which took her at one point across a narrow bridge which spanned a valley of Edenic perfection: a river meandering through lush green shrubbery, from the bouquets of which elegant palms rose and erupted.

Hanalei was quiet. She took her time making her purchases, and by the time she arrived back at Anahola, laden with bags of supplies, she found she had a visitor. Niolopua was sitting on the step, drinking a beer and smoking a cigarette. He got up and relieved her of her cargo, then followed her inside.

"How did you know I was here?" she asked him once the bags had been set down in the kitchen.

"I saw the lights on last night."

"Why didn't you come and say hello?"

"I wanted to get back and tell Mrs. Geary."

"I don't understand."

"Your mother-in-law."

"Loretta?"

"Yes. The old one, right? Loretta. She called me to find out whether you were here or not."

"When was this?"

"Last night."

"So, you came round to look for me?"

"Yes. And I saw the lights. So I called her back and I told her you'd got here safely." It was clear from the expression on Niolopua's face that he was aware there was something odd in all of this.

"What did she say to you?" Rachel asked him.

"Not much. She told me not to bother you. In fact, she said not even to tell you I'd seen you here."

"So why *are* you telling me?"

He looked profoundly uncomfortable. "I don't know. I guess I wanted you to hear what the other Mrs. Geary had said."

"I'm not Mrs. Geary anymore, Niolopua. Please, just call me Rachel."

He made a nervous smile. "Right," he said. "Rachel."

"Thank you for being so honest."

"She didn't know you'd come, did she?"

"No, she didn't."

"Shit. I'm sorry. I should have talked to you first. I didn't think."

"You weren't to know," Rachel said. "You did what you thought was best." He looked thoroughly irritated with himself, despite her words. "Do you want to stay and have something to eat?"

"I'd like to, but should go do some work on my house before the storm." He glanced out of the window toward the beach. "I've only got a few hours before *that* comes in." He pointed to the dark blisters of cloud along the horizon. "It blew up out of nowhere." He kept staring out at the clouds as he talked. "And it's coming this way."

"Well it's nice to know you're on my side, Niolopua. I don't have a lot of friends right now."

He tore his gaze from the clouds and looked at her. "I'm sorry I screwed up. If I'd known you wanted to be here on your own—"

"I'm not here to get a tan," Rachel said. "I'm here because . . ." now it was she who glanced seaward ". . . because I have reason to think he may be coming back."

"Who told you that?"

"It's a long story, and I'm not sure I know how to tell it right now. I need to get some things sorted out in my head first."

"What about Loretta?"

"What about her?"

"Does she know why you're here?"

"It wouldn't be hard for her to guess."

"You know if you want to you could move up into the hills with me for a few days. Then if she sends someone looking for you—"

"I don't want to leave this house," Rachel said. "This is where Galilee expects to find me. And this is where I'm going to be waiting."

# XII

## i

According to the literature on the subject—which is sparse—the raising of storms is at best an uncertain craft. These things have a life of their own; they swell unpredictably, feeding off their own power, like dictators. They veer, they devour, they transform. Though they're subject to behavioral rules based on sound science, there are so many variables in the mix that any computation is at best tentative. The storm is a law unto itself; nobody, not even a power of Cesaria's prescience, may control or predict it once it's in motion.

All of which is to explain how it came about that the disturbance she'd created, stirring the air into life as she had, grew into the tempest that it did.

An hour after the departure from the deck of *The Samarkand* the boat was in dire trouble. The hull, which had resolutely endured some of the worst seas in the world—the Cape of Good Hope, the icy waters of the Arctic—finally cracked, and the vessel began to take on water. Galilee hand-bailed as fast as he was able, having incapacitated the pumps when he'd decided on suicide, but quickly realized he was fighting a losing battle. The question was not whether *The Samarkand* was doomed or not, but rather which of the death-sentences would fall first? Would it be smashed to pieces by the fury of the seas, or spring so many leaks that it sank?

And yet, even as the storm undid the vessel—board by board, nail by nail—it carried him closer to the islands. Sometimes the boat ascended a steep wave from the summit of which he thought he glimpsed land. But in the tumult it was impossible to be sure.

Then, quite suddenly, the winds dropped, and the rain they'd brought mellowed to a drizzle. There was a brief respite—perhaps ten minutes—when *The Samarkand* ceased to roll quite so violently, and Galilee was able to survey the extent of the damage to the vessel. The news was not good. There were three large cracks on the starboard side, and another two on the port; the ruins of the mast, along with the shreds of sails, had been washed overboard but were still attached to the boat by a gnarled umbilical of rope and tackle, which gave the vessel a permanent list.

Nor, of course, had the storm blown itself out. Galilee had experienced this kind of hiatus before: a little window of calm, as though the tempest was gathering its strength for one final cataclysmic assault.

So it proved. After a short time the wind began to rise again, and the ocean to churn and spasm, pushing the boat up ever steeper inches of furious water then dropping it into ever deeper chasms. Resolute as *The Samarkand* had been, it couldn't survive such treatment for long. It began to shudder as though wracked by death tremors, then all at once came asunder. Galilee heard a terrible splintering sound below, as the boards capitulated to the pressure, and the cabin housing cracked and split as great pillows of foamy white water erupted and summarily swept it away.

The water didn't come to take Galilee until the very last. He didn't let it. He clung to the side of the boat while it came undone around him, watching with a kind of wonder the power of the element he'd sailed so carelessly for so long. How it labored, coming back wave upon wave to break what it had already broken, and break it again, the boards becoming tinder, the tinder becoming splinters, and all finally sucked away into the deep.

Only when there were no more such wonders to witness did he finally abandon his vestigial portion of the vessel, and commend himself to the water. He was instantly swept away from the spot where *The Samarkand* had disappeared, his body no more significant to the waves than any other piece of flotsam. He didn't attempt to resist the current: it was a useless endeavor. The sea had him, and it would not give him up again unless it chose to.

But as he went, his body remembered the first time he'd been carried this way: an infant in the grip of the tides of the Caspian Sea, borne away from the shore as he now hoped that he was being borne back to it.

## ii

On the island, preparations for the storm were being made everywhere, from the fanciest hotels to the shabbiest shack. The local meteorologists weren't warning of any great danger to life or property. This wasn't a hurricane, just some heavy weather their charts and satellite photographs had failed to predict—but nor was its proximity to be treated lightly. The islanders had been blindsided before; it was never wise to underestimate the potential vehemence of such conditions. Roofs could be taken off, houses demolished, trees stripped, roads flooded. Along the northeastern coast, where the storm was predicted to come ashore, preparations were made: livestock was herded under cover, children brought home from school early; loose windows were nailed closed, pieces of heavy timber hoisted up onto shack roofs to keep them from being unseated.

As the storm approached the island estimations of its scale grew more pessimistic. It was acting in a wholly uncharacteristic manner, the pundits observed: instead of steadily dissipating, as they had anticipated, the wind velocity continued to climb. Its first effects could be felt on shore by the early afternoon. Trees began to sway; there were speckles of rain in the gusts. Out at sea, pleasure boats that dallied overlong before heading for safe harbor were given a battering, their captains racing to outrun the roiling seas. Three failed. One was lost, overturned with its crew of two and seven passengers all presumed drowned; the other two returned within a breath of disaster, the smaller of them so badly pounded it sank in the harbor.

There was no question: this was turning into a very uncommon piece of weather.

# XIII

### i

Mitchell had not waited for a regular flight out of New York: as soon as Loretta informed him of Rachel's whereabouts he hired a private jet. He didn't call Garrison to tell him what he was doing until he was on his way to the airport, accurately sensing that his brother would not be happy with his decision.

"We said we'd deal with this little problem of yours," Garrison reminded him.

"I'm only going out there to get her to come back with me," Mitchell said.

"Wait until she comes back of her own volition. Wait until she crawls."

"And what if she doesn't?"

"She will. She's got divorce proceedings to finish up, for one thing. She knows she's not going to get a cent out of us unless she plays by the book."

"She doesn't care about the money."

"Don't be so dumb, Mitch!" Garrison suddenly yelled down the phone. "*Everybody* cares about the fucking money!" He took a moment to let his irritation subside, then he said: "Mitch, listen to me. There are other ways to deal with this. Nice, calm, calculated ways."

"I'm perfectly calm," Mitchell said. "And I'm not going to do anything stupid. I just don't want her there. Not with him."

"You don't even know—"

"Give it up, Garrison. I'm on my way and that's all there is to it. I'll call you when I arrive."

*           *           *

Getting to his destination proved more irksome than Mitchell had anticipated. His hired transport had no sooner taxied onto the runway in preparation for takeoff than the radar system servicing the airport ceased operation, grounding every flight and preventing all landings for the next hour and a half. There was nothing to be done but endure the delay. When the glitch in the system was finally fixed, there was of course a large number of circling aircraft which needed to be landed before anybody could take off, and even then progress was slow, with the bigger commercial aircraft being given precedence. By the time the jet was finally airborne, Mitchell had been sitting in his leather seat sipping whiskey and breathing stale air for almost three and a half hours, with a ten-hour flight ahead.

## ii

Garrison had a meeting that evening to finalize plans for the funeral. It was chaired by a fellow he'd never much liked, one Carl Linville, who had organized the momentous events in the family's collective life for thirty years, as his father had done before him. An effete man with a suspicious taste in pastel silk ties, Linville always seemed to know what the most tasteful choice would be under any given circumstance, which skill had always faintly disgusted Garrison. Now more than ever: the idea of what was tasteful and what was not—what flowers, what music, what prayers—seemed profoundly irrelevant. The old man was being put in the ground; that was all.

But he kept his views to himself, and let the ever voluble Linville opine late into the night. He had a sizable audience. Loretta, of course, but also Jocelyn and two of his own staff. There wasn't a detail to be left to chance, Linville insisted; the eyes of the world would be on the event and they all owed it to Cadmus that the funeral proceed with dignity and professionalism. So it went on, with Loretta chiming in now and again to comment on something Linville had said. The only surprising moment in the meeting (and the closest it came to drama) occurred when, in the midst of a discussion about the guest list, Loretta proffered a list of her own, informing Linville that there were two or three dozen names upon it that he would not know, but that had all to be invited.

"May I enquire as to who these people are?" Carl asked.

"If you must know," Loretta said, "several of them are mistresses of Cadmus's."

"I see," said Carl, looking as though he wished the question had never crossed his lips.

"He was a man who loved women," Loretta said with a little shrug. "Everybody knows that. And I'm sure many of them loved him. They have a right to say good-bye."

"This is all very . . . European," Carl remarked.

"And you don't think it's appropriate—"

"Frankly, no."

"—and I don't care," Loretta replied. "Invite them."

"And these others?" he said, a distant chill in his voice now.

"Some of them are business associates from way back. Don't look so nervous, Carl, none of them are going to come dressed as the Easter Bunny. They've all been to funerals before."

There was a little uncomfortable laughter, and the meeting moved on. But Garrison's attention remained with Loretta. She was different tonight, he thought. It wasn't just the black she was wearing, though that did accentuate the precision of her makeup. There was a glitter in her eye; and he didn't like it. What did she have to be so pleased about? It was only when Linville, toward the close of the meeting, mentioned Mitch's function at the funeral, and asked where he was, that Garrison realized why Loretta was looking so smug: she was the one who'd sent him to the island. She was up to her old tricks again, manipulating Mitch, sweetening him, getting him on her side. No wonder he'd sounded so certain of himself on the phone, when a few hours before he'd been a sobbing idiot. She'd given him a pep talk; probably persuaded him that if he did as she instructed she might still get the shopgirl back. And of course he'd fallen for it. She'd always been able to wrap him around her finger.

As the meeting broke up, Linville promising that by midmorning tomorrow he'd have a full itinerary for the funeral in everyone's hands, Loretta came over to Garrison and said:

"When the funeral's over, I'd like you to go down to the Washington house and see if there's anything you want to have for yourself before I put it up for auction."

"How kind of you," he replied.

"I know there's some pieces of furniture there that were brought over from Vienna by your mother."

"I don't have any sentimental attachments to that stuff," Garrison said.

"There's nothing wrong with a little sentiment now and again," Loretta replied.

"I haven't noticed much of it from you."

"I do my grieving in private."

"Well you'll have all the privacy you want when he's buried," Garrison remarked. "I'm surprised you're selling the Washington place. Where are you going to live?"

"I'm not planning to quietly fade away, if that's what you're hoping," Loretta replied. "I've got a lot of responsibilities."

"Don't worry about all that," Garrison said. "You deserve a rest."

"I'm not worried," Loretta said flatly. "In fact, I'm looking forward to getting a better handle on things. I let a lot of details slip in the last few months." Garrison gave her a tight little smile. "Goodnight, Garrison." She pecked him on the cheek. "You should get some sleep, by the way," she said as she departed. "You look worse than Mitchell did."


It was only when Garrison was back at the Tower, and sitting in the chair where he now preferred to sleep (his bed made him feel uneasy, for some reason) that he thought again of the Washington house, and of Loretta's suggestion that he look for some keepsake there. As he'd said, he'd had no great desire to have anything from the house, but if it and its contents were indeed to be auctioned off then he would have to find a day in his schedule to go down and walk around. He'd had happy times there, as a child: in the dog days of summer, playing under the sycamores at the back of the house, where the shadows were cool and blue; Christmases when the place had been warm and welcoming, and he'd felt, if only for a few hours, part of the family. Such feelings of belonging had never lasted very long; he'd always in the end felt himself an outsider. He'd had years of analysis trying to untangle the reasons, but he'd never come close to understanding why. What an utter waste of time that had been: sitting hour after hour with those stale-headed men examining his navel fluff, looking for some clue as to why he felt like a stranger to himself. He knew now of course; now that he could see himself clearly. He didn't belong in that nest because he was another order of being.

It put him in a fine, dreamy mood reflecting on that; and he slipped into sleep sitting in the chair, and did not move until the first sirens of the new day woke him.

# XIV

i

The storm lasted well into the night, veering at the last moment and coming ashore along the southeast coast of the island. The chief town to suffer was Poi'pu, but a number of smaller communities in the area were also badly struck. There was some flooding, and a bridge outside Kalaheo was washed away; so were some small huts. By the time the wind carried the storm clouds off into the interior of the island—where they hung over the mountains for the rest of the night, slowly dissipating—there had been three more fatalities to add to those lives lost at sea.

Rachel didn't retire to bed until after one; she sat up listening to the roar of the wind-filled trees around the house, the palms bending so low that their fronds scraped the roof like long-nailed fingers. She had loved rainstorms as a child—they'd always seemed cleansing to her—and this storm was no exception. She liked its din, its violence, its showmanship. Even when the power failed, leaving her to sit by the light of a couple of candles, she was still quite happy. She had only one regret: that she didn't still have Holt's journal. What a perfect time and place this would have been to be reading the last section of the book. She would never see it again, she assumed: now it was in Mitchell or Garrison's hands, and the chance of her reclaiming it were slim. No matter. She'd find out from Galilee what had happened to Holt. Maybe he'd turn it into a story for her; hold her in his arms and tell her how Nickelberry and the captain and himself had fared together. There wouldn't be a happy conclusion, she guessed, but right now, listening to the downpour lashing against the windows, she didn't much care. It wasn't a night for happy endings: it was a night for the dark to have its way. Tomorrow, when the clouds had cleared and the sun was up, she'd be pleased to hear about miraculous rescues and prayers answered. But right now, in the roaring, pelting heart of the night, she wanted Galilee there to tell her how death had come to Captain Holt, and how the ghost of his child—yes! surely the child came back—had stood at the bottom of his deathbed and called him away, just as he'd called Holt's horse. Beckoned to his father from beyond the grave and escorted him into the hereafter.

The candle flickered a little; and she shuddered. She succeeded in spooking herself. She picked the candle up and ca through to the kitchen, setting it down beside the stove while refilled the kettle. There was a scuttling in the shadowy roof above her head, and she looked up to see a large gecko—the largest she'd seen either in or around the house—scuttling across the wooden slats of the ceiling. It seemed to sense her gaze, because it froze in its tracks and remained frozen until she looked away. Only then did she hear its scrab-blings resume. When she looked up again it had gone.

She went back to refilling the kettle, but in the time it had taken her to look up and see the gecko her desire for tea had disappeared. She put the kettle back on the stove, unfilled, and picking up the candle, she went to bed. She started to undress, but only got as far as taking off her sandals and jeans. Then she slipped under the covers, and fell asleep to the accompaniment of the rain.

## ii

She was woken by an impatient rapping on the bedroom door. Then a voice, calling to her: "Rachel? Are you in there?"

She sat up, the dream she'd woken from—something about Boston, and diamonds buried in the snow on Newbury Street—linger-ing for a moment. "Who is it?"

"It's Niolopua. Nobody answered the front door so I came in."

"Is there a problem?" She looked out of the window. It was day; the sky was a brilliant blue.

"You have to get up." Niolopua said, his voice urgent. "There's been a wreck. And I think maybe it's *his* boat."

She got up out of bed, and wandered across the room, still not fully comprehending what she was being told. There was Niolopua, spat-tered with red-brown mud. *The Samarkand,*" he said to her. "Galilee's boat. It's been washed up on the beach." She looked back toward the window. "Not here," Niolopua went on. "Down at the other end of the island. On the Napali coast."

"Are you sure it's his?"

Niolopua nodded. "As sure as I can be," he said.

Her heart was suddenly racing.

"And him? What about him?"

"There's no sign of him," Niolopua said. "At least there wasn't an hour ago, when I was down there."

"Let me just get some clothes on," she said. "And I'll be with you."

"Have you got any boots?" he said.

"No. Why?"

"Because it's hard to get to where we're going. You have to climb."

"I'll climb," she said, "boots or no boots."


The effects of the storm were to be seen everywhere. The highway south was still awash with bright orange runoff water, the heavier streams of which carried a freight of debris: branches, boards, drowned poultry, even a few small trees. Thankfully, there were very few other vehicles on the road at this early hour—it was still only seven—and Niolopua negotiated both streams and debris with confidence.

While he drove he offered Rachel a short explanation of where they were going. The Napali coast was the most dangerous and beautiful portion of the island, he explained. Here the cliffs rose out of the sea, the beaches and caves at their feet hard to reach except from the sea. Rachel was familiar with images of the coast from a brochure she'd glanced at on the short flight from Honolulu: one of the most popular tourist trips was a helicopter flight over the cliffs, and the narrow, lush valleys between the cliffs, which could only be reached by those foolhardy enough to trek down from the summits. There were rewards for those who dared such journeys—waterfalls of spectacular scale, and dense, virgin jungle—but the trip wasn't to be taken lightly. According to local legend some of the valleys were so hard to reach that until recent times small communities had existed there, completely isolated from the rest of the island.

"The beach we're going to can be reached along the foot of the cliffs," Niolopua told her. "It's maybe a mile from where the road stops."

"How did you find out about the wreck?"

"I was there during the storm. I don't know why I went. I just knew I had to be there." He glanced over at her. "I guess maybe he was calling for me."

Rachel put her hand up to her face; tears suddenly threatened. The thought of Galilee out in the dark water—

"Do you still hear him?" she said softly.

Niolopua shook his head, and his own tears ran freely. "But that doesn't mean anything," he said without much real conviction. "He knows the sea. Nobody knows it better. After all these years . . ."

"But if the boat sank—"

"Then we have to hope the tide brought him in."

Rachel remembered suddenly the tales of the shark lord, who sometimes guided shipwrecked sailors back to land, and sometimes, for his own unfathomable reasons, devoured them, and how Galilee had thrown their dinner into the water that night, as an offering, which she'd thought sweetly absurd at the time. Now she was grateful he'd done so. The world she'd been raised in had no room for shark gods, nor the efficacy of food thrown on water; but of late she'd come to understand how narrow that vision was. There were forces out there, beyond the limits of her wits or education, which could not be contained by simple commandments. Things that lived their own, wild life, unwitnessed, unbounded. Galilee knew them because he was in some measure of them.

That was both her present fear and her present hope. If he felt he belonged to that other life too much, might he not have decided to give himself over to it? To lose himself in that boundless place? If so, she would never find him again. He was gone where she could never go. If, on the other hand, his professions of love had been real—if he'd meant what he said when he talked of all that wasted time, when he should have been looking for her—perhaps the very powers that would claim him if he chose were presently her allies, and the offering he'd made, and the shark god for whom it was intended, had been part of the story that would return him to her.

## iii

The signs of storm damage got worse once they were the other side of Poi'pu; the road was nearly impassable in several places, where the force of the rainwater had washed down large rocks. And once they got onto the beach road, which hugged the base of the cliffs, matters became worse still. The road was little more than a winding, rutted track, which was now largely reduced to red mud. Even driving cautiously, Niolopua several times lost momentary control of the vehicle, as its slickened wheels lost their grip.

Out to the left of the track, on the other side of a ragged band of black rocks, was the shore: and here, more than any other place along their route, was the most eloquent evidence of the storm's power. The sand was strewn with debris from the margin of the rocks to the water's edge, and the waves themselves dyed with the run-off mud. It was like a scene from a dream—the sky cerulean, the sea scarlet, the bright sand littered with dark, sodden timbers. In other circumstances she might have thought it beautiful. But all she saw now was debris and blood-red water: it enchanted her not at all.

"Here's where the climbing starts," Niolopua announced.

She took her eyes from the shore and looked ahead. The muddy track ended a few yards from them, where the cliff face jutted out into the sea; a spit of rock against which the ruddied waves rushed and broke.

"The beach we're headed for is on the other side."

"I'm ready," Rachel said, and got out of the car.

The air, for all the din and motion of the sea, was curiously still close to the cliff. Almost clammy, in fact. After just a minute or so she was sweating, and once they began to clamber over the rocks her head started to throb. Niolopua had left his sandals at the car, and was climbing barefoot, making little concession to the fact that Rachel was a neophyte at this. Only when the route became particularly dangerous did he glance back at her, and once or twice offered a hand up when the rock became steep or slick. In order to avoid having to climb over boulders that were virtually unscalable he led them out onto the spit of rock. Once away from the cliff the air became fresher and every now and then an ambitious wave reached higher and farther than its fellows and broke close to them, throwing showers of icy water against their faces. She was soon soaked to the skin, her breasts so cold that her nipples hurt, her fingers numb. But they had sight of their destination now—a beach that would have looked paradisiacal if it had not been so littered: a long, wide curve of sand bounded on its landward side not by rocks but by a verdant valley scooped from the cliff. The storm had taken its toll here too: many of the trees had been practically stripped by the wind, and the fronds were cast everywhere. But the vegetation was too lush and too impenetrable for the storm to have done more than superficial damage; behind the stripped palms were banks of glistening green, speckled with bright blossom.

There was nobody on the beach, which stretched perhaps half a mile from the spit of rock before it was bounded by another spit, far larger than the one they'd clambered over. At this distance the second spit looked to be impassable: this beach was as far as anyone could go on foot.

Niolopua was already down on the sand, and pointing out to sea. Rachel followed his gaze. No more than a few hundred yards from the shore a whale was breaching, thrusting its almighty bulk skyward, then toppling like a vast black pillar, throwing fans of creamy water up around it. She watched for the creature to rise again, but it was apparently done with its game. She saw only a glistening back, a dorsal fin; then nothing. She looked back at the beach, suddenly heavy with sorrow. He wasn't here; it was obvious he wasn't here. If the wreckage Niolopua had seen was indeed that of *The Samarkand* then its captain was out there in the deep waters of the bay, where only the whales could find him.

She crouched down on the rock for a moment and told herself in no uncertain terms to stop feeling sorry for herself, and finish what she'd come here to do. It was no use avoiding the truth, however painful it was. If there was wreckage here she should see for herself. Then she'd know, wouldn't she? Once and for all, she'd know.

She took a deep breath, and stood up. Then she clambered down over the rocks and onto the sand.

# XV

Mitchell knew where the Kaua'i house was; Garrison and he had talked about it many times over the years. But talking about the place and being there were two very different things. He hadn't expected to feel so much the trespasser. As soon as he got out of the taxi his heart quickened and his palms became clammy. He waited outside the gate for a few moments until he had government of his feelings, and only then did he venture to the step, slide the wooden bolt aside, and push the gate open.

There was nothing here that could do him any harm, he reminded himself. Just a woman who needed to be saved from her own stupidity.

He called her name as he walked up the path to the front door. A couple of startled doves rose from their perches on the roof, but otherwise there was no sign of life. Once he got to the door he called again, but she either hadn't heard him or she was trying to make her escape. He opened the door and stepped into the house. It smelled of old bed linen and stale food; not a bright place, as he'd expected, but murky, its colors muted, all tending toward brown. So much for the feminine touch. Several generations of Geary wives had occupied this house on and off over a period of sixty or seventy years, but the place felt grimy and charmless.

That fact didn't make his heart beat any the less violently. This was the house of women; the secret place, where he'd been told as an adolescent no Geary male ever ventured. Of course he'd asked why, and his father had told him: one of the qualities which distinguished the Gearys from other families, he'd said, was a reverence for history. The past, he'd said, was not always easy to understand; but it had to be respected. Needless to say, this answer hadn't satisfied the young Mitchell. He hadn't wanted vague talk of reverence; he'd wanted a concrete reason for what seemed to him an absurdity. A house where only women were allowed to go? *Why?* Why did women deserve to have such a house (and on such an island)? They weren't the moneymakers, they weren't the power brokers. All they did, to judge by the daily rituals of his mother and her friends, was to spend what the men had earned. He simply didn't understand it.

And he still didn't. There had been times, of course, when he'd seen the strength of the Geary women at work, and it could be an impressive sight. But they were still parasites; their lush, easy lives impossible without the labors of their husbands. If he'd been hoping that entering and exploring this house would offer a clue to the mystery, he was disappointed. As he moved from room to room his anxiety diminished and finally disappeared. There were no mysteries here; nor answers to mysteries. It was just a house: a little shabby, a little stale; ripe to be gutted and refurnished; or simply demolished.

He went upstairs. The bedrooms were as unremarkable as the rooms below. Only once did he feel a return of the prickling unease he'd experienced outside, and that was when he walked into the largest of the bedrooms and saw the unmade bed. This was where his wife had slept last night, no doubt; which fact would not have moved him especially, had it not been for the way the bed was fashioned. There was something about the crude elaboration of the carvings, and the way age had dulled the brightness of the colors, that unsettled him. It was like some bizarre funeral casket. He couldn't imagine why anybody would ever want to sleep there, especially a neurotic bitch like Rachel. He lingered in the room only long enough to go through the contents of her suitcase and traveling bag. He found nothing of interest. With his rifling done, he left the room, closing the door behind him, and turning the key in the lock. It was only then, when he'd put the bedroom out of sight, that he dared bring to mind its other function. It was of course the bridal suite; the place where Galilee had come to visit his women. He stood in the gloomy hallway outside the room physically sickened at that thought, but unable to keep himself from imagining the scene. A woman, a Geary woman—Rachel, Deborah, Loretta, Kitty; all of them in one congealed form—lying naked on that morbid bed, while the lover—his hands as dark as the body he was touching was pale—played and fingered what was not his to pleasure; not under any law in any land: only here, in this godless, gloomy house, where a rule of possession held sway that Mitchell had no hope of comprehending. All that mattered to him right now was to get his wife in his hands and *shake* her. That's what he pictured when he saw them together again: his hands clamped around her arms; shaking her until her teeth rattled. Maybe he could still frighten some sense into her: make her ask him to forgive her, beg him to forgive her, and take her back. And maybe he would. It wasn't out of the question, if she was sincere, and made him feel appreciated. That was the heart of the problem: she'd never been thankful enough. After all, he'd changed her life out of all recognition; snatched out of her trivial existence and given her a taste of the high life. She owed him everything; *everything*. And what had she given him in return? Ingratitude, disloyalty, infidelity.

But he knew how to be magnanimous. His father had always said that when a man was blessed by circumstance, as Mitchell had been blessed, it was particularly incumbent upon that man to be generous in his dealings. To avoid envy and pettiness, which were the twin demons of those who had been denied a grander perspective; to err on the side of the angels.

It wasn't easy. He fell short of those ideals every day of his life. But here was a clear circumstance in which he could apply the principles he'd been taught; in which he could resist the call of envy and vengeance and prove to be better than his baser self.

All she had to do was let him shake her and shake her, until she begged to take him back.

# XVI

"This is part of the hull of *The Samarkand*," Niolopua said, pointing down at a length of battered timber in the sand. "There's another piece over there. And there's more in the surf."

Rachel walked down to the water's edge. There were indeed more lengths of painted wood tumbling back and forth in the waves. And further out, beyond the surf, one or two larger pieces bobbing about, including what might have been a portion of the mast.

"What makes you so sure it's *The Samarkand?*" she asked Niolopua, who'd come to join her at the water's edge.

He stared down at his feet, curling his toes into the stained sand. "It's just a feeling," he said. "But I trust it."

"Isn't it possible the wreckage was washed up here, and he came ashore somewhere else?"

"Of course," Niolopua said. "He could have swum along the coast. He's certainly strong enough."

"But you don't think he did."

Niolopua shrugged. "Your instincts are as good as mine where he's concerned. Better probably. You've been closer to him than I have."

She nodded, looking past him along the littered expanse of the shore. Perhaps her beloved was lying somewhere in the shallows, she thought, too exhausted to make it the last few yards without help. The thought made her stomach turn. He could be so close, so very close, and she not know it. Dying for want of a loving hand.

"I'm going to walk along the beach," she said to Niolopua. "See if there's any sign . . ."

"Would you like me to come with you?"

"No," she shivered. "No thanks."

Niolopua fished in the breast pocket of his shirt, and took out a hand-rolled cigarette and an old-fashioned steel lighter. "Do you want a hit of Mary Jane before you go." he said. "It's good stuff."

She nodded and watched as Niolopua lit a joint up, pulled on it, then passed it over to her. She drew a deep, fragrant lungful then passed it back to Niolopua.

"Take your time with your walk," he told her. "I'm not going anywhere."

She slowly exhaled the smoke, already feeling a pleasant but mild light-headedness, and headed off along the beach. Just a few yards on she found more wreckage—a piece of rope with the tackle still attached; what looked to be the wheelhouse window frame; the façade of an instrument panel, its gauges still intact. She went down on her haunches to examine this last item more closely. Perhaps there was some inscription on it: some sign that would confirm Niolopua's suspicions. Or better still, prove him wrong.

She lifted up the panel; seawater ran out, and a blue-backed crab, secreted in the moist sand beneath it, scuttled away. There was nothing on either side of the panel; not even a maker's name on the face of the gauges. Frustrated, she tossed it back onto the sand, and stood up again. As she did so, the drug in her system played a strange, dislocating trick. She suddenly became acutely aware of how her ears were each receiving radically different information. On her left side, the sea: the rhythmic draw and crash of the waves. On her right, audible only when the sea was momentarily hushed, the sounds of the green. A little breeze had come up since she and Niolopua had started their climb over the rocks, and it gently shook the canopy, moving leaf against leaf, blossom against blossom.

She glanced back toward Niolopua, who was sitting in the sand staring out at the water. This time, she didn't follow his gaze. She wasn't interested in what the sea had to show her. Instead she turned her eyes up the slope of the beach. A few yards from where she stood a small stream emerged from between the trees, carving a zigzag path across the sand on its way to the sea. She started to climb the beach to the place from which it appeared, studying the wall of vegetation as she did so. Another gust of wind moved the canopy, and stirred the colored blossoms so that they seemed to nod at her as she approached.

She slipped off her sandals at the edge of the stream, and stepped into it. The water was cold; far colder than the sea had been. She bent down and let the water play against her fingers for a moment, then— making a shallow cup of her hands—scooped some of it up and splashed it against her face, running her wetted fingers back through her hair. Icy water trickled down the back of her neck, and round and down between her breasts. She pressed her hand against her breastbone to stop the water going any further. She could feel her heart thumping under her hand. Why was it beating so fast? It wasn't just cold water and a hit of marijuana that was making her feel so strange: there was something else. She put her hand back into the stream, and this time she was certain she heard the double thump of her heart quickening. She followed the path of the water with her eyes, up into the green. Another gust of wind, and the fat wide leaves rose all at once, showing their pale undersides, and the deep shadows their brightness concealed. What was in those shadows? Something was calling to her; its message was in the water, flowing against her fingers and up through her nerves to her heart and head.

She stood up again and began to walk against the gentle flow of the stream, until she reached the edge of the vegetation. It smelled strong; the heavy fragrance of blossom mingled with the deeper, more solid smell of all things verdant: shoot, stalk, frond, leaf. She paused to see if there was an easier way in than wading through the stream, but she could see none. The foliage was thick in every direction: the easiest option was simply to keep to the flowing path.

The choice made, she stepped out of the sunlight and into the shadows. After no more than six or seven steps she began to feel clammy-cold; a prickly sweat broke out on her brow and upper lip. Her toes were already starting to numb in the icy water.

She looked back over her shoulder. Though the ocean was only fifty yards from where she stood, if that, it might have been another world. It was so bright and blue out there; and in here, so dark, so green.

She looked away, and resumed her trek. The stream no longer ran over sand now but over stones and rotted leaves. It was a slippery path, made more treacherous still by the fact that the ground was getting steeper as she progressed. She was soon obliged to climb, doing her best to strike out into the undergrowth when the route became too steep, using saplings and vines to haul herself up, then returning to the relatively unchoked stream once she'd reached a plateau and could proceed without the need of handholds.

She could no longer see the beach, or hear the waves breaking. She was surrounded on all sides by greenery and by the inhabitants of that greenery. Birds were noisy in the trees overhead; there were lizards running everywhere. But more extraordinary than either, and more numerous, were the spiders: orange-and-black-backed creatures the span of a baby's hand, they had spun their ambitious webs everywhere, and sat at the heart of their fiefdoms awaiting their rewards. Rachel did her best to avoid touching the webs, but there were so many it was impossible. More than once she walked straight into one and had to brush its owner off her face or shoulder, or shake it out of her hair.

The climb had by now begun to take its toll on her. Her hands, weary with their exertions, were beginning to lose their grip, and her legs were shaking with fatigue. The promising curiosity she'd felt on the beach below had faded. She might go on wandering like this for hours, she realized, and never find anything. As long as she followed the stream she had no fear of getting lost, of course, but the steeper the way became the more she ran the risk of falling.

She found a flat rock, in midstream, to perch on, and from there made an assessment of her situation. She hadn't brought her watch, but she estimated that she'd been climbing for perhaps twenty-five minutes. Long enough for Niolopua to be wondering where the hell she'd got to.

She stood up on the rock and yelled his name. It was impossible to judge how far the call went. Not far, she suspected. She imagined it snared in the mesh of vines, in the hearts of blossoms, in spiders' webs: snared and silenced.

She regretted making the sound now. For some absurd reason she'd become anxious. She looked around. Nothing had changed; there was only green, above and below. And at her feet the burbling stream.

"Time to go back," she told herself quietly, and gingerly took the first step down over the weed-slickened rocks. As she did so she felt a spasm of the same force she'd experienced on the beach passing through her from the soles of her feet.

Instinctively she looked back up along the course of the stream, studying the water as it cascaded toward her, looking for some clue. But there was nothing out of the ordinary here; at least nothing she could see. She looked again, narrowing her eyes the better to distinguish the forms before her. So many misleading combinations of sun and leaf-shadow—

Wait, now; what was that, ten or twelve yards from her, lying in the water? Something dark, sprawled in the stream.

She didn't dare hope too hard. She just started climbing again, though there were several large boulders before her, one of which had fallen like a great log, and could not be climbed around. She was obliged to scale it like a cliff face, her fingers desperately seeking little crevices to catch hold of, while a constant cascade of water rushed down upon her. When she finally clambered to the top she was gasping with cold, but the form she'd seen was more discernible now, and at the sight of it she let out such a shout of joy that the birds in the canopy overhead rose in clamorous panic.

It was him! No doubt of it. Her prayers were answered. He was here.

She called out to him, and climbed to where he lay, tearing at the vines that blocked her way. His face was a terrible color, like wetted ash, but his eyes were open and they saw her, they knew her.

"Oh my baby," she said, falling on her knees beside him, and gathering him to her. "My sweet, beautiful man." Though she was cold, he was far, far colder; colder even than the water in which he'd lain, passing the message of his presence down the stream.

"I knew you'd find me," he said softly, his head in her lap. "Cesaria . . . said you would."

"We have to get you down to the beach," she told him. He made the frailest of smiles, as though this were a sweet lunacy on her part. "Can you stand up?"

"There were dead men coming after me," he said, looking past her into the vegetation, as though some of them might still be lurking. "They followed me out of the sea. Men I'd killed—"

"You were delirious—"

"No, no," he insisted, shaking his head, "they were real. They were trying to pull me back into the sea."

"You swallowed seawater—"

"They were here!" he said.

"Okay," she said gently. "They were here. But they're gone now. Maybe I frightened them off."

"Yes," he said, with that same frail smile. "Maybe you did." He was looking at her with the gratitude of a child saved from a nightmare.

"I swear. They're not coming back. Whatever happened, sweetheart, they've gone and they're not coming back. You're safe."

"I am?"

She lifted his cold face up to hers and kissed him. "Oh yes," she said, certain of this as she'd been certain of little else in her life. "I'm not going to let anything hurt you or take you away from me ever again."

# XVII

### i

He was all but naked, his wasted body covered in wounds and bruises; but when she finally managed to get him up onto his feet—which took five minutes of maneuvering, then another five of her rubbing his legs to restore his circulation—his old command of himself, and the authority of his bearing, started to return. She offered to go down ahead of him and bring Niolopua up to help, but he wouldn't hear of it. They'd make it, he said; it would just take a little time.

They began the descent, tentatively at first, but gathering speed and confidence as they went.

Only once did they halt for any length of time, and it was not because the path became too steep or treacherous, it was because Galilee suddenly drew a sharp, frightened breath and said: "There!"

His eyes had darted off to their left, where the foliage was shaking, as though an animal had just fled away.

"What is it?" Rachel said.

"They're still here," he murmured, "the ones that came after me." He pointed to the swaying foliage. "That one was staring at me."

"I don't see him," she said.

"He's gone now . . . but they're not going to let me alone."

"We'll see about that," she said. "If they've got business with you then they've got business with me. And I'll make them take their sorry asses back where they came from." She spoke this more loudly than she strictly needed to, as though to inform any stalking spirits of her belligerence. Galilee seemed reassured.

"I don't see them anymore," he said.

They began their descent afresh. It was easier now; Galilee seemed to have taken strength from the exchange they'd had, but they were both exhausted by the time they reached the shore, and sat for a little while to gather their breath. There was no sign of Niolopua.

"I'm sure he wouldn't have driven away without me," Rachel said. "I hope he didn't go up in there . . ." She looked back toward the wall of vegetation. As the day crept on the green looked less and less welcoming; she didn't like the idea of going back up the slope in search of Niolopua.

Her fears were unfounded. They'd been sitting catching their breath on the beach perhaps five minutes when he appeared out of the trees further along the beach. As soon as he saw Rachel and Galilee he let out a whoop of happiness and relief, and began to run along the beach toward them, only slowing down when Galilee got to his feet to greet him. Niolopua slowed his approach, halting a few yards from them.

"Hello," he murmured. He bowed his head as he spoke; there was reverence in his every muscle.

"I'm pleased to see you." Galilee replied, with an odd formality of his own. "You thought you'd lost me, huh?"

Niolopua nodded. "We were afraid so," he said.

"I wouldn't leave you." Galilee replied, "Either of you." His gaze went from Niolopua's face to Rachel's, then back to his son.

"We've got a lot to talk about," he said, offering his hand to Niolopua.

Rachel thought he intended it to be shaken, but they had an odder, and in some ways more tender, ritual of greeting. Taking his father's hand Niolopua turned it palm up and kissed it, leaving his face buried in the lines and cushions of his father's immense hand until he had to lift it again to draw breath.

## ii

The hours stretched on, and Mitchell was alone in the house. He was far from comfortable there. Though he was exhausted, nothing would have persuaded him to lie down on any of the beds and sleep. He didn't want to know what kind of dreams came to men who slept here. Nor did he want to touch anything in the kitchen. He didn't like the idea of behaving domestically here; of letting the house lull him into believing it was innocent. It was not innocent. It was as guilty as the women who'd fornicated here.

But as the day passed, he got wearier and hungrier and ranker and fouler-tempered, and by two in the afternoon he was feeling so weak that he realized he was in serious danger of compromising the business he'd come here to do. He would go out and find something to eat, he decided; maybe some cigarettes, and some strong coffee. If his bitch-wife came back while he was away, no matter. He knew the layout of the house now; he could ambush her. And if she was still gone when he returned, then he'd be fortified, and ready to wait out the night if necessary until she came back.

It was a little after two-thirty when he left the premises, on foot. It was a relief to be out in the open air after the confines of the house; his gloomy spirits rose. He knew where he was heading: he'd spotted a small general store not more than half a mile back along the highway from the turnoff down to the house. Meanwhile, there were incidental pleasures along the way: a radiant smile from a local girl hanging out washing to dry; the scent of some flower in the hedgerow; the drone of a jet overhead, and his looking up, squinting against the brightness of the sky, to see it making a white chalk line on the blue.

It was a good day to be in love, and for some strange reason that's how he felt: like a man in love. Perhaps there was an end to his confusions in sight; perhaps, after all, when the shaking and the tears were over, he could settle down with Rachel and live the kind of lush life he knew he deserved. He wasn't a bad man; he hadn't done any harm to anybody. All that had happened of late—the death of Margie, the business with the journal, the chaos attending Cadmus's demise—none of it had been his responsibility. All he wanted—all he'd ever wanted—was to be seen and accepted as the prince he was. Once he'd achieved that modest aim there'd be a golden time again; he was certain of it. Garrison would finally shrug off his depressions, and put his energies back where they belonged, organizing the family business. Old dreams would be realized and new futures made. The past, and all its grimy secrets, would be footnotes in a book of victories.

All these happy thoughts went through his head as he walked, and by the time he reached the store the profound unease that had visited him in the house had been eclipsed. He went about the store whistling; picked up some soda, some doughnuts and two packs of cigarettes. Then he sat outside on the wall of the red-dirt parking lot and drank and ate and smoked and enjoyed the warmth of the sun. After an idling while it occurred to him that perhaps he should return to the house prepared to defend himself. So he went back into the store, and wandered around until he found a kitchen knife that was pretty much to his purpose. He bought it, and went back out to sit on the wall again and finish his little meal. The doughnuts and soda had given him a pleasant sugar buzz; there was quite a spring in his step when he finally started on back to the house.

# XVIII

Galilee's reserves of strength were all used up by the time Rachel and Niolopua got him to the car. He'd become a dead weight, barely able to lift his head for more than a few moments before it sank down again. On the journey back to Anahola he was clearly fighting hard to stay conscious. His eyes would flicker open for a time and he'd speak, then he'd lapse into long periods when he seemed nearly comatose. Even during the periods of consciousness he was barely lucid. Most of what he said was muttered fragments. Was he reliving the destruction of *The Samarkand*? It seemed perhaps he was, the way he'd suddenly shout, his face a grimace. At one point he began to make choking sounds, and for several agonizing seconds his body stiffened in Rachel's arms, every muscle hard as stone, as he desperately tried to draw breath. Then, just as suddenly as it had begun, the attack ceased and he relaxed in her embrace, his breathing quite regular.

After that, they got to the house without further incident. It was almost night by the time they arrived, and the house was in darkness. But Galilee seemed to know where they were, despite his delirium, because as they escorted him up the path, his weight borne almost entirely by Niolopua, he raised his head a few inches, and looked at the house from beneath his heavy lids.

"Are . . . they . . . there?" he said.

"Who?"

"The women," he replied.

"No, baby," Rachel said. "It's just us."

He made the tiniest of smiles, his eyes still fixed on the murky house. "Let me sleep," he said. "They'll come."

She didn't argue with him. If the thought of the Geary women returning here comforted him, then that was fine and dandy. And the prospect seemed to motivate him for those few yards. He made an agonizing effort to enter the house under his own steam, as though there was some point of honor here: that he, who had raised this house, did not want to be seen returning into it with his strength so reduced he could not step over the threshold without help. Once the attempt at autonomy had been made, however, and he was inside, he had no choice but to relinquish himself to Rachel and Niolopua's support. His head drooped again, his eyes closed.

Niolopua suggested they lay him down on the couch, but Rachel had no doubt where he would recover most quickly: upstairs, in the carved, painted bed. It was hard work getting him up the flight of stairs, but Niolopua put his back to the task, and after five minutes of ungainly struggle they got up to the top. From there it was easy enough: along the landing, through the door, and onto the bed.

Rachel tucked a pillow under Galilee's head, and pulled the sheets out from under his body to cover him. He was cold again, as he'd been when she'd first found him, but at least he didn't have the same ashen pallor. His lips were dry and cracked, so she fetched some balm, and applied it thickly. Then she tore away the remains of his vest, and examined the contusions on his torso. None of them were bleeding, so she fetched a washcloth and bathed them, one by one, just to be sure there wasn't any dirt in the wounds. Niolopua helped her roll Galilee over so that Rachel could bathe the cuts on his back. Then she unbuckled his belt and together they removed his pants. Now he lay completely naked on the white sheet, his massive languorous form sprawled on the bed as though he'd fallen there, out of heaven.

"Can I go now?" Niolopua said. He was plainly uncomfortable at being in the room with his father while he lay there in this state. "I'll just be downstairs. Call me if you need me," and off he went.

Rachel went back to the bathroom and washed out the cloths she'd used to clean the wounds. When she came back into the room she couldn't help but stop for a moment and drink in the sight before her. Oh, he was beautiful. Even in this profound repose, with the great mass of his muscle diminished by deprivation, there was still power in him. In those immense arms, which had so effortlessly wrapped her up; in the thick trunk of his neck; in that aristocratic head of his, with its high bones; his mouth, shiny with balm, his brow, deeply etched, his dense, black-and-salt beard. And down past the raked muscle of his belly, the other power here, presently dormant. Lying against his groin in its sleeping state, hooded and huge. She would have a child out of him, she thought, looking at him like this; whatever the risks to her own body, she would have something of him inside her, as proof of their union.

She set to washing the wounds on his thighs and shins; tenderly, tenderly. There was something about his utter passivity that was unbearably erotic. She was wet thinking of what it would be like to sit astride him; to run his flesh in the groove of her sex until it hardened, then take him up inside her. She tried to put the thought away, and concentrate on the business of tending to him, but her mind, and her gaze, returned again and again to his groin. Though he showed no sign of stirring from his sleep, she had the uncanny sense that his sex was aware of her. Wishful thinking, of course; and yet the suspicion persisted. Galilee was lost in dreams, but his cock was awake. Though she was working at his feet now, it stirred and thickened. The hood drew back a little as its head swelled with blood.

She put down the washcloth, and reached between her legs. It knew what she was up to. It saw with the glistening slit of its eye; it luxuriated in the heat off her blushing face. She touched herself, running her fingers over her labia then sliding them up into her body. Then she took the wetness and ran it, oh-so-lightly, up and down the length of his cock. It responded like a stroked animal, rising to press its black spine against her caress, luxuriating in her touch.

She watched his face, half-thinking this was all some subtle seduction he'd engineered, and that he would open his eyes at any moment and smile at her, invite her to climb onto him and be pleasured. But there was no sign of motion, other than that at his groin. His eyes didn't flicker, his mouth didn't twitch. He lay there, as he had from the beginning, in a state of complete quiescence. There was no sign of the man who'd made such intricate love to her on *The Samarkand*, nor of the thug who'd fucked her against the bathroom wall. Only this fat ticking stick, its length as knotted as a vine, its head all but naked now.

There was no resisting it. She undressed, and climbed up onto the bed, still glancing up at his face now and then to see if he stirred. But his breathing was even, slow and soft. He was deep in slumber.

Her own body ached with fatigue, and her hips complained at the effort of climbing astride him. But the pleasure of his body more than compensated for the discomfort. As for any dregs of doubt that she was somehow exploiting his passivity—taking this pleasure when it wasn't freely offered—they drained away the moment he was housed inside her. The chill in his body had gone; his hips, his groin, his cock, were feverishly hot, and knew their duty without prompting. She felt him shift beneath her; then he began to press his length up into her until he won a sob, and another, and another.

She was barely aware of the sounds she was making until they came back to her off the wall, gasps and cries, echoing around the little room. The bed creaked as the rolling motion of his hips escalated; she fell forward, her hands dropping against his chest, which was as burning hot as his groin. She reached down once to feel the place where their bodies met; it was awash with her moisture. The smell of her rose between their bodies. Not fragrant, not perfumed; nothing so delicate. A ripe smell, the smell of her ache and her loneliness pouring out of her and anointing its cure. She felt, as she had never felt in her life before, the primal nature of this act. No words of love, no promises of devotion were necessary: this was the act unadorned by sentiment; a piercing and a possession, her flesh embracing his, demanding its due. If somebody had asked her what her name was at that moment she wouldn't have remembered it; nor his. She—who'd fought so hard not to lose herself—had found her way through the labyrinth in order to come to this place of forgetfulness, where all the Rachels she'd been—the wildling and the sophisticate, the shopgirl and the society wife—were eclipsed.

As she moved on him, she seemed to feel the room around them trembling. The glass in the windows rattled; her sighs and sobs came back from the wall, manifold, as though her noise had woken other voices, their vibrations captive until now. It was not, she realized, simply her appetite for him that had made her so shameless; there was a profounder summons here.

She opened her eyes again, and through a fluttering veil of her pleasure looked down at her lover's face. There was no change in his expression, but his eyes had opened, just a crack, and he was looking up at her.

Then he spoke.

"*We're not alone . . .*" he said.

# XIX

Down on the beach, the surfers had come for a last ride before dark. Their shouts of exhilaration drifted up across the lawn to the veranda, where Niolopua sat smoking the last of his joint. The sight of his father, laid out naked on the bed, had unnerved him. Though he'd known Galilee a human lifetime, he had never seen him so vulnerable. And though he believed Rachel's intentions to his father were good, and her feelings sincere, there was part of him that wanted to take Galilee away from her, away from this wretched house, so full of sad remembrances; take him off to the hills where neither Rachel nor any other Geary woman could ever lay claim to him again. Love wasn't enough; not in this world. Love ended in betrayal or the grave, sooner or later; it was only a question of time.

But the pot put a little perspective on this dour thought. He should not be so pessimistic he told himself. Just because he'd never tasted joy didn't mean it wasn't there to be had. It was just so very difficult, to face the changes ahead. He'd lived a hard life—hidden away in his shack most of the time so that the islanders didn't notice that the years failed to take their toll on him the way they did on others. What little purpose he'd had for himself had been a function of his father's continuing visits to the island. He'd been the go-between, down through the decades; the one who'd sent the message out to his father to tell him that his services were required; the one who'd facilitated each liaison, and more than once stayed to comfort the woman upon his father's departure. He'd never questioned his function, nor his ability to fulfill it. There was a resilient bond between father and son; a bond of minds. It meant that all Niolopua had needed to do was sit in the quiet of his shack and speak his father's true name—Atva, Atva—and Galilee would hear him, wherever he was. No other instruction was needed. Niolopua had only ever called that name when a female member of the Geary had instructed him to do so. And at the summons, Galilee had always come, his skills as a mariner so flawless, and his knowledge of wind and current so profound, that he was sometimes there before the woman whom he'd been called to pleasure had even arrived. It was a dispiriting business, to Niolopua's eye; his glorious father, the great wanderer, brought to heel like a dog. But it was not his place to challenge the ritual. On the one occasion he'd begun to do so, Galilee had told him in no uncertain terms that the subject was not open for discussion. Niolopua had never dared raise the subject again. He wasn't fearful of his father's anger; Galilee had never shown him anything but love. It was the glimpse of his father's pain that had silenced him. He had resigned himself to never knowing why Galilee played the lover to these lonely women. It was simply a part of both their lives.

Would that change now? Did the fact that Galilee's wretchedness had finally come close to devouring him (how else was he to interpret the wretched condition they'd found his father in? Men like Galilee didn't come to such pitiful states by accident. It was self-willed); did that fact mark a radical change in the way their lives would be led henceforth? Was this Geary the last of the women he'd service? If so, what function would be left to Niolopua? None, presumably.

He drew the last draught from the joint, and tossed the remains down onto the lawn. Then he got up and looked back into the house. By now, the last of the day had gone, and the interior was gloomy. He watched for some sign of life, but could see none. Rachel was probably still upstairs, tending his father. Perhaps he should leave, he thought; they had no use for him now. He could come back tomorrow and say his good-byes. He lingered on the veranda for a few seconds longer, then turned about and started down the steps to the lawn.

He didn't see the man coming at him until the very last; there was no time to speak, nor even cry out. The knife was in him too quickly, thrust into his body with such force that all the breath was pushed out of him. He tried to draw another as he pulled away from his assailant, but only one of his lungs would perform the service; the other had been punctured, and was already filling with blood. Before he could raise his hand to ward off a second wound the man was closing on him, thrusting the knife into his stomach. He doubled up from the agony of it, but the man caught hold of his face, the heel of his hand beneath his chin, and pushed him off. He stumbled backward, his hands returning to his body in the desperate hope that he might staunch his wounds long enough to get help. He didn't have the strength to call out; all he could do was make for the house, though every step he took was an agony. From the corner of his eye he could see the knife-wielder three or four yards off from him, just watching now. Stumbling, Niolopua reached the veranda, and started up the steps. He threw himself forward when he reached the top, and for a heartbeat he dared hope that the noise he'd made would bring somebody down from above, and his attacker would turn tail and run. But even as he formed the thought the man came at him again, his form blurry to Niolopua's eye, like a smeared photograph.

Only at the last, when the man was upon him, and the knife buried in his body for the third and last time did he see the face of his killer closely. He knew the man. Not from personal contact, but from the covers of magazines. It was one of the sons of the house of Geary. There was no expression on his handsome features; he looked, in the two or three seconds that Niolopua saw him plainly, like a man in a trance: eyes glazed, mouth slightly open, face slack.

With a little grunt he pulled out the knife, and Niolopua fell forward onto the veranda, his outstretched hand a few inches shy of the door. The Geary didn't attempt to hurt him again; he had no need. He'd done his work. He simply waited on the steps, staring down at his victim. Niolopua had fallen face down, the blood that ran out of his mouth and nose soaking into the boards of the veranda. In the final seconds of his life he did not feel his spirit soaring up to some hurtless place, from which he could watch the scene below, but stayed there in his head, looking down at the grain of the wood on which he lay, as they soaked up the blood issuing from his nose and mouth. His body tried for breath one last, agonizing time, but it didn't have the strength. He shuddered, and made a little moan as the life went out of him; then he was gone.

Mitchell stood looking down at the body, mildly astonished at his own vehemence. He hadn't anticipated the flow of rage he'd feel when he had sight—or *thought* he had sight—of Galilee Barbarossa. He'd almost felt led by the hand which clasped the knife; but oh, the satisfaction he'd felt as the blade had sunk into the man's flesh; the sheer pleasure of the deed. Moments later, of course, he'd realized his error. But those few seconds when he thought he'd killed Galilee were so sweet, so blissful, that he was eager to have the bliss again, this time with the right man.

He went back down the stairs onto the lawn, and crouched down, running his knife into the earth to clean it. A minute ago it had been a cheap little kitchen knife, plucked off a shelf in a general store. But it was on its way to becoming something altogether extraordinary. Initiated now, it was ready for its legendary work. He stood up, and turned to face the house. It was completely quiet, but he had no doubt that the felons were inside; he'd heard his wife earlier, Rachel, sobbing like a whore.

Thinking of the sound she'd been making, he climbed the stairs, stepped over the body of whoever it was his knife had killed, and sliding the door aside, went into the house.

# XX

Galilee's period of lucidity hadn't lasted long. He'd come to the surface of his comatose state to say: *we're not alone*, and then he'd sunk back into it again, his eyes flickering closed. But what he'd said had been enough to make Rachel feel uneasy. *Who* was here? And why hadn't he been distressed at the fact of some other presence in the house? Reluctantly, she slipped him out of her, and climbed off the bed. The moment she was no longer touching him she felt cold; the room seemed almost icy, in fact. She went down on her knees to dig through her bag for something warm to wear. Shivering violently, she pulled out a sweater and put it on. As she did so the door creaked, and she looked up to see a shadow of a shadow, nothing more, flit across the room. It was so subtle a sight she wasn't even certain she'd seen it; and when she studied the place where it had gone, she could see nothing.

She got to her feet, deeply unnerved now. She looked at the bed. Galilee lay inert, his body still aroused, his eyes closed.

She went to the table beside the bed—still keeping her gaze on the place where the shadow had come and gone, and switched on the lamp. The light was strong, but it illuminated the corners where the shape she'd seen had moved. The room was empty. Whatever she'd seen had either gone, or been a figment of her exhausted and overstimulated senses. She went to the door, and opened it. The landing was dark, but there was enough light spilling from the bedroom to allow her to find her way to the top of the stairs. Despite the sweater, she was still cold. Maybe it was simply fatigue, she thought; she'd go and find Niolopua, tell him she needed to sleep, and then go and lie down beside Galilee. As for what he'd said; she would disregard it, there was nothing here.

As she formed the thought something brushed her shoulder, as though an invisible presence were passing her by, walking in the opposite direction. She turned, looking back down the landing to the open bedroom door. Again, nothing. Her body was simply so exhausted, it was playing tricks on her. She started down the stairs. There were no lights on below, but there was sufficient light from the moon to allow her to find the switch beside the kitchen door. As she did so she caught sight of a figure at the other end of the room, close to the front door. This time she didn't doubt her senses. This was no corner-of-the-eye illusion; it was a solid reality. While she watched he finished what he was doing—locking the front door—and then turned back and looked at her. She knew him, even in silhouette. Her heart began to slam against her ribs.

"What are you doing here?" she said.

"What does it look like?" he said. "I'm locking the door."

"I don't want you here."

"You can't be too careful, baby. There's bad people out there."

"Mitchell. I want you to leave."

He dropped the front door key into his breast pocket, and then sauntered toward her. He was wearing a white shirt beneath his jacket, and it was spattered with blood.

"What have you done?" she said.

He looked down at his shirt. "Oh this," he said, lightly. "It looks worse than it is." He glanced past her, up the stairs. "Is he up there?" She didn't answer. "Baby, I asked you a question. *Is the nigger up there?*" He'd stopped walking now; he was maybe three strides from the bottom of the stairs. "Did he try to hurt you, honey?"

"Mitchell . . ."

"Did he?"

"No. He didn't hurt me. He's never hurt me."

"Don't try and cover for him. I know how trash like that think. He gets his hands on someone like you, someone who doesn't know how they work, and he manipulates you. Gets in your head, tells you all kinds of lies. None of it's true, baby. None of it's true."

"Okay," she said calmly. "None of it's true."

"See? You knew. You knew." He tried on one of his smiles; one of those dazzlers he'd lavished on journalists and congressmen. It was designed to melt its recipient. But it simply looked grotesque; a death's-head smile. "That's what I told Loretta. I said: I can still save her, because she knows in her heart that she shouldn't be doing this. You know it's wrong. Don't you?" Rachel didn't reply, so he pressed the point. "*Don't you?*" he said.

She heard the rage, barely concealed, and decided it was best to nod along with what he was saying. His voice became softer. "You have to come home with me," he said. "This is a bad place, baby."

As he spoke his gaze flickered toward the stairs and a look of puzzlement crossed his face.

"All the things that have gone on here . . ." he said, his tone a little distracted now as he watched the stairs ". . . things *he* did . . . to innocent women . . ."

He slowly moved his hand to the pocket of his jacket and pulled out a knife. Its blade had dirt on it.

"It's got to be stopped . . ." he said.

His eyes came back in her direction. She saw the same lunacy she'd glimpsed when he'd come to the apartment and taken the journal; but it was no longer a hint; it was clear as day.

"Don't be afraid, baby," he said. "I know what I'm doing."

She dared a glance toward the stairs, afraid that Galilee had crawled out of bed and was there on the landing. But there was nobody. Just the dim light thrown from the bedroom. It was flickering a little, as though something was moving up there at the top of the stairs; its presence negligible, but its motion strong enough to make the light pulse. She was not entirely sure that Mitchell saw it. Nor did she want to ask him. She didn't want to unseat what was left of his delicate equilibrium. If he went upstairs now, he'd find a completely vulnerable victim. And to judge by the state of the knife, and the blood on his shirt, he'd already done some violence.

Only now did she think of Niolopua. Oh Lord, he'd hurt Niolopua. She was suddenly sure of it. That was why he had that crazed look in his eye; he'd already tasted the pleasure of bloodshed. If her face betrayed this realization, he didn't see it. His gaze was still directed to the top of the stairs.

"I want you to stay here," he told her.

"Why don't we just leave, she suggested. "The two of us."

"In a minute."

"If this is such a bad place—"

"I told you: in a minute. Just let me go upstairs first."

"Don't, Mitch."

His eyes flickered in her direction. "Don't *what?*" he said. She held her breath, aware that his hand was tightening around the knife. "Don't hurt him? Is that what you were going to say?" He moved toward her. She flinched. "You don't want me to hurt lover-boy, is that it?"

"Mitch. I was there when his mother came to the mansion. I saw what she was capable of doing."

"I'm not frightened of any fucking Barbarossa." He cocked his head. "You see, that's the problem—"

As he spoke he jabbed the knife in Rachel's direction, pricking the air between them to make his point.

"—nobody's ever stood up to these people." He was suddenly all reason. "We just gave up our fucking women to that nigger up there, like he owned them. Well he doesn't own *my wife*. You understand me, baby? I'm not going to let him take you away from me."

His empty hand reached out toward her, and he stroked her face.

"Poor baby," he said. "I'm not blaming you. He fucked with your head. You didn't have any choice. But it's going to be okay now. I'm going to deal with it. That's what husbands are supposed to do. They're supposed to protect their wives. I haven't been very good at that. I haven't been a very good husband. I know that now, and I'm sorry. Honey, I'm sorry."

He leaned toward her, and like a nervous schoolboy gave her a peck of a kiss.

"It's going to be okay," he said again. "I'm going to do what I have to do, and then we're going to walk out of here. And we're going to start over." His fingers continued to graze her cheek. "Because honey, I love you. I always have and I always will. And I can't bear to be separated from you." His voice was small; almost pitiful. "I can't bear it, baby. It makes me crazy, not to have you. You understand me?"

She nodded. Somewhere at the back of her mind, behind the fear she felt—for Galilee, for herself—there was a little place in her where she'd kept enshrined the last remnants of what she'd once felt for her husband. Perhaps it hadn't been love; but it had been a beautiful dream, nonetheless. And hearing him speak now, even in this crazed state, she remembered it fondly. How he'd made her feel, in the first months of their knowing one another; his sweetness, his gentility. Gone now, of course, every scrap. There was only the curdled remains of the man he'd been.

Oh Lord, it made her sad. And it seemed he saw the sadness in her, because when he spoke again, all the rage had gone from his voice. And with it, the certainty.

"I didn't want it to be this way," he said. "I swear I didn't."

"I know."

"I don't know . . . how I got here . . ."

"It doesn't *need* to be this way," she said, softly, softly. "You don't have to hurt anybody to prove you love me."

"I do . . . love you."

"Then put the knife down, Mitch." His hand, which had continued to graze her cheek, stopped in midstroke. "Please, Mitch," she said. "Put it down."

He drew his hand away from her face, and his expression, which had mellowed as she spoke to him, grew severe.

"Oh no . . ." he murmured "I know what you're doing . . ."

"Mitch—"

"You think you can sweet-talk me out of going up there." He shook his head. "No, baby. It's not happening. Sorry."

So saying, he stepped back from her and turned toward the stairs. There was a moment of almost hallucinatory precision, when Rachel seemed to see everything in play before her: the man with the knife— her husband, her sometime prince—moving away from her, stinking of sweat and hatred; her lover, lying in the bed above, lost in dreams; and in between, on the darkened stairs, on the landing, those spectral presences, whatever they were, which she could not name.

Mitch had reached the bottom of the stairs, and now, without another word to her, he began to ascend. He left her no choice. She went up after him, and before he could stop her slipped past him to block his passage. The air was busy up here. She could feel its agitation against her face. If Mitch was aware of anything out of the ordinary, his determination to get to Galilee blinded him to the fact. His face was fixed; like a mask, beaten to the form of his features; pallid and implacable. She didn't waste her breath on persuasion; he was beyond listening to anything she said. She simply stood in his way. If he wanted to harm Galilee he'd have to get past her to do so. He looked at her; his eyes the only living things in that dead face.

"Out of my way," he said.

She reached out to the left and right of her and caught hold of the banisters. She was horribly aware of how vulnerable she was, doing this; how her belly and her breasts were open to him, if he wanted to harm her. But she had no other choice, and she had to believe that despite the madness that had seized him he wouldn't harm her.

He stopped, one stair below her, and for a moment she dared hope she could still make him see reason. But then his hand was up at her face, at her hair, and with one jerk he pulled her back down the stairs. She lost her grip on the banisters and fell forward, reaching out to secure another hold, but failing, toppling. He held onto her hair, however, and her head jerked backward. She reached up to catch hold of his arm, a cry of pain escaping her. The world pivoted; she didn't know up from down. He pulled on her again, drawing her close to him, then throwing her backward against the banister. This time she secured a hold, and stopped herself from falling any further, but before she could draw breath he struck her hard across the face, an open-palmed blow, but brutal for all that. Her legs gave way beneath her; she slipped sideways. He caught her a second blow, with sickening force, and then a third, which sent her into free fall down the stairs. She felt every thud and crack as her limbs, her shoulder, her head, connected with stairs and banister. Then she hit the floor at the bottom of the flight, striking it so hard that she momentarily lost consciousness. In the buzzing blackness in her head she struggled to put her thoughts in order, but the task was beyond her. It was all she could do to instruct her eyes to open. When she did she found herself looking at the stairs, from a sideways position. Mitch was staring down at her, grotesquely foreshortened, his head vestigial. He studied her for several seconds, just to be certain that he'd incapacitated her. Then, sure that she could not come between him and his intentions again, he turned his back on her and continued to ascend the stairs.

# XXI

All she could do was watch; her body refused to move an inch. She could only lie there and watch while Mitch went to murder Galilee in his bed. She couldn't even call to him; her throat refused to work, her tongue refused to work. Even if she'd been able to make a sound, Galilee wouldn't have heard her. He was in his own private world; healing himself in the deepest of slumbers. She would not be able to rouse him.

Mitch was three or four steps from the top of the flight; in a few more seconds he would be out of sight. Oh God, she wanted to weep, in rage, in frustration. After all the grand endeavors of the recent past, would it all come down to this? Her lying at the bottom of a flight of stairs, unable to move, and he at the top, just as powerless, while a man with a little knife and a little soul cut the bond between them?

She heard Mitch speak; and tried to focus on him. But it was difficult to see him up there at the top of the stairs; the shadows were dense and they seemed almost to be concealing him from her. She tried to move her arm; to raise herself up a little way, and get a better look at him. As she did so he spoke again.

"Who are you?" he said.

There was distress in his voice; a little panic even. She saw him jab his knife at the darkness, as though to keep it at bay. But it wouldn't be driven off. It seemed to come at him, alive and eager. He stabbed again, and again. Then he took a backward step, loosing a panicked cry as he did so.

"*Jesus!*" he yelled. "What the fuck *is* this?"

With one last, agonizing effort of will Rachel pressed her aching arms into service, and lifted her upper body off the floor. Her head spun, and a wave of nausea rose up in her, but she forgot both in the next moment, as her eyes made sense of what was happening at the top of the stairs. There were three, perhaps four, human forms up there with Mitchell; they moved with gentility, but they pressed against him nevertheless, backing him against the wall. He still continued to jab at them, in the desperate hope of keeping them away from him, but it was clear that they weren't susceptible to harm. They were spirits of some kind; their sinuous forms expressed from the simple convenience of light and dark. One of them, as it closed on Mitchell, looked down the stairs, and Rachel caught a glimpse of its face. Not it; *she*. It was a woman—they were all women—her expression faintly amused by the business she was about. Her features were not perfect by any means; she was like a portrait that the painter had only sketched, leaving the rendering of detail until later. But Rachel knew the face, nevertheless. Knew it not because they'd met, but because this woman had lent the essentials of her features to the generations that had followed her. The sweep of the brow, the curve of the cheekbones, the strength of the jaw, all of these were echoed in the Geary line, as was her penetrating stare.

And if she was, as Rachel guessed, one of the women who'd been with Galilee in this house, then so too were the others. All Geary women, who'd passed sweet, loving times beneath this roof, and who in death had returned here, to leave some part of their spirits where they'd been most happy.

The spinning in Rachel's head retreated somewhat, and as it did so she was able to make better sense of the other forms that moved around Mitchell. Her suspicions were confirmed. One of this number was Cadmus's first wife Kitty, whose picture had hung in the dining room at the mansion. A resplendent woman, with the bearing of an undisputed matriarch, she was here unleashed from her corsets and her formality; her body sensual despite the simple stuff with which it was expressed; as though she'd come back here in the form of the hedonist she'd been under this roof. A woman of pleasure for a few, blissful days, secure in Galilee's arms; loved, even.

That was what these women had come here to find—what she, Rachel, had come here to find, though she hadn't known it at the time—love. Something more than wifely duty; something more than compromise and concealment. A taste of an emotion that struck deep into their being; and offered them a glimpse of what their souls needed to stay bright. No wonder they'd found their way back here; and no wonder they now made themselves visible. They wanted to keep the man who'd offered them that glimpse from harm.

How much of this did Mitchell understand? Very little, Rachel suspected, but there were signs that he was being told. She could hear whisperings coming from the top of the flight—gentle, playful sounds—and the women were pressing themselves upon him as they spoke, their faces inches from his. He'd given up attempting to keep them at bay with his knife; instead he raised his hands to his face and tried to blot them out.

"Leave me alone!" Rachel heard him sobbing. "Leave me the fuck alone!"

But they had no intention of letting him go. They continued to press their attentions upon him, while he cowered in their midst, as though he'd walked into a swarm of bees and having no way to outrun it could only stand there and be stung and stung and stung—

Rachel, meanwhile, had reached for the curve of the banister at the bottom of the stairs, and was doing her best to haul herself to her feet. She was by no means certain she trusted her legs to bear her up, but she knew that while Mitchell's gaze was averted she had a chance to arm herself. She might not get another. But as she was about to rise

she caught sight of another figure up there on the landing. It was
Galilee. He'd risen, naked, from his dreams, and was making his pained
way to the top of the stairs.

Mitchell had also seen him. He dropped his knife hand from his
face and flailed at the spirits around him, loosing as he did so a venomous yell. Then he raised the knife again and pushed up through the
veil of his tormentors to get to his enemy.

From her position at the bottom of the stairs Rachel could not
clearly see what happened next. Mitchell's body blocked Galilee from
view, and an instant later the women in their turn covered Mitchell,
closing around him like a cloud. There was a still moment, when the
darkness at the top of the flight showed her nothing. Then Mitchell
appeared out of the murk, pitched backward with such force that his
feet were off the ground. He missed the top stair, but struck the second,
twisting as he did so. Rachel heard a shout escape him, then a series of
smaller cries as he somersaulted down the flight. At the last moment she
pulled herself out of his path, and he landed face down on the very spot
where she'd been lying seconds before. Almost instantly he raised himself up off the floor, as though he were doing a push-up, and she drew
away from him, certain he was going to renew his assault. But as he
lifted his body she saw that blood was pouring out of him, slapping on
the ground. The knife—that little knife of his—was sticking out of his
chest. Her eyes went up to his face. The mask of his features had
cracked; he was no longer implacable. Tears of pain sprang from his
eyes, his mouth was drawn down to make a pitiful shape. He looked
toward her, his wet eyes wide.

"Oh, baby . . ." he said. "I'm hurting."

It was the last thing he said. His trembling arms gave way beneath
him and he sank down, driving the knife all the way into his flesh; burying it. His gaze was still turned up toward her as the life went out of him.

She stared at him, dry-eyed. There would be tears later, but not
now; now there was only relief that this was ended; that they were finally
done with one another.

She looked up to the top of the stairs. Galilee was standing there,
holding onto the banister for support. He was looking down at Mitch's
body with such a forlorn expression on his face—such a look of *loss*—
that it might have been the corpse of someone he'd loved lying there at
the bottom of the stairs.

"I didn't . . ." he began to say. But he didn't have the will to finish
the thought.

"It doesn't matter," she said.

He sank down, still staring at the body. Behind him, the Geary women stood like a melancholy chorus.

Only one of them broke rank, and moving past Galilee began to descend the stairs. It wasn't until she was halfway down, and had halted, that Rachel realized who it was. It was Margie; or rather some echo of the woman she'd called by that name. Her features were no more finished than those of the other women—perhaps a little less in fact—but there was no mistaking the raised, quizzical brow, nor the sly smile that now came on to her face.

More than a smile; laughter. It wasn't quite the raucous din that had erupted from her in the high times, but it was still recognizably Margie. Who else would have found the sight of Mitchell Geary, sprawled face down in his own blood, funny? The prince was dead, and Margie's spirit stood on the stairs and toasted the sight with long loud peals of laughter.

# PART NINE

# The Human Road

# I

## i

"I'm not a good man," Galilee said. "I've done terrible things in my life. So many . . . very terrible things. But I never wanted this. Please believe me."

They were on the beach, and he was setting a light to the heap of driftwood he'd made, in the same spot where he'd lit that first, fragrant fire: the fire that had summoned Rachel out of the house. As the flames caught, she saw his face. That curious beauty of his—Cesaria's beauty, in the form of a man—was almost too much to see; the exquisite naked-ness of him. Twice on the way out here she'd thought he'd lose control of himself. Once when he came down the stairs, and in stepping over Mitchell's body, set his bare foot in a rivulet of blood. And again when they found Niolopua on the veranda. Great heaving sobs had escaped him then, like the sobbing of a child almost, terrible to hear.

His grief made Rachel strong. She took him by the hand and led him down onto the lawn. Then she went back into the house to fetch a bottle of whiskey and some cigarettes. She'd expected to see the women there, but they'd gone about other business, it seemed, for which fact she was grateful. She didn't want to think about what happened to the dead right now; didn't want to imagine Mitchell's spirit, driven out of the body he'd been so proud of, lost in limbo.

By the time she got back to Galilee, she'd already planned what to tell him. Why don't we go down onto the sand, she'd said to him, taking his hand. We can build a fire. I'm cold.

Like a child, he'd obeyed. Silently gone to collect pieces of drift-wood, and arranged them. Then she'd passed the matches over to him, and he'd kindled the fire. The wood was still damp from the storm; it took a little time for the larger pieces of wood to catch. They spat and sizzled as they dried out, but at last the flames swelled around them, and they burned. Only then did he start talking. Beginning with that simple, blanket confession. *I'm not a good man.*

"I'm not afraid of anything you've got to tell me," Rachel told him.

"You won't leave me?" he said.

"Why would I ever do that?"

"Because of the things I've done."

"Nothing's that bad," she said. He shook his head, as though he knew better. "I know you killed George Geary," she went on. "And I know Cadmus ordered you to do it."

"How did you find that out?"

"It was one of his deathbed confessions."

"My mother made him tell you."

"She made him tell Loretta. I was just a bystander." Galilee stared into the fire. "You have to help me understand," Rachel said. "That's all I want: just to understand how this ever happened."

"How I came to kill George Geary?"

"Not just that. Why you came here to be with the Geary women. Why you left your family in the first place."

"Oh . . ." he said softly. "You want the whole story."

"Yes," she said, "that's what I want. Please."

"May I ask you why?"

"Because I'm a part of it now. I guess I became a part of it the day Mitchell walked into the store in Boston. And I want to know how I fit."

"I'm not sure I can help you with that," Galilee said. "I'm not certain I know where *I* fit."

"You just tell me the whole story," Rachel said. "I'll work out the rest for myself."

He nodded, and took a deep breath. The fire had grown more confident in the last few minutes, cooking away the last of the moisture in the wood. The smoke had cleared. Now the flames were yellow and white; the fierce heat making the air between Rachel and Galilee shake.

"I think I should start with Cesaria," Galilee said; and began.

## ii

Nobody knows the whole story, of course; nobody can. Perhaps there is no thing entire; only that rubble that Heraclitus celebrates. At the beginning of this book I boasted that I'd tell everything, and I failed. Now Galilee promises to do the same thing, and he's fated to fail the same way. But I've come to see that as nothing can be made that isn't flawed, the challenge is twofold: first, not to berate oneself for what is, after all, inevitable; and second, to see in our failed perfection a different thing; a truer thing, perhaps, because it contains both our ambition and the spoiling of that ambition; the exhaustion of order, and the discovery—in the midst of despair—that the beast dogging the heels of beauty has a beauty all of its own.

So Galilee began to tell his story, and though Rachel had asked him for everything, and though he intended to tell her everything, he could give her only the parts that he could remember on that certain day at that certain hour. Not everything. Not remotely everything. Just slivers and fragments; that best universe which is rubble.

Galilee began his account, as he said he would, with Cesaria.

"You met my mother already," he said to Rachel, "so you've seen a little of what she is. I think that's all anybody's ever seen: a little. Except for my father Nicodemus—"

"And Jefferson?"

"Oh she told you about him?"

"Not in detail. She just said he'd built a house for her."

"He did. And it's one of the most beautiful houses in the world."

"Will you take me there?"

"I wouldn't be welcome."

"Maybe you would now," Rachel suggested.

He looked at her through the flames. "Is that what you want to do? Go home and meet the family?"

"Yes. I'd like that very much."

"They're all crazy," he warned.

"They can't be any worse than the Gearys."

He shrugged, conceding the point. "Then we'll go back, if that's what you want to do," he told her.

Rachel smiled. "Well that was easy."

"You thought I'd say no?"

"I thought you'd put up a fight."

Galilee shook his head. "No," he said, "it's time I made my peace. Or at least tried to. None of us are going to be around forever. Not even Cesaria."

"She said at Cadmus's house she was feeling old and weary."

"I think there's a part of her that's always been old and weary. And another part that's born new every day." Rachel looked confounded, and Galilee said: "I can't explain it any better than that. She's as much a mystery to me as to anybody. Including herself. She's a mass of contradictions."

"You told me once, when we were out on the boat, that she doesn't have parents."

"To my knowledge, she doesn't. Nor did my father."

"How's that possible? Where did they come from?"

"Out of the earth. Out of the stars." He shrugged, the expression on his face suggesting that the question was so unanswerable that he didn't think it worth contemplating.

"But she's very old." Rachel said. "You know that much."

"She was being worshipped before Christ was born, before Rome was founded."

"So she's some kind of goddess?"

"That doesn't mean very much anymore does it? Hollywood produces goddesses these days. It's easy."

"But you said she was worshipped."

"And presumably still is, in some places. She had a lot of temples in Africa, I know. The missionaries destroyed some of her cults, but those things never die out completely. I did see a statue of her once, in Madagascar. That was strange, to see my own mother's image, and people bowing down before it. I wanted to say to them: don't waste your prayers. I know for a fact she's not listening. She's never listened to anyone in her life, except her husband. And she gave him such hell he died rather than stay with her. Or at least pretended to die. I think his death was a performance. He did it so he could slip away."

"So where is he?"

"Where he came from presumably. In the earth. In the stars." He drew a deep breath. "This is hard for you, I know. I wish I could make it easier. But I'm not a great expert on what we are as a family. We take it for granted, the way you take your humanity for granted. And day for day, we're not that different. We eat, we sleep, we get sick if we drink too much. At least, I do."

"But you're able to do things the rest of us can't," Rachel replied.

"Not much," Galilee said lightly.

He lifted his hand, and the flames of the fire seemed to leap like an eager dog. "Of course we have more power together—you and I—than either of us had apart. But maybe that's always true of lovers."

Rachel said nothing; she just watched Galilee's face through the fire.

"What else can I tell you?" he went on. "Well . . . my mother can raise storms. She raised the storm that brought me back here. And she can send her image wherever she wants to. I guess she could go sit on the moon if she was in the mood. She can take life like that—" he snapped his fingers "—and I think she can probably give it, though that's not her nature. She's been a very violent woman in her time. She finds killing easy."

"You don't."

"No, I don't. I'll do it, if I have to, if I've agreed to, but no I don't like it. My father was the same. He liked sex. That was his grand obsession. Not even love. Sex. Fucking. I saw a few of *his* temples in my time, and let me tell you they were quite a sight. Statues of my father, displaying himself. Sometimes not even him, just a carving of his dick."

"So you got that from him," Rachel said.

"The dick?"

"The love of sex."

Galilee shook his head. "I'm not a great lover," he said. "Not like him. I could go for months out at sea, not thinking about it." He smiled. "Of course, when I'm with someone, it's a different story."

"No," Rachel said, with a smile of her own. "It's the same story." He frowned, not understanding. "You always tell the same story," she said, "about your invented country . . ."

"How do you know?"

"Because I recognized it when I heard it again."

"Who from? Loretta?"

"No."

"Who, then?"

"One of your older conquests," Rachel said. "Captain Holt."

"Oh . . ." Galilee said softly. "Where did you find out about Charles?"

"From his journal."

"It still exists, after all these years?"

"Yes. Mitchell took it from me. I think his brother's got it now."

"That's a pity."

"Why?"

"Because I think it probably contains the way into L'Enfant. I told it all to Charles when we were going in there together, and he wrote it down."

"Why did you do that?"

"Because I was sick and afraid I'd lose consciousness before we got there. They would have been killed trying to find their way in without my help."

"So now Garrison knows how to get to your mother's house?" Rachel said.

Galilee nodded. "Ah, well. Nothing to be done about it now. Did you read all the journal?"

"Most, not all."

"But you know how we met? How Nub brought Charles to see me?"

"Yes. I know all that." A flurry of snatched pictures passed through her mind's eye: the battlefield at Bentonville, the phantom child on Holt's horse, the ruins of Charleston and the grisly sights in the garden of the house on Tradd Street. She'd seen so much through Holt's eyes. "He wrote well," she said.

"He'd wanted to be a poet in his youth," Galilee said. "He spoke the way he wrote, believe it or not. The way sentences fell from his lips; it was beautiful to hear."

"Did you love him?"

Galilee looked surprised at the question. But then he said: "I suppose I did, in a way. He was a noble fellow. Or at least he had been. By the time I met him he was so very sad. He'd lost everything."

"But he found you."

"I wasn't adequate compensation," Galilee said, smiling ruefully at his own formality. "I couldn't be his wife and children and all the good things he'd had before the war. Though . . . maybe I imagined I could. I think that's always been my big mistake. I want to give gifts. I want to make people happy. But it never ends well."

"Why not?"

"Because I can't give anybody what they really want. I can't give them *life*. Sooner or later they die, and dying's never very good. Nobody dies a good death. People cling on. Even when they're in agony they want a few more minutes, a few more seconds—"

"What happened to Holt?"

"He died at L'Enfant. He's buried there." He sighed. "I should never have let them take me back. It was asking for trouble. I'd been away such a long time. But I was wounded. All used up. I needed somewhere I could heal myself."

"How did you come to be wounded?"

"I was careless. I thought I was untouchable . . . and I wasn't." His hand went up to his face, his fingers instinctively seeking out the scars on his brow and scalp, touching them delicately as though he were reading something there: the braille of past suffering. "There was a woman called Katherine Morrow," he said. "She was one of my . . . what's the word? Concubines? She'd been quite the Southern virgin until she came to be with me. Then she showed her real feelings. This was a woman who had no shame. None. She would do whatever came into her head. But she had two brothers, who had survived the war, and when they returned home to Charleston came looking for her. I was drunk that night. I was drunk most nights, but that night I was so drunk I don't think I knew what was happening to me until I was out on the street, sur-

rounded by a dozen men—the brothers and their friends—all beating
me. It wasn't just that I'd seduced the girl. I was a nigger, and they were
so full of hatred, because that spring all the niggers in America were free
men and women, and they didn't like that. It was the end of their world.
So they beat me and beat me, and I was too stupid with drink and my
own despair to stop them."

"So how was it they didn't kill you?"

"Nickelberry shot the brothers dead. He walked up with two pis-
tols—I can still see him now, just parting the crowd around me, and
blowing holes in their heads. Bang! Bang! Then Charles was there,
threatening to do the same to the next man who tried to land a blow.
That made them scatter. And Charles and Nub picked me up and took
me away."

"Off to L'Enfant."

"Eventually."

"What happened to the people who'd been with you in your . . ."

"Pleasure palace? I don't know. I went back to Charleston a few
years later, to look for them. But they'd all gone their separate ways. I
heard Miss Morrow went to Europe. But the rest . . . ?" He shrugged.
"So many people have come and gone, over the years. So many faces.
But I don't forget them. I never forget them. I see them all still. I dream
about them, as though I could open my eyes and they'd be there." His
voice dropped to a murmur. "And maybe they would . . ." he said.

He halted for a moment, then he got to his feet. "The fire's too
bright," he said. "Walk with me, will you?"

## iii

They walked together, down the beach. Not hand in hand, as they'd
walked that bright day when he'd taken her to see *The Samarkand*, but
a little way from one another. He was so raw, right now; she was afraid
that she'd hurt him, if she so much as touched him.

He continued to talk, but in the darkness he lost the thread of what
he'd been telling her, and now he offered only fragments; disconnected
observations about how his life had been in those distant days. Something about how his homecoming had unleashed a string of catastro-
phes; about horses killing his father; about his sister Marietta protecting
him from his mother's rage; about his other sister's skills with the poultices and pills, which had helped heal him. Rachel didn't press him
with questions about any of this. She just let his mind wander and his
lips report.

Though Galilee made no defense of his actions, I feel that for the sake of veracity I must offer some observations of my own. Though he took the blame upon himself as though every sin committed at L'Enfant in those few grim days were his fault and his alone, this was simply not so. He wasn't responsible for my giving Chiyojo over to Nicodemus; he wasn't responsible for Cesaria's unrepentant rage; he wasn't responsible for the death of his friend Charles Holt, who died by his own hand.

He was, however, responsible for something he didn't mention in his account. When he, Holt and Nickelberry entered L'Enfant, they were followed. Their pursuers weren't common marauders; they were a small group of men led by Benjamin Morrow, the father of Katherine, who had lately lost both his sons to Nub's pistol. He was an old man by the standards of that age, well into his sixties, and perhaps his years made him more cautious and clever than a younger man might have been. Though he and his posse of five God-fearing Charlestonians had several times come close to their quarry as they'd chased them north, Morrow had refrained from attack. He wanted to get to the heart of the unholy power that had so besotted his beloved Katherine that she'd lost every drop of propriety, and gone to be a whore for this nigger Galilee. His caution and his curiosity had saved both his life and the lives of his men. By following in the footsteps of their quarry they'd unknowingly negotiated the traps that would have claimed them had they come into L'Enfant on their own. Once Cesaria realized she had trespassers, of course she descended on them like a fury.

I saw them in their graves, and I will never forget the expressions on their faces. They would have been better served by fate if they'd misstepped somewhere along the way, and perished in one of the traps. Instead they'd looked as though they'd been mauled by a cageful of hungry tigers. But given that they'd been killed by Cesaria, I'm certain even that would have been a kindness.

Anyway, now you know. And I have to say that in some corner of my being I believe the horrors that were visited upon us all soon after the dispatch of the Charleston Six would not have been so disastrous—indeed might not have happened at all—had they been forgiven their error and allowed to leave. Blood begets blood; cruelty begets cruelty. Once the Six were dead, it was all storms, horses and horrors. Galilee wasn't the cause of all that. *She* was; the goddess herself. Though she'd been the one from whom the glories of L'Enfant had come, she was also, in her madness, the architect of its darkest hour.

# II

Rachel and Galilee didn't return to the fire. They went instead to sit on the rocks at the end of the beach. The sea was calm, and perhaps its soothing rhythm made it easier for him to confess what he still had to tell.

"It was Nub got me out of the house," he began, "just as he'd got me in. I think he probably believed Cesaria was going to kill me—"

"She wouldn't have harmed you. Would she?"

"In one of her furies, anything was possible. She'd made me, after all; I'm sure she believed she was quite within her rights as a mother to unmake me again. But she didn't get the chance. Marietta distracted her, and Nickelberry spirited me away. I was delirious most of the time but I remember that night—oh my God, how I remember it—stumbling through the swamp, thinking every sound we heard behind us was her coming after us."

"What about Nickelberry—the things he'd seen. How did he deal with that?"

"Oh Nub was a cool one. It was all too much for Charles, but Nub . . . I don't know, he just took everything in his stride. And he saw power. That was the crux of it. He saw power the like of which he'd never seen before, and he knew that if he had me, he had a piece of that power. He wasn't helping me out of Christian charity. He'd lived the life of an underdog. He'd been brought up with nothing. He'd come out of the war with nothing. But now he had me. My life was in his hands, and he wasn't going to let it slip away."

"Did you talk about what he'd seen?"

"Later. But not for many weeks. I was too sick. He'd brought out medicines that my sister Zabrina had given him, and he promised me that he'd stay with me and make me well."

"What did he want in exchange?"

"At the time, nothing. We made our way out to the shore, and we lived there in the dunes for a few weeks. Nobody came there; we were quite safe from discovery. He made a shelter for us, and I lay in it, listening to the sea, slowly getting well. He was my nurse, he was my comforter; he fed me, he bathed me, he listened to me rave in my fevers. He went out and brought back food. God knows where he got it. What he did to get it. His only concern was to make me well. I know it may sound perverse, but when I look back on that time, I think of it more fondly than any of my time in Charleston. I felt this great weight off me. Like I'd been cured of some sickness. I'd had every excess known to man. I'd made love to so many bodies, had so much beauty in my hands. I'd been so high I thought I'd never come down. And now it was all over. I was living out under the stars with nothing to call my own, just the sea, and time to think. That's when I first began to dream of building myself a boat and sailing away . . .

"Then one day Nub started talking about his own dreams. And I realized it wasn't going to be so easy. He had a friend in me; that's what he believed at least. We were going to work together, when I was well.

" *'This is the perfect time to start over,'* he said to me. *'If we work together we could make a fortune out there.'* "

"What did you say to him?"

"I told him I didn't want to have anything more to do with people. I'd had my fill of them. I told him about my dream of building a boat and sailing away.

"I expected him to laugh. But he didn't. In fact he said he thought it was a very good idea. But then he said: *'You can't just sail away and forget what we've been through together. You owe me something.'*

"And of course he was right. He'd risked his life for me in Charleston, shooting the Morrow brothers. He'd risked his life getting me out of L'Enfant. Lord knows, he'd seen things that would have driven lesser men mad, because of me. And then, when we'd reached the shore he'd tended to me night and day. Without him and Zabrina's poultices I would have been disfigured; maybe died. Of course I owed him. There was no question about it.

"So I asked him what he wanted from me. And he had a very simple answer: he wanted me to help make him rich. The way he saw it there were opportunities to make fortunes out there. Reconstruction was underway. There were roads to lay, cities to rebuild, bellies to feed. And the men who were at the heart of all that—with the wit and the skill to make themselves indispensable—those men were going to be richer than any men in the history of America."

"Was he right about all this?"

"More or less. There were a few oil tycoons and railroad magnates who were already so rich nobody was going to catch up with them. But he'd given the whole business some careful thinking, and he was not a stupid man; not by any means. He knew that as a team—with his pragmatism and my vision, his understanding of what people wanted and my capacity to get the opposition out of the way—we could become very powerful in a very short time. And he was impatient. He'd lived in the gutter for long enough. He wanted a better life. And he didn't care how he got it, as long as he got it." He paused, and stared out to sea. "I could still get myself my boat, he said to me, I could still sail away. That was fine and dandy. He'd even help me find a boat; only the best. But he needed me to help him in return. He wanted to have a wife and kids, and he wanted them to live the good life. It seemed like such a small thing when I was agreeing to it. Anyway, how could I refuse, after he'd done all he'd done for me?"

"We made a kind of pact, right there on the shore. I swore I would never cheat him, or any of his family. I swore on my life that I'd be his friend, and his family's friend, for as long as I lived."

Rachel had a sickening sense of where this was going.

"I think you begin to understand," Galilee said.

"He didn't keep the same name . . ."

"No, he didn't. A couple of days later he came back to the shore in a fine old mood. He'd found a body in a ditch—or what was left of it. A Yankee, who'd died many, many miles from home. In his satchel were all his papers: everything Nickelberry needed to become another man, which in those days was not very much. After that day, he was never "Nub" Nickelberry again. He became a man called Geary."

This was not remotely what Rachel had expected, but as she contemplated the information she saw how the pieces fitted. The roots of the family into which she'd married were deep in blood and filth; was it any wonder the dynasty that sprung from this beginning was in every way shameful and hollow?

"I didn't know what I'd agreed to," Galilee went on. "I didn't realize until a lot later the scale of Nub's ambition, or what he was prepared to have us do to make it a reality."

"If you *had* known . . . ?"

"Would I have agreed? Yes, I would have agreed. I wouldn't have liked it, but I would have agreed."

"Why?"

"Because how was I ever going to be free of him otherwise?"

"You could have just walked away."

"I owed him too much. If I'd cheated him, history would have just repeated itself. I would have been pulled into something else—some other piece of human folly—and had to endure that instead. I would have had to pay the price eventually. The only way to be free—at least this was the way I thought of it—was to work with Nub, and help make his dreams come true. Then I'd have earned a dream of my own. I could have my boat, and . . . off I'd go." Galilee sighed deeply. "It was messy, working for him; very messy. But he was right when he talked about the opportunities. They were everywhere. Of course, to get ahead of the crowd you needed something extra. He had me. I was the one he sent in if he had trouble with somebody, to make sure he never had trouble again. And I was good at it. Once I was in the rhythm I realized I had quite a skill for terrorizing people."

"You get it from Cesaria."

"No doubt. And believe me I was in the right mood to do violence. I was an exile now; I felt free to do whatever crossed my mind, however inhumane. I hated the world, and I hated the people in it. So it made me happy to be the spoiler, to be the bloodletter."

"And Nub—"

"Geary, now. Mr. Geary."

"Geary. He never got his hands dirty? You did all the intimidation, he did all the business?"

"No, he'd get involved when he felt like it. He was a cook. He liked knives and carcasses. Sometimes he'd astonish me. I'd see him do something, so cold, so indifferent to the suffering he was causing, and I'd be . . . I'd be in awe of him."

"In awe?"

"Yes. Because I'd always felt things too much. I'd agonized over things I did. My head had always been filled with voices telling me not to do this, not to do that; or to look out for the consequences. That was why I liked to get drunk, and high; it hushed those voices. But when I was with Geary: no voices at all. Nothing. Silence. It was nice.

"And as the months went by, and I got completely well, and strong again, I began to get a reputation as somebody to be afraid of, and that was nice too. The more of that reputation I got the more I made sure I deserved it. When I needed to make an example of somebody, I was vicious. There was this part of me that was cruel, venomous, and when people saw that in my eyes or heard it in my voice . . . it made them compliant. Often—especially later—I didn't need to lay a finger on them. They'd just see me coming, and they'd be asking what they could do for us, how they could help us."

"And the men who didn't?"

"Died. At my hands. Usually quickly. Sometimes not. Sometimes, if Geary thought an example had to be made of a guy, I'd do something so bad—" He stopped. She couldn't see his face. But she heard the soft sobs that escaped him; and could see his silhouette shake as he was wracked. He took a moment to recover himself and then continued, his voice muted.

"We started to expand our territories, state by state. We went north into Virginia, we went into Tennessee and Missouri, we worked our way through as far as Oklahoma, then down into Texas. Wherever we went, Geary bought up land, most of the time with money he didn't have, but by now he had a name and a reputation; he was this new guy out of Charleston who had a vision and a fast tongue and a way of getting what he wanted, and anyone who said no to him regretted it, so fewer and fewer people did. Fewer and fewer wanted to. They wanted to be in business with him: he was the face of the future, and he always acted as though he had so much money that you'd get rich just by shaking hands with him." His voice was gathering strength again. "The thing was, a lot of people *did* get rich off him. He was a natural; he had a nose for wealth. I think he even surprised himself.

"In a little over three years he was a millionaire, and he decided it was time to start a family. He married a rich woman out of Georgia, who'd taken all her money up north before the war. Her name was Bedelia Townsend, and she seemed to be the perfect match for him. She was beautiful, she was ambitious, and she wanted the world right there, in the palm of her hand. There was only one problem. He didn't take care of her in the bedroom as she would have liked. So I kept her company."

"Did she have children by you?"

"No. They were all his. I was very careful about that. Pleasuring her was one thing, giving her a Barbarossa was another."

"Weren't you tempted?"

"To make a half-breed with her? Oh yes, I was tempted. But I was afraid that would spoil what was between us. I loved being with her. Nothing made me happier."

"And what did Geary think about all this?"

"He didn't care. He was out empire-building. As long as Bedelia produced children, and I was there to play the bully-boy if somebody crossed him, he didn't concern himself with what we did together. It was a busy time for a cook who wanted to be a king. And to be fair to him, he worked, night and day. The seeds of everything the Geary family became were sown in that decade after the end of the war."

"So there must have come a time when you'd paid your debt to him."

"Oh there did. But if I'd walked away from him, where would I have gone? I couldn't go back to L'Enfant. I had no other life besides the Gearys."

"You could have gone away to sea."

"That's what happened, eventually." He paused, thinking on this moment. "But I didn't go alone."

"You took Bedelia?" Rachel said softly.

"Yes. I took Bedelia. She was the first woman to step on *The Samarkand*, and you were the second. We sailed off, without telling Geary we were going. She left a letter, I think, explaining her feelings; telling him she wanted more than he'd given her."

"How could she do that? How could she leave her children?"

He leaned a little closer to her. "You wouldn't have done that for me?" he said.

"Yes," she murmured, "of course I would."

"That's your answer then."

"Did she ever see them again?"

"Oh yes. Later. But she also had another child . . ."

"You had your half-breed?"

"Yes."

"Niolopua . . . ?"

"Yes. My Niolopua. I made sure he understood from the beginning that he had Barbarossian blood. That way he could escape at least some of the claims of time. My father had told me that some of his bastards— the ones who lived in ignorance of who they were—lived ordinary, human lives. Seventy years and they were gone. It was only the children who knew their real nature who could outlive their Biblical span."

"I don't understand," Rachel said. "If you've got Barbarossian blood what does it matter whether you know it or not?"

"It's not a matter of blood. It's a matter of *knowing* who you are. It's knowledge, not chemistry that makes us Barbarossas."

"And if you'd never told him?"

"He'd be a long time dead by now."

"So you and Bedelia go out to sea on *The Samarkand*, and eventually you find your way here?"

"Yes. We came here by chance; the winds brought us here and it seemed like paradise. There was nobody at this end of the island back then. It was like the beginning of the world. We weren't the first visitors, of course. There was a mission in Poi'pu. That's where she had Niolopua. And while she was recovering, I finished work on the house." He looked past her, along the beach. "It hasn't changed much," he said. "The air still smells as sweet as when I was here with her."

She thought of Niolopua as he spoke: of the many times she'd seen unreadable expressions cross his face, and wondered what mysteries lay buried in him. Now she knew. He'd been the dutiful son, watching over the house built for his mother all those long years ago, watching the horizon and waiting for a sail, the sail of his father's boat, to come into view. She wanted to weep, for the loss of him. Not that she'd known him well; but he had been a connection to the past, and to the woman whose love had made so much of what had happened to Rachel possible. Without Bedelia, there would have been no house here in Eden.

"Have you heard enough?" Galilee said to her.

In a sense, she'd heard more than enough. It would take her days to comb through what he'd told her, and put the pieces together with what she already knew: the tales she'd read in Charles Holt's journal, the oblique exchanges she'd had with Niolopua and with Loretta; that last, bitter confrontation between Cesaria and Cadmus. All of it was illuminated by what she now knew; and yet paradoxically was all the darker for that. The pain and the grief, the allegiances and the betrayals, they were so much deeper than she'd imagined. All of which would have been extraordinary enough had it simply been some story she'd heard. But it was so much more than that. It was the life of the man she loved. And she was a part of it; she was living it, even now.

"Can I ask you one last question?" she said. "Then we'll leave it for another time."

He reached out and caught hold of her hand. "So, then, it's not over?"

"What do you mean?"

"Between us."

"Oh God, my sweet . . ." she said, reaching up to touch his face. He was burning hot; as though in the grip of a fever. "Of course it's not over. I love you. I said I wasn't afraid of what you had to tell me, and I meant it. Nothing would make me let go of you now." He was trying to smile, but his eyes were full of tears.

She stroked his brow. "What you've told me helps me make sense of everything," she said. "And that's all I've wanted, since the beginning. I've wanted to understand."

"You're extraordinary. Did I ever tell you that? You're an amazing woman. I only wish I'd found you earlier."

"I wouldn't have been ready for you," Rachel said. "I would have run away. It would all have been too much . . ."

"You had another question," Galilee said.

"Yes. What happened to Bedelia? Did she stay here on the island?"

"No, she missed the social life of the big city, so she went back after three and a half years. Picked up where she'd left off."

"And Niolopua?"

"He went with me for a few years. Out to see the world. But he didn't like the sea very much. So I brought him back when he was twelve, and left him here, where he wanted to be."

One question answered, and another demanded to be asked. "Did you ever see Bedelia again?"

"Not until the very end of her life. Some instinct—I don't know what it was—made me sail back to New York, and when I got to the mansion she was on her deathbed. I knew when I saw her she'd been holding on, waiting for me to come back. She was dying of pneumonia; and Lord, to see her there . . . so weak. It broke my heart. But she told me she wasn't ready to die until she'd seen Geary and me make peace. God knows why that was so important to her, but it was. She ordered him to come up to the bedroom—"

"The big room overlooking the street?" Rachel said.

"Yes."

"That's where Cadmus died."

"A lot of Gearys have been born and died in that room."

"What did she say to you?"

"First she made us shake hands. Then she told us she had one last wish. She wanted me always to be there for the Geary women, to comfort them the way she'd been comforted. To love them the way she'd been loved. And that would be the only service I'd do for the Gearys after her death. No more murder. No more torture. Just this promise of comfort and love."

"What did you say to that?"

"What could I say? I had loved this woman with all my heart. I couldn't deny her this; it was the last thing she was ever going to ask for. So Geary and I agreed. We made a solemn oath, right there at the bottom of her bed. He agreed to protect the house in Kaua'i from any of the male members of his family: to dedicate it to the Geary women. And I agreed to go there when the women wanted me, to keep them company. Bedelia didn't die for another two days. She clung on, while we waited and watched—Geary on one side of her, me on the other. But she never said another word after that; I swear she made us wait so that we'd think about what we'd promised. When she died we grieved together, and it was almost like the old times; like it had been at the beginning, before everything went wrong between us. I didn't go to see her buried. I wouldn't have been welcome in the elevated company which Nub now kept—the Astors, the Rothschilds, the Carnegies. And he didn't want me standing beside his wife's grave, with everyone asking questions. So I sailed away. The day Bedelia was put in the ground I caught the morning tide. I never saw Nub again. But we wrote to one another, making formal arrangements for what we'd agreed to do. It was strange, how it all ended up. I'd been the King of Charleston when he met me; he'd been a wanderer. Our roles were reversed."

"Did you care? That you had nothing, I mean."

Galilee shook his head. "I didn't want anything that he had. Except Bedelia. I would have liked to have taken her with me. Buried her here, on the island. She didn't belong in some fancy mausoleum. She belonged where she could hear the sea . . ."

Rachel thought of the church that she'd visited when she'd first come to the island, and of the small ring of graves around it.

"But her spirit's here, sometimes."

"So she *was* one of the women in the house?"

Galilee nodded. "Yes she was. Though I don't know if I dreamt them or not."

"I saw them clearly."

"That doesn't mean I didn't dream them," Galilee said.

"So she wasn't her ghost?"

"Ghost. Memory. Echo. I don't know. It was some part of who she was. But the better part of her soul has gone, hasn't it? She's out in the stars somewhere. All you saw was something I kept, for company. A dream of a memory of Bedelia. And Kitty. And Margie." He sighed. "I was their comfort when they were alive. And now they're dead, a little piece of them is mine. You see how things always come around?" He put his hands to his face. "I'm all talked out," he said. "And we should make our plans to leave. Somebody's going to come looking for your husband sooner or later."

"One last thing," Rachel said.

"Yes?"

"Is that how I'm going to be one day? Like the women in the house? I'll die, and you'll just dream me up when you're lonely?"

"No. It's going to be different for us."

"How?"

"I'm going to bring you into the Barbarossa family, Rachel. I'm going to make you one of us, so death won't take you from me. I don't know how I'm going to do that yet—I don't even know that I can—but that's my intention. And if I can't . . ." he reached for her, took her hands in his, "if I can't live with you, as a Barbarossa, then I'll die with you." He kissed her. "That's my promise. From now on, we're together, whether it's to the grave or the end of time."

# III

## i

Istayed up through the night writing Galilee's confession. It was in some ways the happiest of labors: I was finally able to unburden myself of portions of this story I've waited a long time to set down; and it was pleasing to interleave my voice with Galilee's in the telling. But it was also the first of many acts of closure that the next few days will bring, and toward the end of the night a distinct sense of melancholy crept upon me. You might think this strange, given how painful many of the demands of this book have been, but for all my complaints, I have been moved and changed by the journey I've taken, and I don't look forward to its being over, as I thought I would. In truth, I'm a little afraid of being finished. Afraid that when I get to the end, and set my pen down, I will have spilled so much of myself onto the page that what remains inside me, to fill the vessel of my being, will be inadequate. That I'll be empty, or nearly so.

My mood lightened somewhat when the dawn chorus started up; and by the time I crawled into bed I was feeling a little happier with my lot. At least I had something to show for my labors, I thought to myself: if I were to die in my sleep, there would be something left behind, besides the hairs in the sink, and the spit stains on my pillow. Something which had come from my hand and head; evidence, if you will, of my desire to make order of chaos.

Speaking of chaos, I realized as I fell asleep that I'd missed Marietta's wedding celebrations. Not that I would have ventured out to attend them; even if the book had not been demanding my attention I would have made some excuse not to go. When I finally travel beyond the perimeters of L'Enfant it won't be to go on a drunken rampage with a bar full of Marietta's lesbian buddies. On the other hand I couldn't help but think that her wedding—assuming it took place—was yet further evidence of how things were changing; and how I, who'd witnessed all these changes, and been their loyal transcriber, was now left behind. A self-pitying thought, no doubt; but sometimes self-pity works better than any lullaby. Bathing in a stew of martyrdom, I fell asleep.

I dreamed again; and this time I didn't dream of the sea, or of the gray wastes of a city, but of a bright burnished sky, and a wilderness of desert. A little way off from me, there was a caravan of men and camels, its passage raising clouds of ocher dust. I could hear the camel drivers yelling to their animals, and the sharp snap of their sticks against the creatures' flanks. I could smell them too, even though they were a quarter of a mile from me: the pungent aroma of dirt and hide. I had no great desire to join their company, but when I looked around I saw that the landscape was otherwise empty in every direction.

*I'm inside myself,* I thought; *dust and emptiness in every direction; that's what I'm left with, now I've finished writing.*

The caravan was steadily moving away from me. I knew if I lingered too long it would disappear from sight. Then what would I do? Die of loneliness or desiccation; one or the other. Unhappy though I was, I wasn't ready for that. I started toward the caravan, my walk quickening into a trot, and the trot into a run, as my fear of losing it grew.

Then, suddenly, I was there among the travelers; in the midst of their din and their stench. I felt the rhythmical motion of a camel beneath me, and looked down to see that I was indeed perched high on the back of one of the animals. The landscape—that aching void of baked earth—was now concealed from me by the dust cloud raised by the travelers in whose midst I rode. I could see the backside of the animal in front, and the head of the animal behind; the rest was out of sight.

Somebody in the caravan now began to sing, raising a voice more confident than it was melodic above the general din. It was, I suppose you'd say, a dream song, wholly incoherent yet oddly familiar. What was it? I listened more carefully, trying to make sense of the syllables, certain that if I concentrated hard enough I'd discover what I was hearing. Still the song resisted; though at times the sense of it was tantalizingly close.

Frustrated, I was about to give up on the endeavor, when something about the rhythm of the song gave me a clue. I listened again, and the words, which had seemed nonsensical just moments before, came clear.

It wasn't a traveler's song I was listening to; it wasn't some exotic paean raised to the desert sky: it was a ditty from my childhood. The song I'd sung in the plum tree, all those many, many years ago.

> *It seems I am,*
> *It seems I was,*
> *It seems I will*
> *Be born, because*
> *It seems I am—*

Hearing it now, I let my voice join in the rendition, and as soon as I did so, other voices were raised around me, all singing the same song. Round and round the words went, like the wheel of the stars; born and being and being born again.

I felt a surge of remembered contentment. I was not empty, despite the tears I'd taken to bed with me. The memories were still there in me, sweet and pungent, like the plums on the branches of that tree. There to be plucked when I needed sustenance. Yes, there were stones at their heart—hard, bitter stones—but the meat around those stones was moist and nourishing. I wouldn't go empty after all.

The singing continued, but the voices of my unseen companions were becoming more remote. I looked back. The camel behind me had disappeared; so had the beast I was following. My fellow travelers, it seemed, had fallen by the wayside. Now I was traveling alone, singing alone, matching the pace of my song to the steady tread of my mount.

*It seems I am,*

I sang.

*It seems I was—*

The dust was clearing, now that there were no animals other than my own to stir it up. Something was glittering ahead of me.

*It seems I will*
*Be born, because—*

A river; I was coming to a broad river, the waters of which had brought forth lush swards of flower-speckled grass and stands of heavy-headed trees. And beyond this verdant place, the walls of a city, warmed by the setting sun.

Now I knew what river this was; it was the Zarafsham. And the city? I knew that too. I had come, by way of a plum tree and a song, to the city of Samarkand.

That was all. I didn't get any closer to the city than that first glimpse. But that was enough. I woke immediately, but with such a strong sense of what I'd seen that the melancholy which had accompanied me to bed had disappeared, healed away by what I'd experienced. Such is the wisdom of dreams.

## ii

It was by now the middle of the afternoon, and I took myself off to the kitchen to find something to eat. I did so without attending to myself whatsoever—thinking that I'd be able to find myself some food and slip back to my study unnoticed. But the kitchen had two occupants: Zabrina and Dwight. They both greeted the sight of me with some alarm.

"You need a shave, my friend," Dwight remarked.

"And some new clothes," Zabrina remarked. "You look as though you've been sleeping in those."

"I have," I said.

"You can take a look through my wardrobe if you like," Dwight said. "You're welcome to whatever I'm leaving behind."

Only now did I notice two things. One, the suitcase beside the table at which Zabrina and Dwight sat; two, the fact that Zabrina's eyes were red-rimmed and wet. It seems I'd interrupted a tearful farewell; at least tearful on her side.

"This is your fault," she said to me. "He's going because of you."

Dwight pulled a face. "That's not true," he protested.

"You told me if you hadn't seen that damn horse—" Zabrina began.

"That wasn't *his* doing," Dwight said. "I volunteered to go out to the stables with him. Anyway, if it hadn't been the horse it would have been something else."

"I gather from all this that you're leaving?" I said.

Dwight looked rueful. "I have to," he said. "I think if I don't go now—"

"You don't have to go at all," Zabrina said. "There's nothing out there worth going for." She reached across the table and caught hold of Dwight's hand. "If you've got too much work—"

"It's not that," Dwight said. "It's just that I'm not getting any younger." "And if I don't go soon, I won't go at all." He gently extricated his hand from Zabrina's hold.

"That damn horse," she growled.

"What's the horse got to do with all this?" I asked.

"Nothing . . ." Dwight replied. "I just said to Zsa-Zsa—" (Zsa-Zsa? I thought. Lord, they'd been closer than I imagined.) "—that seeing the horse—"

"Dumuzzi."

"—seeing Dumuzzi made me realize that I missed seeing things, ordinary things, out there in the world. Except on that, of course." He nodded toward the little television which I knew he'd spent countless hours watching. Had he been yearning to leave L'Enfant all the time he'd been watching that flickering image? So it seemed. But he hadn't known, apparently, how *much* he yearned, until Dumuzzi had appeared.

"Well," he said with a little sigh, "I should be going." He got up from the table.

"Wait until tomorrow at least," Zabrina said. "It's getting late. You'd be better setting off first thing in the morning."

"I'm afraid you'll slip something in my supper," he said to her with a small, sad smile. "And I won't remember why I packed."

Zabrina gave him a small, forbidding smile. "You know I'd never do a thing like that," she replied. Then, sniffing hard, she said: "If you don't want to stay, then don't. Nobody's twisting your arm." She looked down at her hands. "But you'll miss me," she said softly. "You see if you don't."

"I'll miss you so much I'll probably be back in a week," he said.

Zabrina started to shake with sorrow. Tears splashed on the table, big as silver dollars.

"Don't . . ." Dwight said, his own voice cracking. "I hate it when you cry."

"Well then you shouldn't *make* me cry," Zabrina replied, somewhat petulantly. She looked up at him, her eyes streaming. "I know you have to go," she said. "I understand. I really do. And I know you won't come back in a week, whatever you say. You'll get out there, and you'll forget I ever existed."

"Oh darlin'—" Dwight said, leaning down to gather her against him. It was an ungainly embrace, to say the least, Dwight unable to quite get his arms around Zabrina at that angle, Zabrina so desperate to be comforted she grabbed hold of him as though she were about to fall from a great height, and he was her only hope of life. The sobs came loud and long now, though Zabrina's face was pressed against Dwight's belly. With great tenderness he stroked her hair, looking at me as he did so. There was sadness on his face, no question; but there was also a hint of impatience. He'd decided to go, and there would be no changing her mind. Zabrina's clinging and sobbing only delayed the inevitable.

Plainly he wanted me to intervene.

"Come on, Zabrina," I said brightly, "enough's enough. He's not dying. He's just going to go see what's out there in the big, bad world."

"It's the same thing," she said.

"Now you're being silly," I said gently, walking over to her chair and laying my hands on her shoulders. She was momentarily distracted by my touch, which allowed Dwight to pull away from her. She made no attempt to catch hold of him again. She was obviously resigned to his departure.

"You take care of yourself," Dwight said to her. "And you, Maddox. I'm going to miss you too." He picked up his suitcase. "Say goodbye to Miss Marietta for me, will you? Tell her I wish her well with her lady."

He took a couple of backward steps towards the door, but they were so tentative I almost thought he was going to change his mind. And perhaps he would have done so if Zabrina hadn't looked up at him, and with a fierceness that I truly didn't expect from her at that moment, said:

"Are you still here?"

At which cue he turned on his heel, and departed.

# IV

I spent a few minutes attempting to console Zabrina after Dwight left, but I knew nothing I could say was going to comfort her as much as food. So I suggested a sandwich. She didn't brighten up immediately, but the sight of my labors on her behalf slowly dulled her unhappiness. Her sobs faded, her tears dried up. By the time I presented her with my handiwork, which was a minor work of art I may say (freshly sliced ham, cold sliced asparagus, pickles, a little mustard, a little mayonnaise) she had quite brightened up.

Once she began to eat the sandwich I laid out a selection of desserts, and then left her to it. She was so thoroughly engrossed in her edible comforts that I doubt she even realized I'd left the kitchen.

I had made myself a more modest version of the sandwich I'd constructed for Zabrina, and I ate it while I washed, shaved and changed into something more presentable than my sleep-rumpled garb. By the time I was ready for the day, the day was almost over. Dusk was drawing on, so I poured myself a glass of gin and walked out onto the veranda to enjoy the last of the light. It was a sublime evening: a clear sky, not a hint of a breeze. The birds were making a tuneful noise in the magnolias, there were squirrels in the grass going about their last labors of the day. I sipped my gin, and watched, and listened, and thought: so much of what makes L'Enfant beautiful will go on, long after this house has fallen. The birds will still sing, the squirrels will still caper, the night will still descend, and show its stars. Nothing important will pass away.

As I drained the last of my gin I heard laughter drifting across the lawn; distant at first, but getting closer. I couldn't yet see anybody, but it wasn't hard to make a good guess as to its source. This was women's laughter, though it was raucous and raw, and it came, I thought, from at least half a dozen throats. Marietta had brought her wedding party—or some portion of that party—back to the house.

I stepped off the veranda and onto the grass. The milky breast of the moon was rising round and full. Its light wasn't cold silver. It was butter-yellow; and it sweetened everything it lit.

I could hear Marietta's voice now, rising above the laughter.

"Get your asses movin'!" she was yelling. "I don't want anybody gettin' lost."

I watched the dark place under the trees from which her voice had come, and moments later she stepped into view, hand in hand with her Alice. A few steps behind came three more women, one of whom was glancing back over her shoulder, suggesting there were still others following on.

A few months ago I would have been appalled at the idea of Marietta bringing so many strangers onto the grounds of this sacred home. I would have thought it a violation. But what did it matter now? The more people who saw and enjoyed Jefferson's masterpiece before its destruction the better, and it was plain even at a distance that the women, now they had sight of the house, were suitably impressed. The laughter died away; they stopped in their tracks, exchanging looks of astonishment.

"This is where you lucky bitches live?" said one of the women in the party of three.

"This is where we live," Marietta said.

"It's beautiful . . ." said the woman who'd been glancing back over her shoulder. Now she'd forgotten her companions. She walked toward the house with a look of astonishment on her face.

There was more laughter out of the trees, and what I took to be the last of the celebrants came out into the moonlight. One of them was barely dressed, her blouse unbuttoned, her lower half naked. Her companion, an older woman with unkempt gray hair, was dressed more formally, but the front of her dress had been opened up to release her ample bosom. Both women staggered slightly as they walked; and the younger of the two sank down into the grass almost as she saw the house, her laughter fading. I heard her say:

"Oh shit, Lucy . . . she wasn't kidding."

The older woman (Lucy, I assumed) came up behind her, and the younger let her head loll against her thighs.

"How come I never knew this place was here?" Lucy called after Marietta.

"It was our little secret," Marietta replied.

"But it ain't a secret no more," said one of the women in the trio, coming to Marietta's side. "We're going to party all the time, now we know it's here."

"Suits me," Marietta said. She turned back to Alice, and kissed her on the lips. "We can do—" another kiss "—whatever the hell—" another kiss "—we want."

With that, she and Alice made their way across the lawn to the house. I decided it was time to make my presence known. Stepping out into the moonlight I started toward the women, calling to Marietta as I went.

"*Eddie!*" she said, opening her arms to me. "*There* you are! Look at us! We're married! We're married!" I went into her embrace. "Did you bring the minister too?" I said.

"We didn't need no minister," Alice said. "We just said our vows in front of our friends, and God."

"Then we all got drunk," Marietta said. "And we've stayed that way." She leaned close to me. "I love you, Eddie," she said to me. "I know I don't always show it—"

I hugged her again, tighter than before. "You're quite a lady," I told her. "I'm proud of you."

Marietta turned round to face the women. "Listen up, everyone! I'd like y'all to meet my brother Eddie. He's the only man on the planet worth a damn." She grabbed hold of my hand and squeezed it. "Eddie, say hello to everyone. This is Terri-Lynn—" The blonder of the pair who'd followed on Marietta and Alice's heels said hi, with a lavish smile. "And the big ol' gal there, that's Louise, 'cept don't call her that 'cause she'll kick your ass. She prefers Louie. So you've been warned."

Louie, who had the physique of a weight lifter who'd gone to seed, flicked her hair out of her eyes and said hello. The woman at her side, her features as limpid as Louie's were severe, introduced herself without Marietta's prompting.

"I'm Rolanda," she said.

"And I'm pleased to meet you," I replied. She had a bottle of whiskey in her hand, and passed it over to me. "Want a drink?"

I took the bottle, and drank from it.

"And that's Ava and Lucy at the back there," Marietta told me. She took the whiskey bottle out of my hand as she spoke and drinking from it, passed a mouthful of the booze onto Alice.

"I think Ava needs to lie down for a while," Lucy said, "she's kinda out of it."

"Alice'll take you into the house," Marietta said. "I want to have a quick word with my little brother. Go on, honey!" she said to Alice, turning her bride around and patting her on her butt. "Take them in. I won't be long."

"Where do you want us to go?" Alice said.

"Anywhere you like," Marietta said with an expansive gesture.

"Not upstairs," I cautioned.

"Oh, Eddie. She's not going to hurt anyone."

"Who are you talking about?" Rolanda wanted to know.

"My mother."

"Louie'll sort her out. She likes a good fight."

"Cesaria isn't a fistfighting lady," I said. "You just stay downstairs and things'll be fine and dandy."

"Can I have my whiskey back?" Rolanda said to Marietta.

"No you can't," Marietta replied. Rolanda frowned. "You're drunk enough."

"Oh, and you're not?" Rolanda said. She turned to me. "I *know* what you're thinking," she said, with a sly smile.

"Oh and what's that?"

"If only I were a woman, I'd get myself *laid* tonight. And you know what? You would. Big time." She reached down and without a word of warning cupped my genitals. "Pity you got this ol' thing weighing you down." She grinned. I don't think I even attempted an answer. If I did, I stumbled over it, and she was on her way, following the other five.

"So this is your crowd . . ." I said to Marietta.

"Aren't they a riot? They're not always like this, by the way. It's just a special night."

"What did you tell them?"

"About what?"

"About the house. About us. About Mama."

"*Eddie*, will you stop fretting? They couldn't find their way back here if their lives depended on it. Anyway, I trust them. They're my friends. I want to make them welcome here."

"Well why don't we just have an open house for the county?" I said. "Invite everyone in."

"You know that's not such a bad idea," she said, poking me in the middle of the chest. "We've got to start somewhere." She glanced back at the house. All the women had disappeared inside.

"What did you want to talk about?" I said.

"I just wanted to drink a toast," she said, raising the bottle between us.

"To anything in particular?"

"You. Me. Alice. Love." She smiled at me. "It is a pity you've got a dick, Eddie. I could find you a nice girlfriend—" She laughed uproariously at this. "Oh Eddie, I wish I had a camera. You're blushing."

"I am not blushing."

"Baby, take it from me. You're blushing." She kissed my cheek, which was probably somewhat flushed, I'll admit.

"I need to live a little," I said.

"That's our toast, right there," Marietta said, "to being alive and living a little."

"I'll drink to that."

"It's been too fucking long." She put the bottle to her lips and drank, then passed it over to me. I took another swallow, vaguely thinking that I was going to be as drunk as the rest of them if I went on like this. I'd only eaten a sandwich all day, and this was my third shot of liquor, including my gin, in the space of half an hour. But what the hell? It wasn't often a man got to play among wild women like this.

"Let's go inside," Marietta said, slipping her arm through mine. As we ambled to the house she leaned against me.

"I am *so* happy," she said as we got to the door.

"That's not just the whiskey talking?" I said.

"No, it's not the whiskey. I'm happy. I'm deep-down happy. What a beautiful night." She glanced back over her shoulder. "Oh my Lord," she said. "Look at that."

I turned to see what had drawn her attention. There in the middle of the lawn was a quartet of hyenas, their eyes upon us. There was nothing predatory in their stare, I didn't think, but their presence so close to the house was indeed surprising. Their natural nervousness seemed to have vanished. They were suddenly brave. Three of them halted when we stared back at them, but the largest of the four continued to approach, undaunted, and didn't stop until it was perhaps four or five yards from where we stood.

"I think she wants to come in," Marietta said.

"How do you know it's a she?" I said. "I thought you couldn't tell male from female."

"I know a bitch when I see one," Marietta remarked. "Hey, honey," she called to the animal, "you want to come join the party?"

The hyena sniffed the air, then glanced back at her companions, who were watching the whole scene intently, but hadn't come any closer. Deciding perhaps that she needed to study this situation more closely before she took the final plunge and entered the house, the animal lay down in the grass and put her head on her paws.

We left her to her scrutiny. It would only be a matter of time, I thought, and the creature would be over the threshold. Then what? With the wedding party and the hyenas in residence, how long before the foxes came, and the birds? L'Enfant, in its old age, would soon be as busy on the inside as it was out. Perhaps after all my doomy predictions the house would not die a violent death, but be gently brought to ruin by animals that had flourished in its vicinity. Hadn't I even predicted the possibility, many months ago? The thought that my prediction might prove correct was surprisingly sweet.

I left the front door open when we went inside, just to be sure the hyena knew she was welcome.

## i

Why is it so much harder to describe happy times than sad? I've had little trouble conjuring scenes of grief and devastation for the last God knows how many pages, but now—when I come to the simple business of telling you how I passed three or four blissful hours in the company of my darling Marietta and her tribe—words fail me. I was simply content with these women, whose repartee tended toward the ribald, and whose voices—when raised in argument—were deafening. What were the bones of contention between them? I can't remember, to tell you the truth. I know I contributed little or nothing to the debate. I sat and watched and listened to that charmed circle and I swear there was no seduction on earth that would have persuaded me to leave it.

At last, however, the drink and the hour took its toll on even the hardiest of the celebrants, and sometime after midnight the group broke up, and we all went on our way. I'd found a moment to tell Marietta about Dwight's departure, so she invited Rolanda and Terri-Lynn to take his bed for the night. Ava had been tucked up on the sofa since the beginning of the evening, and Lucy went to join her there. Louie stayed where she was, at the dining room table, her head sunk on her hands. The newlyweds, of course, traipsed away to Marietta's bedroom, hand in hand.

As I wandered through the house, heading back to my study, I thought about what was left for me to write. I would have to make an account of how Galilee and Rachel left the island: strictly for neatness' sake; it was an uneventful departure. And then there was the matter of the bodies in the house. I'd have to dedicate a couple of paragraphs to how they were discovered. It was certainly a more interesting anecdote than the details of the lovers' departure, touched as it was by an element of the grotesque. The same blind dog that had wandered up from the beach to be petted by Rachel when she'd first come to the house had been the one to raise the alarm. He had done so not by sitting on the veranda and howling, but by turning up on his owner's porch with a portion of a human foot, chewed off at the ankle, in his mouth. It didn't take long for the police to find the two corpses. Though the body of Mitchell Geary was inside the house, it was his body that was missing the foot. For some reason the animal had stepped over the corpse on the veranda to make dinner of the man at the bottom of the stairs.

The coroner determined that both men had been dead for forty-eight hours. Though the police began a search of the island immediately, it was assumed that the murderer was already long gone; probably back to the mainland. There was plenty of evidence pointing to Rachel, of course: her bags were up in the bedroom, her fingerprints on the banisters, close to the place where Mitchell Geary lay. Later, however, there would be good forensic reasons to doubt her culpability: the general store owner would identify Mitchell as the man who'd purchased the murder weapon; and there would be only one set of prints— Mitchell's prints—found on the knife. But just because she hadn't actually delivered the lethal wound didn't exonerate her. The newspapers were soon full of theories as to what had happened at the house, the most popular being the belief that Mitchell had come to the island to get his wife back, but had suspected that she had some plot laid against his life. He'd armed himself as best he could, killed the man she'd hired to murder him, and then—in some kind of struggle with Rachel—had fallen downstairs and perished in what was essentially a freak accident.

There was no lack of commentary attending this theorizing—a few of the more perceptive journalists commenting on how dysfunctional the relationships between the Geary men and their wives seemed to be. A few even claimed that they'd seen the tragedy coming; that it had been in essence inevitable. *This was a mismatch made in hell,* one of the bitchier society watchers wrote, *and I'm only surprised it's taken so long for it to come to an end. That it has ended so tragically can come as no surprise to the surviving members of the Geary family, in whose ranks the course of love and marriage have seldom run smooth. A cursory glance over the history of the dynasty provides ample evidence that the men have all too often treated their wives as little more than investments with wombs, providing a return in children rather than dollars. Is it any great shock that Rachel Geary apparently resisted this life?*

The family itself made no public pronouncements on the matter, except for a short statement, cautiously worded by Cecil, that put full confidence in the police investigations.

Behind closed doors, there was no gathering of family members to discuss how things went on from here, no stirring speech from Loretta about how this adversity would allow the Gearys to demonstrate their cohesiveness. This was the third death in the family in a matter of months, and it drove everyone into their own private places, to grieve or meditate. Cadmus's funeral was delayed by several days so that Mitchell's body could be flown back from Hawaii, and arrangements could be made to inter Mitchell and his grandfather together. Loretta did not oversee the preparations: she left it all to Carl Linville. Instead she flew down to the house in Washington with Jocelyn, where she locked herself away, taking no calls or visitors, refusing to speak to anyone but Cecil. She had lost her last ally, now that the prince was gone. Whether her appetite for control of the family had been permanently spoiled only time would tell; for now she seemed content to let the world proceed on its weary way without her.

Only Garrison seemed untouched by all of this. No, not untouched, untroubled. When he flew to Hawaii to accompany his brother's body home he strode through the hordes of photographers at the airport like a man who'd been given a new lease on life. It wasn't that he smiled—nothing so crass—but to anyone who knew him, knew the brittle language of his body, and his reticence about being in the public eye, there was plainly a change in him. It was as though Garrison had taken on some of the qualities of his dead brother; inherited at the moment of Mitchell's decease all the confidence that had been the prince's birthright. He parted the journalists like a sea, saying nothing, but dispensing nods to right and left, as though to say: *I am come into power.*

✳     ✳     ✳

When he got to the island his first duty was to go to the morgue in Lihue and confirm identification of Mitchell. This done, he was driven to Anahola to visit the house, which he was allowed to walk around alone. He wanted some time, he said, to pay his respects to the past. The police captain who was escorting him put up no objection to Garrison's request, but when, after half an hour, Garrison had not emerged from the house, he went in to see that all was well. The house was deserted. Garrison had finished with his meditations long since, and was now standing on the beach. He cut a peculiar figure, with his black suit and his slicked hair and his hands thrust deep into his pockets. The sun was blazing; the water turquoise and white. Garrison was staring out to sea, and he stayed there, staring and staring, for perhaps fifteen minutes. When he came back in, he was smiling.

"It's all going to be fine," he said.

## ii

There are no neat conclusions to any of this, of course. All these lives go on, past the end of this book; there's always more to tell. But I have to draw the line somewhere, and I'm choosing to draw it here, give or take a few observations. Tempting though it is to pick at the threads of things I've mentioned in these pages, but left unsewn, I don't dare touch them. Each is a garment unto itself.

So. Let me tell what happened when, having wandered about the house for a while, thinking the thoughts I've just set down, I came to the hallway.

I glanced up the stairs, and there, close to the top of the flight, I glimpsed a motion in the shadows.

I thought perhaps it was Zabrina, who'd been conspicuous by her absence throughout the evening (though she must certainly have heard the noise of the wedding party). I called out to her, but even as I did so I realized my error. The shape on the stairs was small, and even accounting for the fact that it was wrapped in shadow, somehow vague.

"Zelim?" I ventured.

The form rose up from its crouching position, and came a little way down the stairs, its gait hesitant. My second guess had been correct. It was indeed Zelim, or what was left of him. His presence stood to his earlier self as that self had stood to the fisherman from Atva. He was the phantom of a phantom, his substance negligible. Like smoke, I want to say; like a soul of smoke, who only held his form because there was no wind to disperse him. I held my breath. He looked so tenuous that he'd be banished by the mildest exhalation.

But he had sufficient strength to speak: a dwindling voice, to be sure, disappearing with every syllable, yet strangely eloquent. I heard the happiness in him from the first, and knew before he told me that his wish had been granted.

"She let me go . . ." he said.

I dared that breath now. "I'm happy for you," I said.

"Thank . . . you . . ." His eyes, in the last phase of his existence, had become huge, like the eyes of a child.

"When did this happen?" I asked him.

"Just a . . . few . . . minutes ago . . ." the infant said. His voice was so quiet I had to strain to hear what he was telling me. "As soon . . . as soon . . . as she knew . . ."

I didn't catch the last of what he said, but I was afraid to waste a moment asking, for fear of losing him completely in that moment. So I kept my silence, and listened. He was almost gone. Not just his voice, but his physical presence, fading by the heartbeat. I felt no sorrow for him—how could I, when he'd so plainly stated his desire to be gone out of this world?—but it was still a strangely melancholy sight, to see a living soul erased before your eyes.

"I remember . . ." he murmured ". . . how he came for me . . ."

What was this? I didn't understand what I was being told.

". . . in Samarkand . . ." Zelim went on, the syllables of the city like gossamer. Oh now I understood. I'd written about the event he was remembering, I'd pictured it here on these pages. Zelim, the aged philosopher, sitting among his students, telling a story about how God's hands worked; then looking up and seeing a stranger at the back of the room, and dying. His death had been a kind of summons; out of his self-willed existence into the service of Cesaria Yaos. Now that service was ended, and he was remembering—fondly, I thought, to judge by the tender gaze in his eyes—how he'd been called; and by whom. By Galilee, of course.

Did Zelim realize that I was still a little puzzled by what he was telling me, or did he at the last want to simply state how things had come full circle? Which ever it was, he said:

"He's here."

And with those two words gave up his life after death, and went away, smoke and soul.

*He's here.*

That was quite a pair of words. If they were true, then I was amazed.

Galilee, here? Lord in heaven, *Galilee here!* I didn't know whether to start yelling at the top of my voice, or to go hide my head. I looked up

to the top of the stairs, half-expecting to see Cesaria there, demanding I
go fetch him, bring him to her. But the landing was deserted, the house
as still as it had been in the moment before Zelim had spoken his last.
Did she not know he was here? Impossible. Of course she knew. This
house was hers, from dome to foundations; the moment he'd stepped
into it she'd been listening to his breath and to his heartbeat; to the din
of his digestion.

She knew that he'd have to come to her sooner or later, and she
was simply waiting for him to do so. She could afford to be patient, after
all these long, lonely years.

I didn't linger in the hallway, now that Zelim was gone. I headed for my
study, and was a few yards from my study door when I caught the allur-
ing whiff of a burning havana. I pushed open the door, and there, sitting
in the chair behind my desk, was the great voyager himself, leafing
through my book, while he puffed on one of my cigars.

He looked up when I entered, and gave me an apologetic smile.

"Sorry," he said. "I couldn't help myself."

"The cigar or the book?" I replied.

"Oh the book," he said. "It's quite a story. Is any of it true?"

## iii

I didn't ask him how much he'd read; or what he thought of my stylish
eccentricities. Nor did I reply to his perverse question, about the veracity of what I'd written. Nobody knew the truth of it better than he.

We embraced, he offered me one of my own cigars, which I
declined, and then he asked me why there were so many women in the
house.

"We went from room to room," he explained, "looking for somewhere to lay our heads, and—"

"Who's *we*?"

He smiled. "Oh, come on, brother . . ."

"Rachel?" I replied. He nodded. "She's here?"

"Of course she's here. You think I'd ever let that woman out of my
sight again after what we've been through?"

"Where is she?"

His eyes went to the door of my bedroom. "She's sleeping," he
explained.

"In my bed?"

"You don't mind?"

I couldn't keep the grin off my face. "No, of course I don't mind."

"Well I'm glad I've pleased somebody in this damn house," Galilee said.

"Can I . . . take a peek at her?"

"What the hell for?"

"Because I've been writing about her for the last nine months. I want to see—" What did I want to see? Her face? Her hair? The curve of her back? I suddenly felt a kind of *desire* for her, I suppose. Something I'd probably been feeling all along, I just hadn't realized it. "I just want to see her," I said.

I didn't wait for him to give me permission. I got up and went to the bedroom door. A wash of moonlight lit the bed, and there, sprawled on the antiquated quilt, was the woman of my waking dreams. I couldn't quite believe it. There she was: Rachel Pallenberg-Geary-Barbarossa, her liquid hair spread on the same pillow where I'd laid my own buzzing head so many nights, and thought about how to shape the story of her life. Rachel in Boston, Rachel in New York, Rachel convalescing in Caleb's Creek, and walking the beach at Anahola. Rachel in despair, Rachel *in extremis,* Rachel in love—

"*Rachel in Love,*" I murmured.

"What's that?"

I glanced back at Galilee. "I should have called the book *Rachel in Love.*"

"Is that what it's really about?" he said.

"I don't know what the hell it's about," I replied, quite truthfully. "I thought I knew, about halfway through, but . . ." I returned my gaze to the sleeping woman ". . . maybe I can't know until it's finished."

"You're not done?"

"Not now you're here," I replied.

"I hope you're not expecting some big drama," Galilee said, "because that's not what I had in mind."

"It'll be what it'll be," I said. "I'm strictly an observer."

"Oh no you're not," he said, getting up from behind the desk. "I need your help." I looked at him blankly. "With her." He cast his eyes up toward the ceiling.

"She's *your* mother not mine."

"But you know her better than I do. You've been here with her all these years, while I've been away."

"And you think I've been sitting with her drinking mint juleps? Talking about the magnolias? I've barely seen her. She's stayed up there brooding."

"A hundred and forty years of brooding?"

"She's had a lot to brood about. You. Nicodemus. Jefferson."

"Jefferson? She doesn't still think about that loser."

"Oh yes she does. She told me, at great length—"

"See? You do talk to her. Don't try and squirm out of it. You talk to her."

"All right, I talk to her. Once in a while. But I'm not going to be your apologist."

Galilee contemplated this for a moment; then he shrugged. "Then you won't have an ending to your book, will you?" he said. "It's as simple as that. You'll be sitting down here wondering what the hell's going on up there, and you'll never know. You'll have to make it up."

"Jesus . . ." I muttered.

"I've got a point, right?"

He read me well. What was worse than the prospect of going up with Galilee in tow to face Cesaria? Why, the prospect of staying here below, and not knowing what passed between them. Whatever happened between mother and son when they came face to face, I had to be there to witness it. If I failed to do so then I failed in my duty as a writer. I couldn't bear to do that. I've failed at too much else.

"All right," I said. "I'm persuaded."

"Good man," he said, and embraced me, pressing my body hard against his. It made me feel meager, to be sure. I realized as he wrapped his arms around me that I'd hardly expressed with a quarter the passion it deserved what the Geary women must have felt in his embrace. I envied them.

"I'm going to wake Rachel," he said, breaking his hold on me and going to the door of my bedroom. I followed him, as far as the door, and watched him crouch beside the bed and reach out to gently shake her out of sleep.

She was obviously deep in dreams, because it took her a little time to surface. But when her eyes finally opened, and she saw Galilee, a luminous smile came onto her face. Oh, there was such love in it! Such unalloyed pleasure that he was there, at her side.

"It's time to get up, honey," Galilee said.

Her eyes came in my direction. "Hi," she said. "Who are you?"

It felt odd, let me tell, to have this woman—whose life I had so carefully chronicled, and with whom I now felt quite familiar—look at me and not know me.

"I'm Maddox," I said.

"And you're sleeping in his bed," Galilee said.

She sat up. The sheet fell away from her body, and she plucked it up to cover her nakedness. "Galilee told me a lot about you," she said to me, though I suspect this was to cover a moment of embarrassment.

"But I'm not what you imagined?"

"Not exactly."

"You look trimmer than you did when I saw you at the swamp," Galilee said, patting my belly.

"I've been working hard. Not eating."

"Working on your book," Rachel said.

I nodded, hoping that would be the end of the subject. It had never occurred to me until now that she might want to read what I'd written about her. The thought made my palms clammy. I turned to Galilee. "You know I think if we're going to go up to see Cesaria," I said, "we should go soon. She knows you're here—"

"The longer we wait, the more she'll think I'm afraid to come?" Galilee said. I nodded.

"I'd like to at least wash my face before we go," Rachel said.

"The bathroom's through there," I said, pointing the way. Then I withdrew from the room, to allow her some privacy.

"She's so beautiful," I whispered to Galilee when he'd followed me out. "You're a very lucky man."

Galilee didn't reply. He had his eyes cast toward the ceiling, as though he were preparing himself for what lay above.

"What do you want from her?" I asked him.

"To be forgiven, I suppose. No. More than that." He looked at me. "I want to come home, Eddie. I want to bring the love of my life back to L'Enfant, and live here happily ever after." Now it was me who didn't reply. "You don't believe in happily ever after?" he said.

"For us?"

"For anybody."

"But we're not anybody, are we? We're the Barbarossas. The rules are different for us."

"Are they?" he said, his gaze opaque. "I'm not so sure. It seems to me we're driven by the same stupid things that drive everyone else. We're no better than the Gearys. We should be, but we're not. We're just as petty, we're just as confused. It's time we started to think about the future."

"This is strange, coming from you."

"I want to have children with Rachel."

"I wouldn't do that," I said. "Half-breeds are no use to anybody."

He laid his hand on my shoulder. "That's what I used to believe. Anyway what kind of father would I make? That's what I said to myself. But it's time, Eddie." He smiled, beautifully. "I want to fill this old house with kids. And I want them to learn about all the miraculous shit we take for granted."

"I don't think there's much that's miraculous left in this place." I said. "If there ever was."

"It's still here," he said. "It's everywhere around us. It's in our blood. It's in the ground. And it's up there, with her."

"Maybe."

He caught hold of my chin, and shook it. "Look at you. Be happy. I'm home."

# VI

So, up we went, the three of us. Through the dark, quiet house, up the stairs, to Cesaria's chambers. She wasn't there, however. As I went from room to room, knocking lightly, then pushing the doors open, the realization slowly grew that *of course* she wasn't there. She'd gone up one more flight, to the skyroom. The circle was closing, quickly now. The place where all this had begun—where I'd been granted the first visions—was demanding our attendance.

As we turned from the empty bedroom, I heard the click of claws on the floorboard, and saw Cesaria's favorite quill-pig, Tansy, scuttling out from under the bed. I went down on my haunches and cautiously picked the creature up. She was quite happy to be in my arms—and for some reason I found her presence there reassuring.

"Where are we going now?" Galilee said as I passed he and Rachel on my way out of the bedroom.

"Up to the dome," I said.

He looked at me anxiously. "What's she doing up there?"

"I guess we're going to find out," I replied, and led the way, along the passage and up the narrow stairs. Tansy grew more agitated as we went; a sure sign that my instincts were correct, and that Cesaria was indeed awaiting us in the room above.

I paused at the door, and turned back to the lovers.

"Have you ever been in here?" I asked Galilee.

"No . . ."

"Well, if we get separated—" I said.

"Wait. What are you talking about: separated? It's not that big a room."

"It's not a room, Galilee," I said. "It may be that from the outside, but once you get in there, it's another world. It's her world."

He looked decidedly uncomfortable.

"So what should we expect?" Rachel said.

"I'm afraid whatever I tell you, it's probably going to be something different. Just go with the flow. Let it happen. And don't be afraid of it."

"She's not afraid of much," Galilee said, offering Rachel a little smile.

"And as I said, if we get separated—"

"We'll go on without you," Galilee said. "Agreed?"

"Agreed."

With the quill-pig still nestling in the crook of my arm, I turned to the door, and reaching down—somewhat tentatively, I will admit—for the handle, I opened it. There was a sliver of me dared imagine being here would work another miracle upon me. If the first visit had healed my broken body, what might a second do? It was all very well for Galilee to extol the virtue of half-breeds, but I'd found no special glory in that condition; quite the contrary. Was it possible that stepping back into the heart of Cesaria's world I might be cured of my hybrid state? Might be made wholly divine?

That tantalizing possibility made me braver than I might otherwise have been. With just one backward glance, to be sure that I still had Rachel and Galilee in tow, I strode on into the room. At first glance it seemed to be quite empty, but I knew how misleading such impressions could be. Cesaria was here, I was certain of it. And if she was here, then so was the court of visions and transformations that attended upon her. It was just a question of waiting for them to appear.

"Nice room," I heard Galilee say behind me.

There was an ironic edge to the remark, no doubt; he obviously thought I'd overestimated the miraculous nature of the place. I didn't offer any kind of defense. I just held my breath. A few seconds passed. The quill-pig had quieted in my arms. Curious, I thought. I let the held breath go, albeit slowly. Still nothing.

"Are you sure—" Galilee began.

"Hush."

It was not me who silenced him, it was Rachel. I heard her footsteps behind me, and from the corner of my eye saw her walking on past me into the room. She'd left Galilee's side. In other circumstances I might have glanced back over my shoulder and called him a coward, but the moment was too fraught for me to risk the distraction. I kept my gaze fixed on Rachel as she wandered toward the center of the room. That *hush* of hers had come because she'd heard something; but what? All I could hear was the sound of our breathing, and the padding of Rachel's soles on the bare boards. Still, she was clearly attending to some sound or other. She cocked her head slightly, as if she wasn't quite sure whether she was really hearing this sound or not. And now, as she listened, I caught what she was straining to hear. It was the softest of sounds: a sibilant murmuring, so quiet I might have assumed it was the hum of my blood, had it not also been audible to Rachel.

She looked down at her feet. I followed her gaze, and saw that a subtle change had overtaken the boards. The cracks were being erased, and the details of each board, the grain and the knotholes, were shifting. Rachel could obviously feel the effect of this shift against the tips of her toes: the flow of the motion was toward her, out of the heart of the room.

Now I put the sound I was hearing together with the shifting of the boards: the wood was becoming sand; sand blown by a gentle but insistent breeze.

Rachel glanced back toward me. To judge by her expression she wasn't so much alarmed by what was happening as entertained.

"Look," she said. Then, to Galilee, "It's okay, honey." She reached out toward him, and he came to join her, sliding an anxious glance in my direction as he did so. The wind was getting stronger; the boards had now disappeared completely. There was only sand beneath our feet now, its grains glittering as they rolled on their way.

I watched him reach out to take hold of her hand, wondering what place this was, creeping up upon us. The walls across the room had melted away into a gray-blue haze; and I cast my eyes heavenward to see that the dome had also faded from view. There were stars up there, where there'd been a solid vault of timber and plaster. The dark between them was deepening, and their pinpricks growing brighter, even as I watched. For a few giddying heartbeats it seemed I was falling toward them. I returned my gaze to Rachel and Galilee before the illusion caught hold of me; and as I did so the lovers' fingers intertwined.

I felt a subtle shock pass through me, and Tansy jumped out of my arms, landing on the sand in front of me. I went down on my haunches to see that no harm had come to her—strange, I suppose, but there was some comfort in concerning myself with the animal's welfare when the ground was being remade underfoot, and the stars burning too bright above. But Tansy wanted none of my help now. She was off before I could touch her, with that comical rolling gait of hers. I watched her go perhaps three yards from me before lifting my eyes. What I saw when I did so put the thought of her out of my head completely.

There was no apocalyptic scene before me; no vaults of fire, no panicking animals. There was instead a landscape that I knew. I'd never walked there, except in my imagination, but perhaps I knew it all the better for that fact.

Off to my right was a forest, thick and dark. And to my left, the lisping waters of the Caspian Sea.

*Two souls as old as heaven came down to the shore that ancient noon . . .*

This was the place where the holy family had walked; where Zelim the fisherman had left his bickering comrades and gone to engage in a conversation that would not only change his life, but the life that he lived after death. The place of beginnings.

There was no harm here, I thought to myself. There was just the wind and the sand and the sea. I looked back toward the door; or rather the spot where the door had stood. It had gone. There was no way out of here, back into the house. Nor was there any sign of Cesaria's presence along the shore. I thought I could see some hint of habitation in the distant dunes—a new Atva, perhaps, or the old—and there was the skeletal remains of a boat, the bones of its hull black in the starlight, a distance away, but of the woman we'd come here to see, not a sign.

"Where the hell are we?" Galilee wondered aloud.

"This is where you were baptized," I told him.

"Really?" He looked out toward the placid water. "Where I tried to swim away?"

"That's right."

"How far did you get?" Rachel asked him.

I didn't hear his response. My attention was once again upon the porcupine, who having waddled away some distance had now turned round, and with her nose to the sand, was snuffling her way toward the carcass of the boat. Halfway there, she raised her head, made a small noise in her throat, and quickened her pace. She wasn't sniffing her way any longer: she knew her destination. Somebody was waiting for us in the shadows of the vessel.

"Galilee . . . ?" I murmured.

He looked my way, and I pointed along the shore. There—sitting in the boat—was the storm-maker, the virago herself, a scarf of dark silk draped over her head.

"You see her?" I murmured.

"I see," he said. Then, more quietly. "You go first."

I didn't argue. My anxiety had faded, calmed by the tranquillity of the scene. There would be no great unleashings here, I sensed; no forces raging around. Of course that probably meant that my hopes of being raised out of half-breed state were dashed. But nor would I come to any harm.

Following Tansy's tracks in the sand, I approached the boat. The starlight was no longer brightening, but its benediction showed me Cesaria clearly enough, sitting there on a pile of timbers, looking my way. With the ribs of the wreck rising to either side of her she looked as though she were sitting at the heart of a dark flower.

*L'Enfants . . .* she said to us . . . *you took your time.*

Tansy was at her feet. She bent down and the creature clambered up into her embrace, where it perched in grunting bliss.

"We looked for you downstairs . . ." I began to explain.

*I won't be going back there,* she said. *I've shed too many tears down there. And now I'm done.*

She hadn't taken her eyes off me since we'd started toward her. It was almost as though she didn't want to look past me toward her son; didn't dare, perhaps, for fear of shedding the very tears she said she was done with. I could see how close they were; how full of feeling she was.

"Is there something you need from me?" I asked her.

*No, Maddox,* she said, with sweet gravity. *There's nothing now. You've done more than enough, child.*

*Child.* There'd been a time when she'd enraged me with that word. Now it was wonderful. I was a child, still. My life, she seemed to say, was still to be lived.

*You should go,* she said.

"Where?"

*Through the forest,* she said. *The way Zelim went.*

I didn't move. Though I'd heard the instruction, I couldn't bring myself to leave. After all my trepidation, all my fears of what being in her presence might bring, I wanted to stay a moment longer, two moments, three, to enjoy the balm of her eyes and the honey of her voice. It was only with the greatest difficulty that I made my limbs obey me, and turn me toward the trees.

*Travel safely, child . . .* I heard her say.

Lord, but it was hard, walking away, even though in a sense I was being set free. I'd paid for my freedom in words; every thought I've set on these pages has been a ransom against this release. But still, there was a sadness in me, to be going.

I didn't look back until I'd taken perhaps twenty paces. When I did, however, I stopped for a few minutes, just to watch what ensued. This was the moment. Galilee and Rachel, hand in hand, were approaching the boat.

*Brat,* Cesaria said to him. *You took your time.*

"I got lost, Mama," Galilee said. "I got lost in the world. But I'm home now."

*There's nothing left to come home to,* Cesaria said. *It's all gone.*

"Then let me build it again," Galilee replied.

*You don't have the wits, child.*

"Not on my own," Galilee said. "But with my Rachel—"

*Your Rachel,* Cesaria said, her voice softening. She rose from her throne of timbers, and beckoned to Rachel. *Come here,* she said.

Rachel let go of Galilee's hand, and walked toward the boat. Cesaria stepped out between the ribs of the hull and looked her up and down. I was too far from them to see the expression on her face, but I could well imagine how scouring that scrutiny felt. I'd experienced it myself; or some measure of it. Cesaria was looking into Rachel's soul. Making a final judgment as to the appropriateness of this woman. At last, she said:

*Are you sure you want this?*

"This?" Rachel said.

*This house. This history. This brat of mine.*

Rachel looked back over her shoulder. In the long moment that she gazed at Galilee I thought I heard the stars moving overhead, steady and content.

"Yes," she said. "He's what I want."

*Then he's yours,* Cesaria said.

She opened her arms.

"Does this mean I'm forgiven?" Galilee asked.

Cesaria laughed. *If not now, then when? Come into my arms, before you break my heart again.*

"Oh, Mama—"

He went to her then, with such abandon, and pressed his face against her shoulder while she wrapped him in her arms.

"Forgiven?" he said.

*Forgiven,* she replied.

# VII

## i

I did not expect to come to the last few pages of this story following in the footsteps of Zelim the fisherman, but that's what happened. Leaving the reunion to take its happy course behind me I headed for the trees, and stepped beneath their canopy. It was dark, and I very soon gave up any attempt to plot a course for myself; I simply plunged on through the undergrowth, letting accident decide my destiny. I wasn't particularly reassured by what I remembered of Zelim's journey. He'd emerged from this forest only to be raped by bandits. I hoped to be luckier; hoped, indeed, that though I'd left the shore and Cesaria far behind me, she was watching over my progress, and would guide me in my sightlessness.

There was little sign of a guiding hand, however. Just as I was certain the darkness around me was as profound as it could get, it became darker. I was soon reduced to stumbling forward with my arms stretched in front of me, to prevent myself from walking into a tree. That didn't keep my face and hands and chest from being scratched by thorns, or my feet from becoming entangled in the ropes of root across my path. Several times I fell headlong, the breath knocked out of me. So much for Cesaria's final blessing, I thought sourly. *Travel safely*, indeed. If this was her world I was stumbling through, as I presumed it to be, might she not have put a moon up there above me, to light the path?

No, I suppose that would have been too easy. She was never one to be needlessly kind, even to herself. Perhaps especially to herself. Just because her child had been returned to her, she wasn't going to change her ways.

It was too late for me to turn back, of course. The shore had long since disappeared from sight behind me. I had no choice but to wander on—as Zelim had done before me—hoping that the torment would eventually come to an end.

And so, after a long, long time, it did. I caught a glimpse of amber light between the trees, and fixing my eyes on the glow, I stumbled on toward it. Dawn was coming up, ahead of me; I could see layers of tinted cloud, their flat bellies stroked by the emerging sun. And to welcome the light, birds in bright chorus, filling the branches overhead.

My legs were weak by now, and my body shaking with fatigue, but the sight and sound gave me a fresh burst of energy, and within five minutes of first seeing the light I was emerging from the trees.

My night journey had been far more elaborate than I'd realized. Somehow while I'd been blind Cesaria's enchantments had led me out of the house and across the grounds to the perimeter of L'Enfant. That was where I now stood: at the borderland between sacred ground and secular; between Barbarossian territory and the rest of the world. Behind me was a solid mass of trees, the thicket that swelled and blossomed between them so dense that I could see no more than three or four yards, while ahead of me lay a landscape of simple virtues. Rolling hills, rising away from the swampy ground that bounded L'Enfant; scattered trees, uncultivated fields. I could see no sign of habitation.

The birds who'd been greeting the dawn now took flight from the canopy, and I watched them rising up, wheeling around overhead before taking their various ways. I felt suddenly immensely vulnerable, seeing them rise into that bright, wide sky. It was so long since I'd been roofless; I was sorely tempted to turn round and go back to the house. I had unfinished business there, I reasoned: I couldn't just walk out into the world and leave the life I'd been living behind me. A journey like this needed thought and preparation. I had to say goodbye to Marietta, Zabrina and Luman; I had to append a few closing paragraphs to the book on my desk; I had to tidy up my study, and lock away my private papers. There was this to do, there was that to do.

All excuses, of course. I was just trying to find ways to postpone the fearful moment when I actually faced the world again. That was why Cesaria had tricked me into this sudden exile, I knew; to deny me my procrastinations, and oblige me to venture out, under this expanse of sky. In short, to make me live.

I was standing there, facing the empty vista before me, chewing all this over, when I heard a motion in the thicket behind me. I turned around, and to my astonishment saw Luman digging his way out through the shrubbery, cursing ripely as he did so. When he finally emerged from the tangle he looked like some half-crazed spirit of the green, twiglets and thorns in his beard and hair. He spat out a mouthful of leaf, and gave me a fierce look.

"You'd better be grateful!" he groused.

"For what?" I said.

He raised his hands. He was carrying two leather knapsacks, both much battered and beaten. They were packed to the point of bursting. "I brought you some stuff for your travels," he said.

"Well that's good of you," I said.

He tossed the smaller of the knapsacks over to me. It was heavy. It also stank.

"Is this another of your antiques?" I said, looking at the Confederate insignia on the flap.

"Yep," he said. "I got them the same place I got the saber. I put your pistol in there, along with some money, a shirt and a flask of brandy."

"And that one?" I said, eyeing the bigger knapsack.

"Some more clothes. A pair of boots, and you know what."

I smiled. "You brought me my book?"

"Of course. I know how much you love that damn thing. I wrapped it in the ol' Stars and Bars."

"Thank you," I said, taking the second knapsack from him. It was quite a weight. My shoulders were going to regret my verbosity in the days to come. But it felt good to have the thing with me; like a child that I could not bear to be separated from.

"You went into the house for the book," I said. "I know how you hate it in there . . ."

He threw me a sideways glance. "Used to. But it's changin' isn't it? Animals shittin' on the floor. Women everywhere." His face broke into a puckish grin. "I'm thinkin' maybe I'll move back in. Them ladies is mighty fine."

"They're lesbians," I pointed out.

"I don't care if they're from Wisconsin," he said. "I like 'em."

"How did you know where to find me?"

"I heard you walking by the Smoke House, talking to yourself."

"What was I saying?"

"Couldn't make no sense of it. I came out and you jus' walked right on, like you was sleepwalkin'. I kinda figured she'd put you up to this. Old Lady Love."

"You mean Cesaria."

He nodded. "That's what Paps used to call her. '*Old Lady Love, all ice and honeysuckle.*' Didn't you ever hear him call her that?"

"No, I never did."

"Huh. Well, anyhow I figured she'd decided to be rid of you. So I thought I'd just give you something to be going with."

"Thank you. I appreciate it." Luman looked a little uncomfortable that I was thanking him.

"Well . . ." he said, plucking another fragment of leaf from the corner of his mouth. "You've been kind to me, brother."

I wondered, watching him separate leaf and beard, if I'd missed some simple pattern in my investigation of our family; if he wasn't Pan, by another name, and my brother Dionysus, and—

I caught myself in this, and growled.

"What is it?"

"I'm still writing that damn book in my head," I said.

"You'll forget about it, once you get out there," Luman said, his gaze drifting past me to the landscape over my shoulder. There was a certain wistfulness on his face. I thought about our conversation about how he couldn't possibly face the prospect of returning to the world: that it would make too crazy. But I could also see how the idea of risking the journey was deeply tempting to him. I decided to play Mephistopheles.

"You want to join me?" I said.

He didn't look at me. Just kept his eyes on the sunlit hills. "Yeah . . ." he growled. "I want to join you. But I ain't gonna. Least, not today. I got shit to do, brother. I got to arm all them ladies."

"Arm them?"

"Yeah . . . if they're staying—"

"They're not staying."

"Marietta says they are."

"Really."

"That's what she says."

Oh my Lord, I thought: the invasion took place after all. L'Enfant has fallen. But not to the Gearys: at least, not yet. To a tribe of lesbians.

"But you know what you promised—" Luman went on.

"You mean about your kids?"

"You remembered."

"Of course I remembered."

He beamed, his eyes shining. "You'll go look for them."

"I'll go look for them."

He came to me suddenly, and clamped his arms around me. "I knew you wouldn't let me down," he said, planting a noisy kiss on my cheek. "I love you, Maddox. And I want you to take that love along with you, to keep you safe out there." His hug tightened. "You hear me?"

I hugged him back, though it was a messy embrace, with both knapsacks in my arms.

"You know where you're going to start looking?" he asked me when the hugging was done.

"No idea," I said. "I'm just going to follow my instincts."

"You bring my kids back with you?"

"If that's what you want."

"It's what I want . . ." he said.

He fixed me with his gaze for a long moment, and I swear there was more affection in his expression than I'd seen directed at me in many a long year. He didn't linger, but broke the gaze, and turned away, disappearing into the thicket. In four or five strides he'd been eclipsed by the green, and the wall between myself and L'Enfant stood resolute.

## ii

Luman's a lot smarter than a first impression might suggest. He didn't just pack the book, he packed a sheaf of plain paper, some pens, even ink. He knew I'd want to record my departure from L'Enfant; that my farewell to the house would also mark my farewell to these pages.

So here I am, sitting on the roadside maybe three miles from where he and I said our goodbyes, committing these closing thoughts to paper. The day's been kind to me. There's been a gentle breeze blowing since midmorning, and the sun's been warm, but not hot. I came upon this road after a couple of hours of walking, and decided to follow it, though I have no idea where it's going to lead me. In a sense—though I'm a very long way from the Caspian Sea—I'm still following in Zelim's footsteps; traveling blind, but in hope. Of what? Perhaps of a little wisdom; a clue to the question I'd wanted answered by Nicodemus: *what am I for?* It's probably too much to expect; the world grants an answer to that question rarely, I think, and when it does usually makes the recipients pay dearly for the information. The tree of that knowledge has its roots at Golgotha.

In lieu of that, I have no clear agenda. I've been living under a despotic regime for a long time now, with the heel of my own ambition on my neck. Now that it's almost lifted, living free may be satisfaction enough. I am hereafter only the man who told a prodigal's story; who chronicled the return of Galilee and his beloved to the place where they could begin. Forward of that moment is an empty page. And though I will be walking there, I intend to leave no trace of my passing; at least not in words.

All of which is not to say I won't wonder, as I go, how the lives and afterlives of those I've written about here will proceed.

I can see Garrison Geary even now, home from burying his grandfather and his brother, sitting in what used to be Cadmus's sanctum. On his lap, Charles Holt's journal. On the wall in front of him, the great Bierstadt canvas. In his mind he has become the lone pioneer on the crag in the painting; but it is not the plains of the Midwest he imagines possessing. It is L'Enfant. He plans to take it by force. He even knows what he's going to do once he's become the Lord of that house, and it will change the course of history.

In Washington, Loretta is alone; also meditating on what lies before her. Seeing her men put into the ground, side by side, made her wonder if she hadn't been hasty when she'd told Rachel that these mysteries were beyond them all. We're little people, she'd said. We don't have a prayer. But in the dusk, listening to the traffic, she wonders if that's the very thing she has: a prayer; and someone to deliver it to. It will take her a little time to make sense of things; but she's a clever woman, and now she has nothing to lose, which makes her formidable.

Meanwhile, Luman's bastards pass the grimy days in some city I cannot name, the wisest of them expecting nothing; though they may yet be astonished.

And the shark deities move in the clear waters around the islands.

And the dream spirits of the Geary women sit laughing under the eaves of the house in Anahola;

And certain powerful men, weary from their day of politicking, come reverentially into a temple close to Capitol Hill, and pay their sullen respects;

And the gods go on, in spite of themselves; and the human road stretches out before us; and we walk, like wounded children, waiting for the strength to run.

# ACKNOWLEDGMENTS

Thankfully, I did not take this voyage alone. I'd like to offer here a few words of appreciation to those who have accompanied me.

To Vann Sauls, of McGee's Crossroads, North Carolina, for his friendship, his wit, and for the insights he imparted as we explored the Carolinas together. Without our conversations wandering the midnight streets of Charleston, and the woods at Bentonville, where the armies of North and South clashed so calamitously, this book would be much impoverished.

To Robb Humphreys and Joe Daley, who assisted me in my more obscure researches, never failing to find on the library shelves books that contained some vital nugget of information.

To my dear Anna Miller, who along with Robb and Joe runs our film production company here in LA. While I've been at sea with Galilee, she's kept the seductions and the insanities of this town at bay with chair and whip.

To Don Mackay, who did me the great honor of making the typing of this manuscript his only distraction from his true vocation, which is that of actor.

And finally, to David John Dodds, who makes the world in which I live and work run like clockwork, a far from easy task. He has been my friend and guardian spirit for thirteen years. None of this would be possible without his love and faith in me.

C.B.